HEXWOOD

Diana Wynne Jones

HEXWOOD

 Greenwillow Books, New York

Library of Congress Cataloging-in-Publication Data
Jones, Diana Wynne.
Hexwood / by Diana Wynne Jones.
        p.   cm.
Summary: Ann discovers that the wood near her village is under the
control of a Bannus, a machine that manipulates reality, placed there
many years ago by powerful extraterrestrial beings called Reigners.
ISBN 0-688-12488-7   [1. Science fiction.]   I. Title.
PZ7.J684He   1994   [Fic]—dc20
93-18172   CIP   AC

For Neil Gaiman

CONTENTS

PART
ONE

—1—

THE LETTER WAS in Earth script, unhandily scrawled in blobby blue ballpoint. It said:

Hexwood Farm
Tuesday 4 March 1992

Dear Sectéor Controller,

We thought we better send to you in Regional straight off. We got a right problem here. This fool clerk, calls hisself Harrison Scudamore, he went and started one of these old machines running, the one with all the Reigner seals on it, says he overrode the computers to do it. When we say a few words about that, he turns round and says he was bored, he only wanted to make the best all time football team, you know King Arthur in goal, Julius Ceasar for striker, Napoleon midfield, only this team is *for real*, he found out this machine can do that, which it *do*. Trouble is we don't have the tools nor the training to get the thing turned off, nor we can't see where the power's coming from, the thing's got a field like you wouldn't believe and it won't let us out of the

place. Much obliged if you could send a trained operative
at your earliest convenience.

Yours truly,

W. *Madden*

Foreman Rayner Hexwood Maintenance (European Division)

P.S. He says he's had it running more than a month now.

Sector Controller Borasus stared at the letter and wondered if it
was a hoax. W. Madden had not known enough about the Reigner
Organization to send his letter through the proper channels. Only
the fact that he had marked his little brown envelope "URGENT!!!"
had caused it to arrive in the head office of Albion Sector at all. It
was stamped all over with queries from branch offices and had been
at least two weeks on the way.

Controller Borasus shuddered slightly. A machine with Reigner
seals! If this was *not* a hoax, it was liable to be very bad news. "It
must be someone's idea of a joke," he said to his secretary. "Don't
they have something called April Fools' Day on Earth?"

"It's not April there yet," his secretary pointed out dubiously. "If
you recollect, sir, the date on which you are due to attend their
American conference—tomorrow, sir—is March twentieth."

"Then maybe the joker mistimed his letter," Controller Borasus
said hopefully. As a devout man who believed in the Divine Balance
perpetually adjusted by the Reigners, and himself as the Reigners'
vicar on Albion, he had a strong feeling that nothing could possibly
go *really* wrong. "What is this Hexwood Farm thing of theirs?"

His secretary as usual had all the facts. "A library and reference
complex," he answered, "concealed beneath a housing estate not
far from London. I have it marked on my screen as one of our older
installations. It's been there a good twelve hundred years, and there's
never been any kind of trouble there before, sir."

Controller Borasus sighed with relief. Libraries were not places of danger. It had to be a hoax. "Put me through to the place at once."

His secretary looked up the codes and punched in the symbols. The controller's screen lit with a spatter of expanding lights. It was not unlike what you see when you press your fingers into your eyes.

"Whatever's that?" said the Controller.

"I don't know, sir. I'll try again." The secretary canceled the call and punched the code once more. And again after that. Each time the screen filled with a new flux of expanding shapes. On the secretary's third attempt the colored rings began spreading off the viewscreen and rippling gently outward across the paneled wall of the office.

Controller Borasus leaned across and broke the connection, fast. The ripples spread a little more, then faded. The Controller did not like the look of it at all. With a cold, growing certainty that everything was *not* all right after all, he waited until the screen and the wall at last seemed back to normal and commanded, "Get me Earth Head Office." He could hear that his voice was half an octave higher than usual. He coughed and added, "Runcorn, or whatever the place is called. Tell them I want an explanation at once."

To his relief, things seemed quite normal this time. Runcorn came up on the screen, looking entirely as it should, in the person of a junior executive with beautifully groomed hair and a smart suit, who seemed very startled to see the narrow, august face of the Sector Controller staring out of the screen at him, and even more startled when the Controller asked to speak to the Area Director instantly. "Certainly, Controller. I believe Sir John has just arrived. I'll put you through—"

"Before you do," Controller Borasus interrupted, "tell me what you know about Hexwood Farm."

"Hexwood *Farm!*" The junior executive looked nonplussed. "Er—you mean— Is this one of our information retrieval centers you have in mind, Controller? I think one of them *is* called something like that."

"And do you know a Maintenance foreman called W. Madden?" demanded the Controller.

"Not *personally*, Controller," said the junior executive. It was clear that if anyone else had asked him this question, the junior executive would have been very disdainful indeed. He said cautiously, "A fine body of men, Maintenance. They do an excellent job servicing all our offworld machinery and supplies, but of course, naturally, Controller, I get into work some hours after they've—"

"Put me through to Sir John," sighed the controller.

Sir John Bedford was as surprised as his junior executive. But after Controller Borasus had asked only a few questions, a slow horror began to creep across Sir John's healthy businessman's face. "Hexwood Farm is not *considered* very important," he said uneasily. "It's all history and archives there. Of course, that does mean that it holds a number of classified records—it has all the early stuff about why the Reigner Organization keeps itself secret here on Earth: how the population of Earth arrived here as deported convicts and exiled malcontents, and so forth—and I believe there *is* a certain amount of obsolete machinery stored there, too, but I can't see how our clerk would be able to tamper with any of that. We run it through just the one clerk, you see, and he's pretty poor stuff, only in the Grade K information bracket—"

"And Grade K means?" asked Controller Borasus.

"It means he'll have been told that Rayner Hexwood International is actually an intergalactic firm," Sir John explained, "but that should be absolutely all he knows—probably less than Maintenance, who are also Grade K. Maintenance pick up a thing or two in the course of their work. That's unavoidable. They visit every secret installation once a month to make sure everything stays in working order, and to supply the stass stores with food and so forth, and I suspect quite a few of them know far more than they've been told, but they've been carefully tested for loyalty. None of them would play a joke like this."

Sir John, Controller Borasus decided, was trying to talk himself out of trouble. Just what you would expect from a backward hole like Earth. "So what do you think is the explanation?"

"I wish I knew," said the Director of Earth. "Oddly enough, I have two complaints on my desk just this morning. One is from an executive in Rayner Hexwood Japan, saying that Hexwood Farm is not replying to any of his repeated requests for data. The other is from our Brussels branch, wanting to know why Maintenance has not yet been to service their power plant." He stared at the Controller, who stared back. Each seemed to be waiting for the other to explain. "That foreman should have reported to me," Sir John said at length, rather accusingly.

Controller Borasus sighed. "What *is* this sealed machine that seems to have been stored in your retrieval center?"

It took Sir John Bedford five minutes to find out. What a slack world! Controller Borasus waited, drumming his fingers on the edge of his console, and his secretary sat not daring to get on with any other business.

At last Sir John came back on the screen. "Sorry to be so long. Anything with Reigner seals here is under heavy security coding, and there turn out to be about forty old machines stored in that library. We have this one listed simply as 'One Bannus,' Controller. That's all, but it must be the one. All the other things under Reigner seals are stass tombs. I imagine there'll be more about this Bannus in your own Albion archives, Controller. You have a higher clearance than—"

"Thank you," snapped Controller Borasus. He cut the connection and told his secretary, "Find out, Giraldus."

His secretary was already trying. His fingers flew. His voice murmured codes and directives in a continuous stream. Symbols scrolled, and vanished, and flickered, jumping from screen to screen, where they clotted with other symbols and jumped back to enter the main screen from four directions at once. After a mere minute Giraldus said, "It's classified maximum security here, too, sir. The code for your Key comes up on your screen—now."

"Thank the Balance for *some* efficiency!" murmured the Controller. He took up the Key that hung round his neck from his chain of office and plugged it into the little-used slot at the side of his console. The code signal vanished from his screen, and words took its place. The secretary, of course, did not look, but he saw that there were only a couple of lines on the screen. He saw that the Controller was reacting with considerable dismay. "Not very informative," Borasus murmured. He leaned forward and checked the line of symbols which came up after the words in the smaller screen of his manual. "Hm. Giraldus," he said to his secretary.

"Sir?"

"One of these is a need-to-know. Since I'm going to be away tomorrow, I'd better tell you what this says. This W. Madden seems to have his facts right. A Bannus is some sort of archaic decision maker. It makes use of a field of theta-space to give you live-action scenarios of any set of facts and people you care to feed into it. Acts little plays for you, until you find the right one and tell it to stop."

Giraldus laughed. "You mean the clerk and the Maintenance team have been playing football all this month?"

"It's no laughing matter." Controller Borasus nervously snatched his Key from its slot. "The second code symbol is the one for extreme danger."

"Oh." Giraldus stopped laughing. "But, sir, I thought theta-space—"

"Was a new thing the central worlds were playing with?" the controller finished for him. "So did I. But it looks as if someone knew about it all along." He shivered slightly. "If I remember rightly, the danger with theta-space is that it can expand indefinitely if it's not controlled. I'm the Controller," he added with a nervous laugh. "I have the Key." He looked down at the Key, hanging from its chain. "It's possible that this is what the Key is really for." He pulled himself together and stood up. "I can see it's no use trusting that idiot Bedford. It will be extremely inconvenient, but I had better get to Earth now and turn the wretched machine off. Notify

America, will you? Say I'll be flying on from London after I've been to Hexwood."

"Yes, sir." Giraldus made notes, murmuring, "Official robes, air tickets, passport, standard Earth documentation pack. Is that why I need to know, sir?" he asked, turning to flick switches. "So that I can tell everyone you've gone to deal with a classified machine and may be a little late getting to the conference?"

"No, no!" Borasus said. "Don't tell anyone. Make some other excuse. You need to know in case Homeworld gets back to you after I've left. The first symbol means I have to send a report top priority to the House of Balance."

Giraldus was a pale and beaky man, but this news made him turn a curious yellow. "To the *Reigners?*" he whispered, looking like an alarmed vulture.

Controller Borasus found himself clutching his Key as if it were his hope of salvation. "Yes," he said, trying to sound firm and confident. "Anything involving this machine has to go straight to the Reigners themselves. Don't worry. No one can possibly blame you."

But they can blame *me*, Borasus thought as he used his Key on the private emergency link to Homeworld, which no Sector Controller ever used unless he could help it. Whatever this is, it happened in my sector. The emergency screen blinked and lit with the symbol of the Balance, showing that his report was now on its way to the heart of the galaxy, to the almost legendary world that was supposed to be the original home of the human race, where even the ordinary inhabitants were said to be gifted in ways that people in the colony worlds could hardly guess at. It was out of his hands now.

He swallowed as he turned away. There were supposed to be five Reigners. Borasus had worried, double thoughts about them. On one hand, he believed almost mystically in these distant beings who controlled the Balance and infused order into the Organization. On the other hand, as he was accustomed to say dryly, to those in the

Organization who doubted that the Reigners existed at all, that there had to be *someone* in control of such a vast combine, and whether there were five, or less, or more, these High Controllers did not appreciate blunders. He hoped with all his heart that this business with this Bannus did not strike them as a blunder. What—he told himself—he emphatically did *not* believe were all these tales of the Reigners' Servant.

When the Reigners were displeased, it was said, they were liable to dispatch their Servant. The Servant, who had the face of Death and dressed always in scarlet, came softly stalking down the stars to deal with the one who was at fault. It was said he could kill with one touch of his bone-cold finger or at a distance, just with his mind. It did no good to conceal your fault because the Servant could read minds, and no matter how far you ran and how many barriers you put between, the Servant could detect you and come softly walking through anything you put in his way. You could not kill him because he deflected all weapons. And the Servant would never swerve from any task the Reigners appointed him to.

No, Controller Borasus did not believe in the Servant—although, he had to admit, there were quite frequent dry little reports that came into Albion Head Office to the effect that such and such an executive, or director, or subconsul, had terminated from the Organization. No, that was something different. The Servant was just folklore.

But I shall take the rap, Borasus thought as he went to get ready to go to Earth, and he shivered as if a bloodred shadow had walked softly on bone feet across his grave.

—2

A BOY WAS walking in a wood. It was a beautiful wood, open and sunny. All the leaves were small and light green, hardly more than buds. He was coming down a mud path between sprays of leaves, with deep grass and bushes on either side.

And that was all he knew.

He had just noticed a small tree ahead that was covered with airy pink blossoms. He looked at it. He looked beyond it. Though all the trees were quite small and the wood seemed open, all he could see was this wood, in all directions. He did not know where he was. Then he realized that he did not know where else there was to be. Nor did he know how he had got to the wood in the first place. After that it dawned on him that he did not know who he was. Or what he was. Or why he was there.

He looked down at himself. He seemed quite small—smaller than he expected somehow—and rather skinny. The bits of him he could see were wearing faded purple-blue. He wondered what the clothes were made of and what held the shoes on.

"There's something wrong with this place," he said. "I'd better go back and try to find the way out."

He turned back down the mud path. Sunlight glittered on silver there. Green reflected crazily on the skin of a tall silver man-shaped creature pacing slowly toward him. But it was not a man. Its face was silver, and its hands were silver, too. This was wrong. The boy took a quick look at his own hands to be sure, and they were brownish white. This was some kind of monster. Luckily there was a green spray of leaves between him and the monster's reddish eyes. It did not seem to have seen him yet. The boy turned and ran quietly and lightly, back the way he had been coming from.

He ran hard until the silver thing was out of sight. Then he stopped, panting, beside a tangled patch of dead briar and whitish grass, wondering what he had better do. The silver creature walked as if it were heavy. It probably needed the beaten path to walk on.

So the best idea was to leave the path. Then if it tried to chase him, it would get its heavy feet tangled.

He stepped off the path into the patch of dried grass. His feet seemed to cause a lot of rustling in it. He stood still, warily, up to his ankles in dead stuff, listening to the whole patch rustling and creaking.

No, it was worse! Some dead brambles near the center were heaving up. A long, light brown scaly head was sliding forward out of them. A scaly foreleg with long claws stepped forward in the grass beside the head, and another leg, on the other side. Now that the thing was moving slowly and purposefully toward him, the boy could see it was—crocodile? pale dragon?—nearly twenty feet long, dragging through the pale grass behind the scaly head. Two small eyes near the top of that head were fixed upon him. The mouth opened. It was black inside and jagged with teeth, and the breath coming out smelled horrible.

The boy did not stop to think. Just beside his feet was a dead branch, overgrown and half buried in the grass. He bent down and tore it loose. It came up trailing roots, falling to pieces, smelling of fungus. He flung it, trailing bits and all, into the animal's open mouth. The mouth snapped on it and could only shut halfway. The boy turned and ran and ran. He hardly knew where he went, except that he was careful to keep to the mud path.

He pelted round a corner and ran straight into the silver creature. *Clang*.

It swayed and put out a silver hand to fend him off. "Careful!" it said in a loud, flat voice.

"There's a crawling thing with a huge mouth back there!" the boy said frantically.

"Still?" asked the silver creature. "It was killed. But maybe we have yet to kill it, since I see you are quite small just now."

This meant nothing to the boy. He took a step back and stared at the silver being. It seemed to be made of bendable metal over a man-shaped frame. He could see ridges here and there in the metal as it moved, as if wires were pulling or stretching. Its face was made the same way, sort of rippling as it spoke—except for the eyes, which were fixed and reddish. The voice seemed to come from a hole under its chin. But now that he looked at it closely, he saw it was not silver quite all over. There were places where the metal skin had been patched, and the patches were disguised with long strips of black and white trim, down the silver legs, round the silver waist and along the outside of each gleaming arm.

"What are you?" he asked.

"I am Yam," said the being, "one of the early Yamaha robots, series nine, which were the best that were ever made." It added, with pride in its flat voice, "I am worth a great deal." Then it paused and said, "If you do not know that, what else do you not know?"

"I don't know anything," said the boy. "What am I?"

"You are Hume," said Yam. "That is short for *human*, which you are."

"Oh," said the boy. He discovered, by moving slightly, that he could see himself reflected in the robot's shining front. He had fairish hair, grown longish, and he seemed to stand and move in a light, eager sort of way. The purple-blue clothes clung close to his skinny body from neck to ankles, without any sort of markings, and he had a pocket in each sleeve. Hume, he thought. He was not certain that *was* his name. And he hoped the shape of his face was caused by the robot's curved front. Or did people's cheekbones really stick out that way? He looked up at Yam's silver face. The robot was nearly two feet taller than he was. "How do you know?"

"I have a revolutionary brain, and my memory is not yet full," Yam answered. "This is why they stopped making my series. We lasted too long."

"Yes, but," said the boy—Hume, as he supposed he was, "I meant—"

"We must get out of this piece of the wood," said Yam. "If the reptile is alive, we have come to the wrong time and we must try again."

Hume thought that was a good idea. He did not want to be anywhere near that scaly thing with the mouth. Yam swiveled himself around on the spot and began to stride back along the path. Hume trotted to keep up. "What have we got to try?" he asked.

"Another path," said Yam.

"And why are we together?" Hume asked, trying again to understand. "Do we know each other? Do I belong to you or something?"

"Strictly speaking, robots are owned by humans," Yam said. "These are hard questions to answer. You never paid for me, but I am not programmed to leave you alone. My understanding is that you need help."

Hume trotted past a whole thicket of the airy pink blossoms, which reflected giddily all over Yam's body. He tried again. "We know each other? You've met me before?"

"Many times," said Yam.

This was encouraging. Even more encouraging, the path forked beyond the pink trees. Yam stopped with a suddenness that made Hume overshoot. He looked back to see Yam pointing a silver finger down the left fork. "This wood," Yam told him, "is like human memory. It does not need to take events in their correct order. Do you wish to go to an earlier time and start from there?"

"Would I understand more if I did?" Hume asked.

"You might," said Yam. "Both of us might."

"Then it's worth a try," Hume agreed.

They went together down the left-hand fork.

3

HEXWOOD FARM HOUSING ESTATE had one row of shops, all on the same side of Wood Street, and Ann's parents kept the greengrocer's halfway down the row. Above the houses on the other side you could see the trees of Banners Wood. And at the end of this row were the tall stone walls and the ancient peeling gate of Hexwood

Farm itself. All you could see of the farmhouse was one crumbling chimney that never smoked. It was hard to believe that anybody lived there, but in fact, old Mr. Craddock had lived there until a few months ago for as long as Ann could remember, keeping himself to himself and snarling at any child who tried to get close enough to see what was inside the old black gate. "Set the dogs on you!" he used to say. "Set the dogs to bite your leg off!"

There were no dogs, but nobody dared pry into the farm all the same. There was something about the place.

Then, quite suddenly, Mr. Craddock was not there and a young man was living there instead. This one called himself Harrison Scudamore and dyed the top of his hair orange. He stalked about with a well-filled wallet bulging the back of his jeans and behaved, as Ann's dad said, as if he were a cut above the Lord Almighty. This was after young Harrison had stalked into the shop for half a pound of tomatoes and Dad had asked politely if Mr. Scudamore was lodging with Mr. Craddock.

"None of your business," young Harrison said. He more or less threw the money at Dad and stalked out of the shop. But he turned in the doorway to add, "Craddock's retired. *I'm* in charge now. You'd all better watch it."

"Awful eyes he has," Dad remarked, telling Ann and Martin the tale. "Like gooseberries."

"A snail," Mum said. "He made me think of a snail."

Ann lay in bed and thought of young Harrison. She had one of those viruses that were puzzling the doctor, and there was not much to do except lie and think of *something*. Every so often she got up out of sheer boredom. Once she even went back to school. But it always ended with Ann gray and shaky and aching all over, tottering back to bed. And when her brother, Martin, had been to the library for her, and she had read all her own books, and then Martin's— Martin's were always either about dinosaurs or based on role-playing games—she had no energy to do anything but lie and think. Har-

rison was at least a new thing to think about. Everybody hated him.
He had been rude to Mr. Porter, the butcher, too. And he had told
Mrs. Price, who kept the newsagent's at the end, to shut up and
stop yakking on. "And I was only talking—politely, you know—the
way I do with everyone," Mrs. Price said, almost tearfully. Harrison
had kicked the pampered little dog that belonged to the gay boys
who kept the wineshop, and one of them *had* cried. Everyone had
some tale to tell.

Ann wondered why Harrison behaved like that. From a project
she dimly remembered doing at school, she knew the whole estate
had once been lands belonging to Hexwood Farm. The farm
stretched north as far as the chemical works and east beyond the
motel. Banners Wood, in the middle, had once been huge, though
it was hardly even a wood these days. You could see through it to
the houses on the other side. It was just trees round a small muddy
stream, and all the children played there. Ann knew every pretzel
bag under every tree root and almost every Coke ring embedded in
its muddy paths.

But perhaps Harrison has inherited the farm and thinks he still
owns it all, she thought. He did behave that way.

In fact, Ann's real theory was quite different and much more
interesting. That old farm was so secretive and yet so easy to get to
from London that she was convinced it was really a hideout for
gangsters. She was sure there was gold bullion or sacks and sacks of
drugs—or both—stored in its cellar with young Harrison to guard
it. Harrison's airs were because the drug barons paid him so much
to guard their secrets.

What do you think about that? she asked her four imaginary
people.

The Slave, as so often, was faint and far-off. His masters over-
worked him terribly. He thought the theory very likely. Young
Harrison was a menial giving himself airs—he knew the type.

The Prisoner considered. If Ann was right, he said, then young

Harrison was behaving very stupidly, drawing attention to himself like this. Her first theory was better.

But I only thought of that to be fair-minded! Ann protested. *What do you think, King?*

Either could be right, said the King. *Or both.*

The Boy, when Ann consulted him, chose the gangster theory because it was the most exciting.

Ann grinned. The Boy would think that. He was stuck on the edge of nowhere, being a sort of assistant to a man who had lived so long ago that people thought of him as a god. He felt out of things, born in the wrong time and place. He always wanted excitement. He said he could only get it through talking to Ann.

Ann was slightly worried about the Boy's opinions. The Boy was always behaving as if he were real, instead of just an invention of Ann's. She was a little ashamed of inventing these four people. They had come into her head from goodness knew where when she was quite small, and she used to hold long conversations with them. These days she did not speak to them so often. In fact, she was quite worried that she might be mad, talking to invented people, particularly when they took on ideas of their own, as the Boy did. And she did wonder what it said about her—Ann—that all four of her inventions were unhappy in different ways. The Prisoner was always in jail, and he had been put there many centuries ago, so there was no chance of Ann helping him escape. The Slave would be put to death if *he* tried to escape. One of his fellow slaves had tried it once. The Slave wouldn't tell Ann quite what had happened to that slave, but she knew he had died of it. As for the King, he also lived in a far-off time and place, and he spent a lot of his time having to do things that were quite intensely boring. Ann was so sorry for all of them that she had often to console herself by keeping firmly in mind the fact that they were not *real*.

The King spoke to Ann again. He had been thinking, he said, that while Ann was lying in bed, she had an ideal opportunity to observe young Harrison's comings and goings. She might find out something to support her theory. *Can you see Hexwood Farm from where you are?* he asked.

No, it's down the street the other way, Ann explained. *I'd have to turn my bed round, and I haven't the strength just now.*

No need, said the King. He knew all about spying. *All you have to do is to put a mirror where you can see it from your bed, and turn it so it reflects the street and the farm. It's a trick my own spies often use.*

It really was an excellent idea. Ann got out of bed at once and tried to arrange her bedroom mirror. Of course, it was wrong the first time, and the second. She lost count of the weak, gray, tottering journeys she made to give that mirror a turn, or a push, or a tip upward. Then all she saw was ceiling. So off she tottered again. But after twenty minutes of what seemed desperately hard work, she collapsed on her pillows to see a perfect back-to-front view of the end of Wood Street and the decrepit black gate of Hexwood Farm. And there *was* young Harrison, with his tuft of orange hair, sauntering arrogantly back to the gate, carrying his morning paper and his milk. No doubt he had been rude to Mrs. Price again. He looked so satisfied.

Thank you! Ann said to the King.

You're welcome, Girl Child, he said. He always called her Girl Child. All four of her people did.

For a while there was nothing to watch in the mirror except other people coming and going to the shops, and cars parking in the bay where their owners hauled out bags of washing and took them to the launderette, but even this was far more interesting than just lying there. Ann was truly grateful to the King.

Then, suddenly, there was a van. It was white and quite big, and there seemed to be several men in it. It drove right up to the gate of the farm, and the gate opened smoothly and mechanically to let it drive in. Ann was sure it was a modern mechanism, much more modern than the peeling state of the gate suggested. It looked as if her gangster theory might be right! There was a blue trade logo on the van and, underneath that, blue writing. It was small lettering, kind of chaste and tasteful, and of course, in the mirror it was back to front. She had no idea what it said.

Ann just had to see. She flopped out of bed with a groan and tottered to the window, where she was just in time to see the old black gate closing smoothly behind the van.

Oh, bother! she said to the King. *I bet that was the latest load of drugs!*

Wait till it comes out again, he told her. *When you see the gate open, you should have time to get to the window and see the men drive the vehicle away.*

So Ann went back to bed and waited. And waited. But she never saw the van come out. By that evening she was convinced that she had looked away, or dropped asleep, or gone tottering to the toilet at the moment the gate had opened to let the van out. *I missed it,* she told the King. *All I know is the logo.*

And what was that? he asked.

Oh, just a weighing scale, one of those old-fashioned kinds—you know—with two sort of pans hanging from a handle in the middle.

To her surprise, not only the King but the Slave and the Prisoner, too, all came alert and alive in her mind. *Are you sure?* they asked in a sharp chorus.

Yes, of course, Ann said. *Why?*

Be very careful, said the Prisoner. *Those are the people who put me in prison.*

In my time and place, said the King, *those are the arms of a very powerful and very corrupt organization. They have subverted people in my court and tried to buy my army, and I'm very much afraid that in the end they are going to overthrow me.*

The Slave said nothing, but he gave Ann a strong feeling that he knew even more about the organization than the others did. But they could all be thinking about something else, Ann decided. After all, they came from another time and place from hers. And there were thousands of firms on Earth inventing logos all the time. *I think it's an accident*, she said to the Boy. She could feel him hovering, listening wistfully.

You think that because no one on Earth really believes there are any other worlds but Earth, he said.

True. But you read my mind to know that. I told you not to! Ann said.

I can't help it, said the Boy. *You think we don't exist, either. But we do—you know we do, really.*

4

ANN FORGOT ABOUT the van. A fortnight passed, during which she got up again and went to school for half a day, and was sent home at lunchtime with a temperature, and read another stack of library books, and lay watching people coming to the shops in her mirror.

"Like the Lady of Shalott!" she said disgustedly. "Fool woman in that fool poem we learned last term! She was under a curse and she had to watch everything through a mirror, too."

"Oh, stop grumbling, *do!*" said Ann's mum. "It'll go. Give it time."

"But I want it to go *now!*" said Ann. "I'm an active adolescent, not a bedridden *invalid*! I'm climbing the *walls* here!"

"Just shut up and I'll get Martin to lend you his Walkman," said Mum.

"That'll be the day!" said Ann. "He'd rather lend me his cutoff fingers!"

But Martin did, entirely unexpectedly, make a brotherly appearance in her room next morning. "You look awful," he said. "Like a Guy made of putty." He followed this compliment up by dropping Walkman and tapes on her bed and leaving for school at once. Ann was quite touched.

That day she lay and listened to the only three tapes she could bear—Martin's taste in music matched his love of dinosaurs—and kept an eye on Hexwood Farm merely for something to look at. Young Harrison appeared once, much as usual, except that he bought a great deal of bread. Could it be, Ann wondered, that he was really having to feed a vanload of men still inside there? She did not believe this. By now she had decided, in a bored, gloomy, virusish way, that her exciting theory about gangsters was just silly romancing. The whole world was gray—the virus had probably got into the universe—and even the daffodils in front of the house opposite looked bleak and dull to her.

Someone who looked like a Lord Mayor walked across the road in her mirror.

A *Lord Mayor*? Ann tore the earphones off and sat up for a closer look. "Appa-dappa-dappa-dah," went the music in a tinny whisper. She clicked it off impatiently. A Lord Mayor with a suitcase, hurrying toward the peeling black gate of Hexwood Farm, in a way that was—well—sort of doubtful but determined, too. Like someone going to the dentist, Ann thought. And was it a coincidence that the Lord Mayor had appeared just in that early-afternoon lull when there was never anyone much about in Wood Street? *Did* Lord Mayors wear green velvet gowns? Or such very pointed boots? But there was definitely a gold chain round the man's neck. Was he going to the farm to ransom someone who had been kidnapped—with bundles of money in that suitcase?

She watched the man halt in front of the gate. If there *was* some kind of opening mechanism, it was clearly not going to work this time. After standing there an impatient moment or so, the robed man put out a fist and knocked. Ann could hear the distant, hollow little thumps even through her closed window. But nobody answered the knocking. The man stepped back in a frustrated way. He called out. Ann heard, as distant as the knocking, a high tenor voice calling, but she could not hear the words. When that did no good either, the man put down his suitcase and glanced round the nearly deserted street, to make sure no one was looking.

A-ha-ha! Ann thought. Little do you know I have my trusty mirror!

She saw the man's face quite clearly, narrow and important, with lines of worry and impatience. It was no one she knew. She saw him take up the ornament hanging on his chest from the gold chain and advance on the gate with it as if he were going to use the ornament as a key. And the gate opened, silently and smoothly, just as it had done for the van, when the ornament was nowhere near it. The Lord Mayor was really surprised. Ann saw him start back and look at his ornament wonderingly. Then he picked up his suitcase and hurried importantly inside. The gate swung shut behind him. And just like the van, that was the last Ann saw of him.

This time it could have been because the virus suddenly got worse. For the next day or so Ann was so ill that she was in no state to watch anything, in the mirror or out of it. She sweated and tossed and slept—nasty, short sleeps with feverish dreams—and woke feeling limp and horrible and hot.

Be glad, the Prisoner told her. He had been a sort of doctor before he was put in prison. *The disease is coming to a head.*

You could have fooled me! Ann told him. *I think they kidnapped the Lord Mayor, too. That place is a Bermuda triangle. And I'm not better. I'm* worse.

Mum seemed to share the Prisoner's opinion, to Ann's annoyance. "Fever's broken at last," Mum said. "Won't be long now before you're well. Thank goodness!"

"Only another hundred years!" Ann groaned.

And the night that followed did indeed seem about a century long. Ann kept having dreams where she ran away across a vast grassy park, scarcely able to move her legs for terror of the Something that stalked behind. Or worse dreams where she was shut in a labyrinth made of mother-of-pearl—in those dreams she thought she was trapped in her own ear—and the pearl walls gave rainbow reflections of the same Something softly sliding after her. The worst of this dream was that Ann was terrified of the Something catching her, but equally terrified in case the Something missed her in the curving maze. There was blood on the pearly floor of her ear. Ann woke with a jump, wet all over, to find it was getting light at last.

Dawn was yellow outside and reflecting yellow in her mirror. But what seemed to have woken her was not the dreams but the sound of a solitary car. Not so unusual, Ann thought fretfully. Some of the deliveries to the shops happened awfully early. Yet it was quite clear to her that this car was *not* a delivery. It was important. She pulled a soggy pillow weakly under her head so that she could watch it in the mirror.

The car came whispering down Wood Street with its headlights blazing, as if the driver had not realized it was dawn now, and crept to a cautious sort of stop in the bay opposite the launderette. For a moment it stayed that way, headlights on and engine running. Ann had a feeling that the dark heads she could see leaning together inside it were considering what to do. Were they police? It was a big gray expensive car, more a businessman's car than a police car. Unless they were very high-up police, of course.

The engine stopped, and the headlights snapped off. Doors opened. *Very* high up, Ann thought as three men climbed out. One was wealthy businessman all over, rather wide from good living, with not a crisp hair out of place. He was wearing one of those wealthy macs that never look creased, over a smart suit. The second man was shorter and plumper, and decidedly shabby, in a green tweed suit that did not fit him. The trousers were too long and sleeves too narrow, and he had a long knitted scarf trailing from his neck. An informer, Ann thought. He had a scared, peevish look, as if he had not wanted the other two to bring him along. The third man was tall and thin, and he was quite as oddly dressed as the informer, in a three-quarter-length little camel hair coat that must have been at least forty years old. Yet he wore it like a king. When he strolled over to the middle of the road to get a full view of Hexwood Farm, he moved in a curious lolling, powerful way that took Ann's eyes with him. He had hair the same camel hair color as his coat. She watched him stand there, long legs apart, hands in pockets, staring at the gate, and she scarcely noticed the other two men come up to him. She kept trying to see the tall man's face. But she never did see it clearly because they went quickly over to the gate then, with the businessman striding ahead.

Here it was just like the Lord Mayor. The businessman stopped short, dismayed, as if he had confidently expected the gate to open mechanically for him. When it simply stayed shut, his face turned down to the small informer man, and this one bustled forward. He did something—tapped out a code?—but Ann could not see what. The gate still did not open. This made the small man angry. He raised a fist as if he were going to hit the gate. At this the tall man in the camel coat seemed to feel they had waited long enough. He strolled forward, put the informer man gently but firmly out of the way, and simply went on strolling toward the gate. At the point where it looked as if he would crash into the peeling black boards, the gate swung open, sharply and quickly, for him. Ann had a feeling that the stones of the wall would have done that, too, if the man had wanted it so.

The three went inside, and the gate shut after them.

Ann could not rid herself of the feeling that she had just seen the most important thing yet. She expected them to come out quite soon, probably with Harrison under arrest. But she fell asleep still waiting.

—5——————————————

MUCH LATER THAT morning there was a violent hailstorm. It woke Ann, and she woke completely well again. For a moment she lay and stared at thick streams of ice running down the window, melting in new, bright sunlight. She felt so well that it stunned her. Then her eyes shifted to the mirror. Through the reflected melting ice, the road shone bright enough to make her eyes water. But there in the parking bay, mounded with white hailstones, stood the business-man's gray car.

They're still in there! she thought. It *is* a Bermuda triangle!

She was getting out of bed as she thought this. Her body knew it was well, and it just had to move whether she told it to or not. It had needs. "*God!*" Ann exclaimed. "I'm *hungry!*"

She tore downstairs and ate two bowls of cornflakes. Then, while a new hailstorm clattered on the windows, she fried herself bacon, mushrooms, tomatoes, and eggs—as much as the pan would hold. As she was carrying it to the table, Mum hurried through from the shop, alerted by the smell. "You're feeling better?"

"Oh, I *am!*" said Ann. "So better that I'm going out as soon as I've eaten this."

Mum looked from the mounded frying pan to the window. "The weather's not—" But the hail had gone by then. Bright sunlight was slicing through the smoke from Ann's fry-up, and the sky was deep, clear blue. Bang goes Mum's excuse, Ann thought, grinning as she wolfed down her mushrooms. *Nothing* had ever tasted so good! "Well, you're not to overdo it," Mum said. "Remember you've been poorly for a long time. You're to wrap up warm and be back for lunch."

"I shall obey, O great fusspot," Ann said, with her mouth full.

"Lunch, or I shall call the police," said Mum. "And don't wear jeans—they're not nearly warm enough. The weather at this time of year—"

"Fuss-great-potest," Ann said lovingly, beginning on the bacon. Pity there had been no room in the pan for fried bread. "I'm not a baby. *Two* layers of thermal underwear satisfy you?"

"Since when have you had—Oh, I can see you're *better!*" Mum said happily. "A vest, anyway, to please me."

"Vests," Ann said, quoting a badge that Martin often wore, "are what teenagers wear when their mothers feel cold. *You're* cold. You keep that shop freezing."

"You know we have to keep the veg fresh," Mum retorted, and she went back into the shop laughing happily.

The sun felt really hot. When she finished eating, Ann went upstairs and dressed as she saw fit: the tight woolly skirt, so that Mum would see she was not wearing jeans, a summery top, and her nice anorak over that, zipped right up so that she looked wrapped up. Then she scudded down and through the shop, calling, "Bye, everyone!" before either of her parents could get loose from customers and interrogate her.

"Don't go too far!" Dad's powerful voice followed her.

"I won't!" Ann called back. Truthfully. She had it all worked out. There was no point trying to work the device that opened that gate. If she tried to climb it, someone would notice and stop her. Besides, if everyone who went into the farm never came out, it would be stupid to go in there and vanish, too. Mum and Dad really would throw fits. But there was nothing to stop Ann from climbing a tree in Banners Wood and taking a look over the wall from there.

Get a close look at that van, if it's still there, the King agreed. *I'm rather anxious to know who owns it.*

Ann frowned and gave a sort of nod. There was something about this weighing scale logo. It made her four people talk to her when she had not actually started to imagine them. She didn't like that. It made her wonder again whether she was mad. She went slowly down Wood Street and even more slowly past the expensive car parked in the bay. There were drifts of half-thawed hailstones under it still. As she passed behind it, Ann trailed a finger along the car's smooth side. It was cold and wet and shiny and hard—and very, very real. This was not just a fever dream she had imagined in the mirror. She *had* seen three men arrive here this morning.

She turned down the passage between the houses that led to the wood. It was beautiful down there, hot and steamy. Mum and her vests! Melting hailstones flashed rainbow colors from every blade of grass along the path. And the wood had gone quite green while she had been in bed—in the curious way woods do in early spring, with the bushes and lower branches a bright emerald thickness, while the upper boughs of the bigger trees were still almost bare and only a bit swollen in their outlines. It smelled warm and keen with juices, and the sunlight made the green transparent.

Ann had walked for some minutes in the direction of the farm wall when she realized there was something wrong with the wood. Not wrong exactly. It still stretched around her in peaceful arcades of greenness. Birds sang. Moss grew shaggy on the path under her sneakers. There were primroses in the bank beside her.

"Here, *wait* a minute!" she said.

The paths in Banners Wood were *always* muddy, with Coke rings trodden into them. And if a primrose had dared show its face there, it would have been picked or trampled on the spot. *And* she should have reached the farm wall long ago. Even more important, she should have been able to see the houses on the other side of the trees by now.

Ann strained her eyes to where those houses should have been. Nothing. Nothing but trees or green springing hawthorn and, in the distance, a bare tree carrying load upon load of tiny pink flowers. Ann took the path toward that tree, with her heart banging. Such a tree had never been seen in Banners Wood before. But she told herself she was mistaking it for the pussy willow on the other side of the stream.

She knew she was not, even before she came up beside the big leaden-looking container half buried in the bank beyond the primroses. She could see far enough from beside this container to know that the wood simply went on, and on, and on, beyond the pink tree. She stopped and looked at the container. People often did throw rubbish in the wood. Martin had had wonderful fun with an old pram someone had dumped here. This thing looked as if someone had thrown away a whole freezer—one of the big kind like a chest with a lid. It had been there a long time. Not only was it half buried in the bank, but its outside had rotted and peeled to a dull

gray. Wires came out of it in places, rusty and broken. It looked—
well—not really like a freezer, quite.

Mum's voice rang warnings in Ann's ears. "It's dirty . . . you
don't know where it's been . . . something could be rotting inside
it . . . it could be *nuclear!*"

It did look like a nuclear waste container.

What do you think? Ann asked her four imaginary friends.

To her great surprise, none of them answered. She had to imagine
their voices replying. The Boy would say, *Open it! Take a look!
You'd never forgive yourself if you didn't.* She imagined the others
agreeing, but more cautiously, and the King adding, *But be careful!*

Maybe it was the solution to the Hexwood Farm Mystery—the
thing that had fetched all those men to call on young Harrison, the
thing he thought so well of himself for guarding. Ann scrambled up
the bank, put the heels of her hands firmly into the crack under the
lid of the container, and heaved. The lid sprang up easily and then
went on rising of its own accord, until it was standing upright at the
back of the box.

Ann had not expected it to be that easy. It sent her staggering
back down the bank to the path. There she looked at the open
container and could not move for sheer terror.

A corpse was rising up out of it.

The head appeared first, a face that looked like a skull except for
long straggles of yellow-white hair and beard. Next, a hand clutched
the edge of the box, a hand white-yellow with enormous bone knobs
of knuckles and—disgustingly—inch-long yellow fingernails. Ann
gave a little whimper at this, but she still could not move. Then
there was heaving. A gaunt bone shoulder appeared. Breath whistled
from the lips of the skull. And the corpse dragged itself upright,
unfolding a long, long body grown all over with coarse tangles of
whitish hair. Absolutely indecent! Ann thought as the long, spindly
legs rose above her, shaking, and shaking loose the fragments of
rotted cloth wound round the creature's loins. It was very weak, this

corpse. For an instant Ann saw it as almost pathetic. And it was not quite a skeleton. Skin covered it, even the face, which was still far too like a skull for comfort.

The face turned. The eyes, large, sunk, and pale under a gray-yellow hedge of eyebrow, looked straight at Ann. The skull lips moved. The thing said something—croaked something—words in a strange language.

It had *seen* her. It was too much. It spoke. Ann ran. She scrambled into a turn and ran, and her hurtling sneakers slipped beneath her. She was down on the moss of the path, hardly aware of the sharp stone that met her knee, up again in the same breath, and running as fast as her legs could take her, away down the path. A corpse that walked, looked, spoke. A vampire in a lead chest—a *radioactive* vampire! She knew it was coming after her. *Fool* to keep to the path! She veered up the bank and ran on, crunching and galloping on squashy lichen, leaping among brambles, tearing through strident green thickets, with dead branches cracking and exploding under her feet. Her breath screamed. Her chest ached. She was ill. Fool. She was making so much *noise*. It could follow her just by listening.

"What shall I do? What shall I *do*?" she whimpered as she ran.

Her legs were giving way. After all that time in bed she was almost as weak as the vampire-thing. Her left knee hurt like crazy. She glanced down as she crashed through some flat brown briars to see bright red blood streaming down her shin and into her sock. There was blood in the brambles she stood in. It could track her by *smell*, too.

"What shall I *do*?"

The sensible thing was to climb a tree.

"Oh, I *couldn't*!" Ann gasped.

The creature croaked again, somewhere quite near.

Ann found strength she did not know she had. It sent her to the nearest climbable tree and swarming up it like a mad girl. Bark bit the insides of her legs. Her fingers scraped and clawed, breaking most of the fingernails she had been so proud of. She heard her nice anorak tear. But still she climbed, until she was able to thrust her head through a bush of smaller branches and scramble astride a strong bough, safe and high, with her back against the trunk and her hair raked into hanks across her face.

If it comes up, I can kick it down! she thought, and leaned back with her eyes shut.

It was croaking somewhere below, even nearer, to her right.

Ann's eyes sprang open. She stared down in weak horror at the path and the chest embedded in the bank beyond it. The lid had shut again. But the creature was still outside it, standing in the path almost below her, staring down at the scarlet splatter of blood Ann's knee had made when she fell on the stone. She had run in a circle like a panicked animal.

Don't look up! *Don't look up!* she prayed, and kept very still.

It did not look up. It was busy examining its taloned hands, then putting those hands up to feel the frayed bush of its hair and beard. Ann got the feeling it was very, very puzzled. She watched it take hold of the shreds of cloth wrapped round its skinny hips and pull off a piece to look at. It shook its head. Then, in a mad, precise way, it laid the strip of rag across its left shoulder and croaked out some more words. This time the sound was less of a croak and more like a voice.

Then—despite all the rest, Ann still had trouble believing her eyes—the creature grew itself clothes. The lower rags went expanding downward in two khaki waterfalls of thick cloth, to make narrow leggings and then brown supple-looking boots. At the same time the strip of rag on the corpse's shoulder was chasing downward, too, tumbling and spreading into a calf-length robe-thing, wide and pleated, the color of camel hair. Ann's lips parted almost in an exclamation as she saw the color. She watched, then, almost as if she had expected it, the long hair and beard turn the same camel hair color and shrink away. The beard shrank right away into the man's chin, leaving his face more skull-shaped than ever, but the hair halted just below his ears. He completed himself by strapping a broad belt round his waist—it had a knife and a pouch attached to it—and slinging a sort of rolled blanket across his left shoulder, where he carefully fastened it with straps. After that he gave a mutter of satisfaction and went to the edge of the path, where he drew the knife and cut himself a stout stick from the tree nearest the leaden chest.

Even before he moved, Ann was nearly sure who he was. The long, strolling strides with which he walked across the path made her quite certain. He was the tallest of the three men who had come in that car, the one who had made the gate open, the one in the odd camel hair coat. He was still wearing that coat, after a fashion, she thought, except he had made it into a robe.

He came back to the path, carrying the stick. It was no longer a stick, but a staff, old and polished and carved with curious signs. He looked up at Ann and croaked out a remark at her.

She recoiled against the tree trunk. Oh, my God! He knew I was here all along! And now *she* was the indecent one. Comes of climbing trees in a tight skirt. The skirt was rolled up round her waist. He must be looking straight up at her pants. And her long, helpless legs dangling down on either side of the branch.

The strange man below coughed, displeased with his voice, still staring up at Ann. His eyes were light, inside deep hollows. His eyebrows met over his nose, in one eyebrow shaped like a hawk flying. He was a weird-looking man, even if you met him in the ordinary way, walking down the street. You'd think, Ann thought, you'd run into the Grim Reaper.

"I'm sorry," she said, high-voiced with fear. "I—I can't understand a word you're saying—and I don't *want* to."

He looked startled. He thought. Gave another cough. "I apologize," he said. "I was using the wrong language. What I said was, I've no intention of hurting you. Won't you come down?"

They all say that! Mum's warning voice said in Ann's head. "No, I won't," Ann said. "And if you try to climb up, I shall kick you."

And she wondered frantically, How do I get out of this? I can't sit up here all day!

"Well, do you mind if I ask you a few questions?" asked the man. As Ann drew breath to say that she *did* mind, very much, he added quickly, "I've never been so puzzled in my life. What *is* this place?"

Now he was getting used to talking, he had quite a pleasant deep voice, with a slight foreign accent. Swedish? Ann wondered. And he did have every reason to be puzzled. There seemed no harm in telling him what little she knew. "What do you want to ask?" she said cautiously.

He cleared his throat again. "Can you tell me where we are? Where this is?" He gestured round at the green distances of the wood.

"Well," Ann said, "it *ought* to be the wood just beside Hexwood Farm, but it . . . seems to have gone bigger." As he seemed quite bewildered by this, she added, "But it's no use asking me *why* it's bigger. I can't understand it, either."

The man clicked his tongue and stared up at her impatiently. "I know about *that*. I could feel I was working with a field just now. Something nearby is creating a whole set of paratypical extensions—"

"You *what*?" said Ann.

"You'd probably call it," he said thoughtfully, "casting a spell."

"I would *not*!" Ann said indignantly. She might look absurd and indecent sitting dangling in this tree, but that didn't mean she was a moron! "I'm far too old to think anything so silly."

"Apologies," he said. "Then perhaps the best way to explain it is as quite a large hemisphere of a certain kind of force that has power to change reality. Does that help you?"

"Sort of," Ann admitted.

"Good," he said. "Now please explain where and what is Hexwood Farm."

"It's the old farm on our housing estate," Ann said. He looked bewildered again. The one eyebrow gathered in over his nose, and he leaned on his staff to stare about him. Ann thought he seemed wobbly and ill. Not surprising. "It's not a farm anymore, just a house," she explained. "About forty miles from London." He shook his head helplessly "In England, Europe, Earth, the solar system, the universe. You *must* know!" Ann said irritably. "You came here in a car this morning. I *saw* you . . . going into the farm with two other men!"

"Oh, no," he said, sounding faint and tired. "You're mistaken. I've been in stass sleep for centuries, for breaking the Reigners' ban." He turned and pointed a startlingly long finger at the chest half buried in the bank. "Now you have to believe that. You were standing here, where I am now, when I came out. I saw *you.*"

This was hard to deny, but Ann was sure enough of her facts to try, leaning earnestly down from her branch. "I know—I mean, I did see you, but I saw you before that, early this morning, walking in the road in modern clothes. I *swear* it was you! I knew by the way you walked."

The man below firmly shook his head. "No, it was not me you saw. It must have been a descendant of mine. I took care to have many descendants. It was—was one good way of breaking . . . that unjust ban." He put a hand to his forehead. Ann could see he was coming over queer. The staff was wobbling under his hand.

"Look," she said kindly, "if this—this sphere of force can change reality, couldn't it have changed *you* like it changed the wood?"

"No," he said. "There are some things that can't be changed. I am Mordion. I am from a distant world, and I was sent here under a ban." He used his staff to help him to the bank, where he sat down and covered his face shakily with one hand.

It reminded Ann of the weak way she had felt only yesterday. She was torn between sympathy for him and urgent worry about herself. Probably he was not sane. And her legs were going numb and needlish, the way legs do if they are left to dangle. "Why don't you," she said, thinking of the way she had wolfed down that pan of food, "get the force to change reality and send you something to eat? You must be hungry. If *I'm* right, you haven't eaten anything since it got light this morning. If *you're* right, you must be bloody ravenous!"

Mordion brought his skull of a face out of his hand. "What sound sense!" He raised his staff, then paused and looked up at Ann. "Would you like some food, too?"

"No, thanks. I have to be home for lunch," Ann said primly. While he was eating his boar's head, or whatever he got his thing-ummy field to send him, Ann was planning to slide down this tree and run—run like mad, in a straight line this time.

"As you please." Mordion made a sharp, angular gesture with his staff. Before he had half completed the movement, something square and white was following the gesture in the air. He brought the staff down in a smooth arc, and the square thing glided down with it and landed on the bank. "Hey presto!" Mordion said, looking up at Ann with a large smile.

Ann quite forgot to slide down the tree. The square thing was a plastic tray divided into compartments and covered with transparent film. That was the first amazing thing. The second amazing thing was that some of the food inside was bright blue. The third and most amazing thing, which really held Ann riveted to her branch, was that smile Mordion gave her. If a skull smiles, you expect something mirthless, with too many teeth in it. Mordion's smile was nothing like that. It was full of amusement and humor and friendship. It was glowing. It changed his face to something that made Ann's breath catch. She felt almost weak enough, seeing it, to topple off her branch. It was the most beautiful smile she had ever seen.

"It's—that's airplane food!" she said, and felt her face going red because of that smile.

Mordion stripped the transparent top off the tray. Steam rose into the dappled sunlight, and so did a most appetizing smell. "Not really," he said. "It's a stass tray."

"What's the blue stuff?" Ann could not help asking.

"Yurov keranip," he answered. His mouth was full of it. He had detached a spoon-thing from the side of the tray and was eating as if it were indeed centuries since he had last eaten. "A sort of root," he added, fetching a bread roll out and using it to help the spoon-thing. "This is bread. The pinkish things are collops from Iony in barinda sauce. The green is—I forget—a kind of seaweed, I think, fried, and the yellow is den beans in cheese. Underneath, there should be a dessert. I hope so, because I'm hungry enough to eat the tray if there isn't. I might spare you a taste if you care to come down, though it would be a wrench."

"No, thanks," Ann said. But since her legs were going really numb, she struggled one knee onto the branch and managed to pull herself up until she was standing, leaning against the tree trunk, with one arm draped comfortably over a higher branch. Like that, she could wriggle her skirt back down and feel almost respectable. The blood still streaked down her shin, but it was brown and shiny by then.

There *was* a dessert under the hot food. Ann watched, slightly wistfully, as Mordion lifted the top tray out the way you do with a box of chocolates. Underneath, it looked like ice cream, as mysteriously cold as the top course was hot. I am in a field of paratypical thingummies, Ann thought. *Anything* is possible. That ice cream looked luscious. There was a cup of hot drink in beside it.

Mordion tossed the spoon into the empty trays and took the cup up in both hands. "Ah," he said, sipping comfortably. "That's better. Now, I want to ask you something else. But, first, what's your name?"

"Ann," said Ann.

He looked up at her, puzzled again. "Really? I thought—somehow—it would be a longer name than that."

"Ann Stavely, if you insist," said Ann. She was certainly not going to tell him that her middle name was, hatefully, Veronica.

Mordion bowed to her over his steaming cup. "Mordion Agenos.

This is what I want to ask you: Will you help me to make another attempt to break the Reigners' ban?"

"It depends," Ann said. "What are rainers?"

"Those who rule," said Mordion. His face set into the grimmest of death's-heads. Above the steaming cup it looked terrible, particularly surrounded by the bright spring woodland, full of the green of life and the chirping of nesting birds. "There are five of them, and though they live light-years across the galaxy, they rule every inhabited world, including this one."

"What—even inside this thingummy field?" Ann asked.

Mordion thought. "No," he said. "No. I am almost sure not. This seems to be one reason why it came into my head to try to break their ban again."

"Are the Reigners very terrible?" Ann asked, watching his face.

"Terrible?" Mordion said. She saw hatred and horror working under his grimness. "That's too small a word. But yes. Very terrible."

"And what's this ban they put on you?"

"Exile. And I am not to go against the Reigners in any way." Looking up at her from under his long wings of eyebrow, Mordion had a sinister unearthliness. Ann shivered as he said, "You see, I'm of Reigner blood, too. I could defeat them if I were free. I nearly did, twice, long ago. That was why they put me in stass."

Ann thought, Humor him, or I'll never get out of this tree. "So how do you want me to help?"

"Give me permission to make use of your blood," Mordion said.

"What?" Ann backed against the trunk of the tree and pressed farther against it when Mordion pointed to the place in the path where she had fallen over. It had not dried up like the blood on her leg. Down there it was bright red and moist. There seemed to be an awful lot of it, too, spreading luridly among the green mosses and splashed scarlet on the white stone that had cut her. It looked almost as if something had been killed there.

"The field is waiting to work with it," Mordion told her. "It was the first thing I noticed after you ran away."

"What for? How?" Ann said. "I don't agree to anything!"

"Perhaps if I explain." Mordion stood up and strolled over to a spot just under Ann's branch. She felt sick and tried to back even farther. She could see the buds on the end of her branch shaking in front of Mordion's upturned face. She felt as if she were making the whole tree shake. "What was done in the past," Mordion said, "was to get round the Reigners' ban by breeding a race of men and women who were not under the ban and could go against the Reigners—"

"*I'm not doing that!*" Ann almost screamed.

"Of course not." Mordion smiled. The smile was brief and sad, but as wonderful as before. "I've learned my lesson there. It took far too long, and it ended in misery. The Reigners eliminated the first race of people. The second time there were too many to kill, so they killed the best and put me in stass so that I was not there to guide the others. There must be hundreds of their descendants now with Reigner blood, here in this world. *You*, for instance. That's what the paratypical field is showing us." He pointed once more to the bright blood in the path.

In spite of her fear and disgust and complete disbelief, Ann could not help a twinge of pride that her blood was so special. "So what do you want it for this time?"

"To create a hero," said Mordion, "safe from the Reigners inside this field, who is human and not human, who can defeat the Reigners because they will not know about him until it is too late."

Ann thought about it—or, to be truthful, let her head fill with a mixed hurry of feelings. Disbelief and fear mixed with a terrible sadness for Mordion, who thought he was trying the same useless thing for a third time, and horror, because Mordion just might be right, while underneath ran urgent, ordinary, homely feelings, telling her she really did have to be back for lunch. "If I say yes," she said, "you can't touch me and you have to let me go home safe straight afterward."

"Agreed." Mordion looked earnestly up at her. "You agree?"

"Yes, all right," Ann said, and felt the most terrible coward saying it. But what could she do, she asked herself, stuck up in a tree in a place where everything was mad, with Mordion prowling round its roots?

Mordion smiled at her again. Ann was lapped in the sweetness and friendliness of it and weakened in her already wobbly knees. But a small clinical piece of her said, He *uses* that smile. She watched him turn and stroll to the patch of blood, with his pleated robe swinging elegantly round him, and wondered how he thought he would create a hero. His knife was in his right hand. It caught the green woodland light as he made a swift, expert cut in the wrist of his other hand, which was holding his staff. Blood ran freely, in the same unexpected quantity as Ann's.

"Hey!" Ann said. Somehow she had not expected *this*.

Mordion did not seem to hear her. He was letting his blood trickle down his staff, round and among the strange carvings on it, guiding the thick flow to drip off the wooden end and mingle with Ann's blood on the path. He was certainly also working on the paratypical field. Ann had a sense of things pulsing, and twisting a little, just out of sight.

Mordion finished and stood back. Everything was still. Not a tree moved. No birds sang. Ann was not sure she breathed.

A strange welling and mounding began on the path, on either side of the patch of blood. Ann had seen water behave that way when someone had thrown a log in deep and the log was rising to the surface. She leaned forward and watched, still barely breathing, moss and black earth, stones and yellow roots pouring up and aside to let something rise up from underneath. There was a glimpse of white, bone white, about four feet long, and a snarl at one end of what looked like hair. Ann bit her lip till it hurt. Next second a bare body had risen, lying face downward in a shallow furrow in the path. A fairly small body.

"You must give him clothes," she said while she waited for the body to grow.

Out of the corner of her eye she saw Mordion nod and move his staff. The body grew clothes, the same way as Mordion had done, in a blue-purple flush spreading over the dented white back and thickening into what looked like a tracksuit. The bare feet turned gray and became feet wearing old sneakers. The body squirmed, shifted, and propped itself up on its elbows, facing down the path away from both of them. It had longish, draggly hair the same camel color as Mordion's.

"Bump. Fell," the body remarked in a high, clear voice.

Then, obviously assuming he had tripped and fallen in the path, the boy in the tracksuit picked himself up and trotted out of sight beyond the pink blossoming tree.

Mordion stood back and looked up at Ann. His face had dragged into lines. Making the boy had clearly tired him out. "There, it's done," he said wearily, and went to sit among the primroses again.

"Aren't you going to go after him?" Ann asked.

Mordion shook his head.

"Why *not?*" said Ann.

"I told you," Mordion said, very tired, "that I learned my lesson there. It's between him and the Reigners now, when he grows up. I shall not need to appear in it."

"And how long before he grows up?" Ann asked.

Mordion shrugged. "I'm not sure how time in this field relates to ordinary time. I suppose it will take awhile."

"And what happens if he goes out of this parathingummy field," Ann demanded, "into real time?"

"He'll cease to exist," said Mordion, as if it were obvious.

"Then how ever is he supposed to conquer these Reigners? You told me they live light-years away," Ann said.

"He'll have to fetch them here," said Mordion. He lay back on the bank, looking worn out.

"Does he *know* that?" Ann demanded.

"Probably not," Mordion said.

Ann looked down at him, spread on the bank, preparing to go to sleep, and lost her temper. "Then you should go and *tell* him! You should look *after* him! He's all alone in this wood, and he's quite small, and he doesn't even know he's not supposed to go out of it. He probably doesn't even know how to work the field to get food. You—you calmly make him up, out of blood and—and *nothing*, and you expect him to do your dirty work for you, and you don't even tell him the *rules*! You can't *do* that to a person!"

Mordion rose up on one elbow. "The field will take care of him. He belongs to it. Or *you* could. He's half yours after all."

"I have to go home for *lunch*!" Ann snarled. "You know I do! Is there anyone else in this wood who could take care of him?"

Mordion was getting that look Dad had when Ann went on at him. "I'll see," he said, clearly hoping to shut her up. He sat up and raised his head in a listening way, turning slowly from left to right. Like radar operating, Ann thought. "There *are* others here," he said slowly, "but they are a long way off and too busy to be spared."

"Then get the field," said Ann, "to make another person."

"That," said Mordion, "would take more blood—and that person would be a child, too."

"Then someone who isn't real," insisted Ann. "I *know* the field can do it. This whole wood isn't real. You're not real—"

She stopped, because Mordion turned and looked at her. The pain in his look almost rocked her backward.

"Well, only *half* real," she said. "And stop looking at me like that just because I'm telling you the truth. You think you're a magician with godlike powers, and I know you're just a man in a camel hair coat."

"And you," said Mordion, not quite angry, but getting that way, "are very brave because you think you're safe up a tree. What makes you think my godlike powers can't fetch you down?"

"You can't touch me," Ann said hastily. "You promised."

The earlier grim look came back into Mordion's face. "There are many ways," he said, "to hurt a person without touching them. I hope you never find out about them." He stared into grim thoughts for a while, with his eyebrow hooked above his strange flat nose. Then he sighed. "The boy is fine," he said. "The field has obeyed you and produced an unreal person to care for him." He lay back on the bank again and arranged the rolled blanket thing at his shoulder as a pillow.

"Really?" said Ann.

"The field doesn't like you shouting at it any more than I do," Mordion replied sleepily. "Get down from your tree, and go in peace."

He rolled on his side and seemed to go to sleep, a strange bleached heap huddled on the bank. The only color about him was the red gash on his wrist, above the hand clutching his staff.

Ann waited in her tree until his breathing was slow and regular and she was sure he was really asleep. Only then did she go round to the back of the tree and slide down as quietly as she knew how. She got to the path with long, tiptoe strides and sprinted away down it, still on tiptoe. And she was still afraid that Mordion might be stealing after her. She looked back so frequently that after fifty yards she ran into a tree.

She met it with a bruising thump that seemed to shake reality back into place. When she looked forward, she found she could see the houses on the near side of Wood Street. When she looked backward to check, she could see houses again, beyond the usual sparse trees of Banners Wood. And there was no sign of Mordion among them.

"Well, that's that then!" she said. Her knees began to shake.

PART
TWO

—1—

THERE WERE STILL hailstones under the big gray car, but they were melting as Ann hastened past on her way to the path to Banners Wood. She did not stop for fear Mum or Dad called her back. She admitted that setting out to climb a tree in a tight skirt probably *was* silly, but that was her own business. Besides, it was so hot. The path was steamy warm, full of melting hailstones winking like diamonds in the grass. It was a relief to get into the shade of the wood.

Grass almost never grew on the trampled earth under the trees, but spring had been at work here all the same while Ann had been ill. Shiny green weeds grew at the edges of the trodden parts. Birds yelled in the upper branches, and there was a glorious smell in here, part cool and earthy, part distant and sweet like the ghost of honey. The blackthorn thicket near the stream was actually trying to bloom, little white flowers all over the spiny, leafless bushes. The path wound through them. Ann wound with the path, pushing through, with her arms up to cover her face. Before long the path was completely blocked by the bushes, but when she dropped to a crouch, she could see a way through, snaking among the roots.

She crawled.

Spines caught her hair. She heard her anorak tear, but it seemed silly to go back, or at least just as spiny. She crawled on toward the light where the bushes ended.

She reached the light. It was a swimming, milky lightness, fogged with green. It took Ann a second of staring to recognize that the lightness was water. Water stretched to an impossible distance in front of her, in smooth gray-white ripples that vanished into fog. Dark trees beside her bowed over rippled copies of themselves, and there was one yellow-green willow beyond, smudging the lake with lime.

Ann looked from the foggy distance to the water gently rippling by her knees. Inside her black reflection there were old leaves, black as tea leaves. The bank where she was kneeling was overgrown with violets, violets pale blue, white, and dark purple, spread everywhere in impossible profusion, like a carpet. The scent made her quite giddy.

"Impossible," she said aloud. "I don't remember a lake."

"I don't, either," said Hume, kneeling under the willow. "It's new."

Hume's tracksuit was so much the color of the massed violets that Ann had not seen him before. She had a moment when she was not sure who he was. But his brown, shaggy hair, his thin face, and the way his cheekbones stuck out were all quite familiar. Of course, he was Hume. It was one of the times when he was about ten years old.

"What's making the ripples?" Hume said. "There's no wind."

Hume never stops asking things, Ann thought. She searched out over the wide, milky water. There was no way of telling how wide. Her eye stopped with a gentle white welling in the more distant water. She pointed. "There. There's a spring coming up through the lake."

"Where? Oh, I see it," Hume said, pointing, too.

They were both pointing out across the lake as the fog cleared, dimly. For just an instant they were pointing to the milky gray silhouette of a castle, far off on a distant shore. Steep roof, pointed turrets, and the square teeth of battlements rose beside the graceful round outline of a tower. The chalky shapes of flags flapped lazily from tower and roofs, all without color. Then the fog rolled in again and hid it all.

"What was *that?*" asked Hume.

"The castle," said Ann, "where the king lives with his knights and his ladies. The ladies wear beautiful clothes. The knights ride out in armor, having adventures and fighting."

Hume's thin face glowed. "I know! The castle is where the real action is. I'm going to tell Mordion I've seen it."

Hume had this way of knowing things before she told him, Ann thought, gathering a small bunch of the violets. Mum would love them, and there were so *many*. Sometimes it turned out that Hume had asked Yam, but sometimes, confusingly, Hume said she had told him before. "The castle's not the only place where things happen," she said.

"Yes, but I want to get there," Hume said yearningly. "I'd wade out through the lake or try to swim if I knew I could get there. But I bet it wouldn't be there when I got across the lake."

"It's enchanted," said Ann. "You have to be older to get there."

"I *know*," Hume said irritably. "But then I shall be a knight and kill the dragon."

Ann's private opinion was that Hume would do better being a sorcerer, like Mordion. Hume was good at that. She would have given a great deal herself to learn sorcery. "You might not enjoy it at the castle," she warned him, plucking the best-shaped leaves to arrange round her violets. "If you want to fight, you'd be better off joining Sir Artegal and his outlaws. My dad says Sir Artegal's a proper knight."

"But they're outlaws," Hume said, dismissing Sir Artegal. "I'm going to be a lawful knight at the castle. Tell me what they say about the castle in the village."

"I don't know much," Ann said. She finished arranging her leaves and wrapped a long piece of grass carefully round the stalks of her posy. "I think there are things they don't want me to hear. They whisper when they talk about the king's bride. You see, because the king is ill with his wound that won't heal, some of the others are much too powerful. There's quarreling and secrecy and taking sides."

"Tell me about the *knights*," Hume said inexorably.

"There's Sir Bors," said Ann. "He prays a lot, they say. Nobody likes Sir Fors. But they quite like Sir Bedefer, even if he is hard on his soldiers. They say he's honest. Sir Harrisoun is the one everyone really hates."

Hume considered this, with one tracksuited knee up under his chin, staring into the mist across the rippling lake. "When I've killed the dragon, I'll turn them all out and be the king's Champion."

"You have to get there first," Ann said, beginning to get up.

Hume sighed. "Sometimes," he said, "I hate living in an enchanted wood."

Ann sighed, too. "You don't know your own luck! I have to be home for lunch. Are you staying here?"

"For now," said Hume. "The mist might clear again."

Ann left him there, kneeling among the violets, looking out into the fog as if that glimpse of the castle had somehow broken his heart. As she crawled through the thorn brake, carefully protecting her bunch of violets in one cupped hand, she felt fairly heartbroken herself. Something impossibly beautiful seemed to have been taken away from her. She was almost crying as she crawled out from the bushes onto the mud path and stood up to trot toward the houses. And on top of it all she had torn her anorak *and* her skirt, and she seemed to have quite a large cut in her knee.

"Hey, *wait* a minute!" she said, halting in the passage between the houses. She had cut that knee running away from Mordion. She looked from the dried blood flaking off her shin to the small bunch of violets in her hand. "Did I go into the wood *twice* then?"

I don't think so, said the Boy. *I lost you.*

You went out of touch when you went into that wood, explained the Prisoner.

Yes, but did I go in and come out and go in again? Ann asked them.

No, they said, all four of her imaginary people, and the King added, *You only went in once this morning.*

"Hmm." Ann almost doubted them as she limped slowly up the passage and into Wood Street. But the big gray car was still in the parking bay. There were other cars around it now, but when Ann bent down, she could still see just a few hailstones, fused into a melting lump behind the near front wheel where the sun had not been able to reach.

That much is real, she thought, crossing the street slantwise toward Stavely Greengrocer.

In front of the shop she stopped and looked at boxes of lettuce and bananas and flowers out on the pavement. One of the boxes was packed full of little posies of violets, just like the one in her hand. Very near to tears, Ann poked her own bunch in among them before she went inside for lunch.

2

MORDION WAS WORKING hard, trying to build a shelter and keep a watch on Hume at the same time. Hume would keep scrambling down the steep rocks to the river. He seemed fascinated by the fish traps Mordion had made in the pool under the waterfall. Mordion was not sure how it had come about that he was in charge of such a small child, but he knew Hume was a great deal too young to be trusted not to fall into the river and drown. Every few minutes Mordion was forced to go bounding down after Hume. Once he was only just in time to catch Hume by one chubby arm as Hume cartwheeled slowly off a slippery stone at the edge of the deep pool.

"Play with the pretty stones I found you," Mordion said.

"I did," said Hume. "They went in the water."

Mordion towed Hume up the rocks to the cave beneath the pine tree. This was where he was trying to build the shelter. It felt like the hundredth time he had towed Hume up here. "Stay up *here*, where it's safe," he said. "Here. Here's some pieces of wood. Make a house."

"I'll make a boat," Hume offered.

And fall in the river for certain! Mordion thought. He tried cunning. "Why not make a cart? You can make roads for it in the earth here, and—and I'll carve you a wooden horse for it when I've built this shelter."

Hume considered this. "All right," he said at last, doing Mordion a great favor.

For a time then there was peace, if you did not count the thumping as Hume endeavored to beat his piece of wood into a cart shape. Mordion went back to building. He had planted a row of uprights in front of the cave and hammered stakes in among the rocks above the cave. Now he was trying to lash beams between the two to make a roof. It was a good idea, but it did not seem to be working. Bracken and grass did not make good rope.

While he worked, Mordion wondered at the way he felt so responsible for Hume. A small child was a real nuisance. Centuries of stass had not prepared Mordion for this constant need to dash after Hume and stop him from killing himself. He felt worn out. Several times he had almost given up and thought, Oh, let him drown!

But that was wrong and bad. Mordion was surprised how strongly he felt that. He could not let a small stray boy come to harm. Oh, what does it matter why? he thought, angrily pushing his roof back upright. His poles showed a willful desire to slant sideways. They did it oftener when Mordion tried to balance spreading fir boughs on top to make a roof. The whole thing would have collapsed by now but for the long iron nails that, for some reason, kept turning up among his pile of wood. Though he felt this was cheating, Mordion took a nail and hammered it into the ground next to another pole every time his roof slanted. By now each upright stood in a ring of nails. Suppose he were to lash the poles and nails around with bracken rope—

"Look," Hume said happily. "I made my cart."

Mordion turned round. Hume was beaming and holding out a lump of wood with two of the nails hammered through it. On both ends of each nail were round slices that Mordion had cut off the ends of his poles when he was getting them the right length. Mordion stared at it ruefully. It was far more like a cart than his building was like a house.

"Don't carts look like this?" Hume asked doubtfully.

"Oh, yes. Haven't you ever seen one?" Mordion said.

"No," Hume said. "I made it up. Is it very wrong?"

In that case, Mordion realized, Hume was a genius. He had just reinvented the wheel. This was certainly a good reason for caring for Hume. "No, it's a beautiful cart," Mordion said kindly. Hume beamed so happily at this that Mordion found himself almost as pleased as Hume was. To give such pleasure with so few words! "What made you think of the nails?" he asked.

"I just asked for something to fasten the rings of wood on with," Hume explained.

"Asked?" said Mordion.

"Yes," said Hume. "You can ask for things. They fall on the ground in front of you."

So Hume had discovered this queer way you could cheat, too, Mordion thought. This explained the nails in the woodpile—possibly. And while he thought about this, Hume said, "My cart's a boat, too," and set off at a trot toward the river again.

Mordion dived and caught him by the back of his tracksuit just as Hume walked off the edge of the high rocks. "Can't you be careful?" he said, trying to drag Hume more or less out of the sky. They were both hanging out over the river.

Hume windmilled his arms so that Mordion all but lost his grip on the tracksuit. "Hallo, Ann!" he yelled. "Ann, come and look at my cart! Mordion's made a *house*!"

Down below, Mordion was surprised and pleased to see, Ann was jumping cautiously across the river from rock to rock. When Hume shouted, she balanced on a boulder and looked up. She seemed as surprised as Mordion, but not nearly so pleased. He felt rather hurt. Ann shouted, but it was lost in the rushing of the waterfall.

"Can't *hear* you, Ann!" Hume screamed.

Ann had realized that. She made the last two leaps across this foaming river, where there had only been a trickling stream before, and came scrambling up the cliff. "What's going on?" she panted, rather accusingly.

"What do you mean?" Mordion set Hume down at a safe distance from the drop-off. He had, Ann saw, grown a small, curly camel-colored beard. It made his face far less like a skull. With the beard and the pleated robe, he reminded her of a monk or a pilgrim. But Hume! Hume was so small—only five years old at the most!

Hume was clamoring for Ann to admire his cart, holding it up and wagging it in her face. Ann took it and looked at it. "It's a Stone Age roller skate," she said. "You ought to make two—unless it's a very small skateboard."

"He invented it himself," Mordion said proudly.

"And Mordion invented a house!" Hume said, equally proudly.

Ann looked from the cart to the slanting poles of the house. To her mind, there was not much to choose between the two, but she supposed that Hume and Mordion were both having to learn.

"We started by sheltering in the cave," Mordion explained, a little self-consciously, "but it was very cold and rather small. So I thought I'd build onto it."

As he pointed to the dank little hole in the rocks behind the shelter, Ann saw that there was a dark red slash on his wrist, just beginning to look puckered and sore. That's where he cut himself to make Hume, she thought. Then she thought, Hey, what's going on? That cut was slightly less well healed than the cut on her own knee. Ann could feel the soreness and the drag of the Band-Aid under the jeans she had sensibly decided to wear this afternoon. But Mordion had had time to grow a beard.

"I know it gives a whole new meaning to the word *lean-to,*" Mordion said apologetically. He was hurt and puzzled. Just like

Hume, he thought of Ann as a good friend from the castle estate. Yet here she was looking grave, unfriendly, and decidedly sarcastic. "What's the matter?" he asked her. "Have I offended you?"

"Well—" said Ann. "Well, last time I saw Hume he was twice the size he is now."

Mordion pulled his beard, wrestling with a troublesome itch of memory when he looked at Hume. Hume was pulling Ann's sleeve and saying, like the small boy he was, "Ann, come and see my sword Mordion made me, and my funny log. And the nets in the water to catch fish."

"Hush, Hume," Mordion told him. "Ann, he was this size when I found him wandering in the wood."

"But you said, if I remember rightly, that you weren't going to bother to look after him," Ann said. "What changed your mind?"

"Surely I never would have said—" Mordion began. But the itch of memory changed to a stab. He knew he *had* said something like that, though it seemed now as if he must have said it in another time and place entirely. The stab of memory brought with it sunlit spring woodland, a flowering Judas tree, and Ann's face, smudged and green-lit, staring at him with fear, horror, and anger. From somewhere high up. "Forgive me," he said. "I never meant to frighten— You know, something seems to be playing tricks with my memory."

"The paratypical field," Ann said, staring up at him expectantly.

"Oh!" said Mordion. She was right. Both fields were very strong, and one was also very subtle and so deft at keeping itself unnoticed that with the passing of the weeks, he had forgotten it was there. "I let myself get caught in it," he confessed. "As to—as to what I said about Hume—well—I'd never in my life had to care for anyone—" He stopped, because now that Ann had made him aware his memory was wrong, he knew this was not quite the case. At some time, somewhere, he *had* cared for someone, several someones, children like Hume. But this stab of memory hurt so deeply that he was not prepared to think of it, except to be honest with Ann. "That's not quite true," he admitted. "But I knew what it would be like. He can be a perfect little pest."

Hume just then cast down a bundle of his treasures at Ann's feet, shouting at her to look at them. Ann laughed. "I see what you mean!" She squatted down beside Hume and inspected the wooden sword and the log that looked rather like a crocodile—a dragon, Hume insisted—and fingered the stones with holes in. As she inspected the doll-thing that Mordion had dressed with a piece torn from his robe, she realized that she approved of Mordion far more than she had expected to. Mum had tried to make her stay at home to rest, but Ann had set out to find Hume and look after him. It had been a shock to find Mordion was already doing so. But she had to admit that Mordion had really been trying. There were still strange—and frightening—things about him, but some of that was his looks, and the rest was probably the paratypical field at work. It *made* things queer, this field.

"Tell you what, Hume," she said. "Let's us two go for a walk and give Mordion a bit of a holiday."

It was as if she had given Mordion a present. The smile lit his face as she got up and led Hume away. Hume was clamoring that he knew a *real place* to walk to. "I could use a holiday," Mordion said through the clamor. It was heartfelt. Ann felt undeserving because she knew that as presents go, it was not much better than a log that looked like a crocodile.

As soon as Ann had towed Hume out of sight, Mordion, instead of getting on with his house, sat on one of the smooth brown rocks under the pine tree. He leaned back on the tree's rough, gummy trunk, feeling like someone who had not had a holiday in years. Absurd! Centuries of half-life in stass were like a long night's sleep, but he was sure he had had dreams, appalling dreams. And the one thing he was certain of was that he had longed, with every fiber of his body, to be free. But the way he felt now, bone-tired, mind-tired, was surely the result of looking after Hume.

Yes, Ann was right. Hume *had* been bigger at one time. When?

How? Mordion groped after it. The subtler of the two paratypical fields kept pushing in, and trying spread vagueness over his mind. He *would* remember this. Woodland . . . Ann looking horrified—

It came to him. First it was blood, splashed on moss and dripping down his hand. Then it was a furrow in the ground, opening to show a bone-white body and a tangle of hair. Mordion contemplated it. What had he *done*? True, the field had pushed him to it, but it was one of the few things he knew he could have resisted. He must have been a little mad, coming from that coffin to find himself a skeleton, but that was no excuse. And he had a very real grudge against the Reigners, but that was no excuse, either. It was not right to create another human being to do one's dirty work. He had been mad, playing God.

He looked at the cut on his wrist. He shuddered and was about to heal it with an impatient thought, but he stopped himself. This had better stay—*had* to stay—to remind him what he owed to Hume. He owed it to Hume to bring him up as a normal person. Even when Hume was grown up, he must never, never know that Mordion had made him as a sort of puppet. And, Mordion thought, he would have to find a way to deal with the Reigners for himself. There *had* to be a way.

—3

ANN LED HUME away, hoping that the weirdness of this place would cause Hume to grow older once Mordion was out of sight. It would be confusing, but she knew she would prefer it. Small Hume kept asking questions, questions. If she did not answer, he tugged her hand and shouted the question. Ann was not sure she *should* tell him the answers to some of the things he asked. She wished she knew more about small children. She ought to, she supposed, having a brother two years younger than she was, but she could not remember what Martin had been like at this age at all. Surely Martin had never kept *asking* things this way.

They crunched their way up a hillside of dry bracken, littered with twisted small thorn trees, and before they were anywhere near the top, Ann found she had explained to Hume in detail the way babies were made.

"And that was how I was made, was it?" asked Hume.

This was one of the times he pulled Ann's arm and kept shouting the question. "No," Ann said at last, mostly out of pure harassment. "No. You were made out of a spell Mordion worked out of my blood and his blood." Then Hume pulled her arm and shouted again, until she described it to him, just as it had happened. "So you got up and ran away without noticing either of us," she finished as they came to the top of the hill. By this time she was resigned to the paratypical field's keeping Hume as he was.

As they entered woodland again, Hume thought about what he had been told. "Aren't I a proper person, then?" he asked mournfully.

Now she had damaged Hume's mind! Ann wished all over again that the field had made Hume older. "Of *course* you are!" she told Hume, with the huge heartiness of guilt. "You're very particularly special, that's all." Since Hume was still looking tearful and dubious, Ann went on in a hurry: "Mordion *needs* you badly, to kill some terrible people called Reigners for him when you grow up. He can't kill them himself, you see, because they've banned him from it. But *you* can."

Hume was interested in this. He cheered up. "Are they dragons?"

"No," said Ann. Hume really was obsessed with dragons. "People."

"I shall bang their heads on a stone, then, like Mordion does with the fish," Hume said. Then he let go of Ann and ran ahead through the trees, shouting, "Here's the place! Hurry up, Ann! It's inciting!"

When Ann caught him up, Hume was forcing his way through

a giant thicket of those whippy bushes that fruit squishy white balls in summer. Snowball bushes, Ann always called them. They were almost bare now, except for a few green tips. She could clearly see the stones of an old wall beyond them. Now what's this? she wondered. Has the field made the castle a ruin?

"Come *on!*" Hume screeched from inside the bushes. "I can't get it *open!*"

"Coming!" Ann forced her way in among the thicket, ducking and pushing, until she arrived against the wall. Hume was impatiently jumping up and down in front of an old, old wooden door.

"Open it!" he commanded.

Ann put her hand on the old rusty knob, turned it, pulled, rattled, and was just deciding the door was locked when she discovered it opened inward. She put her shoulder to the blistered panels and pushed. Hume hindered in a helping way. And the door groaned and scraped and finally came half open, which was enough to let them both slip through. Hume shot inside with a squeal of excitement. Ann stepped after more cautiously.

She stopped in astonishment. There was an ancient farmhouse beyond, standing in a walled garden of chest-high weeds. The house was derelict. Part of its roof had fallen in, and a dead tree had toppled across the empty rafters. The chimney at the end Ann could see was smothered in ivy, which had pulled a pipe away from the wall. When her eyes followed the pipe down, they found the water butt it had drained into broken and spread like a mad wooden flower. The place was full of a damp, hot silence, with just a faint cheeping of birds.

Ann knew the shape of that roof *and* the shape the chimney should be inside the ivy. She had looked at both every day for most of her life—except that the roof was not broken and there were no trees near enough to fall on it. Now look *here!* she thought. What's Hexwood Farm doing *here?* It should be on the other side of the stream—river—whatever. And why is it all so ruined?

Hume meanwhile charged into the high weeds, shouting, "This

is a real *place!*" Shortly he was yelling at Ann to come and see what he had found. Ann shrugged. It had to be the paratypical field again. She went to see the rusty kettle Hume had found. It had a robin's nest in it. After that she went to see the old boot he had found, then the clump of blue irises, then the window that was low enough for Hume to look through into the farmhouse. That find was more interesting. Ann lingered, staring through the cracked, dusty panes at the rotted remains of red-and-white-checked curtains, past a bottle of detergent swathed in cobwebs, to a stark old kitchen. There were empty shelves and a table with what looked like the mortal remains of a loaf on it—unless it was fungus.

Does it *really* look like this? she wondered. Or newer?

Hume was yelling again. "Come and see what *I've* found!"

Ann sighed. This time Hume was rooting in the tall tangle of greenbriers over by the main gate. When Ann made her way over, he was on tiptoe, hanging on to two greenbrier whips that had thorns on them like tiger claws. "You'll get scratched," she said.

"There's a window in here, too!" Hume said, hauling on the briars excitedly.

Ann did not believe him. To prove he must be wrong, she wrapped her sweater over her fist and shoved a swath of green thorny branches aside. Inside, to her great surprise, there were the rusty remains of a white car hood, and a tall windscreen dimly glinting beyond. Too tall for a car. A van of some kind. *Wait* a minute! She went farther along the tangle and used both fists, wrapped in both sweater sleeves, to heave more green whips aside.

"What is it?" Hume wanted to know.

"Er—a kind of cart, I think," Ann said as she heaved.

"Stupid. Carts don't have windows," Hume told her scornfully, and wandered off, disappointed in her.

Ann stared at the side of a once-white van. It was covered with running trickles of brown rust. Further, redder rust erupted through the paint like boils. But the blue logo was still there. A weighing scale with two round pans, one higher than the other.

It is *a balance*, she said to her four imaginary people.

There was no reply. After a moment, when she felt hurt, angry, and lost, Ann remembered that they had lost her this morning when she went into the wood. Ridiculous! she thought. Behaving as if they were real! But I can tell them later when I come out. So—

Using forearms and elbows as well as fists, she heaved away more briers until she could stamp them down underfoot. Words came into view, small and blue and tasteful. RAYNER HEXWOOD INTERNATIONAL and, in smaller letters, MAINTENANCE DIVISION (EUROPE).

"Well, *that* leaves me none the wiser!" Ann said. Yet for some reason, the sight of that name made her feel cold. Cold, small, and frightened. "Anyway, how did it get this way in just a fortnight?" she said.

"Ann! *Ann!*" Hume screamed from round the house somewhere.

Something was wrong! Ann jumped clear of the van and the briers and raced off in Hume's direction. He was in the corner of the garden walls beyond the water butt, jumping up and down. So sure was Ann that something was wrong that she grabbed Hume's shoulders and turned him this way and that, looking for blood, or a bruise, or maybe a snakebite. "Where do you hurt? What's happened?"

Hume had worked himself into such a state of excitement that he could hardly speak. He pointed to the corner. "In there—look!" he gulped, with a mixture of joy and distress that altogether puzzled Ann.

There was a heap of rubbish in the corner. It had been there so long that elder trees had grown up through it, making yet another whippy thicket. "Just rubbish," Ann said soothingly.

"No—*there!*" said Hume. "At the *bottom!*"

Ann looked and saw a pair of metal feet with spongy soles sticking out from under the mound of mess. Her stomach jolted. A corpse now! "Someone's thrown away an old suit of armor," she said, trying to draw Hume gently away. Or suppose it was only the *legs* of a corpse. She felt sick.

Hume would not be budged. "They *moved,*" he insisted. "I *saw.*"

Surely not? This heap of rubbish could not have been disturbed for years, or the elder trees would not be growing there. Horror fizzed Ann's face and hurt her back. Her eyes could not leave those two square-toed metal feet. And she saw one twitch. The left one. "Oh, dear," she said.

"We've got to unbury him," said Hume.

Ann's instinct was to run for help, but she supposed the sensible thing was to find out the worst before she did. She and Hume climbed up among the elders and set to work prizing and heaving at the earthy mess. They threw aside iron bars, bicycle wheels, sheet metal, logs that crumbled to wet white pulp in their fingers, and then dragged away the remains of a big mattress. Everything smelled. But the strong sappy odor of the elders seemed to Ann to smell worst of all. Like armpits, she thought. Or worse, a dead person. Hume irritated her by saying excitedly, over and over, "*I* know what it's going to be!" as if they were unwrapping a present. Ann would have snapped at him to shut up, except that she, too, under the horror, had a feeling she knew what they would find.

Moving the mattress revealed metal legs attached to the feet and, beyond that, glimpses of the whole suit of armor. Ann felt better. She sprang up the mound again with Hume and dug frenziedly. An elder tree toppled. "Sorry!" Ann gasped at it. She knew you should be polite to elder trees. As it fell, the tree tore away a landslide of broken cups, tins, and old paper, leaving a cave with a red-eyed suit of armor lying in it under what looked like a railway crosstie.

"*Yam!*" Hume yelled, sliding about in the rubbish above. "Yam, are you all right?"

"Thank you. I am functional still," the suit of armor replied in a deep, monotonous voice. "Stand clear, and I will be able to free myself now."

Ann retreated hastily. A robot! she thought. I don't believe this! Except that I *do,* somehow. Hume leaped down beside her, shaking with excitement. They watched the robot brace its silver arms on the railway crosstie and push. The timber swung sideways, and the whole rubbish heap changed shape. The robot sat up among the elder trees. Very slowly, creaking and jangling rather, it got its silver legs under itself and stood up, swaying.

"Thank you for releasing me," it said. "I am only slightly damaged."

"They threw you *away*!" Hume said indignantly. He rushed up to the robot and took hold of its silvery hand.

"They had no further use for me," Yam intoned. "That was when they went away, in the year forty-two. I had completed the tasks they set me by then." He took a few uncertain steps forward, creaking and whirring. "I am suffering from neglect and inaction."

"Come with us," Hume said. "Mordion can mend you."

He set off, leading the glistening robot tenderly toward the door they had come in by. Ann followed, reluctant with disbelief. *What year forty-two?* she wondered. *It* can't *be* this *century, and I refuse to believe we're a hundred years in the future. And Hume* knows *it! How?*

Well, I know the date is 1992, she told herself, and she knew, of course, that there were no real robots then. It was hard to rid herself of the feeling that there must be someone human inside Yam's unsteady silver shape. The paratypical field again, she thought. It was the only thing that would account for those elder trees growing above Yam and the way Hexwood Farm itself was so mysteriously in ruins.

With a sort of idea that she might catch the farmhouse turning back to its usual state, Ann looked over her shoulder at it. It happened to be the very moment when the decaying front door opened and a real man in armor came out, stretching and yawning like someone coming off duty. There was no doubt this one was human. Ann could see his bare, hairy legs under the iron shin guards strapped to them. He wore a mail coat and a round iron helmet with a nosepiece down over his very human face. It made him look most unpleasant.

He turned and saw them.

"*Run*, Hume!" said Ann.

The armed man drew his sword and came leaping through the weeds toward them. "Outlaws!" he shouted. "Filthy peasants!"

Hume took one look and raced for the half-open door, dragging the lurching, swaying Yam behind him. Ann sprinted to catch up. As they reached the door in the wall, more men in armor came running out of the farmhouse. At least two of them had what seemed to be crossbows, and these two stood and aimed the things at Ann and Hume like wide heavy guns. Yam's big silver hands came out, faster than Ann's eyes could follow, closed on Hume's arm and Ann's, and more or less threw them one after the other round the door and into the snowball thicket. As Ann landed struggling among the bare twigs, she heard the two sharp clangs of the crossbow bolts hitting Yam. Then there was the sound of the door being dragged and slammed shut. Ann scrambled toward the open ground as hard as she could go.

"Are you all right, Hume?" she called as soon as she was there.

Hume came crawling out of the bushes at her feet, looking very frightened. Behind him there were shouts and wooden banging as the armed men tried to get the door open again. Yam was surging through the thicket toward them, swaying and whirring. Twigs slapped his metal skin like a hailstorm on a tin roof.

"You're broken!" Hume cried out.

Ann could hear the door in the wall beginning to scrape open. She seized Hume's wrist in one hand and Yam's cold, faintly whirring hand in the other and dragged both of them away. "Just run," she told Hume.

4

MORDION GOT OFF his rock hastily when Ann appeared, breathlessly dragging Hume and the lurching, damaged robot. He found it hard to make sense of what they were telling him. "You went to the castle? Are they still chasing you? I've no weapon!"

"Not exactly," Ann panted. "It was Hexwood Farm in the future. Except the soldiers were like the Bayeux tapestry or something."

"I told them," rattled Yam. His voice box seemed to be badly damaged. "Beyond trees. Soldiers. Me for. Afraid of Sir Artegal. Famous outlaw."

"Mend him, mend him, Mordion!" Hume pleaded.

"So they're not following?" Mordion said anxiously.

"I don't think so," said Ann, while Yam rattled, "Inside. Me for. Famous knight. Cowards."

Hume pulled Mordion's sleeve and shouted his demand. "He's *broken*! Please mend him. *Please!*"

Mordion could see Hume was frightened and distressed. He explained kindly. "I don't think I can, Hume. Mending a robot requires a whole set of special tools."

"*Ask* for them then—like the nails," said Hume.

"Yes, why not?" Ann said, unexpectedly joining Hume. "Ask the parawhosit field like you did for the airplane food, Mordion. Yam stopped two crossbow bolts and saved Hume's life."

"He was *brave*," Hume agreed.

"No," Yam whirred. He sounded like a cheap alarm clock. "Robot nature. Glad. Mended. Uncomfort. Like this."

Mordion pulled at his beard dubiously. If he used the field the way Ann and Hume were suggesting, he sensed he would be admitting a number of things about himself which he would rather not admit. It would be like turning down a forbidden road that led somewhere terrible, to face something he never could face. "No," he said. "Asking for things is cheating."

"Then cheat," said Ann. "If those soldiers go back for reinforce-ments and come after us, you're going to need Yam's help. Or start being an enchanter again if you won't cheat."

"I'm not an enchanter!" Mordion said.

"Oh, blast you *and* your beastly field!" Ann said. "You're just giving in to it and letting it make you *feeble*!" She found she was crying with anger and frustration and swung round so that Mordion should not see. "Come on, Hume. We'll see if my dad can mend Yam. Yam, do you think you can get across that river down there?"

"You know Hume shouldn't go out of the wood," Mordion said. "Please, Ann—"

"I'm . . . *disappointed* in you!" Ann choked. Bitterly disap-pointed, she thought. Mordion seemed to be denying everything she knew he was.

There was a helpless silence. The river rushed below. Yam stood swaying and clanking. There were tears running down Hume's face as well as Ann's. Mordion looked at them, hurt by their misery and even more hurt by Ann's contempt. It was worse because he knew, without being able to explain to himself *why*, that he had earned Ann's scorn. He did not think he could decide what to do. He did not think he had decided anything, until a large roll of metalcloth clanked to the ground at his feet.

"Did *you* ask for this?" Mordion said to Hume.

Hume shook his head, sending tears splashing. Ann gave a sort of chuckle. "I knew you'd do it!" she said.

Mordion sighed and knelt down to unwrap the cloth. He spread it across the earth under the pine tree to find every kind of robotics tool in there, tucked into pockets in rows: tiny bright pincers and power drivers, miniature powered spanners, magnifying goggles, spare cells, wire bores, a circuit tester, a level, adhesives, lengths of silver tegument, cutters. . . .

Yam's rosy eyes turned eagerly to the unrolled spread. To Mor-dion's fascination, a sort of creasing bent the blank modeling of

Yam's mouth. The thing smiles! he thought. What a weird antique model! "Old Yamaha," Yam warbled. "Adapted. Remodeled. Trust. Correct tools?"

"I've seldom seen a more complete kit," Mordion assured him.

"You told me you were old Yamaha before," Hume said.

"Not," Yam rattled. "Gone back. Time you first found me. Think everything. Told for first time. Hush. Mordion work."

Hume obediently sat himself on a smooth brown rock, with Ann on the ground beside him. They watched Mordion roll up the sleeves of his camel-colored robe and unscrew a large panel in Yam's back, where he dived in with some of the longer tools and did something to stop Yam from lurching almost at once. Then he whipped round to the front of Yam and undid the voice box at the top of Yam's neck. "Say something," Mordion said after a moment.

"THAT IS MUCH—" Yam's normal flat voice boomed. Mordion hurriedly twiddled the power driver. "—*better than*," Yam said, and went on in a whisper, "it was before," and was twiddled back to proper strength to add, "I am glad it was not broken."

"Me, too," said Mordion. "Now you can set me right if I get something wrong. You're much older than anything I'm used to."

He went back to the hole in Yam's back. Yam turned and bent his head, far farther than a human could, to watch what was going on. "Those fuel cells have slipped," he told Mordion.

"Yes, the clips are worn," Mordion agreed. "How's that? And if I take a turn on the neck pisistor, does it feel worse or better?"

"Better," said Yam. "No, stop. That red wire goes to the torsor head. I think the lower sump is wrong."

"Punctured," said Mordion. He bent down to the roll of tools. "More fluid. Where are the small patches? Ah, here. Do you know of any more leaks, while I'm at it?"

"Lower left leg," said Yam.

Ann was fascinated. Mordion working on Yam was a different person, neither the mad-seeming enchanter who had created Hume nor the harassed monk trying to build a house and watch Hume at the same time. He was cool and neutral and efficient, a cross between a doctor and a motor mechanic with, perhaps, a touch of dentist and sculptor thrown in. In a queer way, she thought, Mordion seemed far more at ease with Yam than he was with her or Hume.

Hume sat seriously with a hand on each knee, leaning forward to watch each new thing Mordion did. He could not believe Mordion was not hurting Yam. He kept whispering, "It's all right, Yam. All right."

Mordion turned round to pick up the magnifying goggles before starting on the tiny parts of Yam's left leg and noticed the way Hume was feeling. He wondered what to do about it. He could tell Hume Yam did not feel a thing; Hume would not believe him, and that would make Hume just as worried as before but ashamed of his worry. Better get Yam himself to show Hume he was fine. Get Yam to talk about something else besides his own antique works.

"Yam," Mordion said, unscrewing the leg tegument, "from what you said to Hume earlier, I thought you implied you'd been inside this paratypical field for some time. Does it affect you, too?"

"Not as much as it affects humans," said Yam, "but I am certainly not immune."

"Surprising," said Mordion. "I thought a machine *would* be immune."

"That is because of the nature of the field," Yam explained.

"Oh?" said Mordion, examining the hundreds of tiny silver leg mechanisms.

"The field is induced by a machine," said Yam. "The machine is a device known as a Bannus. It has been dormant but not inoperative for many years. I believe it is like me: It can never be fully turned off. Something has happened recently to set it working at full power, and unlike me, the Bannus can, when fully functional, draw power from any source available. There is much power available in this world at this time."

"That explains the strength of the field," Mordion murmured.

"But what *is* a Bannus?" asked Ann.

"I can only tell you what I deduce from my own experience," Yam said, turning himself round to face Ann, with Mordion patiently following him round. "The Bannus would appear to take any situation and persons given it, introduce them into a field of theta-space, and then enact, with almost total realism, a series of scenes based on these people and this situation. It does this over and over again, portraying what would happen if the people in the situation decided one way and then another. I deduce it was designed to help people make decisions."

"Then it plays tricks with time," Ann said.

"Not exactly," said Yam. "But I do not think it cares what order the scenes are shown in."

"You said that before, too," Hume said. He was interested. He had almost forgotten his worry about Yam. "And I didn't understand then, either."

"I have said it many times," said Yam. "The Bannus cannot tamper with my memory. I know that we four have discussed the Bannus, here and in other places, twenty times now. It may well continue to make us do so until it arrives at the best possible conclusion."

"I don't believe it!" said Ann. But the trouble was, she did.

Mordion rolled away from Yam's leg and pushed up his goggles. Like Ann, in spite of not wanting to believe Yam, he had a strong sense of having done this before. The feel of the tiny tool in his hand, the piercing scent of the pine tree overhead, and the harsh whisper of its needles overlaying the sound of the river below were uncomfortably and hauntingly familiar. "What conclusion do you think the machine is trying to make us arrive at?"

"I have no idea," said Yam. "It could be that the people deciding are not us. We are possibly only actors in someone else's scenes."

"Not me," said Ann. "I'm important. I'm *me*."

"I'm *very* important," Hume announced.

"Besides," Ann went on, giving Hume a pat to show she knew

he was important, too, "I object to being pushed around by this machine. If you're right, it's made me do twenty things I don't want to do."

"Not really," said Yam. "Nothing can make either a person or a machine do things which it is not in their natures to do."

Mordion had gone back to work on Yam's leg. He knew he was not in the least important. It was a weight off his mind, somehow, that Yam thought they were only actors in someone else's scene. But when Yam said this about one not being made to act against one's nature, he found he was quivering so with guilt and uneasiness that he had to stop work again for fear of doing Yam damage.

Ann was thinking about this, too. She said, "But machines can be adapted. *You've* been adapted, Yam. And people have all sorts of queer bits in their natures that the Bannus could work on."

That was why he felt so guilty, Mordion realized with relief. He went back to making painstaking, microscopic adjustments on Yam's leg. This machine, this Bannus, had taken advantage of some very queer and unsavory corner of his nature when it caused him to create Hume. And the reason for his guilt was that when the Bannus decided the correct conclusion had been reached, it would surely shut down its field. Hume would cease to exist then. Just like that. What a thing to have done! Mordion went on working, but he was cold and appalled.

Meanwhile, Ann was looking at her watch and saying firmly that she had to go now. She had had enough of this Bannus. As she got up and started down the steep rocks, Mordion left Yam with a driver sticking out of his leg and hastened after her. "Ann!"

"Yes?" Ann stopped and looked up at him. She was still not feeling very friendly toward Mordion—particularly now that it seemed she had been shoved into scene after scene with him.

"Keep coming here," Mordion said. "Of your own free will, if possible. You do me good as well as Hume. You keep pointing out the truth."

"Yam can do that now," Ann said coldly.

"Not really." Mordion tried to explain, before she climbed down by the river where she could not hear him. "Yam knows facts. You have insights."

"I do?" Ann was gratified, enough to pause on one foot halfway down to the river.

Mordion could not help smiling. "Yes, mostly when you're angry."

—5——

ANN DID WISH Mordion had not smiled. It was that smile that had entranced her—she was sure of it—into coming back this afternoon. She had never met a smile like it.

"He thinks I'm *funny!*" she snorted to herself as she made her way home. "He thinks I eat out of his hand when he smiles. It's *humiliating!*"

She arrived home in a pale, shaken sort of state because of it. Or maybe it was being chased by men in armor. At least they hadn't followed them down to the river. Or the Bannus hadn't *let* them follow. Or maybe it's everything! she thought.

Dad looked up at her from where he was relaxing in front of the news. "You've been overdoing it, my girl, haven't you? You look all in."

"I'm not all in. I'm angry!" Ann retorted. Then, realizing that she would never get a plain-minded person like Dad to believe in the Bannus, or theta-space, let alone a boy created out of blood, she was forced to add, "Angry at being tired, I mean."

"This is *it*, isn't it?" said Dad. "You get out of bed just this morning, and off you go—vanish for the whole day—without a thought! You'll be back in bed with that virus again tomorrow. Are you going to be well enough to go to school at all this term? Or not?"

"Monday," said Mum. "We want you well and back in school on Monday."

"There's only two more days of school left," Martin put in from the corner where he was coloring a map labeled "Caves of the Future." "It's not worth going back for two days." Ann shot him a grateful look.

"Yes, it *is* worth it," said Mum. "I just wish I'd paid more attention when I was at school."

"Oh, don't bore on about *that!*" Martin muttered.

"*What* did you say?" Mum asked him.

But Dad cut across her, saying, "Well, if it *is* only the two days, there's no point making her go, is there? She might as well stay at home and get thoroughly well again."

Ann let them argue about it. Mum seemed to be winning, but Ann did not mind much. Two days wouldn't kill anyone. And that would be two days in which the Bannus couldn't use her as an extra in somebody else's decisions. It was good—no, more, a real *relief*— to be back at home with a normal decision being argued about in the normal way. Ann sat down on the sofa with a great, relaxing sigh.

Martin looked across at her. "There's *Alien* on the late film tonight," he said underneath the argument.

"Oh, *good!*" Ann stretched both arms over her head and decided, there and then, that she would not go near Banners Wood again.

PART THREE

—1———————————

ANN KEPT TO her decision next morning. Yam's looking after Hume now, she told herself. He was obviously the nonreal person she had asked the field to provide for Hume when Mordion could not seem to be bothered. But the Bannus had done a lot of fancy hocus-pocus to make Ann believe it was the year two thousand and something, and then more fancy work with the men in armor. It seemed to enjoy making people frightened and uncomfortable.

"I have had *enough* of that machine!" Ann told her bedroom mirror. The fact that she could see the gray car in the mirror over her left shoulder, still parked in the bay, only underlined her decision.

Anyway, it was Saturday, and she and Martin both had particular duties on a Saturday. Martin had to go with Dad in the van, first to the suppliers and then to deliver fruit and vegetables to the motel. Ann had to do the shopping. Feeling very virtuous and decided, Ann dug the old brown shopping bag out of the kitchen cupboard and went dutifully into the shop to collect money and a shopping list from Mum. Mum gave her the usual string of instructions, interrupted by customers coming in. It always took a long time. While Ann was standing by the counter waiting for Mum's next sentence, Martin shot through on his way to meet Mrs. Price's Jim.

"Chalk up one week I don't have to do that for you," he said as he whizzed by.

Poor Martin, Ann thought. His last few Saturdays must have been quite hard work. She had not thought about that while she lay in bed.

"And don't forget the papers," Mum concluded. "Here's another ten pounds to pay the bill—though I don't suppose it'll be that much, even with this new comic Martin got for doing the shopping for you. I want to see some change, Ann."

Trust Martin! Ann thought. My brother will accept a bribe for *anything*. What'll it be like when Martin's grown up and running the country? She was smiling as she went out of the shop. Everything was deliciously normal, wholesomely humdrum, right down to a little sprinkle of rain. The street was safely gray. The other people shopping all looked fretful, which gave Ann a further feeling of security, because this was just as you might expect. She was even able to listen patiently to Mrs. Price chattering away while Ann paid for the papers. Mrs. Price was behaving just as usual, too.

Contentedly Ann heaved up the full shopping bag and set off back home.

And put the bag back down again on the damp pavement to stare at the person coming toward her carrying a sack.

Ann thought at first he was a monk. But the brown robe was not long enough, and it had narrow trousers underneath. And the tall figure looked lopsided because of the rolled blanket-thing over one shoulder. He had a curious strolling walk. Ann knew that walk.

Mordion was smiling to himself as he came. Ann could see all the other shoppers reacting to that smile. Some were startled, some suspicious, but most people smiled, too, as if they could not resist. It gave Ann a very queer shock, which ran all over her skin like soreness, to see Mordion here in Wood Street on a Saturday morning.

"What are you doing?" she said accusingly, standing in his path.

Mordion's smile broadened and became particularly for her. "Hallo," he said. "I wondered if I might meet you."

"But what are you doing?" Ann repeated.

"Shopping," said Mordion. "We were very short of food this winter—until it occurred to me there would be food I could buy here."

This *winter*? Ann thought. She took a quick look at Mordion's left wrist. The cut there was no more healed than her own knee was. She had put a new Band-Aid on it before she came out. The Bannus was playing tricks with time again. "But," she said, "what are you using for money?"

"That's no problem. I seem to have quite a lot," Mordion told her. Ann must have looked disbelieving. Mordion said, "Look. I'll show you." He put his sack down beside Ann's bag. It was one of those green shiny bags with net inside, Ann saw, in which sprouts got delivered to their shop. Her distracted eyes took in potatoes, carrots, onions, lamb chops inside it before they switched to the leather wallet Mordion was taking out of his pouch. "Here," he said, and opened the wallet to show her a big stack of ten-pound notes.

All at once Ann was acutely embarrassed, standing blocking the pavement and being shown someone's wallet as if she were a police-woman asking for ID. She saw people staring. She was just going to ask Mordion to put the thing away when her eye fell on a credit card peeping out of the opposite side of the wallet. Ah, she thought. I can find out who he really is!

"That card," she said, pointing to it, "is even better than money. You—"

"Yes, I know," Mordion said. "I tried it out in the wineshop. It's even got my signature on it. See?"

He held the little plastic oblong out to her. I don't believe it! Ann thought, staring at the raised letters on it. "M. Agenos," they said, and an address in London. She was suddenly exasperated. She looked up into Mordion's smiling, bearded face, like St. Francis or something, except for the diving wing of eyebrow. He looked as innocent as a saint or a baby.

"You've lost your memory, you know," she told him. "Blame the Bannus if you like, but it's *true*! Now you look. Over there." She took hold of the thick wool of his sleeve and turned him to face the parking bay across the street. "That car. The big gray one. You came here in that car. I *saw* you."

Mordion looked at the car with polite interest, but not as if it meant anything to him. "If you say so," he agreed. "I must have come here somehow."

At least, Ann thought, he didn't seem to believe he'd been asleep for centuries any longer. They were making progress. "But don't you think you've got people—family—who must be wondering where you are by now?" she demanded.

"No. I know I've got no family," Mordion said. His smile faded out, and he turned and picked up his green sack. "I must get back. Hume really is starving."

Ann hung on to his sleeve and tried again. "You've no need to live in the wood, Mordion. If you wanted, you could be walking about here in ordinary clothes."

"I like these clothes," Mordion said, looking down at himself. "The style and the color seem . . . right to me. And I like living in the wood, you know. Even if there wasn't Hume to think of, I would probably stay there. It's a beautiful place."

"It isn't real," Ann said despairingly.

"No, that isn't quite accurate." Mordion heaved his sack up into his arms. "Theta-space has genuine existence, even if no one quite knows what it is. Do come and see us there," he added over his shoulder as he set off across the road. "Hume was asking after you."

Ann picked up her own bag and watched him go. He went very quickly in spite of looking as if he were lounging along. "I want to *shake* him!" she said.

In the shop Mum was full of the strange customer she had just served. "I suppose he was a monk or something, Ann. Such a *lovely* smile—and such funny clothes. It seemed odd to see someone like that buying onions."

"I expect he has a screw loose and several pieces missing," Ann said grumpily.

"Oh, no," said Mum. "He wasn't simple, Ann, or mad, or anything like that. But you're right in a way. Something was wrong. I got the feeling of terrible sadness somewhere."

Ann sighed as she unloaded groceries on the kitchen table. Mum was right. *She* was right, too. There was something very wrong with Mordion, and very sad. He seemed to be several pieces of a person that did not fit together. Her sigh was because she was realizing she would have to go to the wood again, not because of Hume but because of Mordion. Mordion needed her to keep dinning the truth into him.

—2—

SHE WENT STRAIGHTAWAY. *Clock me in*, she told her imaginary people as she slipped past the big gray car. It now had pink bud shells all over its sleek roof. *I need to know how long I spend in there.*

I'll try, said the Prisoner, *but I don't have much notion of time.*

The Slave and the Boy were busy, but the King said, as Ann was going down the path between the houses, *I'll time you. By the way, did you ever get another sight of that van?*

Oh, yes—and I forgot because some people in armor chased us, Ann said. *It was a weighing scale. The firm's name is Rayner Hexwood.*

My worst fears conf— The King's voice in Ann's head stopped. Ann's first thought was that she had crossed the boundary into this theta-space the Bannus made. But that could not be so, she realized. She could see Banners Wood in front of her, looking as it always did, and the houses beyond it through the sparse trees. Because it was Saturday, there were little kids all over it, running along all the muddy paths and shouting as they crossed the stream on the tradi-

tional fallen tree and the tree rolled under their feet. Martin and
Jim Price were there, too, comfortably roosting on the branches of
the best climbing tree. But being older, they were simply there to
talk. Martin raised a thumb to Ann as she went underneath them
but did not stop talking to Jim for an instant.

Perhaps the King had simply been called away to a crisis, Ann
thought. And I'm not going to be able to get into the whatsis field
today. The wood's too full.

She was nearly down to the stream by then, passing the yellow
pretzel bag that had been inside the hollow tree for nearly a year
now. No good, she thought. But she went on walking, and it took
her longer than she had expected to reach the stream. When she
did reach it, she was at the top of a high earthy bank. Below her the
stream foamed along as a river, powered by the waterfall on her
right and racing round the big brown rocks by which Ann had
crossed before.

Ann chuckled. As she slid down the bank, she thought, I take my
hat off to that Bannus! It phases the field in so smoothly you simply
can't tell it's doing it.

For a moment, as she climbed the rocks on the other bank, she
thought she was not going to find anyone there by the cave. But
that was because they were all three very busy. Hume was writing,
very carefully with his tongue stuck out, kneeling by paper spread
on a flat stone, using a burned stick to write with. Ann was disappointed to find he was still small. Beyond Hume there was a most
efficient fire pit, where an old iron pot was dangling from a tripod
of tough wood, smelling smoky but enticing. An iron griddle and a
number of Stone Age-looking pots stood in the ashes.

The shelter had walls now, of woven willow daubed with mud.
A homemade ladder led up to the roof. It looked very flimsy, and
it creaked, but it had to be stronger than it looked because Yam was
just climbing the ladder on his big, spongy feet, carrying a mighty
bundle of rushes. Mordion was on the roof, pegging smaller bundles
of rushes into place to make thatch.

"I see you decided to cheat after all," Ann called up at him.

"Only a little," Mordion called down, "and only over the cooking pots."

"Hume must be provided with regular meals," Yam stated. Ann could only just hear him because Hume threw down his burned stick and galloped to meet her, clamoring as usual.

"Ann, Ann, come and look at my writing!"

Ann went and looked kindly at the paper. It was the whitish brown kind of paper that wrapped fish and chips. Hume had done two rows of scribbles and, underneath those, "Yam is on the rufe. He has a lader." It was crooked but quite readable.

"That's very good," Ann said, pointing to the writing. "But I don't think the other two are quite letters."

"Yes, they are," Mordion called from the roof. "He's learning Hamitic and Universal script as well as your Albionese. Yam insisted. Yam, I may tell you, is a real bully."

"The man has to be kept up to the mark as well as the child," Yam pronounced. "That bundle is inefficiently spread, Mordion. Left to himself, Ann, Mordion sits and broods."

"I don't brood," Mordion said, "but I like to sit with the sun on my back and fish. *And* think, of course."

"You idle," said Yam, "and you sleep." He bent his head toward Ann. His face was creased beside his blank mouth, and she supposed he was smiling.

"Draw me a picture, Ann! Draw for me like Mordion!" Hume clamored. He turned the paper over. On the other side Mordion had drawn a beautiful small-headed cat stalking a mouse, a realistic horse—horses were something Ann could *never* get right—and an even more realistic dragon. Each drawing was labeled in the three kinds of writing.

Ann felt most respectful. "I can't draw anything nearly as good, Hume, but I'll try if you want."

Hume did want, so Ann drew him a cow and an elephant and a

picture of Yam on the ladder—Yam turned out far too chunky, but Hume seemed pleased—and labeled each one for him in English. While she drew, she listened to Yam saying things like "You will have to retie all these. Bad work lets rain through," or "That peg is not in straight," or "You must take your knife and make these edges more even." Mordion never seemed to argue. Ann marveled at how happy and submissive he seemed. Yam was so bossy that she was not sure she would have stood for it herself.

After an hour or so Mordion suddenly came down the ladder and stretched. "There is half the roof still to do," Yam said. Ann did not understand how a flat robot voice could manage to sound so reproachful.

"Then you do it," Mordion said. "I've had enough for the moment. I'm flesh and blood, Yam. I need to eat."

"Refuel then by all means," Yam said graciously.

"So you *do* stick up for yourself a bit?" Ann remarked as Mordion came and stirred the iron pot.

Mordion looked up at her from under his eyebrow. "I brought it on myself," he said. "I asked Yam if he knew how to build a house."

"But I wouldn't stand for it even if Yam was human!" Ann exclaimed. "Don't you have *any* self-respect?"

Mordion straightened up over the cooking pot. For that instant Ann knew what it meant when people said someone was towering in his wrath. She backed away. "Of *course* I—" Mordion began. Then he stopped and thought, with his brow riding in over his nose, just as if Ann had asked him something very difficult. "I'm not sure," he said. "Do you fancy I need to learn some self-respect?"

"Er—well—*I* wouldn't let a machine push me about like that," Ann answered. Mordion in this mixture of wrath and humility alarmed her so much that she looked at her watch and found it was time for lunch.

But when she had said good-bye and was halfway down the rocks to the river, it occurred to her that the Bannus was a machine, and she had let that push her about for days now. Talk about the pot calling the kettle black! She nearly went back and apologized, except that she could not bear to look that foolish.

— 3 —————————————————————

SHE WENT PAST the yellow pretzel bag in the hollow tree, sure that she would be at the muddy little stream any second. But when she came to water, it was the river. While she was crossing carefully from rock to slippery rock, Ann could see Yam at the top of the cliff opposite, sitting with his silver chin in his silver hand, contriving to look doleful. By the time she had scrambled up the path that Mordion and Hume had worn going down to the river to wash, she could see Yam was dented as well as doleful. It seemed as if some years had passed.

"What's the matter?" Ann asked Yam.

Yam's eyes glowed mournfully at her. "This is not what I wish," he said. "It is quite against my advice. The correct procedure is to use an antibiotic."

An extraordinary warbling noise, shrill and throbbing, came from the other side of the house. Ann dodged round its walls—it had put out another room since she was last here—and came into the flat space by the fire pit, to find Mordion and Hume kneeling face-to-face there, surrounded by little clay pots and lines drawn in the dusty earth. The noise was from flute-things they were both blowing. These were white pipes with jagged round holes in them. They seemed to be made of pieces of bone. Mordion's beard was inches longer, although his hair, like Hume's, had clearly been hacked off to shoulder length. This, and the fact that Hume was about twelve years old, was so much what Ann expected that she did not think about it until much later. She simply covered her ears against the awful skirling of the pipes.

Hume saw her move and shot her a friendly look between two

throbbing notes. One of his eyes was smaller than the other and very red and runny. Ann was not sure whether she expected this or not. Mordion's deep light eyes turned her way. Next second Ann found herself backing away from a place in the air where everything made a small transparent whirl, like a sort of pimple in the universe.

"If Yam sent you to interrupt us," the whirling pimple said with Mordion's voice, "please don't."

"I—I wasn't going to," Ann said.

"Then just stand there quietly for about five minutes," said the transparent place.

"All right," said Ann.

Mordion had not stopped playing for an instant all through this, and neither had Hume. Ann stood against the flimsy wall of the new part of the house, interested, envious, and wistful. This was the part of Hume's education she most wished she could share. She watched another whirling, transparent place begin to form between the two screaming flutes. This one was long and thin, like an unstable figure of eight. When the thing was properly formed, Mordion and Hume both bent their pipes to it, blowing away for all they were worth, and guided it carefully to stand twirling over one of the little earthen pots. Like charming an invisible snake! Ann thought as the pipes moved the whirling thing on to the next pot, and the next. Before long it had visited every pot in the circle. Mordion and Hume sat back on their heels, piping only very gently now, and watched and waited. The whirling thing hovered for a moment, then made a determined dart for one of the little pots. Ann was not sure what happened then. The whirling thing was suddenly gone, but that particular pot seemed to stand out from the others somehow.

Mordion laid his pipe down. "That's the one then." He took up the pot and carefully anointed Hume's bad eye with the greenish runny mixture in the pot. "Blink it in," he said, "if it doesn't sting too much."

"No, it's all right," Hume said, blinking vigorously. "It's sooth-ing."

"Then that spell worked," said Mordion. "Good. Thanks for being so patient, Ann."

Ann dared to leave the house wall and come over to the fire pit.

"I *wish* I could learn to manipulate the paratypical field like that!" she said yearningly.

"We didn't," said Hume. "We worked pure magic. Look." He blew a warbling scale on his bone flute, and a flight of birds came out of the end of it like bubbles and flew away into the boughs of the pine tree.

"Good heavens!" said Ann. And she asked Mordion, "*Really* magic?"

"I *think* so," said Mordion. "Hume seems very good at it."

"So's Mordion," said Hume. "Wood magic, herb magic, weather magic. Yam hates it. I'll go and tell Yam he can come back now, shall I?"

"If he's not still sulking." Mordion looked at Ann as he said this, and she nodded slightly. She was used to this. Mordion wanted to speak to her privately. Hume knew he did, and Hume had offered to go away in order to let Ann know that he, too, wanted to talk to her. It was odd, Ann thought as Hume bounded away. Both of them seemed to think of her as a sort of consultant.

"What's wrong with his eye?" she asked as soon as Hume was safely out of hearing.

"I'm not sure," Mordion replied. "It's been like that for some time. You must have noticed. I think it's growing wrong. My feeling is that I bungled that eye when I made him. I shan't forgive myself if he grows up with only one eye."

"Sometimes," Ann told him, "you are like a mother hen, Mor-dion. He was perfectly all right when he was older—younger—well, most of the time. Why *should* you have bungled him? It's much more likely that living here in this wood, he's got an infection from lack of vitamins or, well, that kind of thing."

"You really think so?" Mordion asked, anxiously relieved.

"Sure of it," Ann declared.

Mordion picked up the clay pot and turned it round in his hands. "I think we found the correct herb to cure it. There were nine possibles. Magic likes nines. I'll keep using it."

"Can't you teach me wood magic—or whatever it was you just did?" Ann asked.

"I'd like to, but—" Mordion thought, twirling the clay pot. "To learn this sort of magic, you have to be sure you've accepted the wood—wore it round you like a cloak—and you don't, do you?"

"I can manipulate the Bannus field sometimes," Ann protested.

"That's different," said Mordion. "There are two—no, three—sorts of paratypical field here. There's the one the Bannus makes, there's the one the wood makes, with its attendant nature magics, and there's also pure mind magic, though I *think* the three interact quite often. Mind magic's the one you're good at, Ann, and you don't need me to teach you that. So you think Hume's eye is really not my fault?"

Ann assured him again it was not. Though goodness knows why he takes my word for it! she thought, as Yam marched round the house, carrying two dead rabbits.

"Now the hocus-pocus is over," Yam said, "here is some furry fuel."

"Come and play, Ann," Hume said, bounding after Yam.

Ann got up gladly and went with Hume. She liked Hume a lot when he was older. The two of them went racing and leaping upriver, to where the land usually flattened out below the hill where they had found Yam.

"The wood's changed again," Hume called over his shoulder.

"How?" panted Ann. The sole drawback to Hume this size was that he could run much faster than she could. She supposed it was living wild that did it.

"There's a new place by the river," Hume called, receding. "I'll show you."

They came to the place a few bends up, and it was beautiful. Here the riverbank flattened out and ran down to the water like a green lawn, under mighty forest trees. The river was wide here, and shallow, and ran flickering over multitudes of small stones. It was an open invitation to take your shoes off and paddle. Ann and Hume both cast their footgear onto the short grass and galloped into the water. It was icy, and the stones were painful, but that did not prevent a great deal of splashing and fun. When Ann's feet were too numb to go on, she threw herself down on the lawnlike slope and lay gazing at the sky, improbably blue between the amazing young green of the leaves overhead. No wonder Mordion loved this wood so much.

Hume, who seldom kept still if he could help it, became very busy dragging big fallen boughs out of the water and piling them in a heap. "I'm going to build a boat," he explained, "and I'd better make sure of this timber while I can. I can feel the wood getting ready to change again."

This, Ann supposed, was what Mordion meant about wearing the wood like a cloak. She could feel nothing except peace. The huge old trees around her seemed to have been there for centuries and looked as if they would go on growing for centuries more. Change seemed impossible. It was unfair that Hume should feel change coming. "I am not," she said grumpily, "repeat not, going to help you haul that heap to the house."

"Round the house is the only bit that never changes," Hume said, throwing a last branch on the pile. "But please yourself. I can get Yam—though that'll mean arguing for an hour to stop him from chopping it up for firewood. Let's climb a tree."

They climbed the giant Ann had been lying under and scrambled out on a great dipping bough until they were right over the water, where they roosted comfortably, talking—rather as, Ann dimly remembered, Martin had been doing with Jim Price.

"How does my eye look?" Hume asked.

Ann examined it, surprised at how anxious he was. "Better," she said. "Not nearly so red, anyway." It was still smaller than the other eye, but she did not want to worry Hume by telling him that.

"Thank goodness!" Hume said devoutly. "I don't know what went wrong with it, but I've been terrified in case it went blind. No one can be a proper swordsman with only one eye."

"Why do you want to be a swordsman?" Ann asked. "If I had your talent for magic, I wouldn't bother to do anything else."

Hume dismissed magic as just ordinary. "I've got to kill those Reigners for Mordion when I'm old enough," he explained.

"But you can easily do that with magic," Ann pointed out.

Hume frowned, pulling his mouth wide so that his high cheeks stuck out, and thoughtfully watched a wood louse crawl on the branch. "I don't think so. I think Mordion's right when he says using magic to kill sends a person wrong. I get a sort of feel, doing magic, that it would go wrong for later if I tried anything like that. And I owe it to Mordion to get it *right* and set him free properly. I wouldn't want to find I'd used magic to convert the ban to something worse."

Ann sighed. "So how *is* Mordion?"

"He worries me," Hume said frankly. "That's why I wanted to talk to you. I don't even dare read his mind anymore."

Ann sighed again. "That's another thing I envy you for."

"You can tell people's feelings. That's just as—no, better!" Hume said. "You don't have to go inside and—but I'm not going to do that again after the other night."

"What do you mean?" Ann asked.

"Well, you know how Yam always goes on about Mordion being lazy," Hume said, "because Mordion goes off and just sits somewhere, and it takes hours to find him. Well, that's just Yam being a machine. Last time we had to look for Mordion, he was up on those really high rocks downriver from the house, and he looked *dreadful*. Even worse when he tried to smile at me to make me think he was all right. So I took a deep breath. You know how you have to get up courage if you want to say anything personal to Mordion—"

"Don't I just! I can never say personal things to him unless I get angry first," Ann said. It was, she admitted to herself, only anger that could make her ignore the shell of pain Mordion was cased in.

"Yes, I want to shake him a lot of the time, too," Hume agreed, not quite understanding. "But this wasn't one of those times. I breathed in and then asked him straight out what was the matter."

"What did he do?" Ann asked. "Blast you to outer darkness?"

"I—almost," Hume said. "Only it was me that did it. I thought he wasn't going to tell me, so I thought I'd look in his mind. And"—Hume bent a finger and flicked the wood louse off into the water—"it was like—Can you imagine somewhere so dark it's sort of *roaring* and you can *see* the dark, and the dark is like the worst cut or scrape you ever had, so you can *feel* the dark, too, hurting? It was like that. Only huge. I had to stop, quick. And I nearly went away, only Mordion spoke then. He said, 'I'm pure evil, Hume. I've been thinking of throwing myself off this rock into those rapids.' And I took another breath and asked him *why*. It was so awful I—I sort of had to. And he said, 'The Great Balance alone knows why.' What do you think he meant, Ann?"

"I don't know." Ann gave a little shiver as a blue logo painted on a rusting white van passed before her mind's eye. "Maybe it's something to do with the ban."

"Yes. So you can see why I have to break it for him," Hume agreed. "But of course, I couldn't say that to him *then*. He hasn't even told me about the ban or about creating me to break it. Somehow I knew he really would jump off the rock if I brought it up just then."

"So what did you do?" said Ann.

Hume grinned. "I was cunning. I went just as selfish and—and *brattish* as I could, and I whined—actually I probably *sniveled*—that he wasn't to leave me all alone in the wood with his corpse.

On and on." Hume wriggled on the bough, rather ashamed. "I was scared. I *felt* selfish. And it worked. I felt bad. Mordion climbed down and said *he* was selfish. He said I was the one good thing Fate had allowed him to do."

"He's sort of said that to me, too," Ann remarked. "But Hume! Suppose you hadn't found him in time!"

"I used wood magic," Hume admitted. *"He'd* have called it cheating, but I knew it was urgent, and anyway, while I was doing the working, the wood more or less told me I was doing right. And afterward I went and told Yam that he was never *ever* to call Mordion lazy again, and I set him to watch Mordion whenever I wasn't there."

"So Yam's watching him now?" Ann said. That was a relief after what Hume had had to say.

"Yes," said Hume. "Yam's busy, and he can't haul that wood to the house. So you have a choice. You can either help me haul it, or you get bounced off this branch into the water." He began bouncing the great bough they were on, slowly at first, then faster and faster, until the new leaves at the end were dipping into the river at every bounce, while Ann shrieked and implored and scrambled frantically back toward the shore.

Needless to say, she helped Hume haul his timber to the house.

4

PAST THE YELLOW pretzel bag tucked into the hollow tree, there seemed no change in the wood, and Ann could still hear the shrieking of the little kids trying not to fall off the rolling tree that bridged the stream. But somehow she never reached the stream herself. Instead the shrieks seemed to get hoarser, and she came out beside the house on the other side of the river. The shrieks were the shrieks of Hume as he fled round and round the fire pit, pursued by Mordion. Mordion was holding a wooden sword. Hume was all legs these days, considerably taller than Ann. But so was Mordion all legs, and he was gaining on Hume.

"Hey, stop!" she said. "What's going on?"

Mordion stopped. She could not tell whether he was laughing or angry. Hume evidently thought angry, for he took advantage of Ann's interruption to get himself onto the thatched roof. Up he went, with two mighty, striding heaves, where he crouched, ready to flee again if Mordion came after him.

"This," Mordion said, pointing the wooden sword.

Ann turned round to find Yam leaning against the woodpile, rather sideways, with much of his silvery skin flapping round his knees and a whole lot of his works showing. "It was an accident," Yam intoned. "I was not swift enough. It is lucky I am not a human."

"If you were a human, Hume would have got what he deserved and been skewered," Mordion said.

"I would *not*!" Hume said indignantly from the roof.

"Yes, you would. You are getting far too used to taking advantage of the fact that Yam is not allowed to hurt you," Mordion retorted. "Come down off there and see what a real human would do."

"What do you mean?" Hume asked warily.

"What I say," said Mordion. "Yam saw he would hurt you and stopped. You waited for that and carved him open. If you'd been fighting me, I wouldn't have stopped. So come down and I'll show you."

"You mean you—" Hume was clearly astonished. So was Ann. Neither of them had ever seen Mordion do anything remotely war-like.

"I do mean it." Mordion stooped and picked a sword up from the earth. It was a long, gray, beautifully wicked blade. He held it out hilt foremost to the roof. Ann wondered where the sword had come from. Hume had manipulated the Bannus field for it, perhaps? "Here you are," said Mordion. "You can use this and I'll use Yam's wooden one, and we'll see what happens. Or are you scared?"

Hume shifted a little, crouching toward the eaves of the roof. "Well—I—yes. I don't want to kill you."

Mordion laughed. This was another thing Ann had barely ever seen him do. "You," he said, "would be so lucky! Come down and try."

"All right." Hume turned on his stomach and slid down, landing, to Ann's envy, lightly and athletically in front of Mordion. "You're sure?" he said, taking the hilt of the sword.

Mordion nodded. Hume made what seemed a halfhearted slash at him. Mordion promptly knocked the metal sword aside with his wooden one and delivered Hume a decisive thwack to the side of his head.

"Guard yourself," he said. "I've already killed you once. Or maybe just scalped you."

Hume swallowed and came forward again, much more carefully. There was a lightning thwack—CLANG. The metal sword fell to the ground, and Hume received another punishing blow, this time to his leg.

"Dead again," said Mordion. "If you haven't lost that leg, you're busy bleeding to death from it. You've got into some really careless habits, Hume."

Hume was scowling. He picked his sword up and came at Mordion a third time. This time Ann could tell he was really trying. He lasted a little longer anyway. Round and round the two went, leaping and weaving, with, every so often, one of those lightning flurries of action that seemed to leave Ann's eyes a step or so behind. Hume escaped the first two, but on the third he was hit in the ribs with a hefty drub. He staggered backward.

"Third death," Mordion said cheerfully. "Want to stop?"

"No!" said Hume, with his teeth clenched. He rushed in on Mordion and was hit again. This time Mordion did not ask him if he wanted to stop. They just went on, furiously. Ann sneaked round the other side of the fire pit and took shelter beside Yam. She had never seen anything like this, particularly from Mordion. He was so fast.

"Ouch!" she whispered as the wooden sword hit Hume again, smack, on his shoulder.

"This is a somewhat underhanded way to punish Hume," Yam intoned softly. "The damage is only to my tegument and is easily mended."

Ann glanced at Yam and could not help feeling he looked indecent with all those silver twiddly works showing. "I think, though," she said, wincing at another slapping blow, "that Hume probably needed taking down a peg."

"But not this way. It is clear Mordion is a master swordsman," Yam said.

"He is. He's enjoying himself," Ann said. Mordion was smiling as he fought, smiling widely and keenly. Opposite him, Hume's teeth were bared, but it was not a smile. Hume was sweating.

Then it was over. There was another flurry, and Hume was forced to his knees with Mordion's wooden sword pressed against the back of his neck. "This time you're beheaded," Mordion told him, and stood back to let Hume get up.

Hume was nearly in tears. He got up very slowly to give himself time to recover and dusted busily at the knees of his tracksuit. "Swine!" he muttered.

"Actually you'd be quite good if you weren't so careless," Mordion said.

"I *am* good!" Hume said angrily. "I got you once. Look at your left wrist."

Mordion looked at the not-quite-recent red slash there. "So you did," he said. "But you're not as good as you think you are."

"Go and—and *jump in the river*!" Hume snarled at him, and ran away round the house.

Mordion stood for a moment staring at that hardly healed cut. So did Ann. Uh-huh! she thought. How much time *has* passed?

Not much. Meanwhile, Mordion shrugged and leaned the wooden sword against the house as carefully as if it were a real one. "Yam, you're not to let him fight you in future," he said. He sounded distant and chilled. "I'd better teach Hume myself, although—" He stopped then, for so long that Ann thought he was not going to say any more. She moved out toward the fire pit. Mordion looked at her as if he had not known she was there before this. "I have a hideous distaste for anything to do with killing," he said.

"But you *enjoyed* that fight!" Ann said.

"I know. I can't understand it," Mordion said. "Ann, I have to mend Yam yet again. *Could* you go and find Hume and make sure he doesn't do anything stupid?"

"All right," Ann said, hoping Hume had not gone too far away.

He was quite near, only at the bottom of the steep path down to the river, in fact. Ann could see him quite clearly in the unaccustomed brightness down there, sitting brooding in the boat he had made. It was a surprisingly good boat, with a flat bottom and clinker-built sides—not at all the sort of boat you would expect a boy to build—but Ann barely noticed it because of the strange new look of the river. The familiar waterfall was no longer there. The river now flowed in a flat welter of white water split with jagged rocks and fairly roared through the bubbling pools beyond. The homemade floats of Mordion's fish traps bobbed desperately there, like drowning rats. It was wide, and tumultuous, and *flat*. The steep cliffs on either side had been scooped away backward, as if a bomb had hit the place. Ann stared and halted halfway down to stare again.

She was too astonished to consider Hume's state of mind. "Whatever happened to the waterfall?" she said as she reached the shingle where the boat was.

"Don't pretend you don't remember!" Hume growled, and went straight on to his grievance. "Mordion is a total *swine*! What right has he to do this to me? What *right*? And grinning all over his face while he does it, too! Funny *joke*!"

Ann realized she had better forget about the river. Hume's pride was hurting. "Well, he *is* sort of like your guardian, Hume. He did bring you up."

"He's no *right!*" There was an angry grate in Hume's voice that Ann had never heard before. "Guardian, nothing! He just happened to find me in the wood and just happened to feel responsible for me. He has no right to hit me—*and* pretending it was a fair fight while he does! I'll show him rights! I'm going to leave this wood, Ann. I'm going to go so far away that bloody Mordion won't ever be able to find me!"

"I really don't think you should do that," Ann said quickly. Unlike Mordion, Ann had never let herself consider what might happen if Hume went outside the paratypical field. But the instant horror she felt at the mere idea told her that she knew very well, deep down.

"Afraid I'll vanish away, eh?" Hume said harshly. "That's the hold Mordion thinks he's got on me. I don't believe that story any longer."

"It's not worth the risk, Hume," Ann said—no, bleated. She could hear her voice waver.

Hume ignored her. He stared at the rushing white water and said, "Well, at least I cut his wrist. I hope it *hurt.*"

This reminded Ann that very little time had passed, really. She swung over the side of Hume's boat and sat on the gunwale, where she could see Hume's face while he stared, brooding, at the water. If she was right, Hume's eye had been quite badly infected only half an hour or so ago. It ought still to look bad. But look as she would, all Ann could see was a face that looked about sixteen with two healthy gray eyes in it, much the same color as Mordion's. Or was Hume's left eye perhaps a little smaller? That could simply be because Mordion had hit him. There was a white welt along Hume's left cheek, swelling and spreading to a red and blue bruise. Poor Hume. More than his pride was hurting.

"Why are you looking at me like that?" Hume demanded.

"I was wondering if your eye was better," Ann said.

"Of *course* it is! Years ago!" Hume was now looking at Ann as closely as she had looked at him. "I can't help noticing," he said. "Why are you always the same, Ann? I keep growing, and Mordion's begun to go gray in his beard, but you never look any different."

"I—er—time goes slower outside the wood," Ann said awkwardly.

"It's not that I don't like the way you look," Hume explained. "I do. I like your cheekbones—the way they stick out—and your blue eyes with the brown skin. And I like the way you have fair bits on the outside of your hair—the fair shines on the dark wriggles." He put out his hand to take hold of the nearest bit of Ann's hair, and then, before Ann could move, he put the hand awkwardly behind her head instead and tried to kiss her.

"Don't!" Ann said, leaning away backward. This was something she had simply not been prepared for.

"Why not?" Hume demanded, pulling her toward him.

"Because," said Ann, leaning away mightily, "there are other girls you'd like better. I—er—I've got this cousin with bright fair hair. So fair it's nearly white, and the biggest brown eyes you ever saw. Lovely figure, too. Better than mine—I'm dumpy."

Hume let go of Ann with such alacrity that she was quite offended. "Is she nice?"

"Very," Ann invented. "Sweet, clever, understanding."

"Does she live in your village?" Hume asked eagerly.

"Yes," Ann lied. By now she had her fingers crossed behind her back, rather frantically.

"One more good reason for leaving this damn wood." Hume sat back in the boat. Ann did not know whether to be annoyed or relieved. "She sounds just like my dream girl," Hume said. "Talking of dreams, I've been having these dreams lately. I suppose that's why I'm in a bad mood with all—"

Ann climbed out of the boat. She did not want to hear about Hume's dreams, particularly not *that* kind of dream, blonds with hourglass figures and so forth. "Tell Mordion."

"I did. They worried him," said Hume.

They would, Ann thought. "I have to be home for—"

But Hume started climbing out of the boat, too, determined to tell her. Ann gave in and stood on the shingle with her arms folded, resigned. "They're frightful dreams," Hume said. "I'm in this box-thing with wires going in and keeping me alive, and there's supposed to be something to keep me unconscious, but it's gone wrong, and I'm awake. I'm *screaming*, Ann. Beating on the lid and screaming, but nobody hears. It's so awful I have to make myself wake up most nights."

It evidently *was* awful. Hume, from the look of him, had forgotten all about blonds and even about the bruises Mordion had given him. "How horrible," Ann said. She had not the heart to tell Hume that these should be Mordion's dreams—or the dreams from what the Bannus had put into Mordion's head, probably. It was one of the more awful by-products of being able to read minds. She no longer envied Hume.

"Mordion says they should be *his* dreams," said Hume.

"Er—" said Ann.

"Up until today," Hume said, brooding again, bent into a zigzag, half out of the boat, "those dreams were enough to make me *swear* to break the ban on Mordion. But now I'm not sure I *care!*"

Ann thought about it all. "You may be right," she admitted. "It's not fair that you should devote your life to Mordion." At this Hume unbent himself to give her, first, an incredulous look and, then, a huge, grateful smile. "But don't go out of the wood all the same," Ann said. "And now I really must go."

As she began striding from rock to slippery rock on the now much more perilous crossing of the river, Hume shouted after her. She thought the first bit was "—and thanks!" But the next bit, nearly drowned though it was in the roaring of the water, was definitely "—see your cousin!"

"Oo-er!" Ann said as she made the final leap to the earthy opposite bank. "What possessed me to go inventing cousins at him?" She walked into the woodland on the other side of the river with her insides quaking. She simply had not realized that Hume might be like this when he started growing up. She still liked him a lot, but still only as a friend. Nothing else seemed right, considering she had helped *make* Hume. But it made her feel wretched that she had told Hume lies.

She felt so wretched and her insides quaked so that she did not notice where she was until she was starting up the passage between the houses. There she smelled lunch cooking on both sides and broke into a trot. All I need now is Mum mad at me! she thought.

Hang on! she thought, as she came to the gray car. *How long was I in that field this time?* she asked her imaginary people.

About a couple of hours, the King replied.

—5——————————

ANN WAS LATE for lunch. Luckily there was some kind of row going on between Dad and Martin, and Mum was too anxious about that to give Ann more than a mild scold, ending, "And wash your hands at once!"

"Coupled with vengeful hand washing," Ann muttered, running water at the kitchen sink. "I ought to know exactly how Hume feels. Parents!"

From the sound of things Martin had cause to know how Hume felt, too. He had evidently said something that got up Dad's nose properly. All the time Ann was bolting her mixed grill in order to catch up, Dad kept saying, "You'd say anything, Martin, if you thought you could make yourself interesting by it." From time to time he added, "Sure you didn't see a flying saucer, too? Little green men with goggle eyes?"

"I know what I saw," Martin replied sulkily each time. Sometimes he added, "And I wish I'd never told you now."

And the atmosphere became tenser and tenser until finally, as

Ann was clearing the first course away, Martin was goaded into shouting, "You wouldn't believe in *God* if He walked through this door this minute!"

"*Martin!*" exclaimed Mum.

"I can tell real from make-believe, even if you can't!" Dad yelled back. "And don't you shout at me!"

Mum rushed the treacle tart onto the table and tried to soothe things down. "Now, Gary. Martin could easily have seen someone making a film, couldn't he? Treacle tart, Martin. Your favorite." She carved out a thick, trickling slice and realized she had forgotten the plates. "Oh, now look! I'm under stress! Ann, don't just sit there—you're not ill now—pudding plates. They film things all over the place these days, Gary, you know they do!"

Ann slid a plate under the waving slice of tart and put the plate in front of Dad to help with the soothing. "Then Martin shut his eyes when he looked at the cameras and the directors and all that, did he?" Dad asked contemptuously, pouring sugar all over the slice of tart. Dad needed more sugar than anyone else Ann had ever met. He could not eat any of the fruit he sold. He said it was too sour for him. And the marvel was that he never got fat, big as he was. "Nice try, Alison," he went on. "Pity Martin forgot the film crew. I don't know what he saw, but I know *why*. If he hasn't got his nose in a comic, he's watching aliens on TV all night long. He doesn't know truth from fiction, that boy!"

"Yes, I *do!*" Martin got up from the table with a crash, swept past the plate of treacle tart Mum was trying to give him, and banged out of the room, slamming the door behind him.

For Martin to ignore treacle tart was unheard of. Ann was convinced by this that Martin really had seen something strange. After lunch was finished—in subdued and grumpy silence—and Ann had—much too quickly—cleared away, she went to find Martin. He was sitting on the top step of the stairs, glowering.

"About what you saw—" Ann began.

"Don't *you* start now!" Martin snarled. "I don't care what you think. I just know I *did* see a man dressed like Superman, and he *was* climbing the gate into the old farm. So there!"

"*Superman!*" said Ann.

Martin looked at her with hatred. "Yes—only wrong colors. Silver bodysuit and green cape. And I *did* see him."

"I'm sure you did," Ann said. She was too worried and preoccupied even to try to soothe Martin. Could it have been Yam Martin saw? But Yam had never worn any kind of clothes, let alone a green cape. She went out and across Wood Street, fairly convinced that someone else had now entered the field of the Bannus. Or was it—this was the worrying part—that the field was getting larger?

PART FOUR

—1——

"THE FIELD HAS remained stable," said Reigner Five as he came into the pearly hall of the conference chamber in the House of Balance. He waited until the two half-live sentinels at the entry had scanned him and unjoined their hands to let him through, and walked over to the table where the other three were waiting. "That is—as far as my instruments can detect at this distance anyway."

"That's not much comfort," Reigner Three said impatiently. "Reigner Two's been missing for days now. Are we to assume that he and the Servant are still inside the field, or what?"

"I think so," said Five. He sat down and carefully fed the cube he had brought with him into the slot in the arm of his black pearly chair. "This is the processed information from Two's monitors," he told the other three Reigners. "Not that it tells us much. But it shows no record of either Two or the Servant coming *out* of the bannus field. And there are one or two other things it *does* show that I thought you all ought to see. Ready?"

When the three nodded, Five activated the cube. The glassy surface of the table had been showing reflections of their four faces, three young and one old, and all glowing with health from anti-age treatments, but as Five flicked the control, the reflections vanished. The cube's minor theta-field came into being there instead, flickering as it established.

A scene jumped into being on the table, tiny and perfect. Reigner Two, encased in a green tweed suit a size too small for his plumpness and wearing a long striped muffler round his neck, paced irritably in a pearly corridor. The other Reigners recognized the place as just beside the long-distance portal in the House of Balance. Evidently Two was still on Homeworld here, just about to start his journey. He looked solid enough to be picked up, from his pink, petulant face to his big black boots. Figures and signs running along the outer edges of the image showed Reigner Two to be in perfect health at this point, if a little high in adrenaline.

Reigner Four laughed. "Two's counting seconds, as usual! Doesn't he look a fright in that costume?"

"I suppose a robot put him into it," said Reigner Three. "I think we should have a human in charge of costumes."

"We have . . . a young woman called Vierran . . . House of Guaranty," said Five.

Shadows swung on the table, looming on the pearly walls, one shadow advancing, the others hastily getting out of its way. Following his advancing shadow, the Servant lounged into the tiny picture wearing clothes as strange as Reigner Two's.

Reigner Four guffawed. "Mordion looks like a scarecrow! What *is* that yellow thing with buttons?"

"It seems to me," said Reigner Three, "that this young woman in charge of costumes has a sense of humor that could be rather unwise."

On the table the tiny Reigner Two spun round, and his voice rang out of hidden speakers, life-size and perfectly reproduced, with the familiar slight bray on the last word. "And about time, too!"

The tall Servant bent his head apologetically. "Forgive me, sire—"

"And don't call me *sire!*" snapped Reigner Two. "I'm traveling as your servant for security. No one's supposed to know who I am. Let's get going." He snapped his fingers at someone out of range of the monitors. The portal keepers, like everyone else in the House of Balance, were keeping well out of the Servant's way. "Open up, there!"

The portal enlarged from a crease in the pearly wall into a smooth round archway. Reigner Two marched through with the Servant following respectfully. Empty white light filled the table for the second the pair were in transit.

The picture flicked back as the portal reception area of a head office on one of the nearer worlds. Like all Reigner Organization offices, it was open plan and large. Reigner Two and the Servant were emerging into a rather overlighted blaze of whites, greens, and pinks. This was a world that tried to imitate the pearly splendors of the House of Balance. At the edge of the picture a man wearing the neck chain of a Sector Governor, who was just leaving the office with the air of someone wanting his dinner, looked over his shoulder as the portal opened and stopped in his tracks. Awe and dismay came over his face. He whirled round and rushed across to the Servant.

"Reigners' Servant! This is an unexpected pleasure! I see by the strange garb that you're off on another mission. They do keep you busy, to be sure, ha-ha-ha!" He failed to recognize Reigner Two and ignored him completely. The tiny image was clear enough to show that Reigner Two was not sure whether to be pleased that his disguise was so good or annoyed not to be as well known as his Servant. "What can I do for the Reigners' Servant today?" gushed the Sector Governor.

Mordion Agenos smiled that particular smile of his. "I'm surprised you knew me," he said. "We both feel pretty strange in these clothes." Reigner Two looked soothed.

"Oh, I'd know the Reigners' Servant anywhere!" the Governor gushed. Reigner Two scowled.

"I suppose the Servant has got a pretty recognizable face," Reigner Four commented. "Looks like a death's-head."

"It fits the job," said Five.

Reigner Three agreed. "I don't think we've ever had a Servant who looked the part so well."

While they were speaking, Mordion had been explaining where they needed to go.

"Earth—Albion Sector—that's right out on the spiral arm, isn't it?" the Governor said distractedly. He was obviously calculating how much work this would mean and trying to look polite at the same time. "Certainly, certainly. Of course. I'll set it up at once, though it is a long way, you know. I think you'll be able to make three long walk-throughs, but I'm afraid most of the journey will have to be in single hops. That's speaking from memory, of course. We don't often have to set this particular journey up, aside from trade cargo. I'll go and check. And you'd like me to send word ahead of you? I wouldn't want you to be kept waiting any longer than is absolutely necessary."

Mordion bowed his head and seemed to agree to this. The Governor said, "Then forgive me while I go and attend to it personally." He beckoned. There were quite a few lesser executives, managers, and consuls standing about in the overlit space, staring unashamedly. Nearly all of them hurried forward as their Governor beckoned. "Look after the Reigners' Servant," the Governor commanded. "Make sure he has everything he needs. You four come with me." He dashed out of the picture, with his four underlings after him at a trot.

The other lesser ones gathered eagerly round the Servant, except for the last to reach him. That one was crowded out and had to make conversation with Reigner Two instead. Neither of them seemed to enjoy it. Inside the crowd the Servant was talking politely and readily, telling the underlings the latest gossip from Homeworld, refusing offers of food and drink, and making jokes about his odd clothing.

"*He* seems quite at his ease!" Reigner Three remarked. "He never talks like that to us. I was told he never talks to anyone. Who misinformed me?"

"No one. Cool down," said Reigner Five. "He never talks to anyone *here* in the House of Balance. They all keep out of his way."

"With good reason!" said Reigner Four. "But you're wrong, Five. *I* was told he talks to that nasty bit of work who found them those ridiculous clothes."

"Oh?" Three said, mollified, and added with venomous interest, "Nasty bit of work, is she? Doesn't she fancy you then, Four?"

"No," said Four. "Because I'm not her horse. Thank goodness."

All the Reigners laughed.

While they were talking, the Sector Governor must have been setting the journey up with frenzied speed. He came hurrying back, bowing and ushering. The Servant and Reigner Two, still in the crowd of respectful underlings, were hurried across to another long-distance portal and bowed inside it. The image on the table flicked to white again and then flicked back to another Reigner Organization office, this one made of stone and metal in a blank, artistic design. There another Sector Governor, this one better prepared, hurried politely up to the Servant.

"My dear Servant! Do, please, forgive us. We've only just heard you were coming."

After this came an office hung with native artworks, followed by another that seemed to be constructed of hammered bronze. In each, another Governor dashed up to the Servant and fawned upon him.

After the fifth such scene Reigner Three exclaimed, "This is like a royal progress! Nobody's even noticing poor old Two."

"Yes, I thought that would interest you," murmured Five.

"I suppose Mordion *is* our direct representative," Reigner Four said, not sounding too happy about it. "Whenever *he* appears, they all know they're really dealing with *us*."

"Yes, but does our Servant remember it?" Reigner Three demanded.

Reigner One, in his usual way, had up to then been keeping placidly silent. Now he stroked his white beard and twinkled a kindly smile at Three. "Of course he remembers it. I saw to that part of his training with great attention. I assure you he's as humble as he is loyal."

"I still think it's a mistake to send him out unmonitored," said Three. "But for this accident, we'd none of us know how these sector heads behave to him."

"Oh, I would. I do," said Reigner One.

"But just think of the power at the Servant's—" Three began again.

"Shut up, Three," Reigner Five said, flapping an irritable hand. "This next bit coming up is important."

Reigner Two and his Servant had entered one of the long walk-throughs, where several sectors were able to phase their portals together into an avenue stretching from world to world, for light-years across the galaxy. The image on the table strobed from white to picture, to white and back to picture, as the two passed the joins in the portals, but the strobing was fast enough not to interfere with the picture of the tall Servant strolling beside the much shorter Two. It was just a little trying on the eyes. The walk-through looked like a well-lighted tunnel composed of a paler version of the same pearly stuff as the room in which the Reigners sat. Both pearly substances did in fact come from the same source, and that source was, ironically, Earth flint. Only flint imported from Earth was strong enough to stand the strain of a portal. The image reminded all four of the watching Reigners just how important Earth was.

It was clear that Reigner Two had been having the same thoughts as Reigner Three. "You're very polite to all these bootlicking fools," his tiny image said to the Servant in a peevish life-size voice. "Do you *have to* be?"

"I think I do," the Servant answered, considering it. "They're all so mortally afraid they'll offend the Reigners if they offend *me*. It was impressed on me in my training that I'm simply the public face the Reigners show the Organization. This means I have to show them that I'm not in the least offended."

Reigner One shot Reigner Three a humorous look. See? said the look.

"You're probably right," Reigner Two told the Servant grumpily. He was looking nervously around. The tunnel seemed to oppress him. The figures racing at the edges of the image gave his heartbeat as faster and his blood pressure up. Or perhaps he was nervous for another reason. "See here, Mordion," he said suddenly. "I only ever dealt with a bannus once before, and Reigner One did most of it then. Would you mind helping me get some of the points about it straight in my mind?"

A warning look came over Reigner Five's narrow sandy face. He raised a finger to show the others this was the bit he had meant.

"If you wish me to," the Servant said courteously. It was obvious he did not want to. He had, after all, been trained never, ever to pry into any facts the Reigners wished kept secret. "But you will remember, sire, that there may not be a bannus to deal with. The reports were very confused. That letter from Earth to Albion could well be a hoax."

"I know that, you fool!" Reigner Two said, irritated. "But you'll agree that I have to be prepared in case it *wasn't* a hoax?" The Servant nodded. "Right," said Reigner Two. "Then I *order* you to think about the bannus."

There was a gasp from the watching Reigners. Reigner Five smiled sarcastically. For of course the Servant was bound to do whatever a Reigner ordered him.

"What do you think the bannus is?" Reigner Two asked the Servant. "How would you describe it yourself?"

"A machine for making dreams come true," the Servant answered. "At least that's what came into my head when I was first told about it."

"Hmm." Reigner Two plodded down the pearly tunnel, considering this. "Yes . . . in a sort of way . . . that describes quite well the way the bannus makes use of theta-space. One of its functions was to show people—very, far too vividly—whether or not they were making the right decisions."

Reigner Three nodded approvingly. "A prudent half-truth there."

"Wait," said Five.

"So." Reigner Two slowed down until the Servant's strolling stride was forced to become a loiter from one long leg to the other. "So you have a machine that was designed to run through a set of scenes, showing what would happen if you made decision A in a certain position, and then decision B, and so on, until it had shown you everything that could possibly happen. Then, if you'd fed your stuff into it properly, it should stop, shouldn't it? Now, if this isn't a hoax, the evidence says that the thing's still running. Why?"

The Servant loitered along with his hands in the pockets of his outlandish little yellow coat, obediently showing polite interest. "I suppose two reasons. The library clerk could have fed in a lot of stuff. Or he failed to do it properly and fed in something open-ended, which gave the machine no reason to stop."

"Right," said Reigner Two. "Which do you think he did?"

"Well, as Controller Borasus and six Maintenance men—not to speak of the clerk himself—all seem to have disappeared, I suppose it was the second thing," the Servant said. "I *am* right in believing the bannus co-opts living persons for its scenes where possible, am I?"

"Yes." Reigner Two sighed glumly. "And I think it's not a hoax *and* the clerk fed it something open-ended, too. Now you have to add in this: With each person the bannus pulls in, it gets another set of possibilities to work with. This causes it to expand its field and go on working. Where does that lead?"

The Servant shook his head. "There doesn't seem any reason why it should ever stop. Or not until it's taken over the whole planet."

"It could!" Reigner Two groaned. "And I've got to stop it! How am I supposed to do that?"

The Servant gave him a very polite look. "There is no reason for your Servant to tell you that, sire. You have abilities beside which mine are nothing."

"Well—" Reigner Two began frankly.

The four watching Reigners held their breaths, well aware that if the undervest full of gadgets were stripped off Reigner Two, very little would remain, whereas the Servant's abilities were bred into him.

"—yes, you could say I can rely on Reigner powers," Reigner Two said mournfully.

The other Reigners breathed again. The Servant, looking very uncomfortable, said, "Here is the end of the walk-through. The next office will be on Iony."

The sector head of Iony was the most fulsome yet. The watching Reigners were convulsed with laughter at the expression on Reigner Two's face when this Governor offered the Servant dancing girls. "To help pass the time while we connect the walk-through to Plessy," he begged the Servant. "I wouldn't wish Your Excellency to be bored."

The Servant glanced at Two's face and refused the dancing girls with the utmost politeness. Reigner Four was heard to wonder what the Servant would have said if he'd been alone.

"Well, *really!*" Reigner Two said in a shocked whisper when the Governor of Iony had hurried away. He said no more until the two of them were walking down another pearly, strobing tunnel. Then he said, "If the bannus *is* running, I sincerely hope that clerk didn't set it to do anything with dancing girls. I really cannot cope with dancing girls at my time of life!"

The Servant obviously did not know what to say to this. He settled for "Many people quite appreciate dancing girls, sire."

"Don't call me *sire!*" Reigner Two all but shouted.

"Ah," Reigner Four murmured. "Our Servant would have said yes to those girls."

Meanwhile, the numbers speeding at the edges of the scene

showed Reigner Two to be increasingly unhappy. "I wish you'd *understand*," he told the Servant. "It may be centuries since we used the bannus, but I remember the worst part quite clearly. The only way to get that machine to stop is for me to enter into whatever dreadful fantasy the clerk has it running."

The Servant looked startled. "Are you sure? Physically enter, si—er—enter?"

"Of course I'm sure! Here." Irritably Reigner Two pulled a folded fax sheet out of his tweed pocket, paused while it sprang out of its folds, and thrust the smooth white sheet at the Servant. "Take a look at what it says here."

The Servant glanced at the heading and seemed stunned. "This is for the eyes of Reigners only, si—er—Excellency."

"*Read* it," said Reigner Two.

The watching Reigners were nearly as stunned as the Servant. "Two's being impossibly indiscreet!" said Three.

"I know. He wasn't supposed to take that sheet with him," said Five.

"And the Servant can memorize—" began Four.

"The Servant may have a near-perfect memory," Reigner One put in, "but he can be ordered to forget, and he will. The danger is that some other person—say, on Earth—could get hold of that sheet. *May* have done by now."

As the Servant walked along, obediently reading the sheet, Reigner Two was saying, "There. Third paragraph. Doesn't that make it quite clear that I have to go into the field and take command of the action?"

"Yes, it does seem to suggest that," the Servant agreed. He read out: " 'The bannus is so programmed that it will always include itself in the field of action. Usually the bannus takes the form of a cup, weapon, trophy, or similar object. Once the operator has his hands upon this object, the bannus should normally become docile enough to bow to the will of the operator.' I take it this is a safety device? It looks as if you need only enter the field for long enough to recognize the bannus and take hold of it. Then you order it to stop."

"Fight my way through a mob of dancing girls and snatch the dulcimer off the leading damsel," Reigner Two said morbidly. "I can just see myself. I think the fools who invented this thing might have thought of a simpler way to stop it. What's wrong with a red switch?"

"Yes, *why* did they arrange it this way?" wondered the Servant.

"*Oops!*" said Reigner Four.

All the Reigners were greatly relieved when Reigner Two said austerely, "I can't tell you that," and took the fax sheet back. From the look of the Servant, he at once tried to stop thinking about it. "But how do I recognize the stupid thing," Reigner Two complained, "when I *have* wormed my way into some horrible hall of fun? And *then* I have to exercise my will on it. Suppose it doesn't obey?"

"No Reigner need have any difficulty there," the Servant said soothingly.

It was clear that Reigner Two did not have the Servant's confidence. When he trudged through the next portal and found another sector head standing there in full ceremonial robes, with all his underlings, also enrobed, ready to greet the Servant, Reigner Two contrived to look as dismal as any ruler of more than half the galaxy could.

"I'm glad to see," Reigner Three said, "there are *some* things Two's keeping his mouth shut about. Are we into crawling Governors again, Five? How long does this go on?"

"They single-hopped through about twelve major sectors after this one," Reigner Five said. "Governors, consuls, controllers, and all kinds of high executives grovel in all directions for a while."

"Is that the end of Two's indiscretions? Or did he go on?" Three asked.

"There's more. In Yurov, just before they hopped to Albion," said Five. "I can fast-forward it on to there if you like."

"If you can assure us," said Reigner One, "that neither of them said or did anything before that which we ought to know."

"Absolutely nothing," said Five. Reigner One raised Reigner power, looked into Five, and assured himself that Five was not lying. He nodded.

So the four Reigners summoned robots and had them bring food and drink. They set their black pearly chairs to "relax-and-recline" and refreshed themselves, while Five ran the cube forward at high speed. Little figures rushed this way and that on the table. High voices gibbered, even with the sound right down. At last Five recognized the crimson and gold furnishings of the Yurov office and stopped it. He ran it briefly the other way, so that little figures raced backward, squealing more gibberish. Then they were ready to watch again.

Yurov Sector was, itself, some way out along the spiral arm of the galaxy toward Earth. The Reigners writ, of course, ran here, too, but these parts were considered fairly uncivilized. Instead of a Governor, Yurov had a Controller to keep the natives down. And the image was not as clear as it had been, but it was clear enough to show that this office was decidedly opulent. It was hung with silk drapes and divided into rich little areas by worked-gold screens.

The slight blurring of the image caused Reigner Four to remark, "It's a long way off. It must be quite a job getting the consignments of flint through from Earth to where we want them."

"It is," said Reigner Five. "And hellish expensive."

"But worth it," said Reigner Three. "It pays, Four, as you would know, if you thought of anything besides your own wants."

"It pays some of these Controllers, too," Five remarked sourly as the very fat sector head of Yurov pounded into the picture, fetched by a frantic underling, and wove his way among the gold screens and crimson settles. "This one looks to make a pretty good thing of his position."

"And why not?" asked Reigner One cheerfully. "Provided he does an efficient job."

"Great Balance, Excellency!" the Controller of Yurov gasped to the Servant. "I'd no idea you'd be here so soon! We only got the message a minute ago. It takes time to phase to Albion, I'm afraid—there's quite a disjunction out here on the arm."

The Servant smiled at the Controller. "I'm sorry," he said. "We've probably been traveling almost as fast as the message. You may have heard there's a bit of an emergency out in Albion Sector."

The Controller of Yurov gazed up at that smile of the Servant's. He was plainly not sure whether it was as warm as it seemed or whether it was the way the Servant looked at someone he was about to terminate. He managed a wavering, gasping grin in reply. "Yes, I'd heard the Controller there—well, they're saying something's happened to him. Terribly sorry. And sorry you caught us so unready. I'm afraid you're going to have to wait at least a quarter of an hour."

"Whatever time it takes," the Servant said.

The Controller of Yurov seemed to decide the smile was friendly. He said, with much less annoyance and much more real distress, "And I've almost nothing I can offer you by way of entertainment while you wait! We thought we'd have an hour before you came. We were planning to be ready phased when you arrived."

"Think nothing of it," said the Servant. He glanced at Reigner Two, who was shuffling and looking twice the age he usually looked. The symbols and figures streaming at the edges of the scene confirmed that Reigner Two was tired out and low in blood sugar. "All we really need is to sit down quietly somewhere," said the Servant.

"Then please be seated," said the Controller of Yurov, waving to an underling, who hurried to pull forward a red settle. "I really do apologize—"

"I know," said the Servant, "how inconvenient—"

"Wine?" said the Controller. "Can I get you wine? All I have here is some Yurov sangro, but it was grown on my own estate at—"

The Servant looked at Reigner Two's sagging figure and interrupted gratefully. "Thank you. Wine would be perfect."

"I'm glad to see you trained him to be considerate," Reigner Three remarked to Reigner One as Reigner Two sank down onto the plump settle. A swift muttering between Reigners Four and Five ended with the calculation that Two was only eighty years or so younger than Reigner One, and Reigner One, as everyone knew, was coming up to his two thousandth birthday. The celebrations were already being planned all over the Organization.

"Two feels it, poor fellow. I don't," Reigner One murmured. He was smiling at the way the Controller of Yurov was now rushing about among the screens at the back of the picture, giving furious orders about the wine. "And bring it to *me* first," he was heard saying. He had a very penetrating voice. "I shall die of shame if someone gives the Reigners' Servant wine that isn't properly breathed!" Reigner One chuckled.

"What an excellent fellow!" he said.

"I'm perfectly all *right!*" Reigner Two snapped at the Servant in the front of the picture. "I simply need a short rest." He lay back on the settle, looking exhausted.

Shortly an Assistant Controller hastened up with a tray of curious wood inlaid with gold, which had two goblets on it that were obviously solid gold. Another pulled up a gold-topped table. A Consul Manager followed diffidently with another tray loaded with little jeweled dishes of cakes. Finally came the Controller of Yurov himself with a pitcher of sculpted gold from which he filled the two goblets with rich red wine and then stood holding the pitcher, almost prayerfully expectant, while the Servant first thanked him cordially and then sipped the wine. Reigner Two meanwhile grabbed gratefully for the cakes.

The Servant sipped, and his eyebrow moved like wings. "This is *wonderful!*" he said. And smiled.

This time the Controller stretched his own chubby mouth into a smile as warm, though not as enchanting, as the Servant's. He left the pitcher and bustled away, looking thoroughly flattered.

"He certainly knows how to exploit that death's-head grin of his," Reigner Three commented. "Is that what we were supposed to notice?"

"No. Wait," said Five.

Reigner Two drank off his goblet of wine, ate more cakes, poured himself more wine, and sank back with a contented sigh, pulling the fax sheet out of his pocket again as he did so.

"Fool," murmured Reigner Four.

"There's another danger in this bannus business, you know," Reigner Two told the Servant. "You'll have learned up on how we used Earth as a convict settlement before we discovered how rich it was in flint—"

"Not in a sector office, you fool!" Reigners Four and Three said together.

Of course, the image of Reigner Two simply went on talking. "Well, it wasn't only folk who obstructed the Organization we sent there. A number of rebel Reigners were put into exile there, too."

The Servant looked up from admiring the pattern on his goblet. "You wish me to know this?"

"No. Shut up, Two, you fool!" said Four.

"Yes," said Reigner Two. "It could be a factor. I might have to order you to deal with some of these people."

"All right. Stop there," said Reigner Three.

"Surely," said the Servant, with his eyebrow down in a line, frowning, "after all this time, without any old-age treatments, any rebel Reigners would be dead?"

"Don't answer him!" muttered Four.

"Well, there are two problems about that," said Reigner Two. "The exiled Reigners were, of course, put on Earth under a ban as strong as—as I suppose your training is, and forbidden either to leave Earth or to go against the true Reigners—us, you know. One of the standard ways they hit on to get round our ban was to have children. The children would have Reigner blood and powers and so forth and were not under the ban, so they could rebel *for* them. Naturally we sent a Servant—several Servants, in fact—to deal with the children, but they didn't get them all—"

"Didn't get them?" The Servant had gone pale. His face shone like a skull against the crimson settle. "Failed?"

Reigner Two was far too busy with his own worries to care about the Servant's state of mind. "Yes. The training wasn't so good in those days. Just *one* of the things that's worrying me is that there are certainly people with Reigner blood around on Earth. If one of them got near that bannus—suppose that clerk is one—that would be bad enough. But my main worry is those rebel Reigners themselves. I know at least one of them wasn't terminated by the Servants."

The Servant flinched. They saw him look round as if he were hoping someone would come along and interrupt. No one was near. They were all keeping respectfully distant. "Remarkably fine wine, this," the Servant said.

Reigner Two's face was wrinkled with trouble. He took no notice. "The two Servants we had then did their best," he said. "They were outclassed, but they put one rebel—maybe more, I wish I could remember—down into stass sleep somewhere on Earth—"

"That's something," murmured the Servant.

"Yes, but I don't know *where*," Reigner Two continued. "This sheet doesn't *say*." He rattled the sheet irritably. "I wish I'd thought to check before we set out. I've forgotten."

"But this one—or more—is dealt with," the Servant said. He seemed to be trying to console himself more than Reigner Two.

"No, they're *not!*" Reigner Two cried out. "You don't understand! If one of them's near enough to be included in the bannus field, it would fetch him out of stass. I shudder to think what would happen then!"

"Oh, dear," murmured Reigner One. "My dear Two. That you should not have said."

The Servant was shifting around on the settle. His usual relaxed composure seemed to have deserted him. He looked sick. At last, obviously determined to stop Reigner Two, he said, and it could be seen this took him some courage, "Sire, I am sure you should not be telling me things that are not even on the fax sheet."

"I'll be the judge of that," Reigner Two said pettishly. "There are other things about the bannus that—"

"Don't you think the work on these goblets is beautiful?" the Servant interrupted, as if he were desperate. His face shone with sweat, and he was whiter than ever.

"Vulgar, I think," said Reigner Two. "These outer sector heads use their position just to grab money, to my mind. As I was saying, the bannus—"

But to the Servant's evident huge relief, the Controller of Yurov came pelting back, fat quivering all over him and his face speckled with perspiration. "Phased!" he said. "We did it in record time! If you and your man would like to follow me, Excellency."

The Servant unfolded from the settle like someone starting a race. Reigner Two dragged himself up after him, and the two disappeared into yet another portal.

—2—

WHEN THE IMAGE reappeared on the table, it was the sector office in Albion.

"What frightful decor!" said Reigner Three. "Dreadful provincial bad taste."

"They're out in the backwoods now," said Five.

"And it shows!" said Four. "Steak and mustard."

"I thought that was your favorite dish, Four," murmured Reigner One.

The Albion office was lined in yellow shiny wood, crudely paneled, with insets of meaty pink or lime yellow. All the office furniture—and this place was more like an office than any of the others—was the same meat pink and yellow. The effect was even more garish against the emerald green of the robes of the Associate Controller and his assistants, who were sweeping forward to meet the two travelers.

"How come he's only the second one who's had time to get into official dress?" Reigner Four wondered.

"Wears them all the time—probably sleeps in them," Five said.

In fact, the green robes all looked smooth and freshly pressed. They flowed in graceful folds as the entire group bowed as one man. It looked rehearsed. "My name is Giraldus, Excellency," the Associate Controller said to the Servant. "I have had to take this authority upon myself in view of the unfortunate absence of our Controller Borasus. But you find Albion prepared to receive you in spite of our sad emergency."

"Then Controller Borasus is still unaccounted for?" said the Servant.

Associate Controller Giraldus shook his head, with a woeful look that had no woe in it at all. "Not heard of since he stepped through the portal to Earth, I am sorry to say. He never boarded his plane in London. He never made his way to the American conference. But there has been no panic here. We have—"

"The Reigners will be glad to know that," the Servant interrupted politely. A little smug smile curved the corners of Giraldus's mouth, but the Servant did not smile as he went on. "This makes it all the more important for me to get to Earth quickly."

"And you shall!" Giraldus said grandly. Robes swirling, he turned and led the way across the pink and mustard hall. As the picture shifted to follow Reigner Two, the watching Reigners saw that the place was full of office workers, all carefully dressed in Reigner Organization uniform and all doing their best to look efficient and busy. Several hundred pairs of eyes followed the Servant and Reigner Two, awed and curious.

"He must have pulled in the entire staff of Albion Sector," Reigner Five commented. "Or else that office is seriously overmanned."

"I had a hunch that the Reigners would be sending their Servant," Giraldus said, approaching the gray, pearly outline of a local portal. "When I sent my report through, I also took the liberty of requesting hourly updates from Iony Sector. Expensive, I concede, but see how it has paid off. We had ample warning that you were on your way, Excellency. And at that point I decided to go over Earth's head. The Runcorn office has shown that it doesn't know what it's doing, and this is far too important to leave to local idiots. I've calibrated this portal directly to London, which was what our lamented missing Controller did, too, and I've arranged for a car to meet you and drive you straight out to the library complex."

"Most efficient," said the Servant. "Have you money and documentation for Earth, or do I apply to Runcorn for that?"

"Great Balance, no! We leave Runcorn strictly out of this," Giraldus said. He ushered them toward a small meat pink table on which lay a number of flat leather folders. "Provision," he said, "for a large number. We did not know how many colleagues you would be bringing, Excellency." He picked up the largest leather folder and presented it to the Servant with a bow.

The Servant turned the wallet over, musingly, and then opened it to show a thick wodge of paper money and a number of little cards peeping from pockets in the leather. He teased a card forth with his long, deft fingers and examined it. His face went perfectly blank. "This," he said, turning his face, skull-like, toward Giraldus, "is a credit card made out in my own name."

"Yes, indeed," Giraldus said smugly, handing Reigner Two another wallet at random. "I wished everything to be entirely right and accurate. Now please excuse me one moment while I key the portal."

"The names of our Servants," said Reigner Three, "are one of the secrets of the House of Balance."

"Purely for psychological reasons," Reigner One put in.

"It makes no difference," said Reigner Three. "This Giraldus has used his emergency authority to pry."

"Wants to impress Mordion with his efficiency," said Reigner Four. "Aims to get promoted to Controller."

They were relieved to see that as soon as Giraldus turned his back to key the portal, Reigner Two gave the Servant the Sign—with the delay gesture added, meaning that the Servant should terminate Giraldus on the way back. The Servant nodded in reply, very slightly.

"I'm glad to see that Two hasn't lost his head completely," Reigner Three said.

The portal opened. Giraldus swung round and bowed again. "May I wish you a safe and successful journey," he said merrily. "*Auf Wiedersehen*, as they say on Earth!"

"Thank you," said the Servant. Very gravely he added, "I shall see you again on our way back from Earth," and followed Reigner Two toward the portal.

As the table blinked white while the two travelers were in transit, Reigner Four exclaimed, "Our Servant looked *sorry* for him! Is he slipping or something?"

Reigner One twinkled a smile. "No. He always looks like that when he gets the Sign. What made you think he enjoys his work?"

"Well—" Reigner Four thought about it, with his handsome face rather bewildered. "*I'd* enjoy it. I always rather envy the Servants."

"I doubt if you would if you knew," said Reigner One.

Here the table blinked into murky darkness as the two travelers emerged among tall buildings. It was night on this part of Earth, and it appeared to be raining. The monitors enhanced the light so that the watchers could see Two moaning and pulling his muffler round his head. The Servant turned up the collar of his yellow coat while he looked round for the car that was supposed to meet them. It slid up beside them as he looked, and stopped, making fierce yellow bars filled with rain with its headlights.

"I wouldn't care to ride in *that*!" muttered Reigner Four. "Metal turtle."

A heavy man, trimly dressed in a light-colored raincoat, climbed hastily out of the vehicle and hurried round in front of the head-lights. "Reigners' Servant?" he asked, in an angry, abrupt way.

Reigner Five stopped the cube there for a second in order to switch in a translator. Reigner Four stretched his muscular arms and yawned. "Do we need to watch any more, Five?"

"Certain things come out," said Five, "of a different nature."

"We'll be guided by you, Five," Reigner One said placidly.

The image ran again, showing astonishment on the Earthman's large, well-nourished face, as the Servant and Two advanced into the car lights to meet him. The monitors picked up his subvocal comment, which he certainly did not intend anyone to hear. "My God! Where did they get those clothes? The Salvation Army?"

The Servant heard. His ears were as keen as any monitors. A large, amused smile lit his face. Like others before him, the Earthman stared at that smile uncertainly. "Pleased to meet you," the Earthman said, in the same angry way. "I'm John Bedford, Earth Area Director." He held out a broad hand.

The Servant took the hand and shook it. This was obviously an Earth ritual. "And I'm pleased to meet you, sir. We had no idea the Area Director would be here in person."

"No, I'll bet you hadn't!" John Bedford said with energetic bitterness. "I broke all the speed limits getting down here from Runcorn. I was damned if I was going to let Albion go over my head! It was *my* clerk on *my* patch who turned this forbidden machine on, and it's *my* responsibility to see it put right. Earth may be an out-of-the-way hole at the edge of the galaxy, but we do have our pride!"

Reigner Four asked, in some surprise, "Doesn't Earth Organization know how much we depend on their flint?"

"Four, it really is time you took a bit of notice of something besides yourself," Reigner Five told him. "Of *course* they haven't a clue."

"If they knew," Reigner Three explained, "they'd up the price and cut our profits to nothing. Then we'd have to suppress them. As it is, we tell them the flint's used for road rubble and keep Earth busy fighting itself. That way everyone's happy."

"And now you can go back to sleep, Four," said Reigner Five.

While they were talking, the Servant had managed to say something that soothed the angry Area Director. John Bedford was now holding open the rear door of his car and saying quite cheerfully, "It's no trouble really. I enjoy night driving. The roads are empty. Get in. Get comfortable. I want to get through London before the morning traffic starts."

Reigner Two climbed through the door. The monitor image tipped and enlarged to show the interior of the car and its seats covered with a gray, downy substance. Doors banged. The monitors again raised the light level. John Bedford was seated in front of a steering wheel, tipping his head back to tell his passengers to fasten their safety belts. The Servant fastened Reigner Two in and then himself. The racing figures and symbols showed that Reigner Two had almost instantly fallen asleep, even before the car began to move. Reigner Three had to look away as the journey began. The feeling you got from looking at the table, of moving without really moving, was enough to make anyone carsick.

"I've been finding out all about that library clerk," John Bedford said in his abrupt way, tipping his head back as he drove. "Is that the sort of thing you people want to know?"

"Yes, indeed." The Servant hitched himself forward against his straps until he was leaning from the backseat in a hunting crouch. "Anything you can tell me will be most valuable."

"His name's really Henry Stott," said John Bedford. "He gave the name Harrison Scudamore when he first joined us, and that was his first lie. The main thing that's come out is that he's a confirmed liar."

"Oh," said the Servant.

"Yes," said John Bedford. "Oh. You don't have to tell me we boobed. I'm here to tell you I'm prepared to take the rap for it. That's why I came myself. Stott lied about his name. He lied about his family. Here on Earth we have an absolute rule that anyone who joins Rayner Hexwood must have no family to ask awkward questions. We even insist that our people don't marry until they've proved they can keep a secret. I've a wife and kids myself now, but I had to wait ten years and keep poor Fran in the dark about why."

"Is that necessary?" asked the Servant.

"Yes. The higher grades get to travel to Yurov and even beyond," John Bedford told him. "And the rest of Earth is only just starting to think in terms of spaceships. We know this world's just not ready to join the galactic community, so we keep it dark. It wouldn't do at all for anyone to guess we actually trade with other worlds." He laughed. "Actually, back in the days when we used antigravity transports, people were always seeing them and thinking they were flying saucers full of aliens. We had to work hard to discredit the reports. It's a great relief now that we have trade portals."

The Servant meditated on this. The monitors caught him side face, with his eyebrow winging above one deep, bright eye, like a hunting owl. "Go on about Stott," he said after a while.

"He lied," said John Bedford. "He said he was an orphan. In fact, he has both parents living—father breeds pigeons. He lied about his age. Said he was twenty-one, and he turned out to be eighteen. He said he'd had a previous job with an electronics firm, and that was another lie. He's been unemployed since he left school. Then it comes out that he's been in court for stealing from the store where he said he'd had the job. The references, the GCSE certificate, the birth certificate he produced were all forgeries—forged them himself, we think. I suppose he was desperate to get a job, but there's no way *we* should have employed him."

"Don't you have recruiting staff who can see through those kinds of lies?" the Servant asked.

"We're *supposed* to have," John Bedford said disgustedly. "You may be sure I've gone through our Induction Office like a dose of salts. I kicked half of them out into Maintenance, in fact. But they all swear Stott was equal to any test they threw at him. The cocky brat seems to have bluffed his way past everything."

"Weren't they bound to say that?" asked the Servant.

John Bedford barked out a laugh. "Yes, to save their own hides.

That's the problem. But *someone* in Induction had doubts. Stott was only given the lowest level of information and posted to Hexwood Farm—believe it or not, that's supposed to be a place where no one can do any harm! I wish I'd *known* there were dangerous machines stored there. There's no kind of cross-reference to that, even on my Most Secret files. I had to work it out when Albion started asking questions."

"Very few people knew. Albion had no information, either," the Servant said. "So the clerk is a confirmed liar, a thief, and a forger. What are his interests? Pigeons like his father?"

"No, Stott and his dad hate each other. I doubt if they'd agree on anything," John Bedford told him. "I drove over and dropped in on the parents. His pa's a nasty bit of work, too. He thought I was the police at first, and he was scared stiff—I don't think he's on the level, either. Then when he found I wasn't the fuzz, he came the injured father at me and told me he'd washed his hands of young Henry two years ago. Embarrassing scene, with Henry's ma blubbing away in the background about how her Henry was always misunderstood. But Ma came up with something that's definitely worth mentioning. Blubbed on that her Henry was a genius with computers. This is true, too. Runcorn confirmed it—but only when I went back and asked. Apparently he won all the computer games during the induction course and then started showing the other trainees how to hack into my office computer. I had another few hides for that one."

"So he had the skills to start the bannus," the Servant concluded. His dim, owllike profile had the same look, sad and still, as he had had saying good-bye to Giraldus. He knew Stott had to be terminated. "Stott seems to be one who liked to translate his dreams into reality," he added musingly.

"Most crooks are," John Bedford agreed. "But so are a lot of people who aren't crooks. What's achieving your ambition, after all, but just that—dreams to reality? Crooks just take the easy shortcut."

He and the Servant fell to talking about criminals and the criminal mind. They seemed to like each other. Reigner Three shifted about, yawning. Reigner Four stretched again and scratched his curly hair. Reigner One went to sleep, as peacefully as Reigner Two's image on the table. Meanwhile, the car rushed on through growing daylight and patches of green countryside. Reigner Five was the only one who watched and listened closely, with his sandy head sarcastically tipped and his pale greenish eyes hardly winking.

"They're nearly there," he said at long last.

Reigner One woke up so smoothly that it was hard to tell that he had dozed off. Three and Four dragged their attention back to the table. It was quite light in the image now. Houses were going slowly past beyond Reigner Two's bleary, waking face. All four Reigners watched intently as the car stopped and the three men got out into dawn sunlight. They walked slowly along an empty road to an old wooden gate.

And as they reached the gate, the image blanked out into hissing white light.

3

"THAT'S ALL THERE'S been since," said Reigner Five. "From the look of it, something shorted Two's monitors out the moment he got near that gate. It would take an unusually powerful field to do that."

"So you think the bannus *is* running?" asked Reigner Three.

"*Something* is, which could be the bannus," Five answered cautiously.

"Anyone else would say yes," said Four. "The Servant could have handled almost anything else. That's why Two took him along, after all."

"Two should have been able to handle the bannus," Five said irritably. "I certainly hung enough equipment on his fat body."

"Yes, but all the equipment in the Organization won't help a person if his willpower isn't up to it," Reigner Three objected. "Two's isn't. We saw. Bleating at the Servant like that!"

"I always thought he was soft," said Reigner Four. "Ah, well."

There was short silence while the three younger Reigners thought about Reigner Two. None of them bothered to look even as woebegone as Giraldus had looked over Controller Borasus. Eventually Five gave a short laugh and removed the cube from its slot in his chair. The glassy table reflected a puzzled frown growing on Reigner Four's face.

"But couldn't the Servant have handled the bannus?" he asked. "*He* never seemed short of willpower. In fact, this particular Servant never struck me as human that way."

"You're forgetting," Reigner Three told him. "His training will have blocked his will in exactly those places where—"

Here Reigner One made a quiet but decided interruption. "No, my dear. Four has put his finger on it. I very much hope he hasn't, but I fear he has." They stared at him. He twinkled benignly back. "I am afraid we are all in considerable danger," he said blandly, "though I've no doubt we shall survive it, the way we always do. You all know the nature of the bannus. Well. Now consider that Reigner Two not only discussed the matter, almost frankly, with Mordion Agenos but also forgot, as far as I could see, to order him to forget about it." His cheerful old eyes turned roguishly to Reigner Five. "Two *did* forget, didn't he?"

"If you don't count the Sign," Reigner Five said, wary and scowling, "the only orders he gave anywhere on the cube were first to think about the bannus, then to read about it in our private fax. What are you driving at, One?"

"Of course," Reigner One said, "it depends to some extent on what idiot imaginings that clerk set the bannus to work on. Since we now know the clerk was a liar, I'm not sure I believe what that letter said. Making—what were they?—handball teams? Even if that was true, I could still think of a dozen ways the bannus could use to get round my blocks in our Servant's mind. And it will try.

Because—I am sorry to have to tell you this—our Servant is a purebred Reigner."

"*What!*" exclaimed the other three. Reigner Three shouted, "Why weren't we *told*? Why are you *always* doing things behind our backs?" while Reigner Four was bellowing, "But you told us there weren't any Reigners left except you!" and Reigner Five's bitter voice cut across both, demanding, "Does the Servant know?"

"Please be quiet," said Reigner One. His finger was stroking and patting at his silver mustache in a way that was almost agitated. His eyes went more than once to the two sentinel statues at the doorway. They were showing signs of unusual disturbance, jigging, bending, and struggling about on their pillars. "No, Five," he said. "The Servant has no idea—what a preposterous notion! And I am only half Reigner myself, Four. And Three, you were not told because you were only newly a Reigner and somewhat overwhelmed by it when the situation came about. It was when I exiled the last of my onetime fellow Reigners. I kept some of their children back and bred them to be our Servants. The idea pleased me. And you must admit it has been very handy to have someone with Reigner powers at our beck and call. But there always does come a time when we have to terminate them, or"—he gestured toward the agitated statues at the door—"put them to other uses."

Five swung his chair round and stared at the statues keenly. "Excuse me a moment," he said. He got up and strode to the doorway. The movements of the statues became almost frantic as he approached them. Five watched them for a moment, with a bitter, appraising look. Then, with a flash and a dull thump, he put an end to the half-life of the things. "Sorry about that," he said as he came back to the table.

Reigner One waved a cheerful hand at the things, drooping from their plinths. "They were no use to us after this. We can put Mordion in their place as soon as someone fetches him back. As for poor old Two—well, there's no doubt that one of us is going to have to go to Earth."

His eyes, and Three's, and Five's, turned to Reigner Four.

Reigner Four knew that he came only just above Two in the real order of the Reigners. He knew it was important one of them went to Earth. He tried to accept it with a good grace. "So I tackle the bannus?" he said, doing his best to sound willing and competent.

"If you don't," said Reigner One, "you'll cease to be a Reigner. But since we can't trust the Servant any longer, you'd better terminate Two as soon as you spot him—"

"But who runs our finance if Two's terminated?" Reigner Three protested. "One, aren't you forgetting we're an enormous commercial combine these days?"

"Not at all," Reigner One said, at his blandest. "You can all see Two's passed his usefulness. There's that young Ilirion at the House of Interest who's turning out to be even better than Two was once. We can elect him Reigner Two as soon as Four gets back. But Four—even above stopping the bannus and terminating Two, I want you to make it your priority to slap Mordion Agenos into stass by any means you can contrive. Then bring him back. And do it *soon*. If he discovers enough about the bannus, he could be coming back here to terminate us all in a week or so."

"Yes," said Four, willing but puzzled. "But why stass? Killing him would be much easier."

"I haven't bred from him yet," said Reigner One, "and I've got two good girls lined up for it. The annoying thing about this business is that it's putting our future Servants in jeopardy."

"All right." Reigner Four got up. "I'm on my way," he said as he strode out past the dead statues.

"*He's* taking it well!" Reigner Three said, staring after him. "Could it be that my little brother is learning to be responsible— after all these centuries?"

Five laughed cynically. "Or could it be that they're offering people dancing girls on Iony?"

4

REIGNER FOUR COULD not be bothered to go down to the basement to select Earth clothes. He disliked that girl down there—Vierran—too much. He sent a robot down with an order instead, while he took his Earth languages course.

The robot eventually returned with a carefully wrapped package. "Unpack it," Reigner Four said from under the language helmet. He was lying on a couch having his body toned and tuned by other robots. The robot obeyed and left. When Reigner Four at length finished with his treatments and the helmet and strode across his suite, naked, vibrant, and muscular, he found, carefully laid across a pearly table, a pair of red tartan plus fours and a coat of hunting pink. With these, Vierran apparently intended him to wear green high-tops, orange socks and a frilly-fronted white shirt.

Reigner Four scratched his curls and stared at these things. "Hmm," he said. He had an idea that the girl Vierran disliked him at least as much as he disliked her. "I think I'll check," he said.

So while another robot fitted him into the undervest that contained his monitors and the other miniature gadgets that made him the Reigner he was, Reigner Four keyed for a visual of an Earth street scene. It took awhile. The computer had to call in a live archivist, and it was only after a frantic search that she managed to find film of a football crowd leaving a match in 1948. Reigner Four gazed at the hundreds of men hurrying past in their hundreds of long, drab macs and flat caps.

"I'll teach that girl to make a fool of me!" he said. He had a longing to go down to the basement and kill Vierran slowly with his bare hands. He might have done it, too, except that Vierran was, like everyone else who worked in the House of Balance, from an important Homeworld family. The House of Balance had this way of controlling the other great mercantile Houses of Homeworld. They were allowed to trade so long as they did not attempt to compete with the Reigner Organization, and to make sure they knew their place, the Reigners required at least one member of each House to go into service in the House of Balance. Vierran's House of Guaranty was one of the ones who could—and would!—make things awkward for Reigner Four. On the other hand, even the House of Guaranty could not complain if some complete accident happened to Vierran. What if she were to have a crippling fall when she was out riding that beloved horse of hers?

Nice idea. It had the added advantage that Reigner Four would then be able to get near the beautiful cousin that Vierran kept defending from him. Four promised himself he would set that accident up as soon as he got back from Earth. Meanwhile, he dressed himself in the all-over metallic suit he wore when he went hunting and added a long green cloak for the look of it. Reigner Three might preach about the need for secrecy, but let the Earth people stare! Reigner Four still failed to see why Earth had to be kept ignorant. He more or less *owned* Earth, after all. It was time Earth knew its masters.

Clad in silver and green, he strode off to the portal and began his journey. It took him a good deal longer than it had taken Reigner Two and the Servant. He paused in each sector to enjoy the stir he caused there, and when he reached Iony, he turned off his monitors and accepted the Governor's offer of dancing girls. They were very good. They were so good, in fact, that he forgot to turn the monitors on again when he went on. With his mind still on dancing girls, he reached Albion at last, where Associate Controller Giraldus met him with great respect and no surprise at all.

"This *is* sad news, Excellency, sire, about Earth, isn't it? Runcorn is all to pieces. They seem to have lost their Area Director. Hearing you were coming in person, Excellency, sire, I conjectured you would wish to be on the spot with all possible speed to rescue your Servant, and I decided not even to trouble Runcorn for a car. I took the liberty of recalibrating the portal more closely. I can now set you down directly outside the library complex at Hexwood Farm."

"Very good," Reigner Four said genially. The fellow really was too efficient by half and ripe for termination. And he would have to do it himself since the Servant was unavailable. But the dancing girls had put him in a lazy mood. He decided to do it on the way back and simply waved the man over to key the portal.

It set him down in broad daylight in the middle of a road. No one much about. Afternoon by the look of it, on a chilly blue day filled with white scudding clouds. There were dwellings around, but Reigner Four dismissed these with a glance. The place he wanted was clearly behind the large wooden gate opposite. His gadget-augmented perceptions could pick out the circuitry embedded in the woodwork, and—this was pretty annoying!—they were the antiquated kind of lock that his body keys were not equipped to deal with.

Nothing else for it then. He took a run, got his hands to the top of the gate, and swung himself over. He landed, easy and supple, on the other side. There was an empty Earth-type vehicle blocking his path to the door of the building beyond. The litter of twigs on its top and a number of bird droppings showed him it had been here for some time. He pulled down his mouth in distaste as he edged past the thing. It smelled. And surely it was carrying secrecy a bit far to let the house and garden look so run-down! He stooped in under the half-open door of the house.

"Anybody there?" he shouted in his young, carrying voice.

Nobody answered. From the look of the cobwebs and the dust, this room had been abandoned even longer than the van outside. Reigner Four strode through it into a slightly less neglected area beyond. This room held nothing but two stass stores of a type he had thought were all scrapped several centuries ago. It was probably cheaper to dump them on Earth than scrap them. Both were working, one of them with a senile whine that was really irritating. The sound annoyed Reigner Four into slapping the thing, first on its metalloy side and then, when that only changed the noise to a buzz, on its glass front. The thing was labeled in Hamitic script, "Earlyjoy Cuisine," but someone had half covered that with a label written in purple, in Earth script, "Breakfasts." The second stass store was similarly labeled, "Squarefare" in Hamitic and "Lunch & Suppers" in purple Earth script. Reigner Four peered into the second one as he passed and shuddered to see it about one-third full of small plasit trays, each one containing different colored globs of provender.

He found a staircase at the end of the room, leading down into the depths below the house. Since it was carpeted and in good repair, Reigner Four descended unhesitatingly. The room below brought him up short with disgust. It was a bed-sitting-room, and whoever had been living in it must have had the habits of an ape. That clerk, Reigner Four conjectured. The smell from the unwashed bed was appalling. Reigner Four picked his way fastidiously through old beer cans, newspapers and abandoned clothes, orange peel and cigarette stubs, and kicked aside a stack of used stass trays to clear his way to the modern dilating door at the far end.

"Ah!" he said as he came through it.

This was the operations area, and it was actually clean and cared for, if not precisely up-to-date. There were various machines for computing and information retrieval—all about the same age as the stass stores but in much better order—and, stretching away beyond in three directions, numbers of big dark caverns lined with dimly seen books, machinery, cubes, tapes, and even, at the nearest corner, a rack holding parchments. The bannus should be in here somewhere. Now if he could discover how the lights in these caves went on . . .

As he turned back to examine the operations area for light switches, a red light caught his eye, flashing beside one of the display units. Reigner Four discovered, in a leisurely way, which button should be pressed to stop it, and pressed.

He seemed to have got it wrong. The display lit up. A severe face with folds in its eyelids looked out of the screen at him. "At last!" it said. "I am Suzuki of Rayner Hexwood Japan. I have tried contact for two days for book on Atlantis urgently. Now my patience is rewarded."

"This installation is closed for urgent repairs," said Reigner Four. He pressed the button again.

The face failed to disappear. It said, "You are not clerk who is usually here."

"No, I've come to deal with the fault. Get off the line," said Reigner Four.

"But I have urgent message about Bannus," said the Japanese face. "From Runcorn."

"What?" said Reigner Four. "What message?"

"Bannus is at end of record stack straight behind you," said the image.

Reigner Four spun round eagerly, to find that the central dark cavern was now lighted, with a gentle dim glow that allowed him to see no more than a vista of shelves leading off into the distance. He set off down the vista at a fast, swinging stride.

There was a moment of slight giddiness.

—5—————————

REIGNER FOUR FOUND that what he was really doing was riding a horse down a long green glade in a forest.

He had another giddy moment in which he thought he was going mad. Those old-age treatments did sometimes have peculiar side effects. Then his head cleared. He sat upright and looked around him with pleasure.

The horse under him was a great strong chestnut, glossy with grooming and bridled in green-dyed leather. A war-horse. It had armor over its head and mane, which ended in a metal spike between its ears. His helmet hung at his knee against the flowing green saddlecloth, polished steel with a green plume floating off it. His knee, beside it, was also in polished steel. In fact, now that he looked, he found he was dressed in an entire suit of armor, beautifully hinged and jointed. His green shield, with his own personal device of the Balance painted on the green in gold, was slung at his left shoulder. Below it, at his waist, hung a most satisfyingly hefty sword. His other arm cradled a mighty green-painted lance.

This was splendid! Reigner Four laughed aloud as he thudded down the green glade. It was spring, and the sun shone through the tender leaves, and what more could a man ask? Well, perhaps a castle and a damsel or so for when it came to nightfall, he supposed. And almost as he thought this, he came out beside the rippling water of a lake and saw a castle on a greensward across the water. A wooden bridge led across the lake to the castle, but the central portion of the bridge was hauled up to make a drawbridge. Reigner Four thundered along the roughhewn logs of this bridge and drew his horse up near the gap.

"Hallo there!" he yelled, and his voice went ringing round the water.

After a minute or so a man in herald's dress left the castle by a small door and advanced down the green meadow to the other end of the bridge. "Who are you and what do you want?" he called in a mighty voice.

"Whose castle is this?" Reigner Four called back.

"The castle of King Ambitas," the herald shouted. "The king wishes it made known that no man bearing arms may enter this castle unless he first defeats the king's Champions in fair fight."

"Fair enough!" Reigner Four shouted. He hunted daily. He had trained for years in every form of warfare and had absolutely no doubt about his abilities. "Let down your bridge and lead me to your Champions."

They did not let down the bridge straightaway. First, with a tremendous clamor of trumpets, the great door of the castle opened to let men-at-arms with spears and young squires with banners hurry out. These arranged themselves in a wide half circle in front of the white walls of the castle. Ladies came out next, in a beautiful flutter of finery. Reigner Four grinned. This got better and better. Another very solemn fanfare announced the king himself. He was carried through the gates in a sort of bed, by four sturdy servitors, and arranged high up near the gates, where he had a good view of the sloping meadow. It looked as if he were some sort of invalid. Realizing that the king would probably be the last member of the audience to arrive, Reigner Four busied himself with strapping on his helmet, securing his shield to his arm, and feeling the balance of his lance.

Sure enough, the raised section of the bridge came cranking down and crashed into place to make a path to the meadow. As it did, horse hooves clattered in the archway of the gate above. The herald, standing near the center of the field to act as umpire, bellowed, "The first Champion of our noble King Ambitas, Sir Harrisoun."

Reigner Four took a last, pleasurable look around at the bright crowd on the green field, the banners flying, the white castle, and the huddled embroideries of the king's bed. While he did so, he was also taking in, very keenly, the Champion making his way down the meadow. He rode a rangy brown horse and carried a red shield with a curious device of gold with many right angles. The word *circuitry* popped into Reigner Four's mind at the sight of that device. But he dismissed the strange word and went on appraising Sir Harrisoun. The armor was blackish but adequate, and the Champion himself had a strutting, self-confident look—if a person could be said to strut in the saddle—but the Champion's actual seat on his horse looked distinctly shaky. Reigner Four grinned inside the bars of his helmet as he sent his horse clumping sedately over the rest of the bridge and wheeled to face the Champion. He could tell this Sir Harrisoun was no good.

When the herald gave the signal, Reigner Four clapped his heels to his horse and ground his weight down in his saddle. He was sitting rock-steady as he pounded up to the Champion galloping toward him. His lance took Sir Harrisoun firmly in the chest, lifting him off the rangy horse and into the air. Sir Harrisoun fell with a jarring clang and lay where he had fallen. Reigner Four wheeled back to the other end of the meadow, while conversation buzzed in the crowd and people ran to catch the startled horse and haul Sir Harrisoun away.

"The second Champion of King Ambitas, the Right Reverend Sir Bors!" yelled the herald.

"And I hope there's a bit more to him than the first," Four remarked inside his helmet.

Sir Bors's arms were a blue Key on a white ground, and his horse was white. Reigner Four could sense a grim determination in Sir Bors, overlaying a queer lack of confidence. It was as if Sir Bors were saying to himself, "Help! What am I doing here?" But he was determined to make a go of it all the same. He came on at a great gallop, rattling from side to side as he came.

Reigner Four waited, spurred on at the right moment, and wiped Sir Bors out of his saddle as easily as Sir Harrisoun. The crowd above gave out a long "O-o-oh!" Sir Bors lay where he had fallen. Reigner Four saluted the ladies merrily with his lance—there was one lady, standing beside the queen, blond and beautiful, that he had his eye on particularly—while he rode back to wait for the third Champion.

"The king's third Champion, Sir Bedefer!" boomed the herald.

Sir Bedefer, Reigner Four knew at once, was another thing again. He was sturdily built, and he sat his horse as securely as Reigner Four himself. Four squinted down the length of his lance at Sir Bedefer's approaching shield—argent with a cross gules—and knew this was the tough one.

It was. The two met with the crack of two lances squarely in the middle of two shields, and Reigner Four, to his acute astonishment, came off his horse. He landed on his feet, but his armor was so heavy that his legs folded under him and sent him to his knees. Frantically he saved himself from further collapse by digging the edge of his shield into the turf and lumbered quickly to his feet, sure that the Champion would be riding him down the next instant. But both the horses were down near the water. A few yards away Sir Bedefer was also floundering onto his legs.

Reigner Four grinned and drew his sword with a mighty slithering clang. Sir Bedefer heard it and spun round, hauling his own sword out as he turned. The two ran upon each other. For the next minute or so they hacked and clanged at each other with a will. The shouts of the watching folk came dimly to Reigner Four through the belling of steel on steel, but shortly they were drowned by the rasping of his own breath. This Champion was as hard to beat on foot as he was on horseback. Sweat trickled into Four's eyes. His breath made the bars of his helmet unpleasantly wet. His sword arm and his legs began to ache and labor in a way they had not done for years. He began to be seriously afraid he would lose the fight. Unheard of! Pride and panic sent him forward again, dealing smashing blows. The Champion seemed to collect himself. He replied with a similar onslaught. And a lucky blow from Four's sword happened to connect with Sir Bedefer's mailed knuckles, knocking the Champion's sword from his fist.

"Yield!" yelled Four while the sword was still in the air. He made haste to get his heavy foot on the weapon as soon as it clanged to the turf. "Give in," he shouted, standing on the sword with all his weight. "You're disarmed!"

The Champion pushed up his visor, showing a red and irritated face. "All right. I yield, drat you! But that was pure luck."

Reigner Four could now afford to be generous. He pushed up his own clammy visor and smiled. "It was. I admit it. No hard feelings?"

"A few—I'm struggling with them," said Sir Bedefer.

Here Reigner Four became aware of cheering from the crowd and the herald at his elbow, waiting to present him to the king. The herald, at close quarters, proved to be a shrewd-looking weather-beaten man—rather an underbred type for a herald, to Reigner Four's mind. He allowed himself to be led up the hill to shouts of "New Champion! New Champion!" There he clanked gracefully to one knee in front of the king's bed.

"Your Majesty," he said, "I crave admittance to your castle."

"Certainly," said the king. "We admit you to our castle and also to our service. Are you willing to swear fealty to me as your lord?"

Something in the way the king's unwell-sounding voice lifted on the last word struck Reigner Four as familiar. He turned his face up and looked at the king for the first time. An elegant golden coronet surrounded the thinning hair of Ambitas's head. His face, in spite of whatever sickness he had, was plump and lined and pink. Reigner Four had a strong feeling he had seen that face before. A name, or rather a title, flitted through his mind—Reigner Two. But when he considered, it meant nothing to him. Perhaps Ambitas simply reminded him of someone. "Very willing, sire," he said. "But I ride on a quest and cannot be certain to stay here long."

"What is your quest?" asked King Ambitas.

"I seek the bannus," said Reigner Four, because he still knew that this was what he was doing here.

"You have found it," said Ambitas. "It is in this castle, and we are all its guardians. Tell me, what is your name?"

"I am called Sir Fors," said Reigner Four, because this seemed to him to be his name.

"Then arise, Sir Fors," King Ambitas said weakly, but smiling. "Enter this castle as the new Champion of the Bannus."

Then Reigner Four was conducted into the castle with great honor, where he spent his days in joy and minstrelsy and feasting. He led the royal hunt. He had seldom enjoyed himself so much. The one flaw in his enjoyment was that the beautiful blond he had had his eye on always seemed just out of reach. At feasts she was always down the other end of the high table. If he entered a room in search of her, she had always just left by the other door.

PART FIVE

—1———————————————

YAM'S JOINTS WERE frozen. Mordion had propped him up against the wall of the house, where Yam continued to protest. His voice box was, unfortunately, still working. "This is not right. You are taking advantage of my immobility to indulge in hocus-pocus."

"I'm not *indulging*." Mordion looked at Hume's bright face as Hume squatted in the center of the pentagram, bundled in furs. Hume was quite contented—that was the important thing. "Besides," Mordion told Yam, "if you'd taken my advice and stood by the fire pit last night, you'd have been mobile now and able to stop me from exercising my black arts."

"I was not expecting so many degrees of frost," Yam said glumly.

Mordion grimaced because he could not remember ever being so cold. The frost, combined with lack of food, was producing a curious light-headed clarity of mind in him—probably the ideal state for working magic. But Hume was well fed. Mordion had cheerfully stinted himself for Hume's sake. It was all for Hume's sake, this magic. He had been studying how to do this all autumn. Beside him on the frost-dry earth, carefully wrapped in spare tegument from the robot repair kit, was a stack of leather books he had asked the Bannus for. Cheating, he had told Ann, in a good cause.

Mordion smiled. Ann had told him he was obsessed. "You think you're worrying about Hume," she had told him. "Can't you real-

ize that you *like* Hume? And you do magic because you *love* doing it!"

She was probably right, Mordion thought. At the time she had
said it, he had told her crossly to go and play with Hume. His
crossness had mostly been frustration with the old books. They were
full of irrelevant magics, like charming bees or removing chills from
lungs. He had had to work out for himself what rules lay behind
these spells, and where the books did discuss theory, they were
maddeningly obscure and mystical and incomplete. But now, with
this frost-born clarity of mind, Mordion saw exactly what he would
do and how. With nine herbs, and seven herbs, and five, he would
separate the theta-space around Hume and wrap it round Hume's
body in a permanent cocoon. Hume could then take it with him
wherever he went and be safe to go outside the field of the Bannus,
perhaps to the village for a proper upbringing. Mordion himself
would not leave the wood. There was peace here as well as beauty—
two things Mordion knew he wanted above anything else.

"Ready, Hume?" he asked.

"Yes, but hurry up," said Hume. "I'm getting cramp."

Mordion banged his hands together in their rabbitskin mittens to get
the blood going and then took off the mittens. Frost bit at his knuckles.
He took up his polished staff and dipped it carefully in the first pot of
herbs. He approached Hume with the blob of green mixture on the
end of the staff and blue light playing up and down the length of it.
He anointed Hume's head, hands, and feet. As he turned to dip into
the second pot, the corner of his eye caught sight of Ann coming round
the turn of the house. He saw her stare first at his flickering staff, then
at Hume, and then at the icicles hanging from the thatch above Yam.
She shivered and wrapped her anorak around her.

Mordion smiled at her. The Bannus tended to send Ann along
at important moments. This confirmed his feeling that he had got
this magic right. But he did not let it distract him from the anointing.
He put the second set of herbs on Hume and turned toward the
final pot.

"What's wrong with you?" Ann whispered to Yam.

"Frozen lubricant," Yam intoned.

Ann watched Mordion's breath smoke as he touched the flickering staff to Hume's forehead. "That's magic he's doing. What's it for?"

"He is attempting to realify Hume." Yam's voice was much louder than it need have been. Mordion knew Yam was trying to put him off and did not let it distract him. He stood back from the anointing ready to recite the charm.

"Where did you get the fur Hume's wearing?" Ann whispered to Yam.

"Wolfskin," Yam boomed. "We were attacked by wolves. Mordion killed two."

Mordion continued firmly reciting the charm, even though he found his mind slipping off to that furious battle with the wolves. Just at dusk it had been. The beasts had been too hungry to wait for full dark. As Hume and Mordion finished what little food they had for supper, they were suddenly beset by dark, doglike shapes, pouring in upon them, quite silently. Yam, being unable to feel, had snatched a burning branch from the fire pit. Mordion and Hume had defended themselves with sticks from the woodpile. The place was full of animal eyes shining green in the light from Yam's branch. Hume kept shouting, "Use your wand, Mordion! Use your *wand!*"

Mordion knew he could have driven the wolves off by magic or even killed them all with it, but he had deliberately chosen to kill two by normal means. He was astonished at the coolness with which he had singled out the biggest pair and beaten one aside with his stick for the brief instant it took to run his knife left-handed into the other and then drop both knife and stick and break the neck of the other as it sprang. He found himself mentally excusing himself— probably to Ann—for that. Hume had been very cold that winter. They needed those skins. Though it seemed vile to kill a hungry animal, it had been a fair fight. Those wolves had been pitilessly, mindlessly determined to eat the two humans, and there were eight or so wolves. He could still see their yellow, savage, shallow eyes.

They were cunning, too. They saw Yam with his flames as their chief danger, and four of them went for Yam and brought him down. When the battle was over, Yam had climbed to his feet with three-cornered tears all over his silver skin.

The charm was finished. Mordion pointed his staff at Hume. Raised his will. For a short second Hume glowed all over in a greenish network of fire. It had worked! Then—

Mordion and everyone else watched in perplexity the glowing network float free of Hume and rise into the air. It climbed until it met the frosty boughs of the overhanging pine tree. There it vanished, in a strange confusion. The whitened needles surged. Objects rained down. Hume put his arms over his head and fled, giggling, from under a tumbling iron kettle, which landed with a clang inside the pentagram where Hume had been sitting. Mordion dodged a big feather duvet and was hit on the head by a rolled sleeping bag. Two rubber hot-water bottles slapped down on the roof of the house. A fur coat settled slowly across the fire pit, where it began to give out sharp black smoke.

Mordion sat on the nearest boulder and screamed with laughter.

Ann rushed across and dragged the fur coat clear. Her foot turned on a bottle as she backed, towing the smoking fur. She looked down. The label on the bottle said "Cough linctus." "That didn't go quite right, did it?" she said. Her voice quavered. Hume was in helpless giggles. She looked at Mordion on the boulder with his head in his hands and his back shaking. "Mordion! Are you all right?"

Mordion lifted his face. "Just laughing. I let my mind wander."

Ann was shocked at how thin his face was. His eyes, wet with laughter, were in deep bluish hollows. "My God! You look half starved!" she said.

"Food has been very short," Yam boomed. "He fed Hume but not himself."

"Oh, shut up, Yam," said Mordion. "You distracted me on purpose."

Ann hauled the duvet off the ground and wrapped it round Mor-

dion. His shoulders felt all bones under her hands. He had un-
strapped the blanketlike thing he usually wore rolled over one
shoulder and was wearing it as a cloak, but she could feel bones
even through that. "Here," she said. "Make use of this duvet now
you've got it. No wonder that spell went wrong. You look too
weak to think straight. Can't you treat yourself with a bit more
consideration?"

"Why should I?" Mordion said, hugging the duvet round himself.

"Because you're a *person*, of course!" Ann snapped at him. "One
person ought to treat another person properly even if the person's
himself!"

"What a strange idea!" Mordion said. He was suddenly weary to
the point of shaking. He suspected it was because Ann had once
more put her finger on something he did not want to think about.

Ann was in one of her angers by then. "It's not strange, it's
common sense! I wish I'd known you were starving. When I think
of Wood Street full of shops full of food, I could *kick* myself! Ask
the Bannus for some food. Now!"

"I did," said Hume, "but none came."

"I'll go shopping in the village when I've had a rest," Mordion
said to him. "I should have thought of it before."

Ann realized that *this* was when Mordion had got the idea of
going shopping in Wood Street. But he had already *been*, hours
ago, this morning. Really, the way the Bannus mixed up time was
beyond a joke!

"Let's go and play, Ann," said Hume, pulling her arm.

He was quite small again, about ten years old. More mixing up!
Ann was not sure whether she was glad or sorry. She gave him a
friendly smile, and they went off, leaving Mordion sitting on the
stone, wrapped in the duvet.

"Mordion's not really bad," Hume told her defensively as they
went downriver and through the copse where Mordion—or maybe
Yam—had hopefully set out snares for rabbits.

"He's too *good* if you ask me!" Ann answered crossly.

Her crossness vanished when they reached the wider woods beyond. It was true winter here. The trees stood like black drawings against snow. Real snow! In spite of the deep cold, Ann followed Hume in a rush for the open glades where the snow seemed to have drifted. Hume was the size when Ann could still run as fast as he could, but only just. The frozen snow cracked under their flying feet, and their breaths came in clouds. And they ran and ran, leaving mashed blue holes behind them, until Hume found deep snow beyond a bramble thicket by going into it up to his knees.

"There's *masses!*" he squealed, and flung a stinging floury ball of it into Ann's face.

"You little . . . beast!" Ann stooped and scooped and flung—and missed.

They snowballed furiously for a while, until their hair was in frosty spikes and their hands bright blue-red. Ann's anorak was crusted with snow all down the back. Hume's wolfskin jacket was a crazy paving of melting white lumps clinging to the fur. They had both reached the stage where neither wanted to admit they were too hot, too frozen, and too tired to go on when Hume noticed a crowd of rooks rising, cawing, from the trees in the distance. He swung round that way.

"Oh, look!"

Ann looked. Only for an instant. All she saw was movement and an outline, but in that same space something—instinct, intuition— had her dragging Hume by the back of his jacket as fast as she could, out of the blue, trampled shadows of the snowball ground and into cover behind the bramble thicket. "*Down!*" she said, throwing herself to her knees and pulling Hume with her.

"But what—" he said.

"Quiet! Keep still!" Ann hung on to Hume's arm to make sure of him, and together they peered out among the thorny loops of bramble, at a man in armor riding a heavy war-horse across the snowy glades. He was only going at a jog trot, so it took him quite a long time to pass, but they never saw him clearly. He was always teasingly beyond black trees, or the low winter sun caught and dazzled on his armor, making them both wink back tears. And then he would be beyond trees again. The clear air carried the crunch of the horse's great hooves and the faint clink and rattle of tack and armor. Mostly all that Ann saw was the great azure shadow of horse and rider or glimpses of billowing green cloak, but at one point he was near enough for her to feel the ground shake with his weight under her frozen knees. She kept tight hold of Hume then, praying the rider would not notice the blue shadow where they had snowballed and come to investigate. She thought of the man Martin had seen climbing the gate this morning. And her breath went sticky in her throat with real dread.

He was gone at last. Ann relaxed her grip on Hume, and Hume stirred. She looked at him, thinking he ought to be praised for kneeling so still and quiet, and saw that he had simply been stunned with delight. "What—what *was* that?" he said, still barely able to speak. "Another robot?"

"No, that was a knight in armor riding a horse," she said.

"I know the horse, stupid," he said. "What's a knight?"

This is before we found that lake, Ann thought. He knew about knights then. But she was still shaken with dread of that knight. "A knight is a man who fights," she said curtly.

But she might have known it was impossible to put Hume off like that. He clamored questions: Who were knights, what did they do, whom did they fight, and how did someone get to be a knight? So Ann trudged back with him, walking with her legs stiff so that her sodden jeans would not touch her skin too icily often, and explained as they went how you trained to be a knight. She saw no reason not to put in some propaganda here. She told Hume you had to *deserve* to be a knight before you were knighted, and when you were made knight, you had to fight and behave with *honor*.

Then Hume insisted on knowing all about that particular knight. "He lives in the castle, doesn't he? He guards the king from dragons, doesn't he? Does he fight dragons?"

Ann had forgotten how Hume was obsessed with dragons at this age. She said she supposed that the knight did. By this time they were in the copse near the river, and here Hume became, if possible, more excited than ever.

"I'm going to be a knight! I'm going to fight dragons for the king!" he shouted. He seized a dead branch and began hacking at trees with it. And when they came to the edge of the copse and found a rabbit—or maybe a hare—skinny and wretched, caught in the last of the snares there, Hume went half mad with delight. "I'm going to *kill* dragons!" he screamed. "Like this! Kill!" he screamed, and beat the rabbit furiously with his branch.

Ann screamed as well. "Hume, *stop!*" The rabbit was making a horrible noise, almost human. *"Stop it, Hume!"*

"Dragon! Kill, kill, kill!" Hume shouted, battering at the rabbit.

Mordion heard the din as he sat sipping a hot herbal drink. He flung off the duvet and sped to the spot. Ann saw him coming up the path in great loping strides and turned to him thankfully. "Mordion, Hume—"

Mordion slung Hume aside, so that Hume sat down with a crash in a heap of frozen brushwood and, in the same movement, he knelt and put the rabbit out of its agony. "Don't you *ever* do that again!" he told Hume.

"Why?" Hume said sullenly.

"Because it's extremely cruel," Mordion said. He was going to say more, but he looked up just then and saw Ann's face.

She was fixed, unable to look away, seeing again, and again, and again, the way Mordion's long, strong fingers had known just the right place on the rabbit to find and the deft way they had flexed, just the right amount, to break the rabbit's neck with a small final crack. He didn't even have to look! she kept thinking. He was busy glaring at Hume. She kept hearing that weak, clean little snap.

Mordion opened his mouth slightly to ask her what was the matter. But there was no point. They both knew what they knew, though neither of them wanted to.

As for Hume, he sat in the heap of brushwood, and his face passed from glowering to mere thoughtfulness. It looked as if he had learned something, too.

—2—

THE THREE REMAINING Reigners gathered in the conference hall in the House of Balance, none of them in the best of tempers.

"What *does* Four think he's playing at?" said Reigner Three.

"How should *I* know? He turned his monitors off on Iony," Reigner Five snapped. "For all I know, he's still there."

"Nonsense," said Reigner Three. "Iony, Yurov, and Albion all say he passed their portals without any trouble at all. The reports are on the table in front of you."

"But not Runcorn's," said Reigner One. He put a fax sheet down on the glassy surface and let it slowly unfold there.

The other two stared from it to Reigner One's benign old face. "What has Runcorn to do with it?" demanded Reigner Three. "Nobody's taking any notice of them any longer."

"I am," said Reigner One. "They *are* more or less on the spot after all. They have not, of course, heard of Reigner Four, thanks to the zeal of Giraldus on Albion, but they are still mighty concerned about the disappearance of their Area Director. Read the first thing on this sheet." He pushed it across to them.

Reigner Five picked it up, took hold of the split point at the corner, and peeled off a copy for Reigner Three. He read aloud from his own: " 'A party consisting of ten picked men from Rayner Hexwood security, commanded by our chief of security in person and accompanied by three senior observers and two junior executives, has been sent to investigate the library complex at Hexwood Farm. In view of the disappearance of Sir John, it was thought advisable that this party should go fully armed.' Sensible," said Reigner Five. "Though I imagine their weapons aren't up to much."

"Now read the second communication," said Reigner One.

Reigner Three read it out. "Blah blah. 'The armed party sent to investigate Hexwood Farm has not returned and has now been missing for two days. In view of this second set of disappearances, we urgently request advice from Reigner heads and, if possible, armed reinforcements.' Blah, blah, blah. 'Repeat urgently.' "

"Now look at the dates," said Reigner One.

They looked. "Oh," said Three. "These Runcorn people went in *after* Reigner Four got there."

"Precisely, my dear," said Reigner One. "The evidence points to the bannus still being functional and still pulling people in."

"So Four failed," Reigner Five said. "Well, I'm not surprised."

"Not necessarily," said Reigner One. "It does sometimes take awhile to get to grips with the bannus. And bearing in mind that Four had three tasks, we should not leap to the concl—"

Reigner Five got up. "I've had enough of this. *I'm* going in. Myself. Now. It'll be a pleasure to blow that machine up and to wring Two's stupid neck—and Four's, too, if he doesn't do some good fast talking!"

"And the Servant?" asked Reigner Three.

Five answered by giving a sarcastic nod toward the doorway, where all that remained of the two statues were the stumps of their pillars. The entry was now guarded by robots.

Reigner One smiled at Five. "Ah, yes. But our present Servant is mobile. Be very careful, won't you?"

"Why? Do you think I'm senile or something?" said Five. "Stun and stass. What could be simpler?"

"Of course you're not senile," Reigner One replied soothingly. "I simply meant to warn you that our Servant hates us all very deeply."

"I wish you wouldn't joke, One!" said Reigner Three. "It's tiresome. You know the Servant is totally loyal to all of us."

Reigner One turned his soothing, benevolent smile on her. "Of course he was totally loyal, my dear. But the methods I used to make him that way were not at all kindly. I advise Five to keep his distance."

"Your advice is noted." Five strode to the door and shouldered the robots there out of the way. They were just regrouping when Five shouldered them aside again, in order to lean back into the hall and say, "Two days. If I haven't got in touch after two days, you'd better go to panic stations. But I will be."

—3—————————————————

FOOD WAS VERY short that winter in the castle. Sir Fors did not notice straightaway. For one reason the forest was suddenly infested with outlaws. They were said to be under the command of a renegade knight called Sir Artegal. Sir Fors spent much pleasurable time hunting these villains down, either alone or with a band of Sir Bedefer's soldiers. He would dearly have loved to catch Sir Artegal. By all accounts the man was an excellent fighter and would have made a lot of sport. But he was thoroughly elusive. All Sir Fors ever found of him was an occasional camp, completely deserted.

In the castle the Right Reverend Sir Bors had decreed a time of fasting and prayer, in order, he said, to lift the curse of Sir Artegal from the king's realm. It struck Sir Fors as neither very reasonable nor very enjoyable, but he went through with it because everyone else in the castle did the same. He went with the rest of the castle people to the chapel twice a day, and three times on some days, where he stood to watch King Ambitas carried in and then knelt for an hours-long service. It was penitential. It was ludicrous.

"We have all sinned," Sir Bors said, clutching his Holy Key in both hands. Under his rich vestments he was thin and uneasy and weighed down with holy thoughts. "By our sins, the sacred Balance is disturbed, our king's wound remains unhealed, and our lands are plagued with the abomination that stalks the forest in the guise of

Sir Artegal. We can only make amends by praying and fasting and cleansing our minds."

Sir Fors suspected that King Ambitas slept through most of these sermons. He wished he could, too, but he did not have the luck to be carried round in a bed. And when they came out of chapel, it was to a meal of dry bread, thin beer, and lentil hash. Sir Fors's empty stomach started to keep him awake at nights, and he lay listening to more chanting coming distantly from the chapel until well into the small hours.

But at last it seemed to be over. King Ambitas summoned Sir Fors, and Sir Fors went and knelt at the king's bedside. "Well, Champion Fors," the king said, nestling comfortably among his pillows, "all this praying and fasting comes to an end tomorrow, thank the Bannus! I hope the Reverend Bors knows what he's doing, because I don't follow his reasoning at all. I think Sir Artegal would be there whether people behaved themselves or not. And I don't think my great sickness has much to do with sin, either."

"Surely not, sire," said Sir Fors. He was too polite to inquire into the exact nature of the king's illness, but it had never struck him as very severe. The king's face was lined, but it was plump and pink in spite of the fasting.

"Anyway," said Ambitas, "tomorrow brings the yearly Showing of the Bannus, and we are going to have a proper feast. I want it worthy of my lady bride. Let's make it really lavish, shall we? Go and give orders for it, will you?"

Sir Fors bowed and left to order the feast. Twelve courses, he thought, and not a lentil in one of them. But he was much astonished that it was Bannustide again. Two years had gone by in the castle in feasting and mirth, hunting and knightly exercise, as if it were as many days. Not that it worried him. It showed how generally good life was here, although, he had to admit, he had been here long enough for certain aspects of the king's household to irritate him. One thing was Sir Bors's piety, which seemed to get steadily stronger. Another was the king's bride, but the least said about *her* the better. And the beautiful blond lady, Lady Sylvia, was another. She had always just left the place where he was, or she had decided at the last moment not to come a-Maying, or he had given her up and left for the picnic and she had arrived after he had gone. This annoyed Sir Fors considerably. He was an important man in the castle these days. The king relied on him. Everyone else came to him for orders instead of bothering the king.

Sir Fors gave orders for the feast—and immediately came up against the most irritating part of the household of all. The Lord Seneschal, Sir Harrisoun. Sir Harrisoun sought audience with him. Sir Fors could not abide Sir Harrisoun. Sir Harrisoun's unhealthy face, orange hair, and skinny frame grated on him unbearably. There was an aggressive man-to-man familiarity about the way Sir Harrisoun spoke to him which showed that Sir Harrisoun considered himself at least the equal of Sir Fors. This, of course, was utter nonsense.

"Now see here, Fors," Sir Harrisoun began, strutting up to him in a lavish new black velvet tunic, "about this feast you just ordered."

"*What* about it, Sir Harrisoun?" Sir Fors asked coldly. He eyed the gold embroidery on Sir Harrisoun's new tunic. Costly. Though he could not prove it, Sir Fors suspected that Sir Harrisoun quietly helped himself to the king's funds to line his own pockets. He had that greedy look. Everything he owned was as costly as the new tunic.

"Well, I just want to know how you think we can do it, that's all!" said Sir Harrisoun. "It's not just the short notice. I mean, twenty-four hours is a tall order for a full feast, and I tell you straight it's asking a lot of the kitchen staff, though I'm not saying they couldn't do it."

This was what Sir Fors really hated about Sir Harrisoun. The man was a grumbler. No matter what you asked him to do—equip a hunting party, provide a picnic for ladies to take hawking, or even just get supper early—you got this stream of whining complaints.

He had never once heard Sir Harrisoun agree to do something willingly. Sir Fors folded his arms, tapped on the floor with one boot, and waited for a quarter of an hour of solid bellyaching.

"It's asking a lot of flesh and blood," continued Sir Harrisoun, "but the chefs could do it, provided they got the materials. But I tell you frankly, Fors, the materials just are not there this time." And much to Sir Fors's surprise, Sir Harrisoun shut his mouth, folded his arms in a swirl of hanging velvet, and looked Sir Fors angrily in the eye.

"What do you mean?" Sir Fors said, disconcerted.

"I mean," said Sir Harrisoun, "the larder's empty. The buttery's dry. There is not one keg nor one sack of flour left in the cellar, nor even one ham on the beams. The kitchen garden's out, too. New stuff not grown in yet. There's barely hardly enough for tonight's supper, even at the rate Sir Bors has us eating. So—I'm asking you straight—what do we do?"

All Sir Fors could think of to say was "Why didn't you *tell* me?"

"What do you think I've been *trying* to do all this time?" Sir Harrisoun retorted. "But no, you wouldn't listen. Not you. Just order the very best of everything regardless, that's you."

Sir Fors took a turn round the narrow stone room while he tried to digest this. The man *was* a grumbler. But this did not alter the fact that he seemed to have given the wretched fellow a chance to be in the right. It was infuriating. He would greatly have liked to have knocked Sir Harrisoun's orange head off Sir Harrisoun's skinny shoulders. But that wouldn't solve anything. How *did* you have a feast with no food to make it from? For a moment Sir Fors felt so helpless that he almost considered sending for Sir Bedefer and asking Sir Bedefer's advice. But, if he did that, he would be admitting Sir Bedefer was his equal, and ever since that lucky stroke when Sir Fors first came to the castle, Sir Fors had done his generous, laughing best to make sure Sir Bedefer stayed one notch below him in the castle hierarchy. No, he would have to think of something for himself.

He took two more turns round the room and tried not to look at the sneer on Sir Harrisoun's face. "I suppose," he said at last, "that the peasantry must have some supplies left still. Frugal, saving sorts most peasants are. Whereabouts do most of the peasants live?"

From the look on Sir Harrisoun's face, he had considered the peasants even less than Sir Fors had. "Tell you straight," he said, laughing uneasily, "I'm not sure."

Sir Fors pounced on this uneasiness. "You mean," he said incredulously, "that the scum haven't been sending us any tithes?"

"No," Sir Harrisoun said, in a thoughtful, relishing sort of way. "No. I don't think the scum have, to be honest with you." A little smile lit the corners of his mouth.

It was not a smile Sir Fors liked. It was the smile of someone who was going to put the blame on Sir Fors the moment anything went wrong. He ignored it. Something had to be done. "Well then," he cried, "no *wonder* we've no food left! Call to arms, Sir Harrisoun. I'll tell Sir Bedefer to fall in his best squad. You fetch Sir Bors. Tell him it's his holy duty to make sure there's a feast for Bannustide. Meet you in the outer court in half an hour."

"Right you are, Fors," said Sir Harrisoun, and sped away eagerly.

That man has ambitions to replace me, Sir Fors thought. I'll have to watch him. But now was not the time to worry about Sir Harrisoun. The next hour was all lively bustle, shouting orders, strapping on armor, rushing downstairs, commanding horses brought, criticizing their tack, and the men's—the sorts of things Sir Fors most enjoyed doing.

Down in the courtyard Sir Bedefer rode to meet Sir Fors at the head of a smartly turned-out troop of cavalry. There was honest doubt in Sir Bedefer's wide face. "You're sure this is really necessary, Champion?" he said.

"A matter of life and death," Sir Fors assured him, "or I wouldn't have ordered it. These wretched peasants have been denying us our rights for two years now." Sir Bors rode up beside Sir Bedefer while he said this. Sir Fors could see he was seething with religious doubts. To still those doubts, too, he added, "Our strength is as the strength of ten because our cause is just." Now how did I think of that? he wondered admiringly. That's good!

"Twenty men," Sir Bedefer pointed out, "is what we actually have. Do I count them as two hundred?"

Sir Fors ignored him and concentrated on keeping his eager horse quiet while they waited for Sir Harrisoun, who was always late.

—4—

ANN WENT PAST the yellow pretzel bag in the hollow tree. She was beginning to suspect it marked the boundary of the Bannus field. She kept a careful lookout to see just when after that the wood changed. But her attention was caught and distracted by a blue flickering among the trees.

Mordion working magic again, she thought, and broke into a run in order not to miss it. Across the river she went, leaping from stone to stone below the familiar waterfall. She seemed to have done this a hundred times; probably she *had*. And the cunning Bannus had caused her to miss noticing just where its field started yet again. Oh, well. The blue light continued to flicker enticingly on the cliff above. Ann went charging up the path and round the house—which looked weather-beaten and sagging these days—to skid to a gasping halt in the empty space beside the fire pit. Only Yam was there, sitting very upright and disapproving on a stone.

"Mordion is at his hocus-pocus again," Yam said. "He is the most obstinate human alive. He does not attend to my arguments at all. He is making his third attempt to wrap a part of the theta-field round Hume."

"Not *again!*" Ann panted.

"Yes. Again," Yam intoned. "He has given up his herbs, which are harmless, though he calls them inadequate, and his chanting, which the Bannus tends to answer in the wrong fashion, and he is now working with mind power alone." As Yam spoke, the blue flashing was gaining in intensity, dazzling off Yam's silver skin, and giving them both sudden black shadows that leaped across the earthy space, leaped and vanished. The pine tree above the house stood out like a tree in a thunderstorm, alternately a dark mass and then visible in every dark green needle. "He has studied for five years now," Yam said. "I believe he is now working at full strength."

An exceptionally vivid flash made Ann quite sure Yam was right. She dithered in a mixture of curiosity and alarm. "This could hurt Hume," she said. It was partly an excuse to see what was happening. "I'd better go and make sure he's all right."

She set off for the rocks above the house at a run.

Yam's silver hand closed on her wrist. Ann could not believe a robot could be so strong. She swung round in a circle with her own impetus and ended up facing Yam, in another flash so dazzling that it dimmed Yam's rosy eyes. "Stay here with me," Yam said. "It is getting—"

There was an enormous dull explosion.

"—dangerous," Yam said. He let go of Ann and left at racing speed. Even Mordion, running up the path to kill that rabbit, had not moved so fast. Yam went as a silver blur. Ann stared after him, feeling the explosion jarring in her every bone and sure that her eardrums were ruptured. All she could hear was silence. Even the sound of the river had stopped.

But she had barely realized there was silence when there was a monstrous clapping and crashing. Breaking rock. Fragments landed around her. The sound of the river started again, deafening and tumultuous. Ann raced after Yam, horrified, round the house, past the pine tree. As she scrambled up the rocks beyond, everything seemed unearthly, open, and light. The river was roaring, and this roar was mixed with the squealing and rubbly grinding and multiple crashings of more rock breaking. Ann bolted upward, using her hands to help, terrified of what she might find at the top.

It was bright sunlight up there. Mordion was a tumbled brown heap with blood streaming from a gash in his wrist. His blood-covered hand was still obstinately clenched round that wizard's staff of his. Hume and Yam were bending over him anxiously, and to Ann's huge relief, Hume at least had not a scratch on him. Hume was all legs again, taller than she was.

"He's breathing. He's not killed himself," Hume said.

Ann stood, panting and relieved, staring down at the river. The waterfall had gone. There was now a flat white slope of water, roaring and frothing down a chasm that was getting bigger as she looked. A slice of rock as big as a house slanted off the bank opposite and slammed down into the river, sending up high spouts of water that drenched all four of them. The river's sound was almost like a snarl as it tore its way round this new obstacle.

"That wetting brought him round," Yam said.

"What on earth went on here?" Ann demanded. She was now watching the new rockfall sink and spread, break into boulders, and then crumble to flat stones under the white water. Like geology speeded up! she thought. It was as if a giant hand were pressing that rockfall. Beyond, more rock broke and fell, snapping several oak trees like twigs. "What did Mordion *do*?"

"I got it wrong again," Mordion said from behind her. He sounded weak and depressed.

"You didn't, you know," Hume answered. "It was working splendidly. I could feel myself getting wrapped right round in an extra field. Then it sort of rebounded off me and hit the river instead."

"It's still hitting it," Ann said, watching the oak trees disappear in the welter and then bob up again, crushed into hundreds of pieces of yellow splintered wood that went roaring downriver out of sight. "Mordion, I don't think you know your own strength. Or did the Bannus object?"

"*Ann!*" Mordion yelled.

Ann spun round, wondering what the new trouble was. Mordion was sitting up, holding himself steady with both hands on his staff, staring at her as if she was a ghost.

"When did you cross the river?" he said.

"Just now," said Ann. "I—"

"Oh, Great Balance!" The staff clattered to the rocks as Mordion put both hands over his face. "You could have been caught in the explosion!"

"Yes, but I wasn't." Ann went to kneel beside him and jerked her head at Yam and Hume to go away—particularly at Yam, who was no good at this kind of time. Hume nodded and took Yam away, almost tiptoeing with tact. "You're bleeding," Ann said.

Mordion glanced at his cut wrist with his eyebrow drawn to a winged point, irritably. There was no blood anymore. Not even a cut. Ann looked at it wryly. More confusion. Perhaps, she thought, I haven't been so clever, using that cut of his to time things.

"See?" Mordion said, holding his wrist toward her. "I can do this. Why can't I make Hume real?"

"He *is* real, in his own way," Ann pointed out. "After all, what's real? How do you know *I'm* real or if *you* are?" Since Mordion looked as if for once he were trying to think about this, she went on persuasively. "Why is it so important to you to make Hume real anyway?"

"Because, as you're always telling me, I'm fond of him," Mordion said somberly. "Because I set out to use Hume like a puppet—and saw almost straightaway that this was wrong. I want him to be free."

"Yes, you've said that before," Ann agreed, "and it's all true. But why is it *really*? Why do you always think of Hume and never of yourself?"

Mordion slowly picked up his staff, joined his hands round it, and leaned his forehead against his hands. He made a sound that was like a groan. He did not answer Ann for so long that she gave up expecting him to. She knelt and listened to the sounds from the river. Things seemed to have stopped falling and grinding away. It was just rushing water now. She was about to get up and look when Mordion said, "Because I want to be free, too." He added, nearly in a whisper, "Ann, I don't want to think about this."

"Why not?" Ann said inexorably.

There was an even longer pause. This time, before Mordion answered, Hume began yelling from somewhere down by the water. Yam was booming from there, too.

"Curses!" Ann said. "Another crisis!"

"I tried not to damage his boat," Mordion said guiltily, trying to get up.

Since the yells sounded urgent, Ann helped Mordion up, and they made their way down to the house and then, very cautiously, down the cracked and spiky rocks to the river. Yam and Hume were on the shingle at the edge of the new white foaming water, beside Hume's boat, still miraculously there. A true miracle, personally organized by Mordion, Ann thought. But the miracle had been precious close. A big, jagged rock had fetched up on the shingle, right next to the boat, barely a foot away.

Hume was leaning on this jagged rock beckoning, pointing to a big metal staple sticking out from the top of it.

No, it was not a staple, Ann saw as she climbed closer. The bright sunlight was striking red rays off the top of the metal. There seemed to be crimson glass embedded in it.

"What is it, Hume?" Mordion called from above Ann.

"A handle of some kind!" Hume's face was almost wild with mischief and excitement. "Ann, come and pull it. See what happens."

Ann jumped the last way down to the shingle and leaned over the wet brown rock. It was indeed a handle, the metal thing, with a red jewel set into its end. She put both hands to it and pulled. Nothing moved. She tried to pull it toward her, then to push it away. "It's quite solid," she said. "Sorry, Hume."

"Let me," said Yam. He came up beside Ann and wrapped both silver hands round the handle. He pulled. Ann saw his inner works strain against his shiny skin with the effort. "It is fixed," he said, and let go.

Hume pushed them both aside, grinning with joy. "Now let *me*." He jumped up on the boulder, took the handle in one hand, and, without any effort at all, drew a long gray steel sword out of the middle of the stone. Standing there on the rock, he laid the sword across both hands and just stared at it. It was beautiful. The raised rib down the center, instead of being straight, was cunningly worked in a wavy, snakelike, leaflike pattern. "This is mine," Hume said. "The Bannus has sent me my sword. At last!"

Ann laughed. "What's its name? Excalibur?"

Mordion stood some way up the cliff, leaning on his staff, and looked down sadly at Hume, standing there with the legs of his tracksuit wet dark indigo to the knees, and most sadly of all at the joy on Hume's face. "It's a wormblade," he said. "A very fine one. How many times did you pull it out before we came?"

"Only twice," Hume said defensively. "Yam couldn't budge it. I had to have Ann try, though, before I was sure."

"I think," Mordion said, mostly to Ann, "that the Bannus is challenging us. Either I try to change its scenario, or it will play it out as I said I would in the beginning."

"There's writing on the sword!" Hume said. "In Hamitic script. I thought it was just marks at first. It says"—he held the blade out to get shadows across the marks—"it says, 'I am made for one.' " He turned the sword gently, awed by it and afraid of dropping it. "And on this side it says 'Who is Worm's Bane.' "

"I was afraid it might say something like that," Mordion said.

5

SO THAT'S WHERE the sword came from, Ann thought. She was generally thoughtful while she came out through the wood. When she was well past the yellow pretzel bag and starting up the passage between the houses, she asked her imaginary people, *Am I really coming out of the wood this time?*

I can hear you ask, said the King, *for what that's worth.*

Good, said Ann. *Then I want to tell you everything that's hap-*

pened so far. Something's wrong. Something doesn't check out, but I can't see what it is.

Tell away, the King said.

Ann began at the beginning, when she had been ill and watching in her mirror. This was while she was coming up the passage. As she came out and began squeezing among the cars—Wood Street was all parked up, worse than usual on a Saturday—the King interrupted her. *This may be where things do not tally,* he said. *You went into the field of this machine many times while you were ill, too.*

WHAT? said Ann.

Here a bus moved away from the bus stop opposite, and Martin, who had been standing in the bus shelter talking to Jim Price, saw Ann and rushed across the road, weaving hair-raisingly among the traffic. Ann heard the King saying that he had thought she knew or he would have told her, and then falling politely silent, realizing Ann's attention was all on Martin.

"Something else happened while you were out," Martin told her breathlessly. "A lot of cars came. This one you're standing by was one. The others are all up the street."

Ann looked at the car beside her. It was just a car, a more ordinary one than the gray car still down in the bay, and its road fund license had almost run out. "And?" she said.

"A whole crowd of men got out," Martin told her, "looking like police or something. And they waited until they were all out in the road. Then they walked off down to the farm, sort of leaning forward—you know, as if they were really going to *do* something. And they got to the gate, and the one in front banged on it, and it opened, and they all marched in. I saw one fetching out a gun, from under his arm. Like this." Martin mimed it, and his eyes were big at the memory. "Then the gate shut. But we didn't hear any shooting. They're all still in there, though."

"Saying, 'This house is surrounded. Come out with your hands up!' You think? Did you try to see?" Ann asked.

Martin nodded. "Who wouldn't? Jim and I tried the gate when

no one was looking, but it was locked again, so we went round in the wood and tried to get over the wall there. But we couldn't."

"Couldn't how?" Ann asked, seeing Martin looked truly perturbed.

"It was—" Martin kicked the tire of the ordinary car. "You won't believe this. It was slippery—as if it was covered in plastic—and you know how old that wall looks. And we couldn't get up it, not even boosting each other. We just kept slipping off. Then we climbed a tree in the wood, but you can never see in from the trees, not properly. But there was no *sign* of any of those men. Ann, I think there's something really weird going on."

"I *know* there is," said Ann.

"Should we tell Dad?" Martin asked.

Touching faith! Ann thought. And what's Dad supposed to do? "I'll think about it," she said because she simply could not see what else to do. Perhaps Dad or Mum could come up with some idea. "I'll go in and see what sort of mood they're in—and see."

Martin's face cleared, and his shoulders straightened. All responsibility was now shifted to Ann, which was how Martin preferred things. "Thanks," he said. "I didn't fancy trying to tell him, not after the way he was at lunch. But I'll back you up. If you want me, I'll be down in the wood with Jim."

Down in the wood, well out of trouble! Ann thought sourly as Martin whistled Jim over the road just as if Jim were his dog, and the two of them went charging away down the path between the houses. You could trust Martin to keep well clear for the next few hours. Unless, of course, *he* got into the Bannus field, too.

Ann halted and looked back over her shoulder, suddenly worried. But Martin seemed to belong to the real world, somehow, like Mum and Dad. They all three struck Ann as being immune to the Bannus. She went across the road and into the shop.

Tired but cheerful seemed to be the mood in the shop. When Ann came in, her parents were in one of those lulls, just the two of them leaning by the till, drinking a quick cup of tea before the next customer came in.

"Hallo, love," said Mum. "You look a bit tired."

"You have a funny kind of look," said Dad. "What's up? You haven't made yourself ill again, have you? I told you—"

His voice was drowned out, almost from the moment he started to speak, by the furious clattering of horses' hooves that grew louder and louder. Dad swung round irritably. The sound seemed to be right on top of them, mixed with clashing, jingling, and shouting.

"What's *this*, then?" he said, shouting against the noise. "Light Brigade? Local hunt?" He and Ann and Mum all bent down to see under the hanging plants in the window. The window was suddenly darkened by great brown horses, rearing and tossing and scraping iron hooves on the road as they were reined in.

I don't believe this! Ann thought, as she saw men in chain mail and helmets with nose guards dismounting from the horses with a set of deafening crashes.

Dad started toward the door of the shop, half grinning, half annoyed. "Looks like one of those clubs where people dress up and act wars," he said. "Load of idiots!" But before he reached the door, a man taller and wider even than he was came swiftly clanking in, forcing Dad to back away. A green surcoat swirled over this man's mail. His face under its metal helmet was handsome, lordly, and smiling a smile without feeling or friendliness.

"Keep quite still," he said, as if it were obvious that people would do as he said. "Nobody need get hurt. We're only coming to collect what you wretched people owe us."

"What do you mean? We don't owe anybody anything!" Mum protested.

The tall man gave her a brief look that left Mum red as a brick. The look, quite definitely, undressed her and decided she might do if he was desperate. His look went on, round the bags of potatoes, displays of cauliflowers and zucchini, and pyramids of fruit. "I think about two-thirds of this will do for the moment," he said.

"Two-*thirds!*" Dad said, advancing on the man with his chin out and his fists bent. "What do you think you're playing—"

The tall man let Dad come within reach and calmly lashed out with a steel-cased hand. Dad went staggering and arm-waving backward with a rush that ended in a slanted bin of apples, where he landed with a solid squelch. But he was so angry that he was trying to struggle to his feet almost as he landed. Ann, in a terrified, distracted way, noticed that when someone was *that* angry, their eyes really did glitter. Dad's eyes shone wet and dark with fury.

The tall man gave him no chance to move. He raised a heavy metal foot and stamped it in Dad's midriff, knocking him back into the apples again. Keeping his foot there, he drew the great sword that hung in a green scabbard at his waist and pushed the wicked gray point at Dad's throat. "All right, men!" he called. "You can come in now." His eyes flicked to Ann and Mum and decided they were not worth bothering about.

This was enough to make Ann and Mum reach for the heaviest potatoes they could find. As the men at arms rattled in through the door, Mum raised her potato.

"Don't do it," said the tall man. "Any violence from either of you, and I cut your man's throat."

Mum clutched Ann's arm. They both had to stand there miserably and watch the steel-armed men chasing in and out, taking everything that was in the shop. They humped out sacks of potatoes, trugs of mushrooms, flat boxes of tomatoes, bundles of leeks, brown bags of turnips, bunches of carrots, strings of garlic, onions, cabbages, lettuces, brussels sprouts, and zucchini, all tumbled together in baskets. Then they helped themselves to more baskets and chucked fruit into them, lemons, oranges, pears, grapefruit, apples, bananas, and avocados, which they seemed to think of as fruit. From time to time Ann looked dismally out of the window at one of them roping the latest bag or box to a horse's back. Can't anyone outside see what's happening? she wondered. Can't someone *stop* them? But nobody did.

At last, when the shop was practically empty except for the apples Dad was forced to sprawl in and a trodden leaf or so of spinach, one of the men ducked into the shop to say, "All loaded, Sir Fors, sir."

"Good," said the tall man. "Tell the men to mount." He drew back his sword from Dad's throat and casually clanged it against the side of Dad's head. Then he took his foot down from Dad's stomach and strode away through the door, leaving Dad holding his head and almost too dazed to move.

Mum rushed after him, screaming names that normally would have astonished Ann. Now she felt the man deserved every word. She saw Mum stop in the doorway and turn drearily back. "No good. There's a whole army of them," she told Ann helplessly.

Ann was on her way to help Dad, but she ran to the door to look. By this time all the men who had raided them were up on their loaded horses, clattering smartly along the road to join other groups of horses that were also piled with bundles. Most of the riders were laughing as if it were all a great joke. Two doors along, Brian, Mr. Porter the butcher's assistant, was staggering out of the butcher's shop weakly waving a cleaver. The two gay boys from the wineshop were kneeling in the pavement beyond, clutching each other and staring. The bread shop ladies were standing in their doorway, glaring dourly. The fish-and-chips shop had its windows broken, while down the other way Mrs. Price was in tears among milk and burst boxes of chocolate all over the pavement. There was glass from other smashed shops everywhere.

"They've been to *all* the shops!" Ann said. By this time the whole troop of horsemen was riding away with the tall man at its head. Ann dazedly watched one man, who had a white surcoat with a red cross on it, like—and most unlike!—St. George, ride past with most of an ox behind his saddle.

He was the last. After that the riders were gone as suddenly as they had come.

"Help me with your father!" Mum called.

"Of course," Ann said. Dad looked awful. She felt utterly shaken herself. "Oughtn't we to ring the police?" she asked.

"Do no good," Dad mumbled. "Who's going to believe this? This is something we'll have to settle for ourselves. Ann, go and see what they did to Dan Porter. If he's all right, ask him to step along here. And those two from the wineshop, too. Get all of them."

As Mum helped Dad, groaning and wobbling, over to sit on a crate, Ann turned to go out of the shop and nearly ran into Martin coming in. He looked awful, too. He was white as a sheet, with a great bloody, dirty graze down one side of his face. On that side of him, his clothes were all torn, with blood oozing through. "Martin!" she said. "What happened to you?"

"A whole lot of men dressed up in armor riding horses," Martin gasped. "They came charging through the wood like they were mad or something. Me and Jim got knocked down. Jim hit a tree. I think it broke his arm. He—he screamed all the time I was getting him home." His shocked, blank stare slowly took in the empty shop and Dad sitting panting on a crate. "What *happened*?"

"Same damn lot that got you," Dad growled. "That does it! Ann, do as I said, and fetch the rest here. Anyone else who'll come. I'm going to make sure that lot meet trouble if they try this again."

As Ann ran off to Mr. Porter's, all her doubts came back again. Dad seemed so suspiciously ready not to bother the police with this raid. True, it *was* a wild-sounding thing. But it was also armed robbery, or robbery with violence, or something, and the police were supposed to deal with that. Could the Bannus be working on Dad's mind now?

PART SIX

—1

REIGNER FIVE, LIKE Reigner Four, did not bother to go to the basement for Earth clothes. He sent a robot.

Vierran's response was to send the robot back with a monk's robe. Only Vierran and Vierran's private sense of humor knew whether this was a comment on the round bald patch, like a tonsure, in the middle of Five's ginger head, which he kept carefully grafted with carroty hair, or whether it referred to some other aspect of Reigner Five.

Reigner Five had no idea it was a joke. He was preoccupied with the latest reports from Earth and elsewhere. The Organization seemed to have gone to pieces all over Earth, and no flint was coming through. There were outcries and urgent inquiries all over the galaxy. He looked absently at the monk's robe as the robot presented it and saw the garment was ideal for concealing the large number of special gadgets he was planning to take, and he put it on with satisfaction. Five had no intention of letting anything on Earth stop him, including the bannus and the Servant. He had enough under the robe to wipe out London.

His journey was swifter than Reigner Two's and the Servant's, and far, far swifter than Reigner Four's. He was brusque with every Governor and each Controller. He simply demanded the next portal open and went through it, slanting down through the galaxy at his rapid, nervy stride in the shortest possible time. When he reached Albion, he was curter still. He turned his eyes about the office, saw with scorn that the steak and mustard decor was even worse than it looked in the monitor cube, and turned the same look of scorn on Associate Controller Giraldus. This man, he reflected, was slated for termination. It surprised him that Reigner Four had not done it. He had his hand ready raised to terminate Giraldus himself when it occurred to him that this man was at least efficient. He would need someone reliable to open a portal for him on his return. Earth was clearly not to be trusted. They had managed to employ a crooked library clerk. And now they had collapsed in chaos and let vital loads of flint pile up, just because their Area Director and a Security team had gone missing. People like that would probably open a portal onto empty space.

So Five took his hand down, nodded coldly to the bowing Giraldus, and said, "I shan't be long. Keep your portal on standby." Then he let himself be deposited in the road outside Hexwood Farm.

It was early evening. Nobody seemed to be about. Indeed, from the look of the dwellings along the street, it appeared to be the custom to barricade yourself in, in a most untrusting way. Wooden boards were nailed over every door and window, and further nails were strewn, point upward, all over the road. But Reigner Five had very little interest in the peculiar customs of Earth. He swept up to the gate of the farm.

To his surprise and outrage, the gate opened when he touched it. What had Four or Earth Security been thinking of, leaving this gate unlocked? Five edged round the crude land vehicle he found standing outside the house very cautiously indeed, but the gadgets under the monk's robe assured him—and kept on assuring him— that this place was absolutely deserted. By the time he was inside the house, at the head of the carpeted stairs, he was sure his gadgets were right. No one had been near this place for a long time. But the bannus must be here somewhere. He swept on down and did not bother with the squalid room below, since it was just what he expected. In the operations area beyond, a red light was flashing on something, but Reigner Five did not bother with that, either. His gadgets pointed him to one of the software halls beyond, and he went swiftly that way.

The bannus was in some kind of storage section at the end, under jury-rigged cables carrying crude glass light bulbs. The oculus was alive on the front of it, showing the thing was indeed activated. Reigner Five nudged the gadget at his waist up to maximum. It protected him from the thing's field. He halted warily in front of the thing, prepared to handle it with great care. It was taller than he remembered, nearly eight feet high, and square and black. The broken Reigner seals dangled off the two top corners of it like absurd drooping ears.

"Can I do anything for you?" it asked him politely.

As soon as it spoke, all Five's tracers indicated that this was only a simulacrum of the bannus. The real bannus was a short distance away. The thing was trying its tricks. "Yes," he said. "You can show me where the bannus really is."

"Please turn to your right and continue walking," the image of the bannus told him politely.

Reigner Five swung to the right and marched on, farther into the storage bay. It became steadily darker. He adjusted his vision and went on. The floor shortly gave way to irregular wooden planks on which his feet thumped and echoed. Since his attention was all for any further tricks from the bannus, Five did not realize he was on a bridge over a stretch of water until a lighted piece of wood flared in front of him, half blinding him. He readjusted his vision hastily and found that the flaming wood was held in the hand of a man wearing a short embroidered robe, who was standing on the bridge in front of him. The flames sent lapping orange reflections down into the water on both sides. Distantly behind the man was a sturdy, fortlike building that seemed to be dimly lighted inside.

"Out of my way with that thing, man!" Five said. "You'll have this wooden thing on fire if you're not careful."

The man raised his flaming stick high so its light fell wider. He peered at Five and seemed profoundly relieved. "Thank the Bannus you came!" he said. "Now we can eat!"

"*What?*" snapped Five. "A cannibal feast?" Let the bannus dare try that!

"Oh, no, sir," said the man. "Nothing like *that*, revered sir. It's just that our king has decreed that we wait to begin our feast until some marvel or adventure befalls. Very noble idea, sir. But we've been waiting now since sundown, and most of us are getting rather hungry. If you'll just step this way quickly, Your Reverence."

There was a cheer from the long tables as Five was ushered into the castle hall. Sir Fors, waiting by the high table on the platform as impatiently as all the rest, looked up with relief. The marvel was only a miserable, skinny monk, but it would have to do. He could not think what had possessed Ambitas to make this sudden decree. The smell of the feast he had procured with his own efforts, steadily overcooking in the kitchens, was nearly driving him mad by now.

"Driving the cooks mad, too," Sir Harrisoun whispered irritably beside him.

As the monk briskly followed the herald up to the high table, everyone turned anxiously to where Ambitas sat, propped up in his chair with pillows. Surely even the king was hungry enough by now to accept this monk as an adventure? To Sir Fors's dismay, Ambitas was frowning at the monk as if something about the fellow disturbed him. Sir Fors looked at the monk again and found that he was similarly disturbed. The fellow seemed familiar. Where had he seen that high forehead before, with the ginger hair across it in streaks? Why did he seem to know that thin and bitter face?

Ambitas, with kingly courtesy, put aside his doubts. "Welcome, Sir Monk, to our castle on this Feast of Bannustide," he said. "I hope you have some marvel or adventure to relate."

So here are Two and Four! Just as I might have expected! Five thought. Both of them sold out completely to the bannus, the fools! I see now what is meant by having to work through the bannus.

Neither of them is going to listen to a word I say unless I put it in terms of this silly playacting.

"I have both an adventure and a marvel, King," he said. "Your marvel is that I came here from—er—from lands beyond the sun, bringing a message from the great Reigners, who are your overlords and the overlords of all in this place."

"A marvel indeed," said Ambitas coldly. "But I am King here and have no overlord."

"High Rulers, whose rule you share, I mean," Five corrected himself irritably. Old fool. "But they are overlords to *you*," he said, pointing to Sir Fors. I'm damned if I see *you* as an equal again, Four! He searched along the fine company at the king's table. All the ladies and half the men were unreal, inventions of the bannus. Couldn't the idiots *see*? His eye fell on Sir Harrisoun. "They are *your* overlords, too," he said. "And the overlords of you two," he added, pointing to Sir Bedefer and Sir Bors. All of them, Sir Fors included, drew themselves up and glared at Five. "Yes, they are," said Five. "And it is your sacred duty to obey the orders they send. The orders they send concern the adventure I have to relate. Does any of you know of a man called Mordion?"

King Ambitas and Sir Fors both frowned. The name did ring a bell. But not much of one. They shook their heads coldly, like everyone else.

Five had expected this. A large percentage of his gadgets were to warn him if the Servant was anywhere within a mile of him, and they all said he was not. Evidently the bannus was slyly keeping the Servant apart from his rightful masters, no doubt while it worked on the Servant's brain. Well, two could play that game. "This Mordion is the Servant of the rulers beyond the sun, who rule all in this hall," he said. "This Mordion has grievously betrayed and traitorously planned to kill his masters. Therefore, he has grievously betrayed all you in this hall, too. Seek this Mordion out. Put him to death, or he will kill you all." There! he thought. That ought to get through to them.

"I thank you, monk," Ambitas said. "Do you by this Servant intend to name the outlaw and renegade knight Artegal?"

"The name is Mordion," said Five. He was puzzled for a moment until it occurred to him that Agenos and Artegal were somewhat similar names. No doubt this was what Mordion was calling himself now. He opened his mouth to declare that the two names applied to the same man but found he was too late. Ambitas was waving him aside.

"One of our knights will take up this adventure in due course," the king said. "Herald, place the monk at table with our men-at-arms, and then let the feast begin."

Anything Reigner Five might have wished to add was drowned in cheering and a fanfare of trumpets. Five shrugged and let the herald lead him to a table down the hall. He suspected that it was a lowly table and that Two was deliberately being rude to his visitor from beyond the sun, but he did not mind. If he had had to sit near either Two or Four, he thought he would have ended by hitting them. They looked so pleased with themselves and their silly mumbo jumbo. Two particularly. What was supposed to be wrong with him that he had to sit up on pillows? He asked the men at his table.

"Don't you know, Sir Monk? The king has this wound that will not heal until someone comes and asks the right thing of the Bannus," one of them told him. He was real, and so were all the men at this table, somewhat to Reigner Five's surprise. Some must be the Maintenance men, but he was at a loss to account for the others, unless they were the Security men from Runcorn. It did no good to ask them. They looked at him as if he were mad and changed the subject. One of them told him that the Bannus would be showing itself at some time during the feast. It always did on Bannustide, he said.

Reigner Five was pleased to hear this. Just let the bannus wait! The news made this ridiculous feast easier to sit through. Five was always impatient with food. It interrupted his life. And there was course after course of this feast—roasts and pastries, puddings and fruits whipped in cream, pies and roast birds, giant mountains of vegetables, and pyramids of unknown fruit. It was monumental. But most of it was real. The bent yellow fruit he took, expecting its ridiculous shape to mean it was an invention of the bannus, was a true fruit. And the whole roast ox *was* a whole roast ox.

He made cautious inquiries from the soldiers around him. In reply they told him gleefully that they had collected the food as tax from the peasants. It had been such a doddle that they hoped Sir Fors would arrange for them to do it again soon. Have some wine, monk. That was taken as tax, too.

"No wine. My religion does not permit," Five said austerely. He wanted his head clear. He was puzzled. There was something about this real food and this tax raid which made him feel that a few of the facts he was basing his plans on were not correct somewhere, but he could not work out which facts they might be.

While he puzzled about it, the bannus entered the hall.

Five was aware of a hush first and then a sweet scent. It was an open-air scent that seemed to blow away the heavy smells of the feast and fill the hall with an expectation of bluebells, budding oaks and willows, lichen on a heath, and flowering gorse—as if all these things were just round the corner, ready to appear. There was singing, too, faint and pure and far off. Very nice! Five thought. Pretty effect indeed! He swung himself round on his seat to see where it was coming from.

A great chalice was floating up the central space between the tables, shedding its otherwordly light on all the faces near. It was a massive flat cup that seemed to be made of pure gold, wrought in patterns of great intricacy, and it was covered with a cloth so white and delicate that it impeded the light it shed barely at all. The music passed to solemn chords. On the platform the knight with the Key of a Sector Controller was standing up to meet the chalice, and his face was dazzled with reverence.

The bannus floated gently right past Reigner Five. *Got* you! he thought. He pressed the button concealed in his sleeve and released a small-scale molecular disintegrator straight into the heart of the chalice.

For an instant the chalice was wrapped in great wing-shaped flames. There was an explosion.

Reigner Five was congratulating himself when he found that it was he that was wrapped in flames and himself the center of the explosion. For a thousandth of a thousandth of a second he held together, long enough to realize that the chalice was only another image and not the bannus at all. It had fooled him somehow.

Then everything went away, and he was lying on some kind of heath at dawn. His robe was stiff with a ground frost that had turned the heather to gray lace. He was no longer sure of anything very much. But he got up and staggered away. They don't get me so easily! he thought. Not me!

After some hours he found a wood. Because it was easier going downhill, he went downhill through the wood, and after a while there was a trodden path. He followed the path and came to a hut, perched below some rocks beside a river flowing in a small chasm. The hut was old but well made, and quite deserted. However, there were clay pots and leather bags inside containing crudely preserved food—dry, tasteless stuff, but it would keep a person alive.

Why not? thought Five. This was as good a place as any.

—2—

"I THINK FIVE's come to grief, too," Reigner Three said, standing with both hands planted on the glassy table. "Though it's hard to tell. All his instruments cut out the moment he went through the Albion portal."

"The strongest possible instruments, too, you can be sure," Reigner One remarked. "It's certain that Five keeps stuff for himself that he never lets the rest of us see. Dear *me*. Either I'd forgotten how strong that bannus field is, or it's found some way of augmenting itself. I wonder *how*."

"Yes, but Five's had his two days," Reigner Three said impatiently, "and he's not been in touch. What are we going to do?"

Reigner One put his hands on the arms of his chair and slowly heaved himself up. "Nothing for it, my dear. We two have to go ourselves."

Reigner Three's large and beautiful eyes narrowed as she watched him get up. "You really mean that, don't you? There must be quite some danger if *you* bestir yourself."

"There *is* quite some danger," said Reigner One. He wheezed a bit with the effort of standing. "I've suspected for some time that the bannus is challenging me—personally. By its own ridiculous standards, it's quite right to do so, of course, though I thought I'd put a stop to its silly games centuries ago. Drat the thing! I shall have to get a massage and some more youth serum before we can get going."

"But what is the danger?" demanded Reigner Three.

"The confidence of the thing mostly," wheezed Reigner One. "It's not any kind of idiot machine, you know. They used half-life techniques making that bannus that I'd give my ears to understand. You can take it from me that it's very smart indeed. If it thinks it can challenge me and win, then you and I had better get there before it spreads its field any wider. Two touched on the other real danger. I haven't dared think of that yet. You run along now and get some suitable clothes and a course of Earth talk. I shall be ready by this evening."

"What happens to Homeworld if we both leave?" Reigner Three asked, thinking of the other great mercantile Houses. All of them had a smattering of Reigner blood, and some were known to be prepared to move against the House of Balance at the slightest sign of weakness. "Hadn't I better stay here? There's no point in destroying the bannus and then coming home to find we've been taken over."

Reigner One chuckled. "Nice try, my dear. But I'm afraid there's no help for you—you'll have to go slumming on Earth. I need you there. I'll make sure the hostile Houses can't give any trouble while we're gone, never fear. Now you run along."

Reigner One had this way of giving out information only by driblets, Reigner Three thought angrily, stepping into the pearly blue haze of the gravity shaft. "The basement," she ordered it. "Clothing for subject worlds." Cunning old Orm Pender, Reigner One, had kept power for centuries by not telling anyone quite enough. He obviously knew far more about this bannus than he had ever told anyone. If he had told Two, Four, or Five a bit more, the crisis would probably be over by now—but Reigner Three had a shrewd suspicion he had *not* told them on purpose. It was quite likely he had seized the opportunity to get rid of all three. Secretive old—Reigner Three was not to be got rid of so lightly. In fact, *she* would have arranged to do without Orm Pender long ago if she had not been fairly sure that she and the other three would cease to be Reigners the moment anything happened to Reigner One. He had arranged it like that on purpose. Reigner Three, who had once loved Reigner One, had been sick of him for several lifetimes now.

The gravity shaft set her gently down in the basement. She stepped out into dingy caves of dark foundation crete. How dreary! she thought.

Vierran looked up from a gripping book cube about marriage customs on Iony and was astonished to see the tall dark lady picking her way among the racks of hanging clothes. Reigner Three, of all people! Vierran jumped up in a hurry. "How can I help you, ma'am?"

"Who are *you*?" asked Reigner Three. This bannus crisis had made things so hectic in the House of Balance that she had clean forgotten the clothes store would be manned by a human.

"Vierran, ma'am, House of Guaranty," Vierran answered sedately. You did not get on the wrong side of Reigner Three if you could help it—particularly not if you were female.

Yes, of course. Reigner Three remembered now. The one with the unwise sense of humor that Four had called a nasty bit of work. The girl looked too clever by half—well, she was from a brainy House, of course. Pity she hadn't inherited the usual Guaranty good looks. Those prominent cheekbones and that wriggly hair made her look quite a little freak. Vierran barely came up to Three's shoulder, and she was not slender. Must get her looks from whoever the mother is, Three supposed. *Not* a beauty. "I want some Earth clothing, Vierran."

Vierran, with considerable effort, managed to stop her surprise from showing on her face. Reigner Three going to Earth now! What was going *on* in that back alley of the universe that required the personal attention of all the Reigner heads? Whatever it was, Vierran was beginning to suspect it had done for the Servant, or he would have been back by now to return that camel coat and chat to her again. Vierran's lips were pressed together hard as she turned to the control panel and directed it to swing the Earth section out of thetaspace. Again. For the fourth time in ten days.

"This way, ma'am." She led the way to the correct vault, wondering which—if any—of the clothes stored there could possibly be worn by someone as stylish as Reigner Three.

Reigner Three swayed elegantly after Vierran, considering her. Didn't she ever get her robot to style that hair of hers? But—*but*. Reigner Three recalled that this girl was said to be the only person in the House of Balance that the Servant ever talked to. Hard to believe. Three herself kept out of the Servant's way, like everyone else, unless she had to give him orders. That death's-head face of his gave her the creeps. But it might be worth finding out what Vierran could tell her about him.

"You must see our Servant fairly often," she said to Vierran's back.

"Mordion Agenos," said Vierran.

"Who?" said Reigner Three.

"Mordion Agenos," said Vierran, "is the Servant's name. Yes. He comes down here for clothes whenever he's sent to a subject world, ma'am." She went into the vault and swung out the nearest rack of ladies' clothes. No, they were not ladies' clothes—females' clothes, women's clothes, wives' clothes, working girls' clothes, maybe, but nothing for a great lady like Reigner Three, she thought, pushing them along the rack rather desperately. But she would really have *loved* to hand Reigner Three the rayon pinafore dress printed with shrill green and red apples, or the electric blue leotard, and assure Reigner Three with a perfectly straight face that these were the very latest of Earth fashions.

Unfortunately one did not play jokes on Reigner Three, not if one did not want to be terminated. She was said to have no sense of humor at all. And she also had a name for hating women. Vierran had it on good authority—her father's spy network, in fact—that it was because of Reigner Three that the Reigner Organization did not employ a single woman in any of its offices, even on the inner worlds. A very formidable lady, Reigner Three.

"Hmm," said Reigner Three, surveying the pinafore dress, the leotard, and the other clothes on the rack. "So the Servant talks to you when he comes here for clothes?"

Vierran looked at Reigner Three looking at the leotard and hurriedly pulled forward another rack. "Only when I talk to *him*, ma'am. I've never known Mordion Agenos start a conversation himself, ma'am. These clothes on this rack are slightly better quality, ma'am."

Reigner Three surveyed tweeds and moth-eaten furs, and her lovely face was stony. "How are these clothes obtained, Vierran?"

"The House of Balance has an arrangement with various charitable organizations on Earth, ma'am," Vierran explained. "They send us all the donated clothing they can't dispose of—Oxfam, the Salvation Army, Save the—"

"I see," said Reigner Three. "Why does the Servant never start a conversation?"

"I thought at first, ma'am," Vierran replied, "that his training forbade it, but I've come to think that it's because he is sure that everyone hates him."

"These clothes are all hideous," said Reigner Three. "You must revise your method of obtaining them. But everyone *does* hate the Servant, Vierran. Have you any idea what his job is?"

"I was told," said Vierran, with her face as stony as Reigner Three's, "that he kills people on Reigners' orders, ma'am."

"Precisely." Reigner Three slammed the dowdy clothes along their rail. "He's a sort of human robot, designed to obey our orders. I'm surprised he has anything to say for himself. Those years of training were supposed to have left him without any personality at all. But I imagine you've no idea—a child like you—what it takes to train a Servant."

A slight pinkness made its way into Vierran's expressionless face. "I'm twenty-one, ma'am. I've heard a little about the training, ma'am. They say there were six children in training, and Mordion Agenos was the only one who survived it."

This was news to Reigner Three. Here was Reigner One being secretive again! She slammed the tweeds along the rail the other way. "I believe so. Haven't you a solido or cube of Earth fashions I can look at? None of these things will do."

"Well," Vierran said doubtfully, "cube vision hasn't got out to Earth yet, ma'am. They only have two-D on tape and film so far."

"Are you sure?" Oh, what a barbarous place! Reigner Three thought.

"Yes, ma'am. I always make a close study of any world I have clothes for." And so did the Servant, Vierran thought. This was what they mostly talked about. The customs of other worlds were so odd. Last time the Servant had lounged in, with that confident, strolling walk that was really so hesitant if you watched it closely, they had talked of Paris, New York, Africa, handshakes, fossil fuel, flint—and, of course, camels. Vierran tried not to let her face show the grin growing inside it at the memory. Mordion Agenos stood with a bundle of inner clothing over one arm, staining the shadows of the vault scarlet with his bloodred uniform, surveying a row of overcoats. "What *is* a camel?" he had asked. And Vierran had answered, "A horse designed by a committee." Mordion had thought and then asked, "Do you think of me as a camel then?" Vierran had been both embarrassed and confused. Mordion was so sharp. He had indeed been designed by a committee of Reigners, and Vierran did somehow equate him with a horse. But she saw it was a joke—she hoped. "Choose the camel coat, then," she had dared him. And he had.

"Have you got *any* kind of Earth pictures?" Reigner Three demanded.

"Er—only this, ma'am." Vierran rummaged in an alcove and found her a slightly tattered copy of—no, *Teenage Fashion* wouldn't do, nor would *New Woman*—ah! here we are!—*Vogue*.

Reigner Three slipped the jade nail shields off her thumb and forefinger and quickly turned the pages. "This is *slightly* better. Some of these queer outfits are almost elegant. But about our Servant. Perhaps *you* wouldn't talk to him, either, if you knew just how many people he's killed."

"Not at all, ma'am," Vierran answered. Her voice did not exactly change, but there was emotion at the back of it—which she tried to suppress and annoyingly couldn't—as she said, "I've made a complete list of every termination."

"Dear, dear!" said Reigner Three, detecting that emotion. "There's no accounting for tastes, is there? I always think those terminations account for this Servant's singularly horrible smile. Don't you?"

"It could do," said Vierran. She watched Reigner Three go back to *Vogue* and tried not to clench her fists. The high point of her every conversation with Mordion came when she had induced him to give that smile of his. Usually the smile came quite naturally.

But this last time Mordion had been grave. Something about this particular mission worried him. A precognition perhaps. People always said the Servants had near-Reigner powers, and foresight *was* one of those. In the end Vierran was reduced to saying to him, "Smile!" Suddenly. Just like that. Mordion had blinked at her, taken aback, and only produced the slightest vestige of his usual smile. She could see him thinking he had annoyed or depressed her by calling himself a camel. "No, no!" Vierran had told him. "It's got nothing to *do* with camels! Smile *properly*!" At that Mordion's eyebrow lifted, and he did smile, quite amazingly, full of amusement. And it had enchanted Vierran, just as it always did.

"Right," said Reigner Three, handing back the *Vogue*. "Now I'm going to look through all these racks myself. Pull all the racks out."

Vierran did so, quietly and efficiently and a little like a robot. Reigner Three, with equal efficiency, began a swift collection of garments, dumping each one in Vierran's arms as she chose it. You had to hand it to Reigner Three, Vierran thought, looking down at the growing pile. She did have a flair for clothes. Every one of these was *right*.

Reigner Three had a flair for finding what she wanted in other matters, too. As she moved along the racks, she considered what Vierran had said and, more important, the way Vierran had said it. She knew they did badly need some extra, unexpected weapon against the Servant—something to cut down the danger from him at least and leave them room to maneuver against the bannus. There *was* danger from the Servant, and it was probably acute. Reigner One never used words like that unless he meant them. And Vierran might just be what they needed to keep the Servant docile long enough to be stassed.

She went back to Vierran. "I'll send a robot down for these clothes and get them copied in wearable materials," she said. "What do Earth people use to carry clothes? Do they have grav-hoists?"

"Suitcases, ma'am," Vierran told her. "Earth hasn't discovered antigravity yet."

Reigner Three turned her eyes up. "Great Balance! What a hole! Show me suitcases."

Vierran put the heap of clothing down on a work surface and fetched out suitcases. Reigner Three disparaged each one as it appeared as inelegant, or clumsy, or too small. At length, with a sigh, she chose the largest. "I'll have that copied in some color I can bear. Give it all to my robot. Then find yourself Earth clothes, too. I shall need you to come with me as my maid."

Vierran was astounded—and scared. "But—but what about my job here, ma'am?"

"I'll tell the housekeeper to put in a robot temporarily," said Three. "Pull yourself together, girl. You'll have time to take a language course while they're making my clothes, but only if you don't stand around gaping. I want you to meet me at the portal this evening as soon as I page you. Don't dawdle. Neither Reigner One nor I likes to be kept waiting."

Reigner One going, too! As Three went up in the gravity shaft, Vierran sank down on a pile of unsorted clothing, trying to adjust to this sudden change. From being a menial to being a pawn, in one giddy step, she told herself. There was no doubt that something very big was going on. Vierran did not fool herself that Reigner Three had ordered her to Earth just for the color of her eyes. No, she was to be a pawn in something—the Great Balance alone knew what. But Vierran found she was more scared than ever and worried on her own account now, as well as on the Servant's.

As soon as Three's robot had been and gone, Vierran rushed to the basement communicator and requested an outside line. When she had it, she pressed the symbols for her cousin, Siri, with fierce speed. Siri was probably at work—Vierran hoped—but she kept her finger on the "please trace" pad just in case.

To her relief, Siri looked up wearily from a pile of solidos and grinned when she saw it was Vierran calling. "I was afraid it was your father, coming on the line to blast me," Siri said. "We've a right mess going. None of the Earth flint consignments came

through, and almost every House is screaming for a bridging loan.
I've got us almost as overextended as they are, just trying to cover
the urgent ones."

Vierran might have been sitting at that desk, coping with that
selfsame mess, had she not been ordered to the House of Balance
to do menial work for the biggest firm of all. Not that she grudged
Siri. Working for Father was not a bed of roses, and it could equally
well have been Siri who had to work in the House of Balance.
Neither of them had brothers or sisters. They had known from their
childhood that one of them was going to have to serve the Reigners.

"Never mind," Vierran's father had said when the request came
for Vierran and not Siri. "House of Guaranty can use a source of
inside information. Think of it as doing your bit against the Reigners—and I'll get you out of it as soon as I can."

Vierran was glad to do her bit, as Father put it. She had for a
long time known—without being actually *told*—that her father was
high up among those working secretly to overthrow the House of
Balance. And the sooner they did it, the better, in Vierran's opinion.
She had felt quite honored and almost excited to be trusted this
much—particularly when her father insisted on making certain
plans for emergencies. But as the only way she could legally remove
from the House of Balance was by contracting a marriage with
someone outside the Reigner Organization, she could not see her
father getting her out of it quickly. She had been resigned to dreary
years in the basement. Now suddenly everything was changed, and
it was time to call on the emergency arrangement.

She tried to keep the shake out of her voice as she said to Siri,
"Just listen to this—I've been ordered to go to Earth!" She watched
Siri's face sharpen as Siri connected this news with the flint crisis.
"Three and One are going there now. I'm going as Three's maid."

A look of incredulous hope came over Siri's face. Vierran could
see her thinking of the unexplained absence of Reigners Two, Four,
and Five, of accidents at portals, wars on Earth, violent natives, and
a universe ridded of all five Reigners at once. She gave a warning

frown to remind Siri that the line was certainly bugged. Siri tried to turn her expression into a normal smile. "How nice," she said. "None of the poor dears have had a holiday in either of our lifetimes, have they? What an honor for you! I'll tell Uncle for you. When do you go?"

"Later today," said Vierran. "Can you ask him to give me the present he promised me if I was ever honored like this? I'm going for a last ride out in the park in an hour's time."

Siri looked at her timepiece. Vierran's father lived and worked in the House of Guaranty's main holding half the world away. "I'll tell him now," she said. "I think there's just time for him to express you a parcel. I'll ride out and meet you and give it to you if it's come. We can say good-bye anyway. And," Siri added, meaning the opposite, "I do so envy you."

"Thanks. See you. I have to go and get a headache from a double-speed language course now," Vierran said. They grinned at each other, rather tensely, and disconnected.

The language course did give her a headache, but it was not as bad as Vierran expected, and it largely disappeared while she was saddling her beloved horse, Reigner Six. His name was another of Vierran's jokes. As far as she knew, the Reigners took it as a compliment, if they noticed at all. The headache went entirely as Vierran passed under the dark crete of the stable gate and went thudding out across the wide greensward of the great park round the House of Balance. Reigner Six was feeling lazy. Vierran had some fun cursing him in colorful Earth talk, trying to get him to canter. But underneath she was stern with worry. She kept glancing sideways and back at the great luminous looping coils of the House of Balance, a masterpiece in Earth flint. It always reminded Vierran of a model of the inner works of the human ear. Very apt, since the Reigners listened to everything. They might easily have listened to her talk with Siri. And she would only know if Siri failed to turn up.

At least, she consoled herself, Siri would have told Father. And he would be worried sick. Well, she was worried about herself. By now the House of Balance was only a sheen on the horizon. She was sure Siri would not come.

But a bare half mile on, Siri's horse, Fax, and Siri's own shape appeared on the skyline, tall and slender, and Siri's blond hair blew like Fax's mane in the wind. Vierran smiled lovingly. Bless Siri! Siri, in her own way, was quite as beautiful as Reigner Three. She had the Guaranty looks. Vierran had missed those looks, and Mother's, too. Mother called her a throwback. Throwback to *what*? Vierran always wanted to know. A gnome? Mother always laughed and said, No, a throwback to the early peoples of Homeworld. In which case, Vierran retorted, they were right to have died out. But there were drawbacks to looking like Siri. Reigner Four fancied Siri. This was why Siri had a permit to ride in the park. Siri used the permit freely, but only when Vierran told her Reigner Four was out of the way. When she thought of Reigner Four, Vierran had to admit there were some advantages to looking like a gnome.

She waved delightedly at Siri. "You made it!"

"*Eh?*" yelled Siri.

Vierran realized she had accidentally used Earth talk. Serious as this meeting was, she could hardly speak properly for laughing. But Siri, when she came within speaking distance, was too worried to be amused. "How can you laugh? You're mad! Your present arrived. Uncle must be mad, too. This thing must have cost a small estate. Here you are." She handed Vierran a broad jeweled bracelet, the fashionable kind that you wore on your upper arm. Any spy-eye abroad in the park would have registered it as a bracelet—unless it had been specially alerted, of course—and passed on.

Vierran noted the promised microgun disguised in the elaborate gold design, the spare darts for it slotted into the patterned edge and—bless Father!—a tiny message cassette pretending to be part of the clasp. As she clasped the bracelet on her arm, she told herself she felt better. "I'm getting them to send Reigner Six over to you," she said. "Take care of him for me." She wanted to add, "Until I come back," but the words would not come out. Such a gift as this bracelet, as she and her father both knew, was likely to be the very last thing he would ever give her.

—3——————————————

By THE EARLY evening it was all round the House of Balance that Reigner One had had the heads of all the least loyal Houses arrested. Vierran's father was one of the first on the list. But from what Vierran could gather, Uncle Dev and maybe even Siri and Mother had been arrested with him. How stupid, she thought. That business with the bracelet was just too obvious. She had a mad need to throw the bracelet away, or rush to Reigner One's suite and shoot everything she met there, or simply lie with her legs in the air and scream. Instead she packed her bag and went through the pearly labyrinth to the portal when Reigner Three paged her.

Reigner Three was wearing something slender and white, with white fur wrapped across her shoulders, and a broad hat that wonderfully set off her lovely face and dark, glossy hair. She was followed by a robot carrying a suave gray suitcase which, to Vierran's dismay, was nearly twice as big as the one that had been its model. While Vierran looked with foreboding at this enormous piece of luggage, Reigner Three looked with strong disfavor on her new maid. Vierran was wearing trousers with a dark, floppy top, long-sleeved to conceal the bracelet.

"You look like a native of New Xai," said Reigner Three. "Won't they stare at you on Earth?"

"The young people dress like this there, ma'am," said Vierran.

Reigner Three gave this a moment of expressive silence. "Take this suitcase," she said, signaling to the robot to pass it over. "And now I suppose we'll have to wait an hour or so while One finishes arresting people."

But Reigner One was already approaching, followed by another robot with a small valise. He must have had his own private store of clothes. Without going near the basement, he had somehow acquired a dark pinstriped suit, beautifully tailored to his somewhat bulky frame. A white raincoat hung over his arm, and a soft felt hat dangled from his fingers. He gave his mustache an amused tweak as he saw the contrast between Reigner Three and her maid. But the hand fell to his newly trimmed silver beard and tugged when he saw the maid was Vierran.

"My dear," he asked, smiling, "why have you brought the daughter of the House of Guaranty from her duties below?"

"Because I know perfectly well that a robot would cause a sensation on Earth," Three said. "You don't expect me to do without a maid, do you?" She watched the hand on the beard warily. When Reigner One clutched his beard, he was not pleased.

He was not pleased. He weighed the matter up, without altering his bland smile, and decided he would explain to Three later why he was displeased. As to Vierran herself, it could well be an advantage to have her on Earth after all. He had planned to use the blond cousin, but doing things this way would complete the downfall of House Guaranty much more amusingly. He knew all about Vierran. He knew she played at revolution, thinking no one would suspect a girl in her position. He knew about Reigner Six and most of her other interests. And when Vierran, awhile ago, had seemed to busy herself finding out all she could about the Servant, Reigner One had smiled and put information in her way. That, and her sense of humor, amused him, because he knew that very shortly she would have nothing to laugh about at all. He thought he might as well tell her why on the journey.

He took his hand from his beard and signaled them to open the portal. Reigner Three relaxed as she followed him through the pearly arch. Vierran, anything but relaxed, struggled after them with their three bags.

They made an apparently leisurely journey down through the galaxy. But Vierran had good reason to notice that Reigner One never really stopped for an instant. He sauntered steadily onward, beaming genially at Sector Governors and their hurrying underlings, and did not let any of them delay him even for a second. Luckily for Vierran, the hurrying underlings ran to carry the suitcases to the next portal, so she only had to take their weight down the long pearly walk-throughs. That was more than enough. Her hands were blistered and her arms were dragged long before they reached Iony. What a waste! she thought. A great journey like this, and I can hardly notice anything but how heavy these damn things are! By the time they were right out in Yurov, her back ached, and her knees shook.

Reigner One called a surprise halt, here in Yurov. "I hear," he said to this particular Controller, fat and anxiously fawning among his sumptuous gold screens, "that you produce some remarkably fine sangro on your estate here."

"Trust you to remember that!" Reigner Three said tartly. Her feet, in high-heeled white shoes, were killing her. "Does this office have a ladies' room, Controller?"

"Certainly, certainly," said the Controller of Yurov. "Yes and yes, to both matters, Excellencies."

Vierran sighed. Reigner Three would indubitably want her maid there to run round her in the ladies' room. All Vierran wanted was to lie on one of those crimson sofas and rest her aching back. But some kind of look passed between the two Reigners. As a result, Reigner Three went off to the ladies' room like a tall white ship of the line, in a bevy of escorting officials, and Vierran found herself sitting—very upright—on one end of a crimson sofa, with Reigner One lolling easily at the other end.

She was suddenly truly scared. So scared that she realized that her feelings back in the House of Balance had hardly been real. This was real fear. It squeezed her heart and held her in a cold paralysis, almost as if she were in stass. When the bowing Controller handed her a golden goblet of wine, the blistered fingers she took it with were icy, and tight, and withered white.

Reigner One sipped, rolled the sangro round his mouth, and

beamed. "Ah! It *is* wonderful! My Servant has an excellent palate. How ironical that this was something I never thought to breed for! Don't you admire the color of this wine, Vierran? Almost the color of my Servant's uniform, is it not?"

"Not really, sire. The wine's more the color of blood," Vierran answered.

"But I dress my Servant in scarlet to make people think of blood," Reigner One protested cheerfully. "You think it should be a darker red? I believe you take an interest in my Servant, Vierran?"

"I've talked to him, sire," Vierran replied.

"Good, good," beamed Reigner One.

Always smiling, Vierran thought. Why does he *smile*? I ought to use this gun on him. She was surprised to find that her terror left her room for such hatred. It was such fierce loathing, physical, sickening loathing, that if Reigner One had moved an inch nearer to her along the sofa, she would have attacked him with her bare hands.

He knew. He smiled and did not move. He could read her so easily. Rebellion, disgust, murderous hatred, panic terror were all there. He took pleasure in holding her to the spot, so that all she could do was mechanically sip her wine. He doubted if she tasted it. What a waste of a superb wine!

"I've been meaning to talk to you for a long time now, my dear," he said, "and now is as good a time as any. Of course, you may have guessed. You are one of the young ladies I have chosen to breed with my Servant. You and your cousin, Siri, as a matter of fact. But since you are here, we will take you first. You are going to be the mother of my future Servants. Say thank you, my dear. It is a great privilege."

"Thank you, sire," Vierran found herself whispering. No! she thought. No, no, no, *no*! But she could not say it.

Reigner One increased pressure on her, augmented the pressure by his instruments, and continued, "The Servant, as you know, is on Earth, where he seems to have become inadvertently caught in the field of an antiquated machine. When we get to Earth, I am going to send you into that field after him. You are ordered to find him there and breed with him."

Vierran found herself whispering, "Yes, sire."

"Mind you do," said Reigner One. "If you disobey this command, there will be painful consequences for the rest of your family. You are to go into the field and make a child with my Servant. Is that clear, Vierran?"

Vierran struggled against the force she could feel him putting on her. It did no good. All she was able to say was "What fun, sire." Almost as if she meant it.

Resistance. Reigner One's lips pursed. But here Reigner Three came sailing back among the golden screens, and the Controller heaved up from the other side to say the portal was phased and ready. Reigner One let the puny resistance pass. He drained his goblet and got to his feet. "Good, good," he said. "Come along, Vierran."

This casts a whole new light on Father's arrest! Vierran thought as she put down her goblet mostly full and trailed among the screens and the officials to the portal. She wondered what this Controller would do if she seized his pudgy hands and begged him to help her. But she knew she would do nothing. Her fear was gone. In its place was a huge, flat emptiness with voices crying of death faintly in its distances. All she had heard of the mothers of the Servants echoed in those cries. They gave you drugs so that you had as many babies as possible. The babies were taken away surgically. After that you were never heard of again.

The portal yawned in front of her. She picked up the bags and followed the two Reigners through.

4

ASSOCIATE CONTROLLER GIRALDUS was there in Albion to meet the party, more efficient than ever. He knew these were the two Reigners who really mattered.

"Excellencies!" He and his assistants bowed like grass on a green bank waving. "I take it, Excellencies, you wish me to open our local portal for you to Earth. To the Hexwood Farm library complex, will it be, Excellencies?"

Reigner One smiled genially. He wondered why Five had left this fellow alive. One could always get Runcorn to send one home after all. He toyed with the idea of telling Giraldus that they were actually on their way to Runcorn to sort out the flint crisis. He would have to do that anyway—but later. The bannus took priority. And unlike the others, Reigner One intended to approach it with extreme caution. "Well, no," he said. "We want to arrive at what I believe is called a train station. The nearest one to Hexwood, if you please."

Giraldus was not for a moment thrown out. "Certainly, Excellency. Just one moment while I recalibrate the portal," he said, and went with swift, important strides to reset the controls. Reigner One watched how long it took him. Only seconds. The man was too efficient by half. And Vierran, after that resistance of hers, ought to be taught a lesson. Reigner One waited until the portal had opened and Giraldus had turned smugly from the control panel, and terminated Giraldus there and then. He did not watch the smug smile turn to hurt amazement and then to horror as Giraldus realized he had ceased to breathe. He watched Vierran stare as the man's face turned blue. He did not say, "That's what will happen to your father, my dear, if you disobey me." He did not need to. He motioned her politely through the portal after Reigner Three. "After you, Vierran."

Vierran went with her head turned over her shoulder, watching Giraldus choke and fold at the knees. She entered Earth like someone entering an abyss.

Reigner One smiled and gestured with his hat to a taxi waiting outside Hexwood station.

5

THEY DROVE TO the motel on the outskirts of Hexwood Farm estate. "What is *this*?" Reigner Three demanded when she saw the collection of low brick buildings.

"A sort of inn. We own it, as a matter of fact," Reigner One told her.

"Then we own something remarkably like a place to keep pigs in," said Three. She was very discontented. It took Vierran nearly two hours and much patience to get Reigner Three arranged in her room to Reigner Three's liking. Then it took another hour to get Reigner Three changed into the misty sea green draperies she thought fit to wear to eat supper in. Just as well, Vierran thought drearily. I think I might go mad without her to take my mind off things.

"Are you coming to supper? In those clothes?" Reigner Three asked.

"No, thanks. I'm not hungry, ma'am. I think I'll go to my room and rest," Vierran said.

I don't know what One's said to her, but it's certainly pricked her little bubble! Reigner Three thought. About time someone did! She was almost as ripe for termination as that fellow in Albion! Reigner Three took care to be sure that Vierran was indeed lying on her bed, watching something called "Neighbours" on the flat, flickering entertainment box, and then made her way to join Reigner One in a place called The Steak Bar. Here they were served what seemed to Reigner Three a singularly ill-tasting meal.

"This is a hovel," she told Reigner One in their own language. "I warn you—I am not pleased!"

"Neither am I." Reigner One moved his prawn cocktail in order to inspect with wonder the picture of a stagecoach on the mat beneath. "You were not supposed to bring Vierran, my dear. There was a moment when I was quite angry. You see, as it happened I had just dispatched all her family here along with the other disaffected House heads. My aim was to isolate Vierran on Homeworld in order to breed her to the Servant when we bring him back."

"Then you should have *told* me!" snapped Reigner Three. "Whatever did you send the House heads *here* for?"

"To have them under my eye. To show them who is Reigner. And to draggle their fine feathers a little," said Reigner One. "I sent them by the trade routes in an empty flint transport. They should be arriving around now at our factory just north of this place. They will not be served even with such a poor dinner as this."

"Nice!" In spite of her discontent, Reigner Three smiled. These people—or rather, their distant ancestors—had once looked down their noses at her when she was only a singer who was Orm Pender's mistress.

"Yes, but you must on no account tell Vierran that these people are nearby," said Reigner One.

They paused while a rather obtrusive waiter took away their prawn glasses and brought them steak, chips, and coleslaw.

"I apologize about Vierran," said Reigner Three. "What is this white stuff that looks like cat sick and tastes of cardboard?"

"An aberration," said Reigner One, "made of cabbage. Cabbage is a vegetable that came to Earth from Yurov along with the earliest convicts. I accept your apology, my dear. Upon reflection, I saw that this solved at least one of our problems. So on Yurov I ordered Vierran to go into the field of the bannus and breed with the Servant."

Reigner Three actually laughed. "So *that's* what got into her!"

"Yes. Once she has, it will be your task to kill the Servant as quickly as you can. You should enjoy that," Reigner One said amiably. "I was going to put her cousin to him, but I fancy Vierran is better breeding stock. Make sure she's pregnant and then bring her safely out of the field for the appropriate medication, if you would."

Reigner Three looked suspiciously from him to her steak. "What made you change your mind? I thought you wanted the Servant stassed so that you could clone from him."

"Clones are no fun," said Reigner One. "The fun is in breaking in a different set of children each time. No, my dear, we must cut our losses, you and I, and get used to doing without a Servant until Vierran's brood is trained. This one's been too long in the bannus field. We want him finished quick before the real danger arises."

"I wish you wouldn't be so mysterious! *What* real danger?" Reigner Three demanded. But she was thinking, He said "you and I!" He *has* written the other three off. Oh, good!

"I'll show you." Reigner One put a miniature cube on the table between the little cardboard mats on which their wineglasses stood. "Have you finished eating already?"

Reigner Three pushed aside her uneaten steak. "Yes."

Reigner One continued eating placidly. "Here's a map of this area," he said, and activated the cube with a wave of his fork. The picture expanded until it was about the size of the place mat with the coach and horses on it. Three leaned forward and saw the map was of an irregularly shaped island. Rather like an old witch riding a pig, she thought. There were colored dots all over the island. "The key to the dots," said Reigner One, "is something I normally keep only in my head—though I believe if you worked hard, you could put it together from the classified stuff here and on Albion. The blue dots are Reigner installations, including some very secret ones, yellow are the permanent portals, and green, orange, and red are other secret sites of great potential danger."

"Where are we?" asked Three. Reigner One showed her with the tip of his knife. She looked quizzically sideways at the large colored cluster. "About the only thing I *can't* see here is a portal," she said.

"Correct. That would have been asking for trouble," said Reigner One. "Wait, and I'll give you a closer view." The tip of his knife went out and expanded the picture but not the size of the map. The old-witch island sped out of sight at the sides, giddily. It was like plunging nose forward in a stratoship, with the additional giddiness of wriggling contours, mile-wide lettering, and madly branching road systems. Three looked away until it had stopped.

When she looked back, it was at a sort of octopus of roads that gradually melted into square blocks at the edges. Sprawling across it were the symbols HEXWOOD FARM ESTATE. In the lower, octopuslike half, a small green dot beside a blue square seemed to have run and spread a green haze over the wriggle of roads around it.

Reigner One's knife pointed to this. "The bannus. The pale green is its field as my monitors show it at this moment. It's spread a bit since Five went, but not much. Here is our motel." His knife moved to show a small black square toward the top right-hand corner. "We're well out of range, as you see." The knife tip went on to another, larger blue square almost at the top of the map. "That's the Reigner factory I mentioned earlier."

There was one of the bright red dots just beside this large blue square, and two more dots, both orange, spaced out beyond it. Reigner Three looked at them. "And?" she said.

Reigner One's knife indicated the red dot beside the factory, a short stab. "Stass tomb," he said. Then, reluctantly, hating to have the secret dragged out of him, he gave her a name that made Three sit bolt upright in hatred and shock. "Martellian, onetime Reigner One. My predecessor, you might say."

Reigner Three's face went murderous as she thought of their old enemy still there and still, after a fashion, alive. Martellian had been hardest of all to dislodge after Orm Pender had worked his way among the Reigners. Even after Reigners Two and Five had been co-opted, Martellian still hung on, on the other side of Homeworld. It had taken all five of them, using the bannus the way Orm showed them, to dislodge Martellian and force him into exile on Earth. And even there he had continued to cause trouble.

"It gave me great pleasure," mused Reigner One, "to use his own descendants—those two girl Servants, remember?—to put him down into stass."

Reigner Three made impatient tapping motions at the two orange dots. "And these?"

"Stass tombs, too." Reigner One calmly flicked the picture off and summoned the waiter, from whom he ordered coffee and a cigar. Reigner Three waited with one hand clenched so that its pearly red nails bit into her. She would gladly have murdered One if she had been able—particularly when he lit the cigar.

"*Must* you?" she said, fanning with her other hand.

"Among the best inventions of Earth, cigars," he said, and looked at her with placid expectation.

She realized he had expected her to work whatever it was out for herself. She was even more annoyed. "How *can* I understand? You haven't told me all the *facts!*"

"Surely you remember?" he said. "The two orange dots are the most troublesome of Martellian's children. I forget their names. One is from the brood he got when he was calling himself Wolf— the one who wounded Four so badly when we brought in the worms from Lind—and the other is from the second lot, when he was calling himself Merlin."

"You lied!" Three spit at him. "You told us all those children were dead!"

"But these are grandchildren," Reigner One said, calmly blowing smoke. "Or possibly nephews. Martellian did a certain amount of inbreeding, rather as I do with the Servants, in order to breed back to true Reigner traits. These are the two where he succeeded. They are virtual Reigners, and I had to stass them myself."

Three's hand went over her mouth.

"Ah, you're with me now, I see," Reigner One observed.

"*Four* of them, with the Servant!" Three said, husky with horror. "Orm, that's damn near a proper Hand of Reigners!"

"Or could be a whole Hand, if they co-opted an Earthman with the right ancestry," Reigner One agreed. "Like that John Bedford. He seemed to me to have more than a touch of Reigner blood. I didn't like the look of him at all. But there's no need to be so horrified, my dear. The theta-field from the bannus hasn't nearly reached them yet. We got here in time."

Reigner Three's groping hands found a red paper napkin. She tore it tensely to shreds. "Orm," she said, "whatever *possessed* you to park the bannus so *near* them?"

"Then you *don't* understand," One said, carefully detaching the ash off his cigar into the dish provided. "I hope your mind isn't going, my dear, after all this time. The bannus, as you know, is primarily designed to select Reigners—to single out a proper Hand of them and then to elect them. This was in the bad old days when Reigners were legally obliged to be reselected every ten years, one from each of five Houses. Those repeating programs it runs were supposed to test their ability to control it and only secondarily to aid them with their decisions after they were elected. The elected Reigner controls the bannus. Right? But the bannus also has to be strong enough to control the *deselected* Reigners. In fact, it's the only thing that *can* control a Reigner."

"I know all that," Three said, shredding red shreds of paper napkin. "So *why?*"

Reigner One beamed at her. "Two birds with one stone. We had to get rid of the bannus. And the bannus, even under seal, always puts out a small mild field—not theta-space, just influence. We placed those stass tombs just on the edge of that field of influence, and used it to keep the sleepers under. And we double-sealed it so that it could never draw full power. And we left it on Earth, as far away from Homeworld as it could get, so that it wouldn't force us to reselect ourselves every ten years. You owe your long reign to my foresight, my dear."

Three shakily put a handful of red shreds down on the table. "That's as may be," she said. "I'm going to take a look at those stass tombs first thing tomorrow."

"Excellent plan," Reigner One said warmly. "I was going to suggest the same thing myself."

PART SEVEN

—1—

YAM LOOMED OVER Mordion. The newly mended slash in his tegument caught the last of the sun in a jagged orange glitter.

Mordion roused himself with difficulty. He had been sitting here
outside the house for hours now, trying to force himself to a decision.
He knew he was ready to make a move. But what move, in which
direction, when he was unable to think of the reasons for it? All he
knew was that he must advance and that any advance would bring
him face-to-face with things he would rather not know. He sighed
and looked up at Yam. "Why are you standing over me, clanking?"

"It was an error," Yam said, "to worst Hume in battle—"

"He deserved it," said Mordion.

"—because he is now trying to leave the wood," Yam said.

"*What?*" Mordion was on his feet, grabbing for his staff, before Yam
had finished intoning the news. "Which way did he go? When?"

Yam pointed to the river. "He crossed about five minutes ago."

Mordion set off in great leaps down the cliffside and in more
cautious leaps from rock to rock across the white water. Halfway
across, the corner of his eye caught sight of Yam, sedately stepping
from stone to stone, too. "Why didn't you go after him straightaway?" Mordion said as they both reached the opposite bank.

"Hume ordered me never to let you out of my sight," Yam
explained.

Mordion swore. What an obvious trick!

"Many years ago," Yam added. "After you sat on the high rock."

"Oh." Mordion found he was touched—though no doubt Hume was finding that order very useful just at this moment.

He strode forward into the damp half-light of the wood, wondering how far it was to the edge of it this way. They could be too late. Ann had always given him the impression that it was not far. And annoyingly, the wood was now too dark for running. Rustling black-nesses crowded against him and thwacked at Yam's tegument. Both of them stumbled on roots. A branch clawed Mordion's beard. They seemed to have walked straight into a thicket.

A short way ahead Hume yelled. It was only just not a scream of terror.

Without thinking, Mordion raised his staff with a blue ball of light on the end of it. Hawthorns sprang into unearthly green all round. Yam, an improbable glittering blue, swung round beside him and plunged into what was evidently the path they had missed. Mordion squeezed after him among the may blossoms, a heady, oppressive scent, holding his staff high.

Hume was coming toward them down a wider section of path. His head was held sideways in a queer angle of terror. Mordion could see his teeth chattering. Hume was held . . . led . . . pulled by two thorny beings that were insect-stepping along with him on tall legs that ended in sprays of twigs. Each being had a twiggy hand wrapped round one of Hume's upper arms. Their heads seemed to be trailing bundles of ivy, out of which dewspots of eyes flashed blue in Mordion's light.

"Great Balance!" The muscles across Mordion's stomach and shoulders rearranged themselves in a way he absentmindedly recognized as their fighting position. "*Hume!*" he bellowed.

Hume came out of his trance of terror, saw them, and dived toward them, dragging the creatures with him, rustling and bumping on either side. "Oh, thank goodness!" he babbled. "I didn't mean it—at least I did, but I don't mean it now, not anymore!" He flung one arm round Yam and twisted the other into Mordion's rolled cloak. "They came. They rustled. Don't *let them!*"

The creatures appeared to subside to the ground on either side of Hume. Mordion moved his staff jerkily toward the nearest, trying to see it clearly or meaning to fend it off—he was not sure which. The light shone bleak and blue over a small black heap of dry twigs. There was a second heap just beyond Yam. Mordion stirred the nearest pile with his boot. Just twigs.

"The Wood brought Hume back," Yam announced.

"I won't do it again!" Hume said frantically.

"Don't be an idiot, Hume," Mordion said. He was angry with fading terror. "You won't need to do this again. We're going to set out for the castle tomorrow."

"*Really!*" Hume's delight was almost as extreme as his fear had been. "And I can really train to be a knight?"

"If you want." Mordion sighed, knowing that Hume, and maybe Yam, too, thought his decision was for Hume's sake. But Hume had little to do with it. He had known all along, really, that he had to go to the castle and face what had to be faced there.

2

VIERRAN LAY ON her bed in the motel and switched from channel to channel on the flat overbright television-thing, trying to find something that would save her from having to think. There was no escape that she could see. She was alone on Earth with Reigner One's compulsion pressing crampingly on her mind. If she tried to run away, the compulsion would go with her, and Reigner One would follow. And he would give orders to terminate her family. At length she switched the television off and, very slowly, removed the bracelet from her arm. There was always the microgun.

As she unclasped it, her eye fell on the message cassette so cunningly designed to look like part of the clasp. Father really had spent a small fortune on this thing. She could hardly see it for tears. Father and she had always been particularly close. And—it only just now dawned on her—he would surely have sent her a message.

She put the bracelet against her ear and activated the cassette. It whirred irritatingly. Then out of the purring, her father's voice spoke. "Vierran. This is a terrible gift if you're going to use it the way I think you may have to. The darts are poisoned. The choice is up to you. No time for more—I have to get this to Siri. They're just on their way up to arrest me. Much love."

Tears poured down Vierran's face. She sat like a statue with the bracelet still clamped to her ear. Oh, Father. *Worlds* away.

And then, out of the whirring that she now hardly noticed, a second voice spoke, high and trembling, in Earth talk this time.

"Vierran. This is Vierran speaking. Vierran to myself. This is at least the second time I've sat in the inn bedroom despairing, and I'm beginning to not quite believe in it. If it happens again, this is to let me know there's something odd going on."

Vierran found she had sprung off the bed. "Damn *Bannus*!" she said. She was laughing as much as she was crying. "*I'll* say there's something odd going on!"

Four soundless voices fell into her head. It was like getting back the greater part of herself. *You keep blanking me out,* said the Slave, as always the faintest. *Do keep talking,* said the Prisoner. *Go on with the story,* said the Boy, and, *Oh, there you are!* said the King. *What happened? You were in the middle of sorting out what happened in the wood.*

The Bannus interrupted, Vierran told them dourly. *How long ago would you say I stopped speaking to you?*

The Boy said decisively, *Three-quarters of an hour ago.*

In other words, just time for the raid on the shops, followed by the walk back to the motel. *One more question,* Vierran said. *I know it sounds silly, but with that Bannus messing up reality all the time, I have to ask. Who do you all think I am?*

The four voices answered simultaneously, *I think of you as the Girl Child.*

This was not as useless as it sounded. *Not Ann Stavely?* Vierran asked.

I was puzzled by that name, the King said.

The messages from you are not always clear, the Prisoner told her. *Time and space and language interfere. But I was confused by that one.*

Go on with the story, the Boy repeated.

Please, said the King, *I want to hear more. I am currently attending a religious ceremony of unbelievable tedium. I rely on you to amuse me.*

As always, Vierran was uncertain whether they could hear one another. Sometimes, she was sure, they could not, and she had to pass messages between them. But at least her head was back to normal. "I'll *get* you for this!" Vierran promised the Bannus. It had rendered her journey from the House of Balance correctly enough, but it had cut out all the disembodied conversations. Those had been a lifeline to Vierran as she trudged behind the two Reigners laden with luggage. *Think of something else,* the Slave had suggested. *This is what I do. Masters take pleasure in seeing one struggle.* And when Reigner One had smiled and told her of his plans for her, she surely would have despaired but for the Boy riding in her head and saying, *Go on, resist! I know you can!* and the Prisoner surprising and delighting her by asking suddenly, *Who is this Baddydaddy?* Vierran had hung her sense of humor on these kinds of remarks for years now, and during that journey she had hung on to her voices gratefully. Even her shock when Reigner One had terminated that poor Associate Controller had been lifted slightly from her when the King remarked wryly that he wished it had been *that* easy in his day and age.

It was a genuine Reigner trait, having these voices. *My one claim to fame,* Vierran sometimes told the four of them. Mother had hit the roof and wanted Vierran seen by mind doctors when Vierran first confessed to hearing them. Father had quashed that idea. After a long argument, in which he claimed that children often had imaginary companions and that Vierran would grow out of it, he had taken Vierran away into his hushed and air-conditioned study. This had always been a great privilege to Vierran, being allowed in Father's study. And, even more of a privilege, Father had confessed to her, "I've never dared tell your mother—I have voices, too: a woman, two girls, and an elderly man. Don't worry. Neither of us is mad. I've done a lot of research on this. Quite a number of the old Reigners heard voices. There are sworn records of it. In the old days they seemed sure it was rather a special thing."

"Tell Mother you hear them," Vierran had urged him. But Hugon Guaranty refused. She suspected it was because two of his voices were girls. He told her, however, that he had found out about the people who seemed to speak to him, from what they told him of themselves. Two of them he could prove had actually, truly existed on adjacent worlds. One woman, creepily, had left a record of speaking to *him* in her lifetime. This, as he said, suggested that the two he could not trace were equally real.

Together, they had tried to find out about Vierran's people, but they had drawn four complete blanks. The Slave was always very reticent about himself and gave them almost nothing to go on. The Prisoner could have been one of many hundred opponents of the present Reigners. And the Boy and the King were both too far away in space and time to figure in any records that either Vierran or Hugon could find.

"You see, they never give their names," Vierran explained sadly.

"Of course they don't," said her father. "You're not communicating on a level where you *have* names, any of you. You're just 'I' and 'me' to them, and they are the same to you."

Standing in the middle of the motel bedroom, Vierran muttered to the Bannus, "And I'll get you for *that*, too! Making me believe Mother and Father keep a greengrocer's shop!" She had to laugh. What a comedown for the great merchant House of Guaranty! The Bannus had all the details, too: Vierran's loving fights with Mother, and Father's sweet tooth—except who was Martin?

Your story, pleaded the King.

One last question first, said Vierran. *How long ago would you say it was since you made that crack about wishing terminating had been so easy in your day?*

Quite awhile ago. Ten days at least, said the King. *Please, your story, or I shall offend the dignitaries of my kingdom by yawning at holy things.*

Ten days! They had been on Earth ten days, and, Vierran was willing to swear, not even Reigner One was aware of this. Vierran hugged herself about that while she told the King all that had happened in the wood. He deserved to have his boredom relieved, poor King, for telling her this one extraordinary fact. Chalk up one to the Bannus! she thought. It had given her back hope.

But why, she wondered, had the Bannus left her able to talk to her four voices at intervals? Did it perhaps not know about them? No, the Bannus knew so much about Vierran that it had to know about the voices, too. It had to be, she realized, for the same reason that she had been allowed to hear her own message to herself on the cassette. The Bannus *wanted* her to know exactly what tricks it had been playing.

As to why it wanted her to know—by the end of her narrative Vierran was very sober indeed. There was such a difference between the Vierran who now sat down quietly on the motel bed to think and the Vierran who had worked in the basement of the House of Balance. The Vierran of ten days ago, thinking she was plotting rebellion, had played practical jokes on the Reigners and made her careful lists of all the people the Servant had killed and thought she was so *safe*! Then Reigner One had plunged her into the fire she thought she was playing with.

Yes, playing! Vierran told herself bitterly. The Bannus was not the only one who had played—and the Bannus at least played seriously. Vierran had been playing with the feelings of the Servant and her own. Like the high-class sheltered little deb she was, she had been fascinated by violence, murder, secret missions—all the things her life had shielded her from—and she had found these things all the more fascinating because the Servant himself was so quiet and civilized. When he first appeared in the basement in that scarlet uniform—which never suited him!—she had been astonished to find him so mild and shy and surprised to find a human working there instead of the usual robot. Vierran had detected instantly that this Servant found her attractive, unusual—though, she told herself now, this was probably only because she was willing to speak to him. That she had also detected a terrible lonely unhappiness in him she dismissed now with bitter impatience. Pity! Pity was for happy people to look down on unhappy ones with! The fact was, Vierran had come down from her high place—slumming, just like Reigner Three on Earth—and decided she had a crush on the Servant. On the Servant, not the man.

Then the Bannus had neatly got round Reigner One's compulsion. Vierran's face flushed hot, and hotter yet as she thought of herself up in that tree dangling her legs in Mordion's face. She just hoped Mordion had seen her only as the girl of twelve she had thought she was then. Yes, twelve. Ann thought of herself as fourteen, but Vierran well remembered the way the moment her thirteenth birthday was in sight, she had gone round telling herself—and everyone else—"I'm in my fourteenth year now!" So *old*! Little idiot. And the Bannus had got round the Servant's training, too, and shown Vierran Mordion the man—a variety of Mordions, from the one who fussed over Hume to the one who, so easily and expertly, snapped the neck of a rabbit.

Vierran put her hands to her heated face and shuddered. She would never dare go near Mordion again.

Perhaps none of it had happened, she thought hopefully. But it had. If she looked closely, she could see a whole variety of rips and snags in her trousers and her top, from where she had climbed that tree or wrenched herself through thickets. These rents were sort of glossed over with an illusion of whole cloth—no doubt partly for the benefit of the Reigners—but they were there if you knew to look. And—Vierran slowly and reluctantly rolled up her trouser leg—the cut on her knee was there all right. It had been deep and jagged but was now mostly hard brown scab peeling off to leave new pink scar. About the state it would be if it had been done ten days ago. Had Mordion been in that box for a whole week before that, with the Bannus making him think he had been there for centuries? No—she did not want to know. One thing she was absolutely certain of was that she was never going to set eyes on Mordion again.

And no sooner had Vierran decided this than she found she would have to. She had to warn Mordion. If the things she remembered in the wood had truly happened, then the main thing she had seen happening was Mordion slowly making up his mind to go to the castle and confront the Reigners there. Worse, Vierran knew she had unintentionally pushed and bullied him that way herself. She had to stop him. Mordion would think he was going to the castle to face Reigners Two and Four. She did not think he even knew that Five had also come to Earth. He certainly had no idea that Three and One were here, too. And even with the power that could demolish that waterfall, even with the other powers people said the Servant had, Vierran could not see him winning against all five Reigners. Whatever happened to him would be at least half her fault.

Vierran sprang up. She dug her second pair of jeans and her smarter top out of her bag and climbed into them hastily. It was not quite dark yet. There was still time to get to the wood.

She was halfway to the door when Reigner Three flung it open. "Why don't you come when I call, girl? I've buzzed your monitor and I've tried to work that telephone-thing until I broke a nail. Come along. I'm very tired and upset. I need a bath and a massage and a manicure."

—3—

VIERRAN COULD NOT escape the next morning, either. When Reigner Three was upset, she wanted people around to vent her feelings on. Nothing would satisfy her but that Vierran should dance attendance on her everywhere she went. This included following respectfully behind the two Reigners after breakfast, when they set off on foot toward the factory that reared above the houses to the north.

Reigner One said, "Do you really *need* her, my dear?"

"I shall need my feet massaged after walking in these awful Earth shoes," said Reigner Three.

So Vierran, itching to get away and warn Mordion, was forced to trail after Reigner Three—today tall and elegant in skimpy, clinging violet and a wide purple hat—and the shorter, wider, sauntering Reigner One. He was smoking a cigar again and staring benevolently over walls into people's front gardens. Vierran found herself looking at them from an Earth point of view, as if she were Ann again. What a ridiculous pair!

Don't underestimate them, warned the Slave. *Masters are masters.*

It was not far to the factory. They reached it before Reigner Three's tight purple shoes began to give her any obvious trouble and turned along beside a tall green metal fence with spikes on top. Behind the fence twisted metal chimneys steamed above white cylinders with the blue logo of the Balance painted on them. Reigner One beamed at the sight. Vierran wondered why, as Ann, she had never connected the white van with this factory.

The green fence turned a sharp corner beside a grassy, unpaved lane. A sign by the bushy fence opposite said MERLINS LANE. At the sight of the muddy ruts in the lane, Reigner Three gave a cry of dismay and began to hobble.

"Show a little resilience, my dear," Reigner One said, almost impatiently.

This was enough to set Reigner Three limping from rut to rut, holding her hat and looking martyred. But she forgot to limp when the lane turned a corner.

There was a tall grassy mound there, swelling out into the lane. The lane made a swerve to go round it, and the factory fence also made a bend, to go round the back of the mound. But what held Reigner Three rigid, with one hand to her hat, was the way the hedge on the other side of the lane vanished beyond the mound. The lane had vanished, too, into a vista of plowed mud decorated with little orange tags. A big yellow mechanical excavator stood just beyond the mound.

"What is this?" said Three. "I understood that this land was to be left untouched!"

"So did I. But the mound's still there," Reigner One said. "All may yet be well."

Both Reigners went with surprising speed up the smoothly turfed slope of the mound. And all was not well, to judge from their faces.

Vierran came up behind them to find that rather more than a third of the mound was missing on the other side. It had been sliced away into a jumbled, rubbly pile. She was looking down into an old, old square space that had evidently once been lined with blocks of primitive black metacrete. Frayed silvery ends of stass wires curled from the blocks here and there. More wires waved impotently from the heap of rubble, and there, among the earth and stones and broken metacrete, Vierran saw the glint of more than one stass pisistor. Interesting.

More interesting still, people were moving busily in the pit. A man and a girl were working away with trowels and brushes. Another was crouching with a camera and a notebook, and a third man was edging around everyone with a clipboard.

"Excuse me, sir." Reigner One selected the man with the clipboard as the most senior person there. "Sir, has some kind of interesting find been made here?"

The man glanced up in annoyance. He was a worried person

with thinning hair and glasses, who clearly did not wish to be interrupted. But his annoyance melted away as he took in Reigner One's good suit, his silver beard, and his cigar. Reigner One was clearly someone in authority. The worried man responded, harassed but polite. "I'm afraid we're not really sure *what* this is yet. That digger has certainly uncovered some kind of chamber, but it's not clear what it is at all. The factory owners have only given us a week to investigate, more's the pity."

"There's all these wires," said the girl with the trowel. "They're threaded round the whole chamber—almost like an installation of some kind."

"But of course it can't be," said the worried man. He pointed with his clipboard to the sliced-open floor of the square space. "The level of this floor shows this chamber has to have been made something like a thousand years ago. But the wire is some kind of modern alloy."

"Ah," said Reigner One, pulling his beard. "You suspect a hoax." Vierran could feel the pressure he was using to make all the people down there believe it was a hoax. "You'd think," he said, with his eyes keenly on the dark, square hole, "that the hoaxer would have put in a corpse of some kind to help convince you."

The archaeologist looked over his shoulder at the hole, too. "There was," he said. Both Reigners stiffened. "There *was* an imprint as if there had been a body," he went on. "We've photographed it, but of course, we've had to walk on the floor since. The puzzle is that there's no sign of any organic matter in the pit. From the imprint you'd expect there to have been a skeleton, but there's nothing"—he was treading on a broken stass pisistor as he spoke— "nothing but this obviously modern trash," he said, kicking it away.

"Quite so," said Reigner One, working away on the man's mind. "And how long have you been wasting your time on this hoax, sir?"

"We only got here this morning," the archaeologist said.

And under further pressure from Reigner One, the girl who had spoken before smiled and added, "The digger only uncovered it yesterday, you see. And we rushed here from the University as soon as we could."

"Admirable," said Reigner One. "Well, I won't waste your time any further." He beamed at them and marched away down the mound to the lane. Reigner Three beckoned Vierran and followed him. Vierran's last sight of the archaeologists was of exasperation growing on all their faces. They had *known* it was a hoax all along. That was all she saw because she sped after the two Reigners, very curious to know what this was all about.

"He's *gone!*" Reigner Three said, tottering among the ruts.

"He's not been gone long," Reigner One replied. "And he'll be weak as a kitten, all skin and bone for quite a while yet. We're in time, provided we move fast. I'll go after him. You do *your* part, and we'll go after the bannus together when we've both finished." He threw away his cigar into the hedge bottom. "Come along, both of you."

Back they went, past the motel, and on into streets Vierran began to recognize from her time as Ann Stavely. Reigner Three strode impatiently, forgetting about her shoes. Reigner One kept pace with her. Who *was* this man who had been in stass? Vierran wondered. And why had the Bannus given Mordion his memories—because that seemed to be what it had done? One thing was clear. Whoever this man was, she thought, almost having to trot to keep up, he had the Reigners worried enough almost not to notice she was with them. With luck she could slip away soon.

They reached Wood Street at the other end from Hexwood Farm. Vierran blinked as she recognized the row of shops. There was broken glass everywhere. The place was deserted, and it looked ready to stand a siege. Every shop was boarded up. There were barricades in the street and along the pavement. Was this my father who arranged all this, Vierran wondered, or was it really someone else entirely? Whoever had organized things here, it was clear no one was going to stand for any more raids from Reigner Four.

On the corner of Wood Street Reigner One paused prudently and lit another cigar. "You go on," he said, old and worn and out of breath. "I'll catch up."

Reigner Three gave him an impatient look and sailed on, followed quickly by Vierran. Both vanished before they reached the first of the barricades.

"Hmm," murmured Reigner One. "Bannus field's spread a bit in the night. I thought it might." He tossed aside his match and strolled back the other way, breathing blue smoke. He would go and take a look at the other two stass tombs, and then pay a visit to the heads of Houses and other prisoners at the factory. It would pass the time while he considered how best to come at his enemy. Martellian was almost certainly inside the field of the bannus, that was the problem.

He did not see the trees appear behind him, softly springing into existence at intervals along Wood Street and standing in groves in front of the empty shops. For an instant the shops could be seen in glimpses among the green branches. In the road the trees briefly stood on mounds of broken tarmac. Then there was nothing but forest, and old leaves carpeted the ground.

Reigner One paced on obliviously, breathing out smoke, considering his enemy. He had never hated anyone as much as he hated Martellian. Martellian had stood in Orm Pender's way all his life, certainly throughout Orm's youth, maddening Orm with his gifts and his looks, his full Reigner blood, and the easy way the goods of the galaxy fell into his lap. Most maddening of all had been Martellian's pure niceness. Far from despising the young Orm Pender for being a half-breed with an offworld mother, and short, and squat, Martellian had gone out of his way to encourage Orm, to bring him along in the House. Orm hated him for that worst of all. It had given him enormous pleasure to cheat the bannus at the selection trials, to become a Reigner, and then to pry Martellian out of office. It pleased him to make Martellian fight for his life and force him to return vicious blow for vicious blow. By the time he was exiled, Martellian had been forced to fight so hard that he was not nice at all, not anymore. That pleased Orm wonderfully, too. It still pleased him to work out his hatred on Martellian's descendants, on generation after generation of Servants.

Blowing smoke, Orm swung his head. That smell. Martellian's. Martellian was here in the wood, distant but not too distant. He was here. All Orm had to do was find him. He swung in the right direction, farther in among the trees, across a dry brake of brushwood. His long scaled tail slid round the trees after him and followed his great clawed feet over smashed twigs and flattened brambles.

—4———————————————————————

THEY HAD A good journey to the castle. A holiday before things got difficult, Mordion thought of it. He could not let himself think more deeply about what he was going to find. Maybe Hume felt the same. Hume was definitely nervous, and a little tetchy with it. They took Hume's boat, poling it downriver because they all knew that was the right direction, while Yam kept pace with them on the marshy bank, with Hume's precious sword strapped to his back for safety.

Yam had refused to go in the boat. "I am too heavy and too delicate," he said. "You do not treat me with the care I deserve."

"Nonsense," said Mordion. "I never stop tuning you."

"And I refuse to take part in hocus-pocus," said Yam.

"You just be your own charming self, Yam," Hume said, grinning above his doubled-up knees. There was very little room in the boat for two. "We'll do any hocus-pocus there's need for."

"I am not happy about this venture," Yam said, squelching among forget-me-nots and kingcups. "There are outlaws in the wood these days. And worse things."

"Cheerful, isn't he?" said Hume.

Mordion smiled. It seemed to him that the wood was putting

forth its best as they journeyed. Downriver, where the trees closed in, it was floored blue-green with bluebells coming.

5

ANN—NO, VIERRAN, she told herself—went past the yellow pretzel bag and waved it a cheerful greeting. "And I'll get you for that, too!" she told the Bannus. Its field must have been miles outside this all along.

The river, when she came to it, was torrential—white water round all but the tips of the rocks. Vierran went over it very cautiously indeed. Even so, there was one quite horrible bit where she was balanced on a slippery spike with both arms cartwheeling and many yards of torrent between her and the bank. She made it over in a panic rush.

It seemed to be winter still—or at least very early spring—on the other side. No ferns sprouted yet from the cliff, and the bushes near the summit had only the smallest of white-green buds. At the top Ann stumbled over the corpse of a wolf. She backed off, horrified. It had been killed some time ago, very clumsily. Someone had battered its head in with the bloodstained stone that lay beside it. Sickening. This was not Mordion's expert neatness, nor Hume with his sword. Yam? What had *happened*? She avoided looking at the animal's filmy eyes, stepped over it and hastened round the house.

"*Mordion!*"

The hunched brown hairy figure squatting in the yard lifted its head. "Who calls Mordion?"

For one terrible instant Ann thought it *was* Mordion, back to his worst despair. There was a mass of scraggy beard and graying shoulder-length hair. Then the thing lifted its face to her, and she saw it was . . . something else. Something with nearly a true skull for a face, filthy, and eyes as filmed and dead as the battered wolf's. She backed away quickly, with a hand out to tell her when she reached the house.

The thing rose up and stretched bony, bloodstained fingers toward her. "Where is Mordion? You know. Tell me where he is." The voice was hardly a human voice. But the dead eyes saw her. "I must kill him," it croaked. "Then I must kill you." It took a tottering step toward her.

Ann screamed. She found the scratchy mud of the house wall, handed herself along it, and threw herself round the corner just as the thing—corpse, ghost—leaped toward her. Screaming, she ran. Down the cliff she went in great scissoring strides. Rocks falling past her and rattling above told her the thing was still after her. She did not look. She just jumped to the nearest rock that showed above the roaring water, and then to the next, and was across the river almost without slowing down. Behind her, she heard a cawing cry and rocks rolling—was that a splash? She was too terrified to look. She scrambled up the bank opposite, clawing at the mud with her fingernails, and ran again, and ran even after she had passed the yellow pretzel bag.

Behind her in the river Reigner Five stared unseeing upward. His back was broken. The water was forcing his body between the boulders, rolling him onward, pressing him over to drown, too. It took him awhile to give in and admit that he had been dead all along.

PART EIGHT

—1———————————

As VIERRAN ARRIVED panting in the pointed stone archway, wondering how she came to be so late, an agitated lady flew down the stairs toward her, with one hand to the veiling of her pointed headdress and the other holding up her gown.

"Where have you *been*, Vierran? She keeps asking for you! The wedding dress is wrong again!"

Vierran stared up at the lady's worried fair face. "Siri!"

The lady laughed. "Why do you always get my name wrong? I'm Lady Sylvia. But do come on." She turned and hurried back up the stone stairway.

Vierran followed the trailing end of the lady's dress upward, with her mind falling about in a mad mixture of hope and distress and amazement. This really was Siri. The cousin she thought she had invented for Hume. Did this mean the Bannus had somehow worked a miracle and brought most of her family here to Earth? Or were they really other people disguised to make her think so?

"Are you my cousin?" she called up at Siri.

"Not as far as I know," Siri's well-known voice called down.

Was this confirmation or not? Vierran wondered about it as the two of them reached the stone landing and Siri—Lady Sylvia—very cautiously and quietly drew aside the hangings in the doorway there so that they could peep into the bride's chamber beyond.

Morgan La Trey towered in the middle of the room amid a huddle of her other ladies kneeling round her, pinning parts of the dress. It was a beautiful room, with many doors and windows, a vaulted ceiling, and tapestries in dim colors hiding the harshness of the stone walls. It was a breathtaking dress, white with a crusted sheen of pearl embroidery, and its train was yards long. Morgan La Trey looked wonderful in it. But Vierran's eyes ignored all this and flew to the richly dressed young man lounging in the window seat beyond Morgan La Trey.

"The toady's with her," Vierran whispered. "We wait."

She hated Sir Harrisoun almost as much as she disliked Sir Fors. Sir Fors grabbed any lady he found alone, but Sir Harrisoun had this sly way of pawing any female he could get near, whether they were alone or not. And he crawled to La Trey. She used him unscrupulously in all her plots. At that moment she was saying, "And if you can persuade Sir Bors to preach at the king, preferably about sin—get him to say these outlaws are a judgment on us, or something—that is all to the good."

"Shouldn't be difficult, m'lady," Sir Harrisoun said, laughing. "That Bors preaches just asking for the salt."

"Yes, but remember the important thing is to get the king to appoint Sir Fors leader of the expedition over Sir Bedefer's head," Morgan La Trey told him. "Have people pester the king about it. Give him no peace. Poor dear Ambitas does so hate to be bored."

Sir Harrisoun stood up and bowed. "You know your fiancé inside out, don't you, m'lady? Okay. I'll get him pestered for you." He grinned and lounged away to one of the doorways. A gasp and a bobbing among the kneeling ladies suggested that Sir Harrisoun had taken his usual liberties with them.

Morgan La Trey, as usual, ignored it. She turned to the curtained archway. "Vierran! I can see you lurking there! Come here at once. This dress is still not hanging properly."

The wedding of Morgan La Trey to King Ambitas was only three days away now. Morgan La Trey was in a grand fuss about it, probably, Vierran thought, because La Trey knew that Ambitas would postpone the marriage yet again if he saw half a chance of doing so. She seemed to be keeping the king's mind off the wedding by intriguing against both Sir Bedefer and Sir Fors. A cunning lady, La Trey. But then she had been like that as Reigner Three, too.

And I go along with it, Vierran thought, coming to kneel in the space the other ladies made for her. Whatever the Bannus has done to our minds, I still know I could break the illusion if I convinced the right people. But why should I? Everyone's rotten, here in the castle. As she put out her hand for the pincushion one of the ladies was passing to her, Vierran found that her hand was muddy and its fingernails dark with earth. I wonder how I did that, she thought. She rubbed her hand on her dark blue gown before she took the pins. It was like an emblem of life in this castle, that mud. The dirt came off on you. As she took the four pins she saw she would need and put three of them in her mouth, ready, a great sadness came over her. She recalled the first time she and Hume had seen the castle, like a chalky vision across the lake that seemed to promise beauty, bravery, strength, adventure, all sorts of marvels. She had wanted to cry then, too.

Perhaps I was so sad because I knew even then that all that beauty and bravery simply weren't there, she thought, planting the first pin expertly in the waist of the dress. What fun it would be to ram the pin accidentally-on-purpose into Reigner Three—except that her life would not be worth living if she did. I just knew it was an illusion, invented by the Bannus. Maybe beauty and bravery *are* a sham and there are no wonderful things in any world.

Tears got in the way of the second pin. Vierran had to wait for them to clear. While she did, she tried to contact her four voices for some comfort. And as always in the castle, the voices were silent. Damn it! Vierran thought, putting in the second pin, and then the third, quickly. Those four are good people. They *do* exist. It just shows you what this castle does. And suddenly, as if her head had cleared, she was quite sure that wonderful things did indeed exist. Even if they're only in my own mind, she thought, they're *there* and worth fighting for. I mustn't give in. I must bide my time and then *fight*.

She put the last pin in and stood up. "There, my lady, if you have it sewn like that, it should be perfect."

She did not expect La Trey to thank her. Nor did she. The king's bride simply swept out of the chamber to have herself changed into a more ordinary gown.

2

RUMORS FLEW IN the castle all that day. It was said that Sir Bedefer had knelt and implored the king to send his army against the outlaws. Sir Fors strode about, declaring that the outlaws were no danger, and Sir Harrisoun agreed with him, but most people felt that Sir Bedefer was right. The outlaw knight, Sir Artegal, had now been joined by a crowd of rebels from the village, under the leadership of a villain called Stavely, and it seemed possible that the two planned to attack the castle. The Reverend Sir Bors was known to have talked to the king for an hour on this matter.

By midafternoon it was known that Ambitas had given in. Pages and squires raced about, and there were mighty hammerings from the courtyards, where the soldiers were preparing for war. But it was announced that Ambitas had not yet decided how many men he would send nor who would command them. He would give his decision at dinner. This caused some consternation, because as everyone saw, this meant there was a contest for commander between Sir Bedefer and Sir Fors, and everyone in the castle—except Ambitas, it seemed—knew that there should have been no contest at all. Sir Bedefer was the only right choice. People assembled in the great hall for dinner in a state of great doubt and expectation.

"This Ambitas is a feeble fool," Vierran murmured to Lady Sylvia as they filed in behind Morgan La Trey and took their places at the end of the high table.

"It's his wound. He's not well," Lady Sylvia whispered.

"And I shudder to think how much worse things will get when La Trey is actually married to him," Vierran said. "Don't be a dumb blond, Siri. You aren't usually."

Lady Sylvia giggled. "You got my name wrong again. Hush!"

Ambitas was being carried in, and they all had to stand.

Vierran looked sideways at Siri—Lady Sylvia—while the king was being settled on his cushions. Siri was clever. This girl seemed to have no mind at all. Yet Vierran remembered Yam saying that the Bannus could not force any person or machine to act against their natures. Could it be that Siri had always secretly yearned not to be clever as well as beautiful? Or had the Bannus simply obliged Vierran by producing the cousin she had told Hume about? Lady Sylvia *looked* real. Perhaps she was some other girl entirely. Oh, it was confusing.

As soon as King Ambitas was comfortably settled, he gestured weakly for them all to sit. "Be seated," he said. "These are trying times we live in. I have an announcement to make that should cheer us all up." He took a sip of wine to clear his throat. Everyone waited anxiously. "I have decided," said Ambitas, "that we should wait to eat until a marvel presents itself."

Everyone was confounded.

"Oh, not *again!*" groaned Sir Fors. A chef, who had been entering the hall with a boar's head, turned round and carried it out again. Sir Fors's eyes followed him wistfully.

"This is a *treat?*" Vierran muttered, staring at her empty plate.

"I'm sure we will not have to wait long, loyal subjects," said the king. His pink face twinkled roguishly at Sir Harrisoun. Those two knew something.

Everyone's heads snapped round eagerly as the herald, Madden, threw open the great main doors of the hall and advanced up the aisle between the long tables. "Majesty," said Madden, "I have great pleasure in announcing the arrival at the castle of a great magician, sage, and physician who craves the pleasure of an audience with you. Will you be pleased to admit him to your royal presence?"

"By all means," said Ambitas. "Tell him to come in."

Madden stood aside, bowed, and announced ringingly, "Then enter the magician Agenos to the king!"

A tall man in brown, with a brown cloak, strode in, carrying a staff with a mysterious blue light bobbing at the end of it. He bowed with a flourish and then knocked the staff smartly on the flagstones. His assistant, an equally tall youth in shabby blue, entered dragging a wooden boat-shaped cart in which lay a silver man shape with pink eyes.

Vierran swallowed down an exclamation. Mordion! With Hume and Yam! They seemed to have put wheels on Hume's boat. It now somewhat resembled the Stone Age roller skate Hume had made as a small boy. And how *huge* Hume had grown! Vierran's heart battered in her chest. Her eyes shot sideways along the high table to see if anyone had recognized the great magician. At least, she thought, he had had the sense to call himself Agenos. After what that mad monk had said, everyone in the hall was going to remember the name Mordion.

Ambitas clearly did not know Mordion. He looked like a child about to watch a conjurer. Sir Fors frowned a little and then gave it up. His mind was on his postponed supper. Oddly Sir Bedefer leaned forward almost eagerly as if he had just seen an old friend, then sat back, puzzled. But Vierran's eyes sped on to Morgan La Trey, slender and beautiful in a purple gown and headdress, sitting beside the king. La Trey's face was white, and her eyes glared. Vierran could not tell if La Trey knew Mordion or not, but that look of hers was pure hatred. Sir Bors seemed to feel much the same. He made the sign of the Key and looked horrified.

"Will it please Your Majesty to have me display to you my miraculous mechanical man and many other marvels?" Mordion asked.

"Display away, great Agenos," Ambitas said, delighted.

Everyone else would have preferred to have supper first. It said a great deal for Mordion's showmanship that he kept every soul in that hall enthralled for the next twenty minutes. He had Yam rise up out of the boat and dance about, while he pretended to guide Yam with his staff. He had Yam do bends and twists that only robots could. Then before people ceased gasping at that, Mordion gestured to Hume. Hume took up his bone flute and warbled out a flight of butterflies, which Mordion changed to birds, and the birds to blue, to white, to rainbow colors. He gestured the birds up into the rafters in a whirring flight and then made them cascade down from the beams as paper streamers exhaling sweet scents. As they descended around Mordion's shoulders, the streamers became multicolored silk handkerchiefs, which Mordion handed to people at the nearest tables for souvenirs—except for one white one, which he drew out into a line of little flags and sent back to Hume's flute as butterflies again. Everyone clapped. Clever, Vierran thought as she clapped with the rest. It was all so harmless and pretty that she would have bet large money that most people in the hall thought Mordion was really using conjurers' sleight of hand and not magic at all. If they did chance to connect him with the traitor the monk had warned them of, they would not realize that Mordion could defend himself with powerful magics, and he would have a chance to get away. But she *must* warn him about the way Morgan La Trey had looked.

Mordion was now strolling his way up the aisle toward the high table. "For my next piece of magic," he said, "I shall require the assistance of a young lady."

Here's my chance to warn him! Vierran thought. Will he recognize me? She sprang up from her chair at the end of the table.

But Lady Sylvia sprang up beside Vierran, crying out, "Yes, *I'll* help you!" Vierran was then guilty of scuffling with Lady Sylvia in a most unladylike manner, treading on Lady Sylvia's toe and hanging on to her arm. Lady Sylvia won the scuffle, partly by being taller and stronger and partly because her chair was on the outer edge of the table. She jumped down from the dais, pushing Vierran backward as she went, and went speeding toward Mordion. "Here I am!" she said, laughing and flushed from the scuffle.

Hume stared at her. As for Mordion, he put his head on one side admiringly—Vierran had seen so many people do that when they first saw Siri—and a smile of appreciation lit his face. "If you could lend me that pretty girdle of yours for five minutes, my lady," he said.

Vierran's knees let her down. She sat down, with queer pain mowing through her innards and her breath refusing to come. She could gladly have killed Siri—Sylvia—who was now holding her jeweled girdle out and simpering—yes, *simpering*!—while Mordion cut it in two with his knife. The hall seemed dim to Vierran, and she was not hungry anymore.

Oh, damn! she thought. I'm in love with Mordion. Oh, damn! Maybe *this* was why that vision of the castle had once nearly broken her heart. She must have known then, as clearly as she knew now, how hopeless it was to love Mordion.

—3——————————

I DO NOT like the atmosphere in this castle, Mordion thought when he and Hume were seated at one of the humbler tables and supper at last was served. It reminds me too much of—of— The name House of Balance hovered on the edge of Mordion's mind. He pushed it away, back into hiding. Everyone here was on the make, plotting to get the better of someone else, and the center of it all was that dark woman in purple. The conjuring display, besides giving them a grand entry, had been planned so that Mordion could do some unashamed mind reading. The plotting was no more than he had expected, depressing as it was.

While Hume beside him tucked into the best meal of his young life, Mordion explained to the squires at their table that the silver man was not real and did not require food, and went on finding things out.

The outlaws Yam had talked about seemed to be a real threat. Most of the talk was about the renegade Artegal and the villain Stavely and just whom the king was planning to send against them. And it seemed that the king was about to be married to the lady in purple. The king, Mordion thought, had a distinct air of wondering how this had come about. Evidently the marriage was of the lady's choosing. As he gathered this, Mordion was startled to hear his own name. A mysterious monk had appeared on Bannustide, it seemed, and denounced Mordion as a traitor, before touching the Bannus and vanishing in a ball of flame. This, Mordion gathered, had happened quite recently. His name was fresh in everyone's minds. He exchanged looks with Hume, warning Hume to go on calling him Agenos. And he thanked his stars for the odd premonition which had caused him to tell that orange-haired seneschal that his name was Agenos.

As the dishes were cleared away, everyone went expectant. Someone on the dais signaled, and two of the sturdiest squires at Mordion's table rushed up there to raise Ambitas on his cushions so that everyone in the hall could see him.

"We have decided," Ambitas proclaimed, "to send a force of picked men against the outlaws who so basely threaten our realm. The force will consist of the forty mounted men of Sir Bedefer's troop and will leave at dawn tomorrow. It will be commanded by our Champion, Sir Fors." He lay back on his cushions, looking unwell, and signed to his squires to carry him away.

There was uproar for a time. "Forty men!" Mordion heard. "This is mad! There are several hundred outlaws!" During the uproar Sir Bedefer got up and walked out. Sir Fors watched him go with a sympathetic shake of his head and the wry smile of a nice, modest man. It was a smile that kept struggling not to become a smirk. Morgan La Trey gave Sir Fors a look of cool contempt as she beckoned her ladies and sailed out of the hall. After she had gone, but not until then, several people said that the king's decision was certainly her doing and that no good would come of it. She was evidently much feared.

Here a squire appeared at Mordion's elbow and summoned him to the king.

"Get Yam to that room Sir Harrisoun gave us," Mordion told Hume. Yam was lying in the boat over by the wall, pretending to be inanimate. Large numbers of people were trying to prod him to see if he was really a man in disguise. Hume nodded and hastened over there, while Mordion followed the squire.

He was led to a rich vaulted bedchamber with a huge fire blazing in its wide grate. Ambitas lay propped on an embroidered couch close to the hearth. Mordion wondered how the king could stand the heat. Sweat started off him even while he stood in the doorway.

"I need warmth for my great sickness, you know," Ambitas explained, beckoning Mordion to approach.

Mordion loosened the neck of his jacket and threw back his cloak. "How can I serve Your Majesty?" he asked when he was as near the fire as he could bear. The form of his question gave him an uncomfortable twinge. He looked down at the king's pink, ordinary face on the firelit pillows and wondered how anyone could serve such a second-rate little man.

"It's this wound of mine," Ambitas quavered. "It won't be healed, you know. They tell me you're a great physician."

"I have some small skill," Mordion said, quite accurately.

"You certainly *look* as if you do," Ambitas observed. "A sort of—er—clinical look—no offense, of course, my dear Agenos—surgical, you might say. Do you think you would be so good as to look at my wound, perhaps apply a salve—you know—with my wedding coming on . . ." He trailed off and lay looking at Mordion anxiously.

"Of course. If Your Majesty would be so good as to disrobe the afflicted part," Mordion said, and wondered what he would do if the disease were beyond him. Magic, as he had discovered trying to realify Hume, could do only so much.

"Yes, yes. Our thanks." Very slowly, with a number of nervous glances at Mordion, Ambitas drew up his gold-embroidered tunic and the cambric shirt beneath, to display his bulging pink side. "What's your verdict?" he asked anxiously.

Mordion stared down at the large purple bruise over the king's ribs. It was a yellow and red and brown bruise, as well as purple, going rainbowlike the way bruises do when they are getting better. He fought himself not to laugh. It came to Mordion then that there had been many times when he had wanted to laugh at such a man as this, but there had been some kind of physical block—acute nausea that stopped him from even smiling. Now there was no block, and he had a fierce struggle to keep his face straight. He also, to his surprise, remembered how Ambitas had received this so-called wound.

They had gone into the farmhouse, he and this little man, and another, bigger man, where they had suddenly been confronted by a youth—the same orange-haired youth people now called Sir Harrisoun—swinging an enormous sword at the little man. Mordion had leaped to stop the sword—well, anyone would, he thought uncomfortably, remembering the quite inordinate, unreasonable, *sickening* shame he had felt when Sir Harrisoun proved to be coming from exactly the opposite direction. It was as if Mordion had seen the attack in a mirror. He felt true despair at being fooled. He remembered the thwack as the flat of the sword met Ambitas. He remembered whirling round. Then nothing. It was bewildering.

"It's an awful wound, isn't it?" Ambitas prompted him, mistaking the reason for Mordion's bewilderment.

Mordion understood this part of the matter at least. "Indeed it is, Your Majesty," he said, and bit the inside of his cheek, hard, to stop the whinny of laughter he could hear escaping into his voice. "I have a salve here in my pouch that *may* ease it, but I can promise you no healing for such a wound as that."

"But in view of my approaching wedding—" Ambitas prompted him again.

"It would be unfair to both you and your lady to marry just at present," Mordion agreed. He was forced to stroke his beard gravely in order to hide the way his mouth kept trying to spread. He wished he could tell Ann about this! "In view of the seriousness of what I see there, I would advise you to postpone your wedding for at least a year."

Ambitas stretched out both hands and grasped damply at Mordion's wrist. "A year!" he said delightedly. "What a terrible long time to wait! My dear magician, what reward can I give you for this expert advice? Name any gift you like."

"Nothing for myself," Mordion said. "But my young assistant wishes to be trained as a knight. If Your Majesty—"

"Agreed!" cried Ambitas. "I'll give Bedefer orders about it right away."

Mordion bowed and more or less fled from the king's hot bedroom. For a short while he struggled with the whinnies of laughter that kept bursting out of him. Some vestige of decorum made him feel it was not quite right to laugh at the king. Besides, he ought to get to Hume and give him the glad news. But before long he was staggering about. In the end he had to pitch himself into the first empty stairway he came to, where he sat on the stone steps and fairly roared. It seemed to him that he had never enjoyed laughing so much in his life.

4

MORGAN LA TREY stood in the tower room she had discovered and taken as her own. The occult symbols drawn on the walls flickered in the light of the black candles that surrounded her. A pan of charcoal smoked in the center of the round room, filling it with incense and the smell of burning blood.

"Bannus!" she said. "Appear before me. Bannus, I order you to appear!"

She waited in the choking smoke pouring up from the pan.

"I command you, Bannus!" she said a third time.

A brightness came into being behind the smoke—a brightness that was very pure and white, but that cast a dull red light on the groins of the ceiling. The redness seemed to be caused by the scarlet cloth that covered the great flat chalice floating behind the smoke.

Morgan La Trey smiled triumphantly. She had done it!

The smoke and the smell were absorbed into radiant scents of may blossoms and bluebells in an open wood. Under the red cloth the intricate gold work of the chalice was clear and dazzling in its beauty. A voice spoke. It was deep for a woman and high for a man and as beautiful as the chalice.

"Why do you call upon me, Morgan La Trey?"

She was almost awed, but she said, "I must have your help in dealing with my enemy. He has risen from the grave to haunt me again. Tonight he arrived at this castle disguised as a magician, and he's with the king at this moment, poisoning the king's mind against me."

"And what help do you wish me to give you?" asked the beautiful voice.

"I want to know how to kill him—for good this time," she said.

There was a pause. The chalice hovered thoughtfully. "There is a poison," the voice said at length, "clear as water, that has no smell, whose very touch can be fatal to those who have lived too long. I can tell you how to make it if you wish."

"Tell me," she said.

The Bannus told her, while she wrote the ingredients and method down feverishly by the light of it. She noticed, as she wrote, that it floated just where she could not reach it all the time. She smiled. She knew she could always summon it again. But she had things to do before she was ready to seize the Bannus and take command.

—5—

Sir Fors and his company rode away soon after dawn the next day, making a brave show of pennants fluttering, gold on green and red on white, as they thundered over the wooden bridge across the lake. Hume and Mordion watched from the battlements along with most of the other people in the castle.

"I wish I was going!" Hume said.

"I'm glad you're not. I think there are far too few of them," Mordion told him.

"Of course there are too few!" said the man standing next to them. "Even if the outlaws were unorganized, which they're not, they should have sent a decent-sized force and made *sure*."

Mordion turned. It was Sir Bedefer, looking very sturdy and plain in a buff-colored robe. Sir Bedefer stood with his feet wide and surveyed Mordion. Both of them liked what they saw.

"The outlaws don't love us," Sir Bedefer said, turning back to watch the soldiers ride glinting among the trees on the other side of the lake. "We raided them for food. Not what I would have chosen to do, but I didn't have a say." Then, in an abrupt way, which was clearly the way he did things, he said, "That silver man of yours— did you make him?"

"Remade him really," Mordion confessed. "Hume found him damaged, and I mended him."

"Skillful," Sir Bedefer commented. "I'd like to take a look at him if you'd let me. Does he fight?"

"Not very well. He's forbidden to hurt humans," Mordion said, glancing at Hume. Seeing Hume beginning to glower, he added, "But he speaks."

"Doesn't surprise me somehow," said Sir Bedefer. The last soldiers had disappeared among the trees by then. Sir Bedefer looked at Hume. "Is this the lad that wants to be a knight?" Hume nodded, glowing. "Then come with me now," said Sir Bedefer, "and we'll set you drilling."

They walked together along the battlements toward the steps that led down to the outer court. "Think he'll make it?" Sir Bedefer asked Mordion quietly, nodding at Hume.

"I think he'll be wasted on it," Mordion said frankly, "but it's what he wants."

Sir Bedefer raised his eyebrows. "Sounds as if you're speaking from your own experience, magician. You trained once, did you?"

A shrewd man, Sir Bedefer. Mordion realized that he had, once again, in the way Ann always objected to, been confusing his own feelings with Hume's. If Hume were to grow into someone like Sir Bedefer, it would be no bad thing—except that Sir Bedefer was probably wasted on it, too. "Yes, I trained," he said. "It did me no good."

A group of ladies began to descend the steps. "Thought so," Sir Bedefer said as they all stood back politely to let the ladies pass. "Pretty sight, aren't they?" he added, nodding at the ladies.

They were indeed, with their slender waists, floating headdresses, and different colored gowns. Mordion had to admit that this was not a sight you could get in the forest. As the girls rustled past, talking and laughing, he saw that one of them was the pretty blond lady who had lent him her girdle. Hume was staring at her, just as he had done last night. He seemed utterly smitten. The next lady to go past was shorter, plumper, with tip-tilted cheekbones.

"*Ann!*" said Mordion.

He knows me! Vierran whirled round and encountered Mordion's amazed and amazing smile. The hard misery in her innards broke up before a huge, spreading warmth. "My name's Vierran," she said. She could feel her face beaming like Mordion's.

"I always thought it ought to be longer than Ann," he said.

Everyone edged round them and left them standing together at the top of the steps.

"What did it?" asked Mordion. "The name? The Bannus?"

"Damn Bannus!" she said. "I've a bone to pick with it when I catch it!" It was on the tip of her tongue to tell him exactly why, but she looked up into his face and realized he still did not know. The face smiling down at her was not the Servant's, nor was it quite the Mordion of the wood. But he's getting there, she thought. And I'm not going to spoil this moment for *anything*! Instead she said something that struck her as just as urgent. "How old do you think I am?"

Mordion surveyed her, up and down. Vierran was glad to see he seemed to enjoy doing that. "It's hard to tell," he said. "You look younger in those pretty clothes. But I've always thought you were about twenty."

"Twenty-one really." Vierran's face was hot at the memory of herself perched in that tree. "Do you know how old you are?"

"No," said Mordion.

Vierran knew the Servant was twenty-nine. She did not tell him. She picked up the trailing skirt of the pretty dress—which was a terrible nuisance, but if Mordion found it pretty, it was worth it— and began to go down the steps. "Were you just put in the castle, like me?" she asked.

"No, we had to make our way here," Mordion said. "Yam objected, of course. And— Oh, and can we be overheard here? This is screamingly funny." They looked round and found they were quite alone, so as they slowly descended the steps, he told her about the famous wound of King Ambitas. By the time they reached the courtyard neither of them could speak for laughing.

They spent the rest of the day together—or maybe it was several days. As usual, with the Bannus, it was hard to tell. Sometimes they walked about, but most of the time they spent sitting together on a bench against the wall of the castle hall, where someone could find Vierran when Morgan La Trey wanted her. Being called away to La Trey was a great annoyance to Vierran. As far as she was concerned, life centered on that bench in the hall, where things seemed to get better and better and ever more joyful, moving toward something that was even more splendid—though Vierran did not quite put into words what that might be. She just seemed to be waiting for it, breathlessly. When she trudged off to attend to the wedding dress again, she was in a state of suspended animation.

"Keep your mind on what you're doing!" La Trey snapped at her.

"Sorry, my lady," Vierran mumbled around the pins in her mouth.

"You've lost your head to that magician creature, haven't you?" said La Trey. "Don't bother to tell me. I know. How far have you been fool enough to go with him, that's what I want to know. Do you intend to marry the man? *Do* magicians marry?"

Heat surged across Vierran's face in waves. She seemed to have spent most of today blushing. She bent her head to hide it, and considered. La Trey was being bitchy. But as Reigner Three she was probably genuinely trying to find out whether Vierran had obeyed Reigner One's command. It would help Mordion no end if both these Reigners lost interest in him, as they might if they thought there were new Servants coming along. And the Bannus had given Vierran a way to fool them. Hume. Vierran spit the pins out into her hand and raised her head. At the thought of what she was going to do, her face was so red that her neck felt swollen, but who cared if it helped Mordion? "I have made a child with Agenos, my lady," she said solemnly.

"What a perfect little fool you are!" said La Trey. "Run away and don't come back until you can concentrate." And she smiled as Vierran left, in a way that Vierran was not sure she liked at all.

Hume himself was in the hall again when Vierran came back. He had been appearing there from time to time all day, dressed in a squire's cloak and tunic of the same faded blue-purple he always wore. Each time he came in, he was harder and leaner as if he had put in many days of training. Hume was a sore point with Vierran at that moment. She felt shaken and drained and irritable after her confession to La Trey. She looked sourly across the hall and saw that Hume was once again hanging wistfully around Lady Sylvia. He seemed to have had a lot of time to do that. Lady Sylvia was being very kind and adult, keeping Hume at a distance without hurting his feelings. Nice of her, Vierran thought irritably. But then Siri—if not Lady Sylvia—had had a lot of practice.

"How long has today been?" Vierran asked Mordion as she slid back onto the bench beside him.

"Too long," he said, wondering what was the matter. "The Bannus sometimes likes to fast-forward things. We seem to have caught it at it for once."

"Or it's let us see it at it," Vierran said distrustfully. She wished she had her voices to check how long it had been, but there was only silence from them, making a miserable gap in her mind. She realized that she had forgotten to warn Mordion about Morgan La Trey. She turned toward him to tell him, wondering how she would do it without confessing what she had just said to La Trey.

"Your lad's coming along rather well," Sir Bedefer said, sitting down on the bench beside them. "And I had a very interesting talk with that silver man of yours. Hope you didn't mind me hunting it out in your room. It knows a lot, doesn't it?"

Mordion turned to talk cautiously about Yam, though he would much rather have found out what was worrying Vierran. Vierran listened to them talking and tried to be patient. They both liked Sir Bedefer, that was the trouble. But Vierran was certain afterward that her impatience caused her to say what she did.

"I was asking your—robot, did you say the word was?—" Sir Bedefer said, "whether it thought there was any truth in what that mad monk came in here and told us. You know he said we had rulers beyond the stars, or some such rubbish. Called then Reigners and said they ruled Earth. Now your robert-man—"

"But it's true," Vierran said, without thinking. "There *are* Reigners. But they don't rule, they exploit. They take flint from Earth that's so valuable you wouldn't believe, and pay *nothing* for it, and keep Earth primitive on purpose. Rayner Hexwood Earth sells guns to the natives."

"Oh, no, we don't," Sir Bedefer answered, also without thinking. "I like to run a clean ship." Then he blinked and obviously wondered what had possessed him to say that.

Vierran looked uneasily at Mordion. He was sitting very upright and very still. That's done it! she thought miserably. The end of the good times, and I've only myself to blame!

—6—

ORM PENDER WAS hungry by now. Uneasy acids broiled in his vast stomachs. The discomfort became so compelling that he was forced to halt his slow, deliberate progress toward his enemy and turn his great head about to sniff for closer prey.

Ah! Men. From some miles upwind came the appetizing currylike scent of a number of men sweating with effort of some kind. Better still, it was mixed with the more succulent odor of women and the rank, meaty smell of horses. Orm turned, snaking among the trees in that direction, moving faster now, helping himself along in the open glades by spreading his huge, rattling wings. He came to a river in a deep trench and glided across it. When he was nearly over, he almost stooped toward an old human corpse rolling in the shallows there, but that cadaver was too rotten to please him when fresh food was so near. He glided on.

The food was on the farther bank, in the fairly open wood beyond a copse. Orm furled his wings, spread his claws, and came to a silent, raking landing in the copse. He crawled gently among the trees and, trusting to his green-brown mottled scales to hide him, couched cunningly among the bushes at the edge.

Copper blood smells came to him, tantalizingly. There was a battle going on out there. Large numbers of poorly armed men and women on foot were fighting a smaller band riding horses. Annoyingly the warfare had reached the stage where everyone had scattered into small individual struggles, giving Orm no large or easy target. Orm turned his great yellow eyes this way and that, deciding which prey to select. Here a rider crunched the unfurling green bracken, turning and turning his horse to spear at two footmen trying to pull him down. Here another rider thudded in pursuit of several women with longbows. Here other footmen were using the nearer trees as cover, crackling and slipping in brambles as they tried both to fend off a posse of attacking horsemen and to rally others of their people around them. Orm's ears were offended by the hoarse, yelping shouts of these men.

All the same, both the shouting men were tall, meaty types, and others were running to join them. There were a couple of boys with them, one with his arm in a sling. Easy, tender meat for hors d'oeuvres. Orm decided that this group would do. He emerged slowly, slowly from his bushes and crept toward them, swallowing back a belch of hunger as he crawled.

That swallowed sound gave him away—or maybe it was the slight rattle of his wings or the scales of his dragging tail. Orm had forgotten that men, when they are fighting, are abnormally alert. White blobs of faces turned his way. A boy's high voice screamed, *"Dragon!"* It was shrill as a trumpet and carried to all the other fighters. The battling stopped while more faces turned Orm's way.

Orm gave up caution and put on speed, snaking toward his chosen group, belching out his hunger openly in hot, putrid blue clouds. But they were scattering, running away. All over the battlefield his food was throwing down weapons, whipping up screaming horses, and taking to its heels. He broke into a gallop and roared his frustration.

But one of the riders—and only one—who shone in steel and had a lot of green about him, seemed to regard Orm's approach as a challenge. This one reined round his terrified horse, fought it brutally under control, jabbed it with his spurs, and, with a great yell of *"Fors, Fors, Fors!"* came galloping straight at Orm, pointing a long green stick at him.

Orm halted. He could scarcely believe his luck. Food was running straight down his throat. He waited until the galloping pair was only yards away and laughed—laughed out his surprise and scorn in a big rolling billow of flame. Hair and skin sizzled. Orm made a leisured move sideways and let the smoking corpses thunder on under their own impetus. They fell just where he wanted them, beside his great clawed feet. To his annoyance, the rider was still moving inside his blackened armor. He even seemed to be trying to get to his feet. Orm put a stop to that by biting his head off, helmet and all, and throwing it aside with a clang.

Two spears hit him as he did so. Orm reared up, stretching his great neck, hissing his outrage, and rattling his scales to dislodge the things. As the spears dropped off him, he spotted the two who had thrown them, the two tall, meaty men, hastily retreating to either side. Orm lowered his head and sent two rolls of fire after them, to left and to right, which had them both diving for cover. He crawled forward and sent more fire, in a great arc, to discourage any others who might want to creep impudently up on him. The few who were left ran away with most satisfactory urgency.

Orm returned to feast on parboiled horse. He saved the pleasure of picking pieces of the man out of its shell of armor for a second course, when he was not so hungry and could enjoy it. When at last he put out a claw and dragged the delicacy toward him, his eye was drawn to the bright colors of the knight's shield, which had fallen underneath him and was barely more than singed. Two unequally balanced golden pans glittered there on a green field. Orm had a notion that this should mean something to him, but his mind was still on food. He looked irritably round for the detached head, the tastiest part of all. Ah, *there* it was.

"OYEZ, OYEZ!" the herald Madden shouted on the steps of the castle hall. "Know ye that our gracious king, great Ambitas, is once again forced to postpone his marriage to the Lady Morgan La Trey. Being sore troubled with his wound, the king took advice of the noble physician Agenos and by the advice of this same Agenos now hereby makes it known that to his great regret his marriage must be put off for a year and a day."

Morgan La Trey listened to this news, leaning from the window of her tower. She allowed her fury to show only in a long, tight-lipped smile. "Fools!" she said. "Both of them. They have now given me the reason I needed."

The herald had scarcely retired from the steps when the gates were flung open for the twenty-eight remaining horses of Sir Fors's expedition to clatter through. They were all exhausted and foam-damped, and many were carrying two riders. Those poor horses, Vierran thought. The Hexwood Farm Riding School—where those horses must have come from—was going to be twelve short after this.

"It looks just as bad as I feared," Sir Bedefer said, and went down into the front court at a run. After a very few words with the lieutenant, he hurried him to the king. "Worse than I feared. Dragon," he said to Mordion and Vierran as he passed them in great strides, towing the tired lieutenant.

Morgan La Trey raced down the spiral stairs, jubilant. Sir Fors had not come back! One down and three to go. She scooped up Sir Harrisoun as he loitered in an antechamber, and the two of them got to the king first.

Sir Bedefer came back from the king with his mouth crimped shut and his eyes like angry slots. His request to take a large force out to deal with the dragon had been denied. His further despairing suggestion, that they make a pact with the outlaws and ask *them* to kill the dragon in exchange for weapons, had been met with astonished suspicion. Ambitas had expressed doubts about Sir Bedefer's loyalty. "*Mine!*" said Sir Bedefer explosively to Hume. "Let him look at some of the others, I say!"

Hume nodded, puzzled and not willing to be disillusioned about life in the castle. Vierran looked from him to Mordion and thought there was not much to choose between Mordion and Sir Bedefer for grim looks. She wished she knew what Mordion was thinking.

Overpowering disgust, Mordion would have told her. Beyond that he could not and would not think yet.

Minutes later the herald Madden was once more on the hall steps.

"Oyez, oyez! Let all here know that our noble Champion, Sir Fors, did this day meet with a most valiant death at the hands of a vile dragon. Our most generous Majesty, great Ambitas, herewith orders that all in this castle shall now give proper honor to the noble Sir Fors. Every soul within these walls is commanded, on pain of death, to go forthwith and in haste to the field before the castle, there to gaze into the west, where the noble Fors now lies, while the Reverend Sir Bors leads them in both song and prayer to the memory of the said Sir Fors."

"Better go," Vierran said to Hume and Mordion.

They joined the crowds streaming out of the gates in the sunset. Mordion walked pale and upright, struggling with an uprush of notions that threatened all the time to become outright memories if he let them. The worst of it was, he thought, trying not to look at Vierran, was that under the influence of the Bannus, he had completely deceived her. She had no idea of the horrors he had been hiding.

The crowd spilled into a great half circle by the lakeside: pages, cooks, squires, scullions, soldiers, maids, and ladies—all the population of Hexwood Farm estate, Vierran thought wryly—leaving a space by the gates for the nobles, the choir, the king, and Sir Bors. The choir, some of them still struggling into surplices, hastened through the gateway. Sir Bors, standing under the archway, was moving after the choir to take his place when he was stopped by Morgan La Trey. She handed him a small golden flask.

"What is this?" he said.

"Holy water, Reverend," she told him. "For you to sprinkle upon one we both know consorts with the devil."

Sir Bors had long suspected that La Trey herself consorted with the devil. Everyone said she was a witch. He held the flask up to the light and examined it dubiously. It was, he saw, decorated with the device of the Key in hammered gold. His heart was eased. No one who consorted with the devil would have been able to handle such a thing. He thanked her and tucked the flask into the front of his robe. He knew what he had to do.

Morgan La Trey paused under the archway to back up her pressure on Sir Bors by invoking and manipulating the field of the Bannus. It was as well to leave nothing to chance. Then she went sedately out to take her place beside Sir Harrisoun and Sir Bedefer. Ambitas was carried out behind her, and the service began.

This is going to be *so* tedious! Vierran thought, after the first few sentences. She thought with yearning sympathy of her own King, who had to put up with so much of this, and wished for the hundredth time that her voices could speak to her here. She was so bored! She occupied her mind as best she could by admiring the peachy ripples of the lake or looking at the castle people and wondering who they had really been in the Hexwood Farm estate. Some of the soldiers, oddly enough, reminded her of security men she had seen around the House of Balance. And then there were the outlaws. Who were *they*? Not to speak of the choir, she thought, as the choristers started to sing the first of, no doubt, many, many hymns. There was a big church two streets away from Wood Street. Maybe—

Someone tugged gently at her sleeve.

Vierran turned her head. She found herself looking at a dark-haired, shabby boy with a large graze down one side of his face. He was a stranger. Yet she knew him very well. Who—? *"Martin!"* she said, unwisely loud. Martin shook his head urgently at her. "What are you doing here?" Vierran whispered as Hume and Mordion both turned to see what was going on.

"I sneaked in on a horse behind one of the soldiers," Martin whispered back. "Dad told me to try it. Dad and Mum want you with them in the outlaw camp."

Hearing this, Mordion turned his face to Sir Bors again and pretended to be very attentive to the next prayer, but Hume remained turned half round, looking at Martin with puzzled, appraising, friendly interest. Vierran was rooted to the spot, torn. It's not really Mother and Father, she thought. Is it? I *have* to see. But Mordion—

"I'm to tell you the castle's not safe," Martin whispered. "They'll be attacking it tomorrow."

Unfortunately the slight disturbance they were making attracted the roving attention of Sir Harrisoun, who was as bored as anyone there. Even more unfortunately Hume, by turning round, had left a gap through which Sir Harrisoun could see Martin. He stared, with dim memories of a greengrocer's shop.

"Lord! You took a risk!" Vierran whispered. She hovered. "Look, if I come, can Hume and Mordion—"

The right connection clicked in Sir Harrisoun's mind. He took off running and dived through the gap Hume had left. "An outlaw!" he bellowed, seizing Martin's arm. "Here's a filthy little *outlaw* SPY!" Hume jostled at Sir Harrisoun, trying to protest, and Sir Harrisoun kneed Hume in the groin. "Ware outlaws!" Sir Harrisoun roared as Hume doubled up, helpless.

Mordion went into action as Hume fell. He chopped Sir Harrisoun's wrist to free Martin and then hip-threw Sir Harrisoun, who went down on the turf, still yelling. "*And Agenos is another spy! Agenos is a spy for the outlaws!*"

Soldiers and servitors ran at Mordion in a crowd. Mordion smiled. He had little doubt about being able to hold his own. It was a relief to fight, in a way, though without magic he would have been severely hampered by not wanting to kill anyone. No more killing, never again! As it was, he used his staff as a weapon and as a power to hold off the most murderous of his attackers. One soldier who, Mordion remembered, was among the most brutal of the House of Balance security men, he felled with a sizzling blue bolt. He did not see Sir Bors stare at that blue light in horror and then start to make his way over to the fight, but as he jabbed, twisted, kicked, and jabbed again, Mordion did spare a look to see what had become of Martin. Vierran, fluttering artistically with foolish alarm and stupid dismay, managed to get herself and her skirts in the way of the soldiers going after Martin. Martin went off like an eel through the crowd, pushing and ducking, relying on the fact that most people still had no idea what was going on, and Mordion lost sight of him.

While Mordion was looking, a servitor seized the chance to snatch his staff off him. Mordion smiled more widely and felled the servitor, before he turned to take on two soldiers. The staff was nothing, only a useful channel. He saw Vierran run and help Hume hobble clear of the fighting. Hume was hugely annoyed and spitting swearwords Mordion had no idea he knew. Then a fresh crowd of soldiers rushed upon Mordion.

Amid the fury of their beating limbs, Mordion saw Martin break out of the crowd lower down and run along the lakeside with no-where to go. That was stupid! Mordion thought. The bridge was drawn up, and there was no way across the water. Worse, many people had now grasped what was happening. Men from the lower edges of the crowd were running inward from both sides to cut Martin off. Mordion tossed the remaining soldiers away from him in a heap and then used the outflung power he had once used to destroy the waterfall to send Martin instantly as far away as possible. That was not across the lake, unfortunately. He put Martin as far away as he could, behind the castle. At the same time he raised his arms theatrically and called a sizzle of lightning to the spot where Martin had been. With any luck people would think Martin was invisible and look for him in the wrong place. He wondered, as he did it, why he was doing this for Martin. He had no idea who the boy was—except that Vierran cared about him. I'm always defending children, he thought, watching the crowd recoil from the flash of lightning.

He turned round to find himself face-to-face with Sir Bors. The man was shaking and had a look of total horror. "Abomination!" Sir Bors cried out, and poured the contents of the golden flask over Mordion's head.

Mordion was instantly caught fast in a net of pain. The net grew and grew, and he grew with it, writhing, swelling, coiling, heaving, rolling, pawing, clawing, caught and unable to free himself. Dimly he heard Sir Bors crying out, "Behold! Your secret enemy is unmasked! *This* is the abomination that killed our good Sir Fors!" before he blanked out in the agony of it.

Everyone else in the crowd stampeded backward from the great glossy black dragon that heaved and rolled, and gouged out lines of turf with its claws, and shot frantic fire that boiled the lake to steam, until it finally lay still down by the edge of the lake.

Morgan La Trey watched people fleeing past her into the castle. "I don't understand," she murmured to herself. "Is it dead?"

"No," said the beautiful voice of the Bannus in her ear. "You should have got him to drink it."

Here the black dragon roused itself and came crawling up the slope toward the castle gates. Ambitas called frantically to his bearers, who carried him back inside at a run. Morgan La Trey went with them but paused to watch everyone else pouring inside around and behind them. Among the last to come was Vierran, crying and struggling hysterically, so that the new young squire in blue had more or less to carry her.

"Well, that's something, at least," La Trey said, with satisfaction.

Behind her the gates were shut, in hideous haste, only inches in front of the dragon's blank, staring eyes.

PART
NINE

—1—

NIGHT FELL. The net of pain that held Mordion pricked slowly into points of light against the darkness, until his entire huge body was a web of cold sparks stretched half across the night sky. Each speck of fire pierced like a diamond knife, keen as frost and biting as acid. His only choice was to slip from point to fiery point and let each diamond stab him to the soul, or to remain still and experience the blinding pain of all his memories at once. There was no avoiding the memories. They were there, and they existed, implacable and everlasting as stars.

"What did I do," he said aloud, after many centuries of pain, "to deserve what is in my mind?" True, he had walked the galaxy, killing many people, but that seemed like earning his punishment afterward. He had earned it fully, he knew. The form he was in now was his true form. He had known it for years. And the moment he had entered the field of the Bannus and felt the compulsions of the Reigners marginally lifted from his mind, this same form had come upon him—a low, ugly form, smaller than this, and so nasty that he had hidden himself deep in a patch of thorns. Someone had disturbed him there, he remembered. Wanting only peace, he had crawled forward and tried to smile at the boy standing there to show him he wanted only peace. The boy had been Hume, he realized now—Hume before Mordion had created him. That was odd. And

Hume had mistaken the smile, taken it for a threat, and thrown a log into his mouth. It had taken Mordion hours to rid himself of that log, and all the while he was spitting and coughing and pawing at it, he had told himself that it was no more than he had deserved. He had earned this form and this punishment, but he had earned them afterward, and that did not make sense. "I must have done *something* early on," he said.

"You did nothing," said the Bannus. Mordion was aware of it nearby as the outline of a chalice made of stars. He had some thoughts of stretching out his starry tail and wrapping it round the chalice, taking it prisoner and telling it to put him out of his misery, but he saw that would be useless. Here in the sky where they were was in some way also inside the Bannus. The chalice was only an illusion of the Bannus, as empty as the sky behind it, which was also the Bannus. "I can see nothing in your memories that deserves their presence," the Bannus said to him. "Examine them and see."

Mordion wanted to refuse, but since he had only the two choices, he reluctantly exchanged one pain for another and let his consciousness move until he had impaled himself upon the nearest diamond spike. Six children. There had been six children, twin boys, twin girls, and Kessalta. And Mordion. They were all the same age. Mordion had no idea if they were children of the same parents or not. They were all desperately attached to one another because the others were all each had in the world, but since four were twins and Kessalta and Mordion the odd ones out, he and Kessalta were special to each other. She was next to him in abilities. But it was not fair. It never was fair. Mordion had always seemed like the eldest. He was bigger and stronger than the others and could do more things. It was never fair. And the others had looked up to him and depended on him, just as if he were really the eldest.

Always defending children! he thought, and slipped onto the spike of that memory. The six of them were quite small and shut in a room. It was an empty room where they spent much time. Sometimes it was wet and cold in there, sometimes wet and hot. They thought they were put in there to be punished, but they were not sure. This time it was cold and dry, but as always, there were voices whispering in the air. "You are nothing. You are low. Love the Reigners and make yourselves worth something. Honor the Reigners. Please the Reigners." On and on. None of them listened. Mordion, as usual, was keeping them from being too miserable by making up songs and doing magic tricks. One reason he had entered the castle in such a flourish of magic making, he realized now, was the sheer joy of being able to do tricks again.

They were all laughing because Mordion had made a silly image of a Reigner. It was dancing in the air saying, "I've got you! I've got you!" while they all shouted back, "Oh, no, you haven't!" when the door opened and one of the robots that mostly looked after them burst into the room, flailing a strap. "You have displeased the Reigners," it intoned, and went for them with the strap. They all screamed. For a moment they did not know what to do. They were used to robots neglecting them and robots ordering them about, but this was the first time one had attacked them. But when Cation had been quite badly hurt, Mordion pulled himself together and managed to drive the robot into a corner, where he and Kessalta kicked its feet out from under it. But it kept getting up and flailing at them. And it was so strong. In the end Mordion had to pierce its brain with a magic bolt-thing he invented in frantic haste and then tear out some of its works before it would stop.

Their human keepers punished him for destroying a robot, but that had not hurt nearly so much as the memory of those five lost children he had spent his childhood defending.

"Why did you defend them?" the Bannus wondered.

"Somebody had to," Mordion said. He thought the reason he was able to was not so much, in those days, that he was taller and cleverer—which was not fair anyway—but because there were three voices that sometimes spoke in his head. They told him that what was happening was wrong. Better still, they made him aware of wider, happier worlds than the six children knew. Mordion, with intense excitement, learned that these voices came from people many light-years away and that he was speaking with people whose voices had set out for his mind centuries before. He was always sorry that neither the twins nor Kessalta could hear them. They usually spoke, the voices, when Mordion's mind was busy learning all the things they were made to learn. They had lessons and physical training eight or more hours a day. The Reigners wanted their Servants properly educated, they were told. If any of them got restive, robots came. They were all terrified of robots after that one with the strap. And always the whispering in the air that the children were nothing and must love the Reigners. Mordion's voices helped to make all that bearable. But the voices gradually faded away after the Helmets were introduced.

"I am *not* thinking of those!" Mordion groaned. "How often have I been up here, being made to remember?"

"Only this once," the Bannus told him. "My actions ceased to be multiple when you finally decided to come to the castle. You feel you have been here often because those memories were always in your mind. You have been quite a problem to me. I have had to keep much of the action marking time while I induced you to remove the blocks that had been put upon you. It has taken so long that feeding everyone became quite difficult."

"Why did you bother?" Mordion groaned.

"Because you showed yourself able to take command of my actions," the Bannus told him. "First you insisted on taking the form of a reptile. Then, when I induced the Wood to make you become a man again, you insisted on looking after Hume yourself. That was not my plan. Hume was to grow up in the Wood under Yam's care."

He had kept to the pattern of looking after children, Mordion thought. Perhaps it was because it was the only happy thing he had known. But it could have been that he was determined Hume should have a better childhood than his own. Not difficult, Mordion thought. "But I still don't see why you bothered with me."

"I believe I have developed greatly," said the Bannus, "since the days when the present Reigner One cheated me. I had the full use of a large library and learned even while dormant, and when my power was restored, I found the Reigners had done me a great service by constructing portals and message lines throughout half the galaxy. I learned through those, much and quickly. *But* I still have to abide by the rules of my designers. These state that I have to provide everyone capable of it a chance to lay hands on me and take command. I am, as I saw you realized during your conversations with Reigner Two, a device for selecting Reigners. The other candidates are all now prepared to take their chance. Only Hume and Artegal among them caused any difficulty. But you have been so unwilling to come to the point that I had, reluctantly, to decide on this as a sort of crash measure and was forced to exercise considerable chicanery to achieve it."

"Oh, go *away!*" said Mordion.

He had no idea whether the Bannus went or stayed. He was for a long time stretched out along the black interstellar spaces of himself, sliding from point to agonizing point.

Reigner One visited the children often. They adored him. Mordion flinched along his star spaces to think how much they had adored him. When he came, they were allowed good clothes and nice surroundings. He smiled and patted their heads and gave them sweets; they never otherwise had anything sweet to eat. Often the sweets were taken away when Reigner One had gone. "You displeased Reigner One very much," they were told. "You must try harder to be worthy of him." Then Mordion had to comfort the sobbing twins and tell them that they *were* worthy. And they all tried to be worthy of Reigner One. How they tried.

They were given battle training from very early on. Both pairs of twins were slower at this than Kessalta or Mordion, and Mordion was often forced to be very swift indeed to defend the twins from the robots they all so much dreaded. He supposed this was why he eventually lost his fear of robots. He had to disable his own attacker and then turn to help Bellie or Corto with theirs, while Kessalta, slightly slower, helped the other two. And it was the same with instrument detection. Mordion learned to discover what was being used on the others before he even looked at what was attacking him. Then he could shoot the words *spy monitor* or *needle flier* into the minds of Cation and Sassal, quick, while he looked at his own, and those two could stop the instrument before it got to them.

There was another piercing diamond alongside this. When Reigner One later dressed Mordion in scarlet, with the rolled cloak upon one shoulder, and told Mordion he was the Servant now, Reigner One did not seem to know this extreme skill of Mordion's with instruments. He told Mordion that his every act from now on would be monitored. Mordion looked and found that there were times when Reigner One did not bother to do so. But by then there was not a thing Mordion could do about it.

They were not allowed to miss training unless they had bones broken, and they were forbidden to complain of any sickness. They were all forced, to some extent, to learn to heal themselves. Mordion had quite acute asthma whenever the few trees they could see over the walls put out dusty new leaves, and this he could never cure. He learned to ignore it. Cation's twin, Corto, likewise tried to ignore sudden terrible pains in his stomach. They all tried to cure him, but they did not know how. Mordion and Kessalta sat with him all night, helping him ignore it, until, around dawn, Corto died of a burst appendix.

Reigner One arrived in great anger. "You wicked little children," he told them, "this is *your* fault. You should have told someone he was ill."

They did not dare tell him they had been forbidden to. They felt awful. They blamed themselves bitterly. They were made to attend the postmortem on Corto. Anatomy was something they were supposed to know about. They were all sick afterward, and even after that Cation was slower at things than before. He needed all Kessalta's help, as well as Mordion's.

The grief—but not the guilt—they felt about Corto seemed to get smudged out by longer and longer sessions under the Helmets. "I meant not to think about those!" Mordion groaned, but he was impaled on that spike by then.

They all hated the Helmets. The things gave you a headache. But Mordion hated them more than the others because slowly, slowly they shut out his three voices, shut out his ability to do magic, shut down the songs and stories he used to make up. He was forced to console himself with the knowledge that the Helmets did improve the things he was *supposed* to do, like love the Reigners, and fight swiftly and accurately, and obey the instructors' orders, but it was hard. He did not realize that the Helmets could be dangerous until Bellie's twin, Sassal, suddenly went into convulsions under hers and died.

They were not blamed for this death, but they all four kicked and fought and were punished next time they had to put on the Helmets. And there were now two lonely, grief-stricken twins for Mordion and Kessalta to comfort. Mordion thought he might have given up and let himself die in convulsions, too, if it had not been for a sudden new voice that came to him. He called this one the Girl Child. She called him the Slave. She seemed to have got past the Helmets because she was younger than the other voices and came in on a later wave band. She was very young at first. Her cheerful chatter was like a lifeline to Mordion. And she introduced a new notion, almost a new hope. She was very indignant about the life he led. *Why don't you run away?* she said.

Mordion wondered why he had not thought of this himself. The Helmets probably. He started planning to get free. The idea of getting free obsessed him from then on. Naturally he shared the idea with Cation, Bellie, and Kessalta.

Cation went over the wall that same night. He was brought back, horribly mangled. Reigner One came with him. "This is what happens," he said, smiling and pulling his beard, "to naughty children who try to run away. Don't you three even think of it."

Cation died two days later. Here was one more thing Mordion blamed himself for. None of them ran away, but Bellie contrived to hang herself from a pipe in the washroom a month later. Reigner One blamed Mordion and Kessalta for that, but they had expected he would. It was only one more misery on top of grief.

The Girl Child told him not to mind. She was certain he would be free one day. Mordion wished he had never believed her. His captivity and his misery were so much worse after that, that he tried to wrench his consciousness away and only succeeded in falling an another icy spike. Vierran. When he walked into that basement for clothes, expecting only a robot, and found Vierran there instead, there had been something about the way she spoke. Something about her energy and her sense of humor. He felt he knew it. He became convinced, almost straightaway, that Vierran was his Girl Child. He longed to ask her. Several times he had actually started to do so. But he never dared. If he did and he was wrong, then he knew that Vierran would recoil from him like all the other people in the House of Balance. Mordion knew the reason they avoided him, and it was not, as the Reigners thought, because he killed to their orders. It was because they suspected—rightly—that his training had driven him mad. It was meant to, after all. And he could not bear Vierran to think he was mad, as she would if he babbled to her of voices.

"I don't want to *know* any more!" he said.

"I have some fellow feeling for you," observed the Bannus, now in the form of a starry urn. "I am what Earth people would call a cyborg. I was constructed around four thousand years ago from the half-lifed brains of a deceased Hand of Reigners. Five different brains are not easy to assort or assimilate. Meshing them together and then meshing the human parts with the machinery cost me much the same pain as you now feel. Take courage from the fact that I survived it, sanely. Then, like you, I have spent much time closed right down, allowed only to act as a security guard. To judge by my feelings, you have been raging within."

"Yes," said Mordion. "The worst was being forced to be so respectful."

"I am surprised you pick out *that*!" said the Bannus.

"You try being sick every time you want to laugh at someone," Mordion said.

"I understand," said the Bannus. "I suspect you do not believe me, but I do. I have promised myself for centuries this joke I am now playing. I would have allowed myself to rot had I not. And again like you, I am still considerably frustrated. You are held against your will in my field of actions. I am besieged and manipulated by the Wood."

"The wood!" Mordion was truly surprised.

"The Wood," said the Bannus. "The Wood has me in its field. To some extent I have the Wood in mine also. I was placed in it, and over the centuries our two fields have mingled. Maybe I have helped make this Wood more animate than many, but the fact remains that I am in its power."

"I don't understand," Mordion said.

"The Wood," explained the Bannus, "is, like all woods in this country and maybe like woods all over Earth, part of the great Forest that once covered this land. At the merest nudge it forms its own theta-space and becomes the great Forest again. Ask any Earthman. He will tell you how, in this country, he has been lost in the smallest spinney. He can hear traffic on the road, but the road is not there, while there are sounds behind him of a great beast crawling through the undergrowth. This is the great Forest. *You* can deal with the Wood better than I can, for it is magic."

"Can't you control it at all?" Mordion asked.

There was a note of real bitterness in the melodious voice of the Bannus. "I can only compromise. It is ridiculous. I can tap information all over the galaxy, but I cannot communicate with the Wood. It is voiceless, yet it has a will at least as strong as yours. I could only learn, by trial and error, what it would let me do.

Most of what has happened here, including your present form, is according to the desires of the Wood."

"But your field is surely much wider than the Wood's," Mordion said.

"For sure," agreed the Bannus. "It has been quite useful to suggest that the theta-space of the Wood was mine, where in fact, mine was far wider and more subtle. Do not tell me that you have not done the same. You have taken pains to seem all Servant, yet I detect you have kept one portion of your mind almost entirely free of this training you were forced to undergo."

"I was only looking for a way to be free," Mordion said, "although I suppose it kept me sane—as far as I *was* sane."

And he was pitched down upon the sharpest bright points of all.

I *will* be free! he had told himself after Bellie's death. The Girl Child had supported him eagerly. *Of course you'll get free! Go for it!* Mordion had clung to that one small part of his mind where the Girl Child spoke. He made them think he was thoroughly submissive. Although he knew he was submitting to having large parts of his brain closed down, he had let them do it in order to cling to that private corner and the Girl Child's eagerness and her jokes. He was sure the day would come when he could use this to set Kessalta and himself both free.

And the irony of it was that he had simply ended up knowing how deeply he was enslaved.

Kessalta was next to Mordion in strength and ability. She was always special to him, and now more than ever after Bellie died. And somebody noticed. They were kept apart mostly from then on, marched about like prisoners, and only allowed to meet during training. Mordion was glad of that small mercy, and not only because it gave him a chance to see Kessalta. They were training with animals by then, small ones first, then graduating to things as big as those wolves. And Kessalta had what was, in a Servant, a fatal flaw. She could not bring herself to kill anything. Whenever they were put to kill animals, Mordion killed his quickly with his eyes on Kessalta. As soon as she had her hands, or her weapon, in roughly the right position, Mordion terminated the animal for her, Reigner fashion, using his mind. He kept anyone from suspecting Kessalta's failing until they were both fifteen.

Then one day Reigner One turned up to watch their skills. Separately.

After Mordion had passed his own tests, he had an agonized wait in a locked room while Kessalta was tested in her turn. During that time he imagined every dire thing his brain would produce. And the reality was worse. He was called back after several hours. Kessalta was lying on a table, still screaming faintly, while Reigner One washed the blood off his hands. What Reigner One had done to Kessalta was beyond anything Mordion could have imagined.

"Tell Mordion why you were punished, Kessalta," Reigner One said.

Kessalta, still just about able to speak, said, "I can't kill things."

"But Mordion can," said Reigner One. "Mordion, this knack of terminating things that you seem to have developed on Kessalta's behalf would make you an exceedingly accomplished Servant. But you are not obedient, and you are not loyal. You have deceived me, and you shall be punished, too. I've made sure Kessalta will live at least a year as you see her now, and you can be sure I shall not simply leave her alone in that time. You can put her out of her misery now if you want, but you must do it *now*. If you don't, you must think of her living for another year."

Mordion terminated Kessalta on the spot. The pain he knew she was in hurt more than the sharpest diamond spike of his memory. Then he turned away and tried not to be sick.

"Good," said Reigner One. "Now remember this. If you fail to terminate any person as soon as you get the Sign, I shall follow and do this to them."

Mordion had no doubt that Reigner One meant this. He wrestled with two sicknesses, this first one and then the sickness the Helmets

gave you for disobeying a Reigner. "You've made me into a mur-
derer," he managed to say.

"Precisely. And what else can you be, my good Mordion, with a
face like yours?" Reigner One said, and went away chuckling.

Mordion was alone after that for the final years of his training,
and ten years after that, just as he was now, stretched across the
spangled universe of himself.

"No. I am here," said the Bannus. "I conclude you must hate
Orm Pender very deeply."

"That's the wrong word," Mordion said. "Hate is too close and
hot." Now that he saw what had been done to him, it was not hate
he felt, or what mattered. What mattered was that he had been
formed, very cruelly, to carry the guilt the Reigners should have
carried themselves. The Bannus had been clever. Even if it had
been Mordion who had decided to look after Hume, the Bannus
had used Hume very deftly to make Mordion see that he should not
train someone up to do his dirty work for him. And if this was wrong
for Mordion, it followed that it was equally wrong for Reigner One.
What mattered even more was that Reigner One had been doing
this to children for generations and that the next children he would
do it to would certainly be Mordion's.

But there was no way he could move for the blinding pain of his
memories.

"I feel sympathy," said the Bannus. "If you wish, you may attain
peace by remaining always in my field. You may form the constella-
tion of the Dragon in my skies."

The Bannus really seemed to mean this. And it was very tempting.

"No," Mordion said wretchedly. "I must go and stop Reigner
One. It needs to be done. But I'm grateful, Bannus—for that offer
and for the chance you gave me to know Vierran."

Vierran was still the sharpest hurt of all. Mordion knew well
enough what her feelings had been in the House of Balance. It had
been play, and he had been lonely, and grateful for that much. But
now, though Vierran knew she had been Ann, she clearly thought

she was just one of La Trey's ladies in the castle. But she was heir to the House of Guaranty, and Mordion was the Servant. The gulf between them was full of blood and impassable.

—2—

HE WAS ROUSED by a gentle tapping on one of his horny knuckles. Someone seemed to be patting him there. There were whispers around him in the dark.

"Are you sure he'll know you in this form?" A man's whisper.

"Of course he will!" That was Hume's voice and Vierran's together, Vierran's rather hoarse, as if she had been crying. Mordion was sorry about that, but he could not bring himself to stir.

"There's stuff coming out of his eyes!" A boy's whisper.

There was silence, while all four whisperers perhaps wondered what might make a dragon weep. Then the patting began again, persuasively. "Mordion! *Please!*" said Vierran.

Mordion roused himself enough to say, "What do you want?" He felt them all jump back at his deep dragon's voice, resonating from his huge head.

"To see if you were alive, for a start," Hume said.

"I'm alive," sighed Mordion. "And I know you. You needn't be afraid."

"We're *not* afraid," Vierran said indignantly. "But we came to warn you, Mordion. La Trey's sure you're still alive, and she wants you finished off. She's been to the king—"

"And I thought you ought to take Vierran and Martin back to their parents," Hume said. "If you fly away with them over the lake, you'd be safe, too."

Mordion opened his eyes. His night vision was superb. It showed him the four of them clustered round his nose, the boy Martin between Hume and Vierran, and Sir Bedefer bulking behind. He wondered again who Martin was. As Servant he was well versed in the families of the great Houses, and he knew there were no boys in the House of Guaranty. "I didn't hurt you sending you to the back of the castle, did I?" he asked Martin.

"No, though I couldn't think what had happened at first," Martin said. "Hume came and found me and hid me in your room with your robot. He went on about hocus-pocus."

"Yam is a *bore!*" said Hume. "Do you think you can carry two, Mordion?"

Mordion flexed his back and shuffled his wings, testing his strength. "I think so."

"Then I think you should go now," said Sir Bedefer, "before I'm commanded to slay you. But before you go—would you mind answering a couple of quick questions?"

"Ask away." Mordion lowered his body and stretched out a foot. Martin used the foot as a step and slipped nimbly up onto his back. "These spines are *sharp!*" he said. "Go carefully, Ann—er— Vierran."

"Well—um," said Sir Bedefer as Vierran gathered her skirts and started to climb on Mordion, too. "Fact is, Vierran here tells me that you're really something called the Reigners' Servant, and I sort of have glimmerings that way, too—"

Vierran *knew!* Mordion turned his head so quickly to look at Vierran that he almost swept her off his foot.

"Yes, of course I know," Vierran said, hanging on to the spike above his left ear for balance. "The Bannus may have forgotten I have Reigner blood—or it may not have. Anyway, I've known all about everything since yesterday. Mordion, did you know that your eyebrow comes down to a wonderful point between your eyes?"

Sir Bedefer coughed. "Could you just tell me what you know about the Reigners' dealings on Earth? Vierran says you always learn up on anywhere you're sent. She says you can access the Reigners' files. Is that so?"

"Yes, that's true." It looked, Mordion thought, as if Sir John Bedford were beginning to struggle out of the Bannus's hold, too.

"You're not going to like this," Mordion told him. "Vierran told you—" Of *course* Vierran had known he was the Servant! Mordion realized. He could have saved himself much misery remembering what she had said to Sir Bedefer before. But he had been too busy then holding down his memories and his horror to realize. "The flint Earth exports is not for road rubble," he said. "It's the most valuable commodity in the galaxy. Earth has been deliberately kept poor and backward so that the House of Balance can get its flint cheaply—"

"Glass beads for gold nuggets from the ignorant natives, I gather," Sir Bedefer interrupted. "But what I want to know is *how* valuable is our flint."

"Unprocessed, it will be about treble the price of diamonds," Mordion said. "Processed, it's often ten times that, depending on the type of the flint and the current market."

Sir Bedefer, very slowly, seemed to stiffen and enlarge.

"The Reigners hold a complete monopoly in raw flint," Vierran told him from her spiky perch on Mordion's back.

"I see," said Sir Bedefer. "At twopence a ton they surely do make a pretty profit on it. And what about this weapons dealing you talked of?"

"They deal in drugs, too," said Mordion. "Rayner Hexwood has hidden subsidiaries in Brazil, Egypt, and Africa that deal in both weapons and drugs. And half the top secret institutions in Europe are making weapons to use against other subject worlds. I take it you don't know about those?"

"I do not!" said Sir Bedefer, becoming almost entirely Sir John Bedford again. "Be sure they wouldn't exist if I *had* known! Thank you, sir. And where do I find these—these *Reigners?*" He took hold of the sword at his waist as he asked.

"They're all here," Vierran said. At this Sir Bedefer half drew his sword.

"Even Reigner One?" Mordion asked. He swung his head back

and saw Vierran nod from where she sat, just below his neck. "Where was he when you last saw him?" he asked her urgently.

"On the corner of Wood Street," said Vierran.

This meant that Reigner One was inside the Bannus field, too. That altered everything. Mordion weighed up Sir John's obvious intention of trying to kill Reigners with his pitiful steel sword, Vierran's safety, Hume's desires, and Martin's needs. Vierran, it seemed to him, would be safest in the one place he knew definitely Reigner One was *not*. Sir John would be safest where Vierran could not tell him who the Reigners were. Earth had been kept so ignorant that Sir John clearly had no idea what a Reigner could do to him if he tried to threaten one. Martin needed to be out of here. Hume would be safest in the castle, where he wanted to be.

Hard as it was, Mordion changed his plans. Or perhaps made his own plans for a change. "Get down, Vierran," he said. "You stay with Hume in the castle until I come back for you. Get Yam to guard you and keep well out of La Trey's way. I'm going to take Sir John to the outlaw camp with Martin. I think that's where he needs to be."

"I agree with you," said Sir John. "Is that all right?" he asked Vierran.

Vierran climbed down from Mordion without a word. She was determined not to cry, but this meant she could not speak. He's going after Reigner One! she thought. I know he is. And he may not come back.

Mordion relaxed a little as he felt Sir John climb heavily up in Vierran's place. He thought he could trust Yam to look after Vierran. And Earth was going to need Sir John when this was over. He did not expect Vierran to scramble round his face and kiss him on his nose. It made him start backward.

"Oh, don't!" said Vierran. "I *mean* that." Then, having spoken, she was crying. Hume had to take her arm and guide her back inside the castle through the small postern door.

"I'll see you, Mordion," Hume said softly before he shut the door.

—3—

THE DOUBLE LOAD was heavy. Mordion had to use the sloping turf as a runway in order to get airborne, and when he first spread his wings into the breeze over the lake, he was only a few feet off the water. Fortunately the breeze was a stiff one. With a flap and a tilt of his wings, Mordion lifted into it, superbly, and sailed high over the wood.

As soon as he had passed out of sight, Orm stole out from among the trees and glided across the lake to the castle. He had been very patient. Now, as he had hoped, the young black dragon had departed, carrying its prey, and the way to Orm's enemy was clear. He settled down on the turf to wait for him.

—4—

AMBITAS LOOKED ANXIOUSLY round the candlelit hall. There were very few people there, despite his urgent command. And now the people he had sent looking for Sir Bedefer had just come back to say Sir Bedefer could not be found. "There is a dragon at our gates," he said. "One of my Champions *must* kill this dragon. Sir Bors, I command you to undertake the adventure of this beast."

Sir Bors stood forward. "My lord, I beg to be excused. I am weak with fasting and praying to the Great Balance in heaven that it may be restored to hang evenly. Let me instead assist your chosen Champion with my prayers."

Sir Bors did look frail, Ambitas thought, looking at him closely. Foolish business, this fasting. But it did look as if that dragon out there would finish Sir Bors in one bite. "Very well, I excuse you. I command Sir Harrisoun to go against the dragon in your stead."

"*Oh*, no!" Sir Harrisoun stood up from the center of the hall. "Oh, no—no *way*! You saw the size of that dragon. There is no way you are going to get *me* out there trying to fight that thing!"

Then, as far as everyone else in the hall could see, Sir Harrisoun appeared to go mad. He shook his fist at the ceiling. "You there!" he shouted. "Yes, *you*! You just stop this! All I did was ask you for a role-playing game. You never warned me I'd be pitched into it for real! *And* I asked you for hobbits on a Grail Quest, and not one hobbit have I seen! Do you hear me?" He stared at the ceiling for a while. When nothing happened, he shook both fists upward. "*I ORDER you to stop!*" he yelled. His voice cracked high, almost into a scream. The sound seemed to bring Sir Harrisoun to his senses a little. He glared round the hall. "And you're all *figments!*" he said. "*My* figments. You can just carry on playing by yourselves. *I've* had enough!"

Everyone stared after Sir Harrisoun as he stalked out of the hall. "The young man's wit has turned," Sir Bors said sorrowfully.

Very true, and rather embarrassing, Ambitas thought, and it did nothing to solve the problem. "Is there any knight here," he asked without hope, surveying the few frightened faces under the candle-light, "who might wish to gain honor by slaying this dragon?" There was no answer. No one stirred. Ambitas considered. He could offer a reward, but it was hard to think of anything tempting enough. Ah! Wait a moment. He could offer them Morgan La Trey's hand in marriage. No. Better not. On second thoughts, that could get difficult. But on third thoughts, the lady had ladies. He could offer one of those. That beautiful one, the blond. What was her name now? Oh, yes. "If any offer to come forward as my Champion against this dragon," he said, "I will, once the dragon is slain, give him the hand of the Lady Sylvia in marriage."

This caused a tempted sort of stir. But it subsided. Most of the noise, anyway, seemed to have been from a latecomer entering the hall and asking what was going on. Ambitas thought he might as well give up and get them to carry him to bed. Give it one more try. "Will anyone here slay this dragon in return for the hand of the beauteous Lady Sylvia?" he said.

The latecomer surged to his feet, so eagerly that a bench fell over behind him with a clap that made everyone jump. He was a young squire whom Ambitas did not know. "*I'll* fight the dragon for you," he said. He was grinning broadly.

"Then come up here, and we'll both swear to it," Ambitas said, quickly before the youth could change his mind. "What is your name?" he asked as the youngster approached.

"Hume, Your Majesty." The young man seemed to be fighting giggles. Ambitas could not see anything to laugh at. Hume puzzled him by continuing to look unnaturally cheerful, even while he was swearing upon the Key of Sir Bors that he would tomorrow attempt to kill the dragon.

5

OUTSIDE THE CASTLE Orm pricked his spiky ears. There were faint sounds from the rear, carrying clearly over the water. Orm spread his wings and, dark in the darkness, glided round the walls of the castle to investigate. There was a fellow there loading large clinking bundles into a small boat, with every sign of being about to make a hasty getaway. It was not Orm's enemy, which was disappointing, but the fellow did have the taint of Reigner blood to his scent, and that was enough. Orm stooped lazily. As the fellow looked up in horror at the vast dark spread of wings above him, Orm slit his stretched throat with one languid claw. Because he was not very hungry yet, he carried Sir Harrisoun's body back to the front of the castle and laid it on the turf in the corner beside the main gate to wait for breakfast. Then he settled down to wait again.

—6——————————

Mordion, like Orm before him, smelled the corpse in the river.

"What's up?" Sir John asked as Mordion glided lower to investigate.

"Dead body. A smell I know." Talking and flying were not easy to do together. Mordion saved his breath, first for sniffing and then for the hard work of gaining height out of the air currents over the ravine. "Thought so," he said when he was properly aloft again. "Reigner Five. Two of them are dead."

"Then between us we ought to be able to take the other three," Sir John said happily. "I don't mind tackling Reigner One myself."

Mordion did not waste breath trying to convince him otherwise. He sailed on until his nose told him there were large numbers of people hiding in the trees somewhere just below a bare hillside.

"Our camp ought to be down there," Martin said.

Mordion banked round and landed on the hillside, where he thankfully folded his wings. Sir John was heavy. As Sir John and Martin climbed carefully down across his spikes, Mordion said, "I shall need to speak to the outlaws, too."

"Then, er," said Sir John, "I think they might appreciate you more in your usual form."

"So do I," said Martin.

Mordion was sure that if the outlaw Stavely was truly Vierran's father, he would probably prefer to see a dragon, but there were the other outlaws to consider. He bent his head and wondered if it was possible to get out of this dragon's shape.

"Can you change?" Martin asked anxiously.

"I'm not sure." The dragon form, Mordion thought, seemed to be an aspect of this net of pain that still encased him. The knack should be to shrink it round himself. The way to do that ought to be not unlike the way he had tried to wrap theta-space round Hume, only here the theta-space would be himself. Bracing against the pain he knew it would cause him, he wrapped—and pulled. He heard

Sir John and Martin gasp and stumble away backward. From their point of view, he knew, the dragon's black glossy hulk was outlined against the night sky in a thousand tiny blue stars, while the dragon grunted in obvious pain and shrank to blue-glittering man shape. Mordion winced, shortened his beard a little, and said, "Right. Ready."

He wondered whether he ought to warn the two of them that the outlaws were on the alert. His night sight, even in man shape, was good enough to see dim movements down among the trees.

No need, he thought. Dark people sprang up all round them as they started down the hill. All of them were seized and hustled down among the trees. "Hey, it's all right!" Martin protested. "It's me! These two brought me back! Let go!"

"There's a dragon around," someone said.

"It went," said Martin. "We saw it go."

"It could come back," he was told. "We'll let go when we've got you all under cover." And they were hustled on, through carefully hidden paths among brambles and trees, until they reached a clearing where someone was hastily lighting a fire. Into this space the most important among the outlaws were hurrying, some dragging on brown-green camouflage jackets, others wrapped in blankets and barely awake. One of the first to arrive, wrapped in a blanket, was a lady Mordion recognized with some sadness as Alisan of Guaranty. When Alisan saw Martin's face in the new, leaping flames of the fire, she dropped the blanket and ran to hug him. A boy with his arm in a sling sneaked along behind her and banged Martin on the back and then got out of the way as Hugon of Guaranty hastened up to rub Martin's head proudly, as any father might.

"Wonder what my kids think has become of me," Sir John Bedford said.

The Bannus had certainly spread its field wide, Mordion thought. Among the people who arrived to greet Martin and stare cautiously at the two strangers, he recognized numbers from Homeworld, as well as one of the young men from the wineshop where he had used his credit card and the butcher from Wood Street. All the firelit figures had the same look of leadership and purpose, whether they were the lady head of the House of Contract, minor members of the Houses of Accord, Cash, and Measure, or men and women who were strangers from Earth. Hugon of Guaranty—Stavely, as everyone seemed to call him—seemed to be the most powerful and leaderly person there. Or he did until Sir Artegal stood up from lighting the fire.

Sir Artegal was another stranger to Mordion. He was, like Hugon of Guaranty, a tall, well-muscled man with a look of intelligence about him and a strong, commanding feel to him that reminded Mordion of Sir John. In a way those three men were not unalike, except that Sir John was shorter and Guaranty was older and darker. By the firelight Sir Artegal's hair seemed sandy, and his face had a pleasant, open look. You might have taken him for the youngest and least intelligent of the three, unless you looked at his eyes, which were summing Mordion and Sir John up as if he could read them both like a book.

"And what have you two come to us in the night for?" Sir Artegal asked. The mere sound of his voice hushed Alisan of Guaranty, who was anxiously whispering to Martin about Vierran.

"I *told* you!" said Martin. "You heard me tell Mum. They—"

"Yes, but shut up. I want *them* to say," said Sir Artegal.

There was no doubt who was in command here, Mordion thought. As Martin stepped back grinning, Mordion rather envied him his free and easy relationship with this formidable Artegal. He could see why they got on. Both had Reigner blood. So for that matter did Sir John, which accounted for his resemblance to Hugon of Guaranty. Interesting. "I brought Sir John Bedford to join you," Mordion said, "and I think he'll want to discuss attacking the castle with you in a minute. But first, I have to tell you that we are all here in the field of a machine called the Bannus. The Bannus has cast an illusion over us, and though none of what we are doing is precisely false, most people here are not who they think they are.

The reason the Bannus does this is because its aim is to select new Reigners. Its method, as far as I can gather, is to put all its candidates into a field of play where their various Reigner powers can operate without causing severe damage." I sound like the Bannus myself! he thought.

He could see no one believed him. A young man from the House of Cash said, "New Reigners! That'll be the day!"

"You must be mad," Hugon of Guaranty said. "I know who I am. I've run a greengrocer's shop all my life until those robbers from the castle forced us into the woods."

"There's no such machine," said an Earthman with the look of a security guard about him. "Science hasn't advanced that far."

Sir Artegal, still looking keenly at Mordion, said, "No, it's the truth. I know this machine. It came and spoke to me in the form of a large golden cup some time back. It told me to go to the castle. I told it to—well, it doesn't matter, but take it from me, this man is speaking the truth as he knows it. You say this Bannus has deceived us as to who we really are," he said to Mordion. "Who am I?"

"I've no idea," Mordion was forced to say. This, not unnaturally, produced jeering laughs. "But I know you," he said to Hugon. "You are head of the House of Guaranty, and that lady is your wife. You are head of the House of Contract," he said, pointing at her, "and you are the younger nephew of the head of Cash. And you—"

"And who are *you*, thinking you know all this?" Guaranty interrupted aggressively.

Mordion wished he need not say, but he knew of nothing more likely to convince Guaranty. "I am the Reigners' Servant," he said.

Belief hit everyone from Homeworld at that—then disbelief of another kind. "Watch it! It's a Reigner plot!" someone cried out. Swords and knives flashed out into the firelight. A crossbow appeared from under someone's coat, aimed at Mordion's throat. And the outlaws from Earth, seeing that the others really meant it, drew weapons, too.

"Look here!" said Sir John, and Martin said. "This is stupid! I know he's okay."

"Shut up, son," Hugon said. "All go for him together. By all accounts this creature is very hard to kill."

"Don't try it," Mordion said to the finger tensing on the crossbow trigger. He would probably escape, but it would always be like this, he thought, looking at the hatred and hostility in all the firelit faces.

"Put those things away," Sir Artegal said quietly.

"You don't understand!" several voices from Homeworld told him. "This isn't really a man! It's the Reigners'—"

"Just do as I say," Sir Artegal said. There was real force to it.

They looked at him irritably and lowered their weapons.

"Thank you," said Sir Artegal. "Now put every weapon right away. I vouch for this man."

"But—" someone muttered.

Sir Artegal looked at Mordion. "You and I have never met, have we?"

"No," Mordion said regretfully.

"And yet I know you fairly well. Do you know me?" asked Sir Artegal.

Mordion looked at him. As far as he knew, he had never seen Sir Artegal until this moment, and yet—and yet—there was an unaccountably familiar feeling about him. Mordion felt his eyebrow climb his forehead as a possible explanation began to dawn on him. "Not—" he began.

"Voices," said Sir Artegal. "This was long ago for me, you understand, but I remember them very well. You were one of four voices I used to listen to, though you seemed to get fainter and fainter over the years. It got so that you couldn't seem to hear me, though I could hear you. It was whatever they did to your brain, wasn't it? None of us could really contact you except the Girl Child."

"You're—" Mordion began again, but Artegal held up his strong square hand into the firelight to stop him.

"You must listen to this," he said to the staring outlaws. "This man and I have known each other, at the level of souls, where one mind knows another's true nature, and I can thereby assure you that there is nothing to hate or fear in him. At that level you do not know a man's given name. I called him one thing in my mind, and he called me another. To show you this is the truth, I shall whisper to you, Alisan, what he called me and then ask him to tell you all aloud." Alisan was a good choice, Mordion thought, as Artegal called her over and whispered in her ear. She would not cheat, and she was the kind of person who was believed. "Now," Artegal said to Mordion. "Say what you called me."

"You're the King," Mordion said.

"That's what Artegal whispered," Alisan confirmed. "Hugon, you don't believe this, do you? *Hugon!*"

Hugon of Guaranty seemed thoroughly disturbed. He went roving up and down beside the fire, almost snarling to himself. Finally the snarl became a thick growl directed at Artegal. "You're tricking us! You read minds. And everyone says *he* does, too!" He jerked an angry thumb at Mordion.

"I do, to my sorrow, know what's in people's heads when I try," Artegal admitted, "but you must accept my sworn word that neither of us did try. I also whispered to Alisan what *I* called *him*. Will you tell him, or shall I?" he asked Mordion.

Mordion shrugged. "He called me the Slave," he confessed.

Hugon gave out a great, snarling roar and roved up and down again, swearing to himself. "This is terrible!" he said. "Then I think you're one of—all right, all right, I'll have to believe you! I suppose I'll have to vouch for you, too. When I think of all the things you could have put into her mind—and I know you didn't. All right!"

Sir Artegal said soberly to Mordion, "Now, what made you put your head in a noose by telling all of us here these things about the Bannus?"

"Because," Mordion answered, "I think the Bannus has more

power than it is used to from former days, and I think it is getting out of hand. I think the time has come to stop it. If enough of us know what it is and what it is doing, we ought to be able to put an end to its games. My idea was for you people to attack the castle and hunt the Bannus down there. I know it's in the castle somewhere."

"Then we plan war," said Sir Artegal, nodding to Sir John, who nodded back very grimly. "Tomorrow?" he asked Mordion. And when Mordion nodded, Artegal said, "Are you going to join this attack?"

"I'll join you at the castle," Mordion said. "I have one more thing to do first. I hope to get it over sometime during the night."

He left them all gathered round the fire, seriously, although Martin and Sir John both waved to him as he left, and Martin smiled.

He was escorted out onto the hillside by some of the outlaws. When they left him, Mordion paused to gather courage. It made sense to hunt Reigner One in dragon shape, if only because he could see and smell so much more keenly like that, but making the change did most horribly *hurt*. He took a deep breath and thrust the net of fire outward. And it hurt. But not quite so much as before. Mordion knew the pain would be with him all his life, but he began to hope that it might get bearable with usage. He spread his great black wings and took off into the cool predawn air.

He hit the scent over the thick forest and followed it this way and that for some time. To and fro, round and back, like a waiting hawk, Mordion circled. And the scent just seemed to stop in an open glade. Each time he circled, he hoped to pick it up and failed. Dawn came. Mordion watched his huge, vague shadow gliding across trees that were bronzy with dawnlight, and he watched that shadow become smaller and darker as daylight advanced, and still he kept losing the scent of Reigner One. It was almost as if Reigner One had taken wing in that open glade. He was returning to the glade for yet another cast, when Hume's voice suddenly dinned in his head, so sudden and so loud that Mordion dipped sideways and nearly stalled.

"*Mordion! MORDION! HELP—quickly! I've been so STUPID!*"

—7——————————————

THE CASTLE WAS astir before dawn. Vierran was woken in the tiny stone cubbyhole that Yam had found her by tremendous wooden batterings. When she went cautiously out onto the walls to see what it was, she found workmen busy on the walls on the other side of the gate. They were erecting a bank of wooden seats above the battlements there.

"What's this for?" she said.

"It must be so that the king may watch the dragon killed in safety," Yam told her. "Hume is going to kill it."

"*What?*" exclaimed Vierran. She bundled up her skirt and went clattering down spiral stairs into the front court. There she saw Hume in the distance, walking with long, hasty strides toward the armorer. Vierran tucked her skirt up under both arms and pelted to catch him. "*Hume! Are you mad?*"

Hume turned to wait for her. She thought she had seldom seen him looking more cheerful—or so tall. He now towered above her. If one of his eyes was not exactly smaller, then Vierran thought it seemed to crinkle more as he laughed down at her. "Of course I'm not mad," he said. "It's only Mordion out there."

"I know *that!*" said Vierran. "But you're going to—"

"Fake it," said Hume. "Don't be a donkey! I'll tip Mordion the wink as soon as I get out there. Between us we can easily make them think I've killed him."

"But *why?*" Vierran demanded.

"The king offered the hand of Lady Sylvia to the person who killed the dragon," Hume said, "and—well . . ." He trailed off and shrugged, looking much less cheerful. "It's probably the only way I have a chance with her."

"Absolutely right!" Vierran told him roundly. "Apart from the fact that you will have tricked her, which *no one* is going to like when they find out, she is nearly twenty-three, Hume! In real life she holds down a big post in a major interstellar insurance company, and she never did have any patience with lovelorn teenagers. She doesn't even live on this *planet*, Hume, and you—"

"I *know* what I am," Hume interrupted. "And I *don't care!*" He turned his back on her and set off for the armorer again.

"I hope Mordion doesn't come back!" Vierran called after him as loudly as she dared.

Hume called over his shoulder, "Then sucks to you! He *is* back!" and strode on.

Vierran might have followed him, but at that moment Morgan La Trey appeared on the steps of the hall, majestic in black and scarlet. Twenty squires followed her carrying bundles of velvet for the wooden seats, and her ladies followed the squires with armfuls of embroidered cushions. Lady Sylvia tripped along with them, dressed in a bride's fluttering white and looking quite serene at the idea of being handed over as part of a bargain.

"I don't know! Perhaps she thinks he'll lose!" Vierran muttered, backing behind a cart of spare timber. "I wonder where La Trey thinks I am. She doesn't seem to be missing me."

Morgan La Trey, as she passed, had an inward, concentrating look, as if her mind was set on something far beyond such things as missing ladies-in-waiting. When her ladies had also passed, Vierran skipped among the servitors carrying fruit and cakes and mulled wine for the party on the battlements and found herself some bread and sausage in the hall. As the king was carried through, she fled again, back up the spiral stairs to the cubbyhole on the walls. The room was in a tiny tower. From there it was only a step to the battlements and an excellent view of the empty slope of turf running down to the lake.

Vierran leaned on the battlements beside Yam, munching her sausage. "Hume said Mordion's back," she told Yam. "I don't see him."

"The dragon is walking round and round the castle," Yam said.

Vierran craned for a sight of Mordion, unavailingly, and then craned to look at the royal party, banked up above the walls in their brightly draped seats. "That's an awfully silly place to be if it was a real dragon. Don't they know dragons can fly?" She watched the servitors edging along the rows, presenting plates of fruit and pouring steaming drink into goblets. "They're behaving as if this was a concert or something!"

"The dragon is coming," said Yam.

Vierran looked straight downward and caught a glimpse of broad, scaly back slinking along below, glistening like a toad in the early sunlight. Funny! she thought. Mordion looked *black* last night! It must have been the darkness, I suppose. He looks pondweedish by daylight.

A fanfare of trumpets, loud and strident, announced the coming of Hume.

The noise irritated Orm. He spread his wings and glided downhill a short way, where he landed and turned to blare back at the things making the noise. The double din was awful. Vierran was trying to cover her ears with one hand greasy and the other full of bread when Yam's toneless voice penetrated the din. "That is not Mordion. It is a different dragon."

It was, too! Vierran realized. This dragon had a bushy eyebrow tuft over each of its round yellow eyes and further tufts above and below its mouth. These, and a somewhat rounded head and snout, gave its khaki green muzzle the illusion of being the face of a benevolent old man. A bearded old man. The bread fell out of Vierran's hand and plummeted to the turf. She felt sick. If one man could become a dragon, then so could another.

"Yam, I *swear* that's Reigner One!"

There was nothing she could do. The gates had opened during

the fanfare, and Hume was already out there. His precious sword
was in his hand. He had chosen to wear the lightest possible armor,
little of it and that little of hardened leather. It looked impressively
daring when he knew he could not be hurt. His figure looked tiny
as it appeared at the base of the castle walls.

There was a patter of applause from the draped wooden seats on
the wall. "Looks underequipped to me," Ambitas remarked between
sips of hot, spicy wine. "I hope he knows what he's doing."

While Ambitas was speaking, Hume came far enough beyond the
castle gate to see the body of Sir Harrisoun, dumped in the corner
behind the left-hand gate tower. It was probably the worst moment
of his life. He looked at the corpse, its green-white face and the
blood on its throat. He looked in astonished horror downhill at
Mordion. And he knew this dragon was not Mordion.

There was a moment when he wanted so badly to run away, back
inside the castle, that his whole body twitched that way. But it was
no good. He could hear the last of the bars clanging into their locks
behind him. That gate was well and truly shut. By the time they
got it open again, the dragon would be on him, and he would be a
pair to Sir Harrisoun. Besides, Lady Sylvia was up there, expecting
him to fight this beast. He seemed to have no choice.

Mordion created me miraculously for this, Hume told himself.
It's what I'm *for*! All the same, as he made himself move, he did
not feel particularly designed for anything—unskilled, gangling, too
young, too frightened, and, above all, most stupidly in the wrong
kind of armor. But he mustered what little courage he had left and
walked, very slowly and steadily, down toward the dragon with his
sword held out.

The dragon watched him coming with its head inquiringly bent,
as if it took a benevolent interest in this puny creature or as if it
thought the sword was a plaything. But Hume could see the great
muscles of its haunches slowly bunch and the round eyes unerringly
focus. Hume, as he walked, had time to think that perhaps he might
try to exhaust this dragon, and then to reject that idea. It was too

big and too strong. He would be exhausted himself long before the dragon was. But he might just get it to exhaust its fire. He had no idea how much fire dragons had, but they surely must run out in the end. Then he *might* dodge in underneath. Telling himself that the sword he held was a wormblade, designed, just as he was, to kill dragons, Hume kept walking.

The dragon leaped, long before he expected it to. Aided by its wings, it was suddenly above him, reaching with huge claws and six-inch teeth in its gaping mouth. Only the fact that Hume had been watching the bunching muscle alerted him in time. As the dragon moved, Hume moved—forward—and scuttled underneath it in a crouch and out. The dragon ducked its head after him, snaky swift, and spewed murderous jetting flame. Not just flame— poisonous gas, hot, oily smoke, and with those a mental surge of pure venom. Hume rolled aside, coughing, singed, greasy with the vapors of that breath, and got to his feet, dizzy more than anything with the hate that came with the flames. He ran in a circle. Get it to burn itself. Confuse itself with its own hate. He ran hard, and it pursued him, lumbering round with its wings half cocked to points, sending out gouts of its greasy fire. These mostly landed just behind Hume, but once or twice they agonizingly found his legs, right through his thick leather gaiters. With each blast came the same outsurge of utter malice, aimed personally at Hume. It was horrible, but it helped. The malice started fractionally before the fire. Hume ran his third frantic circle, waiting for the hatred, listening for the whirring gust the fire made, then leaped as he ran, and watched the fire shoot beneath him in a black, flaming swath.

Holy . . . gods . . . things . . . above . . . worshiped! he thought, punctuating each thought with a leap. This dragon hated him— *really* hated him! If he had not been so busy, he would have been appalled at being so hated. As it was, he ran in a wider circle and thanked his stars he had been idiot enough to wear such light armor.

"I see the reason for the armor now," Ambitas said, leaning forward to look.

Morgan La Trey swiftly fetched a small phial from her sleeve. While Ambitas's attention was on Hume's racing figure, she tipped the liquid in the phial into his wine. "He certainly is rather good at running away," she agreed, smoothly hiding the phial away.

"This is getting him nowhere!" Vierran whispered, clutching her face.

"The dragon has one more set of limbs," observed Yam, "and a tail in reserve."

"Oh, shut up!" said Vierran.

This is getting me nowhere! Hume thought. His circles had become wider and wider. He was now running in a curve that would have him in the lake on the next circuit. Could he get the thing to quench its fire in the water? Dared he dive in?

He never got the chance. The dragon chased him along the lakeshore, bracketing him with gusts of fire to right and left. *Hisss* went the fire on the water, and *smirrr* on the wet turf. It was playing cat and mouse. Hume knew it. His lungs sawed. His face threw off drops of sweat as he ran.

"This is the most wonderful display of cowardice I ever saw!" Morgan La Trey said, leaning forward delightedly.

"Hmm," agreed Ambitas. "But he's not *killing* it, is he?" He took an anxious sip at his wine. Funny. It did not taste quite as it had before. There was a new bitterness behind the spice. Lucky he had taken only the merest sip. La Trey was still leaning forward to see out beyond the tower, where Hume seemed to have turned and started pelting uphill. Ambitas quietly changed his goblet for hers and leaned forward to watch, too.

Hume knew he had to do *something*. There was a happy air about the dragon's hatred now, as if it were doing exactly what it had always wanted to do. He knew it would play with him until his legs buckled, and then— Don't think of *that*! Hume's life in the wood seemed to be passing in front of his hot, bursting eyes. A memory came to him, out of early days, when he was small. There had been a dragon once then. He could only hope that the same thing would work against this one. He put out a fierce effort and pounded uphill toward the castle. Got to get above it for this.

He made it, largely because the dragon paused on the lakeshore and watched him cunningly. You think you can get away? Hume could feel it thinking. You would be so lucky! Hume gained some ten feet of height above it in the meadow and squatted on the turf to get his breath, giving—he hoped!—the same cunning look back. Come and get me, dragon!

"Now he's just going to *sit* there!" said Morgan La Trey. She took a disgusted pull at her wine. Ambitas watched her with satisfaction. A nice long gulp. Good.

The dragon turned and began a leisurely walk-glide uphill toward Hume. It had him now. Instead of moving, Hume sat where he was and called insults. "Big teddy face—fatso—half-breed—stupid old Orm! Come and *eat* me, Orm! Breakfast!" He had no idea what he was saying. His only thought was that he had to get it angry enough to open its mouth. But it came on almost smiling. "Orm, Orm's a silly old worm!" Hume shouted. "You never could get me—and you never *will*!"

That did it. Orm's mouth opened in a laugh of denial. Fat lot Martellian knew! Breakfast was the word. Breakfast for a long time, in shreds.

As soon as the great mouth opened, Hume flung his sword, accurately, so that it turned over and over in the air and clanged upright between Orm's great teeth. Orm reared up howling, with his mouth fixed open. Fire gushed skyward in clouds. Orm lifted a great claw and tugged at the long cold wedge in his mouth. And came hopping onward on three legs as he tugged, glaring murder at Hume, bringing his spiked tail round in a whistling smack.

Hume stood up and fell away backward just in time. It was not over. And now he was weaponless. He stood up and fell away again, this way and that, as the great tail followed him, smacking and darting. And Orm still has his talons! He only has to hit me once! Hume thought, scrambling away on his back. The tail smacked

again, and he only just rolled in time. Oh, help! His nerve broke.
He screamed for Mordion. It was the most shaming thing, but he
couldn't think what to *do* not to be killed. "Mordion, help! Come
quickly! I've been so *stupid!*"

The shadow of great wings covered him almost at once. Hume
looked up incredulously. How? Instant translocation? Mordion was
coming down from level with the castle's highest tower, fast, with
his glittering black neck stretched.

Vierran did not see him. She was on her way down the spiral
stairs, hoarse with screaming, wrestling to get that bracelet off her
arm. Yam bounded spongily down after her, protesting. "With a
gun like that you will have to be within feet of the dragon to hit it."

"Yes, I know, but the darts are poisoned. It's worth it," she said.
"Shut up and get this postern open for me."

As the wing shadow passed over Orm, he knew the threat instantly. He lodged a claw behind the sword and wrenched. The
sword, and a tooth, flew free in a spray of gray blood and spittle and
clanged to the turf beside Hume. There was no time to get airborne.
Orm reared up high, roaring.

Mordion half folded his wings and came down in a near dive,
calculating distances and what had to be done. Yes, it would work.
If Orm breathed fire, he would roast himself as well as Mordion, so
Orm would not dare. He plunged on, straight on to Orm's raised,
blaring jaws, and locked them with his own.

Vierran burst out through the postern to the flapping struggle of
four mighty wings and trumpeting shrieks from Orm. It seemed to
her at once that Mordion had to have the worst of it. His wing
strokes were clapping like thunder, and he was being steadily pulled
down. She was not sure what good a microgun would do. She
simply ran toward the locked, flapping dragons. As she ran, Mordion
got a clawed hind foot planted behind Orm's shrieking head. Like
that, doubled up and grappled, he took off skyward.

Orm's neck snapped with a crack as precise as the neck of the
rabbit. Vierran could hear it even through the thunder of Mordion's

wings. Hume remembered that incident, too. More shamed than ever, he snatched up the sword, wondering as he did so how he could *bother* that Orm had swallowed the red stone on the hilt, and plunged the blade into Orm's underbelly as Orm's huge body toppled away backward.

Mordion drew in his fiery net and landed beside Hume, in his own shape again, shuddering with the pain.

"Your face is bleeding!" said Hume. "Mordion, I'm *sorry!*"

"It needed doing," Mordion said. "Just a minute." And vanished.

Something had happened, up there on the battlements. Mordion could feel it. It was urgent enough for him to use this new trick of instantaneous travel that he had discovered when Hume called. Using on himself the force he had used on the river and then on Martin, he supposed it to be, in the instant of transit. It was very precise. Mordion arrived in front of the two grand central seats of the wooden stand, one piled with pillows, the other draped with gold embroidered cloth.

He said, with some difficulty, because his mouth was very torn, "What have you done?"

They looked up at him sullenly. "Nothing," said Morgan La Trey. "Should I have?"

"I only wanted a bit of peace," said Ambitas. "She tried to poison *me.*"

Mordion considered them. Reigner Three's face had already elongated into a carven ivory muzzle with scarlet eyebrow spikes. Her hands were forming talons of the same scarlet. Reigner Two was more recognizable, since his snout was puffy and plump, although it was covered with pinkish yellow scales. Mordion could see them both enlarging. Having been a dragon himself, he would have liked to let them be. But Reigner Three was second only in viciousness to Reigner One. As a dragon she would be vicious indeed. Over Two, Mordion hesitated. Two was always so harmless. Yes, Mordion thought, harmless because Two just sat there, knowing exactly what the others were doing and then smugly reaping the benefit. In his harmless way Two was at least as harmful as Reigner Three. As a dragon he would arrange to sit in a cave and have people bring him juicy young women to eat.

Mordion sighed and terminated them both, there and then, and turned away as soon as he had.

Turning, his eye caught a flash of silver against the green turf below. Yam was moving smoothly and speedily along the base of the castle. Mordion did not hesitate. He translocated again.

Vierran had been running toward the dying dragon and Mordion, standing by Hume and holding his sleeve to his bleeding face. Before she had run two yards, Mordion was gone again. She had just located him by the outcry up in the wooden seats when he was not there, either.

Halfway through his translocation Mordion wondered if this might not be cheating, doing it this way. He could, quite seriously, not afford to cheat. Vierran saw him suddenly drop to the turf by the walls, only twenty feet away, and go speeding after Yam in great, sprinting strides.

I'd no idea Mordion could run like that! Vierran thought. She bundled up her tiresome skirts and pelted after the pair of them.

She was still some way off when Yam checked and swerved. Sir Artegal and Sir John were coming round the walls the other way with a posse of outlaws behind them. In order not to run full tilt into them, Yam had to surge aside and dart along in front of their surprised faces. This gave Mordion time to put on a spurt and throw himself into a dive, long and sliding, which enabled him to grab Yam by one of his flying silver ankles. Yam tipped and swayed and by a robotic miracle managed to stay upright. "Let go," he said. "You will damage my delicate interior mechanisms."

"Nonsense!" gasped Mordion, facedown on the grass, hanging on to Yam's leg with both hands. "Give in, Bannus. I've got you."

"You will damage—" Yam intoned, but broke off and said in a much less mechanical voice, "How did you guess?"

"You always knew too much," said Mordion. "But I think I really got suspicious the night Hume ran away and you said, 'The Wood has brought him back.' That struck me as a very unrobotlike thing to say."

"How foolish of me," said Yam. "I admit it. You have me. You may let go now."

"Oh, no." Mordion cautiously pulled his knees under him, still hanging on to Yam for dear life. "Not until you've sorted out this mess. *You* made it, after all."

Yam gave a resigned shrug of one silver shoulder. "Very well. But there is one more thing I wish to do first."

"Then you do it with me holding your leg," Mordion said.

Vierran reached them then. She was not sure what was going on, but the state Mordion's face was in made her clasp her bracelet back on her arm and feel for a handkerchief. She had just found it when neither Mordion nor Yam was there anymore. She looked round in pure exasperation and located them down the meadow beside the dying dragon.

"Where *next?*" she said, setting out once more in another direction.

Orm was not yet dead. Mordion knelt beside Yam with his face turned away. He did not like to think that even Reigner One should suffer in this way. The sword was still plunged into Orm's chest, and his huge head lolled, but his yellow eyes were open and aware.

"Orm Pender," Yam said in the clear, sweet voice of the Bannus, "you cheated me twice, once when you made yourself a Reigner and once when you exiled Martellian. By your cheating you gave yourself an illegal thousand years as Reigner One. It has pleased me very much to cheat you in return. I waited those thousand years, until someone with sufficient Reigner blood was near enough to restore me my full power. I knew this was a statistical probability. As soon as your seals were removed, I spread my field along every communication line and through every portal to the House of Balance, and I brought you here to die. I wish you to know that every one of my six hundred and ninety-seven plans of action was designed to end in your death. And your death now comes." Yam's rosy eyes turned toward Hume. "You may take your sword back now."

Hume put out a reluctant arm and dragged the sword out of Orm.

8

THEY WERE IN a small hollow in the wood. The ground underfoot was squashy and crackling with old leaves. A tree leaned into the hollow, one of those trees that sprout multiple trunks from a central stump. Hume leaned on a chest-high trunk, dangling his dripping sword, with his head bowed. He was still very much ashamed. Mordion crouched beside him, still holding on to Yam, and Vierran at last seemed near enough to pass Mordion her handkerchief.

"This is the best the Wood will let me do for a meeting place," Yam said. "It may become somewhat cramped, for this meeting requires no less than thirty persons of Reigner descent, and this I have been careful to provide. You may let me go now, Mordion Agenos. I am concluding my program. I promise you that this is all I shall do."

Mordion did not trust the Bannus an inch, but he slowly stood up, ready to snatch hold of Yam again if he turned out to be cheating. It was probably among the worst of Orm Pender's misdeeds, he thought, that he had taught what surely should have been a totally fair-minded machine how to cheat. But Yam stood where he was, silver ankles deep in dry leaves. Mordion turned to Vierran. She held the handkerchief out silently. Mordion took it and pressed it to his gashed face, smiling at her round it. She could see the gashes slowly starting to heal. But there was such sadness in the smile that Vierran seized his free hand in both of hers. To her great relief, Mordion's hand curled round and gripped her fingers in return.

Both of them jumped as Sir John Bedford said angrily, "What's going on *now*? We break our necks building rafts and crossing that lake, and next thing we know, we're out in this damned wood again!"

Quite a large number of outlaws were fighting their way through the hazel bushes that surrounded the hollow. The heads of at least five great Houses and numbers of their families came crunching down among the dead leaves, and with them people from Earth, sliding in the mud beneath. Siri, in her white bridal garments, was forcing her way through from another direction. Siri was clearly herself again. When some of Lady Sylvia's floating veils hooked themselves on the hazel rods, Siri gathered them all up in an impatient hand and tore them off her dress. This made Vierran look down at herself. She was in trousers again. Comfortable, thank goodness.

Here Vierran's mother and father descended on her. "Are you all right, girl?" Hugon said anxiously.

"Absolutely and perfectly," Vierran said, beaming up at him. But she saw him realize that she was only sparing one arm to hug him with, and she saw the sour look he gave her other hand, still wrapped in Mordion's. Well, he'll probably come round, she thought.

Her mother saw it, too. "I'm glad to see you yourself again," Alisan said, laughing. "It was bad enough having you as an adolescent *once*."

Since Vierran was not wholly sure that this meant her mother was on her side, she was glad of the distraction the arrival of Sir Artegal made.

Sir Artegal came ducking under the leaning trunks of the big tree and slid in the mud. He saved himself on the chest-high trunk where Hume leaned, and remained there, staring face-to-face with Hume. "I don't believe this!" Sir Artegal said. "It's never—"

Hume looked up, equally astonished. Hume was not a boy any longer or even very young. His face was weather-beaten, almost aging, with rows of lines in its thin cheeks and more lines under his smaller eye. His hair was shades lighter with all the white in it. "Arthur!" he said.

"Merlin," said Sir Artegal, sad and fond.

"Did they get you, too?" said the aging Hume. "Those damned Reigners?"

"They were always going to," Sir Artegal replied, "after you'd gone. We went against them, though, just as I promised you."

"The chronicles report that you went against the emperor of Rome," Yam put in.

"Well, the Reigners were bound to conceal the facts," Sir Artegal said philosophically. "We beat them off Earth, but they came back and—" He broke off and stared at Yam shrewdly. Then he said to Mordion, "So you found the Bannus, Slave."

This made Vierran's head jerk round to look first at Mordion, then at Artegal. Sir Artegal looked at her as she looked at him. Sir Artegal said, "You're my Girl Child!" and Vierran exclaimed, "But you're the *King*!"

Mordion had been looking at Hume, mystified and embarrassed. It was small wonder he had never been able to realify Hume if Hume had been real all along. Now he looked at Vierran again. "Girl Child?" he said. "I so nearly asked you so often if you were!"

"And everyone always forgets about *me*," said Martin. Martin was roosting in the fork of the tree, where all the trunks branched, with his arms folded, looking very comfortable. "Hallo, Slave," he said cheerfully to Mordion. "I spotted you at the castle, but you had things on your mind, so I didn't bother you then." Then he turned, even more cheerfully, to Hume. "Hallo, Prisoner—or should I say Uncle Wolf?"

Hume dropped the sword and trod on it as he whirled round. "Fitela!" he said. "Now by all that's sacred, this is truly amazing!"

Martin hopped to the ground, grinning all over his face. The place that had seemed to be a graze before was now clearly a scar. He was very short, only about Vierran's height, and slightly bow-legged. And he was older, too. He seemed to be only slightly younger than Vierran and as brown and weather-beaten as Hume. "I believe that's my wormblade you're treading on, Uncle," he said. "*And* you've lost the ruby. That's no way to treat a valuable sword."

Hume stooped hastily and picked the sword up. As he handed it to Martin, Hume's face was mahogany color with shame.

Martin brushed away dead leaves that had stuck to the sword and sighted along it. "Do I see correctly?" he said. "This is covered with dragon's blood!" He began to laugh. "Wolf! You never did!"

Hume's face went from mahogany to crimson. "Yes, I *did!*"

"You fought a dragon?" Martin laughed. "I bet you spent the whole time running away, then! You never did have a *clue* with dragons, did you?"

"Martin!" said Vierran. She still felt like Martin's elder sister. "Martin, stop baiting Hume this instant!"

Vierran's mother shook her arm. "Vierran, does this mean he isn't ours? Who *is* he?"

I had not realized, Vierran thought, looking at Alisan's distressed face, that Mother wanted a son so much. "I've always called him the Boy," she said.

"He's one of my descendants," Hume explained. "The Reigners imported dragons from Lind to Earth to kill me, many years ago now, and I bred up a race of my children to deal with them. Fitela is the greatest dragon killer of them all." Martin grinned and bowed to Alisan, very pleased with himself, but Hume's face was still beetroot-colored. "Blast you, Yam—Bannus!" he said. "You were telling me, 'This time kill your own dragons,' weren't you?"

"That is correct," said Yam. "I see I made my point. I am glad to see it. Your rehabilitation was of some concern to me. I was afraid you had damaged your personality irretrievably in the course of your struggle with the previous Reigners. Luckily, after all that time in stass, your body weight was sufficiently reduced for me to circumvent their ban—which I regret to say was imposed through me—by allowing you to believe yourself a child again. And this in turn proved very helpful to Mordion."

"And I was always child-sized," Martin remarked. "Gnomes, both of us," he said to Vierran. "By the way, Wolf, how come you've got two eyes again? Last I saw you, you'd only got the one the dragon didn't get."

"It grew back in the end," said Hume, "but it was always a bit weak."

"And—" began Martin, but he was interrupted by Sir John Bedford, who was leaning against another of the outstretched trunks of the tree and obviously running out of patience.

"If you've all quite done, will one of you tell me why we're all crowded into this mudhole like this?" A murmur from the other people there suggested that they felt the same as Sir John.

"It is quite simple," said Yam. "Four thousand years ago it was felt that the great Reigner Houses on Homeworld would destroy one another unless they were controlled by the strongest possible rulers. For this reason five of the strongest were selected and formed into a new House, which was called the House of Balance. This was because the five chosen were supposed to hold the balance among the rest. But since even then there was strife, I was constructed to make sure that the choosing and the ruling of the Reigners would be absolutely fair and absolutely immutable. The selection process— which has been delayed a thousand years through circumstances beyond my control—has taken place and is now completed. We are met here, with the legal minimum of Reigner candidates, for the Bannus to appoint the new Reigners and name their correct order. For the next ten years Reigner One shall be Mordion Agenos."

For the first time Mordion consciously experienced the strength of the Bannus. It made him know—no, believe—no, made him *be* a Reigner. It would have taken all his strength to refuse, but he would have refused—until he thought of the chaos out there in the galaxy that the absence of the Reigners would have caused. *Someone* had to deal with that. So instead he put out a great effort and said, "Not—not Reigner One. You'll have to call it First Reigner."

"Amended," Yam said, almost approvingly. "You are First Reigner, by reason of your strength of will and considerable knowledge of the House of Balance in its present form. Second Reigner, from much the same considerations, is Vierran of Guaranty."

"What?" gasped Vierran.

"You are very hard to deceive," Yam said, "and you were trained up to run a large commercial concern. Third Reigner is Martellian Pender."

"No!" said Hume, with his teeth clenched. "Not again!"

"That is precisely why you are selected," Yam told him. "You have the experience and the ability, and you are aware of the pitfalls."

"Rather too much so," Hume said ruefully.

"Fourth Reigner," Yam continued, "gave me some trouble to select, which was only solved by other considerations. He is Arthur Pendragon."

"*What!*" said Sir Artegal. "Now I told you—"

"That is why. Only potential Reigners can tell me things," Yam said. "And from your selection, it follows that Fifth Reigner must be Fitela Wolfson."

"*Why?*" said Martin. "Why me? I'm a native of Earth. I don't know the first thing about anything beyond dragons—and besides, I *hate* being responsible!"

"Then you must learn," said Yam. "You have been in communication with the other four for many years—"

"But that was long ago, before they put me in stass," Martin protested.

"This makes a special case, which overrules your incompetence," Yam told him. "Many Reigners in the past have spoken over time and space to others like themselves, but it is very rare for such a Hand to assemble together in the flesh. Past experience shows that a Hand so assembled is unusually successful." His rosy eyes swept round the small, crowded hollow. "So that is settled. You have all seen and ratified the five new Reigners. Now it only remains for us to proceed out of this Wood and to our various homes. You must take me with you to Homeworld, of course."

Hume groaned at this. "It's a man-high box," he told the others, "and it weighs like solid lead."

"No longer," Yam said smugly. "I have just finished refining and transferring all my functions to my present form. Mordion aided me, under the impression he was performing repairs."

"I am," said Mordion, "rather sick of being cheated by you, Bannus."

"You must keep more alert in future," said Yam. "A mobile form is essential to me. One of the ways in which Orm Pender cheated me was by grasping me in his arms before my programs commenced."

"And what were the other ways he used to cheat you?" Sir Artegal asked with courteous sympathy.

"Hocus-pocus," said Yam. "His mother was a witch from Lind." And his eyes swiveled to Mordion with—could it have been?—apprehension.

That is very useful to know, Mordion thought. Sir Artegal said gravely, "That was most unfair." And Mordion felt him give a swift flick at his mind, like a mental wink. Sir Artegal—Arthur—was going to be a pleasure to work with.

But Yam was saying, "We must move now, before the commercial empire of the House of Balance falls apart completely."

"No such bad thing if it did," Mordion said as they all turned to move out of the hollow in the direction Yam pointed.

"Ah, no," Vierran told him. "You can't just let a business slide into ruin."

And Sir Artegal supported her. "That would be causing hardship and ruin to many innocent people," he said.

I am getting a very good taste of the way Reigners work, Mordion thought, forcing a path for himself and Vierran through the hazel bushes. "Then it's going to have a complete overhaul," he said. "I doubt if you know how corrupt it is."

Behind him Hume waited until Siri picked her way near him in her unsuitable white slippers. "Can I give you a hand getting over this ground?" he asked her diffidently.

Siri looked searchingly at his lined face. "If you don't assume anything from it," she said. But she let him take her arm and help her up the muddy bank.

Beyond, the wood was a space of beeches with sunlight glowing through the new green of their leaves. Everyone was able to walk together in a crowd. Vierran walked quietly, listening to the growl and chime of voices, as everyone discussed the decision of the Bannus and tried to get used to it. And it took some getting used to, Vierran thought. She was going to be busy. Overhauling the Reigner Organization was a gigantic task in itself, but then there was Mordion. She looked at him striding ahead in his pale brown version of the Servant's uniform. He was hurting. He always would be. And she would have to try to help. Then there was Hume, who was touchy enough, and not the person she had thought—though she knew him very well as the Prisoner, which might help. Then there was the Bannus. She could tell it was likely to get out of hand if they were not careful. Then there was Martin. Vierran could hear him now, chatting to her parents.

"Oh, no, I *like* these times. There's so much going on. I can't wait to find out more. But"—wistfully—"I shall miss being part of a family. I never did have a family, you know. I was pushed off to fight dragons as soon as I was strong enough."

And darned exciting that was, Vierran knew. But her mother said sympathetically, "You can always consider the House of Guaranty as your family, Martin." And she heard her father giving agreeing sort of growls. Martin was shameless. But it might not be a bad thing for Martin if her parents adopted him. It would save Vierran having to devote half her time to keeping him in line.

But the hardest thing to get used to, she knew, was not having these people talking in her mind anymore. She would be working with them instead, and they would be there every day, but it was not quite the same. Here she looked round to see Yam plodding spongily beside her.

"Why did you always stop my voices when I got into the wood?" she asked.

"That was not me," Yam replied. "That is the Wood. You were speaking to your Hand through space-time, and the Wood, when it forms its theta-space, is timeless. Normal communication is blocked."

Ahead of them Mordion strode across the small muddy stream he remembered and found himself in the sparse trees at the edge of the wood. Here was real life again. But it did no good to run away. He strode with long steps up the passage between the houses and out into Wood Street. Wood Street had a sad, derelict look. The shops were all boarded up, and the road was littered with nails, glass, blowing paper, and leaves from the wood. The surprisingly long line of cars down the near side looked as if every vehicle had stood in all weathers for at least a year.

But normality seemed to be back. Mordion found himself wearing the uncomfortable Earth clothes again, including the short camel coat Vierran had dared him to wear, and when he put his hand to his face, it was not so much bearded as bristly. The gashes Orm had made were healed. He found that, as always, he missed the rolled cloak on the shoulder of the Servant's uniform, so he corrected the clothes back to the ones he had worn in the wood, right down to the grass stains on the front from where he had dived after Yam. But his face— He turned to ask Vierran if she thought a beard suited him.

He was entirely alone.

After a moment, when he stood stunned and lonely, Mordion realized what had happened. It made him smile. The Wood had not finished with them yet. It had let him out. It had given him special treatment, as it always did, even to bringing Hume back when there had been no real need for it, because the Wood knew Mordion wanted this, and it had done it hoping he would understand. Mordion thought he did, but it remained to see.

He went back down the passage between the houses again, with even longer, faster strides, and into the sparse wood. The moment he jumped the little stream, he was in the beech wood again, with green sunlight overhead and pewter-colored trunks in all directions, like pillars in a vast hall. The others were standing in a perplexed crowd a little way off, dull-colored except for the white of Siri at the edge beside Hume and except for the frantic silver figure of Yam.

Yam was running round and round in little circles. "The Wood has taken us prisoner. The Wood will not let us go!" Mordion heard him cry out. "We shall be here forever!"

Mordion was very tempted just to fold his arms and watch the delicious sight of a Bannus that had met its match running round and round on the spot. He let Yam make another circuit and then strolled toward him.

"Oh, there you are!" Vierran said, dashing up to him. "Is this true what Yam's saying?"

"Quite true," Mordion said. Everyone turned anxiously toward him, except for Yam. Yam continued to run round in little circles, crying out. Mordion said, "The Wood has cooperated with the Bannus because it needs something for itself. Now we have to give the Wood what it wants, and it will let us go. I *think* I know what that is. Yam, shut up and stand still and tell me this." Yam surged to a halt in a pile of sherry-colored dead leaves and turned anxious pink eyes on Mordion. "You told me the Wood can form its own theta-space and become the great Forest," Mordion said to him. "Does the Wood only do this when a human being enters it?"

"I had not thought of this," said Yam. "Yes, I believe that when not reinforced by my field, the Wood requires human assistance to change."

"And not all humans will help," Mordion said. "I think what the Wood is trying to tell me is that it requires its own theta-space permanently, so that it can be the great Forest all the time, without having to rely on humans."

"But that cannot be done!" Yam cried out.

"I can do it," said Mordion. "But I shall need help from the Earth people here. And you, too, Hume. You're good with the Wood, too."

He was a little nervous at asking this strange new Hume to help, but Hume came over to him quite willingly. He seemed nervous, too. "I'm horribly out of practice still," he said. "You'll have to take the lead."

"Fair enough." Mordion singled out the twelve or so outlaws from Earth and asked the Homeworld people to stand back. Vierran made a face at him, but she understood, to Mordion's relief. The Earth people came to stand round him willingly enough, but they were nervous, too.

"What exactly needs doing?" Sir John asked.

"The Wood let me experiment," Mordion explained, "with taking a piece of a theta-field and moving it about. It even let me destroy the bed of a river that way. So I think something on those lines is what it needs." The sunny beech leaves overhead rustled excitedly as he spoke. Mordion said confidently, "Hume and I will take this theta-space and spread it as wide as we can and then try to harden it to make it permanent. The rest of you must think with us. First think large, and then, when I nod, think diamond hard. Can you do that?"

They nodded, but they looked doubtful until the young man from the wineshop said, "I get you. Like blowing glass. Is that what you mean?"

"Just exactly!" said Hume. "Ready, Mordion?"

They tried it. It took huge force, so huge that Mordion, who had not meant to be theatrical, found he had to raise his arms to increase the power. Before long the others had their arms raised, too. And all the while the trees around stood as still as if they were a painting. They pushed. And when it seemed impossible, they felt the theta-space give and start spreading, like a balloon being blown up. Then it was only a question of spreading and spreading it, steadily and carefully, until it was as wide as they could get it. Mordion nodded then, and everyone at once thought hardness. Martin was best here. He thought hard steel and frozen snow, adamantine dragon scales, and solid oak. It was so much the right way to think that everyone else found they were following Martin's lead, until they had made a hardness no one had believed possible.

"Right," Hume said at last. "That's the best we can do."

They all took their arms down, feeling unexpectedly tired. The Wood stirred around them and stirred again, until the tops of the trees were making a sound like the deep sea.

"I think we got it right," Mordion said to Hume.

"Permanent hocus-pocus," Yam said sourly. "Anyone entering this Wood from now on is liable to be a long time coming out."

"That won't kill them," said Vierran. She thought about this. "Necessarily," she added.

As they walked in the direction of Wood Street, there were ample signs that they had got the Wood's need right. Nightingales burst into song around them. A herd of deer went in a swift line across their path, and a small wild boar crashed out from a hawthorn beside them and fled into the distance. In that distance a man in green flitted, armed with a long bow. Hume flinched from the great, snaky, glinting coils of a dragon far down an open ride and then flinched again as a row of twiggy figures with wreathed ivy heads went stalking after the dragon. Other people were turning their heads, convinced that they had seen a small man with furry legs dart on little hooves behind the nearest tree, or strange dun-colored women shapes dancing at the corners of their vision. Once Vierran pulled Mordion's arm and pointed. He was just in time to see a small white horse, luminous in the green, with a single horn in its forehead, dash across a far-off glade. And all the time, the branches above gave off a deep, happy surging, like the sea on a good day for sailing.

Before long they were crossing the stream and walking up the passage between the houses.

"Quite a comedown," Hugon said regretfully as they came to Wood Street.

It was very busy there. People were taking down the boards nailed over shopwindows. As the young man from the wineshop raced across the road to help his friend, Vierran noticed that a set of total strangers were at work on Stavely Greengrocer—or not quite strangers. She thought they might have been working in the castle kitchens. All round them and up and down the road, starters were whirring and doors were banging in the neglected cars. Sir John Bedford raced to his own car as soon as they came level with it. The people from Homeworld stood in an uncertain huddle nearby, a very curious, motley crowd, since some of them were in the finery of a great House, others were in camouflage jackets, Siri was in white, and Hume beside her in a threadbare blue tracksuit.

Beyond them the gates of Hexwood Farm swung open, and a white van, covered with twigs and bird droppings, backed slowly out. It was followed by Controller Borasus in a tattered green gown, waving and imploring the Maintenance men for a lift. Madden, who was driving, simply grinned and went on backing the van.

Sir John opened the door of his car. "I've just been through to Runcorn on the phone," he called. "They're going to open a portal there and warn the sectors you're all on your way. You five Reigners hop in, and the robot, too, and I'll drive you there. The rest of you are traveling with the Security team in those other cars. They've been told." Here the baying of Controller Borasus caught his attention. Madden, grinning more broadly than ever, was turning the van to drive away. "Give him a lift, you fools!" Sir John bellowed at the van. "That man's your Sector Controller!"

"When Sir John has finished tidying up Earth," Mordion said to his fellow Reigners, "we'd better make him Controller of Albion."

They looked at Controller Borasus being hauled into the van and agreed unanimously.

—AUTHOR'S NOTE——

Everyone knows who King Arthur was, and that Merlin was the magician who disguised Arthur's father as the Duke of Tintagel and sneaked him in to Arthur's mother, the Duchess of Tintagel. No one says who the Duchess's father was, but she plainly carried remarkable genes: All Arthur's half-sisters were powerful witches. These ladies and Arthur were, of course, part of Martellian's second breeding program, for which he took the guise of Merlin, and this may still be going on today, for Arthur in fact had several sons who do not figure in the best-known stories about him. Martellian's first breeding program was earlier, when he was roaming Northern Europe and calling himself Wolf. In this disguise he was later confused with the god Wotan. As Wolf, he bred a whole race of heroes, the most famous of whom nowadays is Siegfried—but this was not always so. The Anglo-Saxon poem *Beowulf* makes it plain that, in earlier days, the best of Wolf's descendants was a young man called Fitela. Fitela was better at killing dragons than any man alive, but he disappeared from song and story before Siegfried became famous. Fitela, of course, vanished when Reigner One caught him and put him in a stass tomb.

D0010484

The KGB Campaign
against Corruption in Moscow

**Pitt Series in Russian
and East European Studies**

Jonathan Harris, EDITOR

The

KGB

Campaign against Corruption in Moscow

Luc Duhamel

University of Pittsburgh Press

Published by the University of Pittsburgh Press,
Pittsburgh, Pa., 15260

Library of Congress Cataloging-in-Publication Data

Duhamel, Luc.
    The KGB campaign against corruption in Moscow / Luc Duhamel.
        p. cm. — (Pitt series in Russian and East European studies)
    Includes bibliographical references and index.
    ISBN 978-0-8229-6108-6 (pbk. : alk. paper)
    1. Trade associations—Corrupt practices—Russia (Federation) —Moscow—
History—20th century. 2. Corruption—Russia (Federation)—Moscow—
History—20th century. 3. Political corruption—Russia (Federation)—
Moscow—History—20th century. 4. Soviet Union. Komitet gosudarstvennoi
bezopasnosti—History. 5. Moscow (Russia) —Commerce—History—20th
century. 6. Moscow (Russia) —Politics and government—20th century.
7. Soviet Union—Commerce—History. 8. Soviet Union—Politics and
government—1953–1985. 9. Soviet Union—Politics and government—1985–
1991. I. Title.
    HF3630.2.Z9M64 2010
    364.1'32309473109048—dc22   2010009237

Contents

Acknowledgments

I would like to thank Darcy Dunton and Josie Panzuto, who worked on revising the manuscript and translating some sections of the book. I would like to express my gratitude to Ian Gow, Antonino Geraci, and Iuri Klimov, who devoted their invaluable time and energy to reviewing this manuscript and making judicious comments and suggestions. In the discussions I had with them, I truly appreciated their feedback, which definitely contributed toward improving the manuscript. V. Scherrer and E. Piskunova have been exemplary research assistants, selecting the most pertinent data for my research. They provided me with excellent support in translating Russian documents that were not always easy to understand. I would also like to express my thanks to the following people: to D. Atanasov, for his transliteration of Russian terms and his contribution to the preparation of the bibliography; and to Caroline Le Blanc, who skillfully handled the word processing and also contributed to revising the manuscript.

I am also grateful to the Université de Montréal for having provided me with financial assistance so that I could conduct my research on corruption in Soviet Moscow in the 1980s. In addition, mention must be made of the fact that the university's Department of Political Science allowed me to devote considerable time to writing this book. Lastly, I wish to express my thanks to my colleagues at Moscow State University and several prosecutors working in Russian law enforcement agencies, all of whom made it possible for me to have access to substantial, original data and documents about the campaign against corruption in the 1980s.

Introduction

■ By investigating the corruption permeating the internal trade organizations of the Soviet Union—and, more precisely, the Moscow trade network—we can learn a great deal about the Soviet system under the leadership of Leonid Brezhnev from the 1960s until 1982. The rise of the trade organizations' power and political influence reflected in many ways the overall evolution of the Soviet system during the Brezhnev era, and the public exposure of this web of elite privilege and influence would only add to the already developing momentum for change in the Soviet Union. Ironically, it was the sworn protector of the security of the Soviet state, the KGB, that, in the course of its battle to unveil the endemic bribery, unfair practices, and influential favoritism in these trade organs, ultimately undermined its fundamental structure.

This work focuses on the two most important Moscow trade organizations: Glavtorg (Moscow Trade Administration) and Glavka or Glavmosplodovoshprom (Administration of the Moscow Fruit and Vegetable Offices). Despite having constituted an influential social force during the 1970s and 1980s, Soviet trade organizations have been the subject of very few studies in the West. This work addresses that gap.

The study of political economy involves analyzing social groups, the nature of relations among them, and the distribution of resources among them. To examine how social groups in Soviet Russia were favored in the allocation of resources, it is first necessary to draw a distinction between what socialist ideology proclaimed and Soviet law allowed versus the reality of how resources were allocated. I have thus focused on how goods were actually allocated and have made the assumption that corruption largely dictated the allocation process in a system that ultimately favored certain groups over others. This view relates to concepts of economic and political power, in particular, the relationship between economic and political resources. It is logical to conclude that the groups economically profiting from the distribution of goods also had certain political advantages.

The official task of the Moscow trade organization executives was to distribute consumer goods according to government directives, but those executives used a considerable quantity of the merchandise for personal gain. They

acquired power and influence by selling scarce goods at high prices. Although their activities were illegal, they were also tolerated, thus allowing these trade organizations to obtain not only wealth but also power thanks to an entrenched system of corruption. The exchange of resources for support and protection from officials in the higher echelons of the government and Communist Party became systematic.

The Moscow trade organizations became so powerful in the 1970s that they were able to evade Kremlin control. However, it should be noted that not all of the trade executives benefited equally from corruption. Some trade officials benefited more and others less, while some even found the arrangement to be to their detriment. Obviously, certain groups of executives were in a better position to take advantage of resources under their control, depending on the products and the time period. Another factor that came into play was the personal attributes of the individual executives involved.

This book is also a study of the KGB in its attempt to fight corruption in the Moscow trade network. Having access to primary sources held by law enforcement agencies provided me with the opportunity to study the KGB from the inside and to uncover new information about its methods and personnel during the leadership of Andropov, who succeeded Brezhnev. The widespread influence of the Moscow trade network was well established by the 1980s, but the KGB was the only organization that the Moscow trade leaders were not able to buy off. In part, this gap in the systematic corruption occurred because the KGB had also expanded its influence during the 1970s. Soon, these two rising and powerful institutions collided.

The trade network acquired its political strength largely through corruption. Trade executives used calculated defenses in their battle with the KGB, employing the capital they had accumulated to buy not only protection and supplies but also to pay large bribes to have laws passed or altered in accordance with their interests. They also distributed funds to friends and relatives who held important positions and could lobby in their favor. Utilizing these economic and political resources, the trade organizations managed to seriously undermine the KGB and the Soviet system during the years of *perestroika*. As a result, the trade organizations—a conservative force in the Brezhnev era—became a force for change in 1985, lending crucial support to perestroika, but only after Kremlin leaders had turned against them. The three-part theoretical framework used for analytical purposes here is familiar to political scientists. The first part of the framework involves Max Weber's familiar three types of authority. The first of these, the rational-legal type, assumes the supremacy of the law. Representatives of this kind of authority are subject to the law and employ functions that are specified and

restricted by the law. Such representatives include bureaucrats whose activities are dictated by rules that are inspired by universal norms such as rationality and justice. Certain conventions must be in place and accepted in order to guarantee that bureaucrats behave according to these norms. For example, the law must ensure the independence of bureaucrats from politicians and protect bureaucrats from intimidation. Also, while bureaucrats may apply the law, their authority is accepted only as long as they act within the limits of their competence. Further, appointment and promotion in the bureaucracy are decided according to merit and performance. Finally, governing bodies must be in place to ensure bureaucrats' respect for the law and to penalize those who diverge from it.

Weber's second type of authority, charismatic leadership, relies on the exceptional qualities of a leader. People admire charismatic leaders, supporting them and believing that they can significantly improve prevailing circumstances. According to Weber, charisma refers to God-given attributes. Today, neo-Weberians define charisma as heightened political skills, and thus the success of charismatic leaders depends primarily on their political skills and their ability to implement policies that will maintain their popularity. Charismatic leaders know how to persuade and influence their constituents, who in turn view such individuals as the best possible leaders for their society. Finally, while the actions of charismatic leaders are not limited by the rule of law, such leaders are not perceived as taking advantage of the laws for personal benefit.

Weber's third type of authority, patrimonialism (or traditionalism), was the predominant type among the leaders of the internal trade organizations during the Brezhnev era. With this type, the authority of a leader derives from custom, that is, the long-term use of certain practices. In a system of patrimonialism, personal interests determine how a leader will operate. Typically, leaders exhibiting patrimonialsim in a bureaucracy face no legal requirements about how staff members are appointed or promoted, so family or friends become the primary source of staff members. Recruitment does not depend upon merit or performance but is the exclusive prerogative of the leader. Weber identifies sultanism as one form of patrimonialism. It differs from other forms of patrimonialism by the relatively minor role played by nepotism. With sultanism, leaders rely on a group controlled mainly through clientelism. Leaders grant certain advantages to their supporters, who, in return, serve their "sultans" unconditionally.

Weber points out that the three types of authority are abstract notions and that, in reality, we find only mixed categories. This has led neo-Weberians to elaborate the concept of neopatrimonialism, an attempt to update Weber's theory. This concept combines the notion of traditional authority with that of rational-legal authority. It applies to contemporary societies that are dominated by

the characteristics of traditional authority but where practices of rational-legal authority are also present. In this book, the concept of neopatrimonialism is used rather than that of patrimonialism, because the former corresponds more closely to the traditional authority that prevailed in Soviet society.

Among scholars who generally accept Weber's types of authority, the majority of them have focused on patrimonialism. This is not surprising, considering that this type of leader is very prevalent today. (Charismatic leadership, on the other hand, has not drawn much attention in studies of mixed authority types.) I use Weber's types to distinguish different types of leaders in the Moscow trade network even though the patrimonial type was largely dominant.

The trade leaders had various criteria for nominating rational-legal, patrimonial, or charismatic executives. In a given circumstance, they might utilize one type of leader, while another situation might lead them to promote a completely dissimilar executive. The hiring of store managers was also greatly influenced by store type and location (e.g., large grocery store or small shop and downtown versus outlying location). The KGB was cognizant of these types of leadership within the trade network, and their attitude toward them changed with the circumstances (e.g., the security force might shift its focus from apprehending one type of leader to another type).

Another aspect of the theoretical framework for this work is the notion of public choice, which postulates that citizens in society tend to act rationally, although some may behave irrationally. Citizens who behave rationally must, by definition, be motivated by personal interest. While personal interest primarily involves material considerations, there are two other aspects that, while less pertinent, are still significant: thirst for power and desire for prestige. Leaders seek, above all else, to improve their material well-being but also enjoy having authority and dominating others. Leaders also enjoy prestige and the deference that others will show toward them. The public choice approach emphasizes that rational-legal behavior by leaders is based on self-interest, even when they adopt policies that do not appear to be motivated by personal/material interests. Egotistical motives are present within any society or political system, but in a system of rational-legal authority, self-interest is attenuated and limited. In a state defined by the rule of law, the leader will avoid breaking the law due to the high risk of being caught and exposed. Neopatrimonial leaders are heavily involved in corruption when their power is not limited by the law; in other circumstances, however, they will elect to make less of a profit if doing so consolidates their authority. Neopatrimonial leaders would even combat corruption—the personal advancement of colleagues, for example—if doing so could potentially strengthen their political position. The rational-legal leader may make decisions that appear irrational in

the short term but are rational in the long term.

Using the concept of public choice to analyze the leaders of the Moscow trade network also shifts the research focus to the individual instead of the organization. This analytical shift in perspective stems from the understanding that institutions are weaker and less important than their personnel. Public choice theory, with its emphasis on self-interest, is applicable to the situation of individuals in the Soviet Union, who could not appeal to organizations to defend their interests. Use of the public choice approach, with its focus on actors rather than institutions, was rare in Soviet studies of the past due to a lack of information on the middle and lower echelons of Russian society. I have been able to apply this approach here only because of my access to detailed material on the staff and their activities within the organizations that were responsible for food distribution in Moscow.

Public choice holds that the nature of institutions is largely determined by their leaders, since staff loyalty tends to go to the bosses instead of the legal entity. The law specifies the functions of institutions that, in reality, are subordinated to bureaucrats' decisions. A bureaucrat's influence within an organization depends widely on relations with his or her superiors. In the Soviet Union, authority was largely built and maintained by the force of the leaders' personalities—a tendency that was reflected at all levels of Soviet society, from Brezhnev at the Kremlin to communal farm managers.

To bureaucrats, rationality consists of making decisions according to their personal interests, in all situations. Thus, the trade executives adopted a form of traditional domination in the Brezhnev era because it reinforced their positions. This changed with the KGB crackdown in 1982–1985, which ultimately led executives to believe that rational-legal domination better served their interests.

The third aspect of the theoretical framework here—the social capital approach—stresses the importance of social relations to the citizen. In this study, the existence of social capital indicates that the human being is not merely egotistical and is not merely seeking material advantages. It uncovers the fact that individuals may indeed consider mostly their own needs and priorities but, at the same time, remain sensitive to the fate and circumstances of others. The social capital approach attests to the fact that the individual enjoys living with others and is aware that cooperation benefits everyone. This social side of the individual comes from the knowledge that, in certain situations, people can attain important objectives or solve major problems only with the help of other people.

Social capital can be divided into the categories of premodern and modern. Modern social capital consists of formal relations based on trust and collaboration between members of nongovernmental organizations. The modern category

also includes a high degree of trust and cooperation between individuals and the state. Premodern social capital consists of informal relations limited to the promotion of trust and assistance among individuals. One important issue in political science involves the impact of premodern social capital on the outlook of an authoritarian state like Russia. Analysis of this impact raises the issue of how social capital affects political institutions and the intensity of those effects; analysis thus involves measuring the relative strength of the social capital. In this work, it is assumed that premodern social capital contributed significantly to the creation of personal networks, which were a key factor in the growing influence of the Moscow trade organizations. Social capital, in reinforcing the trust and cooperation among trade executives, increased society's support for them. Executives could opt to build upon premodern social capital to the detriment of the modern version, or vice versa, according to time and place. One objective of this book is to show which kind of social capital was promoted by the trade leaders and when and why one type was preferred over another.

My access to the documents and data gathered by the KGB and the Prosecutor General's Office (PGO) during the anticorruption campaign against the Moscow trade network between 1982 and 1986 provided much information on the trade organizations' corrupt activities. This documentation shows the trade organizations in a new light and has allowed me to present a picture of the way the trade executives developed into and functioned like a caste, acquiring almost complete autonomy in the establishment of the norms and regulations within their organizations. These primary sources revealed how trade organization executives made decisions regarding the hiring, promotion, and firing of their staffs and how they were able to obtain for themselves many valuable goods and services—apartments, imported commodities, travel visas, and so forth—from outside organizations. These sources also provided detailed information about who was who within the trade network and about the enormous diversity among the network's members: Russians and members of ethnic groups from the Caucasus region, honest citizens and criminals, the clever and the naïve—groups that were often in competition but, in the long run, complemented each other.

A few caveats about the text and documentation are in order. Because the full names of many of the individuals involved in the trade networks and court cases were unavailable, I have opted for consistency, and thus, with the occasional exception, I refer to individuals by last name only.

Due to the nature of the primary source materials consulted for this study, citations to various documents may not contain all of the detail one might traditionally expect to find there. This is especially true of citations to documents from the law enforcement agencies. Some of these documents are identified by author, title, place, and year; most such documents (e.g., the PGO reports) have

fewer than ten pages. Many citations to these documents do not include page numbers; the original documents were sometimes unpaginated or carried multiple page numbers on a single page.

Citations of testimony from interrogations or confrontations that were videotaped at KGB or PGO headquarters usually mention the date, month, and year the relevant videotape was produced. The citation descriptions of this type of testimony are written in English because these videotaped sources did not have documented titles.

List of Acronyms and Terms

AFPTO: Administration of the Food Product Trade Organizations (Moscow branch)

AGTO: Administration of Grocery Trade Organizations (Moscow branch)

Cheka: All-Russian Extraordinary Commission for Combating Counterrevolution and Sabotage

FSB: Federal Security Service (replaced the KGB)

Galantorg: Central Administration for the Distribution and Retailing of Clothing

GARF: State Archive of the Russian Federation

Gastronom: Grocery store (retail)

Glavka (Glavmosplodovoshprom):
Moscow Administration of Fruit and Vegetable Offices

Glavobshchepitanie:
Central Administration for Public Catering

Glavtorg: Chief administration of trade

Gosplan: Soviet government committee that produced the nation's near-term economic plan

GPU: State Political Administration

GRU: Main Intelligence Directorate

KGB: Committee of State Security

Kontora: Borough fruit and vegetable office

Mosovotshch:
Moscow fresh produce shop

MVD: Ministry of the Interior

NKVD: People's Commissariat for Internal Affairs

Nomenklatura:
Descriptive term for a category of persons in positions of authority

OBKhSS: MVD Department for Combating Speculation and the Embezzlement of Socialist Property

ORPO: Vegetable Wholesale Trade Office

PGO: Prosecutor General's Office (or, in Russian, Prokuratura, RSFSR)

RPT (Raipishetorg):
> District Food Trade Organization

RSFSR: Russian Soviet Federative Socialist Republic

Soyuz plodoimporta:
> All-Union Office for Importation of Fruits and Vegetables

Tsum: Main Store

Univermag: Store selling a variety of goods, including food items

Universam: Store selling only food items

**The KGB Campaign
against Corruption in Moscow**

1

A Force That Eluded Control
The Rise of the Moscow Trade Organizations

■ In the Soviet Union, from the era of Lenin to that of Chernenko, the Communist Party never lost its power to another political force. Nevertheless, its authority was challenged, and some specialists argue that it occasionally lost its grip on Russian society. To support their argument, scholars have pointed to the 1930s and to the period from 1947 to 1953, when the KGB, by creating a climate of terror, accumulated so much power in the Soviet system that it even supplanted the Party. In his memoirs, Khrushchev affirms the validity of this argument.[1]

Other authors assert that the Communist Party lost its power in certain southern republics during the Brezhnev period.[2] Threats to the Party differed in nature depending on the circumstance; for example, during the Soviet military intervention in Afghanistan in the late 1970s and the early 1980s, the army and military-industrial complex undermined the Party's domination.[3]

Due to the pervasiveness of corruption in the 1970s, Soviet trade organizations, which were responsible for the internal distribution of goods, acquired increasing influence, particularly in Moscow. This growth in their influence became a primary concern at the Kremlin, with Gorbachev declaring at the Twenty-fifth Congress of the Communist Party of the Soviet Union that the Soviet system was being seriously challenged in some regions of the country.[4] Gorbachev's concern about the situation had much to do with the fact that Andropov had succeeded Brezhnev as leader in 1982, and Andropov and his protégé, Gorbachev, progressed to the top of the Party hierarchy as champions of law and order. As head of the KGB during the Brezhnev era, Andropov had collected a large amount of evidence pointing to low moral standards among the *nomenklatura.*

1

This study of the Soviet internal trade bureaucracy from the Brezhnev era to perestroika focuses on the Moscow trade network's status and influence. Two key organizations in this bureaucracy were the Moscow branch of Glavtorg (the Moscow Trade Association, which was the central administration for the distribution and retailing of consumer goods) and Glavka (Administration of the Moscow Fruit and Vegetable Offices, or *kontoras*) (see fig. 1.1). Whereas Glavtorg attained the status of a ministry in the Russian Republic, Glavka was not directly involved in commerce because its function was to warehouse and distribute fruits and vegetables to grocery stores. The essential characteristic of these two organizations was that they had been created by the Soviet system under Stalin, meaning that their objectives were determined by the Communist Party and that retail stores belonged to the state. Prices were also state controlled and kept low so that goods would be accessible to all. Centralized decision making in the internal trade organizations was supposed to guarantee adequate supply and fair distribution to the population, but corruption and shortages became widespread. Stalin reacted by initiating campaigns of repression.

The Gosplan, a government committee that produced the nation's near-term economic plan, officially orchestrated distribution, but in reality, it was bribery

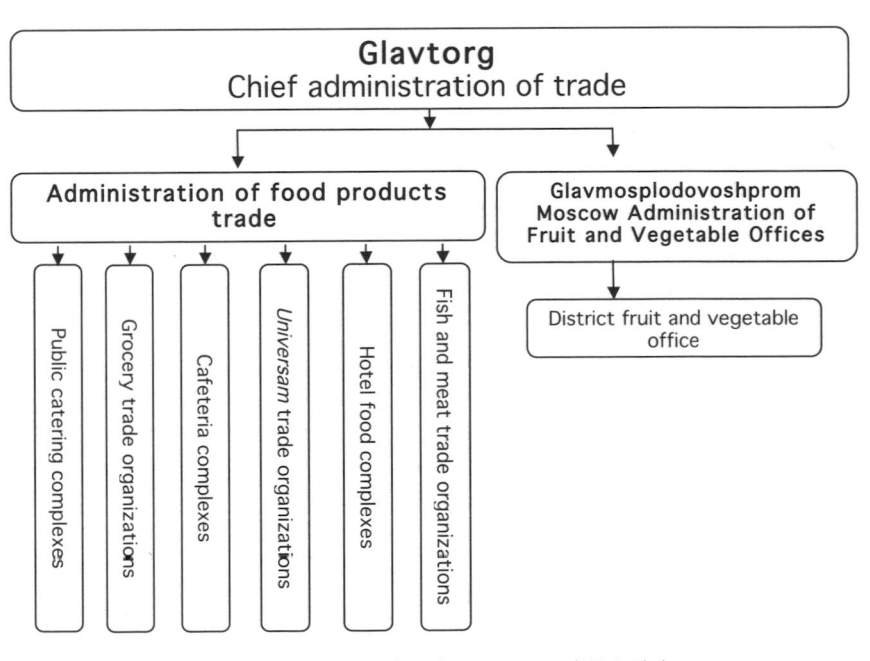

Figure 1.1. Structure of the Moscow Trade Administration (TORG) (5,000 stores– 300,000 employees)

that largely determined the allocation of goods. Employees in the goods distribution organizations were thus engaged in unofficial trade, like their colleagues in Glavtorg. Both Glavtorg and Glavka built up unofficial networks that clandestinely provided them with considerable resources. The power of the Glavtorg and Glavka leaders derived from the fact that they could allocate the goods as they liked. The focus here is on one category of resources in the goods distribution system—food—which the executives of Glavtorg and Glavka were able to transform into political power mainly through personal networks that allowed them to amass considerable sums of money.

Politics can be defined as the battle for the distribution of resources among groups, organizations, or individuals. The more resources a group, an organization, or an individual acquires, the more influential it becomes in the political system. Dennis Mueller proposes that there are three conditions that aid in the acquisition of bureaucratic power: the monopolistic situation that the bureaucrat oversees, the bargaining position the bureaucrat occupies vis-à-vis the organizations that supply necessary resources, and the absence of monitoring, which allows them to conceal both the organizational budget and the expenses incurred.[5]

Executives in the Soviet trade network had access to large amounts of money and resources. Individuals in a society, including bureaucrats who seek material advantages, act out of self-interest to different degrees.[6] This was true of the Soviet internal trade staff, who were typical bureaucrats, that is, always looking for extra revenue despite the risk of punishment. However, another motive played a significant, even predominant role for a sizeable number of executives: they sought positions that conferred power and prestige. This ambition was particularly apparent with older-generation trade managers, because it was less risky than committing economic crimes and because this group was satisfied with a modest standard of living.

The Rules of the Moscow Soviet Trade Network

This description of the irregularities in the trade organizations is not meant to suggest that such abuses were considered minor infractions of Soviet criminal law. Lenin viewed corruption as a highly reprehensible activity that had to be combated with vigor and even given priority over other wrongdoings. He considered bribery and speculation to be major offenses that deserved harsh punishment. Lenin had been very critical of bribery: "If there is such a phenomenon as bribery [i.e., the payment of bribes], it means that there is no point in having political discussions. If bribes are being given, it is pointless even to have political views, and if we have no views, we cannot undertake political activity. The

existence of bribes makes political activity become pointless because all political measures enacted remain in suspended animation. Such measures would produce no results."[7]

Although Lenin set up the theoretical basis of socialism, it was Stalin who instituted the rules and built the structures of Soviet trade. The specific norms he established were modern in that they were universal in character. Moreover, the law defined the functions of bureaucrats in Soviet trade. As Ken Jowitt notes, Stalin lent legitimacy to impersonal laws that applied to all bureaucrats no matter who they were.[8] Transgressions were dealt with severely, so bureaucrats largely observed the rules. On some levels, this aspect of law abidance can be associated with Weber's legal authority type, but in other respects this was not the case. Weberian legal authority implies modernism, that is, the most developed economic and political system: capitalism and the rule of law. On this last point, of course, Stalin and Weber had opposing points of view.

Thus, rules backed by law defined the rights and obligations of every bureaucrat in the Soviet trade organizations.[9] These rules encompassed such matters as salary, hiring, job definition, and customer relations. At the highest levels, Glavtorg leaders were expected to hire employees who fit the attributes of the model executive. Initially, the expectations of the organization were that it would ensure adequate quantities of food for Muscovites so that they would not have to form queues in front of stores. Model managers would first ensure that the neediest citizens received priority care and would also surround themselves with clerks who served customers with sensitivity and care. Executives had to show their competence by successfully executing food distribution plans, and inspectors from the control agencies would thoroughly evaluate the managers. Raids and unexpected visits were a means by which inspectors determined if the assortment of products was adequate, if the employees sold the products at the official price, whether a store was clean, and so forth. If store directors passed such tests, it meant they were working in accordance with Soviet rules. A bureaucrat who broke the law was likely to receive harsh punishment.

At least some trade organization staff members adhered to these rules during the Stalin era because they had no choice. Besides, these Soviet norms seemed reasonable to large sectors of the population due to intensive propaganda. Many executives were patient with the new system and accepted that it needed time to work properly. While many economic crimes continued to take place in trade organizations, harsh repression by law enforcement agencies targeted the violators.

Khrushchev is known as the instigator of de-Stalinization. He denounced Stalin for the reign of terror he had imposed on the country from 1930 to 1953,

but he never directly attacked his predecessor's policy in internal trade matters. Officially, he introduced no major changes to the rules and made no major staff changes at the trade organizations. Still, under his leadership there did emerge certain modifications regarding the management of goods distribution, but they were not immediately apparent and had only an indirect effect on management. After all, Khrushchev represented members of the nomenklatura, including the trade executives. He promoted their interests, allowing them a certain amount of autonomy, and did not directly criticize law enforcement agencies, although he referred in his speeches to abuses committed by the KGB in the 1930s. On the other hand, he demanded that the nomenklatura be more efficient. Unlike Stalin, he did not expect trade leaders, first and foremost, to find and repress "enemies of the people"; rather, he emphasized economic skill and success. This emphasis did not take the form of an official mandate but a tacit pact, one stipulating that, in return for the nomenklatura's strong commitment to improving the standard of living, the Kremlin would allow it almost free rein in the means used to reach that goal. It took years for trade leaders to realize that the Stalinist repression was a thing of the past. Trade staff balked and were afraid to commit economic irregularities because under Khrushchev, although to a lesser extent than under Stalin, such offenses were still treated with severity. Press reports from Moscow about the convictions in 1960 and 1961 of people speculating in foreign currency dissuaded many people from illegal dealings. The nomenklatura appreciated the end of massive physical repression but was still worried by Khrushchev's frequent changes of personnel. In addition, Khrushchev's promise in 1961 that Soviet society would achieve communism in twenty years disturbed the trade staff because it imposed an almost impossible task on them: to considerably increase the quantity of food available to consumers in a short period. Khrushchev's favored policies to achieve this goal required major reforms in agriculture and engendered fierce resistance among the nomenklatura.

Glavka acted to defend its position of strength, which Khrushchev's proposed reforms threatened. The *kontora* (borough fruit and vegetable office) was created in the 1930s as part of the Stalinist agricultural policy. Officially, it was under the supervision of the Ministry of Fruits and Vegetables, but it was very autonomous in its operations. Two features of the *kontora* are worthy of attention. First, its structure gave it total control—through the Ministry of Fruits and Vegetables—over the sale of produce from the *sovkhozes* (state-owned farms) and *kolkhozes* (collective farms). Second, the *kontora,* like many other bodies during this era, was run by a small group of bureaucrats in the capital. This model of extreme centralized administration did not have unanimous support, even among Soviet leaders, and Khrushchev was the first to contest it. To him, agriculture was a

high-priority sector for reform. The Twenty-second Congress of the Communist Party in 1961 announced a program to integrate the *kolkhozes* and *sovkhozes* into agro-food complexes that would process their products for sale in the cities.

If Khrushchev's policies have been attacked for their inconsistencies, there was at least one point on which he acted coherently: he wanted to replace the *kontora* system that prevented farmers from selling their products directly to urban markets. Under Khrushchev's leadership, a first objective was to allow the *kolkhozes* to open stores that would eventually replace the fruit and vegetable offices. The specialists—and there were many who supported the secretary general—were not short of arguments to defend the reform. They noted that the shortcomings, not to say the failures, of Soviet agriculture were largely known. The Soviet regime could not adequately supply its population with food, and the *kontora* system was identified as one of the major weaknesses of the agriculture system. The corruption that weakened the food distribution system was also blamed on the *kontora* system. Khrushchev's proposed decentralization was based on the integration of the agro-food sector, which would give farmers the right to operate stores and would prevent bureaucrats from selling food products to the population via the fruit and vegetable offices.

The way these reforms were implemented was typical of the period. The Kremlin moved slowly and cautiously, so as not to provoke any debate. The first step was to allow the creation of agro-food complexes in certain regions and then wait to see the results. This measured approach, however, did nothing to narrow the gap between the reform's partisans and its opponents, who pointed out that the results were not convincing. The new organizational structures had not ended the shortages in the stores. Still, the reformers did not renounce their project but instead attributed the poor results to sabotage by the nomenklatura, a faction of which opposed the reform precisely because it implied a curtailing of their prerogatives. It implied, too, a loss of some of the profits they made through illegal dealings in the *kontoras*. The *kontora* directors were chosen by top bureaucrats in the Ministry of Fruits and Vegetables and were answerable to them, so *kontora* directors strengthened their positions by involving these influential ministry officials in their corruption schemes.

The attempt to eliminate the *kontoras* as part of the effort to decentralize the Soviet system was substantially weakened by the fall of Khrushchev in 1964. Under the reformist Kosygin, the Kremlin continued to claim that it had not changed its orientation regarding the necessity of improving the distribution of food products, but it became evident after 1964 that the reform had lost its momentum. The reformists adopted defensive measures instead, abandoning the plan to put an end to the *kontoras*, and the conservative faction of the nomenklatura increased its resistance and was not as cautious in defending the *kontoras*.

They did not renounce the agro-food complex but instead undertook to discredit it. The 1970s saw the gradual death of the stores that the agro-food complexes oversaw. In 1976, the poor performance of the new stores provoked a storm of criticism from the media that justified their abolition. Sabotage by the nomenklatura, which cut off funding and support for these stores, was, effectively, the reason for the project's failure.

The failure of the reform revealed the strength of the food distribution bureaucrats and their opposition to any reform that threatened their interests, and it widened the influence of the *kontora* lobbies, opening the door to new violations of the law. If Glavtorg staffers were not officially involved in the conflict between the partisans and opponents of the *kontoras*, they were still very much concerned by it, for the battles of Glavka were also the battles of Glavtorg. The victory of the pro-*kontoras* forces was welcomed by Glavtorg leader Nikolai Tregubov and his colleagues, who had viewed Khrushchev as their prime enemy. The abolition of the centralized network of fruit and vegetable offices would have encouraged the forces of change and increased pressures for additional reforms. For the trade organizations, the principal consequence of the failure of the agriculture reforms was a reinforcement of the conservative trend represented by Tregubov.

Until the 1960s, stores offered only a limited choice of consumer goods, and levels of consumerism were rather modest. Because the majority of citizens shared an ascetic standard of living that highlighted any conspicuous consumption, corruption levels were relatively low. Nonetheless, managers had to give bribes in order to obtain adequate quantities of products for their stores. They did so less for personal gain than because their superiors compelled them to do so. Lower-level store employees felt justified in charging higher prices than the official ones and pocketing the difference because doing so allowed some of them to move from a miserable income to a decent one. Since there were not enough consumer goods to supply every store properly, high-ranking officials often steered scarce goods to managers who offered them the highest bribes and who were extra efficient. Trade officials guessed that the majority of the staff members were engaging in such behavior but rationalized that only small amounts were involved and that circumstances forced staff violate the law. Moreover, trade leaders were indulgent toward those who committed offenses for the store's sake and not for personal gain. For all these reasons, many trade leaders were lenient toward those who committed economic crimes. Executives, however, could not cross the line and were punished if they went too far. As understanding as leaders may have been about the actions mentioned above, they were still expected to denounce colleagues who committed major irregularities. Corruption already existed during Stalin's time, but it increased under his successors due to the decline of repression and the prevailing tolerance of illegal means used to achieve objectives.

The Building of Networks

The role of trade organizations in Soviet society changed significantly in the 1970s because of the political and economic situation. At first glance, the changes did not alter the principle that authority was based on legality; in fact, the tenet was strengthened. Discussions about the necessity and legitimacy of laws became a major issue in the media, and many articles on the importance of improving the laws were published. The elaboration of a new constitution for the country in 1976 was the major legal achievement of the Brezhnev era, but a clear paradox emerged. On the one hand, the Kremlin seemed aware of the necessity of the rule of law, while at the same time, there was some advance toward authority based on tradition. Executives of the trade structures broke the law more than ever before, precisely when they were continually being exhorted to act in conformity with Soviet law.

As many trade organizations, primarily in the food sector, became more powerful, their leaders acquired privileged positions. The foundation of their power lay in their monopoly over the distribution of consumer goods. In the Soviet economy, competition was of course forbidden. Only the Moscow Glavtorg, which had the status of a ministry in the Russian Republic, had the authority to distribute goods to the population of the capital. It was, therefore, a very different system from that operating in the West, where the government attempts to regulate trade organizations in order to collect taxes. While government control appears relatively successful in its oversight of most categories of goods, food regulation has been more difficult. Food is, and will remain, the sector in which it is easiest to avoid government control, regardless of the type of government in power, including the Soviet regime, where executives who distributed food occupied privileged positions.

A major reason that food is difficult for governments to control is its inherent range of quality and its perishablity. Food trade leaders were in charge of setting quality standards for products. Most fruits, vegetables, and meat went through three stages. The first corresponded to their optimum quality (first grade); in the second, the quality was lower, but the food was still good enough to eat (second grade); and finally, the third-grade category was applied to food that had spoiled and had to be thrown away.[10] Many food products are perishable and can thus disappear from inventory through spoilage. But who was in charge of determining the grade of hundreds of kilograms of fruits and vegetables in a store? Who had the power to decide if products had to be sold or thrown out when they were supposedly spoiled? Store directors made these decisions; they were the veritable tsars of the retail concern because there was almost no oversight of their actions. Most store directors had norms that differed from the Soviet trade rules that they imposed on their staffs. Like other executives, irrespective of their levels, they

worked primarily for personal gain, making material profits whenever possible. They could do this because store directors had considerable power in the decision-making process, even though, in general, the executives of the trade network possessed absolute control over the destiny of huge quantities of food. However, objective circumstances helped to provide store directors with wide prerogatives. In many cases, it was not easy for the food quality specialist to decide whether a product should fit into one category instead of another. One investigator said, "We did some experiments; we asked an expert to tell us what grade some herring should be in, and he was mistaken. The standards for determining quality grades are very vague. But if a specialist is mistaken, how can a customer find his way around in this labyrinth?"[11] This confusion meant that store directors could make illegal decisions and appear to be acting in good faith. They were in a good position to manipulate the quantities and qualities of food to their advantage. The first condition stipulated by Mueller for the acquisition of power by bureaucrats, the monopolistic situation, is present here: the Kremlin allowed only Glavtorg executives to distribute consumer goods, particularly food, to the population. Moreover, executives and store managers were in an entirely dominant position with respect to their customers because of the scarcity of many products. As one store manager said, "When I have 100 hats and 99 customers I am nothing, but when I have 99 hats and 100 customers, I am God."[12]

The leaders of Glavtorg had direct control over all consumer goods in the country, while Glavka, the Moscow Administration of Fruit and Vegetable Offices, was responsible for receiving products from the Ministry of Fruits and Vegetables and warehousing them in Moscow before distributing them to the borough kontoras and to the grocery stores. Of course, Glavka leaders allocated products according to the relative generosity of bribe-givers in their district's fruit and vegetable offices. Because the Glavka executives enjoyed a high degree of autonomy, they did not need to offer many bribes to the Glavtorg bureaucrats at the top of the hierarchy and they decided on their own who would receive the best products. The key figures in this bureaucratic structure were Tregubov, Andrei Petrikov, Vladimir Kireev, and Genri Khokhlov of Glavtorg; Sobolev and Eremeev, deputy directors of the Moscow food trade section of Glavtorg; and Korovkin, Sonkin, and Lavrov, directors and deputy directors at the grocery-store level of Glavtorg in Moscow. Others who reaped huge benefits were the directors of the most important grocery stores (fig. 1.2) and the heads of sections in these stores, whose prerogatives were equal to if not greater than those of the directors in many grocery stores.[13]

Founded by the Eliseevski family in the nineteenth century, the top gastronom in the country stood out because of its aesthetics. The Eliseevskis wanted their grocery store to impress customers with its beauty as much as by its assortment of food products. Museumlike, with sculptures and mosaics, the Eliseevski

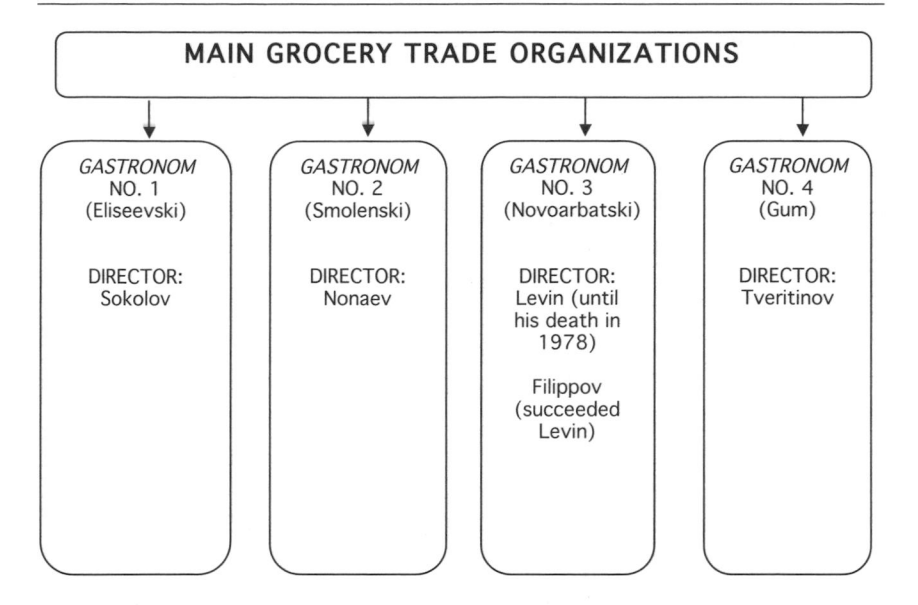

Figure 1.2. Administration of the food product trade organizations and directors of top grocery stores

gastronom figures in the history of Russian commerce as the favorite store of the intelligentsia. During the Soviet period, it maintained its tradition of attracting artists as customers, but the quantity of food in the store window was not always impressive. The Smolenski *gastronom* (the No. 2 grocery store) had a larger-than-average staff. The Novoarbatski *gastronom* (the No. 3 store) was in a similar category; it was usually full of customers, who had fifteen hundred sales clerks at their disposal. The No. 4 store, the Gum *gastronom,* had a thousand employees. There, too, consumer demand was high and expectations, strong.

It should be stressed that all these stores were frequented by very different groups of people. Muscovites were, of course, the primary customers, but tourists and provincials as well came to these top stores for various reasons. Speculators from all over the Soviet Union would assemble downtown to visit stores known for their wide selection of foods. If certain products were not available at one store, people would go to the others, which were close by. The core of the nomenklatura, from ministers to Central Committee members, lived and worked in the area where the stores were located. These influential groups could find very few places that offered quality food, so these top stores were important to them. The Eliseevski *gastronom* was very close to the Central Committee building and to KGB headquarters in Lubianka Square, while the Gum *gastronom*'s advantage was its location on Red Square facing the Kremlin. Gum played the role of a convenience store for the political leaders of the country in the Soviet

era. The relations that store directors had with people in the top echelons of the Party and the government allowed them a large degree of autonomy in the way they conducted their affairs. In any case, few food trade executives paid bribes to people in the nomenklatura, who had their own preferred stores where they had special privileges and could pay with coupons. Bribes did not have to be paid to the leaders of the Ministry of Trade in spite of this ministry's authority over the distribution of consumer goods (with the exception of fruits and vegetables), all of which indicates that the Moscow stores were not strictly supervised either by the government or by the Party.

The situation was different where the fruit and vegetable offices (*kontoras*) were concerned. If Moscow had an advantage over other cities because it received the best products from all over the country and abroad, even there, only a few *kontora*s were well supplied. The *kontora*s in the Dzerzhinski and Babushkin districts and, to a lesser extent, those in the Moskvorets, Baumanski, Leninski, and Sebastopol districts emerged as major distribution centers for black market fruits and vegetables. The Dzerzhinski *kontora* was especially noteworthy, being considered the best in the capital and a model operation offering an abundance of produce and greater variety, including apricots, parsley, and grapes, products that were in high demand and extremely difficult to obtain.[14] Its high status conferred special responsibilities, such as providing food for receptions organized by political leaders. Another role of the Dzerzhinski *kontora* was supplying other types of stores in Moscow: the *mosovotshch* (fresh produce shop), the *gastronom,* the *diettorg* (special diet store), the "specialty bases" (where the elite could obtain products that were in short supply), the *universam*s, Tsum (Main Store), and so forth. Maintaining tight control of the distribution of imported fruits and vegetables, the Dzerzhinski *kontora* leaders likewise invested a lot of time developing relationships of trust and friendship with high-ranking Glavtorg executives.

The Ministry of Fruits and Vegetables directed the distribution of fresh produce for the whole country, employing former leaders of the Moscow trade organizations, who came to dominate the both the Ministry of Trade and the Ministry of Fruits and Vegetables. In 1982, Poliakov, a former head of Glavka and director of the Dzerzhinski *kontora,* was serving as deputy head of the Ministry of Fruits and Vegetables. Kolomeitsev had followed a similar career path: he had been a high-ranking executive in Glavka before being appointed deputy director of Soyuz plodoimporta, the All-Union Office for Importation of Fruits and Vegetables for the Soviet Union. These men not only rose to the top of the two ministries but were also empowered to choose who would succeed them at the *kontora* level. Thus, Poliakov was able to hire his protégé, Mkhitar Ambartsumyan, as director of the Dzerzhinski *kontora,* thus conferring on the latter a reputation as one of the top store managers in the capital. Huge sums of money were amassed through collusion among the leaders of the Ministry of Fruits and

Vegetables, the directors of the Moscow *kontoras* in general, and the directors and deputy directors of the Dzerzhinski and other model *kontoras* in particular. All these officials shared the profits made from selling food products at high prices to the public markets and stores. According to one witness's testimony in the resulting court case,

> Many times in Ambartsumyan's office, I saw orders, which had been pre-pared for Poliakov. All this was supervised by Ambartsumyan. I already said that in 1983, V. T. Roganov sent peaches and tomatoes to our store. I gave the money for that to the driver, who transmitted Roganov's request that I bring a few boxes of peaches and tomatoes to Ambartsumyan. That is what I did. Ambartsumyan said "Thank you." He called Edik (head of Refrigeration Unit No. 35) and with him, we brought half of this order to the cafeteria, but the other half was loaded into Poliakov's car. Edik did the loading. At this time, Poliakov worked at the Soviet Ministry of Fruits and Vegetables. I can even suppose that Poliakov received huge bribes from Ambartsumyan.[15]

Working with Tregubov and other Muscovite trade executives, Kolomeitsev prepared receptions and banquets for Party and government leaders. Top officials of the ministries of Trade and of Fruits and Vegetables, including deputy minis-ters, asked Ambartsumyan for favors. They requested such things as alcohol and even tailoring services. The main advantage enjoyed by the trade executives in this situation was that they could become acquainted with the leaders of these ministries. Their meetings were held under the guise of conferences intended to improve the food supply to the population and to encourage good manage-ment practices. Frequently, high-ranking officials met with model directors and managers to learn from them and apply their methods and experiences all over the country. Ambartsumyan and other model executives were central figures in these conferences and were known as smart managers who could teach their colleagues. The meetings allowed successful managers to build strong personal networks and to win the trust and friendship of many of the participants. They did their utmost to render services to colleagues, and they offered them gifts. The trust acquired on these occasions was useful in strengthening networks, gaining additional support, and justifying the provision of privileged food supplies to the model executives' organizations.

The possibility of traveling abroad was one of the many advantages granted to model executives. They were occasionally selected as members of delegations sent to other countries to negotiate trade agreements. One effect of these mis-sions was to promote the establishment of personal relations, since members of a

traveling delegation were often sharing meals, going on excursions, or arranging negotiations and contracts with foreign firms.[16] Furthermore, each member of a delegation was expected to respect and get to know the other members—people who would not have been there without the support of powerful protectors. The first objective of a delegation member was to be able to continue to enjoy trips abroad, and it was useful for this purpose to befriend all the other members. Therefore, with regard to Dennis Mueller's second condition for acquiring bureaucratic power, that of being in a bargaining position, in Moscow, the managers of the main stores and *kontoras* were not merely in a situation in which they could bargain with their suppliers; they were actually in collusion with many of those suppliers.

A sign of the strength acquired by the nomenklatura during the 1970s and early 1980s was the way in which job stability or tenure developed for executives at all levels. According to Nicolas Werth, "The political stability of the Brezhnev years allowed the blossoming of powerful elites, self-confident and attached to their status and advantages. Elites constituted feudal powers with their hierarchy, their territories, and their clients."[17]

Gradually, according to one of the leaders of the Prosecutor General's Office (PGO), the members of the trade organizations managed to loosen any supervisory control over their activities: "Thus, it came about that inspectors had their 'own' stores, and stores had their 'own' inspectors."[18] Because it was unusual for officials and executives to be fired, they maintained their positions until death. During the 1970s, no grocery store managers in Moscow were prosecuted for corruption.[19] In fact, at every hierarchical level, officials enjoyed a great deal of autonomy; their superiors criticized them less and less, and whether they were criticized or not was of little consequence. The worst that could happen to a director was to receive a reprimand, as in the case of Baigelman, director of the Kuibishev RPT (Raipishetorg or District Food Trade Organization).[20] But even mild penalties were unusual; most of the time, criticism was rather vague and therefore did not threaten anyone in particular. Glavtorg executive meetings ended merely with declarations mentioning that "there are shortcomings in the trade organizations" and emphasizing "the need to intensify the fight against them."[21] Certain weaknesses in the trade network that were denounced concerned the ill-mannered behavior of employees toward customers. Corruption was identified as only one problem among others and, moreover, was only mentioned briefly. Leaders of Glavtorg denounced the tendency of certain employees "to take money from the customers' pockets."[22] However, few formal accusations were leveled, and while some employees were denounced as wrongdoers, no allusions were made to mistakes committed by executives. Because store managers had job security, the nomenklatura could focus on its personal interests and thus enjoyed

good times during the Brezhnev era, when its members had sought, more than ever before, to increase their living standards. The sector of the nomenklatura that benefited the most from this situation was the trade organizations, especially Glavtorg. Of course, the ascendancy of these bureaucrats was due mainly to illegal activities, and since its members had acquired job security and impunity, they became less reluctant to break the law.

The Soviet government encouraged improvements in internal trade in Moscow more than anywhere else. Although the Soviet economy entered a slump in the late 1970s, an expansion in services occurred, as illustrated by the emergence of new grocery stores and the hiring of additional employees.[23] The increase was particularly impressive in the food sector, where some twenty restaurants opened every year. The number of restaurants rose from 243 to 388 (1966–1981) and the number of cafeterias in workplaces and schools increased from 4,008 to 5,645 during the same period.[24] Moreover, in 1980, the Kremlin announced its intention to build *gastronoms* in several factories.

In Moscow, it was difficult for the Kremlin and its law enforcement agencies to control the distribution of resources, particularly food products, because the internal trade staff had several places to sell these resources on the black market. The preferred outlets were the twenty-eight public markets and two thousand food stalls in the Moscow area.[25] Every year, 300,000 kilograms of fruits and vegetables were sold by seventeen thousand individuals in the markets alone.[26] The internal trade bureaucracy also extended to restaurants and cafeterias. The multiplicity of these units increased the opportunities for pilfering, bribery, and speculation. Grocery store employees hid their speculative activities at these points of sale; the police succeeded in catching only a small fraction of the active speculators. Again, with reference to the second condition posed by Dennis Mueller, it can be seen that the effective bargaining position of the trade organization bureaucrats allowed them to increase their budgets, and the additional resources invested in the Moscow trade network reflected the growing influence of Glavtorg.[27] For Glavtorg's leaders, the addition of new food stores increased the possibility of benefits and the opportunity to hire people close to them who would also be willing to pilfer, speculate, and give bribes to their superiors. The food distribution organizations became attractive for the employment possibilities they offered, especially compared to other sectors, where finding jobs was usually difficult. Trade organizations were among the few places where the younger generation could hope to make a career, and the prospect of making money from food trade revenues was an attractive one, even if it required breaking the law. Rather than being put off by rumors of rampant corruption in the trade network, the younger generation saw this as a challenging, even thrilling activity.

Charismatic Leadership, Norms, and Traditional Practices

The personnel in the Moscow food distribution network presented certain marked characteristics. First, the food sector was dominated by Russians, or, more precisely, Muscovites, who were intimately familiar with the workings of the capital. Russians were prevalent in Glavtorg and in the top levels of all the food trade organizations. The leaders of Glavtorg—Tregubov, Petrikov, Kliachin, and Khokhlov—were all of Russian background. All the directors and deputy directors of the *kontoras* were also Russian. Russian deputy directors often succeeded their Russian bosses. The Russian group had an impressive cohesion, built up during the many years they had worked together; moreover, their acquaintance often went back to their participation in World War II. They knew each other well and had learned to work together harmoniously. Their strength lay in their close links with the Moscow Party organizations, links created by the appointment of Party apparatchiks as directors of certain food stores. Tveritinov was an example. He was a Komsomol cadre prior to his nomination as director of the Gum *gastronom.*

Most of the Russians were conservative communists who unconditionally endorsed Brezhnev's policies. No declarations or attitudes cast doubt on their loyalty to the Soviet system. Trade leaders expressed their support of Moscow Party chief Grishin and his team through impressive, exceptional supplies of food and, more generally, consumer products. The best food products were served to participants at conferences or celebrations organized by the Communist Party or the Soviet government. While the Moscow Party organization's tolerance of corruption was a sign of its good relations with the trade leaders, to conclude that such tolerance was the only reason would be simplistic. Most of the leaders of the Moscow trade network were sincere Party members despite their propensity for illegal dealings. A good illustration was Boris Karakhanov, a grocery store director arrested in 1984. He said that one of the worst moments of his life was when he was expelled from the Party. It was the first time he wept in public. He had never felt as ashamed and miserable as in that Party meeting where he was denounced for his involvement in corruption. Karakhanov's arrest made him aware that he had committed reprehensible actions; he had previously believed that the modest sums of money he had given authorities were considered gifts.[28]

The majority of executives in the trade network during this period were World War II veterans, and many had been appointed to their positions specifically because of their military service. They proudly wore their medals on their chests for public show. The veterans occupied a central place in the Soviet system because they were agents of sovietization in the internal trade organizations. Because the

veterans were advocates of the Soviet system and the majority of them were members of the Communist Party, their presence was intended to project a positive image of Soviet trade and present an important example of loyalty to the trade staff.

For Victory Day and other commemorations, the value of the veterans to the motherland was celebrated. Many had been mobilized at a very young age. Sokolov, director of the Eliseevski *gastronom*, the nation's top grocery store, belonged to the generation who had joined the Soviet army at age seventeen and spent the best part of their youth at the front, seeing people die on a daily basis. Many veterans suffered serious injuries during the war or were infected by diseases that affected them for the rest of their lives. Many of them, like Petrikov or Ambartsumyan, who lost a kidney, became disabled or physically challenged. Some had to spend regular stints in hospitals; Eremeev, for example, was hospitalized from September to December 1980.[29] Heart disease was common among the trade staff.

The leadership of the trade network was not lacking in charisma. A few individuals inspired respect and consideration because of their heroic past; they had shown undeniable strength during World War II. They also showed political skill and strong character, qualities that made them highly appreciated by the people around them. During the 1970s, a cult encouraged by the regime boosted the war veterans' reputation. A prototype of the model charismatic Russian director was Rosliakov, the manager of Fruit and Vegetable Store No. 20, who had been an officer of the Soviet army and a civil aviation pilot.[30] He was involved in corruption like his colleagues but was considered to have acted under mitigating circumstances. The KGB took the position that he was not a swindler but rather a victim of the Soviet system; he had taken money because he was a victim of extortion by his superiors. He was popular among his employees, whom he defended against the machinations of corrupt police officers, and his store was reputed to have a larger quantity of products than the majority of stores in the capital. Glavtorg hired many employees like Rosliakov, for obvious reasons. They were seen as models by other employees, in particular by their subordinates. Leaders and executives were expected to observe the law and the rules in front of their employees. This did not imply that they were incorruptible, however. Some, like Sokolov, were hired precisely because they were not afraid to make illegal profits. While some had the reputation of being strong, others had weak characters and could be easily manipulated; it was easy to extort money from them. Thus, staff members had different character traits, and there was the view that executives who were "morally superior to other executives" would balance out other appointments based on self-interest and bribe-taking. Executives with high moral standards were recruited to place limits and constraints on their colleagues' appetite for illegal money. Ambartsumyan, for example, had not entered the trade organization with the intention of making illicit gains. Instead, trade

leaders invited him to work in the Dzerzhinski *kontora* to prevent others from cashing in. Indeed, some trade leaders liked to hire employees who took little because it left more for the others.

Several trade network executives who were considered very competent people, even by officials in the law enforcement agencies, became the "stars" of Glavtorg. According to the KGB, the charismatic Ambartsumyan and Filippov (director of the Novoarbatski *gastronom*) were among the best executives.[31] Executives like Ambartsumyan were praised for having invented new ways of preserving fruits and vegetables. Food trade executives and specialists admired him and came from all over the country to learn about his experiments. Even high-ranking officials of the ministries of Trade and of Fruits and Vegetables attended Ambartsumyan's lectures on how to safely store fruits and vegetables. The charismatic leaders also included Tveritinov and Nonaev, the directors of Grocery Stores No. 2 and 3 (the Smolenski and Novoarbatski *gastroms*), respectively, who shared the reputation of being the most competent directors in their sector, along with Sokolov, who was praised by the president of Glavtorg as "the Eliseevski of our time."[32] Police officers classified Filippov among the top ten managers in the country. In 1978, according to Shimanski, head of the Ministry of Trade, 222 stores in the capital followed the example of the Dzerzhinski *kontora* in the conservation of fruits and vegetables.[33] It was the only fruit and vegetable depot in Moscow to function without huge losses for seventeen years, and during the preceding three years, four other *kontoras* in the capital would imitate it.[34] From 1972 to 1982, the period during which Sokolov was the director of the Eliseevski *gastronom,* according to police reports, the store's revenue increased from 30 million to 94 million rubles.[35]

The star executives of Glavtorg were presented in the media as model citizens and leaders. They accumulated many awards for merit in their work and for their high moral standards. Ambartsumyan received eighteen awards from the state—all prestigious awards, although not the most important ones, and he was not the only one to receive so many honors. Thus, leaders like Ambartsumyan generally projected a positive public image.

The aging members of the Politburo preferred that people of their own generation hold high positions in the various domains of the Soviet system, so older individuals predominated in the top ranks of the trade organizations. The Politburo members wanted executives to reflect their image and to remain in their jobs as long as possible. Certain Party leaders were very well acquainted with the Moscow trade leaders and contacted them regularly. They trusted these executives because they had shown their loyalty on several occasions in the past. Furthermore, conservative Politburo members were suspicious of any reformist trend in society that spread dissidence. With this older generation of trade

leaders in place at the trade organizations, Politburo leaders believed the trade network was well defended against dissidence. Trade leaders were skillful enough to oppose any change in the economic system; they never showed the slightest sympathy for a market or private economy, and their views were pleasing to the Grishin clique of the Party.

While trade leaders might have had good motives for hiring executives with honorable pasts, such as World War II veterans, it was not always advantageous to have lower-level store staff members with these profiles. Most veterans had limited education and similarly limited management qualifications and skill. However, since many activities in the food distribution sector were illegal, the trade organizations needed skilled legal specialists who could shed light on which activities were illegal or legal according to the criminal court, the civil court, or the Comrades' Court, on what constituted a major economic crime as opposed to a minor one, and on several other important issues. On many points, the laws were not clear, and, as a result, some violations were tolerated and others were severely punished. Glavka leaders found a candidate possessing all the education and skills of a law specialist in Volkov, who had risen in the hierarchy after he was named deputy director of the Dzerzhinski *kontora*. Trade leaders also sought out communication specialists. They wanted people trained in journalism who could present good images of the trade organizations throughout Russia. Aging trade executives who had problems expressing themselves orally were even worse off when writing. Sokolov was known to have been hired for his talents as a communicator. Both he and Volkov were very persuasive when defending the trade staff's interests in public. Professionalism and expertise were also required of bookkeepers, who needed to be able to work with data and statistics on store operations. Documents in the trade sector contained considerable masses of data and were very complex. Finding the right person to handle such work was not easy, but occasionally trade leaders did come across suitable candidates.

Food trade employees who proved able to handle these complex tasks were praised in accordance with Brezhnev's policy, which was to reward employees who exemplified Soviet norms by performing well at work and by observing the law. The Party drew up a list of employees and executives in the Soviet internal trade sector who would be given awards and promoted. The Moscow trade sector employees received more honors than any other group. Trade executives took these marks of distinction very seriously; the honors did not always provide material advantages, but they boosted reputations. Trade executives who engaged in corruption needed to build reputations of honesty to compensate for or dissimulate their wrongdoings or rumors of wrongdoings. Awards were also desirable in that they highlighted the recipients' professionalism, and the authorities tended to be more tolerant of corrupt executives who were viewed as competent managers.

Awards to trade organization staff were granted for reasons that appeared contradictory. In reality, these rewards were an integral part of the pervasive graft that existed in the food trade organizations. Corrupt executives were able to rise in the organizations by the very fact that they were deeply involved in illegal dealings. At the same time, executives were rewarded for good performance at work and for promoting Soviet norms in the trade structures. Some executives favored the allocation of products in traditional ways that tolerated redistribution through bribery. Store directors calculated how subordinates could benefit them. In return for bribes, the directors distributed products and services or granted awards or distinctions to whomever they thought was deserving, by, for example, upholding Soviet norms or rendering personal services to the manager. In the top-ranked grocery stores, both criteria prevailed. Thus, in the 1970s, when several complaints were sent to the Ministry of Trade and Glavtorg regarding the cheating of customers and price increases at the Gum, the *gastronom* nevertheless remained a top-ranked store. Its staff received bonuses for their achievements; moreover, the director, Tveritinov, received several awards that qualified him as one of the most competent and successful store managers. Three of his awards conferred particularly high status: the Order of the October Revolution (awarded in 1971), Emeritus Trade Employee of the RSFSR (awarded in 1974), and the Order of the Red Standard (awarded in 1981). Tveritinov was an excellent manager and enjoyed the support of his staff, although his charisma was not at the level of Sokolov's. There were certain shortcomings in his store's relations with consumers, but Tveritinov was not the only one responsible for the problems; some of the issues were structural in nature and existed in most of the stores. These prestigious honors should not have been issued to a director of a store riddled with economic irregularities, but Glavtorg's leaders often rewarded those who served their personal interests, and in this case, Tregubov decided that Tveritinov deserved to be a star among his staff after he had bribed him with eight thousand rubles.[36] Nonetheless, Tveritinov gave this bribe so as to ensure adequate supplies at his stores, not for his own material benefit.

Baigelman, the Kuibishev RPT director, was yet another executive whose reputation was tarnished by grievances, both from consumers and from the ranks of his employees. Even the supervisory body reported arrogance, the insulting of customers by employees, and frequent violations of Soviet trade laws by the RPT. Still, no sanctions were enforced against the Kuibishev RPT director, and no measures were taken to eliminate the abuses in his store. Baigelman was safe because he had the protection of Tregubov; he even received the Order of the Red Standard award.[37] This award boosted his reputation as an honest and highly competent executive, not because he acted in compliance with the rules of Soviet trade but because he fulfilled Tregubov's standards for a model man-

ager. Tregubov himself received his share of awards. As president of Glavtorg, he earned more awards than any other trade executive, and the ones he received were the most important awards. Tregubov was in a category all his own in that he alone among trade executives was chosen laureate of the USSR Council of Ministers, the supreme distinction in trade affairs.[38] These honors reflected the firm support that Tregubov enjoyed at the highest echelon; such support gave official encouragement to his conservative and traditional leadership style and condoned his staff's practices, which included dishonest acts.

One of the dominant norms (that is, legal norms) was the fair treatment of employees. A model director was one whose employees were paid a salary that reflected their job descriptions and who gave employees access to services, for example, housing. This interest in employees' benefits took on different meanings for directors between the Stalin and the Brezhnev eras. Under Stalin's rule, directors treated their employees in a manner that conformed to the boundaries of Soviet law. By the 1970s, sensitivity for the well-being of one's employees meant not only providing them with adequate social services but also tolerating irregularities.[39] Directors and other managers allowed irregularities that would benefit themselves and employees and calculated how to obtain the support of employees who would defend their superiors if they were suspected, interrogated, or prosecuted. However, charismatic leaders were not primarily motivated by material private interests; decent salaries for their employees were a priority for them. They worked principally for the achievements of their stores. At the Dzerzhinski *kontora,* employees were very supportive of Ambartsumyan. One employee said, "A good boss, that's all we can say, a very good boss. Probably there will be no boss like him anymore. That's what he was: a very good boss. We won't see such a boss here at the *kontora* again. That's it. And the gates wouldn't have been broken if he was alive. There was everything in the *kontora.* Everything was in order. In winter there were cucumbers all the time, bananas, apples." Another employee's comments were similar: "What happened, only people at the top know. We are ordinary folks. We knew that to us, he was a good person." A third employee spoke for many when he said, "I have been working here for sixty years. My memories of him are very good; he always provided us with housing."[40]

The employees of the main stores run by charismatic directors had enviable status. Eliseevski employees wore prestigious Bimbar diamonds around their necks and on their wrists; women wore Malika earrings and heavy gold bracelets. Thus, some store employees had access to places like the restaurant or bar of Dom Kino, a venue where celebrities such as film directors, actors, and writers would gather.[41] According to Anatoli Rubinov, Sokolov became a popular figure in the capital among well-known artists and musicians:

The director [Sokolov], with his friendly open face, was proud of his fa-mous visitors who bowed down before him, and he never denounced them. Business cards were always on his desk. Managers, authors, gen-erals, artists, noted physicians, television announcers: their cards were displayed on the table, sometimes in a pile, or fanned out. Visitors could, with a little effort, read the last names on the cards. Some of them, the more trusted ones, called on a direct line without passing through the director's secretary. The visitors could hear the director refuse someone's kindly offer for a cruise on the Mediterranean. "I understand that it is not expensive and that it will be paid for, but believe me I cannot afford to take a vacation." Or tickets for an American film at an elite movie theater. "You know, I already saw it, my daughter and my son-in-law as well, but I am grateful to you." Or tickets for a premiere at the Smolenski Theatre: "You know that tonight I am busy, but I will call you when I am avail-able." Or to go through a tomography scan: "It will be good to do this, but for now I am so busy; although I do realize that we must not neglect our health." Yet another instance was an offer to buy him a new model of Salamander shoes: "Thank you; it is a good brand, but I prefer Topman." Charming to all, Sokolov has become a huge force in Moscow.[42]

Sokolov was a model of how to generate society's support for the trade net-work. He set up four types of privileged relations with famous or influential people.[43] He supplied them through the black market; he sold them high-quality products that were difficult to obtain at official prices and did not require the customer to wait in line; he allocated free food to some individuals; and, perhaps most importantly, he organized receptions for famous members of the intelli-gentsia. The following example, provided by Sergei Semanov, gives a good idea of Sokolov's role:

In fall 1980, a well-known journalist who had worked in the West for a long time returned to work in Moscow. On this occasion, I was invited to a dinner organized at the Aragvi restaurant for him. We had studied to-gether. Everything proceeded normally, but the host particularly shone. He was a middle-aged man, very well-dressed. Everyone there knew him, but I did not know who he was and quickly asked a neighbor at the table. I discovered that this man was Sokolov, the director of the Eliseevski *gas-tronom*. When the guests left the table, they did not go up to the journal-ist, who was the object of the reception, with their business cards in hand, but to Sokolov.[44]

Weber's types of authority are useful when applied to the Soviet trade organizations. While traditional and charismatic types of authority were predominant, legal authority also existed. During the Brezhnev era, this type of authority was in decline; however, in the late 1970s, some measures were taken to reinforce allegiance to the Soviet system. Trade leaders looked for support from other groups in society at this time. For example, the Kremlin, under pressure from the Ministry of Trade in an attempt to improve the food supply, opened grocery stores in several factories. Traditionally, industrial workers were, from the point of view of Soviet propaganda, the leading class of society, and the Party expected support from this group. The trade organizations played a crucial role in fulfilling the needs of the working class. Trade executives did not see these factory stores simply as new places to embezzle but rather as an opportunity to consolidate the leadership under Brezhnev. Wary of Andropov's growing influence in the Party, these officials played a political game by supporting the conservative forces represented by Brezhnev and Grishin against Andropov, the KGB chief. They succeeded in substantially improving the food situation in certain places by inaugurating these factory stores, although for the majority of the population the food deficit continued.

The power of the Moscow trade network can be measured by its capacity for enrichment and the acquisition of resources. Trade executives had access to considerable amounts of money and resources; their influence depended on what they could do with them. At first glance, the Soviet system severely restricted opportunities for them. The ministries of Trade and of Fruits and Vegetables had the support of institutions created by the Kremlin that guaranteed adequate supply to the population. The number of supervisory organs in the country was at its largest since Stalinist times, although they did not have the unlimited power they had held before (see fig. 1.3). The increase in the number of entities during the Brezhnev period can be attributed to the fact that the government wanted to give the impression it was looking after the well-being of the people and that the political system was governed by law and not by arbitrariness. The expansion meant, above all, a commitment to respecting the law in distribution and retail. It would be erroneous to imply that all the control organs, such as the price commission, the union inspection department, and the Glavtorg inspection department were all corrupt or manipulated.

The Transformation of Glavtorg into a Political Force

Leaders in the Ministry of Trade had no leverage when it came to political questions such as constitutional changes, which were the exclusive prerogative of the Communist Party. Trade leaders had no hope of removing the Party from

Figure 1.3. Entities controlling the Moscow trade organizations

power in this nondemocratic system, and without elections, they could not give money to politicians to promote their interests. Thus, while political channels were closed to them, trade leaders could exercise influence on the economic level: in the trade network, the rules were not always respected or enforced. As their authority was not based on law, trade leaders turned to traditional means of protecting themselves. The personalization of power was a deeply rooted practice in Russian society, and, in the 1970s, trade executives consolidated their positions through their personal relations. Superiors decided whether employees were honest and competent or not and when to apply the law. Trade executives' behavior affirmed Mueller's third condition for consolidating bureaucratic power—the absence of monitoring. They eluded control by both Soviet and Party agencies. With money and resources, trade executives at different levels bought political support among Party and government officials and were continuously on the lookout for people to bribe. Colleagues at the district level and the directors of the top *gastronom*s helped them by identifying influential officials to

whom Glavtorg executives could give money or scarce goods. It was thus that Glavtorg became a political force.

Purchasing Political Support in the Law Enforcement Agencies

To become a political force, trade organization leaders had to gain support in the upper echelons of government and Party structures. They could go about this either by working to have their colleagues from the trade network appointed to important positions in these structures or by buying support among political and judiciary officials already in place. In order to carry out these illicit activities without fear of being caught, Moscow trade leaders had to neutralize the entities designed to control their activities. This strategy was exemplified by the actions of Glavtorg chief Tregubov, who represented the trade network in the Moscow Party Committee and, more importantly, was a member of the City Party Committee. Tregubov's strength came chiefly from Moscow Party chief Grishin, who had believed in Tregubov's honesty and competence to the extent that he made him his lieutenant in the trade organizations.

Tregubov and other Glavtorg leaders first looked for support from supervisory bodies within their own ranks. The best way to have the backing of these groups was to involve their leaders in corruption. It became a widespread practice in the inspection staff to take bribes; in return, the inspectors would report that law and order prevailed in the stores. Inspectors could put pressure on managers or employees at any time, and life became impossible for those who were reluctant to meet the inspectors' demands. The inspection department leaders' main function consisted of covering up illegalities and promoting the view that everything was fine in the trade network. Their reports stressed that executives were honest, confirming Glavtorg's reputation as a model organization. If the inspection department claimed that honesty and order were the main features that characterized the trade organizations, it implied that external control was unnecessary. If another control body found illegalities, it would necessarily enter into conflict with the internal trade inspection department, whose leader, Kireev, enjoyed Tregubov's full confidence.

As Brezhnev's authority declined, various organizations won greater autonomy. Broader autonomy in a particular organization meant an increase in its political influence. The strong influence of the Moscow trade organizations was due to a large extent to the power of its chief, Tregubov, as leader of the Moscow trade organizations. His importance in the Moscow Party Committee was made clear in 1972, when investigations by the Russian state price commission disclosed major violations in twenty district stores: "In 156 out of the 193 stores, it turned out that irregularities had been committed. Four out of five customers

had been cheated concerning 51 to 57 percent of prices. Systematic food price hikes were noted in the Proletarski district, where customers lost a total of 32,000 rubles."[45] The president of the commission informed Glavtorg chief Tregubov of these results and told him he had to report on the situation to the Party and the government. Tregubov succeeded in persuading the president of the price commission to allow him to report to the Moscow Party Committee instead and outline the necessary corrections (which he never carried out). I. M. Tiglis, an investigator for the state committee on prices, explained how Tregubov's strategy worked: "Great pressure was placed on me by management, who proposed not to convey the results of the inspection. Soon after, the documents disappeared under mysterious circumstances."[46]

The year 1972 was a turning point: the government control agencies would henceforth have to report trade irregularities to Tregubov. They continued to report many trade network violations to Moscow and even proposed measures to counter them, but it was up to Tregubov to decide what would be done in the end. Moreover, all complaints addressed to the Party Committee about corruption in the trade sector were referred to him. The result was that "in many letters, the organs of the legal and the control system informed Tregubov of the increase, year after year, of incidents of embezzlement, bribery, the cheating of consumers, and other offenses in the Moscow trade network. In these letters to Glavtorg, they proposed to take resolute and efficient measures to eliminate the causes and conditions of [these violations]."[47]

These pressing complaints constituted a threat to Tregubov. Even if he could ensure that the control agencies would not act upon a complaint and although he knew that the political leaders trusted him over the representatives of the agencies, he also needed police support. The law enforcement staff, particularly that of the Ministry of the Interior (MVD), based its legitimacy on apprehending lawbreakers and could lose their jobs if they did not perform. When Tregubov offered them material advantages, police officers would accept only if they were persuaded that it was not risky, that is, if they knew that their bosses were also involved in such practices. Indeed, they frequently had no choice in the matter because their bosses often compelled them to act illegally. The control agencies' staff had to follow the laws that regulated Soviet trade, but in reality, their conduct was dictated by the Glavtorg chief. Tregubov's authority was such that his staff obeyed him even if they risked imprisonment. He was able to buy support from Moscow MVD leaders, who became crucial allies of the trade network leaders. According to Oleinik, who headed the anticorruption brigade and handled the investigation of especially important cases, "When I worked in the Department for Combating Organized Crime, officials reported that inside the State structures, there were a thousand corrupt employees, with 40% in the Ministry of the

Interior and 20% in the courts."[48] According to Petrikov, senior deputy president of Glavtorg, "Tregubov and other leaders of the organization often requested N. T. Mironov, head of the Moscow Department for Combating Speculation and Embezzlement of Socialist Property, not to inform Party and Soviet organizations of irregularities occurring in trade in Moscow, but instead to transfer the information to the Moscow Trade Administration (Glavtorg), which would take measures against it."[49]

According to Petrikov, Tregubov frequently appealed to Mironov's assistant, Maratik, to hide cases of corruption that might have been reported to the police. He said that Tregubov told him, "We [Glavtorg's leaders] had to appeal to Maratik; Maratik would solve the problem." In fact, according to the police report, "During this period, all measures were taken to hide criminal activities in trade." In return, Petrikov revealed that, concerning MVD officials, Glavtorg's leaders "satisfied all their requests and wishes. These requests came not only from Mironov, but also from his deputy heads in the Moscow MVD, I. M. Shutov, V. A. Shashkovski, N. S. Mirikov, and I. A. Minaev. One after the other, they behaved as if they had the right to make various requests of us. Mironov wrote letters to Tregubov and me, letters requesting cars, furniture, carpets, and other things."[50]

MVD officials were very useful to executives in the trade network. According to the law, it was incumbent upon the Ministry of the Interior, and in particular, the MVD Department for Combating Speculation and the Embezzlement of Socialist Property (OBKhSS), to fight corruption in the trade network. If there were irregularities, why should Tregubov be held responsible for them? Under Brezhnev, all information and complaints about wrongdoing in the Moscow trade organizations were referred to OBKhSS. The power of the Ministry of the Interior was, officially, almost unlimited; its officers could arrest and jail any trade employee. MVD officers often wielded their power in another way, however: until 1982, they chose to ignore and even to protect trade executives involved in wrongdoing, receiving in return substantial sums of money and other resources.

MVD officers helped the cause of the trade leaders in several ways. Taking bribes themselves precluded them from opposing this practice, and this put greater pressure on employees to give bribes in general. In taking money, MVD officers reduced the amount of money available to trade executives but increased the number of defenders of wrongdoing in the trade network. The MVD officers' tactic was to extract money from employees and to "embezzle socialist property" rather than to take money from executives. They regularly brought charges against underlings but rarely prosecuted executives. Trade leaders were forced to agree that this MVD police force had to justify its existence and prove its efficiency by prosecuting and convicting some people, particularly when it targeted

trade employees. Managers were not always passive with regard to the relations between law officers and employees: they frequently took the side of the repressors and aided them in practicing extortion. The following case concerns a store manager who reported that two of his employees had been accused:

> Filippov [head of the Babushkin district MVD Department for Combating the Embezzlement of Socialist Property] claimed it was a coincidence, but we knew that he applied some pressure when he needed money, and paying him each month was not possible. We learned that sales clerks Laiushkin and Kasatkin were charged. Their case was not transferred to the criminal court, but to the Comrades' Court. Filippov wanted to stop procedures with 1,000 rubles. I transmitted his proposal to the accused sale clerks, who fretted day and night, asking my help on how to find the money. Filippov told me and my assistants that the sales clerks had to bring the money. I brought the money to Filippov's office. He asked me if the sales clerks knew about it. I said no, and he replied, "Fine, thank you."[51]

The KGB was the weakest link for the Moscow trade leaders. Contrary to what happened with Party officials, trade leaders were never able to place their colleagues in high positions within the security forces. Moreover, law enforcement documents do not mention the names of any KGB officials, even at the district level, who had been bribed by trade executives. This does not mean that the Moscow trade organizations were unaware of the importance of gaining support within the KGB: they expended much effort toward this end, and it eventually paid off. While most trade executives were unable to count on high-ranking KGB officials for support, an exception was Roganov, head of the Sheremetyevo Airport imported food warehouse, who succeed in bringing the KGB officers who worked at the airport onto his side. One trade executive associated with Roganov through illegal activities made the following comment about his colleague: "Besides working at the imported fruit and vegetable warehouse, I do not know how, but Roganov knew almost all of the KGB officers and border guards. He looked like the real owner of the airport."[52]

Occasionally, high-ranking executives, including the directors of the major grocery stores, did find supporters in the KGB. Petrikov mentions that Tregubov once alluded to Sokolov's connections in the security forces. In certain cases, KGB assistance had significant benefits. For example, Tregubov's son would not have entered the KGB if his father had not had friends inside the organization. However, it should be added that Tregubov's connections in the KGB did not extend to the higher levels; moreover, his son was never promoted to a position

of authority in the security force, and Sokolov was not granted a visa to go abroad even after appealing to acquaintances in the KGB intercede for him.[53] In sum, the KGB backed a few trade executives, but this support was not enough for the latter to avoid prosecution when they were eventually charged with wrongdoing.

In general, KGB officers who received favors from the trade organizations were those who worked as volunteers in the food organizations.[54] The KGB volunteers were circumspect, accepting only modest quantities of food, and police documents do not report any instances of KGB intervention on behalf of arrested trade employees. The volunteers were members of the KGB Party Committee in the trade organizations and were therefore accountable to the Party more than to the security forces. Their connections to the upper echelons of their own organization were weak, and consequently, they could not influence KGB actions. However, until 1982, the trade executives were not worried by the fact that they had not bought much support in the KGB, considering that, to all appearances, it was the Party that dominated society. Late in the 1970s, there was no sign that Party hegemony would end in the near future. In this light, it is understandable that the trade executives sought support primarily in the Party.

There was a contradictory tendency in the law enforcement agencies, with part of the staff, concentrated in the KGB, actively combating corruption while another portion supported corrupt trade officials. While it would be incorrect to say that the Prosecutor General's Office was controlled by the trade organizations, widespread corruption at all levels of the Ministry of the Interior indicated that the judiciary organs had been weakened by this division among the ranks.

Purchasing Political Support in the Soviet Agencies

According to the Soviet constitution, the Moscow trade network was under the jurisdiction of the Moscow soviet, as were the ministries of Trade and of Agriculture. Although the Moscow Party Committee controlled the soviet, the latter possessed an autonomy that increased significantly during the Brezhnev era. The Moscow soviet grew in importance due to the privileged status of the city. The influence of this soviet went hand in hand with that of its leader, Promyslov, with his strong personality and impressive authority as mayor of Moscow. Promyslov's status also stemmed from his relations with Moscow Party Committee leader Grishin. Although we have no legal evidence that Promyslov was bought by the trade leaders, there is no question that he belonged to the group that unconditionally supported the trade staff. He demonstrated this support on many occasions.

Moscow soviet leaders did not rule the trade network with exclusivity, but

without their approval, the network was almost powerless. No nomination of a Glavtorg executive was valid without the consent of the Moscow soviet. The situation was the same for other matters, such as determining the quantity of food distributed to stores. The new power acquired by the trade organizations via the support of the Moscow soviet was possible only because trade leaders paid for it. This payoff may have been beneficial for the Moscow soviet leaders in financial terms, but it was prejudicial to the Moscow soviet's institutions, which lost a lot in terms of power. The Moscow soviet leaders thus played a major role in increasing the influence of the trade network. A significant point in this path toward greater influence was Decree 3-59, adopted by the Moscow soviet's Executive Committee in 1971, which widened Glavtorg's responsibilities: "The Moscow Trade Administration assumes the direction of the retail trade in the city, [and] bears responsibility for the state and development of trade and the quality of the services to the population. One of the primary tasks of Glavtorg is to guarantee respect for socialist legality in all spheres of activity in its organizations and enterprises."[55]

Glavtorg's president was assigned additional power in 1973: "The president bears personal responsibility for the accomplishment of Glavtorg tasks and obligations."[56] The Moscow soviet's support for trade executives was based on other considerations as well. For example, the Moscow soviet had jurisdiction over land in the capital. It was responsible for matters related to communication and transport and for the buildings where many stores were located. It thus had to maintain and repair those buildings. Trade executives paid bribes to persuade the Moscow soviet to invest substantially in the improvement of Glavtorg and Glavka structures. Soviet officials allocated certain highly appreciated services, such as housing in apartments and space in garages, to trade executives in return for huge sums of money. Other resources that the Moscow soviet commanded, such as construction materials, were in very high demand on the black market.

The key officials in the Moscow soviet were the deputy directors, and trade executives made it a priority to win their support. One official targeted for such support was Debridin, the first vice president of the Executive Committee and therefore second in importance after Promyslov. Debridin was the effective leader of the staff (he made all personnel decisions) and knew more than anyone else about the illegal activities of his officials. To a certain extent, he orchestrated those illegal matters, and he was Promyslov's confidant inside the Moscow soviet. Trade leaders had bought him and his lieutenants, including Naumenko, his principal advisor.

Trade leaders bribed other vice presidents for various reasons. Each vice president had a particular jurisdiction, and Debridin was reluctant to encroach

upon it. The other vice presidents usually preferred to make deals directly with trade executives because otherwise, if they allowed the first vice president to carry out these operations, they risked losing significant amounts of graft money. Protection from the Moscow soviet was more safely ensured when it involved more than one of its high-level officials, whether that one was Debridin or someone else. Trade executives kept in mind that if one vice president was arrested for corruption, others would have to step in as suppliers and protectors. These officials were the "trade men" within the Moscow soviet, that is, one of their main tasks consisted of consolidating the interests of Glavtorg and Glavka. It should be added here that certain trade organizations were more involved in acquiring this backing than others; many buyers of Moscow soviet support held positions in Glavka, an organization that was riddled with illegalities.

In many respects, the trade executives in the capital offered services to the Moscow soviet's Executive Committee that resembled those provided to the Party Committee. Their contribution was to receive delegations and organize receptions for conferences or meetings. Nevertheless, the proportion of the Moscow soviet staff who regularly received or gave bribes was not as important as the number of MVD officials or district Moscow Party Committee members doing so. Some store managers did not consider the soviet's officials to be as influential as Party or law enforcement officials. They took it for granted that their supporters in the latter organizations were their principal protectors.

Since most of the Moscow soviet officials could not offer as much protection as the other organizations could, they did not expect large bribes. The trade executives were aware of this and occasionally refused to accede to their demands when they involved large amounts of money. However, the Moscow soviet officials had a plan B, which consisted of asking trade executives to deliver free delicacies to them on occasions such as holidays. This demand was more difficult to refuse because, first, it was rather modest and second, some Moscow soviet officials asked so vehemently that their requests could be perceived as threats: "as you give to others, you should give to me too, otherwise. . . ." Moreover, it was hard to refuse such requests when they came from high-ranking persons. Low-risk meetings between trade executives and Moscow soviet officials were frequently held, and during the meetings they would discuss problems and consume illegally obtained food and vodka. Naumenko, the advisor of the first vice president of the Moscow soviet, addressed his requests for goods to Ambartsumyan, the director of the Dzerzhinski *kontora*. In 1982, the two men met five times: twice in restaurants, twice at the Bolshevik baking plant, and once on the outskirts of Moscow. On these occasions, the *kontora* director paid for the food and drink. Nevertheless, apart from deliveries of food, some Moscow soviet of-

ficials demanded additional resources or services, such as repairs to their apartments: "Twice, he wanted repairs to his apartment; once it cost 60 rubles, the second time, 1,000 rubles. Every month, he required food deliveries."[57] When trade executives showed their power by refusing demands made by Moscow soviet officials, even when these came from the upper echelons, some officials complained that the executives did not pay them enough.

The Moscow soviet officials' success varied from one store director to the next. Sokolov, director of the Eliseevski *gastronom,* was more willing to collaborate with them, probably because of his criminal record. (In 1959, while working as a taxi driver, he had been convicted of defrauding customers and was sentenced to one year in a labor camp and fined 20 percent of his annual salary.) The heads of the Moscow soviet contacted the Eliseevski *gastronom* via a special telephone line, a practice that was not usual among officials and that intimidated store directors. Sokolov knew that after receiving a call on this line, he had to raise the amount of a bribe for someone or add some names to his list of bribe-takers.[58] This was part of the price that trade leaders had to pay to remain free of the Moscow soviet's regulations.

Trade executives made particular efforts to buy the district soviet leaders who had accumulated additional power during the Brezhnev era. This was particularly the case in the model districts, where the leaders' authority was reinforced by good management and good results. In the Dzerzhinski model district, Ambartsumyan's achievements earned him an increase in bonuses and honors, some of which went to the district soviet leaders. Illegal dealings also produced extra revenue for the model district soviet's bosses. In addition, the corrupt executives in these districts had powerful protectors and superiors who boosted both their own reputations as excellent managers and those of the district soviet leaders. The trade executives pursued a policy that maximized the importance of the model district soviets, especially with respect to the Moscow soviet. District soviet leaders served trade leaders' interests by buying supporters in the upper echelon of the Moscow soviet. Another tactic of district bosses was to place their colleagues in key Moscow soviet posts. Thus, district soviet leaders helped the cause of the trade staff by corrupting Moscow soviet officials. Trade leaders could buy high-ranking Moscow soviet officials through the intermediary of the district soviet bosses.

Purchasing Political Support in the Party Organizations

One of the trade network leaders' strategies was to gain support among Party officials, something that, at first glance, seemed very difficult. Not all officials were willing to accept illegal resources. However, for the trade executives, finding

support in the Moscow Party organization was a high priority. They attempted to approach officials of Moscow Party agencies who were responsible for inspections. By buying the promise of collusion from apparatchiks, the strength of the trade leaders could only increase, especially in Moscow, where the Party organization was the most influential in the country, if one considers its role as the main recruitment base for the central institutions. The Moscow Party organization also had unusual strength at the middle levels (regional and urban), and because it had such close ties to the central Party structure, Moscow officials naturally rose to the Party's top echelons on a regular basis.

The trade network leaders were successful with their primary tactic, which consisted of turning officials of the Moscow Party structures into bribe-takers. The highest-ranking apparatchik they succeeded in buying was Buchin, who, as president of the Moscow Party Control Commission, was responsible for checking on officials' behavior, and therefore had the final say on whether or not a high-ranking Moscow city official would be charged with corruption. The trade leaders also succeeded in buying support from apparatchiks of the Central Party Committee and the Moscow Party Committee, from the heads of the Trade and Maintenance and the Finance departments, and from the Party secretaries of the Dzerzhinski, Babushkin, Nevski, and Perovski districts. These Party secretaries were very influential and almost independent of the Moscow Party organization because they headed model districts. The Moscow Party Committee's Department of Trade and Maintenance had to deal with the trade organizations in the capital. It did not have to administer trade, a function that was the responsibility of the Ministry of Trade, but it did supervise the trade organizations and was responsible for making sure that they and their staffs were working adequately and honestly. In fact, these officials from the Department of Trade and Maintenance became Tregubov's men after they received bribes from executives in the trade network. Unofficially, their work thereafter was primarily to protect their bribe-givers.

The Moscow trade organizations' secondary tactic for gaining support among Party officials was to offer "gifts" on holidays: "Orders included cucumbers, tomatoes, lemons, oranges, bananas, pineapples. When the amount reached 3 kilograms, it was put in bags. Besides that, such orders necessarily contained Armenian or French cognac, good vodka, good champagne. Also included were dairy products and processed fish."[59]

Because this gift-giving tactic involved less monetary value, it had its advantages, since it did not look like overt bribery and thus did not constitute a serious criminal offense. Another advantage of this practice was that the purchase of the Party officials was achieved at a relatively low price. This kind of "donation" did not imply consent from the receiver, or at least not explicit consent, and it could be given to the targeted person's wife or mother.

One of the major successes of the trade leaders was their purchase of Party support at the Moscow district level. It was through favors to the district soviet and MVD leaders, who were in a position to counter any accusations against them, that the trade leaders consolidated their influence with the district Party secretaries, who also accepted gifts. Whether the favors rendered were actually bribes or true gifts was often a matter of interpretation. While the food given to Party officials was presented as a gift, the amount of food involved was more impressive than what was given to state, soviet, or police officials. The district Party boss received about twenty kilos of a variety of scarce food products, of a value of about a hundred rubles, with lower-status Party officials receiving less. In one police interrogation, the driver for a *kontora* director divulged information about the delivery of such orders:

> *Question:* Do you know how much such deliveries cost?
> *Answer:* For example, an order for the secretary of the Dzerzhinski District Party Committee cost 100 rubles. But the orders were less valuable for deputies and officials of the different organizations, who received no vodka or cognac, but only bottles of champagne.[60]

This generosity was appreciated and even expected by Party officials, but it had its risky side too, because a zealous prosecutor or a new Glavtorg leader could suddenly appear, interpret such gifts as bribes, and put the recipients behind bars or at least cause their expulsion from the Party. But in the Brezhnev era, no one imagined that for such a paltry gesture a Party official would run into problems with the justice system.

Another regular practice was to invite Party officials to the *kontoras*, where they would be volunteers and sort food according to quality. During the Brezhnev era, personnel from numerous organizations performed this work, which was supposed to be unpaid, but in fact Party officials would take some of the best food home with them. Yet another means of distributing favors was to encourage friendships within Party apparatchik circles to create opportunities to meet outside the workplace.[61] One last common practice throughout the Soviet Union in the Brezhnev era was to organize receptions for the guests of high-ranking officials and to look after participants attending conferences, as a trade leader in Rostov recalls:

> When this conference took place, I had to take care of some [Party] secretaries, whose names I have forgotten, from the following districts: Cherossovski, Chenichevski, Brianski, and Riazanski. I had to accompany them, to find a hotel room for them, and to feed them when they were not at their meetings: I had to offer them lunch and dinner in the evening. Moreover, there were souvenirs to give: a scarf that cost 55 rubles, and

a typical vase of the region for 50 rubles; up to 150 rubles for everyone. Also, a bottle of champagne made by the Cossacks in Rostov. Initially, when they told me that the person accompanying them must pay for all this, I wanted to tell them to go to hell. I understood that they would have expelled me from the Party or that I would have lost my job for this. But what did I have to lose? Money, I have enough . . . but I did not refuse.[62]

The Glavtorg leaders in Moscow had to organize more conferences and receptions for high-level officials than did trade organizations in other cities. The importance of their role was magnified because these events were for the Moscow Party Committee, the Moscow soviet's Executive Committee, the USSR Ministry of Trade, and the Ministry of Trade of the Russian Republic. The following account illustrates the role of the Moscow trade leaders in the organization of conferences:

Delegates from all the republics and regions met at the Moscow Party Committee for a conference on the fruit and vegetable supply in Moscow. After the conference, the delegates stayed in Moscow to eat. Tregubov headed this reception. This delightful occasion took place at the Hotel Moskva, in the banquet hall. There were 80 people; for each one, the cost was 15–20 rubles. They were given good cognac, good vodka, good hors d'oeuvres, good caviar, and other delicacies. Of course, we received 200 rubles from the government to organize this delight, but it cost 1,500–3,000 rubles, and maybe more.[63]

Trade executives did their utmost to please Party officials at such gatherings by taking their demands and particular tastes into account, and the goal of serving the correct variety of tempting foods was to compromise the integrity of the maximum number of influential people. The trade leaders knew that certain Party officials were not particularly interested in money but preferred to take part in meetings where good alcohol and delicacies were in abundance. In certain cases, they organized meetings that also included an element of erotic pleasure: "First secretaries of the Dzerzhinski Party Committee, M. A. Ablochin and N. G. Komarov, phoned to tell me that there should be a meeting outside of Moscow, with good food and good alcohol. We also should invite employees from the KGB Party Committee. They told me that the secretaries and deputy secretaries of the district Party Committee would attend this meeting. They were drinking, eating, and kissing. At the end, the unfinished food was packed and brought home."[64]

For Party officials reluctant to take bribes, even gifts in kind, because they were afraid of eventual problems with the law, the trade executives were careful

to find solutions that took such reticence into account. Many officials received "legal" favors, such as being able to skip a long queue of customers when they paid for the best goods at official prices. Even though no law was broken in such a case, the discovery that Party officials had accepted such privileges from a store manager would be serious enough to end their political careers.

Because some trade executives still felt insecure even after buying substantial support among Party apparatchiks, they expended considerable effort in trying to get colleagues appointed to key posts in the Party hierarchy. The practices that trade executives developed at city and district levels to get colleagues into Party and government agencies were very successful and reflected the growing influence of the trade organizations. A report by the Prosecutor General's Office in 1986 stressed that "many who worked before in the trade organizations have reached commanding positions in Party, soviet, and economic structures, where they continue to be useful to their networks."[65]

The appointment of trade executives to the upper echelons of the Party is worthy of attention. The cases of Tregubov and Pospelov are good illustrations. Tregubov reached the post of president of the Moscow Trade Administration after a career in the food trade sector. It was only after he rose to the top of the trade network in the capital that he began a second career as a Party leader. After he was nominated to head the Moscow Glavtorg, Tregubov was responsible for appointing people to the trade organizations, but in the second half of the 1970s, his responsibilities were broadened to include recommending candidates for the Moscow Party Committee's Department of Trade and Maintenance. In 1980, Pospelov, who had made his career in the Moscow Fruit and Vegetable Office, was appointed head of the food section of the Moscow Party Committee's Department of Trade and Maintenance.[66] He emerged as the third most important of the Moscow Party "trade men" after Tregubov and Buchin. All major trade issues were referred to Tregubov, as a member of the Moscow Party Committee, to decide on behalf of the Party. At all levels, the trade leaders enjoyed favored treatment from Party officials, but their representation was the strongest at the district level. District Party secretaries were not afraid to publicly manifest their high consideration for the bosses of the trade organizations. They invited the "trade men" to Party meetings, where they sat with district officials such as the Party secretaries, the president of the Moscow soviet, the secretary of the trade union, and the head of the district MVD. Trade leaders also served as deputies in the local soviet and as members of the Trade Union Committee.[67]

The Moscow trade organizations' success in building networks and controlling and influencing officials in their own and in other spheres was impressive, particularly as they managed to turn entities that were supposed to combat corruption into their allies. These control bodies were mainly law enforcement

agencies; it could be said that the trade organizations' success was relative, since the judiciary organs in the Soviet system were not as strong as they would have been under the rule of law more common in the West. Their most significant influence lay in the diverse echelons of the Moscow Party Committee, which had never been corrupted to this extent before. However, Moscow Party leader Grishin was not involved, although he supported several Party officials who had accepted bribes and knew about their irregularities but only defended most of them after they were accused. He believed in the honesty of most of his officials and was persuaded that the accusations about them were a tactic of his enemies to discredit and replace him and his team. As for their failures, trade leaders never managed to compromise a member of the Politburo, and one factor that should have concerned corrupt trade leaders was that Glavtorg and Glavka enjoyed little support from the KGB.

Social Capital

The trade staff was united by not only corruption but also the sincere friendships that developed within its ranks. The leaders of the trade network worked to build trust among its staff members. Trust was a component of the social capital that was essential to the functioning of the trade organizations. Social capital was situated within the executive's general relations with the rest of society and, more specifically, with colleagues. The more trust that existed among executives, the stronger their positions would be. Furthermore, executives recognized the importance of mutual aid not only with respect to work issues but also personal matters. For example, executives found it important to have their own support system of individuals who could provide assistance in case personal difficulties suddenly arose. After all, citizens could not always count on Soviet institutions for social support.

Trade executives confided in colleagues with whom they colluded in economic irregularities, and these special relationships often extended beyond working hours. Directors did not own their stores but had total control over them during the workday. From eight o'clock in the morning until closing time, store directors invited people to their stores to relax, drink alcohol, or eat with them. This practice was the simplest means of creating social capital. Among the invited guests were high-profile officials who could play the role of protector. Store directors might already be involved with them in corrupt activities, but inviting them for midday socializing would strengthen the personal relationship between them, gain the officials' trust, and through the latter's connections, bring about introductions to even more influential people. For example, according to Rosliakov, A. D. Ulagin told him that "there was no day that MVD leaders did

not come at lunch- and dinnertime to take food, vodka, and beer. Almost every day, V. I. Filippov, deputy director, and V. F. Ivanov, deputy director of the MVD district section, were invited. I've heard that they even got drunk sometimes in Filippov's office. I saw it with my own eyes on certain occasions. I wondered when they found time to work."[68] Directors could not transform their stores into restaurants, but they could entertain guests with good conversation, free delicacies, and the prospect of further illegal gains.

The number of conferences and meetings of all kinds increased significantly during the Brezhnev era. Such meetings, usually organized by the trade agencies, were official functions tied to work matters or to holidays and involved a gathering of small or large groups. Sometimes these meetings were intended for the employees of a single store, other times for the representatives of all the stores in Moscow, and, on occasion, for the directors of different categories of stores in the same district. Each meeting or reception was an occasion to get to know people better, to establish a friendly relationship with them, and to meet new people. The meetings served as a means of collecting information on what colleagues could offer and what they expected in return. Hosting a successful meeting of this type implied that one could expect to obtain access to additional services and products.

Many executives also liked to meet at public baths or country homes. There, they could relax in a familiar and intimate atmosphere. According to Ambartsumyan, "They went for several years to the Sandunovskie bath, the most comfortable bath and the one that provided all services: massage, food, etc. The same circle of friends met there."[69] The executives who colluded in the shadow economy used the baths as a venue in which to discuss their transactions in detail and conclude deals. It was safer to do this in public places other than the workplace, where it might arouse the suspicions of employees. Moreover, several executives had reached an age that made them appreciate the baths for therapeutic reasons. Often, a director would reserve a separate room at the baths. Roganov was one of the executives who discussed major deals with influential people at this privileged venue: "At the central bath, he [Roganov] began to invite other people: store managers with whom he was acquainted, and who frequently traveled abroad." The baths were also a place where gifts could be exchanged: "At the beginning, Roganov, B. G. Nazarev, Beniaminov, and A.V. Kuvaldin went to the baths. Often, an acquaintance of his, a pilot . . . would come and give him souvenirs."[70] Introducing an important person like an Aeroflot pilot had a significant psychological impact on Roganov's colleagues, building esteem and trust among them. Like the other trade executives, he sought to strengthen his network by any means possible. The more impressive the network, the easier it was to attract new adherents and thus increase influence.

Free time was not spent only in business discussions. The executives also liked to socialize with friends. Executives never forgot that one day they might be helping a friend manage some sort of problem and the following day they might be in need of assistance themselves. Furthermore, executives who made profits through corruption found it useful to build friendships with work colleagues, usually their subordinates, who were not involved in bribery in order to make it less likely that the latter would denounce them to the police. So executives sought out occasions to help such friends. Ambartsumyan related this type of relationship with his colleagues: "With Noris A. Mesumian, Roganov, and some other people, we went to the outskirts of Moscow to relax, sometimes for two hours, sometimes more. I knew Noris, his father, and his brother. When his brother died in Moscow, I helped arrange the transportation of the coffin from Domodedovo airport to the city of Tbilisi."[71] Ambartsumyan used his personal connections to offer a service that was theoretically the state's responsibility but that, in practice, was not properly carried out by the state. Here, the accumulation of social capital extended to helping a colleague in a personal matter.

The dacha or country house was another of the trade executives' favorite venues for meetings and building up personal networks. Ambartsumyan said that "the most intensive period in my relationship with Roganov was from 1980 to August 1981. With a small group, we met [at the dacha] every Saturday and ate together."[72] Executives had to dedicate a considerable amount of time to these informal relations in order to succeed in the shadow economy, which was pervasive in nature. Relations became closer and social capital increased with the frequency of these meetings.

Formal invitations to celebrate important events in the lives of the executives provided still more occasions to get together. At executives' birthday parties or the weddings of their children, they had the opportunity to impress their colleagues by displaying their power, and they could expect to receive gifts and bribes. The best restaurants in the capital—the Prague, for example—were favorite places to celebrate. These gatherings could be extravagant. When Sokolov celebrated his daughter's marriage in 1981, hosts and guests drank heavily and acted as if they owned the restaurant. They drew other customers' attention by their rowdiness, even though they were simply following a Russian tradition when they ended their toasts by throwing their glasses of vodka at the wall and on the floor.

In addition to inviting influential officials for pleasure weekends in the region surrounding Moscow, trade leaders took excursions on the Moskva River, even during working hours. High-ranking officials and executives, including Buchin, head of the Control Commission of the Moscow Party Committee; Uraltsev, the director of Glavka; and Bikanov, deputy director of the Dzerzhinski *kontora*, found time to meet as friends and enjoy life, as Ambartsumyan describes: "Bu-

chin, Uraltsev, Bikanov, and I, on the orders of Uraltsev, chartered a yacht, leaving from Klebnikov, a vacation area. We cooked some fish, beef, and chicken on a spit, and we drank heavily. On our way back, Uraltsev fell in the water and got completely soaked. We came back to Klebnikov, where a car was waiting for us."[73]

These pleasure jaunts were opportunities to gain the support of high-echelon officials through friendship instead of by offering bribes, which might be refused. Flattery, awards, and gifts were the means used to win the officials over.

Friendship and trust enhanced the network's cohesion, strengthening links among corrupt trade executives and preparing the ground to recruit new ones. The network also fulfilled needs that had nothing to do with trade matters—for example, the need simply to spend time with friends whom one could trust, to talk things over and ask advice about personal problems, for example, with a divorce or with children. The trust developed in the network could even influence the choice of a marriage partner.

Other considerations influenced the workings of networks. Numerous executives and employees, especially those who had come back from the war in 1945 in a weakened state, worried about proper health care; this need for medical attention explains why many executives stayed on the job for long periods and accepted illegal money. Although illegal practices in stores had further negative effects on their health, their networks gave some of them the chance to receive better care.

Even though many staff members paid bribes to their superiors, some of them desired a minimum of involvement in corruption in order to diminish the amount of risk and the stress it generated. Corrupt executives preferred a network composed at least in part of honest and sincerely friendly colleagues. Some employees attempted to change their relationship with superiors and protectors so that it would be exclusively based on trust and friendship rather than on illegal dealings. Corrupt trade employees knew they were at risk: at any moment, they could be exposed and lose their money and their reputations. Some might be arrested. They knew that an anticorruption campaign would not result in the arrest of all the lawbreakers in the trade organizations because there were simply too many of them. They knew, however, that if they were arrested individually, they were powerless and that the network was their only hope.

During the Brezhnev era, the Kremlin decided that Moscow deserved to be named a "communist city," and it became a model for the rest of the country.[74] Moscow's Glavtorg and Glavka were presented as examples for other trade organizations, and their staffs developed close and harmonious relations with the Communist Party. For example, Gurgen Karakhanov, the Baumanski *kontora* director, received an award in September 1981 for his longtime work with the Baumanski Komsomol Organization, which provided communist youth education.

Trade leaders built up personal relationships with Communist Party officials so that the latter would unconditionally support Glavtorg and Glavka. Thus, city and district Party organizations praised and awarded trade officials and rarely criticized them. Efforts to reform the Moscow trade organizations had effectively ended with the removal of Khrushchev in 1964.

The Party's support of the Moscow trade organizations was due to more than just the involvement of its officials in graft. Grishin, the Moscow Party chief, knew that shortages and corruption did not occur as isolated phenomena in the capital, although he refused to accept that they were generalized.[75] However, he viewed the trade organizations through the eyes of the executive he trusted the most: Tregubov. Grishin believed that corruption was kept under control because of Tregubov's personal integrity. He also held the view, as did Tregubov, that nothing could be done to oppose corruption practiced by high-ranking officials, who included members of Brezhnev's and Foreign Minister Gromyko's families. Corruption, according to Grishin and Tregubov, depended on identifiable factors such as speculators from the south coming to empty the stores in Moscow, which were much better supplied.

Other Moscow Party officials shared their boss's positive view of the activities of the trade organizations, particularly if they had developed good relations with trade executives. They were pleased by the role trade executives played in the preparation of well-provisioned conferences and meetings. Moreover, they appreciated it when delicacies, considered gifts rather than bribes, were delivered to their apartments on holidays or when scarce products were reserved for them. Only personal relations based on discretion and trust could provide perks like these that did not bear an official seal of approval.

The excellent results achieved by the trade organizations, according to data from the Moscow soviet's Planning Commission, confirmed that store managers deserved to be models for the whole country. For all these reasons, Party officials placed elsewhere all blame for the persistent problems in the grocery stores.

The trade leaders also had contacts in the media who would defend their reputations as good managers. In several publications, it was claimed that directors would have been able to supply their stores better if customers and speculators did not come from all over the country to empty them. This affirmation was not entirely false, since stores, particularly grocery stores in the provinces, were not as well stocked as those in the capital. In this sense, Glavtorg appeared to be a victim of its own success. Certain analyses in the media denounced low salaries or inequalities in salary levels as justifications for the trade employees' tendency to work unconscientiously and even their embezzlement of socialist property. The press also attributed the shortages of food products in the stores to negligence rather than corruption.

Other sectors of society supported the trade organizations by making persuasive arguments. Certain scholars defended the trade employees by referring to
social theories, for example, by pointing to the effects of urbanization as reasons
for economic crimes in the trade organizations.[76] These interpretations of food
supply problems were myriad and had some credibility. Along with journalists
and scholars, dissidents had a tendency to exonerate or at least limit the responsibility of the Moscow trade organizations with regard to their shortcomings.
The dissident Medvedev stated that the loss of food through negligence during
its transportation from the villages to the cities was a major factor in creating
scarcities in the grocery stores.[77]

Party officials and members of the media and the intelligentsia had a trust-
based relationship with important members of the trade staff. They were aware
of the material advantages that could be gained from store directors and thus
cultivated friendships with them. However, this trust was more apparent in Party
officials than Party organizations or Soviet laws, which the trade staff officially
endorsed but, in fact, did not respect. On one hand, trade leaders' supporters attempted to minimize and dissimulate violations of Soviet law. On the other hand,
certain supporters sincerely believed in the integrity of their friends in the trade
bodies. With the passing of time, this contradiction—respect for Soviet norms
versus violation of them, or honesty and social justice on one hand versus the
appetite for illegal material gains on the other—would only increase.

Soviet bureaucrats were subject to verification by certain control agencies,
just as their counterparts are in the West. However, executives in the trade organizations, starting with Glavtorg president Tregubov, possessed enough strength
to neutralize these controls, which were managed by law enforcement agencies,
the municipal administration, and the Party under Brezhnev. With their considerable influence, Moscow trade leaders were rarely opposed in higher circles.
The importance of trade executives was attested to by the following fact: after the
1980 Olympics, the Soviet government decided that many trade leaders would
be presented with awards at the Moscow Soviet House. Petrikov revealed that
Sokolov was opposed to this: "Sokolov said, 'Why should it be in the soviet? They
should reward us in the Kremlin.' And it was in the Kremlin. Sokolov, with his
Polaroid, strolled through the Kremlin as if he owned it."[78]

The executives of the Moscow trade structures achieved considerable power
because each of Mueller's three conditions for gaining bureaucratic power was
present. Subject to no control, the executives had a monopoly over the distribution of goods and colluded with their superiors and suppliers. In this privileged
position, the majority of them received considerable sums through bribe-taking.
This explains how Glavtorg and Glavka arose as powerful forces in the 1980s and

could thus bargain from a position of power. A number of former trade executives were either Party officials or enjoyed wide support in the higher echelons of power. Since money and resources were given to many influential people, the trade executives had support throughout Moscow society. And, not surprisingly, due to the lack of control over them, no Moscow trade executives were prosecuted or lost their jobs between 1964 and 1981, despite the deep involvement of many of them in graft.

Regarding Weber's concept of authority types, the neopatrimonial leadership type predominates in the history of Russian bureaucracy, particularly in the trade organizations. In the 1970s, most trade executives had been put in place according to traditional criteria: bribe-giving, nepotism, and other types of favoritism. Those who appointed employees and supervised their activities were deeply involved in corruption, but some portion of the leadership necessarily comprised executives of the rational-legal type, who generally respected regulations in the trade sector. The charismatic type of executive was heavily represented in the Moscow trade network. Such leaders built their power upon the support they enjoyed in society from members of the intelligentsia and the nomenklatura, who appreciated receiving services and scarce goods from the trade executives in a manner that involved a minimum of risk; charismatic executives paid more attention to their needs than did traditional or rational-legal types of executives. However, these two types of leaders were not opposed to the charismatic executives because the bribes they gave and other offenses they committed were for the sake of their organizations rather than for personal benefit.

The trade organizations also featured premodern social capital. Personal relations were encouraged as a means of building trust and solidarity among trade staff members, which increased their capacity to consolidate the organization's interests and its resistance to hostile forces. Through such cooperation, trade leaders found new ways of bribe-taking that helped them accrue greater profits from corruption. Moreover, social capital was intended to decrease the risk that colleagues would inform the authorities about illegal activities. Mistrust of and opposition to the state constituted another element of the social capital prevailing in the trade network, and such attitudes encouraged the taking of resources from the state and the violation of its laws. The social atmosphere of the trade networks thus had a negative impact on relations between civil society and the state because it encouraged hostility between them.

2

Integrity and Efficiency
The KGB's Anticorruption War

■ Andropov's role as longtime KGB chief is an important aspect of the agency's fight against corruption, and a brief review of the KGB's development highlights his ascent.

The KGB and Its Past

The KGB was shaped by the nature of the Soviet regime, which gave it an increasingly important role after 1917, as well as by the character of its leaders. During the first years of the Soviet Union, it constituted a powerful force because the regime had weak support and was in danger of collapse, thus making recourse to repression very appealing. In 1917, Lenin appointed Dzerzhinski the first leader of the Cheka (All-Russian Extraordinary Commission for Combating Counterrevolution and Sabotage). The man had no legal background or qualifications, but Lenin appreciated the fact that he had been hardened by a long jail term and was ready to do anything for the Soviet system. Dzerzhinski tended to see the world in Manichaean terms—as a war between the forces of good (communism) and evil (capitalism), where all means were justified to defeat those who did not adhere to Soviet ideals. Such fanaticism led Dzerzhinski to summarily execute opponents of the regime; he was a zealot whose excesses were denounced even by Lenin. With civil war, economic reconstruction, and other urgent issues demanding attention, the Cheka was viewed as the most reliable ally of the Communist Party, especially in the countryside. It was at the forefront of the battles against the adversaries of communism and addressed the biggest problems facing the regime. Dzerzhinski was appointed president of the com-

mittee combating bribery, considered one of the major scourges afflicting the Soviet Union during this period.[1] The Kremlin also looked to him in emergencies
such as natural disasters and to resolve problems such as homeless children and
working conditions in the mines. In desperate situations, citizens would make
direct appeals to him.

Dzerzhinski's multiple fields of activity made him the obvious person to perform the most important function of the security service: to collect information
for the leaders of the country, who ostensibly needed this information to implement efficient policies. Since the Communist Party needed as much information
as possible to consolidate its power and rule the country, political leaders were, to
a certain extent, dependent on the security service. The Cheka was thus in a position to exert influence on the Kremlin and Communist Party policy by selecting
the information that would be divulged to Party leaders. Such information included negative data, that is, details that exposed the Soviet system's weaknesses.
To uncover such details, security agents made it their business to know what
preoccupied people, who opposed the regime, and what plans those opponents
might be hatching. Agents collected information on the private lives of not only
the regime's opponents but also the nomenklatura, documenting behavior that
may not have been illegal but was considered morally reprehensible. Political
leaders found this information useful for eliminating their opponents, but the security force could also store it for future use against the same officials. The security service's power was accentuated because information did not circulate freely
in the regime, which made it all the harder for politicians to defend themselves
against compromising information coming from the security service.

It is probable that some Cheka agents, even the leaders, were influenced by
the viewpoints and proposals of opponents of the regime. Having a good picture of their society's main problems and possible solutions, agents believed that
the Soviet system was in need of reform and that they possessed the abilities to
become its leaders and address the issues facing the country. In times of weak
leadership at the Kremlin, the temptation to become directly involved in politics
was difficult to resist. Although he was an unconditional Leninist, Dzerzhinski
took a position in favor of economic reform. He was opposed to total state control of the economy; his solution was the market, a concept most of the Party
leaders, including Lenin, rejected outright. Dzerzhinski had political ambitions
and would have preferred to be a leader of the Communist Party instead of chief
of the security service. Thus, like some other Cheka leaders, Dzerzhinski shared
an attraction to reformism and a more political role.

One characteristic of the security force that endured throughout its evolution
was a low level of involvement in corruption. Its members had to meet stringent standards regarding their honesty, and they tended to detest people who

obtained diplomas or job positions through bribery or nepotism. There was also a corporatist interest in avoiding corruption as an institution, particularly since the security force gained power specifically by combating corruption.

Cheka agents had higher salaries than did officials of the Ministry of Interior. They enjoyed a decent standard of living, which meant they had less of a motivation to become involved in corruption. Cheka leaders wanted their agents abroad to project an irreproachable image in the countries where they operated. They believed that, as the agents were closely watched by security services in those countries, corrupt practices would be soon discovered by their Western counterparts. Moreover, the staff of the security force was influenced by its leaders, who were behavioral models they were to follow. Dzerzhinski hired and promoted people who shared his austere lifestyle and modesty. However, in spite of having several traits in common, Cheka leaders were still very different from each other, a fact that was demonstrated by the evolution of the security force from the time of Lenin to Stalin's era.

The 1930s were a transformative period for Soviet institutions, including the security service. While Stalin relied on Dzerzhinski's support until the latter's death in 1926, he could not impose his politics on him. After 1926, Chekists were suspicious of Stalin. The Stalinist campaign for collectivization was unwelcome to Cheka leaders, who favored a market economy, especially in the countryside. To Stalin, security force leaders were a threat, and the Kremlin had already gone after them in the late 1920s. In 1928, Tolmachev, an MVD leader close to the Cheka, was tried and sent to a labor camp for opposing Stalin and sympathizing with Trotskyism. Stalin could not execute Tolmachev at that time, but his arrest and conviction were a first step toward the summary executions that followed.

In the mid-1930s, when the Cheka was absorbed, together with the Ministry of the Interior, into the NKVD (People's Commissariat for Internal Affairs), its authority was undermined by the weakness of its leaders relative to the absolute power of Stalin. Stalin was suspicious of the NKVD, an organization that remained secretive and enjoyed significant autonomy until the mid-1930s, when Stalin learned that the NKVD leader Iezhov had secret dealings with Bukharin, Stalin's chief opponent; it served as a pretext for him to arrest NKVD leaders and have them executed. It was also the signal for him to assign a new function to the NKVD. He transformed the security force into an instrument that he used to consolidate his personal power; more precisely, Stalin needed this organization to be able to carry out an in-depth purge of Party and government staff and replace them with a new generation of managers and executives who were more servile toward him. From 1936 to 1938, Iezhov had been the most powerful figure in the Soviet Union after Stalin, who had used Iezhov to implement the most repressive measures in Soviet history. The role of the NKVD continued to be

expansive under Iezhov's successor, Beria, who led the security force from 1938 to 1953. The odious crimes committed by the NKVD during this period indelibly stained the security force's reputation. After the deaths of Stalin and Beria, its power and influence would diminish considerably.

When the elimination of the market at the beginning of the 1930s led to a degradation of the social and economic situation, Stalin needed the security force to deal with the number-one problem: the food supply. The fact that the peasants were forced to sell their harvest to the state at low prices, together with the appearance of a Soviet retail structure in which state stores sold food products, gave rise to much discontent. Hostility toward the regime first appeared in the countryside and then spread to the cities, including Moscow. Economic crimes such as pilfering ("embezzlement of socialist property") and speculation proliferated. The security force was ordered to gather more information and to intensify repression. The NKVD learned to "spy" on public opinion to an unprecedented extent. Not surprisingly, the Kremlin mobilized the police against the scourge of corruption and shortages in the stores. Their methods included an unforgiving clampdown on store directors in which the director of the most important grocery store, the Eliseevski *gastronom,* was executed. Investigations revealed that graft flourished thanks to the support of high-level managers, several of whom wound up behind bars. The minister of trade himself was imprisoned. Other executives in the food distribution network were indicted based on depositions obtained by the NKVD that bribes had been paid by store directors and speculators to a number of government bureaucrats and Party officials. This severe crackdown coincided with the terror-filled years of the second half of the 1930s. The same evidence gathered against food retailing executives in the campaign against economic crimes served to condemn them to gulags as "enemies of the people," or rather, enemies of Stalin. The heads of the NKVD who had led these investigations were arrested in their turn and vanished into the black eddy of the terror, which weakened the security force in the short term. The experience played in its favor years later, when NKVD agents were seen as victims of Stalinism.

While the impact of the type of leader on the security service's ethics and behavior had been positive in the early period of the Soviet Union, the opposite effect prevailed during the Beria years. Despite this negative aura, Beria resembled previous security force leaders in his political ambitions and his reformist tendencies. Upon Stalin's death, he aspired to be his successor in the Kremlin, unexpectedly presenting himself as a reformist leader. His program proposed to retrocede territory to Japan and to support the reunification of the two Germanies in exchange for economic assistance. His equally liberal ideas for Soviet society included greater freedom for citizens and an emphasis on native language

rights, rather than the mandated use of Russian, in the Union republics. Beria's reformist program showed that he was well versed on the problems affecting the country, which was not surprising for a man who had led the NKVD for a long period. However, Beria's liberal "new look" did not persuade the nomenklatura to let him to take power. Nothing could prevent him from paying for the terrible crimes he had committed under Stalin.

While the Party was divided and hesitated on whether to arrest Beria or not, it was the army that determined the outcome, and Khrushchev defeated Beria in the battle to replace Stalin. Again in 1957, in conflict with the Stalinists, Khrushchev was saved by the army. During these crises, the security force remained silent. Police powers were limited, because Khrushchev wanted a political regime with less repression. In 1954, the Kremlin announced the dissolution of the NKVD and the primacy of the KGB, and measures were adopted to restrict the KGB's role in the judiciary organs and process. After Beria's execution, investigations within the ranks of the security force led to the replacement of forty-six thousand officers. Former Beria colleagues and others suspected of sympathy for him and Stalin were forced to retire. Khrushchev and other Party leaders did not want a KGB leader as general secretary of the Party or even as a Politburo member. They had learned that a police officer should not be allowed to take control of the Party, as Beria had almost done in 1953. Circumspection toward the KGB went further: its leaders were now recruited from outside its ranks, and even candidates with strong personalities were excluded. The Ministry of the Interior was resuscitated and granted wide prerogatives, some of which had previously belonged to the security force. The Prosecutor General's Office was another beneficiary of the restrictions on the KGB's jurisdiction.

At the Twenty-second Party Congress, Khrushchev declared the beginning of a new period marked by the assumption that socialism had definitively triumphed in the Soviet Union. Kremlin leaders proclaimed that it was not necessary to use widespread violence to ensure the security of the country. The KGB had to adjust its modus operandi to the new Communist Party policies. Peaceful means were now preferred as more effective and efficient; the use of forceful methods was substantially reduced and restricted to exceptional circumstances. Henceforth, the battles would be more complex. A greater volume of sophisticated information was required to persuade the people of the superiority of socialism. Violence and war were no longer determinants in relations with the forces of capitalism. However, the battles between capitalism and socialism continued inside and outside the Soviet Union.

The new political atmosphere did not appear to augur well for the KGB at first. The optimism of the Khrushchev period made it seem as if there were no need for the security force, that the Soviet Union had become so strong that

nothing threatened the country or the regime. This optimism was premature: it soon became clear that the Eastern European socialist regimes were not as solid as had been believed. The "Prague Spring" of 1968 was a warning sign that a Soviet bloc regime was not unshakeable. The Kremlin feared that what had happened in Prague was a precedent and that a similar uprising was possible in the Soviet Union. The affirmations that socialism had definitely prevailed and that the adversaries of the regime were too weak to constitute a serious threat were contradicted by increased dissident activities in Russia, particularly in the 1970s. National groups had not manifested separatist aspirations, but nationalist agitation was nevertheless also on the rise. In spite of the improvements in food supply and distribution, especially compared with the 1930s, economic crimes had been increasing since the 1960s, another sign of discontent. The fact that the Party was incapable of countering the above threats with any effectiveness played in the KGB's favor.

Andropov was appointed head of the KGB in May 1967. He replaced Shelepin, who was viewed as too ambitious and independent by Brezhnev. Andropov appeared to be a modest and balanced candidate. He had acquired a reputation of strength and toughness from his preponderant role in the crushing of the Hungarian revolution by the Soviet army in October 1956, although his image as a hawk was nuanced by his support of Kadar in Hungary—the only liberal communist leader in Eastern Europe. During his first years as KGB head, Andropov kept a low profile, avoiding media exposure, but it was not long before his actions attracted favorable attention at the Kremlin. From 1967 onward, he wrote confidential reports to the Politburo on domestic manifestations of Muslim fundamentalism, terrorist plots, extreme nationalism, and major criminal acts. He insisted on the necessity of elaborating and disseminating sophisticated Soviet ideology to combat extremism. He drew up speeches designed to refute and put a damper on the spread of nationalism and other contentious issues.[2] The Party was so pleased by Andropov's performance that its leaders made him a Politburo member in 1973, showing that he had won their trust. Andropov was encouraged to pay attention to more complex, sensitive issues, including the KGB's relations with other judicial organs. One highly placed official opposed him in this enterprise: Shchelokov, the minister of the interior.

Andropov versus Shchelokov

Andropov wanted to appear to be not only a good KGB chief but also the star of the principal judicial bodies of the Soviet Union, and Shchelokov seemed to be a dangerous rival. Authors such as Leonid Mlechin suggest that the bad relationship between the two men acquired major importance in the late 1960s and

1970s.³ The KGB had more powers than the MVD, but Shchelokov had a major advantage in that he was a longtime friend and protégé of Brezhnev. Tension between Andropov and Shchelokov began when the latter took a stand against the KGB's decision to exile Solzhenitsyn. A further point of discord was Shchelokov's opposition to the internal passport imposed by the KGB. Andropov thought that Shchelokov was interfering in the KGB's jurisdiction and was offended by Shchelokov's criticism of the KGB's authoritarianism and attacks against freedom of expression. Beyond their disagreements on the role of the judiciary organs, there was also personal animosity between them. In turning his attention to the problem of corruption in the 1970s, Andropov may have been motivated by the fact that, by doing so, he could weaken Shchelokov's position. Andropov's appointment to the Politburo had already given him an eminent position from which to denounce criminality; he presented it as a dangerous threat to the nation and, by implication, criticized Shchelokov for not doing his job properly. Through an anticorruption campaign, he could take a closer look at the MVD and its leaders and gather compromising information against his enemy.

One criticism of the anticorruption campaign in the Moscow trade network stemmed from the fact that it was conducted by the KGB, an organization that, in principle, had no jurisdiction in this sector. In fact, investigations should have been led by the Ministry of the Interior, which was authorized by the Soviet Constitution to handle economic crimes, speculation, bribery, and the "embezzlement of socialist property," the prosecution of which was the prerogative of the MVD's OBKhSS department. As for the Prosecutor General's Office, its powers with respect to economic crimes included authorizing the detention of suspects and setting time limits for such detentions. The charges had to be serious enough to justify detention, as accused persons could claim *habeas corpus*. The PGO then decided if the evidence was substantial enough to build a case and was subsequently responsible for establishing the person's guilt in court.

The KGB was also responsible for combating economic crimes when these crimes involved foreigners or implied customs infractions and when the sums of money or groups of people involved were considered significant enough to threaten the Soviet system. Drawing a line between one's jurisdiction and the other's was largely a matter of interpretation, and officials with the most influence in the Politburo generally had the best chances of having their point of view prevail. Thus, in the 1970s, Andropov was able to score points against his adversary in this sense, without, however, eclipsing him completely.

According to the law, the Department for Combating Speculation and the Embezzlement of Socialist Property (OBKhSS) of the Ministry of the Interior decided when to act upon rumors or accusations of graft in a store. In the more serious cases, the Party secretary for the city or district would order the OBKhSS to

determine if the suspicions were well founded and would approve its subsequent report. During the 1970s in Moscow, the MVD rejected the great majority of accusations of corruption, for three main reasons: the MVD itself was involved in corruption; MVD agents did not often think they possessed sufficiently solid evidence to indict wrongdoers; and they may have considered an accusation to be well founded but to belong to a category of practices that were widespread in the Soviet Union and had been tolerated for a long period of time. MVD leaders also felt justified in showing tolerance toward reprehensible actions by their agents when their very low salaries were taken into consideration. The police officers responsible for investigating corruption were on the front lines of combat against economic crimes—that is, they were often in the stores and had frequent contact with the personnel. It was inevitable that relationships grew up between agents and store personnel and for gifts or other favors to be offered to agents on special occasions. Good relations developed with store directors, who trusted the MVD agents and who were not always involved in corruption.

The KGB's Growing Influence under Andropov

During the 1970s, the KGB developed expertise in fighting corruption, as Andropov accumulated more information in this area and regularly communicated facts about corruption to the Politburo. Many middle- and high-ranking officials were mentioned in reports as possibly being involved in irregularities; these data were intended to show Party leaders how important a role corruption played in Soviet society. The MVD bosses who were supposed to deal with this issue were almost completely silent about it, while the KGB handled the best-known instances of corruption during the 1970s: notable cases in Rostov, Krasnodar, Moscow, Leningrad, and so forth (table 2.1). The Prosecutor General's Office showed some willingness to cooperate with the KGB (table 2.2). Under KGB supervision, PGO prosecutors brought all kinds of wrongdoers to court: speculators, thieves, murderers, and others.

In the 1970s, the fight against corruption was one of the main preoccupations of the KGB when suspicious activities took place in the non-Russian Union republics or when smuggling was involved. Even within its jurisdictional limitations, the KGB was very busy, particularly in the Caucasus region. In the Rostov and Krasnodar areas, the KGB assembled a considerable amount of information proving that corruption was well rooted in Soviet society, and reports that solidly argued the case were sent to the Politburo. KGB reports also attributed the Polish revolt against the communist system mainly to corruption; whether this explanation was valid or not, it was surely persuasive to the Politburo. In 1980–1981, corruption continued to hold a prominent place on the Kremlin's agenda.

The KGB was sensitive about corruption because the agency believed it posed

a serious threat to the Soviet system and that widespread corruption created an image that was damaging to the country. In 1980–1981, the Western print media reported increasingly often about corruption as one of the main problems of communist regimes. Meanwhile, dissident writings on corruption were becoming more numerous.[4] Both Western journalists and Soviet dissidents claimed that corruption had become a major problem for the Soviet system because of the involvement of high-ranking officials; Soviet Communist Party officials in particular were presumed to be either participating in or passive toward corruption. It was part of the KGB's mandate to inform the Politburo about the perceptions of the Soviet Union abroad; this mandate was a justification to demonstrate to political leaders that corruption was an issue that had to be taken seriously, as Kremlin leaders could not remain indifferent to widespread negative views abroad. However, the main reason that the KGB was so involved in fighting corruption remained the fact that it had already assumed responsibility for the problem during the 1970s. As greater importance was attached to the issue of corruption, the KGB gained influence and was viewed as the organization most capable of dealing with it.

The nomination of the KGB leader as the Party's secretary general in November 1982 gives an idea of how strong the influence of the security force was at that time. Andropov's election as the man to lead the country showed that the

Table 2.1. Major KGB corruption investigations, 1972–1985

Period	Firms and industries	Locations
1972–1982	Svet	Moscow
	Okean	Moscow
	MRKh	Moscow
	Minlegprom (Ministry of Light Industry)	Georgia, Dagestan, Chechnya-Ingushetia, Kazakhstan, the Krasnodar, and Rostov regions
1982–1985	Clothing industry and various local industries	Moscow
	Trade activity	Leningrad, Rostov-na-Donu, Moscow
	Avtotransport	various
	Vneshtorg	Moscow
	Gosnab	Moscow
	Medical and pharmaceutical trades	Moscow and vicinity

Source: Dopolneniia k analizu otdel'nykh iavlenii, obstoiatel'stv, proiavivshikhsia v kontse, 1985 goda i 1986 godu po nastoiashchee vremia (May 12, 1986).

Table 2.2 Cases brought to court by the Prosecutor General's Office

Period	Type of investigation	Entity investigated	Location of investigation
1969–1978	Embezzlement	Dairy industry	Kirghiztan, Kazakhstan
	Embezzlement	Public food facilities	Sverdlovsk
	Bribery	Soviet and judicial organs	Kirghiztan, Uzbekistan, and Dagestan
	Embezzlement and bribery	Light industry	Moscow
1972–1974	Embezzlement and bribery	Light industry	Moscow, Leningrad, Lithuania, Latvia, Ukraine, and Georgia
	Embezzlement, bribery, pilfering, cheating customers	Light industry	Kazakhstan
	Embezzlement, bribery, pilfering, cheating customers	Clothing industry	Moscow, Alma Ata, Petrozasvodsk, and Kazan
1974–1975	Embezzlement and bribery	Kolkhozes, sovkhozes, trade and planning organs	Kazakhstan, Turkmenistan
1974–1975	Criminal tendencies	various	Central Asia, Krasnodar, Urade, Murmansk, Zhdanov, Dnepropetrovsk
	Armed gang attack	Khurtsikavj	Caucasus region
	Armed attacks on police headquarters		Georgia
	Stolen property		Echmedzin, Armenia
	Murder of police captain		Azerbaijan
1979–1988	Various past infractions	Svet stores	Tadjikistan
	Investigation of deputy director	Ministry of Transport, municipal (soviet) level	Oliferenko, Sverdlovsk
	"Leviev case"		Moscow city level
	Fire, Hotel Rossia		Moscow city level
	Pilfering and bribery	Glavtorg and the Moscow Soviet executive committee, in public catering, and in the Moscow City Fruit and Vegetable Office, the Ministry of Foreign Trade, the Ministry of Fisheries, the Okean company, the Moscow Cognac and Wine factories, Samtrest, etc.	
	Murder, drugs and arms smuggling, armed attacks		Moscow region level: Orekhovo, Zuevo, Egor'evsk
	Construction of bridge over Pukino station		Moscow region level
	Collision of passenger and cargo trains at Tcherepanovo station		Novossibirsk rfegion
	Pilfering and bribery	Russian Ministry of Trade	Moscow region and city levels: Tchi, Azerbaijan
	Pilfering and bribery	Russian Ministry of Health and the Union Ministry of Culture	Rostov and Krasnodar regions

Source: Dopolneniia k analizu otdel'nykh iavlenii, obstoiatel'stv, proiavivshikhsia v kontse, 1985 goda i 1986 godu po nastoiashchee vremia (May 12, 19867).

security forces played a fundamental role in Soviet society. This assertion does
not imply that the Communist Party had ceased to be the main power in Russian
society, but it does show that the Party needed the KGB more than before. The
fact that the KGB had again become the main source of appointed Party officials
was equally significant. If incorruptibility was a requirement for a Party official,
it was not surprising that beginning in 1982–1983, the best reference for a candidate was to have a KGB background.[5]

Undoubtedly, the KGB's operations against corruption from 1982 to 1983
and after were very repressive. Analysis reveals the infringement of civil rights,
which was another way the KGB used the situation to increase its influence in
Russian society. However, it did not begin to act in this way without the support
of public opinion. In fact, one of the crucial roles of the KGB had always been to
know the mood of society better than any other Soviet organization and to use
this knowledge to advantage. In 1982, the KGB was well aware that no problem
could irritate the population more than food shortages. In Moscow, popular dissatisfaction was at its peak. Muscovites in particular were troubled by the lack
of food in the stores. Traditionally, Soviet citizens were known to react passively
when confronted by serious problems, thinking that nothing could change. It
was not a new situation to KGB officers, who had been observing civic morale
for a long time. Nevertheless, the KGB and the media had been told over the
previous few years to listen more carefully to people's complaints. The KGB did
so and paid particular attention to complaints about food shortages in Moscow.
In addition, the Party encouraged people to write to the authorities and to the
media if they witnessed instances of corruption.[6] Soviet citizens were also frustrated about having to wait in line in front of grocery stores. By 1982–1983, the
KGB and the Party organs had received millions of letters that denounced cases
of graft in the internal trade organizations.[7] The letters relayed shameful rumors
of blatant corruption. Were these stories true or not? The only way to verify these
accounts was to investigate them. The KGB's weekly reports to the Politburo
about the situation in the country mentioned more and more examples of corruption. The logical move was for the KGB to delve deeper in its inquiries about
corruption.

The KGB as a Model of "Integrity" and "Efficiency" in the Soviet Political System

The KGB's positive image was the result of plans implemented during the
1970s to improve its reputation. While corruption was widespread in the upper echelons of Party and government in the Caucasus region, the KGB had remained upright and had succeeded in bringing corrupt Party and government

leaders to the attention of the law. In Georgia and Azerbaijan, KGB bosses not only cleansed Party and government bodies of corrupt officials but also became the new leaders of these republics.[8] The Soviet press related that corruption was rampant in the non-Russian republics, but, at the same time, it said nothing about a parallel situation in the Slavic republics. In 1981, the Twenty-fourth Party Congress resolved to promote Moscow to the status of "communist city."[9] This status would attribute impressive successes to Moscow in all sectors of activity. As a result, the city could not afford to reveal any significant shortcomings, and even the problem of corruption was presented as marginal. Few cases of corruption were divulged to the public.[10] In other parts of Russia as well, officials talking of their accomplishments boasted that the situation was excellent, and they had little to say about negative phenomena such as graft.

Despite the fact that corruption in the early 1970s was supposedly not a serious challenge to Soviet leaders, and that it was even a forbidden topic of discussion in the media, the KGB had serious grounds for paying close attention to this phenomenon. At international borders, security forces arrested several Soviet citizens and foreigners for smuggling activities.[11] During the investigations, prosecutors gathered material evidence and depositions against middle- and high-ranking Party and government officials; however, the Prosecutor General's Office, not the KGB, was authorized to file charges. All the information uncovered in the investigations was transmitted to the PGO and to the Politburo, which were responsible for the issue. The senior Party and government officials implicated in the investigations were not prosecuted, but data and documents proving their involvement in wrongdoing remained on file.

Late in the 1970s, facts dealing with corruption began to appear in the Soviet press. It was new for millions of citizens to read that incidents were occurring not only in the non-Russian Union republics but in Russia too. The media continued to report cases of corruption in Central Asia and the Caucasus, portraying KGB leaders as champions and heroes in the war against this evil.[12] The press praised Gueidar Aliev, the KGB leader in Azerbaijan who became Party boss of his republic, as a model for other Soviet political leaders to follow. In a 1981 article in *Pravda,* Aliev was given credit for the outstanding success of the economy of Azerbaijan, whereas before, he had been portrayed only as an untainted and competent high-ranking KGB figure.[13] During Aliev's leadership, Azerbaijan drew the attention of Kremlin leaders for an 8 percent economic growth rate, clearly superior to that of other republics. It was a major success for the KGB because it suggested that the security agents could be skillful and successful political leaders. However, Aliev's views on corruption were surprising. In the same article describing his role and achievements in the anticorruption campaign, Aliev affirmed that corruption was still rampant and that only the Central Party

Committee was free of bribery. Aliev's viewpoint was a justification for the grow-ing involvement of the security force in politics.

When corruption charges concerned the customs services, it followed that these incidents should not be handled by Ministry of the Interior officials but by the KGB. These cases involved huge sums of money, and those convicted mostly belonged to well-organized networks in Russia. Moreover, some cases involved the theft of antiques and art objects. All these cases were presented in a very negative and antipatriotic light: speculators were stealing from Russia on many different levels, from food to arts and culture. Corruption was presented in this manner to promote support for the KGB by the nomenklatura and by the Rus-sian people.

During the 1970s, the KGB went to extreme lengths to boost its reputation and to be presented as a model of virtue to the public. First, its prosecutors had to appear very professional in their work. Second, the KGB devoted great efforts to ensuring that there was substantial evidence against suspects. During interroga-tions, KGB agents avoided excessive measures like the use of physical force to ob-tain evidence. They did not attempt to invade sectors beyond their jurisdiction. Most importantly, the KGB took care that its operations occurred under Party supervision. The KGB never showed any inclination to contest Party decisions. Andropov could not be a better example: he submitted everything to Brezhnev, never opposed his decisions, and even became his favorite.[14]

While the KGB possessed the authority to collect data on corruption in the upper echelons, it could not pursue high-ranking officials without the consent of the Party. This restriction was undoubtedly frustrating for the KGB, but the law enforcement agency succeeded, nonetheless, in using this restriction to its advantage. First, the KGB wanted to contrast itself with other organizations by appearing incorruptible. Because it was fighting corruption, it was absolutely es-sential that it stand out as a model with respect to that issue. No other organiza-tion must be perceived as being as incorruptible as the KGB.

As a model leader of the KGB, Andropov was the incarnation of virtue. His private life was irreproachable. While most of the other leaders, including Brezh-nev, had accepted substantial gifts, this was not the case for Andropov.[15] Rumors of enrichment did not circulate about him or his family members. During the early 1980s, no instances of corruption involving KGB officials were revealed. The KGB's reputation as an organization in which high moral fiber predomi-nated was acknowledged in 1981 by the appointment of Andropov as secretary of the important Department of Ideology of the Central Committee of the Com-munist Party. Andropov replaced Suslov, the Party's most important leader after Brezhnev.

Andropov had the reputation of being an efficient leader in the Soviet Union.

Even after his death, the general opinion was that he supported reform. That is why he had such a positive image in society, that and the fact that he was perceived as an honest leader who refused not only bribes but also gifts. He made the KGB into an organization dedicated to fighting corruption. Also contributing to his popularity was his heroic World War II record. Nevertheless, some biographies have recently revealed a darker side to his private life. In order to become a Communist Party leader, one's private life was to be beyond reproach, which meant, among other things, that a man was to keep the same wife, just as Khrushchev, Brezhnev, Gorbachev, and others did. If a member of the Politburo decided to divorce or marry again, he had to gain the approval of his colleagues. The elite knew full well that Shchelokov was attacked and finally dismissed for wrongdoings pertaining to his private life. But despite the fact that Andropov had left his first wife and did not take care of the two children he had with her, his image remained positive among the Russian intelligentsia. Another and more serious negative factor in Andropov's life has been revealed more recently. The son whom Andropov had with his first wife was sent to prison for criminal activities and died at a young age. Andropov would never have become president of the KGB and then leader of the Party had the fate of his son been known. It is quite astonishing that the whole situation regarding his son had been known by neither the public nor his detractors, especially since Andropov was so insistent that a governing officer's private life should be above reproach. Shchelokov is the one person who should have been motivated enough to search for evidence and facts that would have dealt a severe blow to his most dangerous enemy, Andropov. As head of the Ministry of the Interior, he was the one who was most likely to have access to the information that could have put an end to Andropov's career. Yet today it is still an enigma as to why Shchelokov did not find this information. When Andropov threatened to send him to prison for misappropriations and other economic offenses, it would have been logical for Shchelokov to carry out an in-depth investigation into Andropov's private life. Nevertheless, one must not dismiss the possibility that Andropov had taken the initiative to destroy all compromising information pertaining to his son's misconduct. Finally, the sad fate of his son was quite probably a motivating factor in Andropov's dedication to combating corruption and to instigating the campaign against this evil that permeated Moscow society and spread throughout the country. His obsession to fight against corruption, especially corruption within the Ministry of the Interior, may have been motivated by a policy to weaken leaders such as Shchelokov. Nevertheless, this having been said, there is not enough evidence so far to claim that Andropov's campaign against corruption was determined mainly by unfortunate events in his private life.

Andropov's appointment revealed much about the balance of power in the

Soviet system. It confirmed the rising influence of the KGB and that its evolving power was related to corruption. The KGB would not have deemed this issue important unless it had been encouraged to do so by forces that were influential in the Party, even if those bringing their influence to bear were not in the top echelon. While the majority of Politburo members were not inclined to view corruption as a particularly urgent problem, a minority, led by two senior members of the Ministry of Defense and of the KGB, favored taking severe measures to fight corruption.[16]

The army had an influence similar to that of the KGB; both organizations occupied powerful positions just below that of the Communist Party. Neither had been affected by corruption; their shared view was that corruption would damage their organizations. They also shared a nationalistic attitude, wishing to replace the Brezhnev clique with a more competent and dynamic one that would be more effective in the confrontation with the West. There was collaboration between the two in the sense that without the support of the minister of defense, it would have been more problematic for Andropov to become Brezhnev's successor.

These varying attitudes toward corruption determined Andropov's behavior. By reporting more extensively on corruption cases, the KGB seemed to be doing its work, showing the political leaders how serious the issue had become. Information concerning the problem was accompanied by much data and evidence, as the KGB pursued its goal of persuading the Kremlin to increase its oversight in this area. By the end of the 1970s, Andropov enjoyed broader support for this cause. His appeals were highly persuasive because it could not be denied that corruption was flourishing. Certain highly placed officials involved in corruption wanted to prevent him from putting a damper on illegal activity, but some of these were intimidated by the KGB and may have thought that they could benefit more by supporting Andropov than by opposing him. They hoped he would not go after them if they joined forces with him. Other officials may not have not broken the law but lived in fear that the KGB might find compromising information about their lieutenants or their relatives. A curious situation developed: while the Politburo did not change its position of being opposed to corruption in principle, it did not reject the KGB's initiatives. When journalists denounced corruption, with the approval and encouragement of the KGB, a new phase in the approach toward this issue began. Not only was the Politburo informed about the Russian black market but the common citizen was, too. The issue of corruption also became an occasion to depict the KGB as the force capable of opposing wrongdoing. The question of corruption gradually emerged as a central political issue.

Less than a year after his appointment as head of the Department of Ideology, Andropov's ascension in the ranks of the Soviet system culminated in his

appointment as secretary general of the Communist Party in November 1982. Even though Andropov was no longer the leader of the KGB, he benefited considerably from this promotion. As head of the KGB, Andropov had employed people who were not only willing and able to serve the nation but were now also highly reliable instruments for implementing new policies he would put in place as secretary general. Under the guidance of V. Fedorchuk, Andropov's successor as head of the KGB, new rules were adopted by the organization to maximize its positive image. These norms already figured in Soviet ideology but had not often been put into practice by Party officials. KGB agents were required to be socially visible and to project pride in their positions by wearing uniforms representing their status. It was strictly forbidden for them to accept gifts. KGB members were not allowed to own dachas and were expected, along with their families, to declare their assets. KGB members with relatives who broke the law on any level were dismissed from their positions.

Andropov would not have been able to achieve success if he had not built up support for his cause, and the organization he led for so many years was instrumental in his achievement. During the 1970s, Andropov promoted KGB agents who successfully apprehended dissidents. Several of these prosecutors were from outside Russia, a good example being Fedorchuk, who was the KGB leader in Ukraine. Andropov was so impressed by the way Fedorchuk had successfully repressed dissidents in that republic that he chose him as his successor at the KGB.[17] Fedorchuk arrived in Moscow with a team of unconditionally supportive partisans he had assembled in Kiev. In Moscow, Andropov gathered all the necessary information to be able to choose prosecutors who were trustworthy and endowed with integrity. One such prosecutor was Sterligov, recruited from the Customs Department.[18] Andropov's decision to expunge Brezhnevian rule from the KGB and, in the meantime, to lead a campaign against corruption, opened up opportunities for a new generation of KGB officers. Beginning in 1981, many KGB rookies were impatient to acquire experience and to prove to their bosses that they were well trained. However, Andropov's primary source of recruitment was from among the prosecutors who had distinguished themselves in their fight against dissidence in the 1970s. The hunt for dissenters, at least within Russia, had been the KGB's main task during the 1970s. It was through the prosecutors' remarkable success in the battles against dissidents that Andropov had won substantial approval in the high circles of the nomenklatura. The appointment of a KGB chief as secretary general was not the ideal choice from the nomenklatura's perspective; in fact, the majority of them had wanted another candidate. The top leaders of the Party, however, preferred Andropov over the regional Party secretaries.[19] Gromyko and the other leaders trusted Andropov because they had known him for a long time and had noted his willingness to preserve the Party's

leading role. Furthermore, Andropov had always opposed the arrest of high-ranking Party leaders. Among the factors that tended to highlight his image as a leader committed to moderation was the fact that Andropov was elderly and seriously ill; therefore, if he were to aspire to be a new Beria, he would have neither the time nor the strength. The Politburo's intention in 1982 was to choose Andropov the communist, not Andropov the KGB man, as Brezhnev's successor.

The KGB used journalists in the same way that it used scholars and social scientists to mobilize media support. At a first glance, it was surprising that journalists had good relations with the security force, but if we examine this issue from another vantage point, we realize that at the beginning of the 1980s, the KGB had a new image and represented, for some journalists, a source of information on the government that mirrored reality more accurately. Journalists preferred to cull information from the KGB rather than from the speeches and writings of Brezhnev or Grishin. KGB sources were occasionally critical of Soviet reality and supplied journalists with interesting and even sensational stories. In contrast to the monotonous content of the Brezhnevian media, stories of crimes, fraud, and bribery attracted the attention of Soviet readers. Citizens enjoyed reading about corruption because it confirmed their belief that it was widespread in Soviet society. The KGB provided exclusive information about corruption cases to a few newspapers and journalists, and these journalists became the KGB's mouthpieces in the media, manipulating the public without their being aware of it. From 1978 to 1980, journalists made a strong case for the view that corruption was a dangerous evil in Soviet society.[20] They helped undermine Brezhnev's authority by publishing many accounts of cases of corruption involving officials of the Party and the government.

While the Party fell into deeper stagnation with Brezhnev's enfeebled ability to rule, the KGB continued to be one of the few organizations on the rise. Brezhnev relied more and more on Andropov to solve thorny problems. Year after year, under Andropov's supervision, the KGB used its growing influence to enlarge and restructure its staff. The KGB's broader functions in Russian society justified a recruitment based on higher qualifications. It enlisted newcomers from different areas of specialization, including foreign languages, communications, economics, psychology, advertising, computer science, electronics, sociology, and mathematics. While Party and government structures did not change their staffs during the Brezhnev era, the KGB took advantage of its increased autonomy to revamp its personnel.[21] With its highly qualified new agents, the security force was able to gather exhaustive and complex information about Russian society. In the 1970s, employment with the KGB was a sign of prestige: "Leaders of the MVD and officers of the KGB lived much better than their colleagues in the PGO, the Ministry of Defense, the militia, and even the GRU. They received

apartments immediately, after just one telephone call. The KGB all over the Soviet Union benefited from boarding schools, sanatoriums, and rest homes. The
Chekists [KGB members] could go there with their families. Entry to the KGB
opened up brilliant perspectives and opportunities to go abroad, while for common mortals, these roads were closed."[22]

The new staff enabled the KGB not only to collect considerable information
but also to produce analyses of and solutions to the different problems experienced by Russian society. As its staff increased in qualifications, the KGB's reputation as an efficient organization grew, making itself known as a competent
organization in various fields. Thus, the KGB was solicited in almost all areas of
society, and, when not consulted, it intervened when the security of the country
might be an issue. The KGB's traditional image as a repressive force was transformed; by the 1980s, it was perceived, even by certain dissidents, as an organization in which liberalism and reform were equally represented.[23] Some analyses in
the West represented the KGB as Gorbachev's first ally and even as the instigator
of perestroika. Soviet specialists continued to convey the same pejorative image
of the KGB, but a minority of them began to note that the security force did not
oppose limited reforms when they appeared to be the most reasonable option for
the preservation of the Soviet system.

During this period, rumors circulated in Soviet society that Andropov was a
reformer and was partial to Western culture.[24] According to certain sources, there
was some truth behind these rumors, since Andropov appointed advisors who
were known to be progressive and who divulged information about their boss that
suggested he was not a conservative.[25] Other known gossips alleged that some of
the KGB staff showed sympathy toward reform, which helped to increase Russian
society's support for the KGB. Andropov's prestige, which remained unchanged
within the military and the bureaucracy, began to grow among the intelligentsia,
a group traditionally hostile to the KGB. While all this did not mean that the KGB
had become favorable to liberal reforms, it still indicated a sensitivity to the need
for certain changes. It indicated that a significant number of people in Andropov's
circle wanted Soviet law to be enforced throughout society. All the young and
highly qualified individuals recruited by the KGB created an environment that
might be viewed as open to reform. In short, some objective conditions were thus
emerging that promoted interest in the rule of law. Of course, these personnel
changes and the emphasis on integrity and performance did not mean that the
KGB, even the newcomers, wanted democratization of the political system. They
wanted to enforce adherence to the Soviet system, not to abolish it.

The KGB could obtain data that no other organization could, and in very
diverse areas. As Andropov's source of information, the KGB gave him the advantage of being able to intervene in almost any area of society. For example, on
the issue of corruption, the KGB could provide data not only on its extent, forms,

and perpetrators but also on its consequences, that is, its damage to the economy, to the Party, to Russian culture, and so on. It was difficult for other organizations to achieve similarly complete data. During this period, the KGB acquired a reputation for firmness, integrity, and professionalism.[26] Party officials, disappointed by the stagnation of their organization, looked to the KGB. Moreover, the anticorruption campaign, at least in its initial stage, persuaded many honest people to trust the KGB. The crackdown against dissidence drew partisans from the ranks of ideologues and conservatives. Hostility to the Western world, including to liberalism, brought nationalist forces to its side.

Thus, under Andropov's leadership, the KGB developed an aura of competence in Soviet society, even among its detractors. The KGB's policy of hiring young professionals contributed to Andropov's reputation as a force for change; moreover, the recruitment of the sons of the political elite also helped to implement politics in tune with its interests.

Even in the context of severe repression in the Soviet Union at the time, the police were subject to certain constraints in their investigations, and prosecutors were expected to gather sufficient evidence before filing charges, even when the suspect was a high-profile official. In practice, however, the gathering of evidence was often found insufficient, and investigators might face retaliation from their targets. Prosecutors knew this and accordingly often avoided pursuing charges against top officials. For reasons of political rivalry, trade leaders might be directly involved with the investigators who pressured them to inform on upper-echelon leaders.

It was often difficult to convict suspects, especially where bribery was concerned, because there were usually no other witnesses to bribery incidents. The court was expected to decide between the accuser's version of the story and that of the accused. Most of the time, investigators had more difficulty gathering evidence on bribe-takers than bribe-givers because the latter could often rely on the support of important colleagues. Facing these problems, the KGB recruited highly promising candidates from universities to become skillful and well-qualified prosecutors, who were required to bring to trial cases in which the evidence was not readily accessible. In other cases, regardless of the evidence, the goal was to indict suspects by discrediting them and causing their dismissal from the Party.

Tough versus Soft Prosecutors

In order to assess the anticorruption campaign's results, one must examine how competent and objective the police were. The KGB allowed its economic crimes section (table 2.3) to lead the campaign against the Moscow trade network, and this department was under the official supervision of the head of the KGB. In practice, however, the key official overseeing the economic crimes sec-

tion was Alidin, who was head of the KGB's Moscow unit. The economic crimes section was the most important because it was founded in October 1982 to fight corruption. The KGB expected the most from the Moscow section because it was in this city that corruption was the most prevalent. That is why Alidin, the head of the Moscow unit of the KGB, was chosen as the head of the section.

Exemplifying the adage that leaders resemble their organizations, the bulldog-like Alidin was as serious and tenacious as the security force itself. Alidin was ideal for the task of overseeing the anticorruption campaign. Above all, he was discreet, and his reputation established him as a KGB prototype. Alidin was respectful of Grishin, the Moscow Party secretary, but answered primarily to the KGB. Andropov's control over Alidin was total. The KGB double standard of accepting Brezhnev's hegemony while secretly compiling compromising data on the nomenklatura was more risky in Moscow due to the influence of Brezhnev's men in the security force. This was most apparent in Alidin's case: although he had been appointed by Brezhnev, he never contested Andropov's dictates and implemented them even in Moscow. Alidin was motivated by the information he had received in the 1970s on the magnitude of corruption in Russia. He preferred not to divulge the extent of corruption to the public and did not believe that Grishin and his lieutenants were dishonest.[27] Alidin had known Grishin for a long time and trusted him completely, but he realized that if any allegations of wrongdoing were confirmed against the Moscow Party boss, he himself risked being discredited for not having uncovered these illegal actions. Nevertheless, Alidin was pleased by the way his organization was operating; in 1982, when Andropov replaced Brezhnev at the Kremlin, he had a greater voice in the political system. His sense of duty to the KGB was most likely the determining factor in his allegiance to Andropov. Alidin possessed the three attributes of a model KGB officer, as defined by Dzerzhinski: an ardent heart, a cold head, and clean hands. The last requirement was particularly important and was sadly lacking in the early 1980s. Alidin also fit Andropov's expectations of the model employee: he was honest and used correct investigation methods. The result of Andropov's demand that his Moscow team be efficient was that investigations remained hidden and safe from public scrutiny. Alidin's commitment to the KGB should not make us lose sight of the fact that he was, above all, a bona fide communist, which prevented him from filing charges against Party officials. However, in 1984, when there was talk of arresting Tregubov, one of the Party senior officials, he was supportive. Andropov's appointment as the head of the Party's Ideology Department helped to increase, as might be expected, his control over officers like Alidin.

It is not surprising that the KGB asked Trofimov to lead such a critical operation as the anticorruption campaign in the capital. Trofimov was Alidin's main subordinate at the KGB. Had he not been the best in the field, he would not have

occupied this position; he was considered the top prosecutor in Moscow. Tro-fimov was a typical Andropov-era investigator. He was young, ambitious, and intelligent. But he was also a narrow-minded and unconditional supporter of So-viet ideology; after 1985, he was in the pro-Oleinik group, and during the 1990s, when he headed the FSB (which replaced the KGB) in the capital, he remained nostalgic for the good old days, that is, the Soviet era. Trofimov's successful career in the KGB had begun in the early 1970s. At thirty-three years of age, he was ap-pointed head of the Department of Investigation of the Moscow unit of the KGB. Later in the same decade, he was the rising star of the law enforcement agencies, possessing an impressive track record during this period, when he headed the Fifth Department, which carried out the task of suppressing political opposition in the capital. At the end of the 1970s, due to his efforts, dissidence seemed to be in decline. Trofimov's success led to greater responsibilities, and in October 1982, he was appointed head of the short-lived Section of Economic Crimes, becom-ing in effect chief investigator for the KGB. He was given free rein to investigate Sokolov, the famous director of the Eliseevski *gastronom*. No one could compare to Trofimov in the art of obtaining evidence on suspects, and no one possessed his talents and knowledge in the choice of "good" investigators. Litvinenko, a former high-level KGB agent and dissident who immigrated to London during the Soviet period, later said of Trofimov that he had never met such a high-class professional among the KGB staff.[28]

In 1982, Trofimov led the most important KGB investigation in Moscow since the reign of Beria. The Section of Economic Crimes had recruited investi-gators with experience in combating corruption, and under Trofimov's direction,

Table 2.3. Personnel in the KGB's economic crimes section

Agent	Position
Trofimov	Head, Department of Investigation, Moscow KGB section
Kupruchin	Head, Department of Investigation, Moscow KGB section
Sterligov	Senior investigator, Moscow KGB section
Levchenko	Senior investigator, Moscow KGB section
Sorokin	Senior investigator, Moscow KGB section
Matveenko	Investigator, Moscow KGB section
Sharapov	Investigator, Moscow KGB section
Bunakov	Investigator, Moscow KGB section
Put'ko	Investigator, Moscow KGB section
Gulin	Investigator, Moscow KGB section
Shalaev	Investigator, Moscow KGB section
Rodionov	Investigator, Moscow KGB section

Source: Dopolneniia k analizu otdel'nykh iavlenii, obstoiatel'stv, proiavivshikhsia v kontse, 1985 goda i 1986 godu po nastoiashchee vremia (May 12, 1986).

the section patiently drew up a list of the best investigators for the anticorruption campaign. Work on that list began with a review of the main battles against corruption in the entire country and of the investigators who had proven to be the most successful in each case. Trofimov knew which investigators in the capital were trustworthy and which ones were sympathetic to Brezhnev and Grishin. The investigators chosen to work under Trofimov's supervision were compelled to follow strict guidelines.

The KGB decided not to intervene in the trade network before it had solid data on the existence of widespread corruption in Moscow. As early as 1981, prior to Brezhnev's death, Trofimov carried out a preliminary investigation that indicated serious violations of the law were taking place in the trade organizations. Because the KGB was intervening in a sector outside its jurisdiction, its actions had to be justified by sufficient evidence. Trofimov and his team were evaluated according to concrete results: they had to produce irrefutable evidence against accused executives, especially against the higher-ranking ones. The investigators' success depended on their ability to achieve four objectives: (1) obtaining the collaboration of the suspects; (2) acquiring sufficient evidence to charge and convict the accused; (3) finding information that discredited members of the nomenklatura; and (4) recovering the amount of money stolen by the accused.

The results could be attained by following one of two plans. Plan A, the preferable one, involved having a suspect agree to collaborate voluntarily, whether the end result was obtained by manipulation or by persuasion. Plan B involved compelling suspects to reveal all they knew, by using physical violence or by making the conditions of imprisonment particularly severe.[29] If plan B was deployed, it was certainly the more dangerous of the two, since it could easily damage the KGB's public image. At this time, the KGB was sensitive about its image, even abroad, as it was likely that its leader, Andropov, would become the new general secretary of the Communist Party of the Soviet Union. With predecessors such as Beria and Iezhov, any KGB leader entering the political arena had to overcome a certain amount of distrust.

During the1970s, the security force had fought dissidence without worrying about tarnishing its own reputation. Andropov was aware that in Russian society, many were obsessed with the KGB's past and were equally obsessed with not allowing it to regain the power it had held during the Beria period, so he endeavored to present himself as a reformer to quiet these fears. He also required that this image be reflected in the activities of the organization he led until 1982. Guidelines based on preserving a positive image of the KGB were imposed on Trofimov with respect to the anticorruption campaign tactics. Trofimov, and sometimes even Alidin, would visit an important suspect who had just been in-

carcerated.[30] The suspect was invited to collaborate with the investigators in the best interests of justice, the Soviet Union, and for his own sake. The suspect's answers determined which inspectors would be assigned to his investigation.

Investigators had their own styles, some preferring to frighten the suspects, others attempting to persuade and even cajole them into confessing or revealing information. Some investigators were reputed for being honest and had successfully assembled cases against dissidents but still belonged to the traditional school, preferring "plan B" tactics. They were viewed as reliable by the KGB, but their past was suspect. Like good soldiers, they would follow Andropov as the chief of the KGB, but their support of him as secretary general of the Party was uncertain. In some cases, loyalty to Andropov was not the issue: many KGB officers were very conservative and identified too closely with past standards to be able to follow Andropov's reformist strategies for Russian society.

Although Andropov needed the backing of the traditional investigators because of their integrity and their experience in the fight against corruption, he could not rely on them exclusively. He thus devised the plan to hire young professionals more open to change, with reputations untarnished by a record of abusing dissidents. The plan to refresh the KGB staff, beginning in 1980, was never mentioned openly. The newcomers were presumably inclined to adopt more flexible approaches in their investigative methods. Andropov, as KGB head, needed to mold a security force that would complement his political activity as much as possible. The KGB was expected to follow suit and adapt itself to political activities: its members had to become not only efficient and truthful but they also had to take the rights of citizens into account. For corporatist reasons, Andropov also needed a staff qualified in judicial and related matters in society. Because Andropov relied on the KGB as he prepared to lead Russia, he required a staff competent, to a certain extent, in government administration. At the same time, KGB investigators had to be well regarded by the population. This meant that when they investigated the Moscow trade network, inspectors were expected to use methods that were "politically correct." Acceptable investigation procedures involved questioning suspects with skill and persuasion, gathering evidence by moderate means, and rejecting, as much as possible, tactics from the past that could be harmful to the agency's public image. This approach was easier to define than to put into practice, and it contradicted the image of firmness adopted by the KGB.

Andropov's awareness of this situation was apparent in his reorganization of the KGB's Moscow branch and the Muscovite elements in the agency. Andropov chose young and highly qualified candidates, and Trofimov had to integrate these newcomers into his team. The new agents were selected from among the

best candidates, were fully committed to the ideals of the organization, and were eager to prove themselves to their superiors. Their strongly idealistic mentality made them view the campaign against corruption as a crusade against evil.

Andropov's new staff initially had no doubts concerning the wrongdoings of trade executives; they were determined to apprehend them and punish them as severely as possible. Bunakov and Grigorik became the outstanding recruits on the team. They were very hostile to detainees but listened to the details of their declarations for hours on end.[31] While experienced investigators did not always show patience in their meetings with prisoners and even left them alone if they had no confessions to make, the younger KGB recruits listened to them attentively and sometimes had long conversations with them. Evidently, KGB investigators were expected to accumulate all available information on the nomenklatura even if it had no value in court. On a practical level, investigators would attempt to glean from the suspects in Moscow the most complete picture possible of corruption in the Moscow trade network. Some investigators, like Bunakov, also tried to persuade suspects to see the error of their ways.[32] In addition, Bunakov wanted to know all there was to know about corruption in Moscow more generally, which the KGB had not previously attempted to understand in the broader sense.

Less severe investigators, that is, "soft" investigators, were part of the investigative team; they were expected to achieve the same objectives in spite of the differences in their approaches. Such investigators often showed sympathy toward the detainees. They did not view all of them as criminals or dangerous persons and recognized that some of them were competent managers. It was also their point of view that the wrongdoings of some of the detainees should not diminish the fact that they had been courageous fighters during World War II. Undoubtedly, trade employees committed some economic irregularities, but these were not considered comparable to criminal offenses such as murder or rape. Some investigators were sensitive to the conditions of detention; official documents reveal that detainees appealed to the agents regarding daily needs like food.[33] Bunakov said that he gave orders to free a detainee because he was seriously ill. Other documents indicate that a few "soft" investigators intervened to stop some reprehensible practices in Soviet prisons. For example, Bunakov intervened to halt psychiatric tests on some detainees.[34] Some members of the younger generation of KGB officers were not happy when such old-fashioned tactics were used against the accused. The plaintive demands of trade employees—imprisoned, desperate, and ready to commit suicide—moved some new KGB investigators to act humanely.

Several observations can be made about the KGB's new attitude and why it prevailed. Any law enforcement agency has its "soft" personnel, and the KGB was

no exception. It was assumed that lenient investigators were able to obtain better result with some suspects, and, in 1985 and thereafter, KGB staff increasingly differed in their evaluations of trade executives. Representatives of the younger generation, like Bunakov, did not have such a severe attitude toward the executives accused of corruption; therefore, they generally used less repressive tactics. They showed them a certain amount of respect, did not insult them, and did not threaten them. This approach prevailed in the perestroika period.

Lenient investigators also tended to be less involved in the abuse of their authority under the Andropov regime. Still, the lengthy interrogations in which suspects might tell long tales of woe affected the investigators' political convictions and their emotional health. In these drawn-out interrogations, many suspects disclosed cases of bribe-taking by a large number of officeholders. Party officials thus pressured the KGB to stop the investigations, which undermined the young KGB officers' convictions. The new generation of agents remained tough toward executives who had previous convictions and who were clearly swindlers and criminals, but it was another story when they heard the tragedies of Filippov, Ambartsumyan, Eremeev, Rosliakov, and other leaders of the Moscow trade network whom they viewed as victims of the Soviet system. It was difficult for the young agents to view as common criminals men who had been sent to the front in 1941 at sixteen to eighteen years old and who had fought in the famous battles of Leningrad, Moscow, Stalingrad, and Kursk before returning with injuries and infirmities.[35]

After hearing numerous tales of abuse and intimidation from the detainees, some of the new KGB agents were shaken in their political beliefs. Their compassion increased during the Gorbachev era, when criticism mounted in the press concerning the mistreatment of executives arrested by the KGB. Nevertheless, the younger agents did not all belong to the camp of the sympathetic and moderate, just as not all old or middle-aged investigators could be identified with the conservative faction. Sirotkin, a middle-aged man and a PGO prosecutor, always remained calm with the suspects, never threatening them or raising his voice. Not surprisingly, the suspects preferred to meet with him and, in certain cases, even refused to give testimony to other prosecutors. There were other investigators who were reputed to be lenient even after many years of duty in the law enforcement agency. For these reasons, in November 1986, Ambartsumyan agreed to give testimony only to Stirenko.[36]

As a member of the Politburo during the 1970s, Andropov saw the political aspect of corruption. The predominant view on corruption voiced by public opinion was that on the consumer side, it caused product shortages, while on the other side, it created a privileged group of people who received bribes and engaged in black market speculation. A third aspect was that, for many people,

illegal activities supplemented a salary that otherwise would not be enough to provide a decent living. The KGB highlighted the first two aspects when releasing information about corruption to the media. Furthermore, the KGB knew that people believed corruption existed because Party leaders tolerated it and even reaped benefits from it. Moreover, articles in the press reported cases in which the authorities were tolerant of or passive toward corruption. It was significant that, during the early 1980s, critics began paying more careful attention to cases of corruption. This phenomenon can be attributed to the KGB and its strategy of creating the impression that corruption was Russia's primary social problem—a strategy that appeared to have been successful. Corruption in Russia became such a hot issue that dissidents, the press, and scholars in the West all perceived it as the biggest problem needing to be addressed. Since corruption clearly emerged as a major issue in Russian society, we can surmise that the KGB exaggerated the problem or, more to the point, used it to advantage. By presenting corruption as the overriding problem, the KGB put itself forward as the only organization that could remedy it.

Soviet principles suggested that nobody was above the law, even those officers whose job it was to enforce the law and those political leaders who made the laws. Police officers were supposed to arrest citizens who broke the law, regardless of their status, and high-ranking officials were not supposed to interfere in investigations. Judges had to make their verdicts according to the seriousness of the crimes committed by citizens, not according to the defendants' positions or their protectors' status. Police officers and judges could not be accommodating, because if they were, they would become indifferent to corruption. Suspects arrested for economic crimes were to be judged severely, and those involved in bribery would, if the amount of money involved was significant, be sentenced to death.[37] Given the seriousness of the crime as well as the sentence, the KGB considered that only its investigators had the necessary qualifications to do the job. During the 1970s, its official severity toward corruption had provided an unofficial but crucial guideline during investigations, justifying the intimidation and sometimes cruelty to force suspects to confess. This was not the only way to obtain evidence, nor was it the preferred one, but it probably could not have been avoided, particularly during the first stage of the anticorruption campaign, that is, from 1982 to 1984. During this period, the "tough" rather than the "soft" prosecutors prevailed.

Early in the campaign against corruption, the model KGB prosecutor was pitiless in applying the law, recommending severe sentences for detainees indicted for major offenses such as bribery. The KGB leaders reminded their agents to focus on upper-level cadres, whose guilt was considered more serious because of their higher status. But in a campaign whose goal was to show that large-scale

corruption existed, the KGB also knew it was better to err on the side of quantity when it came to arresting people. Without proof of a sufficiently large number of guilty people, it might be thought that the KGB had made a mistake in launching such a campaign, and enough high-ranking officials had to be indicted to justify the KGB's involvement rather than just the PGO or the MVD. The campaign was also an opportunity to shine a positive light on certain rising security force members who wanted to become known not only in the law enforcement milieu but also by the general public. It often happened that once an investigator was convinced of an accused person's guilt, he would stop at nothing to produce the necessary proof.[38] Common methods included detaining the person for an extended period, in fact, until the person confessed, and forging written evidence against the person.[39] Civil society was not overly concerned by this behavior on the part of investigators and prosecutors, as the general attitude was that the arrested person, particularly if he or she occupied a high position, must be guilty, and that any lack of bona fide proof was because the person had powerful protectors in high places who had intervened in his or her favor.

The KGB's standard procedure was to first try to persuade suspects to make a deposition acknowledging their wrongdoings. If they refused, they were detained for an indefinite period and not allowed any visits from relatives. Other measures would follow, if necessary, such as pressuring family members into collaborating with the police. If detainees showed willingness to submit to the demands of the KGB, the agents might transfer the suspect to a more comfortable cell, but if suspects did not cooperate, they might find themselves in worse conditions of imprisonment. Boris Karakhanov, a grocery store manager, described his conditions of detention in the following terms: "They transferred me to a cell intended for five prisoners, but ten were incarcerated there. The atmosphere was terrible: dirty, suffocating air, old men crying, a state of madness. Screaming, weeping, and groaning could be heard all night long. Everyone suffered and was obsessed by talking about his own case, which everyone knew by heart."[40]

Detainees who continued to plead not guilty despite these harsh tactics were sometimes sent to cells occupied by the worst criminals, such as rapists and murderers. There was only one way to escape this nightmare: to cooperate with the law enforcement bodies.

The KGB decided to involve the Ministry of the Interior in corruption cases only after the latter underwent important staff changes. In the early 1980s, many KGB agents with a background in smuggling investigations were appointed to the MVD. A total of 150 KGB officers were appointed to upper management positions in the MVD in 1982–1983; among these, Sterligov was named to head the Moscow MVD's Department for Combating the Embezzlement of Socialist Property and Speculation (OBKhSS).[41] These KGB agents' task was to look

for evidence against trade employees suspected of corruption, and Sterligov was another typical representative of the leaders of the anticorruption campaign. He was an inflexible and ascetic man with a long history of service in the security force.

By fall 1983, the Russian Prosecutor General's Office had established a brigade of prosecutors tasked to bring to trial persons the KGB had arrested for corruption in Moscow (table 2.4). The KGB had never been a substitute for the PGO in court when trying to persuade a judge to convict an accused person. Nevertheless, although this brigade was under the Prosecutor General's jurisdiction, its members were selected by the KGB. Prosecutors directed criminal proceedings against trade employees arrested by the KGB, and the latter demanded that only the most capable and honest prosecutors be selected for this task. The prosecutors who had, over a period of time, drawn the attention of the KGB because of their skill and success in cases regarding economic crimes in the trade organizations were the ones selected most often by the KGB. Their ability to work in a group and in harmony with the KGB was also a criterion for selection. Most of the team comprised investigators from the PGO, but a few officers of the KGB and MVD were also included. All the brigade members were the objects of intense scrutiny and had to act as models in their professional and private lives.

The team of prosecutors was closely supervised by the KGB, since rigorous measures were taken to ensure that the brigade operated with maximum efficiency. Measures for the control and supervision of KGB agents existed but were not applied at the upper levels the way they were within the anticorruption brigade. Also, the KGB did not trust brigade members who had been recruited from outside its ranks because they came from different areas and possessed different backgrounds. Consequently, they were subject to very strict regulations, such as living in a special compound rather than with their families and avoiding any outside contacts. In addition, specific Party and trade union organizations were

Table 2.4. Members of the PGO's anticorruption brigade

Prosecutor	Position
Yemelianov	RSFSR deputy prosecutor general
Oleinik	Head of the brigade
Kupruchin	Head, Investigation Department
L. V. Vovk	Investigator
Burtsev	Investigator
Gavrilova	Investigator
Stirenko	Investigator
Karataev	Investigator

responsible for them and organized programs for their entertainment, such as visits to museums or movie theaters.[42]

In June 1984, the 50 members that comprised the brigade were not enough for its leaders, and by 1985, it had about 80, which was still deemed insufficient. Nevertheless, the leaders were able to augment the staff with officers from the MVD, most of whom had some KGB background. The anticorruption brigade was then divided into groups of between six and ten investigators, with each group being headed by the most experienced member.

Oleinik himself took charge of the investigation of Tregubov, the president of Glavtorg. He had gained a reputation for effectiveness during the 1970s and was the KGB's man in the PGO. At the beginning of his career, the PGO had given Oleinik the difficult mission of ending a revolt in a gulag. His success at that effort led to further important assignments, and in 1972, he was put in charge of investigating a sensational corruption affair involving Communist Party leaders in Kirghistan. He became a model prosecutor to his counterparts outside Moscow and was sought out to solve a wide range of problems.[43] He even occasionally supervised his investigators on the job. Oleinik's success had caught the KGB's attention, especially when, in 1981, he had written a report on a subject that was taboo in the Brezhnev era: organized crime. He thus belonged to a group of prosecutors whose ideas and integrity were noticed and appreciated in Lubianka Square.

The brigade leaders had no doubt that the Moscow trade network staff was deeply implicated in the embezzlement of socialist property and in bribery. In essence, they had decided that trade employees were criminals even before their trials and did not presume innocence before the judge's verdict. Merely because of brigade leaders' suspicions a suspect could be detained, and the pre-trial period was not intended to allow time to build a defense of the accused but rather to enable the prosecutor to gather evidence against him. Isolating suspects sometimes rendered them more willing to collaborate with the police. The Kremlin's message to prosecutors was clear: there were many speculators and swindlers who needed to be exposed and punished. Investigators were evaluated by their superiors according to their skill as "hunters." The highest marks went to prosecutors who collected enough proof to incriminate the leaders of the trade network. The "best" evidence was extracted from suspects who pleaded guilty and collaborated with the police.

The bosses highly appreciated investigators who successfully brought members of the trade staff to trial despite the usual obstacles, such as strong suspicions about an executive but inadequate evidence. Some officials thought that, in this type of situation, the suspect had to be set free for lack of evidence, but the KGB in 1983 felt that in many cases, investigators had to pursue their work nonethe-

less, arguing that the evidence was difficult to obtain because the suspect was a high-profile executive with powerful protectors. Occasionally, an investigation was based on a denunciation by anonymous letter, which was enough to charge but not enough to convict suspects in court. In some cases, KGB investigators thought that this kind of evidence could be made good by persuading witnesses who had been afraid to speak out to change their minds and produce more solid testimony.

Tracking the Caucasus Mafia

The growing power of the KGB initially served as a threat to other law enforcement organizations. Throughout the 1970s, tensions between the MVD and the KGB were apparent. Although the MVD's main task was to fight corruption, the KGB and the PGO had evidence in the 1970s that Shchelokov, minister of the interior, had committed irregularities, such as taking bribes and having luxury goods that were beyond his means. In fact, the MVD departments that dealt with corruption had stopped applying the law in the trade sphere. As we have seen, Andropov's intervention in the battle against corruption gradually improved his position in the Kremlin, to the detriment of Shchelokov. Aliev, the KGB leader in Azerbaijan, became the Party boss of his republic by denouncing corruption and cracking down on many high-ranking leaders. In other words, Aliev carried out a task that was the MVD's responsibility, setting the precedent of the KGB's taking the initiative to make changes in the republic's MVD staff—a direct attack on the MVD's authority.

In the 1970s, the KGB had turned its attention to southern Russia. In the North Caucasus, smuggling activities increased substantially as speculators transformed the Black Sea into the favored gateway to the West. At the same time, in Russia, the same speculators sold imported goods that were not accessible in the markets and hotels, mainly food and clothing. There is a saying in Russia that Odessa is the father and Rostov is the mother of criminality, and some verification about the magnitude of the shadow economy was accomplished in Rostov, a city famous for its high crime rate.[44] Evidence accumulated by the security agencies provided a large amount of data that confirmed the involvement of many elites in corrupt activities.

In 1976, the KGB opened an investigation that dealt with the illegal transporting of an exceptionally large quantity of caviar, and the trail led to the Ministry of Fisheries.[45] The KGB did not have the power to go after the minister himself, but after receiving the authorization to investigate the ministry, KGB prosecutors rapidly collected proof of wrongdoing by the deputy minister, who, aware that serious charges could be leveled against him, decided to reveal the illegal

dealings of the important officials who were colluding with him. The Kremlin responded by sentencing the deputy minister to death and having him executed, all in a very short time, in spite of opposition from KGB prosecutors who wanted to obtain further evidence from him against other highly placed officials.[46] The officials who might have been sent to trial on the basis of the deputy minister's testimony were partly responsible for his death, as they could have spoken out before it was too late. The abrupt end of the case by execution was a major setback for Andropov, but he did not wait long before counterattacking. This time, the battle was concentrated in Krasnodar. Alarmed by the arrest of several speculators and embezzlers of socialist property in Rostov, the dealers of the shadow economy there had decided to relocate their operations to Krasnodar, where they felt safer and where they could rely on the collaboration of Medunov, the strongman of that region.

During the 1970s, the Krasnodar region became a hub for the shadow economy in Russia. Black marketeers chose it as the main transit point for smuggling caviar to the West. The region possessed conditions that encouraged corruption. One of the most important conditions was the presence of a transient population, including foreigners, people from all over the Caucasus, and tourists. Sotchi and other places were very popular with the nomenklatura as venues for vacation or sick leave. In addition, the executives of trade organizations there were deeply involved in the embezzlement of socialist property. The third principal reason for the primacy of corruption in this region lay in Medunov, first secretary of the region and also the main protector of the perpetrators of economic crimes in his territory. Medunov's powerful position depended on his relationship with Brezhnev. He enjoyed the complete confidence of the secretary general, with whom he had developed personal relations over a period of years.[47]

The KGB began to place some of the region's officials on its list of suspects, right alongside the names of smugglers. By putting pressure on smugglers, prosecutors managed to obtain testimony that incriminated these regional leaders. The KGB attacked on several fronts. Even when focusing on the smugglers did not yield solid evidence, some witnesses' accounts disclosed serious offenses in other sectors. The KGB agents became aware that wrongdoing was widespread in internal trade, especially the food trade. These findings came as a surprise, but they were eventually useful to the KGB.

The KGB sent the prosecutor general evidence from their investigations of suspects. The investigators of the security force were convinced that they had collected enough evidence to charge Medunov and his lieutenants, but the outcome of the trial depended on the prosecutor general's ability to prove the guilt of the accused in court. A team from the PGO, headed by Naidenov, the deputy prosecutor general, arrived in Krasnodar to carry out this task. As the team uncov-

ered still more evidence, its expectations for the pending trial grew.[48] Medunov responded to the threat against him by seeking the help of the deputy minister of the interior, Churbanov, who was also Brezhnev's son-in-law. Churbanov trav eled to Krasnodar to try to persuade Naidenov to drop the accusations, but his attempt failed. Medunov decided, as a last resort, to call Brezhnev and complain to him about the harassment of Party officials by the law enforcement agency. His plan succeeded: the team ended its investigation and returned to Moscow. This turn of events was an especially bitter defeat for Naidenov, who died of a heart attack soon afterward.[49]

Although the KGB did not officially react to the outcome of the confrontation between the Prosecutor General's Office and Medunov, the agency staff felt frustrated. Andropov did not admit defeat but called on Brezhnev for the authorization to arrest Medunov:

> One fine day, I [Semanov] was in Leonid Ilitch's office when he received a call from Andropov. When the contact was transferred to the intercom, I understood that I should leave the office, but Leonid Ilitch motioned to me to stay. Iuri Vladimirovich [Andropov] was talking about the first secretary of the Krasnodar region, Medunov. He said that the investigation team had irrefutable evidence that the Kuban Party leader had committed abuses and that corruption flourished in this region. It was usual for Brezhnev to wait for concrete proposals. "What to do?" Andropov answered, "Open a criminal case, apprehend Medunov, and bring him to trial." Brezhnev always agreed, but this time he did not answer for a long time, then, breathing heavily, he said, "Iuri, we cannot do this. He is a leader of a big organization, people believe in him, do things for his sake, and now we send him to trial?"[50]

The appeal to Brezhnev had failed. Nevertheless, the KGB's influence grew steadily after 1975 and was reflected in the decision of the Party Central Committee to closely study the value of the evidence collected by the KGB and the Prosecutor General's Office regarding corruption in the Krasnodar region.

The KGB could not, during the 1970s, complete most of its ongoing investigations on corruption without infringing upon the Ministry of the Interior's jurisdiction, but its agents collected a lot of data on irregularities committed by the elite. The information was often passed to the Politburo, which used the data as it deemed appropriate. One of Andropov's tactics was to inform the Politburo of wrongdoing within the top echelons of the MVD; thus, while discrediting his rivals in the MVD, he also enhanced the KGB's authority. Besides, part of the purpose of Andropov's unofficial campaign against Shchelokov was to win support within the Prosecutor General's Office. The KGB was also required to

transmit to this last organization all the evidence gathered on corruption among officials to be able to bring them to trial. It used this opportunity to disclose that the MVD had acted passively with respect to corrupt executives and may have even aided and abetted them. The KGB also spared no effort in establishing a list of PGO prosecutors and judges who were deemed reliable and therefore capable of resisting pressure from the MVD.[51]

Despite its increasing power, the KGB's actions were still limited by Shchelokov, who in 1980 continued to have considerable influence, a privilege he enjoyed because of personal support from his old friend, Brezhnev. On the one hand, the MVD's influence was maintained through the backing of high Party officials, many of whom were suspected of involvement in corruption. On the other hand, certain top officials were not happy with the growing influence of the KGB in political affairs when they considered the excesses it had committed in the past.

Although the media divulged information more freely on cases in which the KGB had proceeded to arrest smugglers and speculators, it had remained almost silent about offenses in the Ministry of the Interior. Newspapers confirmed public opinion that the MVD was not performing as it should and was even involved in criminal activity. As early as 1980, the KGB began to interfere in MVD operations that were not directly related to corruption but to other crimes. In a carefully prepared move, its investigators decided to tackle the Russian mafia. It was practically forbidden during the 1970s to speak or write about the existence of a mafia in the Soviet Union, but KGB partisans claimed that use of the term had become necessary with the emergence of organized criminal groups in the 1980s. This affirmation was a tactic aimed at refuting the MVD assertion that Soviet criminality was a minor phenomenon in comparison to crime in capitalist countries. The MVD position was that the mafia could not exist in a socialist country. In a move to confirm their allegations, on April 8, 1981, a group of KGB investigators in Moscow arrested Yaponchik. Yaponchik's command of a powerful criminal organization and his connections in the police had previously made him invulnerable. His arrest caused a stir in Russian society and was welcomed by a faction of the nomenklatura because it encouraged a strong hand in the Kremlin. Yaponchik's arrest was not an isolated act; during this same period, the KGB smashed a major criminal group in Tashkent. Its leader, Ladatze, supervised operations by several criminals who stole more than 2 million rubles and who, with guns, artillery, and grenades, had succeeded in cowing the MVD in Central Asia.[52] Although this action was outside the KGB's jurisdiction, it was welcomed by Russian society, which viewed the KGB as its protector against dangerous criminals. The Party's first reaction to the KGB's success against corruption and criminality was to broaden Andropov's responsibilities.

Ever since Shchelokov had attempted to limit the authority of the KGB in the

1970s, Andropov's goal had been to take control of the Ministry of the Interior. Overall, Shchelokov successfully managed to keep the security force from interfering in his jurisdiction, even if on some occasions MVD territory was trespassed upon by its rival. Only the death of Brezhnev and the appointment of Andropov as Party leader created the conditions necessary for the KGB to take control of the MVD. Fedorchuk, the former KGB boss in Ukraine, replaced Shchelokov as the new minister of the interior. This nomination resulted in the appointment of many KGB agents to the upper echelons of the MVD. After Fedorchuk's appointment, the most important one was that of a KGB general, V. Lezhepekov, to head the MVD central apparatus. He played a determining role in the change of staff in 1983, an operation that brought about the replacement of many officials appointed by Shchelokov. The war against corruption within the ranks of the MVD provoked the dismissal and punishment of several police officers. In the Irkutsk region alone, 27 of the 28 district leaders were dismissed, and 56 out of 100 assistants had their positions downgraded. Many MVD officers were charged in court for corruption, notably 135 in Kazakhstan, 78 in Turkmenistan, and 121 in Sverdlovsk.[53]

The KGB proceeded to reorganize the structure of the Ministry of the Interior by eliminating the Organizational and Methodical Center and the Scientific Research Center on the Main Problems of Avant-garde Experiences. These two institutes had been renowned for the seriousness of their research. Very few cases of corruption had been disclosed concerning the intellectuals or researchers who worked there and who constituted a brain trust for the minister. However, in Fedorchuk's view, the institutes were suspicious simply because they had been founded by Shchelokov. Furthermore, their good reputations made their leaders more dangerous because they could attenuate the wrongdoings of the minister by testifying in his favor; thus, they were a potential stronghold of support for Shchelokov and his partisans. Fedorchuk was a suspicious man, and his hostility toward these institutions increased when he realized that there was resistance to his decision to abolish them.[54]

The Hunt for Bribe-Takers in the Moscow Trade Organizations

In Moscow in February 1982, the KGB arrested a man who used to shop regularly at the Beriozka chain of specialty stores. The police considered Russian customers of Beriozka to be suspect because the foreign currency needed to make purchases there was beyond the means of most Soviet citizens. Usually, only people who had relations with foreigners or were involved with dealers of the shadow economy were able to purchase goods from this chain. What ap-

peared to be a routine control for KGB officers turned out to be a major catch. Investigators learned that Avilkina, the suspect's wife, was head of the Fish Department at the Eliseevski *gastronom.*[55]

The KGB was already suspicious about the legality of Moscow trade organizations but could not intervene in a sector outside its jurisdiction. However, in this case, it would be possible to arrest Avilkina for the illegal acquisition of foreign currency. This loophole would, undoubtedly, provide the pretext for the KGB to collect compromising information on the Moscow trade network leaders. Avilkina had been selected as head of a store department for her reliability and strong character by the director, Sokolov, who was confident that even after her arrest, she would say nothing against him.[56]

The KGB investigators proceeded cautiously in the interrogation of Avilkina, who, for a considerable period of time, refused to confess to having committed any irregularities in the store. The KGB used its best investigators for this case and kept her isolated in jail for months. The investigators met with her on a daily basis, renewing their accusations of collaboration and alternating promises of a mild sentence with threats and intimidation. Investigators were aware that she would eventually capitulate after seeing that her friends and accomplices could do nothing for her. During the summer, Avilkina came to the conclusion that she would benefit more by denouncing her superiors than by defending them. This was her primary motive for beginning to collaborate with the KGB by describing in detail the system of corruption at the Eliseevski store. Investigators heard about her bribery of the director and deputy directors of the *gastronom.* Avilkina disclosed rumors she had heard about influential people and celebrities who visited the director and received delicacies or other favors from him. To the KGB, her revelations were the long-sought evidence of generalized corruption in the most important grocery store in the country.

Avilkina also provided the KGB with evidence of deep involvement in corruption on the part of her boss, Sokolov. The KGB's search for information on Sokolov uncovered the fact that he had spent a year in a labor camp. It was shocking to the KGB that a person with a shady past could have acquired the reputation of a competent and honest manager in the premier grocery store of the capital. Another reason for the KGB's hatred of Sokolov was that he was highly esteemed by artists and, more generally, by the intelligentsia, to whom he sold or gave some of his store's best products.[57] For these reasons, Sokolov represented a threat to the Kremlin. Finally, by October 1982, Andropov authorized the KGB to arrest Sokolov. Shortly afterward, several young KGB agents arrested Sokolov in his office after working hours. A team of senior investigators received him upon his arrival at Lubianka, and Sokolov became acquainted with the heads of

the KGB Section of Economic Crimes, who were in charge of the case. The KGB investigators informed Sokolov that he had no choice but to reveal all he knew about illegal activities in Glavtorg. His other option was the death penalty, since the KGB had already found enough evidence to convict him. The investigators emphasized that he deserved to die for the crimes that he had committed. They were relaxed and polite, never raising their voices or showing impatience. Sokolov was understandably surprised by their manner. After weeks of patiently listening to his denials of wrongdoing, the KGB officers seemed to make a concession toward Sokolov. They promised him that if he were to change his attitude, he would be sentenced only to four to six years at a labor camp.[58] The prosecutors persuaded him that they were trustworthy, understanding, and humane. They supplied him with pills for his diabetes and let him know that his relatives were not being harassed by the police and that his wife still held the position of deputy director at the Gum *gastronom*. They told him repeatedly that, because he was a top executive in the Moscow trade network, his testimony would be a turning point in the campaign to reestablish law and order in the trade network, that his invaluable contribution to the investigation would result in his being well treated during detention, that the charges against him would be substantially downgraded, and that no case would be opened against his wife. All these reassurances finally convinced Sokolov that the KGB would keep its promise to save him from the death penalty.

Meanwhile, the prosecutors were watching the evolution of the interrogations. When Sokolov finally opted to collaborate with his interrogators, the KGB's role increased significantly. In his new position of secretary general, Andropov realized that to achieve success during his initial months in power, it was crucial that his strongest weapon come from his former organization. Support from the nomenklatura was not a certainty for him at this early stage, and he needed backing from other sources. It was, at least at the beginning, in the domain of crime and illegal activity that his chances to achieve success were the greatest. Andropov's priority was to bring about significant changes in the judiciary and, by this means, strengthen discipline in society. Through this policy, he expected to increase support among the nomenklatura. Andropov wanted to replace part of his staff with people who were more loyal to him; the difficulty lay in justifying these staff changes.

Above all, Andropov wanted full responsibility for judicial affairs. When he became secretary general, he announced that control over the law enforcement agencies was necessary to reestablish law and order. During the 1970s, the judicial bodies entered into conflict on various occasions; the KGB had a score to settle with the Ministry of the Interior. While the KGB could be mobilized to restore order, it pursued other goals as well. In its crusade for law and order,

the first battle was to identify and punish the corrupt trade executives. The KGB was well prepared to meet this challenge: it had collected, over a long period of time, considerable evidence that provided it with solid reasons to go beyond its jurisdiction to prosecute trade executives. By giving priority to investigations in Moscow, the KGB sought to kill two birds with one stone: to detain corrupt executives of the trade network but also to replace the Brezhnevian staff in the MVD. The success of this operation was crucial because all of Russia looked to Moscow as a model. Besides, Grishin's position was vulnerable to attack; the Party boss in the capital was neither a senior Politburo member nor was he close to Andropov, with whom he had quarreled more than once in the 1970s.

Sokolov's confession and Brezhnev's death in November 1982 marked a new stage in the Kremlin's attitude to corruption; the KGB was now free to tackle the Moscow trade organizations. Sokolov had provided the KGB with enough evidence to confirm its theory that corruption was rampant and posed a serious threat to the existence of the Soviet system; thus, the KGB was justified in continuing and even intensifying its investigations. Although the declarations of a senior executive like Sokolov were crucial and necessary, the KGB needed other executives to corroborate the testimony of the director of the Eliseevski *gastronom*. With this in mind, the investigators obtained confessions from Eliseevski's deputy directors that corroborated those of their boss.

Andropov's ascent to power rapidly produced visible effects on society. The program of the Kremlin's new tenant, with its accent on law and order, made a strong impression on Soviet citizens. It was particularly apparent in the increased presence of police in public places. Foot patrols of soldiers with dogs were frequently seen in the streets. The police multiplied their raids on theaters, public baths, and parks, expelling and fining "lazy" citizens who should have been at their workplaces.[59] The anticorruption campaign was a key element of Andropov's program to reestablish order in the country. The priority given to combating corruption was indicated by Andropov's first public appearance after taking office in the Kremlin, when he addressed a country-wide meeting of representatives of OBKhSS in Moscow in December 1982.

In the meantime, all the preparations for a nationwide anticorruption campaign were being made in KGB headquarters. Late in December 1982, an exceptionally feverish atmosphere animated the Lubianka prison. The cancellation of employees' vacations just a few days before the celebration of the new year suggested that something special was happening. The lights in the office of the KGB's Department of Economic Crimes stayed on all night. The most experienced investigators in corruption and dissidence were appointed to head a new team created especially for a crusade against corruption.

Again, the KGB was on a war footing. The campaign against corruption was

not restricted to Moscow, although the capital was the central battlefield. If successful there, it would open the doors for campaigns in other regions. The KGB leaders did not entirely trust the Moscow section of the organization, and prior to the campaign, major staff changes were made. A special inside investigation of the KGB staff was conducted to find possible links between its members and corrupt trade employees. Inclusion in the team depended on strict requirements. Any inspector who had relatives or past ties with the Moscow trade elite was excluded. This requirement may explain why many people from the provinces were recruited. In December 1982, KGB leaders from the Urals, northern Russia, and the Black Earth region were called to Moscow for briefing. Over the previous few years, they had been ordered to compile a list of the names of their most reliable investigators for possible assignment to special cases. Now, they were asked to recommend their best members for an imminent crackdown on corruption in the capital. They were also warned how important the operation in Moscow was to Kremlin leaders; provincial KGB bosses would be held accountable for the performance of units sent to Moscow. Although the KGB was the only police structure in the capital that had not been bought by the trade executives and nothing compromising had been found among the leaders of the KGB's Moscow unit, it did not mean that the agents could be relied upon completely in a massive investigation of corruption in the Moscow trade organizations. In this kind of operation, officers had to be able to resist strong pressures; if any of the Moscow agents had compromising links within the city's population, they might eventually be subject to the influence of trade employees. For these reasons, KGB military units originally located in the Moscow region were transferred to the provinces, mainly in the North Caucasus, under the pretext of providing better coordination between the center and the rest of the country.

In quiet provinces like Briansk, in central Russia, corruption still existed, but to a lesser degree, so the war against graft there could be waged with a smaller team. When investigators from such areas had less work to do in their own regions, their services could be used elsewhere, for other purposes. Often, as honest and modest employees, the agents from outlying regions were trusted with delicate and crucial operations in the capital. Their dislike and even hatred for Moscow made them tough and zealous executants; these qualities were highly appreciated by KGB leaders such as Fedorchuk. Top KGB officials did not take any chances with security, especially in Moscow; for instance, two elite KGB divisions were transferred to the outskirts of the city. The KGB had always maintained a strong presence in the capital, where the leaders of the country resided, to ensure that the country was well defended against external and even internal threats. As early as 1983, however, the presence of these elite divisions on the periphery of the capital was a warning to MVD units, whose leaders were suspected of having close links with the trade organizations.

The prosecutors were not disappointed by Sokolov's revelations; he had given them more information than they had expected. In June 1983, the investigation reached a new stage. Sokolov's testimony against his colleagues included information on Petrikov, the first deputy director of Glavtorg. Petrikov was the highest-ranking executive mentioned by Sokolov and the one against whom the accusations were the most substantial. Sokolov was close to Petrikov, whom he had known for a long time. Their collaboration in embezzlement went back to their employment by Galantorg.[60] Perhaps no other executive in the Moscow trade network except Sokolov himself was in as bad a situation as Petrikov. As soon as it was known that Sokolov was in the hands of the KGB, Petrikov's days as a free man were numbered. All the odds were against him. The KGB had doubtless been aware of his close relations with Sokolov, whose promotion to the directorship of the Eliseevski *gastronom* would have been impossible without Petrikov's help. Sokolov had carried out his campaign to become director by supplying Petrikov with valuable information that served to discredit his predecessor at the *gastronom*. Sokolov's promise to Petrikov that he would be a very generous provider of bribes was another way to get his friend on his side. Petrikov's appointment of Sokolov as director of the Eliseevski *gastronom* without Tregubov's approval was a clear indication of his power. As soon as Sokolov decided to cooperate with the police, Petrikov was necessarily the most important executive that he could compromise. To the KGB, Petrikov was a key suspect because he was known as one of the top bribe-takers. Sokolov's testimony confirmed this suspicion; therefore, Petrikov was one of the first trade executives to be charged and was, like Sokolov, kept in isolation for months, except during his interrogations by the KGB.

When the prosecutors began to interrogate Petrikov, they figured they would not have any problem compelling him to confess all his crimes, especially since they had enough credible evidence to detain him for a long time. Petrikov confirmed the assumption the prosecutors had about him: shortly after his arrest, he began to collaborate with the KGB.[61] The KGB had thus reached another turning point in the investigation, since Petrikov disclosed the names of several bribe-givers who had given him large amounts of money. In consequence, the KGB was very busy in July and August with the indictment of many Moscow food trade executives, the most important ones being Baigelman, Tveritinov, Filippov, Khokhlov, Kireev, and Korovkin. During this period, the number of executives arrested rose sharply, and those compromised by Petrikov were obliged to cooperate with the KGB investigators. Most of them furnished the KGB with personal lists of bribe-takers and bribe-givers.[62]

In the first half of 1983, the KGB devoted all its efforts to investigating the heads of Glavtorg and Glavka, the body that administered the Moscow *kontoras*. This second institution was attacked first, and more harshly. The circumstances

of the indictment of the Glavka executives showed how powerful the KGB had become. The leaders of the arrest operation did not restrain themselves as far as tactics were concerned.

In the case of the Dzerzhinski *kontora,* for example, the personnel deployed by the KGB put on an impressive display. Ten black Volgas suddenly arrived at the *kontora.* Three investigators stepped out of each car and occupied the offices of the director and the chief accountant.[63] Fourteen leaders of the *kontora* were apprehended on that occasion. In November 1984, fifteen Glavka executives appeared in court and were given lengthy sentences; the minimum sentence was ten years. Among the Glavka leaders who were tried during this period, six were sent to labor camps for lengthy sentences. The sentences were severe but seemed fair, since the evidence presented during the trial was convincing. A crucial factor was that almost all of the accused pleaded guilty and acknowledged their crimes. The impression given by the press in the days after the trial was that justice had been served.

The Kremlin leaders succeeded in making a strong impact on the public, as they had intended. Those guilty of exacerbating shortages in stores—the speculators, embezzlers, bribe-takers, and swindlers—seemed to have received a mortal blow. The large amounts of stolen money and goods convinced the public that the theory suggesting that corruption emptied the stores was true. The message was sent to the law enforcement agencies that the trial was a model to follow. Having closely monitored the case, the KGB determined that subsequent cases would follow the same model: a short trial, solid evidence, and harsh punishment.[64] Witnesses had no chance to review their testimony. Defense lawyers were prevented from cross-examining the PGO's witnesses and could not produce witnesses for the defense. "Solid evidence" implied that only a suspect's confession could establish his or her own guilt. Harsh punishment was intended to impress the public by showing them that the KGB was on their side. The nomenklatura was meant to be dissuaded from wrongdoing by the severity of the sentences and to understand that any bureaucrat who broke the rules would pay heavily, regardless of rank.

Compared to the Glavka cases, those of Glavtorg required more time and effort on the part of the KGB. Many Glavtorg leaders were questioned. Investigators met with the managers of the major grocery stores and tried to obtain information using different tactics. One approach was to tell them that charges would not be filed against them if they divulged incidents of corruption involving their colleagues. Many of them refused to do this at first, but others agreed to do so. In less than a month, prosecutors succeeded in pitting one executive against the other by using an individual executive's testimony to accumulate evidence against the others. By the end of September 1983, the directors and deputy directors of the food trade and the grocery store organizations were behind bars. The only major

executive to avoid detention was Nonaev, director of the Smolenski *gastronom*, who had committed suicide prior to his arrest; after this desperate act, the KGB moved to arrest other main grocery store directors earlier than planned.

The success of the prosecutors reached its peak in the cases against the Glavka and Glavtorg leaders. However, the biggest achievement of the KGB was finding testimony incriminating Grishin and Promyslov, the mayor of Moscow. The evidence came mainly from the testimony of Skil, director of the Sedmoi Nebo restaurant, and Panakov, director of the Moscow Tourist Bureau. Their testimony was the only evidence, but prosecutors were optimistic they would obtain testimony corroborating Skil's.[65] However, prosecutors quickly realized that further testimony was not that easy to get, so they devised other tactics to attain their goal, like promising release or threatening the executives who had close relations with Grishin and Promyslov.

In 1984, the war against corruption entered a new phase. The PGO brigade that was conducting the operations had specific tasks. First, they had to decide which of the employees arrested by the KGB in 1982–1983 should be brought to trial, and then they had to persuade the judges of their guilt. The investigators also had to try to persuade the accused to confess their crimes by promising them that their sentences would be reduced, especially if they divulged compromising information about high-ranking executives. This time, the brigade leaders were ready to respect their promises. Of the executives behind bars who agreed to testify against high-profile figures, many were freed or had their sentences reduced.

Another initiative taken by the brigade was to imprison suspects who had been denounced in an investigation. In the absence of sufficient proof, the prosecutors would detain these suspects while they verified the accusations against them. Investigators had to check all the allegations of bribery mentioned in the testimony of the detained person. The ruling principle here was that everybody was equal before the law, and any employee who broke the law would face justice. Thus, investigators could file charges against every suspect, no matter how numerous they were, regardless of the suspect's rank. Above all, they were looking for evidence against high-level executives, the most important being Tregubov, the Glavtorg chief. The measures the investigators used were often illegal but were presented as exceptional and justified by the circumstances. Prosecutors knew from experience that after months and even years of imprisonment with almost no contact with the outside world, the suspect would usually admit to the charges. Oleinik, the leader of the brigade, justified these questionable investigation methods by suggesting that the dangerously pervasive extent of corruption necessitated them.[66]

As a first step, prosecutors hoped to gather prejudicial evidence against the head of Glavtorg from lower-level executives. From 1982 to July 1984, the KGB

suspected Tregubov of corruption but was unable to prove it. Finally, they arrested him after obtaining testimony that implicated him in bribe-taking. In jail,
Tregubov was confronted by Petrikov and Tveritinov, who had claimed to have
bribed him. This was the most famous case of bribery in the history of the anticorruption campaign against the Moscow trade organizations. The representatives
of the prosecutor general had to prove that the persons who claimed to have paid
Tregubov were bribe-takers themselves. This was the case with Petrikov, who had
received bribes from several Glavtorg officials. He gave wide-ranging testimony
about the bribes he had taken and about the people who had bribed him, explaining that he had decided to bribe his boss, Nikolai Petrovich Tregubov, "so he
would depend on me, so he wouldn't denounce me as a bribe-giver. As he knows
that I dealt in these dirty tricks, he may know this. But I repeat once more: never
did Nikolai Petrovich tell me or another person directly about this. All these
things were done ambiguously, ambiguously, and ambiguously again." In reply to
one of the investigator's questions, Petrikov elaborated on other reasons that led
him to bribe his superior: "I was afraid that Nikolai Petrovich, with his cunning
character, would decide to ask me to retire. I was afraid of it, I was worried, and
I did not want it. If he became dependent on me materially, I thought that he
would not do that. The third reason was my intention and my desire to change
my apartment. It was not complicated, but it was not so simple either. I had a
two-room flat, and I wanted to have a better, larger, more comfortable one."[67]

The circumstances in which money was given to Tregubov were an important part of the accusation. When Tregubov and Petrikov confronted each other
in court, the latter described the first bribery incident in detail, including his
boss's reaction to his "gift":

> I went to sit down at the conference table. You came near me and said,
> "You understand that you can go to jail for this kind of behavior." I an-
> swered, "Nikolai Petrovich, I understand all this, but don't worry. There
> is no risk, because no one will ever know about it. I have never spoken to
> anyone about it. . . . Why? You know me. I am a human being and I am
> not ungrateful." You told me, "Wait a minute," and I stopped. You took
> my envelope from your papers and tried to give it back to me, but I did
> not come toward you. I immediately left your office.[68]

Tveritinov, the manager of the Gum grocery store (facing the Kremlin), was
the second witness who incriminated Tregubov, claiming that he too had bribed
the Glavtorg chief executive. The first time, Tveritinov had offered him a thousand
rubles, a sum that was not considered enough by his boss. Tveritinov returned to

Tregubov's office with eight thousand rubles. Tregubov, who complained to him on the occasion of the first bribe attempt that the money was not for him alone, said that the second gift was "still nothing." The grocery store director described his thoughts after this second meeting as follows: "I said to myself, Nikolai Petrovich has many friends at higher levels and it is good to help him, so that it is all in the nature of things." In addition, Tveritinov bought Tregubov a gold watch. In contrast to Petrikov, Tveritinov invoked unselfish motives for his illegal actions. It seemed that Tveritinov's only intention was to improve the performance of his store, and he asserted that his superiors at Glavtorg obliged him to break the law. He stated that if he did not give them gifts, his store would not have been treated fairly: "I thought of only one thing: that there should be a fair and objective approach toward the Gum collective, considering all its unsolved problems."[69]

Tregubov's defense plea lost credibility when he stated that no one ever came to see him at his office without the consent of his secretary, who, moreover, listened to every conversation he had with his guests; however, a bribe-taker had to come before or after working hours, as Petrikov probably did. Although Tregubov denied the accusation that he had obtained an apartment for Petrikov and insisted that the City Department for Housing had allocated the apartment, the fact remained that he had sent a request to this organization for a new apartment for his first deputy director. Shortly after this request was sent, Petrikov had moved to a larger flat. Nonetheless, Petrikov's testimony revealed some weaknesses: investigators obtained much corroborating evidence that he had taken large sums of money, but none confirmed the allegations he had made about giving bribes to his boss. Tregubov continued to deny accusations concerning situations where there were no witnesses. He resisted for more than six months, but the investigators' perseverance paid off when he finally acknowledged the validity of the accusations in February 1985, perhaps in hopes that he would be granted a lighter sentence if he cooperated with the police.[70] Although Oleinik had been only half successful in his interrogation of Tregubov, it encouraged the police to intensify the anticorruption campaign.

By the end of 1984, the number of suspects in jail awaiting trial had risen significantly, and at a higher rate than the investigators had expected. The leaders of the brigade were helped by the KGB and by OBKhSS, which was now controlled by former members of the KGB. Although the number of staff members in the anticorruption brigade was quite impressive in 1983–1984, its leaders complained about being short-staffed because they wanted to intensify their operations.[71] The fact that thousands of trade employees were arrested in 1984 showed that corruption was extremely widespread. Brigade leaders viewed these results as confirmation that corruption had reached a level that seriously threatened the

Soviet system and that it had rotted away the core of their society, penetrating the highest levels of the regime. It was clear that corruption could not be eradicated quickly and that its perpetrators and beneficiaries could not be easily removed.

In 1984, the high number of arrests caused some agitation and anxiety in Russian society, giving rise to criticism of the KGB for its abuses and of the brigade for arrests on insufficient evidence and violations of prisoners' rights. The information about civil rights abuses in prison had a considerable impact because many of the detained people had recently been employed in the trade organizations and had acquaintances among the elite. Elites who had been involved in the corruption schemes were frightened when they learned of the conditions of detention they might face in the future. Brigade leaders surmised that certain pressure tactics, like complaints in the press about irregularities by investigators, had been initiated by high-ranking officials who wanted to put a stop to the investigations before they themselves could be compromised. However, the harsh situation in jail and the disturbance it caused in society were not enough to impress the minister of the interior, Fedorchuk. The KGB's response was to ask for more resources and more investigators and to file more charges against trade staff members.

Fedorchuk's zealous attitude led the KGB to intensify its campaign. His prosecutors emphasized the negative effects of corruption, citing the incompetence of the trade executives and attributing it to the corrupt hiring policies of the trade leaders. Fedorchuk's firmness received the support of the majority of the prosecutors appointed by the KGB to head the brigade and who were committed to respect for the law. They wanted first to bring to trial all the suspects against whom they had obtained testimony. In their zealous pursuit of suspects, they wanted to punish the trade elite for being so dismissive of the rule of law. However, the brigade tended to attack all shortcomings in trade staff behavior, whether legal or illegal. Thus, everything that contradicted the ideal behavior of the cadre was denounced. Brigade documents contained considerable information about the executives' dubious morality, citing nepotism, favoritism, alcoholism, marital infidelity, and paying prostitutes for sex. One practice that was criticized was the hiring of people with criminal records. The prosecutors pointed out more than once that a person with a criminal past had been appointed to run the premier grocery store in the country. Trade executives were also criticized for their incompetence. Prosecutors reproached Glavtorg's leaders for not hiring and promoting staff members according to criteria of competence and merit. They reported that the trade leaders preferred to appoint to the better positions relatives or those who were involved in economic irregularities instead of qualified people. Thus, although there were fifty employees with a high level of education and two hundred with a medium level of education in eighty-seven district food

establishments, only three of the first category and twenty-one of the second category held management positions.[72] Indeed, the brigade reported cases of store managers who barely knew how to write.

The campaign against corruption focused on the trade agency's executives. But, as of 1983, the Soviet press began to accuse tolerant Party officials with corruption, as the following quote shows: "Certain leading officials in the district illegally obtained automobiles for their personal use, spent large sums of state and collective farm money to hold anniversary celebrations, weddings, and other festivities, and violated norms by keeping livestock in personal auxiliary farming operations."[73] These practices were not as much crimes as they were abuses at the limits of legality. More often than not, crimes were not committed. Nevertheless, their exposure in the media would contribute to undermining Party official's positions.[74] Gorbachev preferred to denounce these practices instead of sending the officials to jail, the main reason being that to prosecute them would likely lead to the intervention of the KGB and a boost in its influence. The precedent created in 1982 by the arrival of Andropov to power haunted Party leaders.

The principal blame for the rampant corruption in internal trade was laid upon the managers and employees of the grocery stores, that is, the retail end of the food distribution system. Indeed, these people were the most widely and deeply involved, and the KGB easily gathered a large volume of incriminating evidence against them. As they were less influential than Party officials, it was less of a risk for the KGB to accuse them of wrongdoing.

A number of Party cadres in Moscow were forced to resign or retire in 1982 and the following years, for reasons that included tolerance toward corruption. They were criticized for their passivity or lack of vigilance toward the phenomenon, although few were accused of corrupt practices themselves. This situation contrasted with that in the provinces, where cases of graft were reported more frequently, and in the non-Russian regions, where Party officials were accused and even convicted of having committed economic crimes such as bribery. In Moscow, however, Party cadres were supposed to be models of integrity, and it was out of the question that they be exposed for corruption, especially in the media. Law enforcement bodies, including the KGB, were meant to observe this unspoken rule and avoid taking on Party officials under any circumstances. In fact, however, the KGB was the only entity that possessed a formidable weapon against the Party: its long-established authority to systematically gather, sift, and classify information on the country's leaders, including Party heads. In the context of the anticorruption campaign, the KGB was in a good position to find out who was bribing whom in the retail sector of the food trade network, and it could use this knowledge to intimidate and pressure perpetrators into revealing their higher-level protectors.

In 1984, the conviction of Pospelov, the head of the food division of the Moscow Party Committee's Department of Trade and Maintenance, created a precedent. This case was a sensation because the sentencing of such a high ranking Party official to many years of imprisonment would have been impossible during the Brezhnev era.[75] It reflected a weakening of Grishin's leadership of the Moscow Party Committee. Henceforth, the law courts could rely on this precedent to file charges against Party officials anywhere. Pospelov's sentence affected people's confidence in the Party. It was logical to assume that, if Pospelov was a major bribe-taker, then some other Party officials probably were, too. One lesson learned from this episode was that whether people believed in communism or not, they were all in agreement that Party officials had to be held accountable for their actions. Whenever a corrupt senior Moscow Party official was denounced, there was an increase in the number of citizens writing to the media and to Party agencies about cases of abuse on the part of officials and executives. The KGB had undermined Party authority by arresting Moscow Party officials in 1983, but until the perestroika years, no officials other than Pospelov were actually brought to trial. Even this single conviction was enough to cause anxiety about the KGB among certain Party leaders. The KGB had broken the unwritten rule that the police could not go after middle-ranking Party bosses, and it now posed a serious threat to the Party's authority.

When the KGB initiated the campaign against corruption in the Moscow trade organizations, it was primarily looking for information to discredit the Grishinist nomenklatura. In Moscow, Grishin was the KGB's number-one enemy between 1982 and 1985. Most of the city leaders were on Grishin's side, a fact that may explain why the Moscow Party boss remained at his post until 1986, more than three years after the beginning of the anticorruption campaign. Grishin still had considerable influence throughout this period, as shown by the fact that Gorbachev defeated him by only one vote in the election of the new secretary general held by the Politburo in February 1985. Furthermore, Grishin remained the Moscow Party boss after this defeat. Having had twenty-one years to place his people in key posts, he was able to maintain his strong position.

In his struggle to strengthen his authority, Gorbachev brought in new officials and created new policies that became known by the term *perestroika*. Gorbachev was obliged to seek support from groups opposed to the status quo, such as intellectuals, who demanded respect for civil rights and limits on Party domination. Many reform-minded intellectuals were appointed Party officials. A second group consisted of people employed in the economic sphere; more specifically, it included a faction in the trade network. In the history of the Soviet Union, this group had had limited influence and its demands for change had been modest, but during the perestroika era, the acrimonious feelings of this group toward the

Soviet system came to the fore (see chapter 1). Irregularities had been rampant in the trade organizations because of the Kremlin's tolerant stance, but the situation began to change in 1982 with the advent of the harsh crackdown that affected many members of the trade staff.

The officials newly appointed by Gorbachev wasted no time fulfilling his expectations. The new policies were elaborated in such a way as to be significantly distinguishable from previous ones, thus justifying the changes in staff, particularly the removal of the Grishinists in Moscow. The new Party officials had no choice but to introduce changes and reforms that would consolidate their authority. Some middle-ranking officials without any manifestly liberal tendencies were frustrated by the stagnation that had blocked their ascension to the top of the hierarchy and saw Gorbachev's promotion to secretary general as an opportunity to rise in the Party. In the capital, many Grishinist partisans were removed between 1983 and 1985 and replaced by KGB leaders and men close to them. While the departure of the Grishinists was welcomed, Gorbachevians were not always happy with their successors. With Gorbachev in power, the KGB gradually became as much a target as the Grishinists had been. Gorbachev and his partisans wanted to make substantial changes but were not willing to risk damaging the Party's authority to the advantage of the security forces. In their view, the solutions to the Soviet Union's problems should not have been decided at KGB headquarters but by the Central Committee, nor should the solutions have come from prosecutors and investigators but rather from reformists and intellectuals, many of whom were appointed Party officials under Gorbachev. The Kremlin's new strategy was based on the principles of the decentralization of government, the participation of the population, and a bridging of the gap with the West.

Although it could not be openly stated, many members of the nomenklatura shared Gorbachev's worry that the anticorruption campaign had allowed the security force to assume an overly dominant role in Russian society. From 1983 to the end of 1985, the prerogatives of the Ministry of the Interior and the Prosecutor General's Office were severely limited by the KGB. Many KGB officials had been transferred to the top echelon of the MVD, and even if the anticorruption brigade was officially under the jurisdiction of the PGO, it received its orders from the KGB. The success achieved by the KGB with respect to the MVD and the PGO encouraged the security force to try to do the same thing with respect to the Party. With the justification that Party authority had been damaged by corruption, the KGB attempted to transfer part of the Party's prerogatives to itself.

After the brigade had imprisoned thousands of Muscovite trade executives implicated in corruption between 1982 and 1985, the KGB planned to shift the anticorruption campaign toward the Party and government officials suspected of having conspired with the trade leaders. Party apparatchiks like Gorbachev were

aware of the peril in this plan. Gorbachev knew that the majority of Party officials shared the habit of accepting gifts and had committed other abuses. Fedorchuk's move to redirect the anticorruption campaign from trade organizations to the Party leadership would clearly mean a major reconfiguration of power: if Fedorchuk's suggestions were accepted, the Party's Central Committee, which had monitored the actions of Party officials until 1985, would be obliged to transfer this function to the law enforcement agencies and, in this case, directly to the KGB.

The Party reacted to this attempt to limit its authority by taking quick action. For example, Sterligov, the former KGB official transferred in 1982 to head OBKhSS, was dismissed for his attempt to charge the secretary of a district Party committee with corruption.[76] Even some Politburo members who were reputed to be honest had a stake in curbing the KGB's power. Gromyko and other high-level Party officials had used the influence of Promyslov, mayor of Moscow, to acquire goods or services, such as garages and apartments for his relatives.[77] If the campaign against corruption were prolonged and expanded to target Party officials, people would learn of these violations.

On December 24, 1985, Boris Yeltsin succeeded Grishin as leader of the Moscow Party organization, considerably increasing the strength of the reformers who were now in a better position to renew the Moscow leadership. However, the promotion of Yeltsin to Party secretary in the capital also engendered new divergences within the reformist forces. At this time, Yeltsin supported the continuation of the anticorruption campaign in the capital, even if it did not correspond to the general policies of the Party. He had good reasons for opting for this position, because until then, his anticorruption stance had been profitable for him in terms of popularity. Yeltsin had received information about Moscow Party and Soviet officials' implication in corruption from the KGB and the brigade. His skill in politics became apparent when he introduced a major change in the anticorruption campaign. During 1985, he had realized that the campaign was losing the popular approval it had enjoyed in its earlier stage. Aware that investigators had occasionally committed abuses and that the campaign was causing popular dissatisfaction, Yeltsin deferred to the liberal intelligentsia who constituted his main support and who were generally hostile to the campaign because they saw it as a KGB tactic to increase its standing in society.

Therefore, the campaign had to be reoriented and presented from another perspective. The Communist Party or, more precisely, its staff in Moscow appointed by Grishin, was now targeted as being mainly responsible for the widespread culture of corruption. In 1985, Yeltsin began to publicly pair corruption and official abuses with his criticism of the privileges enjoyed by Party officials.

He attacked the elite sector for its materialist values—its taste for luxury, foreign goods, and so on. He insisted that the pursuit of material benefits derived from the nomenklatura's involvement in corrupt dealings. Indeed, the nomenklatura's attraction to consumerism had been stimulated by all the money and resources accumulated in the trade organizations and redistributed to Party officials. During this period, Yeltsin thus waged a war against privilege.[78] He liked to present himself as a Party official who was capable of refusing favors. It was well known at the time that he traveled by subway and that his wife waited her turn in line at the grocery stores. Yeltsin always wore shoes made in Russia instead of the more stylish Italian imports. He proclaimed that officials who broke the law would have to face justice regardless of their rank in the Party.

Yeltsin approved of the brigade's operations, since their purpose was crucial to his quest for power. While he consolidated his support from the intelligentsia by identifying Party officials as the target of the anticorruption campaign, he simultaneously gratified the KGB and specifically the anticorruption brigade by allowing them to continue their investigations despite the limits he imposed on their operations. Prosecutors now had Yeltsin's backing if they wanted to arrest Party officials; moreover, they were made aware that they should concentrate their search on Party cadres while minimizing the repression of trade executives, who were now perceived as victims of the Soviet system. The permission to target Party officials indicated that Yeltsin was hostile to only one faction of the nomenklatura. In the same vein, by presenting the trade leaders as victims of the system, it implied that he was a defender of some factions of the nomenklatura that had been oppressed by the Communist Party and was willing to make peace with any Party officials who wanted to join his camp, whatever their political convictions had been in the past. After all, this was the path he himself had followed in his career.

Gorbachev, for his part, believed that, since the anticorruption campaign had carried out much of its mandate under Andropov, it should now be reined in and its pace slowed. Gorbachev was willing for the campaign to continue because he was loath to antagonize his colleague, Ligachev, a member of the Politburo and leader of the conservative faction in the Party during perestroika. He consented to have Ligachev appear to be the principal defender of this policy, with himself in the role of simple supporter. Gorbachev progressively distanced himself from the campaign as criticism against it mounted. Since he depended on support from the nomenklatura to maintain power, the campaign was a double-edged sword for Gorbachev. He wanted to use the campaign to pressure the nomenklatura to accept his reforms—and doubtless wanted to force part of this group out of the corridors of power—but without carrying out an inquisition or bringing

Party and government officials to trial, which could lead to the loss of his principal support base.

Yeltsin was more openly critical of the nomenklatura. Nevertheless, the differences between Gorbachev and Yeltsin in 1985–1986 should not be exaggerated. Gorbachev valued radical partisans who could lead frontal attacks against the Party's adversaries and counterbalance the influence of the most conservative elements in it. The hypothesis that Gorbachev tried to use Yeltsin to remove Grishin is credible. Gorbachev had brought Yeltsin to Moscow to fulfill specific functions, one of which was to hold a radical discourse that would help Gorbachev's cause. Yeltsin represented the tribune that Gorbachev needed to attract the section of the intelligentsia and the youth that supported radical reform. Upon arrival in Moscow, Yeltsin did show himself to be interested in winning support among those groups, but that this was a matter of personal conviction is doubtful. His repeated attacks included the following type of appeal:

> Why have we been unable for so many years to eradicate bureaucratic excess, social injustice and abuses? Why, even now, is the demand for radical change getting bogged down in a stratum of time-servers with party membership cards? Poor supervision of the work of cadres, who have been resting on their laurels for years, and the lack of initiative on the part of a number of Party Committee first secretaries, increasingly frequent deviations and abuses, the absence of self-criticism and genuine collective leadership: these are the reasons for slumps and failures in the work of entire regions.[79]

Yeltsin lost little by attacking the nomenklatura. However, his seeking support in public opinion did not mean he was a sworn enemy of the nomenklatura. Yeltsin had climbed the steps to Party power in the Ekaterinburg (Sverdlovsk) region precisely because he had been supported by the local nomenklatura. Arriving in Moscow and depicting himself as a champion against corruption, he was attempting to build up a base of popular support. The population was very sensitive to the issue, especially when it concerned the link between product shortages in the stores and corruption, a point stressed by Yeltsin.[80] This public opinion helped both him and Gorbachev in the power struggle in Moscow. However, Yeltsin's objective was also to win over the partisans in the nomenklatura, who he needed to gain power at the center. An apparatchik like Yeltsin was quite at ease among members of the nomenklatura and knew how to get what he wanted from them. He was not as familiar with the intelligentsia and with youth, groups that were less stable and more difficult to satisfy. His appeal to popular support was made essentially so that the nomenklatura would view him in a more favorable light. Yeltsin's ambition to rise in the ranks of the Communist Party would

have been difficult to predict in 1985, due to the fact that the Party organization in the capital was dominated by conservatives. His anticorruption discourse was intended to win him support among certain groups in the nomenklatura, including the army, heavy industry, and nationalists, who believed that the country had been seriously weakened by corruption. More than once, Yeltsin was heard to insist that corruption and the resulting social ills would not be so extensive if the judicial bodies, the brigade in particular, were given free rein during their investigations. These statements naturally pleased those people in the law enforcement bodies who were urging a more rigorous application of the law.

Yeltsin was not a member of the Moscow elite, and, as an outsider, he had no choice but to rely upon the law enforcement agencies. In 1985, he knew little about the political situation in Moscow and about corruption among the capital's elite. He became close to the anticorruption brigade leaders and met with them on a weekly basis. The brigade leaders contributed significantly to the formation of his opinions on the political situation in the capital. They even exercised considerable influence on his strategy to replace Grishin, and it was from the anticorruption brigade that Yeltsin received most of the weapons that he used to discredit the Grishinists. In turn, Yeltsin encouraged the brigade to pursue the investigations into the food trade organizations, and he defended it against those who wanted to limit its powers, presenting cogent reasons to continue the campaign.

In 1986, the brigade was opposed to a faction of the PGO that wanted to put an end to an investigation that it considered had gone far enough, while the brigade insisted that their job remained unfinished. The information the brigade later transmitted to Yeltsin revealed that economic irregularities and embezzlement continued to proliferate in the trade network as late as 1987, when the illegal pricing of fruit and vegetables by disguising their inferior quality was still a common practice. The brigade agents queried why the anticorruption campaign should end when corruption was still so widespread and even on the increase.[81] They insisted that as long as highly placed individuals were above the law, corruption would continue to exist on a large scale. These law enforcement officers had an interest in prolonging the campaign for career reasons, but more than that, they were well aware of the pervasiveness of graft from the information that the KGB had gathered and therefore knew that they possessed solid evidence against the personnel in the retail end of the food distribution network.

The Attack on Party Officials

During perestroika, Oleinik became Yeltsin's ally, as both men were interested in uncovering evidence against top Party officials and both were convinced of Grishin's misconduct in public office. The consequence was Oleinik's politi-

cal involvement on two levels: first, within the law enforcement agencies, as he advocated a preponderant role for the KGB, and second, on a social level, as he emphasized the responsibilities of Party leaders regarding corruption in the trade organizations. Perestroika brought hard times for Oleinik because those in the nomenklatura who were suspected of corruption were very hostile to the anticorruption brigade. Media criticism of those who led the campaign against corruption represented something new that was impossible before 1985. This factor made the situation more difficult for Oleinik and his investigators and was a primary reason why Oleinik's perception of Gorbachev changed for the worse after 1985. He attacked Gorbachev, believing that Gorbachev had destroyed the progress Andropov had made: "It was Andropov and not Gorbachev who began perestroika in the U.S.S.R. High-level officials of the nomenklatura were denounced and criminal charges were laid against them in Moscow and in the southern parts of the country. But the battles against criminality became less relevant after the beginning of perestroika. Apparatchiks of the Party have skillfully diverted the blow that threatened them, targeting instead those who fought against criminality."[82]

However, the Oleinik who backed Andropov because he had wanted a state under the rule of law, along with respect for that law and fair justice, did not match the Oleinik known as the champion of harsh sentences for trade leaders, who he had from 1982 to 1985 described as the most ignoble of criminals. Furthermore, the Oleinik who had been accused of mistreatment and even cruelty toward Filippov, Sokolov, and other executives of the Moscow trade network now rehabilitated the same people, who were presented as martyrs: "I tell you frankly that several directors of the main food stores suffered in this affair. I do not want to name them now, but if necessary, I will name them—the heads of the kontoras, and executives at all levels. Basically, they were scapegoats of this terrible, corrupt system."[83]

Oleinik was among those in the law enforcement bodies who proposed some reforms in the economy, including the consumer trade network. This move may be seen as an effect of Andropov's policy of refreshing his staff during the 1970s: a significant portion of this new, more open generation was willing to support perestroika. Political reform that might lead to the overthrow of the Soviet regime and the advent of liberal democracy had few partisans among KGB agents, even though the majority of them desired changes in the political system that would ensure the equal application of the law to everyone—in particular, to Communist Party officials. Oleinik was a partisan of reforms in the justice system that would guarantee its independence from political influence and may thus be characterized as a legal leader according to Max Weber's definition. In

Oleinik's view, everyone is equal before the law, and representatives of law agencies, such as judges and prosecutors, are nominated according to standards, such as competence and performance. Oleinik adhered to these principles all his life, although in practice he was not always consistent.

The above discussion should not be taken as highlighting the fact that Oleinik's beliefs were inspired by his desire to keep the highly sought after posts he had occupied during the Brezhnev and Andropov period. Oleinik was aware of his popularity and also knew that by going after various communist officials he might reinforce his appeal, since to accuse such officials of corruption was well regarded among the law enforcement staff. From this perspective, we can understand Oleinik's conversion to reformism, which enjoyed growing support among people and one faction of the nomenklatura during the early period of perestroika.

But the priorities of Oleinik and his brigade remained the same until 1987. They wanted to prove that corruption prevailed inside the Moscow Party Committee but unfortunately were unable to prove it. That proof was harder to obtain during perestroika is understandable because citizens had more rights to defend themselves. Moreover, the brigade was handicapped by the fact that, between 1982 and 1984, lesser amounts of credible evidence were transmitted by investigators. For one thing, the evidence accumulated by KGB during the Andropov era was considerable, but its value decreased in 1985 and thereafter because of the methods by which it was obtained. Another factor was that the political intervention of high Party and government officials put an abrupt end to the judicial process vis-à-vis corruption case. The effect was that the confidence of the reformist trend in the Soviet justice system decreased considerably. The members of the brigade did not find enough evidence against high-ranking Moscow Party officials; nevertheless, they were not indifferent to the discovery that many Communist Party officials had low moral standards, tolerated corruption, and protected corrupt officials.

Sterligov, the KGB officer appointed head of OBKhSS in the Moscow MVD, commented on the impact that the campaign against irregularities in Glavtorg and Glavka had had on him and on many of his KGB colleagues: "Three years in this job opened our eyes a great deal. . . . Being so close to the national economy and economic crimes, we realized the falsehood of what was being done officially for the well-being of the people, and how people from the Party structures dissimulated what they did against them. They behaved as if they were above the law."[84] Investigation leaders, such as Sterligov and Oleinik, criticized the actions and attitudes of the Party and its representatives: "Party apparatchiks thought they were justified in interfering in all aspects of the law. They pushed for the

repression of minor offenses committed mostly by young sales clerks; they pressured us to sentence them severely, but at the same time, they protected the real criminals, the big crooks."[85]

Disillusionment with corruption in Party organs was particularly prevalent among the younger generation of law enforcement personnel; they preferred Yeltsin's intransigence over Gorbachev's ambivalence and indecision. Bunakov and several other members of the KGB's younger contingent constituted a force of change in the law enforcement agency. Moreover, the soft prosecutors, more respectful of the rights of the suspects, did not have to worry that Yeltsin's reforms would lead to tougher interrogation requirements.

Yeltsin was willing to support the brigade in 1985 and 1986 in his attempts to discredit Party conservatives associated with Grishin. However, inculpating Party officials was less necessary for Yeltsin after he replaced Grishin as first secretary of the Communist Party in Moscow. Discrediting Grishin was taken care of by journalists who were enjoying a new freedom of expression thanks to perestroika. Newspaper articles on corruption among the nomenklatura proliferated, and Party officials were not spared. Media exposure became a much more effective way of destroying politicians' reputations than confessions obtained by the KGB. The word *corruption* had acquired less of a legal meaning and more of a political one. A large sector of the population believed that Grishin had been guilty of corruption even though it was never proved. It was clear that in this societal shift, the KGB had lost ground in favor of the media. Yeltsin maintained the reputation of a strong fighter against corruption, but he no longer linked the problem to the judicial organs. Nonetheless, he continued to treat the KGB as an important player, realizing that his climb to power would be much more difficult without the support of the KGB, or at least of a significant faction within it.

The dilemma for Oleinik and other reformist investigators was whether it was more advantageous for them to favor Yeltsin or the KGB. Their natural inclination went to the latter, whose interests and working methods they shared. However, they would accept almost any political system that would maintain their positions. Oleinik's choice likewise depended on the situation. As the influence of the KGB decreased gradually during perestroika, he tended to lend more support to Yeltsin. Since he exhibited a preference for a powerful leader, like Yeltsin, he would therefore adopt a more reformist approach. To make the transition toward a state under the rule of law was easier for Oleinik for different reasons. He was more influenced by the West, by virtue of his relatives in America. Oleinik had also developed relations and contacts with journalists and law specialists in the West, never hesitating to give interviews to foreign journalists and specialists. A man who liked to be in the public eye, Oleinik was considered a specialist and scholar by members of the judiciary for his publications and lectures on law and

crime. Finally, he knew how to express himself in the media. All these attributes made Oleinik not only a real leader in the law enforcement agencies but also one of Yeltsin's most valuable allies.

Yeltsin's interest in corruption coincided with that of the law enforcement agencies: they all wanted to get rid of the Grishinist elite and believed that the KGB could provide compromising information on them. Yeltsin's emphasis on the fight against corruption helped him gain support among the KGB staff, and he was good at making friends and allies in law enforcement agencies, especially in the security force. He brought some KGB officials onto his side by giving them important posts, and others were invited to join the ranks of his candidates for the 1989 election. Some young KGB officers who stood up for him were eventually rewarded by being given important positions in the police. Generally, these young officers who supported Yeltsin were motivated by career considerations. Perestroika and the rise of Yeltsin signaled the possibility of advancement, particularly for the younger generation. Some middle-aged representatives of the law enforcement agencies who already held high-ranking posts also hoped that their adherence to Yeltsin could result in opportunities for more prestigious jobs.

Just as it was with PGO criminal investigators, the KGB had its own confidential agents among the judges. The KGB's stable of judges was very useful in the campaign against corruption because they were quite harsh when sentencing retail trade leaders and did not hesitate to reach agreements with members of the KGB on the verdicts they would issue. The KGB fully trusted these judges and gave them the most prominent cases. They collaborated closely with Oleinik during perestroika after the KGB was forced to withdraw from the war against corruption. Many of those judges sided with the Yeltsin camp, which brought together those who represented the judiciary powers that adhered to Yeltsin's reforms. The most prominent of these judges was V. V. Demidov, who was the presiding judge in the corruption trial of Sokolov, the most renowned retail trade leader in Moscow.[86] After Yeltsin came to power in August 1991, Demidov was appointed judge at the Supreme Court while Oleinik became judge of the Constitutional Court.

If Bunakov, the KGB investigator, had not given support to Oleinik's investigation in the Ambartsumyan case, he would not have been subsequently appointed to lead a major investigation in Moscow on corruption in the furniture stores.[87] Also, Yeltsin occasionally recruited KGB officials who, like Sterligov, had no interest in reform but were opposed to Gorbachev. After Sterligov and Oleinik, Trofimov was the highest-ranking prosecutor to join Yeltsin's camp. He belonged to the group of KGB agents who had been criticized and dismissed late in 1985 upon the arrival of new leaders in the PGO. Trofimov was dismissed for his zeal and excess in the investigation that he led against corruption in the

Moscow trade structures, but, more importantly, the liberals had viewed him as their number-one enemy because he led the antidissident Third Department. Essentially, the liberalization of the Soviet system undermined Trofimov's authority and influence. The rise of Gorbachev could have ruined his career and even resulted in charges being brought against him for his repression of dissidents, but in the confusion of perestroika, he was saved by Yeltsin, who, after 1987, invited him and other tough prosecutors to join the ranks of his partisans. Trofimov returned in full force with the rise of Yeltsin. Another reason why Trofimov was trusted and appreciated by Yeltsin was Trofimov and Sterligov's willingness to file charges against Party officials, notwithstanding the consequent bad relations with the Kremlin in 1985. In addition, Trofimov's hostility toward Gorbachev explains why Yeltsin appointed him to a high position in the security force. Sterligov was given a similar appointment during perestroika but was dismissed soon afterward. Yeltsin did not hesitate to replace people when they ceased to be useful to him.

The KGB's influence in the political system grew in the 1970s chiefly due to the anticorruption battles it led, especially in the Caucasus region. Those early campaigns gave the KGB the opportunity to acquire experience and to train its personnel in the struggle against economic crime, a phenomenon that became widespread in the Brezhnev era. The anticorruption battle greatly helped to boost the KGB's reputation as an institution based on rational-legal authority. Under Andropov's direction the security service extended its influence in the political system as a force dedicated to respect for the law. Most of its representatives were viewed as competent and incorruptible.

The KGB launched its anticorruption campaign against the Moscow trade organizations in 1982, a most propitious time for such a move. Late that year, Andropov succeeded Brezhnev as secretary general, and the frustrations and complaints of the population regarding corruption reached their zenith. Less than two years after the beginning of the campaign, KGB leaders could declare that their mission had been accomplished. Almost all the leaders of the Moscow *kontora*s and of the Moscow Trade Administration (Glavtorg) had been arrested on the basis of significant evidence. The campaign had also achieved its main political goal: discrediting the Grishinist Party officials, even though the Party officials charged were not numerous. It took more time—until 1986—for the KGB and the anticorruption brigade to uncover evidence on a significant number of district Party officials, although very few of these were in the higher echelons, since Grishin, Promyslov, and most other high-ranking apparatchiks avoided criminal proceedings. The incomplete nature of this campaign could have been partly due to the fact that the prosecutor's mandate was limited to investigating

the trade structures. More significantly, after Andropov's death and the Grishin-ist defeat, the anticorruption campaign had less of a raison d'être. Moreover, some KGB and PGO officials joined the forces hostile to the campaign because they thought it would be beneficial to their careers. As a consequence, the KGB's role diminished because of divisions within its ranks—one faction siding with the conservatives and the other, with the liberals.

3

Who, How Many, and How Much?

Corruption in the Moscow Trade Organizations

■ From analyzing the impact of the KGB's crackdown on the trade organizations, we now turn to an analysis of those who were suspected, accused, and convicted of corruption and to the scope of bribe-giving as a form of corruption in the Moscow trade network, scope being a reference to the number of people and the amount of money involved. Among the published analyses of the different facets of this corruption, none has yet given concrete details on the employees in the trade organizations who gave or accepted bribes. The focus here is primarily on the food sector because that is where most of the available data were.

During the first months of 1983, the KGB was at the zenith of its power, and the political outlook in the country could not have been better for it. The KGB effectively controlled politics, the economy, and law enforcement and enjoyed broad popular support. The media had helped the KGB by printing many articles on how corruption was a serious threat to society. Even intellectuals looked to the KGB to establish a greater measure of law and order, joining in the consensus that such a move would solve problems and lead to improvements in several areas of society. Andropov's actions met with approval when, in the first months of 1983, the KGB, taking advantage of its favorable position, unleashed its campaign, which hit hard and high. Tactics were carefully practiced, and the best officers were mobilized. The investigators knew that simply arresting the trade leaders would not put an end to the corruption. It was true that the KGB would make a splash by targeting giants like five-star hotels Kosmos and Russia, considered foreign oases, and factories reputed to be in the hands of gangs

that produced difficult-to-obtain products, such as alcohol. However, its central objective was to attack and destroy the whole network of graft in the trade organizations. They systematically investigated one store after another, one warehouse after another, beginning with the most important and interrogating and incarcerating thousands of people.

Officials and Organizations Involved in Bribery

Records of the KGB's investigation of Glavtorg (the Moscow Trade Administration) provide a considerable quantity of data on corruption in the Soviet trade organizations in Moscow. Such a large-scale investigation had never been undertaken, and it required a long period of evidence collection, from November 1982 until the end of 1985. There were twenty thousand people employed at Glavtorg, which had direct jurisdiction over five thousand stores.[1] Within Glavtorg, the RPTs (District Food Trade Organizations) managed two thousand food stores.[2] The KGB inquiry began with the Glavtorg administration, twenty-nine of the thirty-one RPTs, and fifty of the more important *gastronoms*.[3]

Glavtorg directed the distribution and sale of consumer products in the capital. Its president, Tregubov, was surrounded by a bevy of vice presidents: Deputy President Petrikov; Second Vice President Khokhlov, who headed the personnel department; Third Vice President Kireev, head of the inspection and control department; and Fourth Vice President Kliachin, in charge of accounting. It did not take long before the heads of Glavtorg, with the exception of Tregubov, admitted their guilt. Each of them had amassed large amounts of money from bribes: Petrikov with 84,400 rubles, Khokhlov with 33,209, and Kireev with 17,500. It was from the directors of three of the four top Moscow *gastronoms* that the KGB obtained the most impressive results, with 300,000 rubles in Sokolov's possession, 50,000 for Tveritinov, and 171,300 for Filippov among those who had profited enormously from corruption. Sokolov had received even higher amounts than the heads of Glavtorg. The police data show that cases of bribery were uncovered in twenty-nine RPTs and that five thousand employees had committed reprehensible acts.[4] The directors of the Pervomaiski, Volgogradski, and Kuibishev RPTs and the Sokol'niki *universam* were jailed mainly because of the privileged relationship they had with Glavtorg president Tregubov. Baigelman, the director of the Kuibishev RPT, admitted to being one of those who had received a very large amount of money, a confession that enabled him to leave prison camp earlier than expected. The investigators gave details on the kind of life that Kantora (a relative of the mayor of Moscow) had been living. Searches carried out at Kantora's fifteen-bedroom secondary residence revealed that he possessed objects worth 900,000 rubles and gold worth 500,000 rubles.

The investigators claimed that they would have been able to bring evidence against many more people if they had had more staff members and more time. They cited the case of the Perovski district, where they said they held solid proof against hundreds of people besides those who were brought to trial and eventually found guilty.

Most of the main grocery stores' directors as well as a number of restaurant managers were incarcerated following the presentation of damning evidence against them. The evidence was often extracted from the testimony of the leaders of the Administration of Grocery Trade Organizations or AGTO, who were also imprisoned. According to the data, the directors of the RPTs were the principal sources of bribes given to the heads of the AFPTO (Administration of Food Product Trade Organizations), and the amounts involved were high. The heads of the AGTO enjoyed the greatest generosity in terms of bribes, with Sonkin receiving 208,000, Larionov 105,000, and Korovkin 71,600 rubles, respectively.[5] The heads of the AFPTO received large amounts as well, although not approaching the sums amassed by heads of the AGTO. In 1983, the KGB had succeeded in obtaining confessions from the leaders of the AFPTO and the AGTO, and their statements included comprehensive information about the different amounts they had received in bribes and which RPT directors had bribed them. However, the investigators' job was far from over, because some of the RPT heads denied the accusations against them. Supplementary proof had to be found, and uncovering it would be a lengthy task, given the huge number of RPTs. However, the heads of the AFPTO and the AGTO had provided considerably less information that was relevant to the KGB's primary interest, that is, implicating highly placed officials. There may have been a lot of information on a few Glavtorg leaders, but there was nothing on its president, Tregubov, and very little on officials in the upper echelons of government and the Party. The higher the investigators went in the Glavtorg hierarchy, the more difficult it was for investigators to gather evidence. Also, the information obtained at the upper levels was sometimes of doubtful legal value. At the level of the AFPTO, in the revelations concerning the deputy director, Eremeev, bribery often could not be distinguished from legitimate gift-giving. Moreover, the information given by Eremeev on the bribes he received was rarely confirmed by the people he implicated.[6]

Gathering the necessary data on corruption in Glavka did not take as long as it did with Glavtorg, and not only because the latter was a larger organization. While proof against Uraltsev, the Glavka president, accumulated very rapidly, no such stockpile of evidence developed in the Tregubov case. The inquiry into Tregubov's activities covered a longer period: while Uraltsev had become Glavka president in 1976, Tregubov had occupied his position since the 1960s. In addition, according to KGB priorities, the investigation of Tregubov had to be more

thorough, since he was presumed to have compromising relationships with more important people. The Glavtorg vice presidents denied having given bribes to their boss; only Petrikov finally confessed to having bribed Tregubov, after denying it for several months. The dearth of evidence had consequences, including the fact that it took investigators longer to find less convincing evidence against the Glavtorg leaders. Occasionally, they had suspicions about the guilt of certain accused persons and the seriousness of their crimes but could not uncover any actual evidence against them. In the case of Ambartsumyan, director of the Dzerzhinski *kontora,* the KGB agents believed that he had pocketed much more than sixty thousand rubles, the estimate made by the judge at his trial, but they were never able to prove it.

Graft was not limited to the food distribution system; investigations into the automobile sector in Moscow resulted in judicial procedures against fourteen upper management cadres.[7] Hundreds of employees of the Moscow Central Tourist Bureau also faced charges. Rozanova was the director of Galantorg (Central Administration for the Distribution and Retailing of Clothing) until she was indicted for accepting bribes in 1983. The head of furniture inspection and the directors of eleven stores in this sector were also arraigned for trial.[8] However, since the KGB was given the resources and the mandate to concentrate their inquiries within food distribution and sales, they could not, in principle, carry out systematic investigations in other sectors. Nonetheless, results obtained in preliminary inquiries showed that those sectors had also been subject to massive illegalities.

The Importance of Bribe-Takers and Tregubov

Statistics from the investigations reveal that the number of bribe-givers in food distribution and sales diminished at the higher levels of the administrative hierarchy. This is where the strongest contrast between bribe-givers and bribe-takers can be seen, with the bribe-takers occupying positions in the top strata. Their influence and power made it more difficult for investigators to gather evidence. Going after bribe-takers often implied going after their networks, which usually included people who held key posts in the regime. The network was typically composed of a group involved in corruption and another made up of their friends and bosses, often Party and government officials who would defend the members of the first group when necessary, vouching for their integrity and competence and always ready to help them get out of difficult situations.

Not everyone could benefit from such loyal protectors. One had to occupy a relatively prestigious job, and such jobs were not plentiful, even in Moscow. In food distribution and retail, this type of position was limited to the directorships

of the four celebrated downtown *gastronom*s: Eliseevski, Smolenski, Novoarbatski, and Gum. In Glavtorg, those whose positions guaranteed the protection of networks included the directors and the vice directors of the AGPTO and of the AGTO stores. Certain personal qualities characterized the executives within the executive hierarchy: anyone who was named to a higher position had to have a certain amount of experience in management and graft and to have demonstrated the proper techniques of giving and taking bribes. He or she could move to a higher position only by being recommended by superiors who were themselves masters in the art of diverting funds into their pockets.

Sokolov, director of the Eliseevski *gastronom*, had the most influential protectors. Before being named to the top management job at this prestigious store, he had proved himself at the Galantorg clothing stores. He was able to rise in the Glavtorg power pyramid only after becoming an associate of Petrikov during his time at Galantorg. Once he became director of Eliseevski, Sokolov consolidated his network, becoming a friend of Galina Brezhnev and Mrs. Tregubov and creating close relations with Filippov, the director of the Novoarbatski *gastronom*. He drew investigators' attention by the large number of highly placed cadres (more than twenty-nine of them), including Party, government, and union officials, who benefited from his largess. It had taken Filippov only four years as *gastronom* director to establish this list.[9] Sokolov's execution and Nonaev's suicide gave greater importance to Filippov's testimony. Tveritinov, director of the Gum *gastronom*, could not boast of a list of protectors as long as Filippov's or of one that included as many highly placed protectors as Sokolov's. On the other hand, Tveritinov was one of the few executives to have bribed Tregubov, and he also belonged to the select group that Tregubov had gathered around him for travel outside the country. Moreover, according to the investigators, Tveritinov gave gifts to high-level officials of the regime, although he was never indicted for this activity. We do not have a list of the people bribed by Nonaev, the director of the Smolenski *gastronom,* due to his suicide.

The directors of the Dzerzhinski and Sheremetyevo *kontora*s stood out for the importance of their protectors, who were leaders in the ministries of Trade and of Agriculture and directors of the central *kontora* that served the entire Soviet Union.

The real strength of the directors of the four most prestigious Moscow *gastronom*s lay in their political support networks of Party and government officials.[10] Likewise, the directors of the model *kontora*s had the support of the Party and soviet chiefs of their respective districts, to whom they had given bribes. Directors of the other *kontora*s, however, did not have the same kind of close relations with their district chiefs, even though they often gave them gifts, and

the AFPTO and AGTO directors paid out considerable sums of money, but only to Glavtorg leaders. For this reason, their networks were not as strong as those of the Glavtorg and model *kontora* heads.

Tregubov emerged as the most important bribe-taker, not because of the amount of money taken but because of his influence, as Glavtorg leader, on the attitudes of the trade staff in general and on corruption in particular. With his charismatic leadership qualities, he was able to rise to the top of the hierarchy in the trade sector. People were impressed by his imposing stature, his unbridled energy, and his passionate manner. He exuded confidence, so with his personality and the power he accumulated, he was intimidating; few people challenged him. Tregubov submitted to Grishin but to few others, even if they were members of law enforcement bodies. He was defiant and even arrogant toward the prosecutors interrogating him and remained convinced that the KGB could do nothing to him. When Prosecutor Oleinik went to Tregubov's office to interrogate him, the latter mentioned that if Oleinik liked to dress well, he, Tregubov, had some nice suits in his stores.

In Tregubov's early years in the trade organization, his personality naturally drew attention, but he also skillfully presented himself to superiors as a dynamic employee. He was not careless or indifferent on the job and had not decided to pursue a career in the trade sector because he had failed at other occupations or at school, like many other trade employees had. He wanted to work in the trade sector because he liked it. Because he always appeared to be genuinely interested in his work and in the problems of the trade sector, he always made an excellent impression on his bosses. Tregubov often intervened in meetings, but not only to justify the choices made by upper management, even though his views often matched those of his superiors. With his impressive physique, he was imposing in public even though he was not a formidable orator. He could not have been promoted to head of the Moscow trade network in 1969 if he had not successfully gone through a KGB investigation establishing his honesty—an obligatory practice for such an important appointment.[11] While this seal of approval did not mean that Tregubov was not involved in illegal activities, it at least explains why the amounts of money he acquired tended to be modest. Tregubov likely took food, gifts, and even bribes. Later, when he was under suspicion in 1983–1984, the police obtained information that he had taken bribes while working in the food transportation department, but no solid evidence supported this allegation.[12] He lived modestly, even after his appointment as Glavtorg chief, and none of his relatives were ever appointed to management positions.[13] Thus, Tregubov could not be viewed as a traditional-type leader, because he was not motivated by personal interests.

Tregubov, who knew very well how to please his superiors, was able to impress them by criticizing shortcomings in the trade network. He knew that his boss, Grishin, was intolerant of and obsessed with dissidents, including those in the economic sector. He even occasionally sensed dissidence where none existed. Since the capital potentially harbored more dissidents than anywhere else in the country, the Kremlin expected Grishin to be vigilant and to guarantee that the city was an island of loyalty to the regime. It may have been Tregubov's greatest achievement to have ensured obedience within Glavtorg. In fact, during Tregubov's tenure, not a single executive openly criticized Glavtorg or proposed changes in favor of a free-market economy or privatization. This loyalty was especially welcome in a sector of the economy that was confronting significant problems. Trade leaders were a conservative force, and their long years in power had made them attached to traditional management methods. They tended to trust and appreciate conservatives like themselves, people who were older and whom they had known for a long time. They feared that new managers would bring in methods that challenged their authority. However, Tregubov knew how to gain and keep the trust of his superiors, and the food store near Grishin's home consequently always offered an impressive assortment of goods.[14] Tregubov's bosses also trusted him because he was highly respected by the Glavtorg staff, even though he often publicly criticized and even humiliated his executives for misconduct or mistakes. Nonetheless, there was another side to Tregubov, who considered his executives to be like members of a family.

Another of Tregubov's talents was his ability to build strong support within his staff. He was aware of how difficult it was to work in the trade sphere, with all its attendant problems, and he knew that bribery was a long-standing practice. Officially, Tregubov sided with his superiors, but in practice, he was often supportive of his staff, although there were limits to what he could do for them. Thus, although Tregubov severely criticized his chief accountant more than once for neglect and drunkenness at work, he did not dismiss or demote him.[15] Tregubov could have asked his bosses to provide decent salaries and to improve the quality of food products, which would have been legitimate requests, but he knew that generosity toward the trade network depended on standards that had nothing to do with the Soviet system. Trade Ministry leaders often gave extra resources to managers who bribed them, even though their official declarations spoke of rewarding high-performing store managers by supplying a good assortment of products. True, Trade Ministry leaders acknowledged that there were still many problems in their sector, but the solutions they prescribed, including the constant refrain to work better, were not new and were largely meaningless.[16]

Tregubov's attitude did not always conform to Soviet norms, but on several occasions he showed that one of his main concerns was to protect his executives.

He defended the RPT directors, although the people who had complained about them kept their jobs. Tregubov's appointment as head of Glavtorg meant that the Moscow leaders wanted stability in the trade organizations, just as they wanted it for society overall. The nomenklatura had been stressed by the many changes Stalin and Khrushchev had introduced into Soviet society, so their desire for continuity in politics was what had led them to choose Brezhnev to succeed Khrushchev. Brezhnev was cautious, flexible, tolerant, and had a weak character by Soviet standards. His program was simple: by giving autonomy and stability to the cadres, their effectiveness would increase accordingly.[17] In fact, Brezhnev believed that increased production constituted the key element needed to resolve the problems of Soviet society. In terms of the trade network, this view meant that the distribution of additional consumer goods was the best solution to the major trade problem: shortages. Tregubov and the other trade officials could only agree with this policy, because it was an idea they had always attempted to put in practice. From 1964 to 1975, the Brezhnev approach seemed to bear fruit: the standard of living of the Soviet citizen improved, despite being low in comparison with that of the West.[18] The successes achieved during this period explain why the same policies were followed after 1975 and why people remained in the same posts in all the domains of society. Why change cadres if they have performed well?

Although people were generally not being removed from positions, Tregubov did often promote people he knew personally. Their loyalty to him was a decisive factor in his decision to promote a person. Another criterion for promotion was mastery of the tactics of the shadow economy; one mark of success in this area was to be able to make profits through graft without being arrested. Also, Tregubov welcomed any proposals for appointments from his friends and protectors in the higher echelons. In this system, almost all the different organizational levels had autonomy: the borough, the store, the department, and so forth. The boss of each unit had considerable room for maneuvering and exercising power. He or she decided on the allocation of resources and on staff assignments, suffering little interference from the outside. The staff had usually been in place for a long time, and the bosses could trust them insofar as no employee or executive dared to take initiatives that were contrary to those of management. In any case, trade executives were generally too conservative to be innovative; they had succeeded as managers by complying with Brezhnev's standards.

The Moscow trade network had been granted a specific status within the Ministry of Trade, enjoying a high degree of autonomy even before Brezhnev's ascendancy at the Kremlin. In the 1970s, the Moscow trade staff transformed Glavtorg into a clique that had a considerable amount of resources at its disposal and an army of employees to distribute them. The resources had to be distrib-

uted in a certain way, according to precise formal regulations; in reality, however, Glavtorg staff allocated them according to their own rules. The trade executives succeeded in accumulating huge sums of money to defend and promote their interests. Not all trade employees, however, were able to enrich themselves; the majority of them still lived poorly. Pilfering in the workplace increased their standard of living, but their net gains were actually rather modest because they had to pay a heavy tribute in bribes to their superiors in order to continue the petty thievery. There was one category of employees able to generate large revenues by selling products on the black market. However, the risks were higher for them, as police occasionally arrested these individuals. If, under Tregubov, store managers and high-ranking executives were above the law prior to 1983, this was not the case for their subordinates. The OBKhSS branches had to demonstrate that they were fulfilling their mandate, and as they could not charge the store directors, they went after the employees, mainly those who speculated on the black market. Some OBKhSS officers regularly extorted money from such employees but avoided attacking the executives. Most of the employees were powerless and without protectors; those who were victims of extortion would appeal to their superiors in the store, but to no avail. The superiors would frequently recommend that they pay bribes, since they themselves were colluding with OBKhSS agents.[19] Tregubov probably did not know what happened to all of the sales clerks in these cases, since he could not supervise the thousands of stores in the capital personally.

Tregubov's management style was as strikingly efficient in illegitimate activities as in legitimate ones. Basically, those executives who ensured a good assortment of products for their stores were praised and promoted. These same model executives not only committed irregularities for their own personal benefit but also bribed their suppliers and protectors. Likewise, they knew how to supply their superiors with scarce goods. They were generous and solicitous in meeting their superiors' needs in the matter of apartments, vehicles, vacations, and so forth. Tregubov had worked long enough in the trade organizations to realize that his staff could not survive without illegally acquired supplementary resources.

Tregubov was appointed a Party official only after obtaining the top job in the Moscow Trade Administration (Glavtorg). He was also a deputy in the Supreme Soviet and a delegate at the Twenty-fourth Congress of the Communist Party of the Soviet Union in 1981. As a delegate, he was considered a model Communist Party member, and his power was typical of an official during the period of stagnation. His position was secure, and like many others, he remained in office for a long time, until 1984. The Party relied on him in all trade matters, the key factor being that he enjoyed Grishin's confidence. No one could challenge him.

Despite the corruption in Glavtorg, Tregubov appeared to be a successful

leader with a reputation as a remarkable manager. His main objective as a bureaucrat was the growth of his organization. In this light, Tregubov was also tremendously successful, especially when one considers that internal trade was one
of the few sectors that actually progressed in the 1970s. The number of trade staff
increased substantially, and several new retail establishments—especially grocery stores, cafeterias, restaurants, and hotels—appeared in the capital.[20] While
the quantity of products in the stores registered a spectacular leap forward in the
1970s, shortages remained a major issue in the capital. But the impression one
got from reading the Soviet press of that time was that the Kremlin was aware of
the problem and taking serious measures to combat it. For instance, the decision
to open food stores in factories could be viewed as a new effort to better serve the
population. Naturally, in large part, Glavtorg and its chief, Tregubov, took credit
for creating the factory food stores. But in the late 1970s, the public's attitude
toward the food stores changed, and not for the better. On the one hand, the supply of groceries did not meet the needs of the population. On the other hand, the
KGB's efforts to expose failings—especially corruption—in the trade organizations had begun to produce results. It was not that the KGB had begun to attack
the Moscow trade organizations; in fact, it had been careful to avoid doing so.
But the public's impression was that the KGB would go after the trade organizations sooner or later, and this was good news for the general public.

Late in the 1970s, after Tregubov had been at the head of Glavtorg for several years, the shortcomings in this trade sector became increasingly apparent.
Tregubov's tolerance of corruption contributed to its considerable growth. The
embezzlement of property, the giving and taking of bribes, and other economic
crimes proliferated in the second half of the decade, probably to a greater degree than even Tregubov considered tolerable. In these circumstances, executive
autonomy expanded as never before. Tregubov tried to counter criticism of his
staff. He had always been understanding of his executives, but in the second half
of the 1970s, he criticized them even less than he had before. When Tregubov
took bribes from his first deputy, Petrikov, in 1976 and thereafter, it was likely a
turning point for the Glavtorg chief. After accepting bribes from his first deputy,
Tregubov could not criticize Petrikov and had to change his position on hiring,
promotion, and the supervision of staff conduct. After 1975, a paradox emerged.
On the one hand, Tregubov and other executives were praised and awarded on
several occasions for being competent and successful managers. On the other
hand, criticism of shortages in the food sector skyrocketed in the same period.
Because of this turn of events, Tregubov lost some of his authority and charisma
to the extent that it is more realistic to define him as a traditional leader at the
end of the 1970s. He was not challenged and continued to be popular with his
staff, but in the stores, the directors and their deputies did practically whatever
they wanted.[21]

Tregubov supported some of his executives even when he should not have done so. The executives felt so secure that many of them dared to increase their illegal activities. Thus, over the years, the threshold of Tregubov's tolerance for corruption rose. For example, Churin, the director of the Sports Trade Organizations (Moscultorg), committed several offenses, including bribe-taking, and lost his job but was later appointed director of an automobile sales center on Tregubov's recommendation. Gorbunov, an instructor of the Moscow Party Committee, also lost his job for taking bribes, but Tregubov proceeded to hire him as head of the AFPTO. Gorbunov was dismissed again, but a month later, he entered a job at the Trade Ministry, again due to Tregubov's intervention.[22]

By 1983, Tregubov's competence was not in question, but his authority had been undermined; some of his executives even began to make fun of him.[23] After all, they had been subjugated by Tregubov for a long time, and the situation had changed. He faced resistance from three of the major grocery store directors, who rejected his suggestion, made after Sokolov's arrest, that they retire. Tveritinov had answered jokingly, "What, you dreamed that I should quit my job?" Nonaev's reply to Tregubov was more elaborate but no less negative. To Petrikov, who was delivering Tregubov's message that the store directors should retire, he served a glass of cognac and prepared for him a sandwich with caviar. Nonaev covered the glass with the sandwich and said, "Listen, my dear colleague, if you take the sandwich, I will understand that you want to drink from the glass. How can I quit my job? People will think I am implicated. Drink, my dear friend, and please forget what you have suggested to me." Filippov gave the simplest answer: "Petruccio, all I know how to do is manage a big store. I cannot lose this job, absolutely not."[24]

Party Officials

At first, it seems odd that little mention is made of the Party in the mass of documents gathered by the KGB on corruption in internal trade and that there were so few Party cadres among the thousands of accused persons. One explanation is that KGB investigations did not concern cases outside the retail sphere. Nonetheless, the names of two important Party officials did emerge: Tregubov and Pospelov. Tregubov, besides being president of Glavtorg, was the chief Party representative in that organization until July 1984; Pospelov was head of the fruit and vegetable section in the trade department of the Party in Moscow, and in 1983 and 1984, the KGB made a concerted effort to inculpate the staff members of this department. Both Tregubov and Pospelov were eventually dragged before the courts, where they were viewed as trade milieu cadres who had risen to key positions in the Party through corruption. The Party was thus perceived to be

a victim of corruption and of the heavy influence exercised by grocery stores and other trade organizations during the Brezhnev years. The fact that corrupt retail trade cadres occupied choice positions in the Party may have been due to Grishin's tolerance toward corruption. The lack of data on corruption in the Party was also related to the rule that any law breaking by Party cadres was subject to judgment only by the Party. The rule existed because Suslov (a member of the Politburo), Brezhnev, and even Andropov believed that allowing Party representatives to be judged for their faults in the courts like any other citizen would discredit and weaken the Party. This attitude prevailed until 1985, when, under Gorbachev, it became a critical source of division in the Party.

Furthermore, cadres in the Moscow Party may have been involved in corruption to a lesser extent because of the privileged nature of their positions. Prestige and authority appealed to them more than the possibilities of enrichment offered by managing stores or depots. They seem to have been more attached to Soviet ideals, laws, and principles. The low statistical involvement in graft may also indicate that the top executives of Glavtorg and Glavka saw no need to grease the palms of Party officials because Glavtorg and Glavka were not really supervised by the Kremlin.

Nepotism

For diverse reasons, the family was the most reliable institution for promoting and protecting the interests of the trade executives. Those employed in trade structures who were seeking to improve their situation could try to move up through nepotism; this strategy worked with the typical traditional leader, who usually preferred to hire relatives. Nepotism was the safest way to benefit from certain advantages without breaking the law, but it was accessible only to those who were fortunate enough to have an influential relative who could obtain a job or a promotion for them.

For a few years during the 1970s, when anticorruption activity had abated, many trade executives who frequently gave or received bribes did not run into any problems with the justice system. Most of the Moscow food trade managers accumulated significant amounts of money (despite their support for the Soviet system), and the fact that executives generally remained in their posts for a long time made it increasingly easy to hire relatives. Many executives were under the illusion that the good times they were experiencing would last forever. For some, however, fears of exposure and repression persisted, leading them to hire relatives who would be more likely to put up a solid defense in the advent of an anticorruption crackdown.

Family support took various forms, and the nature of nepotism was influ-

enced by culture. Among those from the Caucasus region, reliance on relatives was practically obligatory, as there was little support in governmental or Party structures, especially in a Russian city like Moscow. Russians working in the trade network were older and better established and felt secure; at the same time, they were under pressure from the younger generation. Fathers had a strong sense of responsibility toward their children, who were frustrated during the Brezhnev era by the lack of access to essential services and facilities such as apartments, and the fact that the older generation monopolized job positions, thus restricting career opportunities for the young. As a result, trade executives redoubled their efforts to appoint their sons and daughters to prestigious posts during that period.

The woman at the head of the Perovski *universam* was a relative of the deputy mayor of Moscow, and she was among the top bribe-takers. Law enforcement agencies were aware that if they charged her, it would be perceived by the Moscow soviet leaders as an operation directed against them. Sokolov, director of Eliseevski, the top *gastronom,* had his wife appointed deputy director of the entire Gum retail enterprise. Thus, the Sokolov family was in a position to create the most impressive network of all. Sokolov already had a solid network, and with the inclusion of his wife, it became even stronger. As deputy director of Gum, Sokolov's wife was the direct superior of the store's *gastronom* or food section manager, Tveritinov, a person she knew very well. Gum's strength derived from its proximity to the Kremlin. It served as a kind of convenience store for Kremlin leaders on their way home from work and was a place where they picked up goods they had forgotten to buy or had not had time to buy at their special stores. Their assistants also visited Gum to buy gifts for guests.[25] Tveritinov and Sokholov's wife received these special customers with marked attention and consideration: such customers did not have to wait and were offered the best products. The principal advantage for the Sokolov family was that they could put the best goods in the country at the disposal of these clients. The elite knew very well that even the scarcest consumer goods could be obtained by the Sokolov family and would be delivered to them in a timely fashion. Sokolov and his wife complemented each other because they served different clienteles at the two stores: Eliseevski attracted more members of the intelligentsia, while Gum mainly received representatives of the nomenklatura. Sokolov supplied delicatessen items while his wife provided other consumer goods. He would pass on certain requests from influential consumers to his wife and vice versa, and she would send some of her special clients to her spouse's store.

Executives could easily appoint a relative who would support them, and if a son, for example, was hired in the same area of specialization as his father, they could both benefit from being part of the same network. Being so close, how-

ever, was not necessarily desirable: everyone in the workplace would be aware of the relationship, which could stir up jealousy and even result in denunciations. The appointment of Ambartsumyan's son as director of the Dzerzhinski ORPO (Vegetable Wholesale Trade Office) reflected the vast authority that his father wielded in the Moscow trade network, as this type of request would normally have been refused and could have proved detrimental to the son.[26] However, Ambartsumyan felt confident enough in his power and position to indulge in this kind of influence peddling. It must be added that because his son's position was so closely connected to Ambartsumyan's own, the son could learn more and become as powerful as his father in a relatively short time.

On the other hand, if close relatives worked in another field or district, it could create the impression that they had obtained the post on the basis of merit alone. In many cases, executives used their relations to appoint relatives to coveted positions in another organization. This was the case of the Dietorg director, Ilin, who had one of his sons appointed as a department head in the Novoarbatski *gastronom* after giving a bribe to Petrikov.[27] Ilin's behavior was a more typical case of nepotism: he gave the bribe in secret and his son was hired at a store where nobody, even the son, was supposed to know about the circumstances of the appointment.

Employees willing to steal had their best opportunity to do so by having a relative in the law enforcement agencies, especially in the Ministry of the Interior. Azarova, who was appointed head of Warehouse No. 24 in the Dzerzhinski *kontora,* was a relative of an MVD official from the same borough. She denied that her appointment was a case of nepotism, although it was confirmed by substantial evidence.[28]

Among the specialized law enforcement agencies, the most important player remained the OBKhSS. Chances were slim that a relative in the KGB or even in the Prosecutor General's Office would be involved in corruption. In contrast, many OBKhSS officials colluded with trade staff in breaking the law or closed their eyes to economic crimes. Those who embezzled socialist property felt safe when they had OBKhSS officials on their side, as Azarova did. However, the situation could change rapidly and radically, depending on the reliability of a person's protectors. This is what happened in 1983, when officers who had previously been above the law gradually became the targets of virulent criticism.[29] Trade executives who had enjoyed the support of the OBKhSS increasingly became subjects of suspicion because of those same ties. Among other instances of nepotism, the manager of the Sokol'niki store owed his appointment to Promyslov, the president of the Moscow soviet who was also his relative; however, no proof of collusion between them was ever established. Tentser, another influential deputy director, helped his brother become director of a food store.[30] Other trade execu-

tives attempted to place their relatives, but not in the trade network. Without his father's help, Tregubov's son would not have been hired by the KGB.

The family was also useful for hiding money. Pospelov gave his wife a large part of the money he had acquired illegally. According to an investigator in the Tregubov case, the decision not to pursue his daughter, who had hidden the money and other items received as bribes by her father, was based on the idea that the arrest of family members would make the KGB look bad.

The KGB's attempts to find money or evidence within family circles sometimes did not lead to the expected outcomes, especially in the case of families from the Caucasus region, who demonstrated more cohesion and solidarity. In addition, Russian women did not always display strong loyalty to their husbands when the latter were arrested for economic crimes. When he was apprehended in 1983, Eremeev lost his freedom, occupation, and reputation. What was more, his family abandoned him and he had to find another apartment.[31] (In the 1980s, he recovered his liberty but not his health, and until his death he fought unsuccessfully to be rehabilitated.) It was hard for a wife or other relatives to resist pressure from the KGB to confess where money was hidden. Sometimes the arrested husband would ask his wife to cooperate with the investigators. Pospelov's wife returned money to the government after her husband requested that she do so. In contrast, women in families from the Caucasus persisted in refusing to cooperate. Ambartsumyan's wife would not make a deal with the police even though her imprisoned husband asked her to do so.[32]

Age and Gender

Grishin knew that corruption existed in the trade organizations, but he believed that it was still quite modest in scale. To Grishin and the Kremlin, the older generation, represented by Tregubov, was critical to containing corruption because there was awareness that the younger generation lacked enthusiasm for socialist values in general and for Soviet trade rules in particular. Since the Kremlin bosses considered the older generation to be more reliable, the trade organization leaders took advantage of the Party's confidence in them and profited handsomely. With each passing year, however, the health of many executives declined, and they became more vulnerable. Older executives were worried that their superiors would pressure them to retire and replace them with younger, more efficient managers. Their bosses could point to the fact that the executives had worked long enough and that the time had come to make room for new blood, or they could claim that because of health problems, it was in the cadre's own interest to retire. Nonetheless, trade leaders had reasons to appreciate aging employees and to keep them in their posts. It could even be more profitable to

keep an old employee than to hire a new one; a boss might allow aging executives to continue working after they agreed to pay a bribe in return for staying on.[33] Some older executives suffered from chronic diseases and spent long periods in the hospital, but showing them the door was out of the question. Leaders were reluctant to dismiss these sick employees, since their World War II service was often viewed as the cause of their health problems.

There were various reasons why these older veterans of World War II had been appointed to management positions in the trade organizations. The first was that it had seemed unlikely that these "good" people would allow rampant corruption in the stores they ran. Second, the police did not suspect them and therefore would have needed evidence in order to follow up on any accusations against them. Third, many veterans holding high-level positions in the trade network still believed that the Soviet system had a debt toward them and that they deserved the right to extra revenue, even if it was illegal. The veterans had served the Soviet system during the war and had shown courage and self-control during this period, two necessary qualities in the shadow economy. Still another factor favored the aged employees and veterans: in order to be hired, an employee had to demonstrate other abilities, such as having been involved in black market activities for a long time without being caught.

Trade executives expressed loyalty to both the regime and their families, even when this was contradictory. Family loyalty meant that they occasionally had to comply with the requests of relatives, which seemed legitimate enough, given the very low standard of living of most of the population. Their decisions were frequently determined by self-interest. Ken Jowitt explains this ambiguity: "Corruption refers to an organization's loss of its specific competence through failure to identify a task or strategy that practically distinguishes between rather than equates or confuses (particular) private interests with (general) national interests."[34] This dual loyalty within the system was a setback for the regime. After the war and in the 1950s, loyalty had often been exclusively directed to the regime, but later, the state had to tolerate other rather incompatible values. The problem reflected the emergence of social groups that were not as supportive of the regime as the older generation. It signaled the emergence of a generation gap.

During the years following 1945, the trade staff had endured hard times. Many executives lived on miserable salaries, and while those working in food distribution had access to additional food in times of severe shortages, in general they did not try to enrich themselves after the death of Stalin in 1953. The mass of trade executives lived as badly as the rest of the population, even during the Khrushchev era. Only in the 1970s could trade executives finally hope to live more decently. They were willing to take advantage of the modest improvement in the consumer economy after the many lean years of shortages. Since the Soviet

system had demanded so many sacrifices and privations of them, they now had no hesitation in committing economic crimes in order to live better. After a long period of being abused and earning miserable wages, many of them were more than willing to become the new abusers.

Nevertheless, trade leaders kept store and RPT managers in check. It was one reason why the latter often tended to take only modest sums of money: if a portion of it was diverted for personal gain, the rest was earmarked for other goals such as receiving delegations or organizing receptions for Party and Moscow soviet conferences and commemorations. Tregubov testified, "I did a lot for trade at the time. Overall, the bribes I took were not for me. There were several delegations from many countries. This money was also used to travel abroad. Of course, we had to find money. The sums that I received from the government were enough, but I wanted everything to be perfect."[35]

During the stagnation years, successfully finding the money to pay for these celebrations took on political significance: it could consolidate the executives' positions in the upper echelons of power. In addition, the events were an opportunity to become friendly with high-ranking officials.

While many store managers accepted bribes less for personal gain than to improve the performance of their stores, they gave bribes in turn to avoid accusations and to ensure a better supply of goods to satisfy their customers' demands. Executives might also agree to take part in illegal activities only after their superiors had done so, thus setting a precedent. Lower-level officials believed that their superiors, who were often their friends as well, had good reasons to engage in illegal behavior. The higher-level managers believed that the low salaries of their staff justified allowing them to appropriate extra revenue, even though it was expressly forbidden by law.[36] The attitudes outlined above were typical of the neopatrimonial leaders who predominated in the 1970s.

These typically neopatrimonial executives were suspicious of hiring managers with backgrounds different from their own. New executives had to be trained in how to engage in irregularities and had to be introduced to the bribe-takers and bribe-givers. Problems sometimes arose during this orientation period. The newcomers might try to establish some practices of their own, ask for higher rates, or seek a larger number of bribe-givers. These newcomers who, for the most part, came from the younger generation, were perceived as materialistic. Trade leaders were aware that newcomers often took more and had selfish motives. Overall, the young executives did not show the same respect and loyalty as the older generation. They often had impersonal relations with the trade leaders.

In Soviet Russia, women played an important role in the trade organizations. Making up the vast majority (70 percent) of the labor force in the trade organizations, many of these women were praised in the press and in meetings. They

also frequently received awards and distinctions for their good performance at work. The journal *Sovetskoe Torgovle,* the principal publication in the trade sector, gave wide coverage to women and would frequently feature on its front page photos of women celebrated as work heroines. Soviet newspapers gave the impression that women were treated fairly in the trade organizations; in fact, the positions held by women seemed appropriate for most of them. Many jobs in the trade sector did not require the physical exertion that jobs in other sectors did. Furthermore, employees who were dissatisfied with their workplace could easily apply for positions in other stores because of the staffing shortages that prevailed in this sector.

Although women constituted the majority of the staff, they were as underrepresented in the upper echelon of the trade organizations as they were in that of other sectors. Several factors lay behind women's absence in the higher ranks. For one, men generally had more time to invest in their careers. In the Soviet Union, this difference was accentuated in psychological and material terms: women who were mothers and wives spent a lot of time waiting in lines. For another, women were aware of not only the advantages but also the dangers of holding an executive position during the stagnation era. At the top echelon, employees had the opportunity to make substantial gains, but since it was often by illegal means, they might easily be apprehended. From this perspective, many women, perhaps because of their caution, were not as interested in career advancement as men were. Also, the view persisted that it was the man's duty, as the chief provider of the family, to support his wife and children. Men had to assume certain risks when necessary and would take on a well-paid job even if it included illicit activities more readily than a woman would. The opinion prevailed that positions with the best opportunities for making money in the trade agencies should be assigned mostly to men. Thus, the low representation of women in the upper echelon may have been due to their decision to play it safe.

Nevertheless, because of food shortages, some women found grocery stores, cafeterias, and fruit and vegetable warehouses very attractive places to work because they provided easier access to food products. One of the basic Soviet tenets was that women and men had equal rights and that these rights must be reflected in the proportion of women employed at the higher echelons of power. In consequence, leaders in the trade organizations admitted that women working there should earn more and have access to high-ranking positions. The difficulties encountered by women in this sector of the economy were presented as temporary, since the Party was supposedly taking measures to correct the problem. The Party Congress was the supreme occasion for leaders to reiterate their commitment to bridge the gap between men and women.[37]

Party leaders at all levels were obliged to take steps in the right direction,

toward gender parity, and many women were appointed to executive positions after receiving praise for being model employees, based on the Soviet values of diligence, teamwork, and honesty. Demonstrating possession of these values was the first way that women in the trade organizations could improve their status, as trade leaders promoted candidates who exemplified these norms.

Many female employees who believed that adherence to Soviet principles was one of the most efficient ways to improve their situations thought that they should denounce law breaking and negligence. Denouncing individuals engaged in such activity was a second means of promoting themselves within the trade organizations. The efficiency of this strategy depended on the circumstances prevailing at the time, and it was viable during an anticorruption campaign like that of 1982–1985, when problems in the trade structures were imputable, above all, to the embezzlement of socialist property. The repression of corruption, which led to the dismissal of thousands of employees, provided wide promotion opportunities for employees who collaborated with the police. This means of ascent was limited, however, by the authorities' tolerance of corruption. While some employees denounced corruption through anonymous letters, others denounced it openly. An employee of one RPT had enough of her boss's corrupt activities and decided to tell the Glavtorg director about it: "The witness, I. A. Glotova, stated that she worked in the Kuibishev RPT, and was often repelled by the offenses committed by the Torg director, Baigelman, about whom people often wrote complaints, but who continued to rule with a tight fist. She did not address her complaints to Baigelman, but one day, she decided to go to Glavtorg to tell Tregubov about Baigelman's abuses."[38]

Not all employees were under pressure to break the rules, since corruption may not have been a widespread practice in their stores; nevertheless, in general, both executives and employees faced corruption in the workplace. Anticorruption campaigns were rare and relatively short, but tolerance toward corruption lasted for long periods of time. In the case of Glotova, her complaints to Tregubov did not bring about the expected outcome: "There [at Tregubov's office], they asked her why she wanted to see Tregubov. She answered that she had come to complain about Baigelman, the director of the Kuibishev RPT. Shortly after, they told her that Tregubov could not receive her because he had to leave for an emergency."[39]

Another woman, Sarkisova, when appointed head of a store, refused to give bribes. She complained to Tregubov about extortion attempts:

> The witness, N. S. Sarkisova, indicated that when she was a store director in 1977, she faced widespread instances of bribery. She fought this system of corruption. In July 1978, she was received by Tregubov, the director

of Glavtorg, and told him about the bribery, saying that without bribery, the products would not be delivered. She spoke of bribery on the part of Kuzmenko, director of the Volgogradski RPT, and his deputy director, Rakhmanov. Tregubov promised to settle the matter, and he did settle it: he dismissed her as director of Store No. 24, the Volgogradski RPT. She was moved to the Pervomaiski RPT, where she again found a system of bribery in operation. Nemtinov, the Torg director, behaved like a prince. In 1981, she was compelled to give him 500 rubles.[40]

Thus, most of the women who had been promoted by Soviet standards would, sooner or later, be confronted with corruption. The cases of Glotova and Sarkisova were not isolated; they demoralized those who believed in Soviet trade and led even them to transgress the law. While a few women remained honest after their promotions, others—the majority—agreed to participate in corruption after their appointments to higher positions. Compliance with Soviet norms did not necessarily lead to improving the status of employees in the Soviet trade organizations and even produced the opposite effect.

For women working in the trade organizations, denouncing corruption did not usually bring improvement to the overall situation. Shortages continued, illegalities were as frequent as before, and the same corrupt and abusive managers, male and female, continued to occupy their jobs. Most of the women had a low opinion of colleagues who had jobs that provided considerable sums of illegal money; they wanted to see such people punished. At the same time, they envied and admired their corrupt colleagues and were encouraged by their success. While they saw and approved of the fact that some of those colleagues were denounced in public and imprisoned, they were also aware that other women in their milieu had taken advantage of opportunities to enrich themselves illegally without being caught by the police. The stance of the Glavtorg leaders toward corruption also affected the attitudes of women employed in the trade organizations: at meetings and in the media, these leaders often praised directors who combined talent in management with skills in committing fraud, for example the directors of the Eliseevski, Smolenski, Novoarbatski, and Gum *gastronoms*. Several managers involved in illegal activities enjoyed a reputation for excellence. Honest women who hoped to improve their situation in the trade network through observing Soviet norms were disappointed and soon saw that to rise in the hierarchy, other means were necessary. The belief spread throughout society that the trade network offered opportunities that did not exist in other sectors of the economy.

During the Brezhnev era, the executives' materialistic appetites grew at the same rate as their profits. It became fashionable to have access to imported prod-

ucts and to sexual favors on demand. For female employees in the trade organizations, sex constituted the third means of improving their situation, whether
they were willing participants or not. Trade executives' pressure on women for
sex was hard to resist, given the economic difficulties of the period. Coerced into
submitting to their bosses, they tried to make the best of a bad situation. The
exchange of sexual services for extra resources and positions was widespread.
Documents from the KGB and the PGO reported many cases of women being
compelled to live with store directors. One indicted executive declared, "I heard
that in the grocery store organizations, there was an obligation for women employees to live with the leaders if they wanted to keep their jobs."[41]

These women knew that their bosses were untouchable because of their powerful protectors. Moreover, very few women reported sexual harassment because
it implied personal and intimate relations that they were ashamed to talk about,
even to the police. To disclose economic crimes was difficult enough, but to report sexual wrongdoing led to even more difficulties. The women's reluctance was
aggravated by the fact that there were almost no female investigators in the law
enforcement agencies. One investigator queried, "Why did these wives, mothers,
and daughters keep silent? Even when they did talk about it, they did so reluctantly." The answer was: "They were afraid to lose their jobs. Some revenue in the
trade network did not derive from work. And to whom could they complain?
It is known that all store managers have protectors. We cannot complain to the
Glavtorg personnel because they take bribes. Directors have good reputations in
the borough organizations. Women have no possibility of complaining. They are
scared to lose their jobs."[42]

In return for sex, some women accepted material rewards and protection.
One employee who lived with her store director declared, "I work in the *univermag*. I live with the director. As an individual, he's a bastard. I mean, considering
his mind and age, I see nothing good in him. But I have an apartment." The reaction of the investigator to this woman's statement was to comment, "But you lived
in a dirty way." The woman replied, "A person can get used to anything, even to
dirtiness."[43]

Women were rarely satisfied with the conditions imposed by their directors,
but many resigned themselves to the situation. Another female trade employee
who had been subjected to sexual exploitation by her director said, "They told
me straight out, if you don't accept our conditions it will be very difficult for you
to work, because this system of relations between people is built on the principle
'You scratch my back and I'll scratch yours.'"[44]

Women might have been able to refuse their directors' propositions without losing their jobs, but to depend exclusively on the official salary would have
meant a miserable life for them. Thus, certain women living with their directors

accepted money from them. One woman implicated in corruption in the trade organizations stated, "I did not think about where his money came from; this question was of little interest to me. What we received in the legal way was not sufficient." The investigator asked her, "Tell us, do you think that many directors belong to the same category as yours?" Her answer was: "I think there are a lot like that."[45]

The woman's director/lover was expected to protect her from repression and harassment by other executives. However, if a woman decided to play it safe and take a lover in the top echelons, this choice had its drawbacks. The higher the rank of the lover, the more power he had over her.

Despite the difficulties, some women were able to find lovers who could effectively provide strong protection and patronage. Perova made a "good choice," at least in terms of material benefits, by becoming the mistress of Roganov, head of the most prestigious imported fruit and vegetable distribution warehouse in the Soviet Union, the Sheremetyevo Airport *kontora*. Perova owed her entire career to Roganov, who was married and let her know that he had no intention of leaving his wife for her. In this respect, Perova may not have gotten all she wanted, but she still received important advantages from him. She was appointed the warehouse vice director, the second most important job after Roganov's. It provided the highest possible revenue on the black market, as the products distributed through this *kontora* were the most difficult to obtain. However, the trade staff did not approve of Perova's relations with Roganov, which showed that a woman who took a married man as a lover was not likely to enjoy a good reputation among her colleagues. The situation could be even worse if colleagues got the impression that the sexual relationship was based solely on the prospect of profiting through illegal activity.[46]

Perova had risen through the hierarchy of one of the Glavka warehouses. She was known to have a bad temper, which caused problems for Roganov. Perova would stand up to bosses and colleagues and was not afraid to quarrel with them, as one witness reported: "Roganov was never like this before the arrival of Perova in his warehouse. Roganov personally recommended her for appointment as the officer in charge of the conservation of products in the warehouse. But I must say that she did everything to bring about a general deterioration in relations with Roganov's friends. It began with A. Kasumov, then B. G. Nazarov, and after that, with me and with others."[47] Roganov's friends and colleagues did not appreciate the fact that he systematically lied to his wife. They were confused when the wife called them to say that Roganov was not where he was supposed to be. Moreover, Perova interfered in the administration of the warehouse and managed it as if it was her own fief. She made decisions and took initiatives without Roganov's consent, even in areas outside her jurisdiction. She had a

strong character, which contrasted sharply with that of Roganov, who was a true crook, but a weak-willed one.

The few women employees of the law enforcement agencies mostly worked in product control; thus, they had something in common with the women working in the grocery stores in that their jobs concerned food. The most influential lovers of these women held posts at the highest level of the OBKhSS. Zinaida Kirillova and L. V. Krimskaia were fortunate to have as protectors and lovers the men in charge of clamping down on economic wrongdoing in the borough.[48] The women working in the Moscow stores rarely found lovers as well placed in the bureaucracy as Filippov and Sapoinikov, who were, respectively, the heads of the MVD section and the OBKhSS of the Babushkin borough. No accusation of economic wrongdoing could be brought against a trade employee without the approval of these two men. Kirillova in particular knew exactly how to take advantage of this situation. She had worked as a fruit and vegetable inspector in the OBKhSS for several years and was promoted from inspector to captain. Women in mid-level positions in the MVD seemed to play a more important role in the pervasive corruption of the trade sector, and Kirillova made substantial profits from her illegal activity. Like Perova, she was an intelligent and self-confident officer and an OBKhSS boss in one of the districts that was the most successful in the shadow economy. She was part of a powerful network that included executives reputed to be the best in all of Moscow, among them Ambartsumyan, celebrated as a model executive in food and vegetable conservation and distribution. Kirillova showed toughness and even cruelty in carrying out her duties; she did not hesitate to have sales clerks arrested and jailed for committing minor offenses. The manager of a vegetable store described Kirillova's style when she led a control operation in his store: "My first meeting with Kirillova was when she made an inspection with a group of volunteers in the cheese section. We attempted to persuade them that I had only been working in the store for two months, that I was merely executing orders, and that the operation was highly damaging to sales clerks. How would it look to the RPT director? None of my arguments had any effect. One sales clerk was sentenced to three years' detention." Kirillova also systematically used extortion when she visited stores. She was reputed to have forced sales clerks to pay tribute: "Kirillova also dealt in extortion—'Aren't you bringing in products?' All the sales clerks were put behind bars."[49]

It was not unusual for an inspector to extort money for her superiors; moreover, extortion within the law enforcement agencies was widespread. Subalterns knew how to please their bosses, and they knew they had to bribe them. To become an OBKhSS agent, Kirillova had to go through a training session under her boss, Polevaia, which included learning how to fulfill her boss's needs by illegal means: "How could she fulfill her duties without controlling the store? When

she entered the store, she suddenly wrote a good report, took a bag of apples and bottles of vodka for Polevaia, and left."[50]

Kirillova inspired respect and submission from store managers. She was responsible for inspecting a particular group of stores and would receive food from the store managers in return for a lenient inspection. She also extracted substantial sums of money and other material advantages from managers; in turn, she made sure that the managers obtained immunity from prosecution. Kirillova's activities provided her family with a high standard of living: a spacious apartment, good furniture, and a car. Her main asset was having Filippov as her lover. Managers tried to stay on good terms with Kirillova and lavished attention on her, although Filippov would remind them that she was *his* lover and that they should keep a certain distance from her. Filippov did not want to leave his wife and his four children, but he let everyone know that he had exclusive sexual rights over Kirillova. According to a witness, "One boss said to me: 'I know you sometimes go to the house of Z. P. Kirillova. Try not to lose your head. Kirillova is the mistress of V. I. Filippov.' At that time, I did not know Filippov. Subsequently, when I became acquainted with Filippov, he reminded me on several occasions that Kirillova was his mistress."[51]

Kirillova eventually faced major problems. Investigators began looking into accusations that she was committing economic crimes, and as a result, her furniture was seized and she was forced to resign. However, the investigations eventually stopped, likely because of her protectors in the MVD. Kirillova was then appointed to another job, where she was able to continue committing economic irregularities. Moreover, after her resignation from the OBKhSS position, she was replaced by Krimskaia, who engaged in the same illegal behavior. In written declarations, Krimskaia admitted taking bribes for Sapoinikov.[52] She was as tough as Kirillova in extorting and intimidating food store managers.

Another means that female employees in the trade organizations used to improve their circumstances consisted of committing minor economic crimes, like pilfering, the most common offense committed in stores. These activities did not pay big dividends but were a means of survival for the women and often meant being able to maintain decent living standards for their families. Female employees engaged in minor crimes such as pilfering more often than their male counterparts, largely because they had no choice, but store managers and other trade executives took advantage of their subservient roles and of the shortages in stores to abuse women employees who were in need of scarce products, protection, and promotion. When executives acquired job security in the Brezhnev era, few of them hesitated to practice extortion; bribery was less risky in the stagnation period. Impunity caused an increase in the number of executives looking for bribes; it also provided new opportunities to abuse women. Bosses were not

as afraid to pressure and intimidate their employees for bribes; they were also in a position to be less generous than they had promised. Nevertheless, female employees gained some advantages from pilfering. The modest amount of money or food stolen meant that the cases were classified as minor offenses and referred to the Comrades' Courts instead of the criminal courts; thus, their chances of avoiding detention were relatively good.

The majority of women employees were not victims of extortion by male executives or sexual harassment, but they usually had to pay tribute to the heads of store departments, many of which were run by women. High-profile male executives would not usually interfere in extortion and bribe-taking, preferring to let their deputy directors and department heads take care of these matters.

Women were well represented among department heads of stores, and they had the most influence at the top stores, which had better products. The process of departmentalization was observable at all levels of the Soviet economy, so even grocery store departments had significant autonomy. Department heads had direct legitimate and illegitimate relations with the stores' suppliers. Some department heads had protectors at the top level of Glavtorg and were not accountable to store directors. They enjoyed more support and protection than many store directors. However, women at the heads of departments were still in a weak position with respect to sexual harassment and extortion.

Although there were some female store managers who were not involved in corruption, other women sought and obtained positions of authority that allowed them to receive bribes from their employees, yet another means women used to make gains in the trade organizations. Such women possessed strong characters and high intelligence, which enabled them, even in the male-dominated world of the trade organizations, to gain access to enviable positions and the possibility of substantial illicit benefits. In competition with male colleagues, their primary tactic consisted of personalizing relations with their bosses. Women would draw the attention and consideration of their bosses by giving them large bribes. They had to develop special relations with their superiors by providing resources or services superior to those offered by their colleagues and had to persuade their bosses that female employees would give larger bribes if they were promoted. For the women, it was a matter of assembling all the elements necessary to present themselves as the best candidate when the time came for the director to select an employee for a promotion. A good example of someone who rose to prominence in this manner was Garina, appointed director of the Olympiki *universam* in 1981 after having served as director of a grocery store and of the *universam* No. 39 from 1971 to 1980—and after giving her bosses huge sums of money. She became the main organizer of the illegal economy in the Gagarinski district, although she did not have high-powered connections. Garina's position in

the district was not as advantageous as it appeared, however. Her appointment as director of the *universam* should have placed her in a strong position in the shadow economy, but it did not; one year after her appointment, Moscow was hit by the anticorruption campaign. Garina was ill prepared for it because her main protectors were only mid-level officials in the Gagarinski district department of investigation and OBKhSS.[53]

Female representation was rare at the top level of the Moscow trade structure. A few women succeeded despite the discrimination and obstacles that were set before them. Zara Sumbatovna, a high-profile official in the Moscow soviet (Mossoviet), was one example. The importance of an official did not depend only on his or her rank in the hierarchy; in Sumbatovna's case, her influence lay in the fact that she was responsible for making the list of top officials who would receive bribes and gifts on holiday occasions. It was she who decided to whom the stars of the Moscow trade organizations, such as Sokolov, must give bribes and how much they had to give; this role established her as one of the leaders of the shadow economy. Sokolov was said to "fear only one person, Zara Sumbatovna, who works for the deputy president of the Mossoviet. She calls him on his direct line, the one which rarely rings, and the director asks her to repeat what she is saying to make sure he has not made a mistake in the family name of the person he will henceforth have to treat in a loving way."[54]

Women who held posts in the Moscow soviet, the political institution the least repressed by the anticorruption brigade, and women who had relatives in this entity could expect help in reaching prominent positions and then enjoy the highest level of protection and assistance. Sumbatovna and Cheliuk were among these. Second in importance were women who, like Sokolov's wife, relied on protectors outside the trade structures or who had protectors in key positions in the Moscow soviet and among the intelligentsia. These networks were useful in different ways, such as for securing a promotion and gaining protection against bribery charges. In the case of Sokolov's wife, this outside network helped her avoid charges and even keep her job, despite the law enforcement agencies' claim that she was involved, with her husband, in economic crimes. Third in importance were women who held senior OBKhSS posts in the model boroughs. In the cases of Kirillova, Krimskaia, and Polevaia, protection was ensured by lovers who were leaders of the district MVD section. In addition, the mistresses of the two top leaders of the MVD were related to each other. Nepotism was rampant in the borough, as revealed by Sapoinikov, Krimskaia's lover and the brother of a woman who headed Warehouse No. 24 of the Dzerzhinski fruit and vegetable office. In fourth place were women directors of grocery stores who relied on protectors in Glavtorg, that is, directors or deputy directors of AGTO. Accordingly, they did not exert as much influence as the women mentioned above. Fifth in

importance were the women heads of departments and warehouses who were obliged to give bribes to their directors, their sole protectors. (The data obtained concerned the department heads of the two most important grocery stores in Moscow [see table 3.1].) Finally, female employees whose main defenders were department heads had to rely on the weakest link in the protection chain, and they made the least profits. The economic crimes they committed were not usually the object of harsh punishment.

Innovators and Neopatrimonial Trade Leaders in the Shadow Economy

Several executives in the trade organizations had criminal records and thus should not have been hired in the first place. Roganov, Sokolov, and Khokhlov, who were the best-known operatives in this category, were nevertheless very valuable to trade organization leaders. These men were willing to take greater risks than others. The trade network leaders had to infiltrate agencies or structures where black market opportunities could be found; at the same time, however, such agencies were dangerous places to commit economic crimes. Intrepid, unscrupulous people in influential positions who were willing to take additional risks were required. In return, they were rewarded by the possibility of making big profits.

Khokhlov was the ex-convict with the highest-ranking position in the Moscow trade network. He was deputy president of Glavtorg, in charge of organizational matters, and the third man in the hierarchy, after Tregubov and Petrikov.

Roganov had the necessary qualifications in that he was the epitome of the clever, experienced thief. His job as head of the imported fruit and vegetable warehouse at Sheremetyevo Airport meant that he controlled the most difficult-to-obtain goods in the country. Control of the international airport was crucial for any government, including the Soviet regime, and for this reason, many KGB agents worked there. Despite this, Roganov stole and speculated in imported fruits and vegetables with impunity for many years. His success in the fruit and vegetable black market encouraged him to go further into the shadow economy. As he became more confident, he began to trade in other products, becoming a vendor of video recorders, television sets, and other electronic items. According to Ambartsumyan, "Roganov dealt in the trade of VCRs and television sets. I bought a VCR for my eldest son for 2,500 rubles and another for my younger son through Roganov. I bought eight television sets for myself, for my relatives, and for Uraltsev. In the last ten years, Roganov bought four cars: one through the Dzerzhinski *kontora* and three from friends."[55]

There is no doubt that the expansion of Roganov's activities increased both

Table 3.1. Glavtorg women executives convicted for bribery in September 1986

Name	Birth date	Position	Amount of bribe (rubles)	Sentence
Sapronova, Nadezhda Sergueevna	12/5/1940	Head, Fruit & Vegetable Dept., Branch No. 2, Novoarbatski gastronom	900	Community service, 1 year
Ponomareva, Galina Nikolaevna	10/26/1933	Head, Fruit & Wine Dept., Branch No. 2, Gum gastronom	10,000	Prison, 9 years
Polovinkina, Vera Arsentievna	10/3/1939	Head, Dairy Products Dept., Novoarbatski gastronom	11,900	Prison, 8 years
Otvechikova, Valentina Savelievna	11/15/1939	Head, Fish Dept., Novoarbatski gastronom	16,950	Prison, 8 years
Nosova, Nina Linichna	12/4/1934	Head, Confectionery Dept., Novoarbatski gastronom	2,400	Community service, 1 year
Kalinkina, Evguenia Nikolaevna	12/16/1933	Head of Fish Dept., then of Delicatessen, Branch No. 2, Novoarbatski gastronom	28,850	Prison, 9 years
Guseva, Valentina Andreevna	9/28/1926	Head, Food Dept., Novoarbatski gastronom	13,950	Prison, 9 years
Gulevskaia, Tamara Petrovna	7/27/1929	Head, Fruit & Vegetable Dept., Novoarbatski gastronom	33,950	Prison, 9 years
Golenaeva, Zoya Aleksievna	8/8/1941	Head, Fish Dept., Gum gastronom	8,850	Prison, 8 years
Fetissova, Iraida Petrovna	12/23/1929	Head, Meat Dept. & Delicatessen, Novoarbatski gastronom	3,900	Prison, 4 years
Bairamova, Galina Petrovna	4/16/1932	Head, Food Dept., Novoarbatski gastronom	17,500	Prison, 8 years

Source: Prigovor sudebno kollegii po ugolovnym delam Verkhovnogo Suda RSFSR po delu Tregubova N. P., Petrikova A. A., Khokhlova G. M., Kireeva V. P., i drugikh, delo no. UK PI-85 II, Moscow (September 8, 1986).

his profits and the risk level he assumed. His ambition soared as he decided to accept invitations from abroad, which enabled him to get a visa and travel to the West. He may have decided on his own to increase the range of products he dealt in, or he may have been pushed in that direction by high-ranking trade leaders. Roganov was subject to the iron rule of the illegal economy: the more profits he made, the more bribes he had to give to his superiors and friends. In the meantime, as he extended his operations, his protectors become more dependent on him, which prompted him to enter into new deals. Roganov thus became one of the most powerful figures in the shadow economy. The leaders of the black market could depend on him for services that, at first glance, seemed almost impossible to obtain. To import or export goods illegally for Soviet citizens was not easy and was fraught with dangers, but for Roganov, it became an ordinary operation. In the 1970s, he created a special network for foreign trade, comprised mainly of grocery store managers who frequently traveled abroad, returning to Moscow with many products that they then sold to customers. Roganov himself relished the opportunity to travel outside the country and bring back imported goods to sell at fabulous prices. He simply had to pay his dues to the leaders who allowed him to travel. Roganov and his friends were sent abroad to enhance the network, namely, to find new supporters and to obtain products for officials who were already in collusion with them. Thus, Roganov traveled to Paris on short notice, not forgetting to take large quantities of caviar with him. Once in Paris, he spent a lot of time with high-level officials at the Soviet embassy, to whom he sold the caviar and with whom he ate in good restaurants.[56] His stay in Paris included time to buy products that were highly sought by the nomenklatura as well as gifts for the KGB officers and border guards who welcomed him upon his return at Sheremetyevo Airport.

Sokolov, the manager of the Eliseevski store, was another ex-convict. Though it was less intensively monitored than the airport, this store was under constant surveillance by two KGB officers. Trade organization leaders appreciated colleagues like Sokolov and Roganov, who both displayed unparalleled generosity; because their pasts made them vulnerable, they needed strong support from higher up and therefore tended to be more generous when bribing. The fact that trade network leaders could appoint people with previous convictions to management positions in the premier *gastronom* and as heads of such key national security facilities as the Sheremetyevo Airport said a lot about their influence.

Trade executives with previous convictions were also appreciated by their colleagues because they were among those who stole the most, and they had many opportunities to do so because many of them managed important stores or offices. Since the potential for stealing quality goods was greatest in these places, those managers were also expected to pay a heavy amount of tribute to

their superiors. These men and others like them were thus models in the shadow economy for two reasons. First, they had achieved success by reaching top ranks in the trade organizations even though they had served time. Their arrests and their stays in labor camps had not broken them or prevented some of them from reaching the highest echelons of power. Second, their achievements showed the trade staff, including newcomers, that this type of leader had powerful connections in the political system. Moreover, the trade organizations made it clear that even if one of their executives were to be charged and sentenced, they could still get him out of prison and into a powerful position.

Executives with previous convictions were not necessarily criminals, however. Those who had committed economic crimes could be divided into two categories. The first consisted of people who had been convicted for minor offenses such as a one-time attempt at speculation involving modest quantities. Most of them had been charged in the more lenient Comrades' Court. The second group included employees who had committed economic crimes involving large amounts of money as well as repeat offenders. Sokolov was in the first group: he had been sentenced only once, for speculating in alcohol, a minor infraction committed by at least 20 percent of the population. Roganov, on the other hand, belonged to the second, more serious category.

Among the most admired executives were individuals who had made long careers in the trade network, speculating and embezzling socialist property without ever being caught. Those who had stolen successfully during the difficult World War II period were particularly venerated. In 1942, Roganov was appointed head of a warehouse, where he applied all his energy to stealing. Except for Roganov himself, every member of the group of criminals to which he belonged was eventually arrested and executed.[57]

A prerequisite for membership in this exclusive group was innovation in committing illegal acts. Certain executives did not fall short of expectations: they discovered new ways to steal more, using new methods that were very difficult for the police to detect. Tentser's endeavors in this field made him a hero in the trade network. He stole for a long period of time without encountering any problems with the justice system and became famous for devising new techniques to use in stealing from the food sector. Under Tentser's direction, these techniques were first applied systematically in the 1960s in the model Dzerzhinski *kontora* and in the Babushkin *kontora*. A food delivery would consist of a certain quantity of specific products, but the delivery receipt would list completely different commodities, a much smaller quantity of goods, or a lesser quality of goods. Another embezzlement tactic was to exaggerate the quantity of spoiled food. Tentser's first innovation consisted of getting workers who were supposed to destroy spoiled products to transform this food into preserves or sausages. His second innova-

tion in the day-to-day business at the Dzerzhinski *kontora* concerned first-grade fruits and vegetables intended for hospitals and orphanages: these goods were actually sold in public markets at inflated prices, while second-grade food would be delivered to the institutions in question. Tentser developed a third procedure, which was probably the most profitable of all. Several imported products were officially allocated to the *kontora* because of its model status among the food and vegetable distribution warehouses. These products did not pass through the government-regulated process at the *kontora*. Instead, a portion of them would be sold illegally in the markets at the highest prices. The executives in charge of destroying spoiled produce were paid to declare that the imported food products received had been thrown out because of their poor quality.[58] Tentser's innovations at the Dzerzhinski and Babushkin *kontoras* were so successful and appreciated that they soon spread throughout the entire Moscow trade network.

Other executives also showed creativity in the shadow economy. Here again, the Dzerzhinski *kontora* leaders set the example. Ambartsumyan, Tentser's boss, was highly praised within the shadow economy for having found an ingenious way of stealing.[59] A container full of fruits and vegetables that were in short supply would arrive at the *kontora* for sale to consumers. The produce would be sold very quickly, and if an inspector appeared, he would be shown the bill of sale. If no inspector came, the container would again be filled with fruits and vegetables and the bill for the first load would be used for the second one. The money from the sale of the produce from the first container would go into the pockets of the depot managers and was lost to the state. Black marketeers also learned innovative tactics in bribe-giving and bribe-taking at the Eliseevski *gastronom*.[60]

The International Connection

Trade network leaders further consolidated their positions by incorporating representatives of ethnic minorities, mostly those from the Caucasus region (see table 3.2). They knew that in the southern areas of the Soviet Union the demand for consumer goods was high. Huge profits were made selling to dealers who belonged to ethnic groups from the Caucasus, and several of these dealers belonged to the diaspora in Moscow. Their ethnic background did not take away from the fact that they were first and foremost Muscovites. Many were Armenians born in Moscow or who had lived in the city for many years. Some had never been to the Caucasus and could not even speak their ethnic language. One reason for their integration into Moscow society was the fact that they were veterans of World War II and shared this defining experience with other Muscovites. The Soviet people accepted them as their true compatriots. They were trusted by the authorities for the same reason, and their illustrious past was a positive factor

Table 3.2. The Caucasus connection

Name	Position
Nonaev	Director, Novoarbatski *gastronom*
Sarkisyan	Director, Brezhnevski RPT
Sagyan	Director, *gastronom* nos.17, 59
Kandichyan	Director, Tushinski RPT
Ambartsumyan	Director, Dzerzhinski *gastronom*
Karakhanov, G. B.	Director, Baumanski *kontora*
Karakhanov, B.	Director, store no.54
Miltonyan	Director, Kalininski *kontora*
Oyanesov	Director, *gastronom* no. 26
Chaverdov	Director, *universam* no. 19
Baigram-Ogli	Director, *gastronom* no. 27
Tairov	Director, Lublinski RPT
Gabolaev	Director, vegetable store no. 37

whenever there was an executive-level job opening in the trade network.

Armenians were the best-represented ethnic minority in the Moscow trade organizations in the early 1980s. Ambartsumyan and his son were, respectively, the uncle and cousin of Karakhanov, a store manager who was arrested in 1984. Armenians were known for not betraying their relatives or colleagues. The money accumulated by Armenians in Moscow could easily be hidden by their relatives in the distant and inaccessible Caucasus, making it much more difficult to gather evidence against the embezzlers or their superiors. Armenians who were afraid of being arrested could disappear into their home region, which served as a haven. Through their contacts, Armenian colleagues could find trustworthy and rich compatriots to bribe the Moscow trade leaders. Armenians constituted a sizable proportion of the black market entrepreneurs, and they served as intermediaries between the Moscow trade organizations and the leading business figures of the shadow economy in the south. They were also used by the Moscow trade leaders to counterbalance the influence of certain other ethnic minorities from the Caucasus—Chechens and Azeris, for example—who also held strong positions in the capital in the late 1970s. The trade agencies preferred Armenians, however, in whom they had greater trust. Moreover, the trade leaders knew that many Armenians had connections in the West to relatives and friends. This connection was important; no other group in the trade network was as successful in developing networks abroad. Armenians were also strongly represented in Soviet organizations beyond the U.S.S.R. borders, for example, branches of Intourist and Aeroflot. Ambartsumyan had succeeded in his efforts to find positions for his two sons in Aeroflot offices in Western Europe thanks to Armenian cronies in the countries concerned.[61]

As the shadow economy expanded in the trade organizations, it inevitably also spread abroad. Food products from abroad were the most coveted consumer goods on the black market, but almost any imported goods were in high demand. Increasing demand for foreign goods meant that people in the Soviet Union who had a lot of money were willing to spend it on such products. It also meant that trade executives making increased profits from these highly desired foreign items had to pay more to their bosses and protectors. They were willing to take this step because they were more confident and had the surplus amounts necessary to pay for more protection. Some executives also had experience speculating in foreign goods, and executives skilled in paying effective bribes could obtain a better assortment of products and services abroad, which helped strengthen the support they received from their protectors and enhanced their ability to find new ones.

The demand for foreign currency rose significantly at the end of the 1970s as more travel visas were issued to Soviet citizens. With citizens traveling more frequently, they could use foreign currency to purchase Western products in special stores. Currency speculators became very active, often in public places, changing currency for the thousands of tourists who were beginning to visit Moscow. Those dealers who operated in the shadow economy were encouraged by the large profits they made but less satisfied with the limited choice of items they could buy with rubles compared to the greater variety available to those with foreign currency to spend.

Executives who had grown rich off their illegal activities in the Moscow stores began to face competition from street speculators. Executives and officials did not want to be under the control of street speculators, so they had to offer equivalent or better products to their friends and protectors. To do so, they needed access to foreign currency and imported goods within their organizations, and, therefore, they needed executives who could obtain foreign products and currency at a lower risk and at lower prices.

The food trade executives thus began to forge connections with corrupt officials in civil aviation. In the 1970s, key civil aviation leaders, including those of Aeroflot, Intourist, and the Moscow airports, were involved in the shadow economy. They sent their cronies abroad as representatives of Intourist in the United States, Great Britain, and other countries. One individual who benefited from this practice was Grigory Mirzoyan, a high-ranking civil aviation official in Baku who became deputy director of civil aviation at Sheremetyevo Airport before moving to London to serve as the top Aeroflot executive there. He later returned to Moscow as deputy director of civil aviation.[62] After his return to Moscow, Mirzoyan was also busily engaged in reselling clothes he bought in the West, but his most lucrative activity was selling Aeroflot jobs abroad. One buyer was Ambartsumyan, whose son was studying at the Trade Institute at the time. Am-

bartsumyan agreed to provide Mirzoyan with considerable quantities of valuable goods in exchange for a prestigious Aeroflot job in London for his son. He sent Mirzoyan "deliveries of fresh fruits and vegetables every week over a five-year period for a total of 5,800 rubles."[63]

Armenians preferred to make deals with their compatriots but also agreed to provide contacts in the West for high-ranking trade leaders. The Armenians provided executives with broad opportunities, such as customers in the West and privileged access to foreign currency. Making money at the international level was more complicated, but it could bring in handsome returns. More importantly, the Armenians created networks that enabled Soviet citizens to escape repression by leaving the country. For the Soviet trade executives, the Armenians represented a door to the West.

The Accumulation of Capital

Just as the number of employees and executives involved in corruption was certainly larger than what was proven in court, the amount of money diverted to the black market was certainly larger than could be documented in court. This statement is hardly contestable, but estimating the actual sums accumulated through the black market is another matter. According to Western specialists, only 5 percent of the economic crimes involving bribes are ever proven in court. This figure is comparable to similar estimates made by Russians with respect to the proportion and scope of corruption there. Besides, bribes were not the only way to steal from the state. According to the Soviet Ministry of the Interior, at the end of the 1980s, only 5 to 10 percent of economic crimes went before the courts.[64] This last assessment is probably close to the truth because the amount of money accumulated was likely ten times greater than what was reported by investigators, excluding money stolen through other practices, such as fraud and the falsification of documents. The data are too incomplete to permit an accurate evaluation of the amount of capital accumulated on the black market, but the numbers reported by the KGB in 1983 are likely close to reality. The numbers reported by the KGB are based on the considerable amount of information collected during the anticorruption campaign. Collecting that mass of data was possible because no limits were imposed on the investigators after KGB head Andropov became first secretary of the Communist Party, and many agents worked full-time on the anticorruption assignment. The more evidence they found, the better it was appreciated. Several members of the KGB were transferred to the Ministry of the Interior and the Prosecutor General's Office and given the task of unmasking corrupt officials at all levels. It was difficult for the accused persons to resist; their only hope to improve their situation was by collaborating. The KGB

investigators had a free hand since they did not have to fear any Party interference, or at least not as much as before, and, besides, the public approved of the anticorruption campaign. However, this period was also dangerous for the KGB because their data on corruption was suspect; some was based on testimony obtained under duress and intimidation and some was based on rumor.

There is no reliable method for precisely gauging the amount of capital accumulated by the trade agencies. Gurov was a competent senior Russian law enforcement official who had access to primary police sources. According to him, in 1988, during perestroika, Moscow soviet leaders took 20 million rubles in exchange for the creation of private cooperatives. Gurov's revelations are not entirely credible, as he did not cite his sources; however, because he held a position in the top echelon of the Ministry of the Interior, his numbers are probably not far from the truth.[65]

The Medvedev brothers wrote excellent biographies of Andropov in which they highlighted the wealth accrued by the directors of the central Moscow *gastronom*s. Their favorite target was Sokolov, director of the Eliseevski *gastronom*.[66] However, their descriptions of the relations between Sokolov and Galina Brezhnev, like many of their affirmations, are not confirmed in any documents. Sukhanov was probably a more direct source for their descriptions.[67] As a former member of the Party Central Committee, he had access to confidential information, but even so, one has the impression that his data were based on rumors generated by the population or within the Central Committee. While few of the above-mentioned statements can be confirmed by data from the law enforcement agency archives, they nonetheless indicate that the Moscow trade staff acquired a lot of money.

In the Ochakovo food complex, directors Chmireva and Drugova and their assistants received bribes totaling 300,000 rubles. The director of the Mosrestaurant organization colluded with the deputy director of the Hotel Russia food complex, the Sofia restaurant, and the Riga food complex. The hotel complex was one of the most lucrative bases from which to accumulate money, generated by the presence of many tourists and foreigners. The demand for foreign currency was strong in the whole Soviet Union, and the hotel in Moscow was the most convenient place for the exchange of rubles on the black market. Foreigners were openly and frequently solicited for this purpose in restaurants and bars, and even in their hotel rooms, despite the presence of the KGB agents who were assigned to suppress the practice. In a period of only two years, the Mosrestaurant director stole a total of 700,000 rubles and accepted 200,000 rubles in bribes. Between 1982 and 1984, at the immense Hotel Kosmos, which boasted 28 floors and 1,177 rooms, the director and his two assistants received from their employees in the food complex bribes totaling 155,000 rubles.[68] The

only reason investigations were not undertaken or completed in all the restaurant or hotel food complexes was the sheer volume of the task. The situation that prevailed in these places was representative of the reality in all the trade organizations.

As for exact amounts of money illegally acquired, the only figures known are those recorded by prosecutors. Executives who were charged had good reasons to undervalue the amount of money they had received. The more misdemeanors they admitted to, the more likely they would receive a heavy sentence. In jail, they could do nothing for their families except provide them with the money they had accumulated illegally (which the wife usually had in her possession). Prosecutors needed to know the actual amounts involved and to uncover all the offenses committed by suspects to be able to prove their guilt. In some situations, however, prosecutors dropped the charges against suspects in return for testimony against other people. Furthermore, prosecutors did not have enough time or staff to investigate all the irregularities committed by the trade employees.

In Moscow during the second half of the 1970s, more bribes were being given, and being given by more individuals. Executives who had not received bribes before 1975 now began receiving them, and those who regularly received bribes began to demand larger amounts. The result was an increase in the accumulation of capital and a new generation of bribe-takers willing to take even more because the experience of previous years showed that the risks were slim and because, in the upper echelons, officials wanted more money.

The Ambartsumyan case was a good example of just how much a Moscow trade executive could accumulate. As head of the model Dzerzhinski *kontora,* Ambartsumyan made bigger profits than the directors of other *kontora*s during the Brezhnev period, receiving large amounts of money for the fruits and vegetables sold to the markets and the big grocery stores in central Moscow. It was the best-supplied district fruit and vegetable distribution warehouse in the entire country, thanks to the payment of generous bribes to Glavka leaders. As detailed in his sentence, Ambartsumyan gave 60,000 rubles and received 400,000 rubles in bribes. However, the investigators said they had obtained testimony that he had given a total of 900,000 rubles to senior officials. Moreover, the same investigators claimed to have recovered 1.1 million rubles from Ambartsumyan.[69] They simply did not need to use all of the evidence collected against him. Besides, some of the testimony against Ambartsumyan would have required further investigation. If they already had enough evidence to prove that Ambartsumyan was a major bribe-taker, why waste time trying to find more? Another factor that clouds the determination of amounts taken was that prosecutors covered up evidence, dropped accusations, or stopped further investigations concerning Ambartsumyan in order to obtain his collaboration against other executives. A

final reason was related to nationalities, as Armenians in particular were reputed to be good at hiding money. Ambartsumyan's wife, with his money, was hidden by his family in Georgia following his arrest. Police were also frustrated by their fruitless search for money in the case of Ambartsumyan's nephew, Karakhanov.

Relatives in the Caucasus region were not the only ones who guarded large sums of money; many Russians were also successful in keeping illegally acquired cash. The police suspected Tregubov's daughter of hiding the gains he had amassed from bribery. Pospelov's wife, in the court confrontation with her husband, rejected accusations of having much of his illegally acquired money in her possession. Later, however, after prosecutors pressured her, she confessed to having received the money and then handed it over to the KGB. Sometimes, the people who were supposed to hide money for sentenced executives might simply keep it for themselves. Arrested and sentenced trade executives occasionally denounced the relatives or neighbors who had received their money, and they in turn usually denied the accusations. When the money was finally traced, with supporting proof, it reverted to the state. On the whole, however, huge sums acquired by the dealers in the shadow economy remained in their control, despite the assiduous efforts of the law enforcement agencies to recover it.

Rent-Seeking

Rent-seeking refers to the dividends paid to government officials in exchange for services, contracts, or other advantages.[70] Soviet bureaucrats, as we have seen, were keen on acquiring material advantages, especially in the trade sector. The time, energy, and resources they devoted to extracting favors from the trade staff constituted huge losses for the state. While these payments and advantages generated profits for the trade executives, they also affected them in a negative way. The problem was that model organizations ended up paying a significant percentage of their money to maintain their privileged position and ever-larger sums of money had to be spent on bribes. Trade executives also wasted a significant amount of time performing tasks that had nothing to do with their work, such as meeting the nomenklatura's diverse and multiple needs, finding specialists who could make high-quality products, or obtaining visas to go abroad, among other things.[71] Providing money, resources, and services became a heavy burden for the model executives. Their superiors in the trade hierarchy and even officials the law enforcement agencies made frequent demands of them. The deputy minister of trade asked an executive to find someone to make a suit for him; a district MVD leader asked a grocery store director to give free food to his mistress; a grocery store executive had to find a visa for an official to go to the United States, and so on. Ambartsumyan said the following about certain executives:

I had to order meals for 20 people. I placed the order, but did anyone think of paying for these meals, which cost 400 rubles? Ivanov, inspector in the Moscow Party's Department of Trade and Maintenance, demanded bribes when he had a high-level job in the Moscow Party Committee. The first time, I gave him 200 rubles. He said that it was not much. Over a period of five years, until his retirement, he received a sum of 12,000 rubles. V. A. Naumenko, advisor to the Moscow soviet deputy president, asked to have his flat repaired. The first time, it cost 600 rubles; the second time, it cost 1,000 rubles. He requested that he be paid by 48 deliveries per month over a period of four years, which cost a total of 2,800 rubles. Over a period of ten years, the Dzerzhinski district MVD section head regularly came to the *kontora* to ask that orders of fruit, vegetables, and alcohol be delivered to his home. Every year, he asked for material to upgrade his bathroom. Every month, he received approximately 50 rubles.[72]

Payments or services solicited by high-ranking officials cut substantially into trade executives' profits. As the number of bribe-takers grew, so did the risk of one of them betraying or denouncing someone to the police. While amounts rose, the executives' benefits diminished. Many paid so much money and took such high risks that it became less advantageous for them to keep their positions; the number of officials to bribe was simply too high. Some managers criticized the extortion that was being practiced. They refused certain requests or envisaged doing so. The director of Grocery Store No. 28, Rosliakov, complained that his superiors demanded too much and that the system had been pushed so far that there were almost no profits to be made in the early 1980s. He announced to one of his bosses his intention to retire: "When he [G. V. Nichkin] became a trade organization director, I had a friendly relationship with him; he had been a fellow civil aviation officer. I let him know what I had written about Kirillova, and said, 'Genadi Vasilevich, it has become impossible to carry out the distribution of products. Ambartsumyan and M. V. Bikanov are practicing extortion. If you don't give them [bribes], you don't receive fruit.' Nichkin answered, 'I know all this. It's been that way for a long time in the trade sector. Do you think it's any better for me?'"[73]

Rosliakov's words reflected the state of mind of many executives who were dissatisfied with their jobs despite having made substantial money in Soviet trade. They complained that there was no point in making money if they had to pay most or all of it to their superiors. Executives complained for other reasons as well. Lepeshkin, one of Ambartsumyan's lieutenants and the head of the Dzerzhinski warehouse, made considerable profits in the shadow economy, but

he protested that, with the exception of alcohol, he could not turn the wealth into any benefits for himself. Others like him were frustrated because opportunities to spend money were so limited in the Soviet economy.[74]

In the anticorruption campaign, prosecutors collected evidence on thousands of employees and several senior executives. The campaign, aimed at discrediting and ultimately removing Grishin, the Communist Party first secretary in Moscow, was successful, and the evidence presented was sufficient to put many store managers and RPT heads, including the most important ones, behind bars. The typical executive targeted in the crackdown was from the older generation and had held the same job for a long time. Such executives were Brezhnev-style managers, that is, their organizations were not run according to objectives and standard rules; rather, the personal element dominated in the relations among staff members and between employees and consumers. A good example of such a manager was Tregubov, chief of the Moscow trade organizations. He governed his kingdom in the same way Brezhnev led the country: he was reputed to protect his clique. He gave his lieutenants and managers wide-ranging autonomy; he trusted and supported them if they committed irregularities. He allowed his assistants to make use of broad prerogatives, such as appointing or promoting personnel. Tregubov focused on the positive aspects in the trade agencies, on achievements rather than shortcomings. The Tregubov style reigned supreme in all the trade agencies.

The Tregubov style was evident in the role of deputy directors in the stores. The deputy director sought to reconcile an illegal phenomenon with the requirements of the store and benefits to the staff. The secret of their success was that they managed to satisfy two important groups, and corruption helped them a great deal in this enterprise. Through graft, they were able to increase the earnings of personnel and suppliers, while increasing the amount of goods in their stores. Corruption was more beneficial to certain groups than others, however. Trade executives of Armenian origin profited the most from corruption because of their connections abroad. They were an important force, being heavily involved in the extortion of huge sums of money within the network.

Corruption was the principal means of the accumulating of capital in the trade organizations. While the police were remarkably successful in punishing corrupt trade staff, at the same time, they eliminated the Brezhnev-style trade personnel. The capital accumulated higher up in the trade bodies was another matter. The law enforcement agencies succeeded in seizing modest amounts of the money stolen during the Brezhnev era, but many executives, particularly those with origins in the Caucasus, were able to hang on to large sums despite the severe crackdown. Soviet internal trade, even in the period of stagnation,

suffered serious setbacks that adversely affected trade executives, even those who were deeply involved in the embezzlement of socialist property and in bribe-taking. More precisely, the risks and costs of making money in the Soviet trade network increased significantly in the early 1980s. Many executives were open to reforms in the economy, even if they were not allowed to say it openly, as they hoped to make higher profits without the risk of a police investigation. Such executives typically came from the younger generation.

The War the KBG Lost

■ The Moscow trade network was already a political force in the Brezhnev era, having acquired considerable influence during the 1960s due to its increasing autonomy in the allocation of resources in the capital. Its political successes were most apparent in the food sector. The leaders of the Moscow trade organization used their influence to promote their interests and were quick to defend the interests of their organizations whenever they were threatened.[1] This was particularly true in the 1980s, when the KGB launched its anticorruption campaign against the Moscow trade network.

The campaign ran from 1982 to 1987, although, after 1985, at a lesser level. It comprised distinct phases, the first, in late 1982 and in 1983, being the toughest for the Moscow trade staff, whose resistance was then at its weakest. The KGB had a free hand after the appointment of Andropov as leader of the Communist Party, and the population, including the nomenklatura, was afraid of the security forces and did not dare to show any opposition. In addition, the KGB benefited from prevailing attitudes in Russian society at this time for different reasons. Initially, the anticorruption operations in the capital represented a change, and people may have believed that cracking down on corruption was the best way to eliminate the problem. The KGB had built up a stock of sympathy during the 1970s and enjoyed the trust of the population. In contrast, the trade organizations, especially the food sector, were not well thought of by the public, and their staffs were suspected of being deeply involved in irregularities. The embezzlement of socialist property by trade employees was seen as the main cause of shortages in the grocery stores. Mindful that popular dissatisfaction was high,

the KGB had been closely watching the grocery stores since the beginning of the 1970s. Thus, in 1982, the KGB had at least two reasons to attack corruption in the food sector in particular. First, it already knew a lot about the situation there and possessed evidence on trade leaders, and, second, because of the popular frustration with respect to this sector, it hoped to generate wide political support for Andropov. The KGB, in the first year of its war against corruption, arrested several trade employees and gathered evidence incriminating them, but it was not empowered to prosecute and try people, a rather complex task that was under the jurisdiction of the Prosecutor General's Office. Furthermore, in 1983, the KGB filed charges against middle- and high-ranking trade executives, who were easier targets than their higher-level counterparts—the senior Party and government officials.

Many executives arrested in 1983 arrived at the conclusion that their only option was to capitulate to the KGB's requests to corroborate all the accusations against them. Hoping that their sentences would be substantially decreased if they collaborated, executives were ready to submit to the KGB's prosecutors and divulge evidence that compromised their superiors. The executives inclined to cooperate with the KGB were those who knew the most about the wrongdoings of high-ranking executives or officials. It happened, however, that arrested employees willing to serve the KGB were sometimes misled: their apologies and the acknowledgment of their guilt did not necessarily improve their situation. In fact, employees often received severe sentences whether they cooperated with security forces or not. Ambartsumyan, for example, was executed even after having provided more testimony than any of his colleagues. Petrikov's testimony led to the disgrace and eventual arrest of Tregubov, but he was still sentenced to ten years in a labor camp (table 4.1). Distrustful and experienced organizations like the KGB were aware that suspects might testify in detail and denounce many officials to save their own lives rather than do so for the good of the society. Thus, the slanderous information on high-ranking officials obtained in this context could not only compromise the friends and protectors of the accused but also worsen the arrested person's situation. For example, after having refused to divulge the identity of his bribe-takers, Sokolov changed his mind and decided to cooperate with the KGB when they promised to reduce his sentence. The result was of no benefit to Sokolov, who was soon executed anyway.

The Moscow Trade Leaders Counterattack

Not surprisingly, the trade executives were the most vehement defenders of their accused colleagues; their own fears of being imprisoned spurred them to help those who had been arrested. Also, the detainees would be less likely to

Table 4.1. Indicted Glavtorg executives

Executive	Sentence in 1984–1986	Status in 1990
Sokolov, I. K.	Death penalty	Executed
Ambartsumyan, M. A.	Death penalty	Executed
Tregubov, N. P.	15 years	Detained
Bikanov, M. V.	15 years	Detained
Mugurdumov, M. V.	14 years	Detained
Nemtsev, I. V.	14 years	Detained
Petrikov, A. A.	12 years	Detained
Filippov, V. I.	11 years	Detained
Iakovlev, V. F.	14 years	Released
Svezhinskaya, N.V.	11 years	Released
Tveritinov, B. C.	10 years	Released
Khokhlov, V. P.	10 years	Released
Guseev, V. A.	9 years	Released
Kalinkina, E. N.	9 years	Released
Ponomareva, G. N.	9 years	Released
Baigelman, M. Ia.	8 years	Released
Bairamova, G. P.	8 years	Released
Berbasov, B. F.	8 years	Released
Golenaeva, Z. A.	8 years	Released

denounce colleagues who expressed support for them. Many arrested trade employees asked for help from friends or relatives. Sometimes, an executive suspected of having committed offenses would be promoted to a higher position as
a protective measure, to make that executive less likely to inform on colleagues if
investigators came calling. Even without rumors that a person was under suspicion, higher-level executives were often convinced that these suspicions were not
sufficient to convict their friends. Frequently, a suspect's confession was enough
to bring about a conviction or at least greatly facilitate the conviction; suspects,
however, were hesitant to confess as long as they could count on the help of
friends. While a sudden promotion suggested that the superior was the employee's accomplice, the superior might still decide that taking the risk and moving
the suspect to a higher position would make it more difficult for law enforcement
agencies to charge him or her. This tactic had proven successful in the past, based
on the premise that leaders of the trade network were simply carrying out their
responsibilities in promoting their staff. The arrest of this type of executive by the
KGB, therefore, gave the appearance of an abuse of power. Another tactic was for
the superior to simply assign a suspected employee to a new position.[2] While it
was in the director's best interests to provide assistance to a person with whom he
was in collusion, it still happened that an appointment to another position would

be decided by a boss who had never been involved in illegal dealings with the employee but merely believed in the suspect's competence and honesty.

Examples of high-profile executives under suspicion who were helped by their superiors in this way included Ivan Kolomeitsev, a senior official of Glavka who was hired in 1983 as head of Soyuz plodoimporta in the Soviet Ministry of Agriculture. Kolomeitsev was promoted during the period when the KGB indicted several leaders of the Moscow Fruit and Vegetable Office. The minister of agriculture's decision was intended to suggest that Kolomeitsev should not be arrested and that, in the eventuality that it was to happen anyway, his new bosses would do their utmost to save him. Another example was Trepelkin, head of Warehouse No. 1 at the Dzerzhinski *kontora,* who was appointed director of the Moldovan Food Quality Inspection Committee. The Dzerzhinski *kontora* was in turmoil because of intensive investigations that culminated in the arrest of its managers. Trepelkin's nomination to a new post at that time demonstrated a vote of confidence in him: the message sent to the KGB was that there was no reason to consider him a criminal, the proof being that he had even been promoted. In another instance, Sokolov's wife remained deputy director of Gum even after her husband was sentenced to death. While she was not promoted, she still held an enviable position in Glavtorg. Sokolov's bosses had thus succeeded in saving her, but it must be pointed out that Sokolov paid enormous sums of money—almost 200,000 rubles—in bribes to the Glavtorg leaders.[3] Volkov, head of the personnel department at the Dzerzhinski *kontora* until May 1983, was promoted to manager of the Products Department of the Ministry of Agriculture. Volkov was not, however, as lucky as Sokolov's wife, as his appointment to the Ministry of Agriculture did not prevent him from being sentenced to a labor camp.[4] This heavy sentence could be partly explained by the fact that his protectors were not as influential as those of Sokolov or Kolomeitsev.

Trade executives were constantly aware that they could be sanctioned for their wrongdoings, even in a stagnant period like the Brezhnev era. They knew that the best way to protect themselves was to place their colleagues at all levels of power. It was crucial to have protectors at higher levels, but they were aware that that was not enough in itself; they knew from experience that the secretary general in the Kremlin could be replaced at any moment. During the Brezhnev era, the trade leaders became increasingly preoccupied by this eventuality as they watched the secretary general's health declining. To counter this threat, they adopted different means, one of which was very effective.

Store directors' assistants, especially the deputy director, had to be selected primarily for their trustworthiness. The director could not be surrounded only by close partisans, however, as this gave rise to suspicions of shady dealing. A circle of partners in crime at the upper echelon was necessary but not enough by itself

to prevent problems; the director had to have partisans in the lower levels as well. This is not to suggest that all trade executives were involved in corruption with their store directors; a certain number practiced austerity and abstained from economic irregularities. Nevertheless, the great majority were unconditional supporters of their corrupt store directors. The network of those involved in the irregularities was set up for flexibility. Directors relied on diverse categories of henchmen according to different scenarios, keeping in mind the eventuality that the police might accuse them and their assistants and arrest them. Some would defend their directors and were the people most likely to replace them, since they had the necessary experience to manage the stores. Therefore, the directors wanted to help themselves to illegal gains, but they were also obsessed by the idea that they could be put behind bars. So, devising a sort of "plan B," the directors hired employees who stole less or even not at all. These kinds of people would be able to succeed their directors. Directors surmised that the KGB could not have all employees dismissed; the store had to continue to distribute its products even when corrupt employees were apprehended. Staff continuity was necessary or the allocation of food in the society would seriously deteriorate.

Trade executives placed some of their key collaborators in the lower levels of the hierarchy to ensure that, if ever they were indicted and their protectors removed, strong support would remain. Low-ranking executives had a good chance of being appointed to higher positions if police began arresting the higher-ranking staff. The Eliseevski *gastronom* was a good example of how this system worked and of how difficult it was for the police, even the KGB, to combat the trade organizations. The KGB obtained enough evidence to arrest the leaders of this *gastronom*: the manager, deputies, and department heads; however, at the lower level, it allowed Glavtorg to decide who could keep their jobs. As a result, some deputy heads of sections were promoted to *gastronom* managers because they were honest, while others were allowed to keep their jobs even if they had been involved with Sokolov and his associates in bribery and the embezzlement of socialist property.[5] These new leaders were very helpful to their former bosses, who were behind bars, and were very active during perestroika, trying to obtain favors for their arrested comrades. The situation of the Eliseevski store was not an isolated case; there were similar situations in several other stores.

Tregubov worried in particular about the arrest of Svezhinskaya, head of the fish department of the Eliseevski *gastronom,* when she was arrested in 1982. At first glance, the indictment of the head of a department would not be a source of preoccupation for a boss, but this was, after all, Tregubov's Moscow Glavtorg, an organization that was a model for the country, and the Eliseevski *gastronom* was the most prestigious grocery store in Russia. What troubled Tregubov most was that when Svezhinskaya was arrested by the KGB, the arrest appeared to be

a destructive blow aimed at his power and reputation. Tregubov was backed by years of experience, and he knew that Svezhinskaya was not the first executive to be charged and would not be the last. As the head of Glavtorg, Tregubov was the backbone of the trade network, and, if something went wrong, he would be the first to have to deal with the situation. The centralization of the system was also visible inside the trade structure. Tregubov was the boss and protector of all the executives. Thus, after Svezhinskaya's arrest, Tregubov's assistants and managers drew closer to him because of their need to be reassured. Tregubov had solid reasons to avoid panic and calm them down. First, Sokolov assured him that Svezhinskaya was loyal and that no matter what pressure was put on her by the investigators, she would refuse to testify against her superiors.[6] Sokolov's assumption seemed credible because many weeks went by without further arrests.

This confident outlook was shaken in August 1982, when Sokolov was denied a visa to travel to Yugoslavia. Tregubov's fears from the spring were revived. It was not likely that the KGB investigation could have continued if they had not found some evidence against Sokolov. Nevertheless, Tregubov believed that the situation was under control and that Sokolov's arrest could still be prevented, although it would require a fight. After all, the executives knew that, at any moment, they could be accused of irregularities, so they needed to develop a strategy to counteract the KGB's accusations. It was crucial to defend Sokolov, and it seemed possible to do so, considering that he had built a network that was stronger than those of his colleagues. Tregubov could not believe that Sokolov, with such powerful protectors, could remain long behind bars. Tregubov was so confident that, when Sokolov was refused a visa, he told him to use his connections in the KGB to have the decision reviewed.[7] Sokolov's arrest, three months later, changed Tregubov's view of the situation: it was more serious than he had thought. In the beginning, Tregubov was not sure about the real intention of the KGB; different scenarios could have explained its strategy toward him. The KGB may simply have chosen not to go after him, until November 1982, that is, when the KGB finally prioritized its plans to target corruption. It was still not allowed to deal with matters outside its jurisdiction, however. Thus, Svezhinskaya's arrest might simply have been understood by Tregubov as an operation within the KGB's normal jurisdiction, since she had purchased imported products in stores reserved for foreigners, where one could pay only in foreign currency. Tregubov rejected the idea that the KGB would go further and engage in a war against corruption in the Moscow trade network.

In any case, Tregubov and the other executives endured a terrible year in 1982. Ominous events happened one after another. The worst was at the end of that year: the announcement of Brezhnev's death and his succession by Andropov, a change that was a severe blow for the trade organizations. The first

lesson that Tregubov and other trade leaders drew from the setbacks of 1982 was that their men in the KGB had not been able to ensure that the agency would tolerate corruption in Moscow. As a result, the trade leaders appealed to their high-ranking protectors for help. Tregubov's first move, however, was to inform the executives of the danger of the situation and of the necessity of taking certain measures immediately. The first of these measures was for store managers to put an end to irregularities in their establishments. Tregubov's second decision was to pressure certain managers to either retire or to shift to other functions. In the beginning, the response to these initiatives was not generally positive, which was understandable, given that the executives were confident that their boss was powerful enough to protect them from arrest. None of Tregubov's measures was unusual, given the circumstances. These same means were often employed successfully as the first line of defense against the arrest of trade employees. Besides, when high-ranking executives or officials were suspected of serious misconduct, they were rarely sent to trial. Instead, the person in question was usually made to retire or was transferred to another position. Therefore, Tregubov expected that his initiatives would have the same effect as in the past.

In 1983, Glavtorg's executives were not the only victims of the KGB, nor were they the most repressed; the leaders of Glavka were in a worse situation. It was clear that the latter were not as influential as the former, since the KGB put almost all of them behind bars and prosecuted them the following year. In the case of the Glavtorg executives, their initial reaction to the investigations was to deny the accusations against them. Their resistance did not last long, however, and in a month or two, they all capitulated to their interrogators. The protectors of Glavka's leaders in the ministries of Trade and of Fruits and Vegetables did not intervene on their behalf, either in public or in private. On the contrary, they denied any association with the accused people. The only area in which the executives of Glavka refused to collaborate with the KGB was that concerning the sums of money they had received illegally. The police were never able to recover most of this money, primarily because many of the indicted people belonged to the ethnic groups of the Caucasus, whose families assisted them in hiding the money in their homeland. Even when the arrested executives divulged the identities of those who had received money, it was rarely recovered. In another area, too, the investigation of Glavka had its limits: the KGB gathered evidence against the executives of the Moscow Fruit and Vegetable Office more expeditiously because its leaders, apart from Pospelov, were not associated with Party or government leaders. This factor explains why they were quickly apprehended and convicted and, moreover, why the KGB was more interested in the Glavtorg executives, as they were supposed to have ties to Grishin and other Moscow political leaders.

When the members of the Politburo named Andropov first secretary in 1982,

they knew that he was not in good health, but they still expected him to remain at his position for a few more years. Later that year, however, Andropov was too ill to return to the Kremlin, and it was clear he would not recover; in August, he was running the country from his hospital bed, but by December he could no longer perform the duties of secretary general. The ensuing power shift to other members of the Politburo had a major impact on the KGB. It seemed that this would be negative for the KGB leader, Fedorchuk, although as late as the end of 1983, his authority did not yet appear to have been affected by what was happening in the Kremlin. Fedorchuk's campaign against corruption continued as before, but it was only a question of time before it would run into major difficulties.

When Sokolov, the manager of the country's premier *gastronom,* was arrested, the last period of his life was filled with torment. Sokolov's nightmare during his period of detention would ultimately be shared by several of his colleagues. It was not long after Sokolov became a "guest" at the KGB's Lubianka Square headquarters that he realized the hopelessness of his situation. In fact, his unhappy end could have been predicted by his employees, who knew of his many wrongdoings. Still, his periods of pessimism alternated with moments when he believed that things would return to normal and that he would once more be allowed to run his store. Sokolov continued to struggle to obtain his freedom like a drowning man clutching at straws. He denied having committed any wrongdoing and continued to assert that, as the star of Glavtorg, he did not have to worry, since he had enjoyed the consideration and favors of influential and respectable people over many years. Sokolov had been more generous with bribes than any other executive in the Moscow trade organizations and was in contact with the most powerful bribe-takers. It was inconceivable to him that such good and influential friends could forget their sponsor. After all, he had given more than 200,000 rubles in bribes, so that if one day he was in trouble, he would be rescued immediately.[8] Sokolov told himself that all these bribe-takers would not have accepted the money had they not been willing to save him if the need arose.

After weeks of hope, not even one bribe-taker or friend showed up to support Sokolov. He grew to realize that he was in dire straits and that his only choice was to go along with the prosecutors' proposals. As soon as he accepted this notion, his confidence abruptly collapsed and his sole obsession became to escape the nightmare and to see his wife and children again. The only person from the outside with whom he had contact was his lawyer, who advised him to refuse any deals with the KGB.[9] Sokolov's collaboration would have been the equivalent of pleading guilty to all the crimes of which he was accused and would thus justify the most severe punishment. His lawyer, Artem Sarumov, insisted that the KGB did not yet have enough proof against him, but Sokolov decided not to listen to him. Instead, he blindly placed his trust in the KGB's good faith, his last resort.

Sokolov's lawyer knew that he had a good reputation among friends in the elite, but he also knew they would abandon him and even turn against him if he testified against them. Sokolov's credit and connections within the nomenklatura were his best assets. In retrospect, confessing was not the best option for him, but it was undeniably a turning point in the KGB investigation of the Moscow trade network. Subsequently, the crackdown would be intensified, and more people would be arrested.

Sokolov surrendered, but his partisans did not. His supporters could not obtain his release, but they provided money to his family and pursued the battle for his rehabilitation. As mentioned previously, his wife avoided prison and retained her high-ranking position. Despite the fact that Sokolov's defenders possessed solid reasons to support him and that his colleagues strongly opposed his conviction, he was the first senior trade executive to be convicted. In the matter of the death sentence, his defenders failed in not being able to prevent his execution, but they were more successful on the question of civil rights. His lawyer had a strong point when they argued that no legal basis could justify a death sentence for a person accused of corruption. Sokolov's best defensive move had been in choosing Sarumov as his lawyer, considering that that latter was reputed to be the best defense lawyer in Moscow at the time. Still, the effort to exonerate Sokolov during the Andropov period had, as we have seen, little success. His lawyer did not have the opportunity during the trial to use his skill on behalf of his client, but he still managed to mark some points for him. He attacked the judge for his prejudices against the accused and requested the right of his client to change his plea, arguing that the initial testimony had been made under pressure and intimidation. These tactics were not enough to save Sokolov, but in pointing out the unfairness of the trial, the lawyer created a precedent that stimulated the resistance of his trade network colleagues in their subsequent trials. Sarumov's defense of Sokolov would introduce another force in support of the Moscow trade staff: setting the tone for the defense of other trade executives. To capitulate to the KGB was revealed not to be the best option, and pandering to the KGB had its negative impacts for the indicted executives, like having the elite turn against them. During perestroika, the eloquence and brio of Sarumov and other defense lawyers in court and in interviews with the media helped create a trend that favored the cause of their clients accused of corruption.

Eremeev, vice director of the Moscow food trade office (a section of Glavtorg), was another high-profile executive who was arrested, but his reaction to the KGB differed from that of Sokolov. Whereas the latter had capitulated, the former put up a fierce resistance. Eremeev had worked for the KGB in the past; thus, as soon as he was arrested, the KGB did its utmost to persuade him to provide valuable information on the trade leaders and, even more importantly, on

its own organization. Eremeev announced his willingness to disclose all he knew but asked for the necessary time to give accurate testimony. He then dedicated all his attention to writing meticulously about his job in the top echelon of Glavtorg. Eremeev not only wrote about the Moscow trade network but also tried to meet the expectations of the KGB agents by writing out a long list of suspects, including some who were purely the fruits of his imagination. In creating so impressive a list, Eremeev used the trade executives' directory and even added the names of some executives who had died.[10] In some instances, he named executives who had given such small amounts of money that they resembled gifts rather than bribes. These admissions about small amounts of money received from store managers were welcomed by the KGB because they discredited the Grishinist nomenklatura; however, under perestroika, they would no longer be viewed as minor offenses. Eremeev's list of suspects also included the names of people who were only rumored to have committed bribery. Even if Eremeev told the truth much of the time, many of his written statements contained outright lies.

Eremeev played a dangerous game: instead of revealing the wrongdoings of officials for the sake of justice, he did so to improve his chances of survival. As long as he said or wrote things that interested the KGB, he expected favors in return. As head of the Moscow food trade organization, Eremeev had supervised the training of thousands of cadres. His work experience with the KGB gave him an edge over other executives.[11] He knew about the KGB's obsessions and its insatiable appetite for information on the elite. Eremeev had a prodigious memory and revealed this quality to the investigators. Because his responsibilities as a deputy director consisted of monitoring the trade staff, he learned, on a daily basis, the secrets, good or bad, of his staff. Eremeev also used his considerable knowledge of the situation in Glavtorg to boost his credibility when dealing with KGB investigators. He amended Sokolov's and others' accusations and successfully persuaded the investigators to drop some of the accusations of bribe-taking against him. Other accusations against him were also withdrawn after he proved that he could not have been with his accusers on the day that the infractions had allegedly occurred.[12]

Eremeev's story was typical of the stories of executives who never capitulated to the KGB. These executives continued their combat against the KGB, regardless of their suffering. They denounced injustices in labor camps, and, even after their release, they continued their campaign against repression until the last days of their lives in hospital beds.[13] Eremeev was among those suspects who responded skillfully in interrogations: while they divulged a considerable amount of information on the elite, their evidence had low value in court. This situation was particularly true during perestroika, when this kind of testimony was practically useless to KGB prosecutors. The KGB undermined its reputation with the Ere-

meev case; its agents committed the error of detaining the suspect for four years without trial. The competence of the security force was also on the line, considering that most of the testimony collected against Eremeev was excluded for lack of credibility. After Eremeev's four years of detention, the judge rejected the charges against him, but he received no compensation for damages.

Executives used all possible means, from the most sophisticated to the simplest, to resist the law enforcement agencies. Levtonov, director of the Dzerzhinski RPT, was in the category of employees who were the most vulnerable—the ones who gave in during the first interrogation. Levtonov collaborated with the investigators by confessing all he knew, and even more. The problem with a suspect like Levtonov was that he wanted to fulfill the expectations of investigators but could not because he was too honest. For example, he told investigators that he had bribed Tregubov, but, later, he felt remorseful and denied having done so.[14] In these circumstances, individuals like Levtonov were at a disadvantage. They did not have influential protectors to help them avoid repression, and they could not deliver the desired testimony incriminating high-level officials. Worse, they sometimes lost the money they had accumulated. This was the case with Levtonov who, moreover, suffered three heart attacks in 1983, doubtless brought on by stress and heavy smoking in detention.[15] Understandably, he was not in a position to bargain with the security force. Executives like Levtonov had one last hope: to elicit sympathy in the hearts of the investigators; some of them were even successful in this effort. As if their torments in prison were not enough, several arrested executives suffered because their family members failed to support them, while for others, the family was their main support. Executives had committed irregularities for the sake of wives and children who, even knowing the circumstances, abandoned their husbands and fathers when they were imprisoned. On the other hand, some detainees lost both their families and the money they had gained through corruption. A significant number of executives, who had endured the most hardships, lost everything, including their health.

Tveritinov received a harsh sentence, one intended to keep him in a labor camp for at least a decade. The manager of the Gum *gastronom* had had influential acquaintances; his network must have been impressive for him to be appointed head of the No. 4 *gastronom* in the country, a much-desired position in the capital. According to the law enforcement agencies, a good number of high-ranking officials, even some from the Kremlin, were clients at his store. The proof of Tveritinov's social skills was that he had joined Tregubov's inner circle and accompanied him in delegations to Western countries. He had taken money, but not as much as Sokolov or Ambartsumyan, and he had succeeded in persuading the judge that most of the bribes he had given were not for his personal benefit but so as to obtain better products for his store.[16] Tveritinov had offered

his complete collaboration with the KGB agents, bringing significant evidence against the most important suspect in the trade network, Tregubov. He had made a traditional self-critique in his confrontation with Tregubov, which could only satisfy the investigators. He had apologized to the court and to the Party for his corrupt activities. He still received the harsh sentence but was released after serving four years of his sentence, due to the intervention of friends to whom he had distributed scarce goods. (He had even consistently made written declarations incriminating these Party officials and the high-level government officials he had served.)

Tregubov's first deputy director, Petrikov, was in the category of accused trade personnel who collaborated with the police but were more valuable to the KGB than Levtonov was because they could compromise high-ranking executives and disclose information on the entire Muscovite nomenklatura. Also, he was very coherent in his statements and, therefore, was credible, in contrast to Levtonov. Above all, the investigators appreciated the fact that Petrikov was very persuasive in court. The outcome of a case was not determined solely by the collaboration of suspects or by the quantity of information they disclosed but also by the articulateness and clarity of their testimony.

Another category of suspects was willing to provide any testimony that might improve their situations. Not surprisingly, the accused people wanted to save their skins, and some were willing to go further than others, falsifying their declarations to incriminate former colleagues. Ambartsumyan and Sokolov, who received the heaviest sentences, fit this category. They confessed to having committed many wrongdoings in collusion with highly placed officials, but the two also accused several officials of acts that were not always criminal offenses, according to the law. Ambartsumyan, for example, admitted to having offered particular individuals free meals and alcohol on several occasions at receptions or for holiday celebrations.[17] This type of testimony was often dropped for its lack of value in court.

The employees most intimidated by the KGB were those incarcerated between January 1983 and September 1983. During this initial stage, the accused did not benefit from the sympathy of the public. On the contrary, the KGB's popularity rose to its highest with Andropov's appointment as Kremlin leader. Some executives were vulnerable because they were aged and were convinced that the Communist Party would forgive and release them. They did not even consider defending themselves by insisting on their civil rights and denouncing police abuse. But the trade executives who suffered the worst consequences were those who pleaded not guilty. They were, for this reason, the first to be tried and were subsequently sentenced to death, if we consider that long-term sentences in labor camps led to premature death. The most notorious cases in this category

were those of Larionov and Kliachin, who were so frightened that they went insane, becoming incapable of understanding what was happening to them. The gap between being employed at the highest echelon of the Glavtorg and occupying a cell in Lubianka Square was too wide for Kliachin who, seventy-two years old and ill, was easy to break, especially when he lost all hope of surviving his fourteen-year sentence in a labor camp. Kliachin, absent-minded and incoherent during his trial, was aggressive toward the judge and refused to admit to any irregularity.[18] Seen by the judge as a man who defied the law and insulted the court, Kliachin, it seemed, was more in need of medical assistance than punishment. Larionov was also hit hard and was unable to answer the questions of the tribunal. Whereas Kliachin was impulsive and angry, Larionov's interventions were rare and consisted of senseless remarks.

Lidia Tomashevskaya was one of the many executives of the younger generation who rose in the trade organizations.[19] She was successful in her studies at the Trade Institute and then was hired at the Dzerzhinski *kontora,* where she drew her superiors' attention by her professionalism and hard work. She climbed rapidly in the organization and soon became head of a warehouse. Tomashevskaya did not choose to work in a trade organization for the opportunity to make illegal money. When she discovered that illegal practices were taking place, her superiors explained to her that the depot enjoyed a special status and privileges due to its good performance and therefore, certain practices that were not permitted elsewhere were accepted, including violations of the law. Moreover, the impression was created that these offenses were acceptable because nothing was done to combat them for many years.

Certainly, Tomashevskaya earned extra money on the side, but most of it went to grease the palms of suppliers. Her arrest in 1983 was unexpected and even more so was her sentence of ten years in a labor camp. At only thirty years of age, she was powerless, having accumulated little money and no links to an influential network.

The law enforcement agencies gained almost no benefit from detaining this kind of executive. On the contrary, many such executives came to be viewed as innocent victims of the KGB during perestroika.

The case of Boris Karakhanov, the manager of a fruit and vegetable store, is less interesting for the transgressions that sent him to prison than for his being connected to the directors of the Baumanski and Dzerzhinski *kontoras.* The detectives believed that Karakhanov belonged to an influential network; consequently, he was held in prison for years for questioning. Like many other suspects questioned for infractions that concerned them, he was also cross-examined for knowledge of highly ranked officials, such as Tregubov. The detectives believed that Karakhanov might know compromising details on these officials, or, lacking

these, they did not exclude the possibility that if he could not supply testimony against high-ranking officials, Karakhanov could at least divulge the names of those employed in the business, as a means of inculpating those in command. The police did not think they would come away from the Karakhanov investigations empty handed; however, Karakhanov did not fulfill their expectations and denied having given bribes to well-placed officials. He also refused to sign any written statement that could be used against his family members, claimed that his interrogators were biased against him because of his ethnic roots in the Caucasus, and subsequently revealed their mistreatment of him. Karakhanov also later disclosed that there were two types of prison cells, the first one being the one most difficult to withstand in terms of harsh conditions and reserved for those who refused to cooperate with the police. The second type of prison cell accommodated those who were willing to provide information to the investigators. Without the coming of perestroika, Karakhanov's situation might have worsened; consequently, his sentence, and that of others in similar circumstances, was reduced.

The crackdown on Moscow trade executives significantly affected their perception of society because they realized that even their network of connections, including high-level officials in the political structure, had not prevented the KGB from targeting them. In 1983, all the gifts, meals, and bribes they had given to high-ranking officials no longer seemed to have been advantageous investments; now, all that time, attention, and care appeared to have been wasted.

In some cases, trade executives were denounced by colleagues. People who were supposed to be their supporters now produced evidence against them. In short, their networks were damaged or destroyed and no longer provided adequate protection. It was a terrible situation for these aging executives, as the option of building up new networks was too radical for them. They continued to place their trust in the old networks and to believe in their protectors even after the latter had lost their influence. The arrested executives hoped for a *retour en force* by their old buddies. They were unable to see that the changes occurring in society went beyond simply fighting corruption. Moreover, a movement emerged to use the anticorruption campaign to replace the old executives with a younger generation, and even the latter were obliged to create new networks.

The trust that the older executives were clinging to, even in the face of its ineffectiveness, was based on personal relations and reflected a culture of premodern social capital that dominated until the advent of perestroika. This culture would be replaced by one based on modern social capital, which consisted in 1985 and thereafter of trust in the state and its institutions. To use Kenneth Newton's terms, Soviet society was in transition from a "thick" trust to a "thin"

trust.[20] The new trend was to look toward other groups for cooperation and then work with them to influence the government rather than rely on individuals in personal networks.

This tendency in favor of the rule of law could even be found among trade executives, who sought to reinforce their positions with respect to the state in general and regarding the suspicions or the accusations of corruption against them in particular. With perestroika, trade executives found increased opportunities to defend their cause. The advent of the rule of law in Soviet society could provide political dividends. While citizens were deprived of their political rights and submitted to the dictates of the Communist Party during the Soviet period, under the rule of law, the trade executives could produce their own political power by using the institutions of the new regime: parliament, the media, nongovernmental organizations, and civil rights. In court, the trade executives took advantage of the presumption of innocence for all it was worth. Members of parliament (or "deputies") enjoyed impunity; therefore, they were protected against intimidation and arbitrariness. The deputies of the new parliament possessed significant powers to adopt new laws and grant licenses. They could lobby for their stores and some associations. The deputies were also in a position to influence the political forces in the achievement of certain objectives. Under the rule of law, the elections would no longer be controlled by the Politburo but would be transformed into a competition among political forces and leaders. Money would replace the Communist Party as the decisive factor in election campaigns. In addition, the deputy's importance brought certain privileges: the pay is high and the role comes with a comfortable apartment in the capital. The parliament is a strategic place for the deputies to influence public opinion, since its activities are largely covered by the media. But there were other institutions that offered trade executives occasions and places to consolidate their interests.

Generally speaking, the trade executives needed to improve their public image, their priority being to rebuild a reputation that had been tarnished by involvement in corruption. Thus, it was important for them to use the parliament and the elections in their project to discredit the KGB and the former Soviet system, presented as the real culprit behind their transgressions of the law during the Brezhnev era. It should be emphasized that the managers of the major grocery stores and many other top trade executives were also parliamentary representatives. While these positions were mainly honorary in the Soviet system, in a pluralist system the deputies would play an important role. The adoption of the rule of law would give trade executives who were also deputies greater influence. It was also beneficial to trade executives to be able to rely on the protection given to citizens' rights in a state operating under the rule of law and the guarantee that they could take abusive government officials or police agencies to court. At this

point, however, pressures for the rule of law were just beginning, and they mainly concerned the economy.

The trade executives' new approach was primarily determined by their personal interests; their rejection of the Soviet trade system had no ideological basis. It was rather their observation that trade leaders and party officials were no longer effectively able to defend their cause. In the same vein, they did not prefer the rule of law because of their political convictions but believed it would offer better protection against the law enforcement agencies' efforts to clamp down on bribery and the embezzlement of socialist property. The principal advantage of a regime under the rule of law was that it could reinforce their cause and unite them with other forces opposed to the KGB and its practices. Alliances with other organizations provided the best chance to persuade the government to put an end to criminal proceedings against trade executives as well as to release those who had already been incarcerated. Consequently, the trade executive was invited at all levels—district, store, and so on—to encourage the development of networks with representatives of other organizations. Cooperation presupposed, obviously, the building of relations of trust with officials of all groups opposed to the KGB. The establishment of good relations with different organizations did not necessarily mean formal and closed alliances. Instead, the leaders of the different organizations were united by their support for the rule of law and their opposition to the KGB. It was up to every executive, at the different levels, to decide what concrete form this cooperation with representatives of other organizations would take.

As the winds of change swept over Russian society, the economy was subjected to a wave of criticism that did not spare the trade organizations. The issues of the Soviet economy had occasionally been dealt with openly before 1985, but that year and thereafter, the analysis became increasingly critical. Trade organizations received more attention than ever before as specialists and journalists debated the measures needed to improve the situation. Most of the changes proposed in 1985 were not new; nevertheless, new approaches defended by a minority of the public slowly surfaced. A private market economy was not adopted as a solution, despite the fact that the pros and cons were evaluated in a balanced way. That solution was considered relevant for some socialist countries, Hungary, for instance, while Soviet specialists were slow to voice an opinion on its pertinence in the Soviet Union. Nonetheless, capitalism and the shadow economy received more attention. The Moscow trade network initially began to address perceptions of capitalism and the shadow economy, and, as early as 1980, Tregubov had written articles on the success of consumerism in Hungary. While Tregubov did not propose to adopt the Hungarian model in the trade network, the mere fact that he praised it was significant. Naturally, it would have been beneficial

for trade leaders to adopt some parts of the Hungarian model, as it would have minimized the offenses they committed in their stores.

In 1985–1986, a consensus existed in the media that the Soviet economy needed major readjustments. The debate on this issue was not confined to specialists, and the question of what to do became a hot issue, especially in the trade organizations, due to the arrest of thousands of employees. Between 1983 and 1986, many executives were convicted for activities considered criminal offenses according to the Soviet trade laws, but this approach was challenged as perestroika gradually presented a privatized economy in relatively positive terms. Questions were raised about the accusations made against many trade executives. The issue became crucial because it involved thousands of Muscovites. Within the discussion, divergences appeared. One point of view denounced the media for having presented the crackdown on the staff of the food trade organizations as a fight against the corruption in this sector.

A growing number of trade cadres affirmed that their mediocre salaries had led them to break the law. E. Khiller, the director of a fruit and vegetable store, attempted to persuade the judge that the accusatory document did not reflect the reality of the situation. It was a state store, but it paid such miserable salaries to its employees that their children suffered from hunger. "We had to ensure that they had something to eat for their lunch—but where could we get the resources for that?" Khiller added that he needed money for "fire insurance," "special funds for transport," "a reserve to pay fines," and so on.[21] Even in the judicial sphere, some of the major changes were perceptible; as a defendant in court, Khiller, like many others, could defend his position and not remain silent or admit his guilt under the pressure of the KGB. The KGB was not as dominating in court as it had been before, and some defendants challenged it.

A considerable amount of the evidence used in the trials of the trade executives rested on testimony of questionable validity. While most testimony was obtained through persuasion, some of it was acquired through pressure tactics, even physical pressure. The methods of the KGB at that time did not compare to those employed by its predecessors in the Stalin era, but although the use of physical pressure was not widespread, it had not disappeared altogether. The KGB employed this tactic in a few cases concerning key suspects. All means were valid if a detainee was presumed to possess incriminating information on high-level Grishinist officials. Roganov was in this category: as head of the most important warehouse in the country, he was suspected of being acquainted with these officials. A healthy man until his arrest, Roganov was unable to walk or even stand up at his trial. He claimed he had been tortured by the KGB. In jail for a year and a half, he had seen a doctor only once officially, to treat a cold, despite the fact that he was sick for a long period.[22] However, Roganov's case was an

exception, as very few depositions by suspects mentioned physical intimidation. The prosecutors had tactics at their disposal that may have excluded physical pressure and torture but were still very intimidating. For example, detainees were obsessed with the prospect of being sent to a psychiatric hospital. The comments of incarcerated trade employees who were forcibly interned in psychiatric institutions did nothing to quell their colleagues' fears. Serguei Belaev, an employee at the Hotel Kosmos who was indicted for corruption, told of his experience in a psychiatric hospital: "I was escorted in alone, and I saw my brother's coat hanging in the corner, soaked in blood. Behind me the guards were saying, 'It's a pity: yesterday's guy couldn't take it—he died.' My hair rose on end: why my brother? I couldn't understand it; was this their 'psycho-rehabilitation' or 'psychoanalysis?' Then I heard knives being sharpened and a voice from behind the wall or the ceiling, saying, 'Now we'll cut him and he'll talk.' Another voice asked, 'Should we send in the rats?'"[23]

One of the KGB agents promised the suspect that the higher the amounts in bribe-giving he confessed to, the lighter his sentence would be: "Investigators insist on large sums of money, saying that the length of the sentence depended on it."[24] Other KGB agents told suspects that Kliachin, the chief Glavtorg accountant, had been warned that he would receive a sentence of fifteen years behind bars if he persisted in his refusal to cooperate with the police. KGB agents admitted that they had a good opinion of Filippov, getting his sentence diminished because he provided investigators with credible written declarations on corrupt officials. The investigators were accused of using the illnesses of some detainees to force them to testify against their superiors; for example, it happened that prosecutors refused to give Sokolov the pills he needed for his diabetes until he had complied with their requirements.[25]

It was often during their initial interrogations that imprisoned executives tended to be easily intimidated into signing declarations to please investigators. Later on, they realized that the KGB was not as terrible as they had imagined. In the detention centers, they grew acquainted with other trade executives in situations similar to their own. Some had been behind bars for quite a while and had accumulated face-to-face experience with the KGB. These detainees told the newly arrived executives that prison conditions were difficult, of course, but it could have been worse, as the KGB did not usually torture them. They told the new prisoners not to pay attention to KGB threats and not to believe in promises to reward them if they collaborated. There was no guarantee that their sentences would be diminished if they confessed all they knew about the irregularities committed in the trade network.

Late in 1983, the indicted trade employees were encouraged by the news that the agents of the PGO anticorruption brigade would replace their KGB col-

leagues in the interrogation of suspects. However, the trade staff soon realized that the anticorruption brigade simply continued the investigations in the same way as the KGB, employing typically Soviet methods. Many trade employees were imprisoned for months and even years without trial and were not allowed to see their relatives.

Gorbachev not only instituted new policies but also justified his changes by attacking the policies that had been in place. This criticism led the new leadership in the Kremlin to reexamine the past with new eyes, a reevaluation that affected the justice domain in a major way. What followed was a wave of criticism, which progressively took on the air of a campaign to destroy the KGB's reputation. The investigations of the retail trade, which had previously been well received by Russian civil society in 1982 and 1983, were now denounced. During this period, the media began to expose the many cases of abuse by the KGB. It was as though trade organizations had found a major weakness in the armor of the KGB. The employees of the trade organizations could not erase the accusations of corruption, especially since there was convincing proof of their deeds. By 1985, however, those in the trade organizations who had been accused were able to shift the focus onto the KGB and its strong-armed interrogations, prolonged periods of imprisonment, and repressive treatment of prisoners. Those tactics, pointed to as current practices of the KGB, were viewed as serious human rights abuses. Thus, as of 1985, media attention focused less on the proof of corruption submitted by the KGB and more on the means by which the proof was obtained.

The KGB's methods of investigation often appeared to be gross violations of civil rights, which made their perpetrators vulnerable to attack. Many trade employees did not deny their guilt concerning economic offenses; nonetheless, they realized that the new political atmosphere offered them the opportunity to use the excesses of the anticorruption campaign against its authors.

Its public image already tarnished, the KGB saw its situation worsen as its methods were scrutinized by the watchful eyes of those who had, until then, been its most faithful followers. As a matter of fact, a new divide appeared, this time a chasm separating the KGB from the judges. In a state operating under the rule of law, the judges can administer justice fairly only when certain conditions exist. The judges must be competent and impartial and must be able to make decisions independently, without pressure from any group or organization. The judges who conducted trials and rendered verdicts involving the Moscow trade organizations in 1984 were not always impartial, particularly in high-profile cases. Some of them later claimed to have been pressured by the KGB.[26] The bias of the judicial system could be seen in the trial of Sokolov and his four assistants, which did not take place in the court of the Baumanski district like it should have, since it concerned speculation; instead, the KGB decided that the Supreme Court must

hear the case. This move was the KGB's first action in the campaign that violated the constitution, but many others occurred during the first trials of members of the Moscow trade network. Sokolov's trial was conducted without regard for criminal law, and the trials that followed were similar. Sokolov and his lawyer were denied the opportunity to present new evidence during the trial and were compelled to deal with the testimony given during the interrogations by KGB investigators when Sokolov had begun to collaborate with them. The judge was partial to the KGB and the prosecutors and showed his partiality more than once. He commented on Sokolov's previous conviction (for alcohol speculation), despite the fact that the law did not allow reference to a conviction after an amnesty. Moreover, he altered biographical information on the accused, replacing the term "injured" during World War II with "slightly injured" when he had no legal basis to do so. The judge referred to the sum of 300,000 rubles taken by Sokolov, without mentioning that he had given a large part of this amount, more than 200,000 rubles, to superiors in bribes.[27] It would have been more appropriate for the judge to state that the accused had kept only 100,000 rubles for himself.

In addition, prior to their trials, many of the detainees had solid grounds to protest how their cases were being handled. The KGB major who orchestrated the confrontation between Tregubov and Petrikov in July 1984 was very biased against the former, as shown in his interventions, although he was supposed to show impartiality.[28] The tribunal was a place that was supposed to carry out justice but was turned into a branch of the security services. When the judge sentenced Sokolov to the death penalty, applause broke out. After a moment, a group of young people left the room; it appeared that the KGB had brought them in. They played the role of intimidating the executives who attended the trial, and their applause was intended to force the other people present to follow their example. Some store managers were compelled by the KGB to attend the trial so they would know what awaited them in the future if they did not cooperate. The Soviet Supreme Court's decision to reject Sokolov's appeal to annul the capital punishment verdict against him was yet another occasion that demonstrated the violation of procedures. In Sokolov's case, a bureaucrat signed the rejection of the appeal despite the fact that only the prosecutor general or the president of the Supreme Soviet was authorized by the constitution to do so; according to the *Rossiiskie Vesti*, the KGB asked the bureaucrat to sign because the president of the Supreme Soviet was opposed to the death penalty.[29] Suspects rarely criticized or disagreed with the judges, but a few of the accused did attack the judge's partiality despite the risk of a severe penalty. A witness reported Ambartsumyan's behavior at his trial: "'Pick up the file in front of you,' Mr. Ambartsumyan once said in irritation to the judge. 'It was written beforehand how much should be given to each of us.'"[30]

In 1983 and 1984, many trade executives who were arrested did not have access to a lawyer. For months, they were incarcerated and isolated. Some defense lawyers in the Glavka cases requested the appearance of certain witnesses who could attest to their clients' innocence. They also insisted that the KGB's witnesses come to court to corroborate their testimony as had been promised and to be subjected to cross-examination. Both these requests were refused. In addition, defense lawyers argued that persons could not be arrested simply because their names were mentioned in a suspect's written declaration. This was a major point for the lawyers of the indicted executives, and it was used to try to prevent the KGB from opening criminal proceedings against Party or government officials merely because they had been denounced during an interrogation of a suspect. The lawyers questioned the motives of these suspects; they knew that some of the jailed trade employees would confess to anything with the hope of being released. In this way, the lawyers who defended the faction of trade staff indicted for corruption were also the defenders of those absent from the court—top leaders who, after having been mentioned in certain written declarations by suspects, mobilized all possible resources in their favor to stay out of jail.

Lawyers defending high-profile trade leaders brought whatever arguments they could to court. Ambartsumyan's lawyer talked of his client's honorable service during World War II. According to him, Ambartsumyan, a war hero, did not deserve to be executed because he had taken bribes. The law stipulated that a detainee could be sentenced to death only if he was a security risk to the state, which Ambartsumyan definitively was not. Ambartsumyan's lawyer, after the Prosecutor General's Office recommended the death sentence for his client, responded, "What country are we living in? A war hero who participated in the victory celebration on Red Square, Ambartsumyan spent the whole war with weapons in his hands. He was at the front from 1941 to 1945 and was injured twice. He was awarded a cavalry medal, but still, the Moscow prosecutor recommends the execution of this war veteran on the eve of Victory Day."[31]

The executives of the trade organizations, especially those who were imprisoned, had the most to gain from the social and political changes. They considered 1985 the most opportune time to request a review of their sentences; the social reforms that were in progress encouraged them to hope for change. High-ranking officials who had been detained or condemned for corruption were in the most advantageous position to ask for their freedom. They had the support of the best lawyers in Moscow, attorneys who, during this period, would be the most likely to be able to help. These lawyers requested their clients' freedom or acquittal by relying on the impressive number of documents that detailed the abuse and illegal practices of the KGB from 1982 to 1984. Numerous testimonies from 1982 to 1983, they argued, had been obtained by questionable methods,

namely through physical pressure. Because of the shady practices of the KGB, many officials under arrest registered pleas of not guilty. Those who appeared before Supreme Court judges were former leaders of the retail business who had been condemned for having broken laws within that same sector. Notably, the vice mayor of Moscow and two agents of the business inspection service retracted their testimonies by claiming that they had been obtained under duress. In addition, two officials of Glavobshchepitanie (Central Administration for Public Catering) accused the KGB of having used coercive methods to obtain testimony against Tregubov and Grishin.[32]

Furthermore, not all retail business officials enjoyed the same amount of credibility in the judicial setting. Officials who had a criminal record were less credible; thus, the mutability of depositions could be attributed to the investigators' questionable interrogation tactics. It is not unlikely that some officials changed their statements when they realized that they could shorten their sentences or even be freed. Roganov, the head of the Sheremetyevo Airport warehouse for imported fruits and vegetables, was a typical example of an official who compromised his credibility by changing his testimony. His attitude toward the KGB was influenced more by personal interest than by fear of the law. In 1983, he played the informant on his colleagues with the sole purpose of bettering his situation. By 1985, however, he had denounced the KGB for having mistreated him in order to obtain information.[33] Knowing that perestroika guaranteed more leniency from the judges, Roganov changed his testimony. However, his allegations of torture at the hands of the KGB were not taken seriously in court because his credibility was in question.

Upon their lawyers' advice, most of the trade executives who had capitulated to the KGB in 1983 decided to plead not guilty in 1985. Perestroika created favorable circumstances for the lawyers, who could now contest the legality of the investigation methods used by the KGB during Andropov's time. At the end of 1985, pressure on the Kremlin to make changes to the justice system was high. Several executives claimed to have testified under threats and intimidation and went as far as denouncing the violence against them. One after the other, they appealed to the Supreme Court to have the charges against them annulled. The judge also rejected a few other accusations of bribe-taking by Tregubov. Other cases came to haunt the prosecutors. Eremeev, incarcerated in 1983, personified a flagrant instance of injustice. Over a period of five years, Eremeev submitted to a hundred interrogations based on the denunciations of twenty-seven people; of these, the tribunal upheld the charges stemming from the testimony of ten people.[34]

For the prosecutors, the problem often lay in the details. Defense attorneys claimed that small errors were significant and called the credibility of the entire

body of evidence into question; they argued that a single mistake in one aspect of the investigation was enough to cast doubt on all the rest. For this reason, the KGB was rigorously thorough in terms of evidence. In the absence of witnesses revealing details and circumstances, the decisive factor became which one, the bribe-giver or the bribe-taker, was telling the truth. The more persuasive of the two antagonists was the one who could describe the circumstances of the offenses in greater detail. Defendants had to discredit the veracity of the accusation, and if they managed to raise doubts on at least one point of the deposition, it could determine the outcome. Of course, the more precise the testimony, the greater the possibility that it would contain inaccuracies and contradictions. Another advantage for the accused was that an irregularity committed a long time ago was more likely to leave holes in the evidence; it was harder to remember with exactitude and in detail. The KGB, nevertheless, was equally demanding with suspects when violations of the law had occurred several years previously. A further factor working against the prosecutors was the advanced age of many of the trade executives, who often had problems remembering details. These elements could only play in favor of the accused in court. During perestroika, defense attorneys focused on these weaknesses in the prosecution and no longer showed restraint, as they had prior to 1985, when they were still intimidated by the KGB. However, even under Andropov, a few of them had been brave enough to either openly complain in court or voice their disapproval indirectly, with sarcasm.[35]

The law enforcement agencies were criticized for their lack of firmness, but during perestroika, inspectors were attacked mainly for their abuse of the suspects' rights. Kotova, the deputy director of the Dzerzhinski borough trade organization, was arrested and isolated in jail for bribe-taking. Investigators ransacked her house in search of evidence but were unable to obtain any proof of wrongdoing, so the police released her. However, the matter was not closed, as Kotova sued the government for material and moral damages and won her case in court. The court decision created a precedent for the defense, encouraging lawyers to intensify their battles on behalf of trade employees. Interventions (to have charges dropped or to obtain compensation for damages) proliferated in court against the KGB and the brigade investigators. The veracity of testimony was attacked in many cases and not without success. It was revealed in one case that an individual accused of bribe-taking had been dead for two years while another suspect, accused of the same type of offense, had retired before the event had supposedly occurred.[36]

Many of the suspects' relatives preferred to remain quiet and even appeared to forget about them. For others who tried to provide help and were ready to take risks, the result was rarely conclusive, except when the relatives in question were influential people. Kantaria, a man who had gained fame and immense

celebrity as a Soviet soldier during World War II, came to the defense of his relative, Kiut, the former director of a grocery store, when the latter was taken into custody. The leader of the PGO brigade, responsible for launching the anticorruption campaign, wrote to his staff that Kantaria's actions would have a negative impact on public opinion and, therefore, on the case. He was not wrong: Kiut was released not long afterward. Interventions from people other than relatives brought mixed outcomes. For example, a police report denounced Sokolov's popularity among the artists and journalists of the capital, as well as the attempts of some of them to intervene in his favor. These initiatives did not save Sokolov.[37] Tregubov was one of the high-profile officials who had influential friends, and he was released after having spent a quarter of his sentence in a labor camp.

Trade employees who had not been arrested were a key force in the resistance. The indictment of many employees and the publication of numerous articles in the media about corruption in the trade network led to a deterioration in morale among store employees. Staff changes and police investigations created an atmosphere of suspicion, and staffing shortages in the trade agencies increased due to the negative image of the agencies projected in the media during the anticorruption campaign. The technical courses established to train specialists in the consumer trade also had difficulty recruiting candidates. The trade staff voiced frustration and dissatisfaction with the Kremlin's decisions to appoint executives from the provinces. Rumors of irregularities committed by these new high-ranking Glavtorg executives spread rapidly.[38] There was no evidence to prove the rumors, but they contributed to the developing impression that the newcomers were no better than their predecessors. The partisans of Tregubov were still numerous in Glavtorg, and they launched a campaign against the crackdown on their organizations. Not without reason, they demanded that the investigations be fairer, by covering not only the period from 1976 to 1985 but also the preceding period. The authorities were also criticized for charging only the staff of the food organizations, while the other sectors (furniture, construction, gas, clothing, etc.) had been subjected to only a few isolated inquiries. Several Glavtorg managers received harsh sentences, while the leaders of the ministries of Agriculture and Trade avoided accusations. The following passage from the *Rossiiskie Vesti* expressed the feelings of several trade executives in 1985–1986:

> If we decide to uphold order and integrity in trade, why do the battles against crimes occur only in some stores, when embezzlement is rampant everywhere else? Trade ministries of the RSFSR and the USSR have been shaken by little eruptions, but these volcanoes occurred only in private, local, and closed places. Why have we not attacked local trade if every

city has its own Eliseevski, which secretly supplied the elite? Why has the
Trade Ministry been spared from the fight against crime as if all the embezzlement and secret economic privileges did not originate in it?[20]

The trade leaders claimed that irregularities continued for years after the anticorruption campaign. They said that the situation in this sector had not improved
with the KGB crackdown but had instead been aggravated. New executives in the
food sector seemed to be no better than their predecessors.

The impression was widespread in society that law enforcement crackdowns
were not a solution to trade problems. In private interventions directed at political leaders from 1983 to 1985, complaints were made about the persecution of
many trade employees. Hostility toward the crackdown increased substantially
with the advent of perestroika, which provided an opportunity for the trade executives to multiply their interventions in court and to expose their opinions to
larger groups. The trade leaders were not afraid, as they had been before 1985,
to voice their grievances, and they took some actions that would have been forbidden previously. They dispatched delegates to authorities at city and borough
levels, in Party organizations, trade unions, and at Soviet headquarters to argue
on behalf of colleagues who had been arrested.[40] Speeches were no longer moderate. Some delegates threatened to stop working if the police did not end their
meddling in the affairs of the stores. They said openly that corruption would
continue to be rampant in their sector as long as major changes were not made
within the Soviet economy. These delegates publicly challenged the KGB, claiming that most of their colleagues sentenced for corruption were innocent. They
repeated that it was time to stop using the trade executives as scapegoats for the
mistakes of the Soviet system.

One of the corollaries of increased criticism in society was pluralism. During the mid-1980s, tolerance of different points of view emerged on the public
front. At first, this critique derived from the milieu of the intelligentsia and from
members of the trade organizations. Criticism also assumed larger dimensions
because members of a faction of the nomenklatura, namely, the directors of retail
businesses and their associates, also contributed to the discourse. The underlying ideas behind these critiques can be identified as liberal because they sought
to gain liberties for the citizens of the Soviet society. This liberalism, however,
was relative in that it was not to be associated with the values of a democratic
system of government. Aspiring for greater liberties, this faction of the nomenklatura essentially wanted to protect or restore the rights and privileges that had
been threatened by the campaign against corruption. The faction had a liberal
approach on certain issues, despite the fact that, fundamentally, it remained con-

servative. During the first years of perestroika, members of this faction of the nomenklatura did not blame their problems on the existence of the Soviet regime;
rather, they confined themselves to asserting their right to increased protection
from the law enforcement agencies' arbitrary measures, and they drew attention
to cases of flagrant injustice against their colleagues behind bars. They wanted a
wider forum in which to defend their point of view, and they urged more freedom for the media. Some executives had, in effect, been sentenced to long-term
incarceration in labor camps for having acted like capitalist managers. Here, the
meaning was that the manager in the Soviet economy should have more freedom. Tregubov was found guilty by the Soviet court of running Glavtorg with a
"liberal" approach.[41] Many trade executives admired managers in the capitalist
economy. The granting of greater economic liberties constituted the first measure the trade executives wanted; a reform of that type would be a prerequisite
for the granting of liberties in other sectors of society.

Several trade managers claimed that, during the anticorruption campaign,
they had been condemned for actions that would have been considered normal in a capitalist economy, as illustrated during Sokolov's trial, when the judge
said that the accused had "provided the heads of warehouses with advantageous
products under advantageous conditions."[42] After the trial, supporters of the
trade executives quoted statements from the trial to prove their point.

After 1985, not all of the population wanted a complete shift to a Western
economy, but the majority wanted an economy that had some market-oriented
features. Society, even the government, no longer viewed capitalist-style management as a criminal offense. The trade leaders and their supporters emphasized civil rights and freedom of speech and saw connections between a private
economy, democracy, and efficiency. Highlighting these aspects of a private
economy was an effective strategy for resisting the repression of the trade organizations because it provided the best rallying cry for mobilizing large segments
of the population. Trade leaders were avenged by the halting of the crackdown
and by the release of all their jailed former colleagues. They sought the freedom
to criticize the police without being punished for it. In this way, the trade leaders advocated the principle of freedom of the press.[43] Many executives had been
arrested, and many others were afraid to suffer a similar fate if the anticorruption campaign continued. Like many of the Party and government officials who
had colluded with them, they wanted to discredit the investigators and, more
particularly, the KGB. It was also easier for them to overtly criticize the security
services because the number of organizations manifesting hostility to the KGB
was increasing.

The Communist Party Fights Back

Many Party and government officials protested the arrests of trade executives and leaders, and some of them telephoned the prosecutors to request the release of detainees. The leader of the anticorruption brigade investigating the trade area related how difficult it was to resist these pressures, which initially took the form of threats implying that highly placed officials would take repressive measures against them. Then, the tone would change, with interveners stressing the fact that trade employees were unfairly and falsely accused.

> Bear in mind that if it happens, the resistance will be very strong. Some-one coined the expression "telephone law." It operated at peak capacity. Whom didn't I get calls from! Don't think me immodest, but a certain fortitude is needed to resist this. We had to appeal to higher Party bodies in order to remove certain obstacles in the way of investigations. Now there are fewer calls. Their nature has changed, has become softer: "Isn't that slander? Aren't you violating socialist legality? We have to take care of our cadres." Many people are lying low and waiting until the campaign ends, hoping that they will be rescued. After all, there are people who are not personally involved in crimes but who shut their eyes to them; they're still at their posts, and some have been promoted. Yes, some were punished, but privately, with no publicity.[44]

As the secretary of the Moscow Party Committee, Grishin was aware of the corruption existing in the trade network because he received indisputable in-formation about it. He spoke on this subject more than once with Trushin, the head of the Moscow MVD. Trushin, an honest and competent official, admitted that the phenomenon was not rare but said he could not counter it. He knew that abuses were committed by Politburo members and their relatives, includ-ing some senior ministers (e.g., Shchelokov, the minister of the interior), who were reputed to have stolen large amounts of money. Even the reputedly honest minister of foreign affairs, Gromyko, committed abuses of power in obtaining apartments and garages for his relatives and friends.[45] Like Trushin, Grishin was aware that he did not have the power to wipe out the corruption, but he could at least limit it. He also knew that as long as Shchelokov remained minister of the interior, he could not rely on the Department for Combating Speculation and the Embezzlement of Socialist Property (OBKhSS) to do its job. It was, however, Grishin's responsibility to control the leaders of the Moscow trade network. More than once, he requested that the KGB check on Tregubov's integrity.[46] The results

of this operation allowed him to continue to believe that Tregubov was in no way involved in corruption.

However, not all of the law enforcement leaders believed in Tregubov's honesty. The KGB spent the last two months of 1983 preparing the evidence to convict those trade executives they deemed guilty, especially Tregubov. The prosecutor general initially reviewed and assessed the importance of the information and evidence gathered on the Glavtorg executives. The operation was supposed to find convincing proof for the arrest of thousands of employees and especially the "most wanted" in 1984, Tregubov. This time, Tregubov had to face justice, and his fate depended largely on Sokolov, who, if he decided to talk, could send Tregubov, with whom he had been acquainted for many years, to jail. Tregubov was aware, however, because of his experience, that the investigation and indictment of Sokolov could take another direction, considering that the Moscow Party boss had to approve all decisions regarding Sokolov. The KGB and Grishin endorsed Sokolov's arrest and conviction, but for opposing reasons. The former wanted Sokolov to divulge compromising data on the Moscow elite, while the latter wanted to sentence him to death for corruption and for having defamed the Soviet nomenklatura. Grishin wanted, as early as possible, the death of an executive whom he accused of having denigrated the elite merely to please the investigators who promised to save him from the death penalty. The outcome was that Grishin's point of view prevailed over that of the KGB. Consequently, Sokolov hesitated at first but then gave testimony that incriminated Petrikov. Investigators had to be a little more patient with Tregubov, but after Sokolov had divulged the names of high-ranking officials as his bribe-takers, he was sentenced to death. Grishin and the PGO were persuaded that Sokolov had not told the truth but had only tried to save his life. For this reason, Sokolov was executed a short time after the verdict, and, more importantly, the declaration he had written against Tregubov mysteriously disappeared, as did most of the depositions from high-ranking officials. The effect of Sokolov's death was to make it more difficult to file charges against Tregubov, as the investigators had lost their prime witness in the case. As a result, Tregubov's arrest was delayed for a few months, and it took more than a year to gather enough solid evidence to bring him to trial. Had Sokolov testified against him, there likely would not have been such controversy and doubts surrounding Tregubov's guilt. The court revelations about irregularities between Sokolov and Tregubov came from Petrikov's testimony and, for this reason, were not as credible as disclosures by Sokolov himself would have been. In this scenario, the Party, through Grishin, succeeded in neutralizing Sokolov and protecting Tregubov. This setback did not discourage the KGB in its efforts to find evidence on Tregubov, though. Grishin had won a battle but not the war in this case.

The Moscow Party Committee constituted another important front in the battle to prevent Tregubov's arrest. In 1983, the KGB received two incriminating witness accounts concerning the Glavtorg leader. They were not sufficient to indict him, but they did energize the investigators, who intensified their activities in the case. In 1984, the investigators paid more attention to this case than they had before. They interrogated almost all the executives and promised various favors to whomever would reveal Tregubov's wrongdoings. Their efforts finally paid off when they obtained a seemingly very credible third witness account: that of Petrikov. With this testimony, Tregubov became the obsession of the investigators, who now considered that they had enough proof to indict him. The challenge in this new phase of the case was to succeed in arresting Tregubov despite Grishin's opposition. The prosecutors realized that filing charges against Tregubov would not be that simple, since he denied all the accusations. By 1984, the KGB was convinced that Tregubov was deeply involved in corruption in the trade network and, therefore, disagreed with Grishin, who firmly trusted his chief of staff in the trade network and opposed his arrest. Several times in 1984, the PGO unsuccessfully requested the Party Control Commission's permission to charge Tregubov. Gorbachev was sure that Grishin was defending Tregubov because he himself had committed offenses, probably bribe-taking and bribe-giving. If Tregubov was prosecuted, he could have compromised Grishin, providing a good reason to get rid of him.

The KGB's problem in Tregubov's case was that it had not collected enough data in 1983 to arrest him. The prosecutor's only hope was that Petrikov, his first deputy director, would testify against him. Petrikov was the most likely person to have given Tregubov bribes, but when he was arrested, he refused to acknowledge any wrongdoing involving his former boss. Finally, Tregubov was indicted in July 1984 on evidence that has remained controversial to this day. Investigators wanted to arrest Tregubov that year, after Petrikov changed his testimony and claimed to have received twenty-one thousand rubles from his boss. They needed Grishin's approval, but he refused to grant it. The investigators also had to obtain the authorization of the Party Control Commission, which had refused to do so in 1983. In fact, the Party Control Commission based its decision on the recommendations of the Moscow section, which was headed by Buchin, a Grishin partisan who insisted on Tregubov's innocence. None of the three witnesses' accounts accusing Tregubov of bribe-taking looked very credible. Since the evidence collected was convincing enough to indict Tregubov but not to convict him, the prosecutors unsuccessfully sought additional testimony.[47] Until his death, Tregubov denied taking any bribes, and his partisans insisted that Petrikov, after a year behind bars during which he denied having given bribes, had changed his mind only because he was subjected to intimidation and false

promises by the KGB's prosecutors. The investigators never found the money allegedly taken by Tregubov, who lived modestly. Even though the prosecutors had no doubt that Tregubov had taken bribes, they could not prove that it was for his personal enrichment. The problem remained for the prosecutors to find further evidence. Since 1983, the anticorruption brigade had been seeking evidence against high-level officials, especially in the Moscow Party Committee. As its investigators did not obtain any evidence from Tregubov against Grishin, they turned their attention to other upper-echelon officials. The most important Party official against whom the KGB collected evidence was Buchin, the president of the Control Commission, but this evidence did not seemed credible enough: According to Ambartsumyan, "After meetings with Uraltsev, we delivered orders worth 100 rubles, six times; twice we took deliveries from Gastronom No. 3; we sent four orders to Uraltsev's office, where they would prepare four deliveries for Buchin. We gave it all to Uraltsev's main driver, who came to the fruit and vegetable office. Uraltsev explained to me that it was for Buchin. I do not know if he transmitted it or not; I cannot confirm it."[48]

Buchin was a critical obstacle for the KGB, since his Party Control Commission had to authorize the arrests of senior executives like Tregubov. The KGB wanted compromising material on Buchin so that it could remove him and then make it possible to arrest Tregubov. Furthermore, if the KGB agents could find enough evidence to file charges against Buchin, it would discredit Grishin as well. As the likelihood of being able to use Tregubov against Grishin decreased, the prosecutors decided to substantially expand the list of suspects, and Buchin became more important to them. In 1984, they did not have enough evidence against Buchin to arrest him, although they were encouraged by what they had already found out about him. However, a year later, times had changed with perestroika, and more solid evidence was needed to charge officials. What had looked promising as evidence now seemed insufficient in Buchin's case, as in many other cases. The accusations against Buchin seemed to concern gifts rather than bribes, and the brigade was obliged to direct its attention elsewhere.

Tregubov would never have been arrested if he had not committed a fatal mistake during his interrogation. In order to better argue in his favor, his defenders from the Central Party Commission, without authorization, had showed him the prosecutor general's request to the Central Party Commission to charge him. Tregubov inadvertently told his interrogators that he had seen all the evidence presented to the Control Commission for the justification of his arrest.

The investigators decided to indict Tregubov only after Grishin left Moscow on vacation. After his arrest, on one occasion, Tregubov acknowledged having received bribes, but later he claimed that his statements had been written under duress. He reported that the intimidation tactics included subjecting him to psy-

chiatric tests, a practice usually viewed as the prelude to a death sentence. After he acknowledged having received bribes, Tregubov explained that the money had not been for his personal use but rather to pay for receptions during conferences of the Moscow Party Committee and to host delegates from other regions of the country and abroad. Tregubov said of the executives from whom he had received bribes that "they received no special service from me; I did nothing special for them."[49]

After Tregubov's arrest, Grishin was unable to obtain his release, and he even officially condoned Tregubov's detention. This turn of events was a clear indication that the Grishinists were in decline, and their power to intercede in favor of arrested trade executives diminished in consequence. What had been an asset to Tregubov in 1983–1984—his connections in the Party—became a liability for him after the election of Gorbachev as secretary general in February 1985. As Grishin's man in the trade network, Tregubov was vulnerable and an easy target. Officials with whom he had links spurned him as soon as he fell out of favor with the Kremlin.

The advent of perestroika worsened the situation for the Communist Party. Emerging freedoms in the political system made it harder for the Party to maintain its monopoly of power. Criticism gradually extended to traditionally forbidden zones, like the politics of the Communist Party and the actions of its political leaders. By 1985 and 1986, it was more accurate to say that criticism was mounting against the Moscow Party Committee because of its domination by Grishin and his partisans, who represented the past and more conservative values. Grishin had run the city for more than twenty years, and he became the target of criticism as early as 1985. His resignation in 1986 did not mean, however, that the fight against the conservatives was over; a large number of officials of the Grishinist era continued to hold their posts. Not all of these officials could be identified as holding Grishin's values, since they had divergent points of view among themselves regarding trade matters. They observed the anticorruption campaign with apprehension, because they sensed how vulnerable they were.

The group of Grishinist officials in the Communist Party who had committed economic crimes was the easiest target. A second group had praised or promoted store managers who were now charged with corruption; such actions did not constitute crimes because those officials may not have known about these employees' corrupt activities at the time, but they were discredited all the same. Their reputations were put into question by the public, causing some to lose their jobs and even be criticized in the press. Politically, this exposure significantly weakened the Grishinist position. The third and largest group of compromised Grishinists consisted of Party officials who had accepted gifts. Many Communist Party members did not accept the harsh criticisms of the Soviet system, which

they considered to be a kind of welfare state. They were persuaded that a social contract existed: that the Kremlin provided social security in the way of stable prices, job security, and so forth, and, in return, the regime was expected to tolerate, to a certain extent, corruption, to include some practices like giving gifts to officials. This corruption has mostly, but not exclusively, negative aspects. Corruption helped some people have access to goods and services that the government was not able to provide adequately.[50] The vast majority of district Party secretaries and Party factory leaders received free packages of delicacies during the holidays. The tradition placed them in a thorny situation. Prior to 1985, they had no reason to avoid this practice, since it was tolerated in the country at all levels. Party officials had no reason to fear that they would be prosecuted even if they were dismissed when their practices were too flagrant. By 1985, however, the anticorruption brigade was taking a different stance. Brigade members claimed that gifts, even low-cost ones, constituted dissimulated bribes if they were accepted several times. Prosecutors may have been right to consider such gifts to be bribes, especially when they were of considerable value. Communist officials who had accepted gifts had good arguments on their side as well. For example, why decide now that this practice was equivalent to a crime when it was tolerated before? Was it fair to file charges only against Moscow Party officials, when the tradition of exchanging gifts was practiced all over the country? The accusations represented a serious threat to the Moscow Party staff. Now, they could not only lose their jobs but charges could also be filed against them and they could be taken into custody. Not all of them were necessarily Grishinists and dishonest, and some of them may even have sided with Gorbachev; however, almost all of them had accepted gifts in the past. The jailed Party officials were in the most difficult situation. To get them released was almost impossible. The fourth category of Grishinist officials who had committed economic crimes included those who had been dismissed for infractions but were allowed to remain free. People in this group could comfort themselves with the thought that they had never been charged or incarcerated, but they were still very worried because they were acquainted with people who had been indicted. In the fifth and last group were officials who saw no future in the Party because of their long association with Grishin. Some members of this group were attracted to business activities because of their connections in the trade organizations and within government circles involved in corruption. They intended to leave the unstable and insecure political arena for the economic sector, where they expected to be able to make substantial money. The Zagorsk Party secretary and certain Moscow Komsomol leaders, such as Khodorskovski, followed this path after 1986. Several Party cadres had left the Party earlier to avoid the fate of their comrades who had already been arrested.

The cases of trade executives arrested and often sentenced to long jail terms in the Andropov era were reassessed in 1987 and later. These executives were now viewed either as culprits or as victims of the Soviet system, and they found new allies to their cause in Yeltsin, his partisans, and the brigade carrying out the crackdown against corruption in the Moscow trade network. The sudden compassion for the convicted trade employees did not extend, however, to those who were closely linked to the Communist Party. This underlying motive in the softening of the attitude toward the trade employees was to shift the focus onto Moscow Party apparatchiks. As Grishin's partisans entirely dominated the Moscow Party staff, the attack against the Grishinists was effectively transformed into a charge against the Moscow Party organization. In the press, communists gradually became the object of severe criticism, along with those associated with them in the trade network. If, on one hand, Grishin and other city Party officials were losing their grip on the Moscow Party Committee, on the other hand, few were charged due to the lack of evidence of bribe-taking or other wrongdoing. The situation was quite different at the district echelon, where Party staff had close links with trade executives suspected of corruption.

The organization of the Communist Party of Moscow did not have any choice but to defend itself from the attacks coming out of the districts. At meetings and conferences of the Communist Party, the favored topic of conversation and discussions focused on police repression. Some officials were arrested while others questioned by the police, but news of the suicide of the secretary of the Communist Party of the Kiev district in November 1986 marked a turning point. The communists seemed to have found their martyr. This occurrence stimulated their opposition to the legal system; consequently, they accused Yeltsin and the legal force of having pushed the Kiev secretary to commit suicide. What had really happened, however, was that he had been interrogated by the police in October 1986 for having solicited the favors of woman near a Moscow metro station.[51] The police had not arrested him but had subjected him to close questioning regarding corruption in the trade organizations. Even today, the circumstances of this case remain unclear. What is clear is that in testimony to investigators, some of the indicted individuals had mentioned his name in relation to corruption in the Kiev district. It is probable that the secretary of the Party committed suicide to avoid having to live through the scandal that would have ensued over the solicitation of a woman, rather than for having been harassed by the police. At Party reunions, the late secretary of the Communist Party of the Kiev district was regarded as a martyr, as someone who had been the victim of police brutality. Some delegates at the nineteeenth conference of the Party affirmed that the former secretary of the Party in Kiev, like many others, had had to face defamatory accusations that had been pieced together by the police. They claimed that

Stalinist practices were being revived. The director of the Dzerzhinski factory ended his address to the conference by positing the following question, "If we compare, how is 1986 better than 1936?"[52]

Numerous letters were sent to the media and to Party organizations denouncing the illegal arrest of several district-level officials. These complaints often originated from the district where repression was most widespread: "In the middle of 1980, the Russian Prosecutor General led an unjustified repression against communist officials at all levels. In three months in the Soviet borough, thousands of communists were detained; many of them died; hundreds became disabled."[53] In the past, there were no precedents to the stringent persecution of Party officials by the legal system. Officials of the lower echelon surely suffered more blows, but higher-level persons in charge of the party did not think they were safe, estimating that the investigations would reach the upper echelon as well. As a counterpoint, it must be said that numerous Party officials attacked the police force like they had never done in the past. Soon, rebellion against the police force brought about conditions that led to the detention of Party officials. This was hardly surprising because, in 1986, respect for citizens' rights occupied a central place in political debate. The Party had already been accused of not respecting the rights of individuals in the past; at this point in time, many of these officials used this motif to further their interests. During this time they also asked delegates at the Party conferences to see in person the inhumane conditions of custody reserved for numerous higher-level officials of the Party: "I requested the conference president to allow the delegates to go with Vinogradov, the Soviet district Party secretary, and me, so that we could show them the isolated section of the prison where the interrogations took place."[54]

Communist officials could no longer rely on immunity. Membership in the Party did not provide the benefits that it had in the past; on the contrary, it became almost a handicap. Nevertheless, the officials still had influential relations in government structures because they had previously appointed, rewarded, or protected certain officials who had needed Party recommendations to hold middle-level and high-level positions in Russian society. During the Brezhnev period, they had occasionally rewarded and promoted executives or officials who were deeply involved in corruption. These relations were very useful during perestroika as events unfolded prior to the collapse of the Soviet regime. A few Communist officials quit the Party and found a niche with the help of friends who still held key jobs in industry, government, or elsewhere. Those who continued to work in the Party or had no support outside it had to face harsh criticism. Other Party members opposed the mass arrests of trade employees even if they were in favor of Gorbachev. As long as the KGB continued its crackdown against corruption, the majority of Communist Party officials did not feel safe. This is

why a large number of them approved denunciations of corruption among Party officials but did not agree with the idea of filing charges against them. They
claimed that corruption was primarily a political issue and not the KGB's responsibility. At this time, the reformists became preponderant at the head of the Party,
but at the lower echelons, the majority remained conservative and Grishinist.
Reformists like Gorbachev wanted to renew the state apparatus and purge it of
its conservative wing, but not by judicial measures.

The Moscow Soviet, Winner of the Campaign against Corruption

The decline of Party authority could only benefit the Moscow soviet. Perestroika, embodying a trend against authoritarianism, in its first stage began to
limit the power of the law enforcement agencies. This trend had existed in the
past, but it strengthened in the 1980s in reaction to the expansion of KGB influence in the political system. Civil society had begun to express a desire to curtail
repression. The demands of the perestroika movement prioritized respect for
the constitution and the rule of law. The groups that wanted these changes were
heterogeneous, and indeed, they occasionally defended conflicting interests, but
they united under the leitmotiv of respect for the constitution. The Soviet constitution was far from democratic, but, for many Soviet citizens at this time, it
had the advantage of being realistic and provided the framework for a first step
in the right direction. The gap between what was stated in the constitution and
reality was huge. Emphasizing respect for the constitution was the only way to
significantly undermine the power of the law enforcement agencies, primarily
the KGB. The Moscow soviet was the institution that could reap the most benefits
by implementing the constitution, which, in effect, stipulated that the Moscow
soviet was the organ that was supposed to govern society.[55] The election of its
leaders invested the soviet with the legitimacy to govern the country, and the
government adopted many laws in the 1960s and the 1970s defining and reinforcing the role of the Moscow soviet in the management of the trade network.

It was not the first time that high-profile leaders moved to widen the prerogatives of the soviet. Khrushchev's desire to reform the political system by boosting
the responsibility of the soviet led to its being perceived during the Twenty-first
Congress of the Communist Party of the Soviet Union in 1961 as the main organ
to lead society to the communist stage.[56] The reformers claimed that modern-
izing the system by increasing the authority of the soviet was consistent with
a constitution that considered this institution the main instrument of popular
participation in the political system. The promotion of the soviet was associated
with democratization of the system because it referred to the political, economic,

and religious rights of citizens, in contrast to the Party, the selective structure of which engaged only those sectors of the population that adhered to Marxist ideology. The soviet possessed another virtue in that it was associated with de-centralization and, therefore, with the necessity of conceding vast autonomy to the inhabitants of large cities like Moscow.

The promotion of the soviet implied the immediate need for the Party to delegate power to the soviet and to shift additional resources to the soviet, to the detriment of the Party. From this perspective, the soviet staffs, particularly in the trade sector, were the winners in the outcome of these reforms.

It should be stressed that the soviet in the capital was at a great advantage in this process. The resource distribution centers were located in Moscow and would be restructured to the convenience of the new leaders in the Kremlin. In spite of the general trend in favor of decentralization during this period, many products, especially imported ones, still had to pass through Moscow before be-ing distributed in the rest of the country. In practice, then, a huge quantity of products spent a given amount of time under Moscow's control, which allowed the Moscow soviet staff to use their strategic positions to promote their personal interests.

Another post-1985 tendency was the progressive placing of store managers under the supervision of the soviet, while Party interference was reduced to a minimum. In this new era, the soviet would oversee the establishment of plural-ism in the economy by instituting different sorts of property. At this stage, it was necessary to be careful not to exaggerate the differences between Party staff and those working for the soviet. Prior to 1985, most of the personnel in the two structures had worked in both places at different times and cooperated instead of competing. They also shared similar methods of management in compliance with the primacy of centralism, collectivism, and statism.

However, leaders of the Moscow soviet also had to defend certain interests. They were involved in the corruption that spread throughout the trade network, although few of them were arrested. They were saved by the advent of perestroika and the Kremlin's decision not to extend the anticorruption campaign beyond the trade structures, as had been proposed by the KGB. Thus, many of the Mos-cow soviet bosses eluded interrogation and arrest. Instead of suffering repression, they were given wide autonomy in the launching of economic reforms and used those reforms to reinforce their own positions. On one hand, by legalizing the private economy and cooperatives, they at least partly rehabilitated the trade em-ployees who were victims of repression. They helped their acquaintances in the shadow economy to make more profit and to legally secure their assets. On the other hand, the leaders of the Moscow soviet were aware of the trade employees' interests in the political sphere. In the initial stage of perestroika, they supported

transformations in the political system that would not endanger the monopoly of power held by the Communist Party. Their attachment to the Party can be explained by the control they exercised on this organization through their networks. When faced with the collapse of the Party, however, these leaders adopted another position, gradually adapting to and even supporting the disintegration of the state and the destruction of the Soviet system. The end of the centralized state had its advantages, allowing the leaders of the Moscow soviet practically free rein in the running of the economy. The soviet contributed to the weakening of the law enforcement agencies by dismissing many of their representatives. Furthermore, it introduced elements of a private economy but did nothing to change the law to reflect those new economic features. The powerlessness of the state allowed the trade leaders to make decisions that served their corporatist interests. With the fall of the Party and the destruction of the center in the last years of perestroika, the Moscow soviet enjoyed more power than ever before. New money-making opportunities for its staff appeared in the form of licensing stores, the sale of state assets, extorting money from cooperatives, and more, with the final stages of perestroika legalizing private economic enterprise.

The Revolt by the Ministry of the Interior

While Tregubov continued to insist upon his innocence, after February 1985, the prosecutors decided to look for further evidence against him. One direction the investigation took was to intensify the anticorruption campaign at the district level. Prosecutors turned their attention to an executive who interested them, less by the fact that he was the manager of the Sokol'niki RPT than by the fact that he was a relative of Promyslov, the mayor of Moscow; they were convinced that he was involved in corruption and had colluded with Tregubov and Grishin. Similarly, prosecutors showed interest in the Sebastopol *univermag* manager, Cheliuk; where they had not succeeded with Tregubov and Buchin, they could hope to succeed by compromising these store managers. To obtain material against them was therefore a priority.

Moscow had thirty-three districts, and each one had become a power center during the years of stagnation. The Grishinist nomenklatura had transformed almost every one of them into a kingdom of sorts. Most of the district officials had held their positions for a long time and had not only learned to live together but also to create networks that were difficult to break through. The district Communist Party secretary ruled his kingdom through reliable people he appointed himself. Under Grishin, the city and the district nomenklaturas improved their situations by achieving increased autonomy and gaining access to resources. At the same time, district trade leaders reinforced their positions through the distri-

bution of products. This phenomenon could be seen with senior trade executives and managers such as Baigelman, Cheliuk, Sokolov, Filippov, and Tveritinov: the districts and stores that they ran offered a greater choice of products. District Party and MVD leaders were very much under the influence of the heads of the trade organizations that bribed them with resources. Therefore, an anticorruption campaign meant an attack against the networks run by the leaders of the nomenklatura in the districts. After taking over the task of collecting evidence of corruption in 1983, the prosecutors of the anticorruption brigade, still monitored by the KGB, charged several trade employees and executives at the district level; they gathered so much information that in almost all the thirty-three districts, irregularities were uncovered. The trade leaders responded by taking preventive measures to avoid ending their lives in prison. One of these measures was to take advantage of the hostility of the Ministry of the Interior toward the KGB. High-profile executives from Glavtorg and those of the ministries of Trade and of Fruits and Vegetables encouraged executives at all levels to resist. As long as their leaders and protectors were not prosecuted, the lower-ranking executives continued to challenge the authorities.

The Ministry of the Interior, and especially OBKhSS, was a major supporter of the trade executives. In several districts, the MVD was supportive of trade organization executives and even did its utmost to prevent their indictment. Whether it backed them because it was implicated in corruption or because it believed that the evidence was insufficient to charge them, it remained that MVD intervention made the brigade's task more difficult. The brigade not only had to prove the trade executives' guilt but also prove MVD wrongdoing. By doing so, the brigade came into conflict with leaders of the Moscow MVD district units. MVD officials also reacted negatively to what they considered to be an abuse of power by the KGB, because the latter had gone beyond its jurisdiction by investigating the trade network. The brigade and the Ministry of the Interior also clashed on the methods of investigation. The MVD questioned the legality of the interrogations conducted by the KGB agents, the nature of the evidence collected, and the wide-scale detention of trade staff. The MVD considered trade matters to be within its jurisdiction, not the KGB's.

In December 1982, MVD investigators in the Perovski district arrested an employee for cheating consumers out of considerable sums of money. OBKhSS investigator Stebletsov refused to charge anyone, despite the fact that evidence had been collected against the manager of the food section of the Perovski *univermag*. In contrast, when the brigade entered the scene, fifteen people working in this store were arrested and convicted. In 1983, leaders of the food section of Universal *univermag* were accused of the embezzlement of socialist property. Investigator Stebletsov intervened and the decision was made, with the MVD's

approval, to annul the charges "for not having established that consumers were cheated by the employees of the *gastronom* and in the absence of proof of deceit."[57] There was, therefore, no reason to continue legal proceedings.

Brigade prosecutors faced serious problems in their investigations, especially in the Moscow trade districts and in the different agencies of the Ministry of the Interior. They could not prove that MVD inspectors were acting illegally without witness accounts of bribe-taking, which was due to a second factor that greatly complicated investigations in the Perovski district. Brigade reports told of mass involvement in economic offenses among sales clerks, workers, heads of sections and departments, district Party officials, and leaders of the district soviet. The prosecutors stated that hundreds of people were involved in criminal infractions, which meant that many more law enforcement representatives would be needed to arrest so many individuals. More than once, anticorruption brigade leaders requested a larger number of investigators.

When the brigade prosecutors charged a large number of trade employees in the mid-1980s, among them was Stebletsov. It took investigators nearly three years, from 1984 into 1986, to research his case, which was ultimately dismissed, all of which suggests that he had many defenders. Furthermore, circumstances improved for Stebletsov and others, who began to suspect that there was a lack of sufficient evidence to indict executives, especially after the press began to expose excesses committed by the law enforcement agencies. It was frustrating for the brigade not to possess any compromising material on suspected district MVD officials, but the investigators still did not show any signs of giving up in the Perovski district.[58] They were not able to increase the size of their staff, but they took the initiative of requesting the intervention of Party leaders. Burtsev, with Oleinik's help, obtained the permission of the Moscow Party leaders to file charges against certain Party and soviet leaders in the Perovski district. This unusual procedure was intended to prevent Buchin and his Control Commission from blocking charges against district Party leaders.[59]

Prosecutors also faced difficulties in the Zheleznye Dorogi district of Moscow, but they achieved some limited success in their investigation of corruption among MVD officers there. In 1983, Chupakin, head of the district OBKhSS, took bribes from trade executives Khokhlov, Nikolaev, and their accomplices, who were not sentenced until 1985 and 1986. According to the prosecutors' reports, "This was due to an unhealthy atmosphere in some MVD districts, whose leaders and employees were involved for a long time in criminal collusion with crooks and bribers who committed various crimes in office."[60] In the Sebastopol district, the MVD defended accused trade executives with some success. Chebulaev, head of the district OBKhSS, was arrested in 1981 for having accepted bribes. Only by 1986 was there enough evidence to try and convict him. Accord-

ing to police reports, Chebulaev knew that Cheliuk, director of the Sebastopol RPT, had carried out "various machinations regarding fruit and vegetables" and had committed major offenses, yet he did not take actions against her for taking bribes.[61]

The brigade suspected that other investigators were involved in bribery, but they were unable to prove it. Cheliuk kept her job until 1984, when she was accused of having continued to commit offenses under MVD protection after the anticorruption campaign had begun. The brigade denounced this state of affairs, saying that if economic irregularities continued to proliferate after 1982, it was because the MVD investigators had tolerated it. Here, too, KGB and brigade reports revealed pilfering by employees at more than one hundred stores.[62]

On another level, it was not only corrupt MVD officers but also many other people who prevented the law enforcement agencies from making mass arrests. Cheliuk did not help the prosecutors. She was incarcerated but never confessed to the charges filed against her. In addition, she refused to give testimony concerning her brother-in-law, the deputy president of the Moscow soviet's Executive Committee. Apparently, she stubbornly believed that her connections would save her. In the end, the brigade achieved a mixed success in this operation: Cheliuk was indicted, but her influential brother-in-law avoided judicial proceedings.

In the Kuibishevski, Babushkin, Pervomaiski, Perovski, Proletarski, Volgogradski, and Sebastopol districts, which were, with Dzerzhinski, the most organized districts as far as black market activities were concerned, prosecutors succeeded in finding enough evidence against several trade organization leaders and officials to send them to labor camps for long-term sentences. This success was, however, far from complete, since no compromising facts were disclosed against high-ranking Party and soviet officials. This shortcoming was not because the prosecutors had not put all their efforts into the investigation but because Party leaders in these districts sided with the trade executives and opposed their arrest. Their names were even mentioned in the executives' testimony and written declarations. Many RPT and *gastronom* managers, before their arrest, received awards and promotions from Party officials, who nevertheless avoided being charged. The KGB was unable to prosecute these officials and many others due to the attitude prevailing in the Ministry of the Interior and, more precisely, to that of OBKhSS. The MVD refused to collaborate in what it considered an infringement of the suspects' civil rights.[63] Moreover, trade executives had the backing of the people whom they supplied illegally, notably members of the Moscow MVD, who refuted the accusations as incomplete and unconvincing and defended the integrity of the suspects. Progressively, the conflict between the KGB and the MVD grew beyond the context of the anticorruption campaign.

The brigade arrested Suskin, the leader of the Leningradski district MVD, for

having sold false documents from 1978 to 1980. Nonetheless, until 1984, Suskin remained in his position due to the support of his superiors. The fact that "many times, Suskin received support from the MVD city management" could explain why the MVD resisted the brigade's very insistent requests for incriminating evidence on him in 1983.[64] During the same period, Suskin was given a promotion by his bosses, which placed him in the Moscow city section of the MVD.

The MVD's resistance to the KGB was weakened in 1983 by the arrival of Sterligov at the head of the Moscow city OBKhSS. Even so, during that same year and thereafter, officials of the Moscow district's OBKhSS were able to stop the prosecution of some trade executives. In the meantime, some MVD district units continued to oppose similar criminal proceedings against friends in the trade organizations. The MVD officers were helped in this by prison wardens who had been bribed by trade executives. The prison warden occasionally allowed prisoners to receive unauthorized visits from colleagues and even suppressed evidence for them. Veselkin, the director of one Moscow detention center, was sentenced to six years in a labor camp: "For criminal, personal interests, he systematically broke the law and the norms during the preliminary hearing, as specified in decree NVDSSR No. 0056 - No. 0030, 1976. For doing this, he received bribes of more than 30,000 rubles from inmates and their relatives." The police report added that, even after sentencing Veselkin, wardens continued to be bought: "Until now, in practice, no measure has been adopted concerning the sentences of the guilty parties, particularly as serious violations took place in other Moscow detention centers as well."[65]

Prosecutors of the brigade were obliged to give priority to investigations on MVD officials and prison wardens in many boroughs, which caused a delay in criminal proceedings against corrupt executives. This delay saved several of them, since the emergence of new leaders in the Prosecutor General's Office at the end of 1985 slowed the anticorruption campaign and, as a consequence, many of the accusations involving trade affairs were dropped.

In 1983-1984, every trade employee interrogated was asked to disclose Tregubov's illegal dealings, but very few responded positively. The prosecutors' major disappointment was in the Sebastopol district, which was of primary interest to them. Investigators there found it easier if executives admitted their wrongdoings, especially in cases of bribery, as there were rarely any eyewitnesses. We must keep in mind, however, that in the Sebastopol and Zheleznye Dorogi districts, the accused executives denied their guilt and denounced unfair treatment by investigators. The brigade charged several MVD officers, but these were mainly in OBKhSS. Moreover, the KGB's accusations that the MVD had been too lenient in 1983-1984—when many MVD district leaders insisted that the

evidence was not sufficient to arrest trade officials—played against the KGB in 1985 and later, when this point of view came to prevail in society.

One of the most serious shortcomings of the brigade was that it failed to prove the guilt of the Moscow MVD leaders. Trushin, the Moscow boss of the MVD, who had never been subjected to corruption investigations, was nevertheless aware that corruption was rampant in Glavtorg and in other Moscow trade organizations. He could not fight it effectively due to protection at top political levels. Several MVD agents were involved in illegal activity, but Trushin was not in a position to respond to it when the minister and deputy minister of the interior were Shchelokov and Churbanov. He also knew that members of his staff were under the influence of the Moscow trade executives. The MVD frequently considered evidence offered by the KGB and the brigade as insufficient when it involved accusations of corruption, tending to perceive as gifts what their rivals called bribes and taking the attitude that receiving products without waiting in line was reprehensible but could not be classified as a criminal offense. The MVD also cast doubt on the validity of testimony. We should consider, too, that in the context of that time, Party leaders at different echelons were not only above the law but took the place of the police in the implementation of the law. In this context, the nearly powerless MVD agents had no alternative but to close their eyes to corrupt practices.

While the Ministry of the Interior had once been seen as tolerant and even complacent toward economic crimes, after 1985 it fulfilled its constitutional role as the uncompromising upholder of justice, particularly where civil rights were concerned. Reformers at the Kremlin progressively rehabilitated the MVD as a necessary step in their attack on the KGB. They had no choice but to prefer the MVD over the KGB. The liberals who denounced the KGB unhesitatingly promoted the Ministry of the Interior, preferring Trushin to Fedorchuk; their comments on the anticorruption campaign resembled those of the MVD. They, too, criticized the KGB for charging trade employees without sufficient evidence and for sending many executives to prison for years after their conviction for minor offenses. The media continued to attack Shchelokov and other MVD agents but stressed that the bulk of the MVD staff was competent and honest.

KGB officers appointed to top positions in the Ministry of the Interior did not have long or successful careers there: they were all dismissed after brief periods because of their authoritarian ways and excessive methods of repression. The criticism of the KGB that arose with perestroika can be perceived as an attempt to weaken its influence; the investigation into the Moscow trade organizations provided the occasion to launch this attack on the KGB.

Under the influence of liberal reformers, the media sent out the message

that investigators needed additional proof, and especially from 1985 onward, the court imposed more stringent requirements on investigators. Following the media criticism, judges focused particularly on the accused trade executives and the violation of their civil rights by prosecutors in the Andropov era. With perestroika, investigators were obliged to amass additional evidence: in 1985, the evidence upon which executives had been convicted two years earlier was considered inadequate, and KGB or brigade investigators had to reopen some cases that had been deemed closed in 1983. The proper handling of cases in 1985 and afterward meant not only having to persuade the judge by presenting credible proof but also showing that acceptable investigative methods had been employed. Although it was true that the majority of trade employees had resorted to illegal practices, almost all the investigators, even those associated with the democratic forces represented by Gorbachev and Yeltsin, had also broken the law during the Brezhnev years. With the advent of perestroika, the question of the investigators' methods took on as much and even more importance than the evidence itself in the trade employees' trials. Accordingly, it was hardly surprising that the investigators' attitude and approach turned out to be a determining factor in establishing the relative credibility of the Moscow trade staff.

One consequence of the criticism of the KGB was a change in attitude regarding the MVD's actions throughout the stagnation period. MVD investigators who had refused to charge trade employees during that period were now viewed as victims of the KGB. The trade leaders benefited from the rehabilitation of the Ministry of the Interior, since many of them had developed contacts and even friendships with MVD officials. They supported the reformist demands that the MVD, not the KGB, should investigate the trade organizations. In the face of the excesses of the KGB in the campaign against corruption in the trade organizations, the MVD was the only alternative law enforcement agency. Thus, the discrediting of the KGB and the tolerance manifested by the MVD toward the Moscow trade network in the past became an advantage for the latter after 1985. The emergence of a stronger MVD was a boon to trade executives, who could expect greater freedom with the return of the Ministry of the Interior as the main organization overseeing their activities.

Although prosecutors succeeded in indicting many grocery store managers through their employees' testimony, they failed, most of the time, to find employees who would compromise Tregubov and other senior Moscow Party and soviet officials. Several trade organization leaders were sentenced in 1986, but only in the Perovski, Pervomaiski, Babushkin, Volgogradski, and a few other districts. Even in these districts, investigations took a long time—up to several years—and were far from complete in 1986 because of the trade executives' support from the MVD.

To be able to replace the principal MVD officers in OBKhSS, the brigade and the KGB had to obtain solid evidence against them—not an easy task, which explains why so many executives were still not sentenced in 1986. Moreover, investigations of the trade organizations' leaders could be concluded only after the corruption of some districts' MVD officials was proven. In 1986, a directive from the prosecutor general admitted that the war against corruption had not been won: although many executives had been brought to trial for corruption, many more remained free. The prosecutor general used the word "complex," which, in communist terminology, was associated with failure:

> Only neglect in the work of cadres, together with the offenses committed in the management of the MVD districts, explains the fact that even after the disclosure by the KGB of a criminal system in the trade network, and the opening of preliminary proceedings by the brigade regarding the criminal activities of officials and the revelations of criminal groups, the situation concerning the investigations in the trade network remained complex in the following districts: Kievski, Leningradski, Moskvoretski, Kuibishevski, Dzerzhinski, Sverdlovski, Pervomaiski, Sokol'nicheski, Babushkinski, Sebastopol'ski, Gagarinski, Perovski, Krasnogvardeiski, and Proletarski.[66]

The criticism of the KGB culminated in 1986 with a major change of staff in the law enforcement agencies, a change that favored the Ministry of the Interior and led to Trushin's return in force. Also that year, the Kremlin decided to recruit a new team at the head of the Moscow OBKhSS, based on references by Trushin. Experienced MVD officers, many of them from the district level, received promotions, and most of them had already worked in the field of economic crimes. Some senior investigators who had been particularly recommended by Trushin and who had proven their competence in the investigation department also benefited from the restructuring. None of the promoted officers had any previous involvement in the anticorruption brigade, and according to its leaders, most of these new MVD bosses were known for their tolerance of corruption or for their resistance to the anticorruption campaign in the food distribution system. Oleinik denounced these staff changes because they were directed against the KGB and the brigade.[67]

The Revolt in the Prosecutor General's Office

Emelianov, the prosecutor general of the Republic of Russia until the beginning of 1986, was associated with Andropov, and he endorsed the anticor-

ruption campaign. He unhesitatingly accepted the KGB's intrusion into sectors outside its authority and instructed the PGO staff to look to the KGB as a model of firmness. Emelianov approved the creation of the anticorruption brigade even though it was removed from the authority of the PGO. Moreover, he never questioned the KGB's harsh investigation methods; he saw firmness where others saw police abuse. Emelianov made no secret of his views. On the contrary, the campaign could not have been characterized by such severe tactics on the part of KGB and brigade agents had Emelianov not explicitly condoned them. He was among those who had no doubt that Sokolov and other trade executives had made unfounded accusations against other leaders in order to avoid the death penalty.[68] Emelianov was aware that Sokolov's trial and his harsh sentence had set a precedent that other judges would follow in subsequent corruption cases.

However, by the end of 1985, the Kremlin had decided to take measures that increased the authority of the Prosecutor General's Office, to the detriment of the KGB. The first move by the Kremlin was to replace the deputy prosecutor general, Namestinov, who was associated with the KGB, with an executive more in favor of perestroika. The Kremlin also made it a priority to reassign the investigators working on the trade network cases. Some KGB agents were part of the brigade, and its involvement in the crackdown on trade network staff members was considerable. The brigade began the campaign in 1982, and until October 1983, the KGB gathered evidence on trade employees suspected of corruption, before transmitting it to the PGO. In 1985–1986, this evidence was suddenly considered suspect and of little value because it had been obtained in dubious circumstances. In 1986, the Kremlin decided to dismantle the KGB's economic crimes section, founded in November 1982. Another Kremlin directive announced that the anticorruption brigade would no longer include KGB agents, who were now forbidden to investigate corruption in the trade organizations. It was not a true purge, but it was more than just a change in staff.

The leaders in the Kremlin seemed to seize the crackdown on the trade organizations as an opportunity to review the role of the KGB in the political system, which could explain the Kremlin's decision to attack some Moscow KGB leaders. Some of those who headed the security agencies' operations in the capital during the Brezhnev era were dismissed. The crackdown on the trade network was not the only reason for their eclipse: the revision of their past actions extended to other areas, such as politics. Certain senior KGB officials who had led the repression against dissidence during the 1970s and who subsequently led the anticorruption campaign in Moscow were now vulnerable to criticism. Trofimov was the most important of these high-ranking officers who conducted the war on these two fronts, and he was also the first to be compelled to resign.

The PGO agents who were in collusion with the KGB found themselves in an

uncomfortable position. This was the case for Oleinik and several other leaders of the anticorruption campaign, who nevertheless did not lose their jobs. They were able to continue their investigations, but their powers were significantly limited. The PGO closely supervised their activities, and the brigade's mandate was significantly reduced. In addition, the brigade was notified of an effective deadline applied for their investigations because at the end of December 1986, the brigade was slated to be dissolved. The brigade's staff was also cut, from eighteen to six members, in September 1986. The anticorruption brigade in Moscow managed to avoid dissolution in the winter of 1986, however, because it enjoyed the political support of Boris Yeltsin. His position made the chiefs of the PGO very prudent with regard to the brigade. The office of the general prosecutor could not bureaucratically squeeze them out as long as Yeltsin favored them. However, the second half of 1986 was marked by serious clashes between the Prosecutor General's Office and the brigade leaders.

Zemlianouchin, the new deputy prosecutor general, and his partisans were determined to make some reforms.[69] Upon being nominated, Zemlianouchin did not waste time distinguishing himself from the former deputy prosecutor general. His first measures showed a sensitivity to civic rights and a determination to eradicate the abuses of the law enforcement agencies. In addition, the new deputy prosecutor general was mindful of having to deal with personnel whose methods conformed to the changes brought about by perestroika. Prosecutors were commanded to "strictly observe the law concerning the investigations of officials."[70] This command was a reaction to the numerous complaints of abuse committed by certain members of the prosecutor general's personnel. The complaints were not necessarily all justified. Some emanated from executives who claimed their innocence in spite of the apparently solid evidence against them.

The new deputy prosecutor general wanted, furthermore, to distance himself from the former management by announcing that the behavior of investigators would be henceforth subject to strict surveillance control.[71] This last directive raised suspicions with respect to the work of the prosecutors; it implied a low level of trust in certain agents and put pressure on the prosecutors to change and improve their work methods.

The office of the prosecutor general expected to adopt better measures by showing that it would not accept good intentions or general statements. It also decided that it would enforce these measures by intervening in cases that were controversial or concerned higher-level officials. Late in 1985, the Soviet Supreme Court examined the cases of Tregubov and other Glavtorg leaders, as well as those of certain store directors. The judges taped the declarations of the accused and the testimony presented by the Prosecutor General's Office. The Court also demanded verifications of the accusations and confirmations of the declarations

presented to it. Among the accused were Skil, a restaurant director, and Panakov, head of the Moscow Tourist Bureau, both accused of bribing Tregubov. They had also testified that they had given bribes to Grishin and to Promyslov, mayor of Moscow. The Supreme Court procedures served to confirm the accusations. Under Soviet law, the accused had almost no other choice but to acknowledge the documents presented by Oleinik, considered one of the top prosecutors in the country.

Once perestroika and a new deputy prosecutor general were in place, however, witnesses felt free to change their testimony. Skil and Panakov now denied that they had bribed Grishin, Tregubov, and Promyslov. They were not alone in changing their stories, but early in 1986, they also added allegations that the brigade had used violence and drugs to extract confessions. Skil was the first to challenge the accusations by the brigade; his declarations also drew attention because accusations of corruption against leaders of the trade sphere, the Moscow soviet, and the Moscow Party Committee were so rare. Opponents of the brigade fired new salvos and many trade executives vehemently defended themselves, but Skil and Panakov were among the few to attack Oleinik and his brigade directly. Moreover, Skil denounced the harsh treatment of the trade employees and Party officials imprisoned for corruption. Oleinik and the KGB, who had made Skil and Panakov key witnesses, were embarrassed by the men's *volte-face*. Because Oleinik and his team had emphasized the integrity and credibility of Skil and Panakov regarding the testimony against Tregubov and Grishin, they were not in a good position to attack Skil after he changed his declarations. The decision of the PGO to nominate A.K. Rozanov, the secretary of the party committee for the PGO and one of its top officials in the capital, to investigate these new charges gave more importance to the review of the case. This nomination also represented more bad news for Oleinik because it was evident that this initiative by the PGO in 1986 was intended to prove that Oleinik had not respected the rights of detainees in the campaign against corruption. But there was more at stake: the PGO wanted to halt the work of the brigade and needed reasons to justify it. The PGO's other objective was to transfer Oleinik to another position, at a lower level. Another consequence of the allegations by Skil and Panakov was that other executives decide to follow their example and openly attack Oleinik and other members of the brigade. Eventually the investigation ended, and the charges against Panakov and Skil were dropped. However, the Court rejected the accused men's assertion that the investigators had subjected them to violence and forced them to take drugs. Ultimately, the Court acquitted Skil and Panakov of giving bribes to Tregubov, moreover the PGO sent a directive to investigators prohibiting the arrest of officials mentioned in the depositions of the accused but that did not appear in cases for the prosecution. Their case thus set a precedent:

they showed that it was possible to win in Court against the law enforcement agencies. Their relative success against Oleinik made them heroes among the trade staff, and their assertions highlighted the injustices suffered at the hands of the KGB and the anticorruption brigade.[72]

The cases of Skil and Panakov shed some light on illegalities committed by the KGB and the anticorruption brigade as they pressured trade executives to denounce high-ranking officials in exchange for better conditions during or release from detention. In some cases, executives who had committed serious crimes were released for denouncing colleagues, while others were released in exchange for testimony that was ultimately of little legal value. Some high-ranking officials were arrested on the basis of unverified accusations or gossip. Those who feared they would die in detention because of mistreatment or illness were prepared to say anything to gain their freedom or better conditions. The brigade's tactics thus backfired, because they led to the release of many executives who had been indicted only because they had agreed to denounce high-ranking officials. To be accused of bribe-giving by just one person was sometimes grounds enough to arrest suspects, interrogate them, and place them under house arrest or in jail. Thus, all officials were vulnerable; anyone could be subject to punishment because of baseless accusations. Oleinik admitted that he sometimes had not respected the law but added that he was justified in acting as he did because of the difficulties of the campaign. The PGO reacted in other ways to these excesses, forbidding its staff to accuse or to detain upper-echelon officials without the authorization of the Party Control Commission or the PGO.

Even with the new orientation of the PGO, which took seriously the trade employees' reports of police brutality, the KGB continued to claim to be above reproach. The PGO also received complaints about the brigade directed by Oleinik (whose power at the PGO had, by this time, declined because of his past liaisons). The prosecutor general possessed many files and documents on the transgressions committed by the police force, but the KGB and the brigade had also compiled a considerable quantity of data and testimony to justify their behavior in the fight against corruption in 1982–1984. In Ambartsumyan's case, the brigade believed it could prove, with supporting documents, how corrupt Party and state officials were, and Ambartsumyan's own testimonies provided the best evidence of their argument compared to those of other cases. Oleinik and his prosecutors emphasized that Ambartsumyan was not an exception and that there were other detained managers who could provide powerful testimony against high-level officials. Brigade leaders also affirmed with great conviction that Sokolov knew more than what he was saying but that the nomenklatura would have executed him before he could reveal more. Sokolov's ultimate fate was a chilling reminder to other suspects, who were all too aware of what lay in

store for them if they were to reveal what they knew of certain members of the nomenklatura. In addition, brigade leaders did not want history to repeat itself, which explains why brigade leaders asked on different occasions that Ambartsumyan be kept alive.

Brigade leaders were certain that some concessions granted to Ambartsumyan after his arrest in 1983 would be justified without bending any rules. The first means by which they could accomplish this was to overturn his death sentence. The advantages of this decision could have been to influence Ambartsumyan to reveal more compromising details on higher-level officials. The result would have been that these officials incriminated by Ambartsumyan would, under pressure, have provided further testimony on the corruption of the nomenklatura. Consequently, it would send a message to other suspects that they should cooperate with the police, an added advantage to brigade leaders. Those prisoners who provided testimony under these circumstances would be compensated for helping police officers. Oleinik believed in justice; respect for the law was a fundamental issue for him. He was certain that corruption was a principal weakness of the elite and that this evil was spreading toward the state, even in the direction of the Communist Party. Oleinik, thus, never doubted that Grishin had accepted bribes although police officers never managed to prove it.[73] Even in 1986, Oleinik believed in Andropov's view that the solution to the country's number-one problem lay in eradicating corruption and establishing the rule of law.

Would Oleinik have had the same hostile attitude toward the nomenklatura had he not had Yeltsin's support? Yeltsin occupied an important position at the end of 1985. He was Gorbachev's protégé and a rising political figure, to the point of replacing Grishin as manager of the Moscow Party, and the campaign against corruption had made him popular; it was the factor that made him known and appreciated by public opinion. In Moscow, a city where Yeltsin was less known, it was a little more difficult for him, especially since he initially ran up against a bureaucracy that was increasingly threatened by Gorbachev's reforms and that rapidly became hostile to him. Yeltsin, a newcomer in the capital in 1985, needed support, which he initially found in the police force. It was Yeltsin's paradox to propose an expansion of citizens' freedom within the political system and, at the same time, in 1985–1986, to sponsor the campaign against corruption in order to create political capital. His first allies were the anticorruption brigade leaders, with whom he met on a weekly basis in 1985. Soon, he adopted the fight against corruption as his own. The brigade supplied him with exhaustive information on the corruption of the nomenklatura in the capital. Brigade members were honest, but they presented the campaign against corruption when it was most opportune to their cause (making themselves known to the public at the same time),

and they started off by exaggerating the dangers of corruption and the benefits of overcoming the phenomenon. The brigade's continuation of the fight against corruption and the opposition to the PGO on this issue made Yeltsin's support of the brigade crucial. On his end, Yeltsin did not disappoint; he provided not only firm support but also encouraged the brigade to investigate highly placed officials of the Party and the government.[74]

Oleinik could not ask for more because that would have necessitated getting Yeltsin to side with the brigade against the PGO. Yeltsin's support served to foster the eagerness of brigade chiefs in their battle against corruption despite the opposition of the PGO. It also explains why they wanted Ambartsumyan's testimony: they sought to reinforce Yeltsin's cause by providing him with compromising information on highly placed members of the nomenklatura. If brigade investigators discovered cases of corruption within the higher echelon of the nomenklatura, the result would have been to weaken its position and strengthen that of their ally, Yeltsin.

It is significant that, by the fall of 1985, the new policy of perestroika had already expanded the rifts in the political system. Stable for numerous decades, the political system had now been stirred up by its contradictions, which were being revealed more and more publicly. By the fall, these contradictions intensified and began to affect the legal sector, long known for its conservatism. The tensions between the KGB and the PGO appeared alongside the tensions between the KGB and the MDV, which were already present under Andropov's rule. What was even more troublesome to the legal system was that the Party was experiencing growing difficulties in conciliating and arbitrating the conflicts between its many factions. These factions eventually saw the need to compromise, given the continuing dominance of the Party. Reaching agreement, however, took a long time, and this agreement reached seemed tenuous.

Tensions rose within the ranks of the PGO. In November 1985, the PGO initiated hostile measures against the brigade, requesting that it shed more light on Ambartsumyan's testimony concerning bribery "to officials of the Party, the Soviet, Glavmosplodovoshprom, the Ministry of Fruits and Vegetables, the Ministry of Trade, the Ministry of the Interior, and other [entities]."[75]

Fulfilling the brigade's request could bring to court many high-level officials of the Moscow soviet as well as many Moscow Party officials.

The leaders at the Prosecutor General's Office were persuaded that these accusations of bribery were unfounded. However, there was also a political dimension to the accusations. Kremlin officials were suspicious of the KGB's intentions. The question was, why had the KGB been so active in the Ambartsumyan case in 1983 and 1984? One explanation could be found in the agency's determination

to put an end to corrupt practices by the elite. However, another explanation was that its agents were primarily motivated by a thirst for power. The consequence of the trials and convictions of high-ranking officials would be the opening of new posts in the government and in the Party—posts that could be filled by people with convictions similar to those of the KGB. Understandably, the PGO gave more credit to the second explanation. Another factor to take into consideration is that the men who orchestrated the anticorruption campaign—Burtsev, Oleinik, and Sterligov—were closely connected; their victory in the Ambartsumyan case would boost the already expansive power of the KGB in 1983 and 1984. At this time, the PGO had no choice but to accept control by the KGB, with the attendant frustrations and humiliation.

However, in 1985, circumstances changed for the KGB with the advent of perestroika, which implied that the principles outlined in the constitution had to be taken seriously. In the Ambartsumyan case, it meant that the PGO, not the KGB, had to verify the legality of the actions taken by law enforcement agencies and the judiciary staff. The deputy prosecutor general, Zemlianouchin, demanded proof that the brigade prosecutors had done their work properly. In this context, the KGB and the brigade became vulnerable. The KGB had a long history of repression and domination among the law enforcement agencies. Although, on the surface, the KGB of the 1980s appeared quite different from the agency of the 1930s, its methods had not changed much, as the anticorruption campaign made clear.

Oleinik and the KGB did not renounce their effort to find evidence of corruption among Party and high-ranking government officials, but the debacle over Sokolov, Skil, and Panakov led them to focus their attention on other suspects. The KGB and the brigade believed that they had a key witness to prove the guilt of high-level officials: Ambartsumyan, who, since 1983, had been willing to denounce a number of highly placed officials to avoid execution. He was a senior executive and had been in contact with many of these officials. Oleinik wanted Ambartsumyan to provide them with substantial evidence in a short time because, by 1986, there were complaints that the anticorruption campaign had gone on long enough and should be brought to a close. It was also pointed out that, after three years, the guilt of most of the leaders in Moscow suspected of corruption had still not been proved. Oleinik had not accomplished what he had promised at the beginning of the campaign, particularly with regard to the indictment of Grishin. The observation was made that, if these leaders had not been proven guilty of corruption, it must follow that they were innocent. Still worse, Oleinik and the brigade had lost their battle against Skil and Panakov. That made Ambartsumyan's testimony crucial for Oleinik. However, this testimony had its weaknesses. Oleinik's tactics were traditional, with brigade members encourag-

ing suspects to denounce high-ranking officials in return for their freedom. Was this the wrong tactic? It did not seem so at first, when government officials were arrested on the flimsiest evidence. However, while the accused officials were detained, the brigade took a long time to obtain evidence to bring them to trial. This unreasonable delay led to protests among the trade staff and prompted the PGO to issue a warning to Oleinik that the case needed to be concluded.

The pressure put on the brigade to achieve more success can explain why the brigade increasingly relied on Ambartsumyan to produce solid evidence regarding corruption among the elite. The leaders of the brigade took a risk: obtaining the evidence would reinforce their position and ensure the continuation of the investigation, but if they failed with Ambartsumyan, it could be the beginning of the end for their careers.

The prosecutor Sheremetev was appointed by the Prosecutor General's Office to revisit the Ambartsumyan case. Officially, Ambartsumyan demanded that his death sentence be commuted to a lesser punishment. The brigade backed him up on this request and hoped that a reversal of his death sentence would allow them to continue investigating the case. Sheremetev focused on what he considered the low credibility of the Ambartsumyan testimonies. To prove his point, he indicated that Ambartsumyan was seriously ill during his questioning, which also put him under great pressure. Sheremetev had to suspend his verification of the Ambartsumyan case for almost a month because of the trade official's bad health. According to Sheremetev, it was difficult in November and December 1985 to obtain precise information from Ambartsumyan since he suffered from memory loss and was unable to confirm past testimonies; oftentimes his testimony undermined what he had previously affirmed. Many of Ambartsumyan's allegations involved the distribution of food delicacies to officials during the 1970s. Given that he was ill, it was difficult for him to provide precise answers to questions that required him to remember things from more than ten years in the past. For instance, some of the details expected of him were the time of day he met a certain person, the color of his or her pants, or a description of the location where they met. Ambartsumyan admitted to Sheremetev that he had given Kolomeitsev a package of delicacies for the amount of three thousand rubles. In June 1984, however, he had paid another sum, this time thirty-six hundred rubles. In this case and in others, even if the investigators put in a lot of effort, it was not always sufficient to lend credibility to someone's testimony, considering that the distinction between a gift and a bribe when dealing with food baskets is rather blurred. Another weakness of Ambartsumyan's testimony was that his statements also repeated what other witnesses had said about certain officials accused of bribery. Sheremetev's main point was that Ambartsumyan was motivated by personal interest and was ready to testify indiscriminately to avoid execution. He added

the qualification that "considering that [Ambartsumyan] is sentenced to death, he bears no responsibility for giving false testimony."[76]

Although Sheremetev never mentioned Oleinik, he indirectly attacked him and his brigade when he claimed that Ambartsumyan was ready to say anything that would please the investigators. At this time, Oleinik was criticized for his investigation methods and his role in the anticorruption campaign launched by the KGB in 1983. His detractors, mostly the reformists, attempted to limit the influence of the KGB and its supporters, particularly Oleinik. Oleinik had managed to gather incriminating evidence against numerous highly placed officials of the trade organizations, but he lacked evidence implicating senior officials of the Party and the state. In fact, he had not been able to accumulate enough evidence to bring leaders of the Moscow Party, including Grishin, to court at all. What Oleinik and the KGB needed most during this period was evidence against high-profile officials in the Party and the government, and Ambartsumyan was one of the rare detainees who could deliver it. Sheremetev did everything he could to undermine Ambartsumyan's credibility, harping on the major offenses he had committed for so long as a food depot manager. He also insisted that Ambartsumyan had made false declarations in 1986 when the latter suddenly revealed that he knew several high-ranking Party and government officials who were involved in bribery and that he would give all the pertinent details if his death sentence were commuted. Although he disclosed the identities of a few of these top officials, Ambartsumyan could not produce any solid evidence corroborating his denunciations. Sheremetev finally made the point that the glaring weakness in Ambartsumyan's testimony was that it was unlikely that he would have or could have withheld such supposedly significant evidence during three years of detention and interrogation.[77] Sheremetev concluded that this last argument invalidated the whole body of Ambartsumyan's testimony. Sheremetev's report, issued in March 1986, countered the brigade's request to continue investigating the detainees' cases by stating that Ambartsumyan's testimonies lacked precision and coherence. In addition, the request that the death sentence be commuted was denied.

Sheremetev's report confirmed the new orientation of the Prosecutor General's Office. He had accepted Ambartsumyan's testimony when it concerned bribe-taking by Glavka leaders and other high-level Moscow trade executives but not when it concerned highly placed Party and government officials. He agreed with the PGO's new bosses that the brigade's mandate was limited to investigations inside the Moscow trade organizations, and therefore inquiring about Party or ministry officials was out of the question. Sheremetev had to choose between the rights of the third parties who had been denounced in interrogations and court testimony and the rights of the detainees and witnesses. By undermining

the credibility of the indicted individuals, Sheremetev sided with the high-level officials. The verification of the brigade's investigation methods meant focusing on the sensitive issue of civil rights; it also meant defending the interests of the nomenklatura, which had been threatened by accusations of corruption. This approach was not new with respect to the past: the law enforcement agencies would not change their politics to avoid charging upper-echelon officials. The Ambartsumyan case was similar to that of Sokolov. It was out of the question that a high-ranking executive should be able to compromise representatives of the nomenklatura. The case was thus viewed as an attempt to defame the Communist Party and, therefore, it was a serious offense. The officials Ambartsumyan accused may not have been the most important ones, but approval of the brigade's investigations would encourage a further search for testimony, and if high-echelon officials were charged, they would likely expose still others who had colluded with them. Thus, if the anticorruption campaign continued to expand, it would reach higher levels.

Sheremetev's recommendation that Ambartsumyan be executed without delay was thus well received by the PGO, which felt that the Ambartsumyan case had gone on long enough and should end soon. However, the PGO quickly realized that Sheremetev's report did not allow any leeway for a change in Ambartsumyan's sentence, and it then decided to make certain concessions in his case. It deferred his execution until a last chance could be given to the brigade to discover irrefutable evidence against Party and government representatives. This last delay gave the brigade until the end of September to complete the inquest on Ambartsumyan.[78] The PGO agreed to let investigators focus on the gifts received by the higher-level officials of the Party, the state, and the police. The police would gather testimony against the higher-level officials, especially those living in Moscow. In addition, prosecutors sought authorization to confront Ambartsumyan and Kolomeitsev, a manager for the office overseeing the importation of food products into the Soviet Union.   This delay in the Ambartsumyan case did not help to minimize friction within the ranks of the PGO. The confrontation between Kolomeitsev and Ambartsumyan confirmed that the former, via the latter's utterances, had received bribes from the latter; accusations were also made regarding the excesses committed by the leaders of the Moscow Party Committee. However, Kolomeitsev did not divulge any infractions or the names of highly ranked leaders. Moreover, he denied all of Ambartsumyan's accusations. Ambartsumyan had also revealed the names of many officials in his districts (Dzerchinski and Babushkin districts) who had received baskets of scarce food items. These accusations revealed two weaknesses in the case. First, providing the gift baskets as bribes was contestable; this practice had long existed among the nomenklatura. A second weakness was that these accusations mostly

concerned officials of two of the Party's Moscow districts. This type of excess on the local level was already known and of less interest to the prosecutor, who expected the brigade to unveil, as promised, proof against higher-echelon officials, especially those of the Moscow Party Committee. It is true that Ambartsumyan revealed the identity of certain highly placed managers of the ministries of Trade and of Agriculture and of the national office for importing food products.[79]

In his confrontation with Kolomeitsev, Ambartsumyan describes the unacceptable behavior of highly placed officials; the value of this testimony in court remains questionable, however. Ambartsumyan alluded to the gifts given to high-level officials, but his accusations appeared too vague to serve as conclusive evidence once presented to the courts. His most sensational declaration was to accuse the officials of the Moscow Party Committee of corruption: "At the fruit and vegetable office in the Dzerzhinski borough, extortion came from upstairs: you had to give to the Moscow Party Committee: you had to give here and there; you had to give to Glavtorg; you had to give to Glavmosplodovoshprom. The result of all this was that I became the scapegoat: they have to execute me to re-establish order in the trade networks."[80] Here, however, Ambartsumyan did not divulge any names, nor did he make a precise accusation. This was his most serious accusation of all, the one that could have been a determining factor for his execution. As a matter of fact, his general denunciation attacking the Party looked slanderous and demonstrated, as even Sheremetev was aware, that Ambartsumyan was prepared to do anything to avoid being executed.

The outcome of the Ambartsumyan case was a victory for the PGO and a defeat for the KGB. The brigade assembled by the KGB sought to continue the anticorruption campaign, but a central question divided the law enforcement agencies. The brigade, and the KGB behind it, after having carried out its task of convicting the leaders of the trade organizations, now wanted, in a second stage, to direct its investigations toward the Party and government officials who had been denounced by the trade executives. The PGO objected to this however and decided to abolish the brigade despite opposition from the KGB. The PGO did, however, give Oleinik a final chance to find evidence against high-ranking officials, which is why it accepted the confrontation between Ambartsumyan and Kolomeitsev. Ultimately, the PGO was convinced that a continuation of the investigations would produce many accusations but little evidence to support them. Prior to 1986, the conflicts between the PGO, the brigade, and the KGB never appeared in public. But in 1987, the PGO criticized the leaders of the brigade for having overstepped their authority: they had accomplished their task of investigating the Moscow trade network, but they did not have the mandate to extend their inquiry to Party and government circles. It was a setback for the KGB; it lost its main support in the PGO after Oleinik was forced to resign.

The Mobilization of Intellectuals against the KGB

Communist Party officials hoped they could continue to avoid the focus of the anticorruption campaign as they had in the past, and until the end of 1985, very few Party representatives were accused of corruption. In 1986, however, this state of affairs changed when the anticorruption brigade proposed to check up on trade employees' testimony regarding wrongdoing by Party officials and high-level officials in ministries. Rumors circulated in Party circles that the brigade already possessed considerable evidence regarding certain Party leaders. The KGB agents had gathered a significant amount of information on abuses by apparatchiks, but they were persuaded that trade executives knew much more on the subject than they had indicated so far. For the above reasons, the Party feared the KGB. Party officials realized that they might well have to endure the same fate as the thousands of trade employees against whom charges had been laid. They wanted to take initiatives to stop the KGB before it was too late. Certain measures had to be taken, but the priority was putting an end to the crackdown.

One consequence of what occurred after 1982 was that the KGB's influence could still increase if Party and trade leaders did not find some other source of support in Russian society. The Party was not, at that time, in an optimistic frame of mind regarding Gorbachev. The new secretary general had not yet established his authority with respect to the conservatives in Moscow represented by Grishin and who dominated at every level of the Party organization. Gorbachev's authority was weak; he had defeated Grishin by only a narrow majority, and the conservatives still dominated the lower echelons of the Party. From 1982 to 1985, Andropov and Gorbachev made frequent staff changes in the Party, replacing incompetent and corrupt personnel with conservative and morally sound newcomers. While these newcomers mostly wanted to undermine the Grishinists, they occasionally attempted to impose their point of view on Gorbachev.

Gorbachev worked with conservatives close to the KGB in his first year at the Kremlin and implemented some policies inspired by their approach. The Party prioritized respect for the law as its primary means of solving the main problems in society. After Andropov took office in the Kremlin, tighter control was exercised on workers, and there was a crackdown on wrongdoing in factories; even the consumption of alcohol was frowned on and drunkenness was punished. Thus, a new impetus was given to the anticorruption campaign. All of these policies were marked by a central goal: to establish law and order in society as a precondition for stimulating its development. However, it was already clear by late 1985 that these policies had not produced the desired outcome: the conservative policies Gorbachev had implemented had caused a stir, but he needed to consider other methods. He turned toward new policies that were inspired, this time, by a reformist approach.

Gorbachev had no choice but to find support in another group. He chose the intelligentsia because it was relatively easy to rally this group to his cause. Gorbachev did not want to appoint people with convictions similar to those of his enemies in the Party, and the intellectuals could provide what he was looking for. We usually associate Gorbachev with the intelligentsia because of his inclination for reform and liberalization, but other factors brought Gorbachev closer to the intellectuals. The crackdown on the trade network in the mid-1980s was determinant in the intelligentsia's attitude toward the Kremlin: many intellectuals went further than simply expressing sympathy for the threatened trade staff, and the two groups established close links during the Brezhnev era.

During this time, the trade executives began to seek support in the media. Already in the 1970s, they had paid journalists to write articles favorable to them. According to the Prosecutor General's Office, "Criminality began to exercise pressure on the media during the 1970s. The price varied from 10,000 to 20,000 rubles for each published article."[81]

The two groups also exchanged favors. A certain number of intellectuals earned high salaries and had the opportunity to travel abroad. They were therefore able to buy scarce products on the black market. In the 1970s, the prestigious Dom Kino bar and restaurant, reserved for filmmakers and actors, counted many trade employees among its clients. In return, it received goods from grocery stores in the form of orders sent to cultural organizations for holidays and receptions. The trade organizations had used this practice to increase their support in society, but as an experiment, at the beginning of the 1980s, Glavtorg leaders tested the waters by sending newspaper editors, television and radio station managers, and theater directors innovative orders of products—packages that would normally have been too expensive to deliver to most members of the intelligentsia. This tactic on the part of trade leaders to reinforce their support among the intelligentsia was a response to the KGB's success in recruiting certain journalists to support their fight against corruption in the late 1970s. The most illustrious representatives of Glavtorg were solicited to supply influential members of the intelligentsia. Sokolov was the best known of the trade executives involved in this scheme; he became very popular among those receiving the favors because he supplied his special clients with their preferred delicacies. Sokolov implemented the policies of his superiors, who were less interested in satisfying the needs of the population than in giving priority service to the groups who could promote their interests.

Literaturnaya Gazeta related a typical case of these deliveries during the Brezhnev era. A reporter from this newspaper accompanied a Moscow Trade Department inspector on a visit to the Eliseevski *gastronom* after receiving letters

from Muscovites complaining about corruption in the store. The inspection of a few "special delivery" packages disclosed food products that had been in short supply for many years. These special deliveries were destined for people working for the Moscow soviet, newspapers, and film production houses. The day before the article was supposed to appear, the newspaper received telephone calls from leaders of the Moscow soviet and prestigious journalists, as well as other representatives of the media, asking that the article not be published. Sokolov's protectors won the day and the article was never printed.[82]

Some members of the intelligentsia were able to improve their living conditions thanks to the trade executives, but the same cannot be said for the KGB. The media gave an edge to the trade staff, projecting a favorable image of this group, while the trade executives provided services and scarce products in return.

The intellectuals were conscious that the KGB's battle against corrupt trade executives could provide a pretext for increasing the limitations and even the repression of the intelligentsia. The evolution of the campaign and the KGB's arrest of thousands of employees increased their apprehension. Worse, even after large numbers of trade employees were indicted in 1986, the KGB, through the brigade leaders, asserted that the crackdown on the Moscow trade network would be intensified, and it criticized the insufficient number of agents assigned to the investigation. Certain members of the intelligentsia who were implicated in economic crimes imagined that their turn to face justice would come soon. Other intellectuals had no fear of being indicted for this kind of irregularity, but as dissidents, they had been harassed more than once by the KGB. They knew that certain prosecutors leading the anticorruption campaign had been appointed for their record of zeal and brutality against dissidents in the past. Intellectuals feared the KGB more than any other organization; while it had not played a role as sinister as it had in the days of Beria before 1953, it was still the principal agency that limited and violated civil rights. The KGB, not the Party, decided whether people could obtain visas to go abroad or move from one part of the country to another. More importantly, the KGB had free rein regarding any sign of opposition to the Soviet system. Among the citizens hostile to KGB, a significant number were descendants of the millions murdered by Beria and other KGB leaders. Most of them had been quiet and obedient, sometimes even conservative, but deep inside their minds, resentment toward the KGB was still alive.

The intellectuals had to devise a strategy that maximized their chances of success. The promotion of freedom was the best tactic to unite and mobilize the intelligentsia, as most of them were in favor of individual civil rights. Concretely, they wanted guarantees against charges by the police, and they spent much effort and energy to achieve this. Their goal was to weaken the KGB's role in society as

much as possible, and the battle with the KGB was seen as a fight for democracy. The insistence on individual freedoms implied that Soviet society suffered a deficit in this area and that it was a priority to improve it. Very few people objected to this ideal, and liberalization suited the interests of the trade staff above all. In the mid-1980s, the timing was good to fight for a broadening of individual rights and for the victims of repression, and the trade executives were positioned to be the main beneficiaries of this situation.

The trade executives found it difficult to defend themselves against accusations of corruption in 1982–1983. The judges showed bias toward the prosecutors, but in any case, the defense of the suspects was almost an impossible mission, even if the trials had been fair. Much of the evidence was obtained by unacceptable methods; however, numerous written declarations against trade leaders did exist, including damning confessions by the detainees themselves. Moreover, the trade executives could hardly refute the charges of corruption because, in truth, many of them had committed serious violations of the law. This impasse lasted from 1982 to 1985, not only because the rights of the suspects were not respected but also because the suspects made mistakes during their own defense. In 1985, the defense strategy changed substantially when it began to stress the infringement of the suspects' civil rights instead of the nature of the accusations. This reorientation in arguments for the defense of the trade executives constituted a turning point. It became an offensive based on attacking and undermining the KGB, presenting it as a dangerous enemy of freedom. A number of cases regarding the security force's disrespect for the individual rights of trade employees were disclosed to the public.

Gorbachev and other Party leaders backed the executives and their superiors who criticized the infringement of civil rights by the KGB. They encouraged people to denounce practices such as imprisoning executives for long periods of time without trial and preventing inmates from seeing their relatives or lawyers. The death penalty for bribery was no longer viewed as acceptable. More importantly, the idea that trade executives had simply accepted gifts instead of what the prosecution defined as bribes became more acceptable. Giving free packages of delicacies to government, media, and Party officials on holidays may still have been viewed as morally reprehensible, but it was no longer enough, from a legal point of view, to charge executives with economic crimes. Moreover, most of the cases of bribery disclosed in public appeared to involve people who had been subjected to extortion by high officials. Evidence given by detainees who agreed to testify against high-profile suspects in return for promises of freedom was no longer accepted. Testimony of low credibility was also denounced by the media; nevertheless, it was still accepted by the judges in certain cases.

Criticism of the KGB spread from the Kremlin to the media in a move in-

tended to rally public opinion. It was a key element of Gorbachev's strategy to seek support from civil society; he counted on the force of public opinion when dealing with the KGB. Journalists were the principal beneficiaries of this development, with the media gaining influence during the period of liberalization. Criticism of the security force increased in intensity in articles on the violation of civil rights, with some journalists going so far as to accuse the KGB of cruelty. New reasons were found to criticize the security force, and soon, no domain was immune from attack. It was not long before the KGB's competence was under fire. Under Andropov, the KGB had maintained a reputation of effectiveness, even among its detractors, but now, newspapers reported on cases in which the wrong person had been convicted and published stories of people sentenced to long terms in labor camps on false testimony. One newspaper article reported that an MVD police official, falsely accused of corruption, had been obliged to go into hiding for years in order to avoid imprisonment. Another instance that came to light was the case of an MVD boss in the Irkutsk region who had been suspected of corruption; for several months, he was the object of harassment by security forces.[83] He was dismissed from his job and subjected to multiple interrogations and strong pressure to confess. Other newspaper articles on the KGB's misconduct built up the impression that the security force must be subjected to strict societal control of its activities. Finally, during perestroika, the denunciation of the KGB's crimes during the Stalin period became a hot topic in the media.

The Moscow trade staff did not remain passive in the face of repression by the KGB. Trade leaders initially used their Party connections to resist, but the Party was weakened by divisions in its leadership, including conflicts over the anticorruption campaign. Due to other factors, the Party's reformist wing, headed by Gorbachev, who began to dominate the Communist Party in 1985, took a favorable stand toward the trade staff. However, Gorbachev and his team did not have the authority to impose their views on the KGB at that time, and, consequently, the trade executives had to appeal to other forces for help. They needed allies in the judiciary and especially from the Ministry of the Interior, an organization that dealt with legality in general and with violations of the law in the trade agencies in particular. The MVD did help the accused trade employees, but this assistance was not sufficient to halt the crackdown. A third force provided major assistance to trade staff, although, again, it was not decisive. The leaders of the Prosecutor General's Office, contrary to those of the Ministry of the Interior, had not been corrupted, and their opposition to the anticorruption campaign derived from the pressure of the Communist Party's liberal faction. The main motivation of the PGO, however, was its hostility toward the KGB's actions to control it. In

weakening the KGB's authority, the PGO also helped the cause of the trade staff. It is clear that the trade leaders' problems could not have been solved through the intermediary of the PGO alone. Without the help of the intelligentsia and the media, the balance of power in society could not have shifted in a direction that was advantageous to trade staff. The change was marked by the release of several incarcerated former trade employees, by the withdrawal of charges against many of their colleagues, and even by changes in the criminal law. The trade leaders were able to checkmate the KGB's anticorruption campaign because of the support of all these forces.

Conclusion
Changes in the Moscow Trade Organizations

■ The nomination of Andropov to be leader of the Communist Party in 1982 was a clear sign that the KGB had regained a level of power in the Soviet political system that it had not had since the 1930s. The security force's influence had increased during the 1970s, primarily through its battle against lawbreakers—speculators and smugglers, among others—a battle in which, by Soviet standards, the KGB was successful. These operations enlarged the KGB's responsibilities, particularly when it was mandated to remove corrupt senior leaders and expose the "caviar mafia" in the southern Caucasus. The KGB enhanced its image in society during that decade by presenting itself as a force dedicated to ensuring the implementation of Soviet law. It focused on the principle that everyone is equal before the law and that all citizens are accountable for their actions. By 1982, the KGB was in charge of applying this norm and punishing transgressors, whatever their position in society might be. The principle was important to the KGB, which presented itself as the only organization in the country that could successfully fight corruption.

This study focuses on Moscow because the dominant faction of the nomenklatura and the greatest concentration of resources in the Soviet Union were found in the capital. The central state apparatus in Moscow determined the allocation of resources for the whole country. The capital was also a place where the demand for goods was harder to meet, because it was where the political elite, with their more cosmopolitan tastes, lived and had to compete with other elites for the same scarce goods. For these reasons, corruption existed on a large scale in Moscow, but although regions such as Krasnodar and Rostov also experienced high rates of corruption, data for those areas were not as complete or as accessible as the data for Moscow, and the original sources could not be consulted. Nonetheless, this study shows that the major difference between Moscow and the regions was that in the capital, the leaders of the central power and the security services in particular were generally less tolerant toward corruption than their counterparts in other regions.

The launching of an anticorruption campaign—enforcing the rule of equality before the law, which was being flouted—was an enterprise that would clearly

pay political dividends, widening the KGB's influence in the political system. The challenge was huge: punishing the authors of infractions at the upper echelons meant attacking the elite. It was not certain that the KGB could win against the group that controlled the resources and could therefore put up the strongest resistance.

The phenomenon of corruption can be explained in different ways. It was perceived by many Communist Party officials as the major cause of food shortages in the internal trade network, and therefore, the Party was hoping that the KGB could significantly improve the situation. The KGB provided the Party with information that gave credibility to its assumption that corruption was the main cause of the problem. Moreover, by allowing the KGB a free hand to tackle corruption, the Party could disclaim responsibility if the operation failed. If, as both these organizations believed, corruption was a major cause of the problems in the distribution of resources in the Soviet Union, especially in the area of food, it was also a consequence of those same problems. The latter view is widespread among scholars, but, of course, it was unacceptable to the Kremlin. It was necessary to find another explanation that did not discredit the Soviet system and would hide the real causes of the shortcomings in the trade sector.

Did KGB leaders fabricate the urgency for an anticorruption campaign with the aim of enhancing their political influence? Whatever we may think of this suggestion, it remains true that in 1980, corruption preoccupied many people in Soviet society. Some members of the nomenklatura deplored the fact that corruption was so widespread that it posed a threat to the power of the state. Consumers were frustrated by the shortages in stores. Even some dissidents pointed to corruption as society's primary problem. These groups were not opposed to the anticorruption campaign, at least not in its initial stage, although the fact that the campaign was spearheaded by the KGB did not make for unanimity. The majority of Soviet citizens supported the principle of punishing lawbreakers, irrespective of their rank.

The KGB's operations should be appraised objectively. This book emphasizes the zeal and abuses in the KGB's actions with numerous examples and illustrations, but it should be pointed out that the KGB under Andropov was very different from the KGB under Beria. The severity of the methods of KGB agents in 1983 was undeniable, but there is little evidence that trade employees were victims of torture; the suspects who made such accusations were few and far between and were not always reliable. Only two executives were sentenced to death. Among the trade executives who were given long-term sentences that were considered equivalent to the death penalty, several were released a few years later under perestroika. The KGB rarely went after the relatives of the accused in the trade network, even when it had gathered considerable evidence against them. The

indicted persons kept the apartments they had acquired in relation to their jobs. For instance, Ambartsumyan, the director of the Dzerzhinski fruit and vegetable depot, was sentenced to death on corruption charges, but his family remained in possession of the sumptuous apartment he had received because of his position.

In some ways, the KGB agents obtained impressive results in their campaign by amassing evidence on thousands of employees and putting many of them behind bars. It was a confirmation of Russian public opinion. By the end of 1983, KGB data, including proof against the heads of the trade network, indicated that corruption extended to so many levels that it effectively posed a threat to the Soviet system. The KGB used the media to provide maximum coverage of the campaign and of wrongdoing by corrupt employees to confirm the widespread nature of corruption in the trade agencies. The revelation of corruption's rampant expansion was justification for the KGB's renewed authority to combat it and for the KGB's expanding role in the political system.

Indeed, the campaign promoted the image of the KGB as an efficient organization devoted to respect for the law and capable of hunting down those who broke it whatever their rank; the campaign also legitimatized the KGB's incursion into the trade network, a domain outside its jurisdiction. Nonetheless, while Andropov's KGB was not as repressive as that of Beria, its anticorruption activities engendered a certain amount of opposition. The fear was that through the acquisition of additional prerogatives, the security services would revert to what it had been in the 1930s.

The KGB's anticorruption operations were to be carried out in two steps. The first was to indict a large number of trade employees at different levels. The rate of convictions of staff at higher levels was much lower than for those of the lower echelons of Glavtorg. Facing increasing difficulty in compromising the trade organizations' leaders, the KGB claimed that these executives were being protected by high-ranking officials and that it therefore needed to widen its investigations. Obtaining a mandate to pursue its operations beyond the trade network was the second step the KGB hoped to take, and it would constitute a turning point in the strategy. However, before long, the balance of power in society changed, the supporters of the KGB being supplanted in influence by its opponents. While the victims of corruption sympathized with the KGB, its opponents, although less numerous, were extremely influential. The KGB had the advantage over the trade network through its monopoly over violent means and its role of law enforcer, but the trade staff held the trump cards through its connections in the media and in state structures. The nomenklatura felt threatened by the anticorruption campaign, and the KGB's plan to expand the crackdown beyond the trade sphere exacerbated those fears. Party officials had not been affected by this type of campaign in the past and thus had not opposed them. But in the 1980s, the

nomenklatura had no alternative but to counterattack. For the first time since the Stalinist era, Party officials, although they were not indicted, were being interrogated and harassed

The main tool the trade executives used to defend their interests was their network. The KGB's attack on the trade staff and their cronies united the network as never before. Trade leaders had supporters in important nerve centers: the different law enforcement agencies, the Party, and certain ministries. The most supportive officials were those who received bribes, but there were also plenty of partisans who received gifts, promotions, awards, or other favors. These supporters were present in all sectors of society, including customers who bought scarce products at the official price but without waiting in line.

The network comprised high-echelon trade executives of varying levels of importance, starting with those who might be categorized as charismatic leaders. They had risen to the top and held their influential positions due to their political skills. Tregubov, Sokolov, Ambartsumyan, Eremeev, and others were renowned for their astute decisions in the appointment of personnel. They had implemented a number of internal trade policies that had made them popular with their staffs and among certain groups in society. They were masters in the arts of communicating and persuading, and they knew how to win support from influential people who were impressed by their personalities. These charismatic executives were viewed as exceptional managers and even humanists. They took money, but they did so only to improve the performances of their stores rather than for personal benefit. The second category of individuals in the trade officials' network was the rational-legal executives, who took Soviet law seriously and, overall, respected it. They were close to Communist Party officials through the exchange of mutual advantages, offering gifts to officials and occasionally accepting favors from them, not for self-enrichment but mostly because it was such a deeply rooted habit in Russian society. This category was the weakest in terms of influence, especially in the late 1970s, when corruption was increasingly tolerated. The neopatrimonial executives, who constituted the third category of individuals in the trade network, differed from the charismatic and rational-legal leaders in that personal enrichment was their principal motivation. They possessed all the characteristics of one who maintains a traditional dominance in relation to others. Their authority was not limited by the law, and they acted according to their personal interests. They considered the store or trade organization as their private property, and their management style was to favor certain groups and to cultivate support through nepotism and clientelism. However, these executives were not strictly patrimonial but also behaved in conformity with the law. For example, while store directors might pocket a significant sum of state money, they were well aware that the rest of the money and resources had

to be allocated legally, and they generally respected these norms in managing their stores. This category of high-echelon executive recruited their relatives or their accomplices for higher positions, but they also hired competent candidates at different levels. The majority of the executives in the Moscow network were neopatrimonial leaders deeply involved in corruption.

Networks are like the *matrioshka,* the famous Russian doll, often being interconnected. The network had existed for a long time in Russia, even prior to the Soviet system, but it was in the Brezhnev era that it truly flexed its muscles, and nowhere was this as evident as in the Moscow trade organizations. The network's strength lay in its vertical axis, with bribe-takers at the top and bribe-givers at the bottom. The horizontal axis was also crucial, consisting of support from different organizations, particularly those of the Communist Party. The network favored certain Party organs, augmenting their influence tremendously. To give one example, the Party Department for Trade and Maintenance acquired a progressively dominant position through its influence on the distribution of resources. Its members were favored in the quantity of products received, and they wielded decisive power in the allocation of goods. A sign of the trade leaders' power in this aspect of the network was that they often chose the heads of this Party organ.

At the beginning of the 1980s, the trade network boosted its power through the disposal of a surplus of resources that it generated in different ways. It took some of these resources from ministries, a practice that did not conform to the law. Supervisors believed staff members when they claimed that the illicit resources had actually been wasted due to negligence. Another way of obtaining extra resources was to give awards to those executives who supposedly performed well at their jobs; these awards were usually accompanied by resources. A third way was for supervisors to take bribes from employees who wanted preferred treatment.

The network invested money to build up trust among its members. Additional resources were used to multiply the occasions for trade staff to meet during the 1970s, with parties organized to celebrate the successes of employees or stores. Since the network in Moscow was considered the best in the country, there were many pretexts for holding celebratory meetings to congratulate trade staff and make their successes known. The money was invested mainly to raise trade leaders' influence at the top political levels. A huge amount of money was directed toward providing services such as housing for high-ranking officials. Trade leaders were continuously investing money to find new ways to please the top officials of the country.

The network continued to expand until 1982, when the KGB took steps to curtail it. Trade personnel had to elaborate changes in their strategy with respect to the evolving situation during the 1980s, which began with the transition from

the Brezhnev era to the Andropov regime. This shift necessitated modifying the approach to the KGB and to Party leaders. The KGB's anticorruption campaign prepared the ground for the trade leaders' later defense strategy in which they argued that the KGB had abused its authority and violated the trade leaders' civil rights during interrogation and detention.

The KGB started the process of disparaging the Communist Party in 1983–1984, even though the arrests of apparatchiks were rare at that time. KGB agents denounced the view that Communist Party officials were above the law and encouraged the media to criticize them, which caused those officials to find themselves in a vulnerable situation with respect to the KGB. The Party was divided whereas the KGB was not; it was harder to identify liberals and reformers in the security force than in Party ranks.

Thus, the trade staff changed its strategy toward the Party when the latter began to decline in influence. Trade leaders wanted to replace the Brezhnev-Grishin leadership with one that would be more attentive to their interests. Their close relations with the Party and the favors granted to Party representatives had enabled the trade leaders to avoid repression for a lengthy period, with a guarantee of impunity for them despite their involvement in corruption. This period ended in 1982 with Andropov's ascendancy at the Kremlin, and it was followed by the indictment of thousands of members of the trade staff. The Party officials who had colluded with trade personnel did not prevent the massive crackdown on the latter. Certain Party leaders had lost their power, and indeed, being acquainted with them could only make the trade executives' situation worse. A few of the officials who still occupied their posts attempted to rescue their colleagues in the trade organizations. Some officials promised to put pressure on the law enforcement agencies or take other initiatives, but they noted that circumstances were not favorable at the time. When officials did intercede, the result was often unexpectedly discouraging, and the trade executives came to the conclusion that the old methods—giving favors and offering bribes—were no longer efficacious; high-ranking officials made themselves scarce when corrupt practices became risky. Moreover, the amounts of the bribes to be paid rose sharply during this same period.

The reserve of social capital in the trade network trickled away during these years. Trust and cooperation that had been built up over the years was seriously eroded by the KGB investigations. Allegiances and loyalties were put into question or were reversed. Suspicion took the place of trust when many employees and executives were forced to cooperate with the KGB; treachery and denunciations predominated over cooperation in the food stores. The crackdown hit the network hard. It started with the elimination of the charismatic leaders at the top echelons of Glavtorg and Glavka, with the consequence that by 1984, the

trade network had lost several of its most competent leaders. Without its most dynamic elements, the network began disintegrating.

Going on the offensive was revealed to be the best defense for arrested trade executives: they emphasized the Party's and even the KGB's role in corruption and revealed the extortive practices of Communist officials toward them as the primary cause of bribery. During perestroika, the latter issue became the preferred plea the trade executives' lawyers offered in court. A second key point in the defense of trade executives concerned the tribute or gifts given to Party officials on holidays; these accusations were controversial because Soviet law is rather vague regarding these offenses. Moreover, the judiciary was supportive of the Communist officials in question, considering that in the past, such accusations did not often lead to convictions. But what had been previously viewed as gifts offered to Party leaders were now, under perestroika, perceived as bribes. The accusations launched in 1985 and afterward were highly effective in political terms, contributing significantly to the undermining of the Communist Party's legitimacy.

During perestroika, Soviet trade underwent a long period of agony, leading to the end of the state monopoly and the leading role of the Party. Dominant forces in society were active in this process, including the trade staff, which, after having taken advantage of the Soviet system, turned against it in reaction to the anticorruption campaign and publicly blamed the system for promoting wrongdoing in the stores. The crackdown on corruption in the Moscow trade organizations produced a frenzy of charges, detentions, and gathering of evidence, all of which discredited the Soviet economy. Paradoxically, the KGB's operation was also detrimental to itself, due to the abuses committed by its prosecutors. Moreover, along with the KGB's excesses, its "successes" as it delved into the activities of the nomenklatura provoked mounting hostility and fear. During perestroika, it became a priority to weaken the role of the state, including the law enforcement agencies, with respect to the economy. In particular, there was the assumption that the KGB had gone too far into areas outside its jurisdiction, notably in its crusade against corruption in the trade organizations. The outcome was that during perestroika, the trade sector increasingly escaped control and regulation by the organs of the Soviet system. Gradually, the Soviet economy was freed from the domination of state and Party, even though the economy did not become a free one as a result.

During perestroika, the defense pleas of trade leaders and their partisans were based on the rule of law. This emphasis on the supremacy of law was set in contrast to the civil rights violations by the police. The KGB's abusive investigative methods were seen as a legacy of the practices of the Stalin era, and critics pointed to the whole history of repression by the KGB. As early as 1986,

the media began reporting many cases of the suspension of individual rights by the state, thus broadcasting a negative image of the police. The denunciation of repression concerned political and religious freedoms, but it soon extended to other spheres of society. It was inevitable that trade leaders would use this situation to their advantage. Some points of view emerged in the press and in the declarations of certain political leaders creating a rapprochement between politics and the economy, acknowledging that there were grounds for dissidence in the latter domain as well as in the former, that the laws governing the Soviet economy were repressive, and that the trade employees indicted for corruption were actually victims of repression, condemned for actions that would be legitimate in a market economy. The intelligentsia had good motives for endorsing the trade staff's position. Applying this principle of the rule of law to the economy implied a privatized, market-run system, instead of an economy run by the state and the politicians. Also, if the KGB observed the letter of the law, its functions would be strictly limited to security. Thus, on the matter of the application of the law, the intelligentsia and the trade staff had convergent points of view. In the confrontation between conservatives and liberals between 1985 and 1987, the intelligentsia welcomed any group that strengthened its case.

The liberal camp in this period of perestroika equated the rule of law to respect for the Soviet constitution. Trade staff members and intellectuals in particular emphasized respect for Soviet law. It had been unusual in the Soviet Union to call for lawbreakers inside the law enforcement agencies to be exposed to public censure. A new era began in which members of the law enforcement agencies were to be treated like any other group in society and would be held accountable for their actions. Reading the Moscow print media at that time, one got the impression that the representatives of the judiciary were, more often than not, respecting the law. The Kremlin's sensitivity toward the law was not exclusively intended to discredit the authors of the anticorruption campaign, but doing so was surely one of its main objectives. The review of the cases of many convicted trade executives did not often lead to lighter sentences, but the investigative methods and court proceedings were criticized. This insistence on respect for the law led to serious consequences.

The staff changes, which had begun with Andropov's ascendancy in the Kremlin, continued after 1985 and at all levels, indicating an attempt to correct some of the mistakes made during the Brezhnev era. The most important adjustment occurred within the judiciary: if the changes made during the Andropov era were characterized by the strict application of the law in the stores, after 1985, the new prosecutors and their leaders focused more on respect for the law by the investigators, and the prosecutors themselves, in their work. The new prosecutors of the PGO and the MVD were not as harsh as those who had acted during

the anticorruption campaign; some of them had even been attacked in the past for their lack of firmness. Judges and defense attorneys enjoyed a certain degree of independence; in particular, it was stressed that they should be free from interference by the security service. Of course, the Kremlin did not encourage them to oppose the KGB and the PGO; however, many law enforcement representatives were dismissed at that time for abuses of office under the new leadership of the PGO and MVD.

In this power shift, the city government of Moscow (the Moscow soviet) was the winner with respect to the Party and the police. According to the law, the Moscow soviet was the body authorized to manage Glavtorg. Corruption had seriously undermined the legitimacy of the Party and the KGB with respect to taking the lead in the trade sector. The elite worried about the broadening of the KGB's role and, seeking protection against it, showed a greater commitment to the constitution and more interest in promoting laws that would give greater independence to certain categories of people, including journalists and dissidents and particularly judges, lawyers, and the staff of the Prosecutor General's Office and the Ministry of the Interior who had been subjected to arbitrariness, humiliation, and repression by the KGB. The judiciary had been the institution most invaded and colonized by the KGB between 1982 and 1985, and thus, it could be counted on to work to diminish the KGB's role and influence, thus regaining the influence it had enjoyed prior to 1982. For the trade leaders, the task was to rebuild their network by replacing Party officials and KGB agents with MVD and PGO prosecutors. MVD investigators in particular had been sympathetic to the trade executives; they were more willing to accept bribes or gifts.

There were many losers in the battle for the control of resources during the 1980s. Trade leaders had been the winners before they were attacked and repressed in the 1980s, during the Andropov and Chernenko years; they remained the losers until it was the KGB and the Communist Party's turn to see their authority undermined in 1985 and thereafter. The main winner during perestroika was the Moscow soviet, which filled the vacuum created by the setbacks that hit the Communist Party and the KGB. If we take the Soviet constitution seriously, there is no doubt that the Moscow soviet had the legitimacy to govern. The Communist Party, which had, in fact, governed the city since Stalin's time, was now too discredited to carry out this role in exclusivity. The Moscow soviet represented democracy, while the Communist Party was elected by Party members only. The reputation of the Moscow soviet had remained unassailable throughout the 1980s; the anticorruption campaign had exposed very few cases of its high-ranking officials being involved in major offenses. The anticorruption campaign tended to corroborate the public's view that the staff of the Moscow soviet was relatively honest. Even if this had not been the case, the fact that the campaign's

primary targets were the Party and the law enforcement agencies strengthened the Moscow soviet's position. It was true that the soviet did not play a key role in the capital, and the trade staff paid less attention to it since its support was not so important. The soviet's power was strengthened when Communist Party officials were criticized for their defense of the trade executives accused of corruption. Moreover, many believed that the law enforcement agencies, specifically the KGB, should withdraw from matters that were officially under the jurisdiction of the soviet. Naturally, the Moscow soviet's staff could only be in favor of this development.

The trade network watched the growing importance of the Moscow soviet closely. It needed to boost its relations with the soviet, now that the latter had replaced the Party as the principal political organ to which it was accountable. After years of declining influence, the trade leaders finally had an opportunity to promote their own interests and rebuild the network that had been weakened by the repression and the loss of crucial supporters in the law enforcement agencies and in the Party. It could now regain its previous influence by recruiting newly influential Moscow soviet leaders or by giving more to the soviet employees and executives who were already part of the network. The maneuvering of the trade staff to have a Moscow soviet more amenable to its interests was obvious. The trade organizations had had a conservative political outlook as long as the strategic elements of their network consisted of Party officials; then, when this was no longer the case and they had to select officials from the Moscow soviet as the mainstay of the network, they changed their outlook to harmonize with the prevailing respect for the rule of law. The Moscow soviet, as it had before, offered protection in exchange for money; now, it could do even more, by changing the law, creating non-state companies, and legalizing personal profit.

The trade executives' declarations in favor of the supremacy of the law were based on the defense of their corporatist interests and were related to the fate of the charismatic executives in the trade network. These executives had contributed to development of modern social capital in Soviet society. Their policies and strong personalities had generated trust and cooperation between the Moscow trade staff and the population, and even with the state. Furthermore, the management approach of the charismatic trade executives was, to a certain extent, reform minded; its approach was to destroy that trend that prompted the anticorruption campaign, which had targeted the trade executives as a priority. When the charismatic leaders were crushed, the leadership vacuum was filled by relationships of traditional authority. Another consequence was that the new leadership in the trade network wanted the adoption of laws and measures that would, overall, maximize their benefits. They encouraged every step in this direction. They supported the independence of civil society and the extension of

the rights of individuals and of associations. They also supported the right to criticize. In this period, the promotion of civil rights led to the weakening of the state and an end to its monopoly and its arbitrariness. The trade staff would be in a better position with respect to the state, weakened as it was by the loss of considerable resources and attributes. After the severe repression they had undergone, the trade leaders wanted the state to be as weak as possible.

During the 1980s, the trade executives had faced a harsh crackdown, one that hit certain subgroups harder than others, especially those with roots in the Caucasus. Despite this crackdown, many trade executives were rehabilitated during perestroika. The development of good relations between the internal trade organization leaders and the bosses of the Moscow soviet was not the single factor explaining this rehabilitation: there was also the Caucasus-origin executives' efficient resistance to KGB repression, which ended with their return in force to Moscow. Several of them had been able to hide in the Caucasus, together with their illicit gains, thanks to the unconditional support of their relatives. A further factor that helped them was diminished control in Moscow after the liberalization of the Soviet political system, from 1985 onward. By the beginning of the 1990s, the Caucasus-origin groups occupied dominant positions in the trade network in the capital.

Appendix

Officials Charged with Bribing Deputy Directors of the Administration for Food Product Trade Organizations

Individuals charged with giving Sobolev a total of 86,000 rubles, 1979–1983

Name	Position	Amount taken (rubles)	Data status
Zerchaninov	Deputy director, Kuibishevski RPT	13,300	
Litvin	Deputy director, Kalininski RPT	7,300	
Rakhmanov	Deputy director, Volgogradski RPT	3,600	
Levtonov	Director, Dzerzhinski RPT	1,800	
Sonkin	Deputy director, grocery trade organizations	1,700	
Demkin	Deputy director, Brezhnevski RPT	1,000	
Polishchuk	Director, Union of Perovski univermags	500	
Sokolov	Director, Eliseevski gastronom	500	
Kozlenok	Director, Tushinski RPT	300	Not verified
Maranov	Director, Oktyabrski RPT	900	Not verified
Sidorenko	Vice director, Krasnogvardeiski RPT	2,000	Not verified
Sarkisyan	Director, Brezhnevski RPT	2,400	Not verified
Gilyarov	Director, Krasnogvardeiski RPT	800	
Samokhin	Director, Krasnogvardeiski RPT	200	Not verified
Savinov	Director, store no. 70, Proletarski RPT		Undetermined
Kuzmenko	Director, Volgogradski RPT	300	Not verified
Karasev	Director, store no. 14, Proletarski RPT		Undetermined
Lebedev	Deputy director, Pervomaiski RPT		Undetermined
Sorokin	Director, store no. 81, Proletarski RPT		Undetermined
Ivanov	Deputy director, Baumanski RPT		Undetermined
Belova	Deputy director, Leninski RPT	500	Not verified
Avramich	Deputy director, Tushinski RPT		Undetermined
Valueva	Deputy director, Kirovski RPT	1,500	
Vizhonskii	Deputy director, Frunzenski RPT		Undetermined
Bazhenov	Director, store no. 6, Proletarski RPT		Undetermined
Bronshtein	Director, store no. 16, Proletarski RPT		Undetermined
Drozdov	Director, store no. 12, Proletarski RPT		Undetermined
Gusenkov	Deputy director, Sokol'nicheski RPT	1,400	Not verified
Dorozhkin	Director, store no. 30, Proletarski RPT		Undetermined
Dergachev	Deputy director, Timiriazevski RPT		Undetermined
Zhilochkin	Director, store no. 78, Proletarski RPT		Undetermined
Kotova	Deputy director, Dzerzhinski RPT	4,500	
Lavrov	Deputy director, grocery trade organizations	4,000	
Malyshev	Director, Moskvoretski RPT	3,300	Not verified
Pronin	Deputy director, Krasnopresnenski RPT		Undetermined
Popov	Deputy director, Liublinski RPT		Undetermined
Pronin	Deputy director, Sovetski RPT		Undetermined
Ryazanov	Deputy director, Proletarski RPT	3,100	Not verified

Chukhin	Vice director, Krasnogvardeiski RPT	Undetermined
Shimko	Vice director, Tushinski RPT	Undetermined
Kharchenko	Vice director, Sverdlovski RPT	Undetermined
Filippov	Director, Novoarbatski gastronom	000

Individuals charged with giving Eremeev a total of 42,600 rubles, 1965–1983

Name	Position	Amount taken (rubles)	Data status
Sonkin	Deputy director, grocery trade organizations	3,000	
Levtonov	Director, Dzerzhinski RPT	2,500	
Larionov	Director, grocery trade organizations	600	
Baigelman	Director, Kuibishevski RPT	500	
Smirnov	Director, Voroshilovski RPT	300	
Kotova	Deputy director, Dzerzhinski RPT	300	
Polishchuk	Director, Union of Perovski univermags	300	
Goncharova	Deputy director, Dzerzhinski RPT	150	
Korovkin	Director, grocery trade organizations	100	
Vasilenko	Director, store no. 35, Dzerzhinski RPT	100	Not verified
Volodkin	Director, Leningradski RPT	400	Not verified
Ilin	Director, Sokol'nicheski RPT	200	Not verified
Klimov	Director, Krasnopresnenski RPT	600	Not verified
Kotenkov	Director, Perovski RPT	100	Not verified
Kandichyan	Director, Tushinski RPT	200	Not verified
Lukinov	Director, Babushkinski RPT	500	Not verified
Nemtinov	Director, Oktyabrski RPT	2,000	
Nikonorov	Deputy director, Baumanski RPT	600	Not verified
Nychkin	Director, Babushkinski RPT	100	Not verified
Perov	Deputy store director, vegetable trade organizations	200	Not verified
Peshkov	Director, fish trade organizations	200	Not verified
Sobolev	Director, Proletarski RPT	100	
Seliukov	Director, Gagarinski RPT, former deputy director, Dieta (store no. 45)	200	Not verified
Sorokin	Director, Timiriazevski RPT	800	Not verified
Smirnov	Vice director, vegetable trade organizations	200	Not verified
Tairov	Director, Liublinski RPT	400	Not verified
Tavyrin	Director, Zhdanovski RPT	450	Not verified
Cheliuk	Director, Sebastopolski RPT	300	Not verified
Chumakov	Deputy director, vegetable and fish trade organizations	100	Not verified
Shkodin	Director, vegetable trade organizations	200	Not verified
Shishkov	Director, Kuntsevski RPT	200	Not verified
Shvachkin	Store director, Dzerzhinski RPT	250	Not verified
Tsatskin	Store director, Dzerzhinski RPT	250	Not verified
Valueva	Deputy director, Kirovski RPT	200	Not verified
Gusenkov	Deputy director, Sokol'nicheski RPT	800	Not verified
Kuzmenko	Director, Volgogradski RPT	1,500	Not verified
Kozlenok	Director, Tushinski RPT	300	Not verified
Samokhin	Director, Krasnogvardeiski RPT	300	Not verified
Litvin	Deputy director, Kalininski RPT	250	Not verified
Maranov	Director, Oktyabrski RPT	200	Not verified

Murashko	Director, store no. 4, grocery trade organizations		Undetermined
Malinina	Director, Leninski RPT		Undetermined
Solntsev	Director, meat trade organizations		Undetermined
Sulin	Director, Leninski RPT	300	Not verified
Alekseev	Director, Kuntsevski RPT	300	Not verified
Aleksandrovski	Director, unidentified store, vegetable trade organizations	200	Not verified
Belova	Deputy director, Leninski RPT	100	Not verified
Bondash	Director, Kievski RPT	300	
Borgor	Director, meat trade organizations		Undetermined
Gradov	Director, Perovski RPT	200	Not verified
Gabolaev	Director, store no. 37, vegetable trade organizations	225	Not verified
Semenov	Vostok gastronom	200	Not verified
Malyshev	Deputy director, Moskvoretski RPT	200	Not verified

Source: Spravka po delu o vziatochnichestve v sisteme torgovli g. Moskvy, L. Volk, sledovatel' sledstvenno' brigady prokuratury RSFSR, pp.1–3, GARF, ProkuraturaRSFSR, ugolovnye dela.

Notes

Chapter 1. A Force That Eluded Control

1. N. Khrushchev, *Memoirs* (Moscow, 1971), pp. 84–85, quoted in Vladimir Nekrasov, *Trinadtsat' "zheleznykh narkomov"* (Moscow: Izdatelstvo Verst, 1995), p. 204.

2. See Zhores Medvedev, *Andropov* (Oxford: Basil Blackwell, 1983), p. 66.

3. See Cornelius Castoriadis, *Devant la guerre* (Paris: Fayard, 1981).

4. "At some stage, we placed certain republics, territories, provinces, and cities outside the zone of criticism. In local areas, this led to a situation in which a species of untouchable districts, collective farms, state farms, factories, etc., began to appear." In "Political Report to the Twenty-seventh Congress of the Communist Party," *Pravda,* February 27, 1986, in *Current Digest of the Soviet Press,* March 1986, p. 34.

5. Dennis C. Mueller, ed., *Public Choice II* (Cambridge: Cambridge University Press, 1989), pp. 248–51.

6. W. A. Clark, *Crime and Punishment in Soviet Officialdom: Combating Corruption in the Political Elite* (Armonk, NY: M. E. Sharpe, 1993), p. 29.

7. V. I. Lenin, *Polnoe sobranie sochinenia,* vol. 44, p. 173.

8. K. Jowitt, "Challenging the Correct Line: Reviewing Katherine Verdery's *What Was Socialism and What Comes Next?*" *East European Politics and Society* 12, no. 1 (1998): 96.

9. Max Weber, *Economy and Society* (London, 1989), p. 215. See also Max Weber, *Max Weber on Law in Economy and Society,* ed. Max Rheinstein (Cambridge, MA: Harvard University Press, 1969), pp. 336–37.

10. G. Dolgov, "Gnil," *Kriminal,* no. 1 (1991).

11. Quoted in Y. Seosanov, "Moscow Trade Abuses No Longer Isolated," *Izvestia,* May 30, 1986, quoted in *Current Digest of the Soviet Press,* July 9, 1986, p. 2.

12. Quoted in V. I. Sukhanov, *Sovetskoe pokolenie i Gennadiĭ Ziuganov* (Moscow, 1999), p. 298.

13. See Luc Duhamel, "The Last Campaign against Corruption in Soviet Moscow," *Europe-Asia Studies* 56, no. 2 (2004): 187–213.

14. Zaiavlenie ot podsledstvennogo V. K. Rosliakova nachal'niku Sledstvennogo otdela upravleniia KGB po g. Moskve i Moskovskoĭ oblasti podpolkovniku A. V. Trofimovu (May 15, 1983), p. 1, GARF, Prokuratura RSFSR, ugolovnye dela, delo Mkhitara A. Ambartsumyana.

15. Ibid., p. 2.

16. Zaiavlenie ot podsledstvennogo Mkhitara A. Ambartsumyana, nachal'niku

Sledstvennogo otdela UKGB SSSR po g. Moskve i Moskovskoĭ oblasti A. V. Trofim-
ovu, st. sledovateliu po OVD UKGB po g. Moskve i Moskovskoĭ oblasti V. I. Bunakovu
(June 21, 1983), pp. 8–9, GARF, Prokuratura RSFSR, ugolovnye dela, delo Mkhitara A.
Ambartsumyana.

17. Nicolas Werth, *Histoire de l'Union soviétique* (Paris: Presses Universitaires de
France, 1990), p. 480.

18. Y. Seosanov, "Moscow Trade Abuses No Longer Isolated," *Izvestia,* May 30, 1986,
quoted in *Current Digest of the Soviet Press,* July 9, 1986, p. 2.

19. Ibid.

20. *Moskovskaia Pravda,* April 26, 1977.

21. Spravka, O nekotorykh prichinakh i usloviakh, sposobstvovašhikh razrastaniu
v Moskovskoĭ torgovle prestupnykh posiagatel'stv na sotsialisticheskuiu sobstvennost'
vziatochnichestva, koristnykh zloupotreblenii dolzhnostnym polozheniem v period
1969–1983 godov (July 11, 1986), pp. 4–6.

22. Ibid.

23. *Moskva v tsifrakh* (Moscow, 1984), p. 134.

24. Ibid. At the end of the 1970s, two enormous hotel complexes, Ismailov and Kosmos, were built for the Olympic Games in Moscow. They became strongholds for dealers
of the shadow economy.

25. *Izvestia,* August 4, 1988.

26. *Sotsiologicheskoe Issledovanie,* June–July 1977, pp. 107–14.

27. Mueller, *Public Choice II,* p. 252.

28. Boris Karakhanov, interview by author, Moscow, February 5, 1999.

29. Jaloba v sudebnuiu kollegiiu po ugolovnym delam Verkhovnogo Suda RSFSR,
ot Eremeeva Aleksandra Matveevicha, osuzhdenogo k 4 godam 7 mesiatsam 125 dniam
lishenia svobody, na prigovor Moskovskogo gorodskogo suda (May 6, 1988), p. 3. This
document can be found at the Association for the Defense of Economic Freedom and of
Persons Convicted of Economic Offenses, Moscow.

30. V. Bunakov (KGB investigator in the Ambartsumyan case), interview by author,
Moscow, February 23, 2000.

31. Bunakov said that Ambartsumyan was a very good specialist. Bunakov interview, February 23, 2000. Eremeev reported that KGB agents considered Filippov one of
the best store managers in the trade organizations. Jaloba v sudebnuiu kollegiiu po ugolovnym delam Verkhovnogo Suda RSFSR, ot Eremeeva Aleksandra Matveevicha (May 6,
1988), p. 35.

32. V. Oleinik, interview by author, Moscow, February 10, 1999.

33. Zaiavlenie ot podsledstvennogo Mkhitara A. Ambartsumyana (November 29,
1985), GARF, Prokuratura RSFSR, ugolovnye dela, delo Mhkitara A. Ambartsumyana.

34. Ibid.

35. Anatoly Rubinov, "Soblaznennyĭ i rastreliannyĭ," *Literaturnaya Gazeta,* November 22, 1995.

36. Prigovor sudebnoĭ kollegii po ugolovnym delam Verkhovnogo Suda RSFSR po

delu Tregubova N. P., Petrikova A. A., Khokhlova G. M., Kireeva V. P., i drugikh, delo no. UK PI 85 II, Moscow (September 8, 1986), p. 46.

37. Ibid.

38. Ibid.

39. See Jowitt, "Challenging the Correct Line."

40. *Les rubans du KGB,* documentary film (Montreal: SRC [Canadian Broadcasting Corporation], June 1999).

41. Document on videocassette, from the Russian Prosecutor General's Office (Moscow, 1986), GARF, Prokuratura RSFSR, ugolovnye dela, delo Tregubov, Petrikov, Khokhlov, Kireev, i drugikh, 1986.

42. Rubinov, "Soblaznennyĭ i rastreliannyĭ."

43. Ibid.

44. Sergei Semanov, *Andropov* (Moscow, 2001), p. 264.

45. *Moskovskaia Pravda,* September 14, 1986.

46. Quoted in ibid.

47. From a letter of the Moscow soviet to Tregubov with the resolution "to take necessary actions." Prigovor sudebnoĭ kollegii po ugolovnym delam Verkhovnogo Suda RSFSR po delu Tregubova N. P., Petrikova A. A., Khokhlova G. M., Kireeva V. P., i drugikh (September 8, 1986), p. 10.

48. Oleinik interview, February 10, 1999.

49. Spravka, O nekotorykh prichinakh i usloviakh, sposobstvovavshikh razrastaniiu v moskovskoĭ torgovle prestupnykh posiagatel' stv na sotsialisticheskuiu sobstvennost', vziatochnichestva, koristnykh zloupotreblenii dolzhnostnym polozheniem v period 1969–1983 godov (July 1986), p. 8, GARF, Prokuratura RSFSR ugolovnye dela.

50. Ibid.

51. Zaiavlenie ot podsledstvennogo V. K. Rosliakova (May 15, 1983).

52. Zaiavlenie ot podsledstvennogo Mkhitara A. Ambartsumyana (June 21, 1983), pp. 8–9.

53. Nikolai P. Tregubov–Andrei A. Petrikov confrontation on videocassette, Moscow (July 1984), GARF, Prokuratura RSFSR, ugolovnye dela, delo Tregubov N. P., Petrikov A. A., Khokhlova G. M., Kireeva V. P., i drugikh.

54. Zaiavlenie ot podsledstvennogo Mkhitara A. Ambartsumyana (December 16, 1985).

55. Prigovor sudebnoĭ kollegii po ugolovnym delam Verkhovnogo Suda RSFSR po delu Tregubova N. P., Petrikova A. A., Khokhlova G. M., Kireeva V. P., i drugikh (September 8, 1986), p. 49.

56. Ibid.

57. Zaiavlenie ot podsledstvennogo Mkhitara A. Ambartsumyana (June 21, 1983), pp. 8–9.

58. Rubinov, "Soblaznennyĭ i rastreliannyĭ."

59. Zaiavlenie ot podsledstvennogo Mkhitara A. Ambartsumyana (December 16, 1985), p. 3.

60. Spravka o doprosakh Ambartsumyana v nastoiashchee vremia i o pokazaniiakh lits, na kotorykh on sylaetsia, Kuznetsov, B. N., sledovatel' sledstvennoï brigady prokuratury RSFSR, (September 25, 1986), pp. 2-3.

61. Ibid., p. 3.

62. Document on videocassette from the Russian Prosecutor General's Office (Moscow, 1986).

63. Mkhitar A. Ambartsumyan–Ivan N. Kolomeitsev confrontation on videocassette (Moscow, November 1986), p. 2, GARF, Prokuratura RSFSR, ugolovnye dela, delo Mhkitara A. Ambartsumyana.

64. Zaiavlenie ot podsledstvennogo Mkhitara A. Ambartsumyana (November 29, 1985).

65. "Korruptsiia eto seriozno" (1985), GARF, Prokuratura RSFSR, ugolovnye dela, delo o vziatochnichestve v sisteme torgovli, g. Moskvy, pp. 2-3.

66. See Zaiavlenie ot Pospelov O. O. k nachal' niku Sledstvennogo otdela UKGB SSSR po g. Moskve i Moskovskoï oblasti A. V. Trofimovu (1983), GARF, Prokuratura RSFSR, ugolovnye dela.

67. The case of Ambartsumyan is typical. Zaiavlenie ot podsledstvennogo Mkhitara A. Ambartsumyana, nachal'niku Sledstvennogo otdela UKGB SSSR po g. Moskve nachal'niku Sledstvennogo otdela UKGB SSSR po g. Moskve i Moskovskoï oblasti A. V. Trofimovu (1983).

68. Zaiavlenie ot podsledstvennogo V. K. Rosliakova (May 15, 1983), p. 2.

69. Zaiavlenie ot podsledstvennogo Mkhitara A. Ambartsumyana, p. 10.

70. Ibid., p. 10.

71. Ibid., p. 11.

72. Ibid., p. 10.

73. Dopolnenie k "Zaiavlenie ot podsledstvennogo Mkhitara A. Ambartsumyana" (July 21, 1983), p. 2.

74. Sukhanov, *Sovetskoe pokolenie i Gennadiĭ Ziuganov,* p. 296.

75. "Neizvestnyĭ Grishin," *Vzgliad,* no. 37 (1993).

76. See V. M. Kogan, "The Content of World and Anti-Social Behavior," *Soviet Sociology,* summer 1986, p. 44.

77. Medvedev, *Andropov,* p. 131.

78. "Korruptsiia eto seriozno," 1985, p. 2, GARF, Prokuratura RSFSR, ugolovnye dela, delo o vziatochnichestve v sisteme torgovli g. Moskvy.

Chapter 2. Integrity and Efficiency

1. Nekrasov, *Trinadtsat' "zheleznykh narkomov,"* pp. 66-67.

2. Oleg Khlobustov, *Neizvestnyĭ Andropov* (Moscow: Izdatelstvo Ėksmo, Iauza, 2009), pp. 248 49, 230 32.

3. Leonid Mlechin, *Andropov* (Moscow: Izdatelstvo Prospekt, 2009), pp. 301-4.

4. On scholars' growing interest in corruption at that time, see the issues of *Soviet Studies* from 1982 to 1985.

5. Z. Medvedev, *Andropov,* pp. 80–81.

6. At the Twenty-fourth Party Congress, in 1981, the Soviet Communist Party encouraged citizens to write letters to the media to express their criticism.

7. Z. Medvedev, *Andropov,* p. 143.

8. Georgia's Shevardnadze was not a KGB official, but he was still associated with the security forces.

9. Sukhanov, *Sovetskoe pokolenie i Gennadiĭ Ziuganov,* p. 296.

10. Moreover, the cases that were divulged mainly concerned low-ranking officials.

11. For example, the Soviet press exposed cases of smuggling in Rostov.

12. Z. Medvedev, *Andropov,* p. 143.

13. Ibid., pp. 117–18.

14. R. Medvedev, *Neizvestnyĭ Andropov* (Rostov-on-Don, 1999), pp. 257–58.

15. F. D. Bobkov, *KGB i vlast'* (Moscow, 1995), pp. 203–4.

16. Z. Medvedev, *Andropov,* p. 121.

17. Fedorchuk's promotion indicated that Andropov appreciated conservative cadres even if they had served for a long time and supported Brezhnev unconditionally.

18. See A. Sterligov's *Opal'nyĭ general svidetel'stvuet* (Moscow, 1993), pp. 5, 233.

19. Ibid., p. 11.

20. See Semanov, *Andropov.* On the utilization of journalists, see Z. Medvedev, *Andropov,* p. 67.

21. Oleg Blotskii, *Vladimir Putin* (Moscow, 2001), p. 284.

22. Ibid.

23. This image was put forward most effectively by the brothers Medvedev.

24. Z. Medvedev, *Andropov,* p. 68.

25. Two of these advisors were Iuri Arbatov and Fedor Burlatski. For more about the latter, see Fedor Burlatski, *Russkie Gosudari epokha reformiatsii* (Moscow, 1996), pp. 163–91.

26. Blotskii, *Vladimir Putin,* p. 284.

27. This assertion is based on what Oleinik related to the author on more than one occasion.

28. Anatoli Trofimov was murdered by hired thugs in 2005.

29. Boris Karakhanov, "Perovka, v Butyrki, Dalee," *Zashchita Ekonomicheskikh svobod i Kommercheskoi deyatel'nosti* [ZEK], no. 3 (1987): 42.

30. Both prosecutors led the interrogations of top Glavka executives, including Ambartsumyan, Pospelov, and Rosliakov.

31. Bunakov, interview by author, Moscow, March 1999. See also a published interview with Bunakov in G. Dolgov, "Gnil," *Kriminal,* no.1 (1991).

32. Bunakov interview, March 1999.

33. Ambartsumyan's written declarations mention requests he made to KGB agents regarding his material needs.

34. Bunakov interview, March 1999.

35. In their interrogations with KGB agents, detained individuals insisted that, as veterans of World War II, they could not be held as criminals.

36. Raport zamestiteliu nachal'nika sledstvennoĭ chasti prokuratury RSFSR, starshemu sovetniku iustitsii V. Oleiniku ot V. Andreeva, sledovatelia sledstvennoĭ brigady Prokuratury RSFSR (November 26, 1986), p. 2, GARF, Prokuratura RSFSR, ugolovnye dela, delo Mkhitara A. Ambartsumyana.

37. This was the case for Ambartsumyan and Sokolov, who were sentenced to death for taking bribes.

38. Vladimir Oleinik, interview by author, Moscow, March 1999.

39. Jaloba v sudebnuiu kollegiiu po ugolovnym delam Verkhovnogo Suda RSFSR, ot Eremeeva Aleksandra Matveevicha (May 6, 1988), p. 3.

40. Karakhanov, "Perovka, v Butyrki, Dalee," p. 42.

41. A. Sterligov statement quoted in Leonid Mlechin, *Predsedateli KGB* (Moscow, 1999), p. 233.

42. V. Oleinik, V. Pegrebko, and V. Shevkov, "Nekotorye voprosy i nekotorye rassledovaniia ugolovnykh del po khishcheniiakh i vziatochnichestve v sisteme torgovli (iz opyta rassledovaniia dela v sisteme Glavnogo upravleniia torgovli Mosgorispolkoma)" (Moscow, 1988), unpublished manuscript, pp. 4-11.

43. See Goratsii Misharin, *Prigovoreny k vyssheĭ mere* (Perm: Izdatel'stvo Ural LTD, 1998).

44. Luc Duhamel, "La stratégie des cadres en Russie pour contrer les accusations de crimes économiques," *Revue d'études comparatives Est-Ouest* 2, no. 3 (1991): 5-21.

45. On corruption in the Ministry of Fisheries, see Z. Medvedev, *Andropov,* pp. 139-40.

46. Ibid.

47. Leonid Mlechin, *Brezhnev* (Moscow: Izdatelstvo Prospekt, 2008), p. 265.

48. Arkhady Baksberg, "Le troisième infarctus du procureur," *Sputnik,* June 1988, pp. 78-82.

49. Ibid.

50. Semanov, *Andropov,* p. 194.

51. See Oleinik, Pegrebko, and Shevkov, "Nekotorye voprosy i nekotorye rassledovaniia."

52. Vitaly V. Fyodorchuk, http://dbpedia.org/resource/Vitaly_Vasilyevich_ Fyodorchuk; L. Shinkarev investigation, *Izvestia,* December 6, 1988, in *Current Digest of the Soviet Press,* January 4, 1989, pp. 26-28.

53. Ibid.

54. Ibid.

55. O. Basilevski, "Neizbezhnyĭ krakh," *Moskovskaia Pravda,* September 12, 1986.

56. Ibid.

57. Rubinov, "Soblaznennyĭ i rasstreliannyĭ."

58. Ibid.

59. R. Medvedev, *Neizvestnyĭ Andropov,* pp. 368-69.

60. Serguei Glazunov, "Khoziaĭnoĭ gorod," *Shchit i mech,* January 1991.

61. Still, for six months Petrikov continued to deny having given bribes to Tregubov.

62. L. Volk, "Spravka po delu o vziatochnichestve v sisteme torgovli g. Moskvy," pp. 1-3, GARF, Prokuratura RSFSR, ugolovnye dela.

63. Stanislav Volkov, "Tenevniki, naden'te ordena," *ZEK sbornik* (Moscow, 1993), p. 74.

64. Ibid., 73–75.

65. Dopolneniia k analizu otdel'nykh iavlenii, obstoiatel'stv, proiavivshikhsia v kontse, 1985 goda i 1986 godu po nastoiashchee vremia (December 12, 1986).

66. Ibid.

67. Nikolai P. Tregubov–Andrei A. Petrikov confrontation, on videocassette (Moscow, July 1984), GARF, Prokuratura RSFSR, ugolovnye dela, delo Tregubov N. P., Petrikov A. A., Khokhlova G. M., Kireeva V. P., i drugikh.

68. Ibid.

69. Nikolai P. Tregubov–Boris S. Tveritinov confrontation on video cassette (Moscow, November 1984).

70. Stenogramma, doprosakh Tregubova (Moscow, February 1985), GARF, Prokuratura RSFSR, ugolovnye dela, delo Tregubov.

71. Dopolneniia k analizu otdel'nykh iavlenij, obstoyatel'stv, proiavivshikhsia v kontse, 1985 goda i 1986 godu po nastoiashchee vremia (December 12, 1986).

72. Ibid.

73. *Pravda,* April 17, 1983.

74. Ibid.

75. Investigator V. Burtsev, interview by author, Moscow, May 1993.

76. Dopolneniia k analizu otdel'nykh ipravlenii (December 12, 1986), p. 2.

77. "Neizvestnyĭ Grishin," *Vzgliad,* no. 37, (1993): 1.

78. *Moscow News,* September 24, 1986.

79. Quoted in *Pravda,* February 27, 1986.

80. Archie Brown, "The Gorbachev Era," in *The Cambridge History of Russia,* vol. 3, *The Twentieth Century* (Cambridge: Cambridge University Press, 2006), p. 326.

81. Spravka, 1986–1988 (Moscow, 1988), pp. 1–2, GARF, Prokuratura RSFSR, ugolovye dela.

82. Oleinik interview, March 1999.

83. Ibid.

84. Sterligov, *Opal'nyĭ general svidetel'stvuet,* p. 5.

85. Ibid.

86. A. Kolesnikov, "Kak ubili russkogo sovetskogo Eliseeva?" *Rossiiskie Vesti,* August 27, 1994.

87. See the interview of Bunakov by G. Dolgov in "Krovat' dlia gospodina grabitelia," *Kriminal,* no. 2 (1991): 83–84.

Chapter 3. Who, How Many, and How Much?

1. Oleinik, Pegrebko, and Shevkov, "Nekotorye voprosy i nekotorye rassledovaniia," pp. 10–11.

2. V. Oleinik, interview, "Pochemu oni nas ne boiat'sia?" *Rossiiskie Vesti,* August 27, 1991.

3. Spravka, O nekotorykh prichinakh i usloviiakh, sposobstvovavshikh razrastaniiu v moskovskoĭ torgovle prestupnykh posiagatel'stv na sotsialisticheskuiu sobstvennost',

vziatochnichestva, koristnykh zloupotreblenii dolzhnostnym polozheniem, v period 1969–1983 godov (Moscow, July 1986), 5, GARF, Prokuratura RSFSR, ugolovnye dela, p. 5.

4. Ibid.

5. Ibid.

6. Ibid., pp. 6–7.

7. Ibid., p. 6.

8. Ibid., p. 4.

9. Ibid., p. 14.

10. Ibid., pp. 18–19.

11. "Neizvestnyĭ Grishin," *Vzgliad*, no. 37 (1993).

12. According to the prosecutor general, Tregubov was already receiving bribes when he worked in transport. Vladimir Oleinik, interview by author, Moscow, January 2000.

13. According to Grishin, Tregubov lived too modestly to be accepting bribes.

14. Reported by Oleinik, interview by author, Moscow, October 17, 1991.

15. Tregubov-Petrikov courtroom confrontation on videocassette (Moscow, July 1984), GARF, Prokuratura RSFSR, ugolovnye dela.

16. See Oleinik, Spravka, O nekotorykh prichinakh i usloviiakh, sposobstvovavshikh razrastaniiu v moskovskoĭ torgovle prestupnykh posiagatel'stv na sotsialisticheskuiu sobstvennost', vziatochnichestva, koristnykh zloupotreblenii dolzhnostnym polozheniem, v period 1969–1983 godov (July 1986), p. 5, GARF, Prokuratura RSFSR ugolovnye dela.

17. By promoting the stability that the nomenklatura craved, Brezhnev solidified his popularity with this group.

18. After 1975, however, there was widespread economic stagnation in the country, and Brezhnev's popularity suffered as a result.

19. See Zaiavlenie ot podsledstvennogo V. K. Rosliakova (May 15, 1983), p. 7.

20. See chap. 1, note 24.

21. It was at this time—this turning point—that Tregubov also took bribes from Tveritinov. Prigovor sudebnoĭ kollegii po ugolovnym delam Verkhovnogo Suda RSFSR po delu Tregubova N. P., Petrikova A. A., Khokhlova G. M., Kireeva V. P., i drugikh (September 8, 1986), pp. 38–39.

22. Tregubov-Petrikov courtroom confrontation on videocassette (July 1984).

23. Ibid.

24. Glazunov, "Khoziainyĭ gorod."

25. Oleinik interview, October 17, 1991.

26. According to Bunakov in Dolgov, "Gnil'," *Kriminal,* p. 35.

27. Prigovor sudebnoĭ kollegii po ugolovnym delam Verkhovnogo Suda RSFSR po delu Tregubova N. P. (September 8, 1986), p. 18.

28. Prigovor sudebnoĭ kollegii po ugolovnym delam Moskovskogo gorodskogo suda po delu, Ambartsumyana M. A., Azarovoi A. M., Bikanov M. V., Gotloiba I. M., Gurianova V. A., Hiller A. M., Kats A. M., Kokomva P. R., Mugurdomova G. G., Tatintseva A. S., Rosliakov A. S., Lepeskina I. V. (Moscow, October 25, 1984). This document can

be found at the Association for the Defense of Economic Freedom and of Persons Convicted of Economic Offenses.

29. Oleinik in Spravka, Dopolneniia k analizu otdel'nykh iavlenii (December 12, 1986).

30. Zaiavlenie podsledstvennogo Ambartsumyan Mkhitar Adamovich nachal'niku Sledstvennogo otdela UKGB, SSSR, po g. Moskve i Moskovskoĭ oblasti Trofimovu A. V. st. sledovateliu po OVD UKGB po g. Moskve i Moskovskoĭ oblasti Bunakovu V. I. (July 1983), p. 1, GARF, Prokuratura RSFSR, ugolovnye dela, delo Mkhitara A. Ambartsumyana.

31. Aleksandr Eremeev, interview by author, Moscow, February 1999.

32. Women with family roots in the Caucasus typically thought of their children first, then their husbands. Ambartsumyan's wife wanted to keep the money for her children and thus defied her imprisoned husband's request to give it back to the state.

33. For example, Petrikov, deputy director of Glavtorg, bribed his boss, Tregubov, to let him continue working despite the fact that he was old and ailing.

34. Quoted in Werth, *Histoire de l'Union soviétique,* p. 480.

35. Interrogation of Tregubov by PGO prosecutor V. Oleinik and KGB major Grigorik, on videocassette (Moscow, February 1985), GARF, Prokuratura RSFSR, ugolovnye dela, Moscow.

36. Oleinik, Pegrebko, and Shevkov, "Nekotorye voprosy i nekotorye rassledovaniia."

37. See the Program of the Communist Party of the Soviet Union, Twenty-second Congress (Moscow, 1961), pp. 100–101.

38. Prigovor sudebnoĭ kollegii po ugolovnym delam Verkhovnogo Suda RSFSR po delu Tregubova N. P. (September 8, 1986), p. 43.

39. Ibid., p. 43.

40. Ibid., p. 50.

41. Videocassette (Moscow, 1986), Prosecutor General's Office, GARF, Prokuratura RSFSR, ugolovnye dela, delo Tregubov N. P., Petrikov A. A., Khokhlova G. M., Kireeva V. P., i drugikh.

42. Ibid.

43. Ibid.

44. Ibid.

45. Ibid.

46. Zaiavlenie ot osuzhdennogo M. Ambartsumyana, nachal'niku Sledstvennogo otdela UKGB SSSR po g. Moskve i Moskovskoĭ oblasti A. Trofimovu, st. sledovateliu po OVD UKGB po g. Moskve i Moskovskoĭ oblasti V Bunakovu (Moscow, August 28, 1983), p. 10.

47. Ibid.

48. Zaiavlenie ot podsledstvennogo V. K. Rosliakova nachal'niku Sledstvennogo otdela upravleniia KGB po g. Moskve i Moskovskoĭ oblasti podpolkovniku A. V. Trofimovu (May 15, 1983), p. 4, GARF, Prokuratura RSFSR ugolovye dela, delo Mkhitara A. Ambartsumyana.

49. Ibid.

50. Ibid.

51. Ibid.

52. Ibid.

53. Spravka o nekotorykh prichinakh i usloviiakh, sposobstvovavshikh razrastaniiu v moskovskoĭ torgovle prestupnykh posiagatel'stv na sotsialisticheskuiu sobstvennost', vziatochnichestva, koristnykh zloupotreblenii dolzhnostnym polozheniem', v period 1969-1983 godov (July 1986), GARF, Prokuratura RSFSR, ugolovnye dela.

54. Rubinov, "Soblaznennyĭ i rasstreliannyĭ."

55. Zaiavlenie ot osuzhdennogo M. Ambartsumyana, nachal'niku Sledstvennogo otdela UKGB SSSR po g. Moskve i Moskovskoĭ oblasti A. Trofimovu, st. sledovateliu po OVD UKGB po g. Moskve i Moskovskoĭ oblasti v Bunakovu (August 28, 1983), p. 10.

56. Ibid.

57. Information from published interview with Bunakov in Dolgov, "Gnil," *Kriminal,* p. 43.

58. Ibid.

59. Ibid.

60. Ibid.

61. Ambartsumyan's two sons received advantages from Armenians working in Aeroflot. Information from published interview with Bunakov in Dolgov, "Gnil," *Kriminal,* p. 39.

62. Zaiavlenie ot podsledstvennogo Mkhitara A. Ambartsumyana, nachal'niku Sledstvennogo otdela UKGB SSSR po g. Moskve i Moskovskoĭ oblasti A. V. Trofimuvu, st. sledovateliu po OVD UKGB po g. Moskve i Moskovskoĭ oblasti V. I. Bunakovu (June 21, 1983), pp. 8-9, GARF, Prokuratura RSFSR, ugolovnye dela, delo Mkhitara A. Ambartsumyana, p. 111.

63. Ibid., p. 111.

64. *Izvestia,* March 29, 1990.

65. A. Gurov, *Krasnaia mafia* (Moscow, 1995), p. 176.

66. Z. Medvedev, *Andropov,* p. 189.

67. Sukhanov, *Sovetskoe pokolenie i Gennadiĭ Ziuganov.*

68. See Spravka o nekotorykh prichinakh i usloviiakh, sposobstvovavshikh razrastaniiu v moskovskoĭ torgovle prestupnykh posiagatel'stv na sotsialisticheskuiu sobstvennost', vziatochnichestva, koristnykh zloupotreblenii dolzhnostnym polozheniem', v period 1969-1983 godov (July 1986), p. 5, GARF, Prokuratura RSFSR, ugolovnye dela.

69. Burtsev interview, May 1993.

70. Mueller, ed., *Public Choice II,* pp. 229-30.

71. V dopolnenie k zaiavlenie podsledstvennogo Mkhitara A. Ambartsumyana, nachal'niku Sledstvennogo otdela UKGB SSSR po g. Moskve i Moskovskoĭ oblasti A. V. Trofimuvu, st. sledovateliu po OVD UKGB po g. Moskve i Moskovskoĭ oblasti V. I. Bunakovu (June 21, 1983), pp. 8-9, GARF, Prokuratura RSFSR, ugolovnye dela, delo Mkhitara A. Ambartsumyana.

72. Rosliakov, in Zaiavlenie ot podsledstvennogo V. K. Rosliakova nachal'niku Sledstvennogo otdela upravleniia KGB po g. Moskve i Moskovskoĭ oblasti podpolkovniku A.

V. Trofimovu (May 15, 1983), p. 4, GARF, Prokuratura RSFSR ugolovye dela, delo Mkhitara A. Ambartsumyana.

73. Ibid.

74. Bunakov in Dolgov, "Gnil," *Kriminal,* p. 43.

Chapter 4. The War the KBG Lost

1. O. Bazilievich, "Neizbezhnyĭ krakh," *Moskovskaia Pravda,* September 12, 1986.

2. See *Izvestia,* July 9, 1986.

3. Bazilievich, "Neizbezhnyĭ krakh."

4. Volkov, "Tenevniki, naden'te ordena," pp. 68–83.

5. Bazilievich, "Neizbezhnyĭ krakh."

6. Ibid.

7. Nikolai P. Tregubov–Andrei A. Petrikov confrontation on videocassette (Moscow, July 1984), GARF, Prokuratura RSFSR, ugolovnye dela, delo Tregubov N. P., Petrikov A. A., Khokhlova G. M., Kireeva V. P., i drugikh.

8. Kolesnikov, "Kak ubili russkogo sovetskogo Eliseeva?"

9. Ibid.

10. Vladimir Sergeev, "Sazhaem vsekh," *Rossiiskie Vesti,* April 27, 1995.

11. Jaloba v sudebnuiu kollegiiu po ugolovnym delam Verkhovnogo Suda RSFSR, ot Eremeeva Aleksandra Matveevicha (May 6, 1988), p. 3.

12. Ibid.

13. The author met with Eremeev in February 1999, when he was already very sick.

14. Interrogation of V. N. Levtonov by PGO investigator S. G. Rodionov.

15. Interrogation of V. N. Levtonov by Oleinik.

16. Nikolai P. Tregubov–Boris S. Tveritinov confrontation on videocassette (Moscow, November 1984).

17. Spravka o doprosakh Ambartsumyana v nastoiashchee vremia i o pokazaniiakh lits, na kotorykh on sylaetsia (September 23, 1986).

18. Dopolneniia k analizu otdel'nykh iavlenii, obstoiatel'stv, proiavivshikhsia v kontse, 1985 goda–1986 godu po nastoiashchee vremia (May 12, 1986), p. 4.

19. Volkov, "Tenevniki, naden'te ordena," p. 74.

20. Kenneth Newton, "Social Capital and Democracy," in *Beyond Tocqueville: Civil Society and the Social Capital Debate in Comparative Perspective,* ed. Bob Edwards, Michael W. Foley, and Mario Diani (Hanover, NH: University Press of New England, 2001), p. 228.

21. Volkov, "Tenevniki, naden'te ordena," 74.

22. Ibid., p. 69.

23. Ibid., p. 72.

24. Jaloba v sudebnuiu kollegiiu po ugolovnym delam Verkhovnogo Suda RSFSR, ot Eremeeva Aleksandra Matveevicha (May 6, 1988), p. 3.

25. Ibid.

26. Eremeev interview.

27. Kolesnikov, "Kak ubili russkogo sovetskogo Eliseeva?"

28. Nikolai Tregubov–Andrei A. Petrikov courtroom confrontation, on videocassette (July 1984).

29. Kolesnikov, "Kak ubili russkogo sovetskogo Eliseeva?"

30. Volkov, "Tenevniki, naden'te ordena," pp. 72–73.

31. Ibid., p. 74.

32. Oleinik, Dopolneniia k analizu otdel'nykh iavlenii, obstoiatel'stv, proiavivshikhsia v kontse, 1985 goda–1986 godu po nastoiashchee vremia (May 12, 1986).

33. Ibid.

34. Jaloba v sudebnuiu kollegiiu po ugolovnym delam Verkhovnogo Suda RSFSR, ot Eremeeva Aleksandra Matveevicha (May 6, 1988), p. 3.

35. Kolesnikov, "Kak ubili russkogo sovetskogo Eliseeva?"

36. Sergeev, "Sazhaem vsekh."

37. Kolesnikov, "Kak ubili russkogo sovetskogo Eliseeva?"

38. Ibid.

39. Ibid.

40. Oleinik, Spravka (1988), p. 8, GARF, Prokuratora RSFSR, ugolovnye dela, delo o vziatochnichestve v sisteme torgovli gorod Moskvy.

41. Prigovor sudebnoĭ kollegii po ugolovnym delam Verkhovnogo Suda RSFSR po delu Tregubova N. P., Petrikova A. A., Khokhlova G. M., Kireeva V. P., i drugikh, delo no. UK PI-85 II (Moscow, September 8, 1986).

42. Kolesnikov, "Kak ubili russkogo sovetskogo Eliseeva?"

43. *Izvestia*, in *Current Digest of the Soviet Press,* May 10, 1986, p. 17.

44. Ibid.

45. "Neizvestnyĭ Grishin," *Vzgliad,* no. 37 (1993).

46. Ibid.

47. The anticorruption campaign leaders ordered investigators to root out witness evidence on Tregubov.

48. V dopolnenie k zaiavleniiu (June 21, 1983), Zaiavlenie ot podsledstvennogo Mkhitara A. Ambartsumyana, nachal'niku Sledstvennogo otdela UKGB SSSR po g. Moskve i Moskovskoĭ oblasti A. V. Trofimovu, st. sledovateliu po OVD UKGB po g. Moskve i Moskovskoĭ oblasti V. I. Bunakovu, GARF, Prokuratura RSFSR, ugolovnye dela, delo Mhkitara A. Ambartsumyana.

49. Interrogation of Tregubov by PGO prosecutor V. Oleinik and KGB major Grigorik, on videocassette (Moscow, February 1985), GARF, Prokuratura RSFSR, ugolovnye dela, Moscow.

50. Regarding the relationship between social contract and corruption, see Stephen E. Hanson, "The Brezhnev Era," in *The Cambridge History of Russia,* ed. Ronald Grigor Suny (Cambridge: Cambridge University Press, 2006), pp. 301–3.

51. Oleinik, Spravka, Moscow (1988).

52. Chikirev, as reported by Oleink, Spravka, Moscow (1988).

53. Telegram sent by N. E. Shkil to the Twenty-ninth Congress of the Soviet Communist Party, July 2, 1988.

54. Ibid.

55. The Twenty-first Congress of the Communist Party of the Soviet Union (CPSU) in 1959 emphasized the increasing role of the soviets with the entrance of Soviet society into the communist stage of political development.

56. See the proceedings of the Twenty-first Congress of the CPSU.

57. Spravka, O nekotorykh prichinakh i usloviiakh, sposobstvovashikh razrastaniiu v moskovskoĭ torgovle prestupnykh posiagatel'stv na sotsialisticheskuiu sobstvennost', vziatochnichestva, koristnykh zloupotreblenii dolzhnostnym polozheniem v period 1969–1983 godov (July 11, 1986), pp. 4–6.

58. Ibid.

59. See chapter 2 on Tregubov.

60. Spravka, O nekotoryhh prichinakh i usloviiakh, sposobstvovavshikh razrastaniiu v moskovskoĭ torgovle prestupnykh posiagatel'stv na sotsialisticheskuiu sobstvennost', vziatochnichestva, koristnykh zloupotreblenii dolzhnostnym polozheniem, spravka v period 1969–1983 godov (July 11, 1986), pp. 14–15.

61. Ibid., p. 18.

62. Ibid.

63. Ibid.

64. Ibid., p. 17.

65. Ibid., p. 20.

66. Ibid., p. 12.

67. Oleinik, in Dopolneniia k analizu otdel'nykh iavlenii, obstoiatel'stv, proiavivshikhsia v kontse 1985 i 1986 godu po nastoiashchee vremia (May 12, 1986).

68. Reported by Eremeev, in Jaloba v sudebnuiu kollegiiu po ugolovnym delam Verkhovnogo Suda RSFSR, ot Eremeeva Aleksandra Matveevicha (May 6, 1988).

69. See Oleinik, in Dopolneniia k analizu otdel'nykh iavlenii, obstoiatel'stv, proiavivshikhsia v kontse 1985 i 1986 godu po nastoiashchee vremia (May 12, 1986).

70. Ibid., p. 2.

71. Ibid.

72. Zaiavlenie ot osuzhdennogo Mkhitara Ambartsumyana (October 25, 1984), GARF, Prokuratora RSFSR, ugolovnye dela, delo Mkhitara Ambartsumyana.

73. Oleinik, in Dopolneniia k analizu otdel'nykh iavlenii, obstoiatel'stv, proiavivshikhsia v kontse 1985 i 1986 godu po nastoiashchee vremia (May 12, 1986).

74. *Moscow News*, September 24, 1986.

75. V. Kravtsev, Zamestiteliu prokurora RSFSR, gosudarstvennomu sovetniku iustitsii 3 klassa B. Namestnikovu (October 4, 1985). On the Ambartsumyan case, see also Luc Duhamel, "Justice and Politics in Moscow, 1983–1986: The Ambartsumyan Case," *Europe-Asia Studies* 52, no. 7 (November 2000): 1307–29.

76. Postanovlenie ob otkaze v vozbuzhdenii ugolovnogo dela, st. prokuror sledstvennoĭ chasti Prokuratury RSFSR, Sheremetʹev (March 28, 1986).

77. Ibid.

78. Spravka, O sostoianii rassledovaniia materialov ugolovnogo dela, vydelennogo v otdelʹnoe izvodstvo iz dela Glavtorga v otnoshenii dolzhnostnykh lits kontroliruiush-chikh, sovetskikh i partiĭnykh organov (November 13, 1986).

79. Mkhitar A. Ambartsumyan–Ivan N. Kolomeitsev confrontation during interro-gations (Moscow, November 17, 1986), p. 2.

80. Ibid.

81. V. Oleinik, interview by author, Moscow, May 1993.

82. Rubinov, "Soblaznennyĭ i rasstreliannyĭ."

83. L. Shinkarev investigation, *Izvestia,* December 6, 1988, in *Current Digest of the Soviet Press,* January 4, 1989, pp. 26–28.

Selected Bibliography

The bibliography includes brief descriptions of the original material used in my research. These unpublished, previously inaccessible documents produced by various entities in the Soviet judiciary made it possible to follow the rise of the internal trade bureaucracy in Moscow as a political force during the 1980s. Also listed here are secondary sources, including works written in the West that analyze the forces or groups that profited from corruption in Russia, as well as works presenting theoretical approaches that help provide insight to anyone studying corruption in Russia. Other works included are those that were published after the advent of democracy in 1991 and that deal with corruption in Russia during the 1980s.

Russian-Language Sources

Documents and data related to investigations of corruption in retail trade in Moscow, 1982–1987:

Minutes from trials concerning the executive personnel of the Moscow Trade Administration (Glavtorg), the Moscow Administration of Fruit and Vegetable Offices (Glavka), the Dzerzhinski Fruit and Vegetable Office (*kontora*), the Eliseevski *gastronom*, and other organizations

Documents from the Prosecutor General's Office and the KGB: statements, interrogations, and courtroom confrontations of executive personnel from the Moscow Trade Administration, the Moscow Administration of Fruit and Vegetable Offices, the Dzerzhinski and Kievski Fruit and Vegetable Offices, the Eliseevski *gastronom*, and other organizations, as well as directives, interrogations, and comments by executive personnel and prosecutors in the KGB and the Prosecutor General's Office

Author interviews with executive personnel of the Prosecutor General's Office, the KGB, the Retail Trade Administration, the Dzerzhinski Fruit and Vegetable Office, and the Eliseevski *gastronom*

Bobkov, F. D. *KGB.* Moscow, 1995.
———. *KGB i vlast'.* Moscow, 1995.
Burlatski, Fedor. *Vozhdi i sovetniki: o Khrushcheve, Andropov i ne tol'ko o nikh.* Moscow, 1990.
———. *Russkie Gosudari epokha reformatsii.* Moscow, 1996.
Chaadaev, S. G. *Ugolovnaia politika i prestupnost'.* Moskva, 1991.
Churbanov, Iuri. *Raskazhu vsë, shto bylo.* Moscow, 1993.

Dokuchaev, M. S. *Moskva, Kreml', Okhrana*. Moscow, 1995.

Dyshev, S. *Rossiia ugolovnaia: ot "vorov v zakone" do "otmorozkov."* Moscow, 1998.

Dzhafarov, S. A., and V. N. Riabinin, *Za chuzhoĭ schet, borba s parazitichevkim obrazom zhizni*. Moscow, 1986.

Gdlian, T., and E. Dodolev. *Mafiia vremen bezzakoniia*. Yerevan, 1991.

Gladkov, Teodor, and Oleg Mosokhin. *Vozhdi, Menzhinskiĭ intelligent s lubianki.* Moscow: Izdatelstvo Ėksmo, 2005.

Grishin, V. V. *Ot Khrushcheva do Gorbacheva*. Moscow, 1996.

Gurov, A. *Krasnaia mafia*. Moscow: Kommercheskii vestnik, 1995.

Khlobustov, Oleg. *Neizvestnyĭ Andropov*. Moscow: Izdatelstvo Ėksmo, Iauza, 2009.

Kraskova, Valentina. *Kremlevskaia doch' Galina Brezhneva*. Moscow: Sovremennyĭ literator, 1999.

Kriuchkov, V. *KGB SSSR, Lichnoe delo*. Parts 1 and 2. Moscow, 1996.

Maĭsurian, Aleksandr. *Drugoĭ Brezhnev*. Moscow: Vagrius, 2004.

Medvedev, R. *Neizvestnyĭ Andropov*. Rostov-on-Don, 1999.

———. *Lichnost' i epokha: politicheskiĭ portret L. I. Brezhneva*. 2 vols. Moscow: Novosti, 1991.

Minutko, I. A. *Bezdna (mif o Iurii Andropove)*. Moscow, 1997.

Misharin, G. *Prigovoreny k vyssheĭ mere*. Perm: Izdatel'stvo ural LTD, 1998.

Mlechin, Leonid. *Andropov*. Moscow: Izdatelstvo Prospekt, 2009.

———. *Brezhnev*. Moscow: Izdatelstvo Prospekt, 2008.

Nekrasov, Vladimir. *Trinadtsat' "zheleznykh narkomov."* Moscow: Izdatelstvo Verst, 1995.

Oleinik, V., V. Pogrebko, and V. Shevkov. "Nekotorye voprosy i nekotorye rassledovaniia ugolovnykh del po khishcheniiakh i vziatochnichestve v sisteme torgovli (iz opyta rassledovaniia dela v sisteme Glavnogo upravleniia torgovli Mosgorispolkoma)." Moscow, 1988. Unpublished manuscript.

Osnovy borby s organizovannoĭ prestupnost'iu. Moscow, 1996.

Osokina, Elena. Za fasadom "stalinskogo izobiliia." *Rossiĭskaia politicheskaia entsiklopediia*. Moscow: Izdatelstvo Rosspėn, 1998.

Semanov, S. *Brezhnev*. Moscow: Izdatelstvo Veche, 2002.

———. *Andropov*. Moscow: Izdatelstvo Veche, 2001.

Sharonin, Viacheslav. *KGB-TSRU*. Moscow, 1997.

Sinitsin, Igor E. *Andropov vblizi: vospominaniia o vremenakh "ottepeli" i "zastoia."* Moscow: Rossiĭskaia gazeta, 2004.

Skaredov, G. I. *Uchastie prokurora v sledstvennykh deĭstviiakh*. Moscow, 1987.

Sokirko, V. V. *Summa golosov prisiazhnykh v poiske graneĭ ėkonomicheskoĭ svobody*. Moscow: Izdatelsvo RosKonsult, 2000.

Sterligov, A. *Opal'nyĭ general svidetel'stvuet*. Moscow, 1993.

Sukhanov, V. I. *Sovetskoe pokolenie i Gennadiĭ Ziuganov*. Moscow, 1999.

Teshkin, Iuri. *Andropov i drugie*. Part I. Yaroslavl: Verkhniaia Volga, 1998.

Timofeev, Lev. *Chërnyĭ rynok kak politicheskaia sistema*. Moscow, 1993.

Volkov, S. "Tenevniki Naden'te ordena." In *Zashchita Ėkonomicheskikh svobod i Kommercheskoĭ deiatel'nosti*, pp. 74–78. Moscow: Obshchestvo zashity osuzhdennykh khozaiistvennikov i ėkonomicheskikh svobod, 1993.

Zashchita Ėkonomicheskikh svobod i Kommercheskoĭ deiateľ nosti. Moscow: Obshchestvo
   zashity osuzhdennykh khoziaistvennikov i ėkonomicheskikh svobod, 1990–1995.

English-Language Sources

Andrew, Christopher, and Vasili Mitrokhin. *The Sword and the Shield: The Mitrokhin
   Archive and the Secret History of the KGB.* New York: Basic Books, 1999.

Bacon, Edwin, and Mark Sandle, eds. *Brezhnev Reconsidered.* New York: Palgrave
   Macmillan, 2002.

Boobbyer, Philip. *Conscience, Dissent, and Reform in Soviet Russia.* New York: Routledge,
   2005.

Brown, Archie. *The Gorbachev Factor.* Oxford: Oxford University Press, 1996.

———. *Seven Years That Changed the World: Perestroika in Perspective.* New York:
   Oxford University Press, 2007.

Clark, W. A. *Crime and Punishment in Soviet Officialdom: Combating Corruption in the
   Political Elite, 1965–1990.* Armonk, NY: M. E. Sharpe 1993.

Coleman, James S. *Individual Interests and Collective Action: Selected Essays.* Cambridge:
   Cambridge University Press, 1986.

Cook, Linda. *The Soviet Social Contract and Why It Failed: Welfare Policy and Workers'
   Politics from Brezhnev to Yeltsin.* Cambridge: Cambridge University Press, 1993.

Deriabin, Peter, and T. H. Bagley. *KGB: Masters of the Soviet Union.* New York:
   Hippocrene Books, 1990.

Dininio, Phyllis, and Robert Orttung. "Explaining Patterns of Corruption in the Russian
   Regions." *World Politics* 57, no. 4 (July 2005): 500–29.

Duhamel, Luc. "The Last Campaign against Corruption in Soviet Moscow." *Europe-Asia
   Studies* 56, no. 2 (2004): 187–213.

Felbrudge, F. J. "Government and Shadow Economy in the Soviet Union." *Soviet Studies*
   36, no. 4 (1984): 528–43.

Fukuyama, Francis. "The Great Disruption: Human Nature and the Reconstitution of
   Social Order." *Atlantic Monthly*, May 1999, 55–80.

———. "Social Capital, Civil Society, and Development." *Third World Quarterly* 22, no. 1
   (2001): 7–20.

Garceron, Marc. *Revolutionary Passage: From Soviet to Post-Soviet Russia, 1985–2000.*
   Philadelphia: Temple University Press, 2005.

Gibbs, Joseph. *Gorbachev's Glasnost: The Soviet Media in the First Phase of Perestroika.*
   College Station: Texas A&M University Press, 1999.

Gregory, Paul R., and Robert C. Stuart. *Russian and Soviet Economic Performance and
   Structure.* Boston: Addison-Wesley, 2001.

Greif, Avner. "Cultural Beliefs and Organization of Society: A Historical and Theoretical
   Reflection on Collectivist and Individualist Societies." *Journal of Political Economy*
   102, no. 5 (1994): 912–50.

Hanson, Philip. *The Rise and Fall of the Soviet Economy: An Economic History of the
   USSR from 1945.* New York: Longman, 2003.

Head, Tom, ed. *Mikhail Gorbachev.* San Diego: Greenhaven Press, 2003.

Hedlund, Stefan, and Niclas Sundstrum. "Does Palermo Represent the Future for Moscow?" *Journal of Public Policy* 16, no. 2 (1996): 113–55.

Heywood, Paul. "Political Corruption: Problems and Perspectives." *Political Studies* 45, no. 3 (1997): 417–35.

Hoffman, David E. *The Oligarchs: Wealth and Power in the New Russia.* New York: Public Affairs, 2003.

Holmes, Leslie. *The End of Communist Power: Anti-Corruption Campaigns and Legitimation Crisis.* Oxford: Oxford University Press, 1993.

Hutchcroft, Paul D. "The Politics of Privilege: Assessing the Impact of Rents, Corruption, and Clientelism on Third World Development." *Political Studies* 45, no. 3 (1997): 639–58.

Hyden, Goran. "Civil Society, Social Capital, and Development: Dissection of a Complex Discourse." *Studies in International Comparative Development* 32, no. 1 (1997): 3–30.

Kantidey, Harendra. "The Genesis and Spread of Economic Corruption: A Microtheoretic Interpretation." *World Development* 17, no. 4 (1989): 503–11.

Katsenelinboigen, A. "Coloured Markets in the Soviet Union." *Soviet Studies* 29, no. 1 (1977): 62–85.

Keeran, Roger, and Thomas Kenny. *Socialism Betrayed: Behind the Collapse of the Soviet Union.* New York: International Publishers, 2004.

Kotkin, Stephen. *Armageddon Averted: The Soviet Collapse, 1970–2000.* Oxford: Oxford University Press, 2001.

Kramer, John H. "Political Corruption in the USSR." *Western Political Quarterly* 30, no. 2 (1977): 213–25.

Lambert, Nick. "Law and Order in the USSR: The Case of Economic and Official Crime." *Soviet Studies* 36, no. 3 (1984): 366–85.

Lane, David. "The Gorbachev Revolution: The Role of the Political Elite in Regime Disintegration." *Political Studies* 44, no. 1 (1996): 4–23.

Ledeneva, Alena. *Russia's Economy of Favours: Blat, Networking, and Informal Exchanges.* Cambridge: Cambridge University Press, 1998.

Marples, David R. *The Collapse of the Soviet Union, 1985–1991.* Harlow, England: Pearson Longman, 2004.

Medvedev, Zhores. *Andropov.* Oxford: Oxford University Press, 1983.

Melvin, Neil. *Soviet Power and the Countryside: Policy Innovation and Institutional Decay.* New York: Palgrave Macmillan, 2003.

Mueller, Dennis C. *Public Choice II.* Cambridge: Cambridge University Press, 1989.

Newton, Kenneth. "Social Capital and Democracy." *American Behavioral Scientist* 40, no. 5 (1997): 575–86.

Ogushi, Atsushi. *The Demise of the Soviet Communist Party.* London: Routledge, 2008.

O'Hearn, D. "The Second Consumer Economy: Size and Effects." *Soviet Studies* 32, no. 2 (1980): 218–34.

Ostrom, E. "Social Capital: A Fad or a Fundamental Concept?" In *Social Capital: A Multifaceted Perspective,* edited by Partha Dasgupta and Ismail Serageldin. Washington, DC: World Bank, 2000.

Passas, Nikos. "Global Anomie, Dysnomie, and Economic Crime: Hidden Consequences of Neo-liberalism and Globalization in Russia and around the World." *Social Justice* 27, no. 2 (2000): 16–44.

Philip, Mark. "Defining Political Corruption." *Political Studies* 45, no. 3 (1997): 436–62.

Pierson, Paul. "Increasing Returns, Path Dependence, and the Study of Politics." *American Political Science Review* 94, no. 2 (2000): 251–67.

Rose, Richard. "When Government Fails: Social Capital in an Antimodern Russia." In *Beyond Tocqueville: Civil Society and the Social Capital Debate in Comparative Perspective*, edited by Bob Edwards, Michael W. Foley, and Mario Diani. Hanover, NH: University Press of New England, 2001.

Rosefielde, Steven, and Stefan Hedlund. *Russia since 1980: Wrestling with Westernization.* Cambridge: Cambridge University Press, 2009.

Seliktar, Ofira. *Politics, Paradigms, and Intelligence Failures: Why So Few Predicted the Collapse of the Soviet Union.* Armonk, NY: M. E. Sharpe, 2004.

Spulber, Nicolas. *Russia's Economic Transitions: From Late Tsarism to the New Millennium.* New York: Cambridge University Press, 2003.

Tompson, William. *The Soviet Union under Brezhnev.* Harlow, England: Pearson Longman, 2003.

Weber, Max. *Economy and Society.* London, 1989.

———. *Max Weber on Law in Economy and Society.* Edited by Max Rheinstein. Cambridge, MA: Harvard University Press, 1969.

Wittlin, Thaddeus. *Commissar: The Life and Death of Lavrenty Pavlovich Beria.* New York: Macmillan, 1972.

Yeltsin, Boris. *Against the Grain.* London: Cape, 1990.

Zubok, Vladislav M. *A Failed Empire: The Soviet Union in the Cold War from Stalin to Gorbachev.* Chapel Hill: University of North Carolina Press, 2007.

Index

Note: Page numbers in *italic type* indicate tables.